GOLDEN CHAINS

By David I. McCaskey

For Bart

D.P. McCaskey
9/11/14

This book is dedicated to my friend John, who told me of a Western State Hospital patient allowed to keep bees on the hospital grounds many years ago; and to my friend Jean, who suggested that I invent the man's story when the official record was found to be closed because of the medical privacy laws.

1. THIS HAPPENED EARLY ON IN RAYMOND'S LIFE

The little boy followed the old man across the lot between the barn and smokehouse to the mixed row of sectioned tree trunks and white boxes just at the east edge of the woods, where the light and warmth of the sun hit them first thing every morning. The old man was in his everyday farming clothes, but had a length of tulle wrapped around his face and neck, turbaned around the brim of his straw hat and up over its crown. The boy was bare-headed and bare-foot, holding his grandfather's work-hardened hand. "Step easy and move slow," the old man said, "and I'll show you something, those golden chains we talked about last night."

They eased up beside one of the white boxes, set up on a stand of rocks, careful not to put themselves in front of the straight lines of flying honeybees, one going out from the flat board at the front of the box, the other coming in, both made up of bees spaced pretty evenly, at least as far as you could make them out. The old man eased the top off of the box, opened his pocketknife and slid the blade between the two sides of a pair of the horizontal bars just visible to the boy over the rim, twisting it when he got to each end to free things up. Ever so gently he pulled the bar and its suspended rectangular frame up and out, holding it down to where the boy could see.

"There they are!" the boy whispered, "the golden chains!" On both sides of the comb that the bees were drawing out into cells there were vertical chains of bees, holding onto the comb one above another, holding onto each other one above the other when the old man tilted the frame a little. "That's what I was telling you about on the porch last night," Grandfather said, talking lower than his usual outside voice, "that's how they build the comb, the one on the bottom takes a bit of wax from between the plates on her belly, chews it soft, and passes it up to her sister, who adds her flake and passes it on, up to the top of the chain where the builders take it and press it into just the right shape to make a cell, a cell for honey, for pollen, or for the queen to lay her eggs in."

2. THIS HAPPENED SHORTLY BEFORE THE END

The kid in sneakers, jeans, and a t-shirt followed his new friend out of the carpenter shop where his grandfather worked and where he got to come some days in the summer, up across the grass to the small, fenced-off area where there were four stands of white bee-boxes. "Go easy Johnny," Raymond said, "you ain't got no tiger-hunter's hat" tapping the brim of his hat, molded out of paper to look like a British colonial pith helmet, but with thin gauze fastened around it with an elastic cord, draped down over his face and neck and tied around his chest by another string, "just," he'd said back in the shop as he tied it tight, "like your granny ties her apron, can't nobody tell you how, your fingers gotta teach themselves behind your back. Go easy and those bees won't care about you -- I'm the one that's messing with them. Stand to the side away from their line of fire and I'll show you what we were talking about."

Raymond eased the top off of the bee box, leaning it behind the stand without any vibration. He took his little crowbar and wiggled it at each end of one of the wooden bars visible in the box, once on each side, then stuck the bar into his back pocket. Grunting a little, he pinched the bar with the fingers of each hand and pulled, easing it up to reveal the rectangular frame, half built out with honeycomb and with several vertical rows of bees clinging to each side. He tilted the frame and the chains of bees would swing out and back, out and back as he repeated the motion. 'Golden chains'. 'Golden chains', that's what Granddaddy called them back in Carolina. That's how they make their wax, the bottom one pulls a little flake out from the scales on her belly, chews it and passes it up. Passes it up to her sister who does the same thing, and by the time it gets to the top its big -- kinda like chewing gum under the edge of the table -- and the builder bees press it into cells, some for honey, some for pollen, and some for the queen to lay her eggs in."

Just then a loud electric bell rang on the side of another building. "You scoot, now," Raymond muttered, "I gotta go." Easing sideways to avoid the flying bees Johnny ran back to where his grandfather was working. Looking back over his shoulder he could see Raymond replacing the frame and lid a lot faster than he'd taken them off, but still moving easy, unstung by the bees coming and going in their two even lines. Away from the hive, Raymond pulled the hat and veil off and swung into his peculiar, rolling gait, which favored his right leg, and clearly relied on the homemade walking stick in his left hand, headed towards the building where he lived -- it was time to trade his beekeeper's hat for the engineer's cap he habitually wore and then to go to supper.

3. WHAT FOLKS BELIEVED THEY KNEW ABOUT

RAYMOND'S WAR

After a day and a half pitching around on the transport, guys seasick and puking everywhere and the heads overflowing, it was almost a relief to swarm down the cargo nets into the Higgins boats. Pretty soon all hell was going to be breaking loose, shells from their own ships screaming overhead, formations of high-flying bombers with white bars on their wings, and incoming shells from the shore batteries starting to explode around them, bracketing for range. Everybody'd been told what to expect, it just hadn't quite started yet. His unit had been crowded into a part of the ship where he couldn't see out, and when he got on deck he was amazed at the number of ships all around and the even larger number of boats crowded against them with men moving en masse down the nets into them. Not individuals climbing, but whole platoons crawling together, down into the little Higgins boats. Raymond told folks that the GIs moved down like the wild swarms of bees moved in a glistening sheet from the broken-off branch where they'd gathered into a new box at his Grandfather's command, except that they weren't as happy as the bees once they got there. They'd been a complaining bunch jammed into a pitching ship, seasick and puking, now they were jammed into a flat-bottomed landing craft, seasick again even if they'd gotten used to the ship, complaining, puking, and wet with saltwater spray.

Because they were going in before the main force of soldiers, Raymond's unit had been loaned three landing craft from the Brits with some metal on the sides. Not so much that anyone called it armor, but enough to provide them with a little more protection in the exposed part of the long run in to the beach. They climbed down the nets and got as settled as they could, waiting. On the troopship's signal a lone, blacked-out destroyer eased out of the fleet and passed close by, heading inshore. The Boson swung the boat away from the netted wall, hollered into the engine hatch, and the boys down there gave her everything they could to pull in behind the protective bulk of the passing ship. Their mission was to go in, climb the cliffs above the steep shingle beach at Port du Hoc where aerial reconnaissance showed artillery that threatened one of the main landings on Omaha beach. The Germans had to realize that something was up, but it couldn't be much, one destroyer coming in towards an area where an infantry landing was impossible. The planners of their raid were counting on Rommel's shore batteries to be under strict firing discipline not to reveal their exact location by blowing a lone, probing destroyer out of the water. The ship took them in as far as the depth allowed and the three boats passed it running towards the beach at full speed, their crews poised to power down as soon as they hit the shingle, drop the ramp for the men to disembark, hauling their ladders, then hold fast in position and listen for the two rockets rigged with grappling hooks and light line to fire from the launchers in the troop well of each boat. The Boson's directions were to give the line a few seconds to clear the boat as the rockets and grappling hooks flew up and over the edge of the cliff above the beach before giving his crew the order "up and full astern", take advantage of the area near the beach masked from enemy fire to turn about, then give her all they could to get away and seek shelter behind the destroyer that had brought them in and which would stand off at a distance determined by the depth of the sea and provide what support it could once the real fight began.

Nobody in Raymond's unit had a basic infantryman's load. Part of a Ranger battalion, they were heavy with ropes, ladders, ammunition and explosives. Their mission was to get onto the beach, scale the cliff, and silence the guns threatening Omaha beach. They didn't have a radio, although one of their lieutenants was lugging the bulk of an ancient heliostat and tripod that he'd thought of but nobody had ordered. At the last minute their Colonel had disobeyed orders to stay behind and had slipped into the last boat. "Just one more Ranger," he'd proclaimed, subordinating himself to the established chain of command. Because of their extra gear, and because of the climbing, most of them had chosen to carry Thompsons and a vest of thirty-round stick magazines rather than Garands. All with satchel loads and most of the others carried .45's as well. Everyone had grenades, both fragmentary, for fighting, and demolition, for their mission against the guns. The grenades gave everyone distorted-looking legs from long patch-pockets filled with them. They were loaded down with ropes, grappling hooks, satchel charges, and ladders. They even had a couple of extension ladders from a London fire brigade to attempt a head start on the climb and full-length rope ladders to pull up for the real work once they'd got a man up at least one of the six lines thrown by the rockets.

One or more of the hooks was expected to catch hard enough to hold one man's weight. If not they'd just have to let their best man climb up unaided, feet scrabbling and a knife to jamb into chinks in the stone in one hand. They had some Banglores for whatever wire they couldn't deal with using the cutters spread throughout their ranks. The chart-reading fellows were pretty sure that they'd hit shingle with no significant water beyond, but you could never be sure about the sea. Many weighty items for those who might have to try to swim, guaranteed awkward burdens for those who made it to the bench and then had to climb. Duplicate equipment was spread throughout the platoons, squads, and individuals so that a functioning amalgamation of men and material would survive the trip in to assemble and begin the ascent.

4. HOW HE'D GOT THERE, TO WAR

Raymond'd turned eighteen late in the summer, youngest in his class but for his cousin Carolyn, who, of course, didn't have to go to the county seat to register with the Selective Service. Drove to town by himself on his birthday, climbed the stairs, and proudly, cluelessly, signed the forms Miss Alice typed for him. Funny how he was so elated about turning eighteen that it didn't register at the time how sad she looked as he turned away, but he saw it and remembered it later. Remembered it and realized that she was sad because she'd typed those forms for too many boys with no idea what they really meant, many of whom were already dead, and would type so many more before it was over. He'd remembered her sadness later, later and until his dying day.

When he got his notice, Raymond had taken the bus to the induction center in Charlotte with about thirty other guys from the County. The service had done its selecting, and none of them had an articulable basis for deferment; no sole surviving sons, no defense workers--no defense plant in the county--and the farms were mostly like Raymond's family's, small, a couple of old men on the place, and a couple of kids and sisters coming up to help with the crop, so that there were few farm deferments. The only thing that happened at the center was a lackadaisical physical that any country boy was bound to pass, except for a couple of guys who'd caught a rock in the eye as kids. The first of them was told to hold his hand over the good eye first, so that he was rejected; the second read and memorized the next-to last line on the chart while the man in charge was fussing with some papers, drew the bad eye first, and upheld his masculinity by rattling off what he'd memorized before he was told to switch hands, oblivious to the potentially high price of salvaged pride and inclusion in the pool of the normal.

Sent to one of the posts paradoxically named after a general on the losing side of "the War", because the populace and their elected representatives would tolerate no reminder of either the victors or the ensuing occupation when new United States Army posts were needed in the South, Raymond and his buddies learned to soldier; to march, to shoot (Christ, they already knew how to do that, they thought). Learned the Army way, everything "by the numbers", and mostly to come to accept that life, what you did, and how you did it ("Men, there's the right way, the wrong way, and the Army way!"). When you did it, was dictated by the sergeants, no questions asked. Adjusting to some northerners who inexplicably were sent down by train and really had most of the adjusting to do themselves made things amusing, and since he'd been schooled to unquestioning obedience to his grandfather and father-- even when their instructions were contradictory -- the sergeant business wasn't all that difficult to deal with.

Basic training ended with a big parade, and because of his size, apparent soldiering skills, and whatever else they were looking for, he'd been singled out from the rest of his company, brought in front of the Captain, and told that he was being offered Ranger training. Raymond wasn't real clear what that was, but the First Sergeant's comments as he was being ushered in to see the "Old Man", led him to believe that this was an honor, that he really didn't have any time to consider the question, and that after the formality of exchanging salutes with the man behind the desk, he'd damn well better answer up "Yes, Sir, thank you, Sir," shake the hand if offered, salute again, do an about face, come back to the First Sergeant's desk, sign where he was told to sign, take his printed orders, get his barracks bag, and get the hell home for a few days leave that nobody else had before reporting to Ranger training. It sounded ok to him. The "Old Man", a Captain, thin, maybe all of twenty-six and relying on a cane seemed like a nice enough sort. He had the little orange "Ranger" diamond below the division crest on his left arm, right above where his stripes'd start if he were a sergeant.

Back in the company street on the way to the barracks to get his gear, he met his platoon sergeant, who filled him in. "Those Rangers," he said, "are hard men. They're scattered around in lots of units, and there's a couple of battalions they keep together, just in case there's something special."

5. LEAVE

He got home on leave and found that everyone was doing fine. The younger boys and his sister were working out on the farm after school, and the bees were settling into their late-fall routine -- pushing the drones out to starve and freeze at the first frost.

Grandpa spoke a great deal about Mosby's Rangers exploits during The War, but said very little about Quantril. Soon enough Raymond would learn about the Revolutionary War roots of the United States Army's Rangers, the Green Mountain boys from Vermont and the Southerners at King's Mountain, and how their style of fighting won the war, pressing the British back into the peninsula at Yorktown.

Leave over, headed south on the bus, he mulled over Grandfather's last story about Mosby. Seems he got through the war without serious wounds, went home and prospered but was driving a horse and buggy when he let the lines slip over the dash. Reached down to get them and the horse kicked him in the head, killed him dead.

6. RANGER SCHOOL

As usual, the Sergeant had been right. The Rangers were hard men, and their school made him hard, too, harder than the farm ever had. Hard in crazy ways like marching for days without sleep only to stay awake another half a day, waiting in ambush. He learned more ways to use a rope than sailors cowboys dared dream of. Everything was a weapon. The days began and ended in the sawdust fighting pits, and his knife became an automatic extension of either hand. He trained to work with others, but learned the certainty, too, that if he were the last man, he could move silently through the night, find his objective, and complete any mission. The Jody calls that they sang as they marched, though, never had any lines about coming back. The fiddler's green was not, apparently, part of Ranger lore.

7. RAYMOND TOLD FOLKS SOME MORE ABOUT HIS WAR

He didn't take all the stuff about the Germans in the Jody calls personal, it was just part of the rhythm of training. On the troopship and landing boat, he didn't take the little bit of extreme range machine gun fire that they fell under personal -- they were after the boats, not Raymond McCleary. It got personal later, headed up the ladders. No sonofabitch in a kraut uniform had sighted down a barrel at Raymond Lewis McCleary, but whoever was pulling the pins on grenades up above and holding them for a second or two to insure that they exploded along the ladder's length rather than down on the beach was after him.

The rocket men, who had been busy tearing the greasy protective paper off of their gear as the troops offloaded, pulled the covers from the tubs of light line set up to trail after each shot, used Kentucky windage to set the launchers' angle, and let go. Raymond glanced back into the troop well and could see that line unspooling like thread from a silver bobbin dropped from his mother's sewing machine to the floor as the men who'd just fired the rockets grabbed their weapons and leapt off of the ramp towards the beach.

First off of the boat, the men with London's ladders threw them against the cliff to see how they'd go. They didn't. The steep beach was so deep with pebbles that with every adjustment and every additional man's weight the ladders slipped hopelessly out of position and were abandoned as useless. Looking back on it later, Raymond wondered if anyone, perhaps the crew of one of the landing craft, thought to gather them up and return them.

As each line slapped against the cliff, several men grabbed the line and pulled, hoping to set the hook. In an effort to discourage German tampering with the hooks, they'd wrapped them with slow fuse, lit off before firing, so that observed on the ground the hooks were sputtering smoke and sparks, looking like they were something trying to explode. When a hook held, a climber started up. Some of the hooks slipped, sliding the climbers down the face of the cliff until the points grabbed some new, unseen purchase above; some of the hooks let go completely, but most held. The cliffs were, according to the maps twenty-seven meters high-- ninety feet. Where the hooks didn't hold firm but didn't come tumbling back over the cliff, a climber went up anyway, without much help from the rope, fingers and bayonet probing for a hold in the stone, feet scrabbling. A man getting to the top that way meant that the rope that hadn't been much help in climbing could be used to pull up a rope ladder, hooks set so that he was sure that they'd hold. When a climber hit the top he found out if he was lucky. Luck meant some cover from the machine guns, or at least concealment from the gunners. The unlucky hardly had an opportunity realize it, catching a round as soon as they cleared Fritz's horizon.

The fortunate climbers didn't unlimber their weapons, but checked their hooks, repositioning them and adding another if necessary, to insure that they'd hold the weight of more than one man. Keeping low, they hauled in the line that their companions had attached to a rope ladder that they hoped to ascend two or three at a time. Once he'd gotten the ladder up and secured to the hook, the climber lay down over the edge and waved for the number of men he thought the hook would hold at the start, spacing out the load and figuring that the weight of the men on the ladder would dig the hooks in more solidly. If the climber didn't make it back to the edge, another man went up; ready to signal once he'd got the situation in hand.

As soon as ladders rose into position, the main body of Rangers started up, every man slinging his gear the way he could climb with less impediment and start fighting as soon as he cleared the top. It hadn't taken the appearance of more than a couple of climbers for the Germans to understand that the unlikely assault was underway and start some rifle fire on the cliff top against the Americans, fire which was returned as the Rangers made it to the top, grouped into fighting units and started to move on the artillery emplacements.

The strongest resistance that they encountered was from machine gun crews positioned and dug in to protect the flank of the artillery position or to fire on the beach. The gunners were dug in, but dug in to protect against an attack from inland, with any fields of fire seaward directed at great distances, the source of the ineffective firing on the landing craft. So positioned, none of these guns were able to sweep the edge of the cliffs with fire, as the cliffs were considered sufficient protection on the ocean side.

Some of the German gun crews had moved out in front of their positions, exchanging small arms fire and grenades while their comrades struggled to reposition the guns. They were close enough at a couple of ladders that the grenades overshot the Americans they could see, sailed over the edge of the cliff and exploded on the way down, slashing some climbers with deadly shrapnel, and hitting all of them with the concussion of detonation. It became a grenade fight as the defenders realized that they were slowing the climbers and might even get lucky and sever the ladders. It didn't take long, though, as the danger posed by the Rangers became evident, for a couple of the heavy machine guns trained on the beach to be horsed around inside the bunkers and brought to bear on the ascension points. By the time Raymond started up it had been established which ladders could support the most men and get them off into an area not yet covered by a machinegun. Probably a dozen grenades went off above, below and beside him during the minutes of is climb -- his head rang and he could feel each detonation in his gut. Amazingly, the protective protuberances of the cliff were where he needed them to be and the vagaries of munitions manufacturing resulted in chunks of hot steel whose shape propelled them elsewhere, not into him. Not everyone was as fortunate. Climbing up meant holding on as men fell around him and working his way past the wounded, slowed or just hanging on in place.

Once on top he unlimbered his weapon, found a bit of cover, the looked for where he could be most useful. Smoke pouring from the nearest bunker showed that the deadly leapfrog of clearing the headlands had begun. Some small groups of men, having survived the ascent together, were, amazingly, functioning in their designated squads, moving forward by fire and maneuver. Others had, by virtue of their training, formed into equally effective groups, the sappers with their satchel charges working forward as the others provided the opportunity for advancement with bursts of fire and grenades. Some individuals were working their way along behind the German positions, turning their connecting pathways and bunkers into a surprise highway of death.

In those first moments, Raymond reflected and decided that his trip up the ladder was about like everyone else's. Not something he cared to remember, but he felt victorious, they'd achieved something that Field Marshall Rommel had considered impossible when designing the defenses and allocating his troops. He had to put the concussed blur of faces, names, and bodies behind him and get on with the mission. There was about forty yards to a spot from which the next bunker looked to be within grenade range, a little further to a nook from which a satchel charge could be flung. Raymond got several of his grenades out of the baggy pockets of his field pants and hooked them by their spoons on the top of his ammo carrier and caught the eye of a couple of guys behind the next outcropping. One of them had a satchel. The Nazi gunner at the next bunker had found it necessary to shift into an awkward, exposed position to get them under fire, but was brave enough to stay there, firing controlled three-or four-round bursts whenever he or his ammo man spotted a Ranger's movement or place of concealment.

Raymond signaled to the riflemen that he and the sapper were ready to try for a better position, closer to the bunker. The riflemen started some suppressive fire, trying to get the gunner's head down. Raymond and the sapper took off, heading towards the rear corner of the bunker from where they could skirt the edge of the German's field of fire and either get within hurling distance of the position or, if they were lucky, spot some weak point that would allow them to attack from behind.

8. CATCHING A ROUND

The climb had been arduous, but Raymond couldn't remember ever expending so much energy in so short a period of time as he sprinted over the uneven grassy ground towards the bunker, just a few yards behind the sapper, not even when he was twelve and the bull had got after him in the orchard. He'd made the fence that time, just barely, but this time the bull's horn caught him. Hard. The Jerry gunner wasn't a fool, knew that he had to brave the small-arms fire if he was to stay alive, and put his head up long enough to get off another burst. Just at his extreme left field of fire he saw two Americans pass where his aiming peg would have been if he'd set things up as a drill for his sergeant rather than having had to come crawling half out of his position to deal with the enemy who came from where it was supposed that they couldn't. He fired a burst and got his head back down. The first two rounds went harmlessly between Raymond and the sapper, the third, a tracer, caught him in the right thigh, hit the bone, and threw him just like that Holstein bull would have, spun him around, but amazingly just far enough so that he was beyond the gun's immediate traverse and depression. All the wind knocked out of him, he was flat on his back, looking up, when he heard the roar and saw the flame and smoke as the explosion of the sapper's charge flamed from the embrasure. The German machine guns were silent and the Rangers still coming up the cliff now had some room to organize and swiftly pass him by to move on the artillery positions.

9. HOW EVERYBODY ELSE UNDERSTOOD WHAT HAPPENED NEXT

The fighting part of his war hadn't lasted long. Hardly lasted all morning if you didn't count the part on the boats. The round had gone into his right thigh, struck the bone and probably broken it, and glanced off, exiting on the outside, up towards the hip. His leg and trousers were bloody as hell, but not getting rapidly worse, so he figured that the bullet had missed the artery. A couple of guys moving up pulled him up from his back against a hillock so that he could see what was going on, pulled the rags of his pant leg off of the wounds, and tied their three bandages as tightly around his leg as they could to slow the bleeding. They took his grenades and most of his extra magazines for the Thompson, figuring they needed them more than he did. Raymond felt weak and, never having had any significant injury in his life up until now, figured that he was justified in concluding that what he was experiencing could be called extreme pain. He hoped that no Germans showed up, and was real glad that he'd taken those grenades out of the pocket the bullet came through!

Not too much longer more Americans covered the headlands as the beach exits were cleared and fully-organized units began to both sweep inland and convert the backsides of the German line into defensive positions to be ready for nightfall. A genuine medical corpsman appeared, approved the bandaging job, and gave him a shot of morphine, using his index finger to outline a bloody "M" on Raymond's forehead so that they'd know at the next step along the line what he'd been given. The laying on of the finger made Raymond think of the time his Aunt had been real sick and the Dunkard preacher had come to pray and anoint her, using his thumb to smear what looked suspiciously like hair wax out of a little tin above her eyes. As the morphine hit, Raymond gave in to his fatigue, falling to sleep, thinking, oddly enough, of the chains of bees in his grandfather's hives, except that instead of individual bees making wax, it was a swinging string of orangeish ranger tabs strung along a cliff side ladder.

Before nightfall the litter bearers and another medic came. Another shot, another "M"; this time his last thoughts were of the amazing stack of thick steel spring leaves, like pages in a book, that made up the suspension of the Dodge Power Wagon ambulance passing in front of his eyes as he was carried around the side to be slid into one of the racks in the back for transport to the just-established medical holding area.

At the holding area, the triage officer saw that Raymond wasn't bleeding profusely, had some color and a pulse, and assigned him to that fortunate third whose duty was to hurry up and wait.

Raymond eventually got his turn on the trestles under the bright light. His bandages were cut away, his wounds debrided and evaluated; dosed with a sulfa compound minimize the chances of infection, he was re-bandaged, splinted in an effort to minimize the agonizing grind of bone on bone at the break, and tagged for transfer to a real hospital. Included in multiple rows of men on litters in a huge tent, he was sequentially visited by nameless men and women who, after checking the notations on the tablet strung around his neck and lying on his chest, gave him water and a little something to eat; checked to see if he corpsmen who had picked him up had missed relieving him of any firearms (Funny how careless they were at taking them away after months of counts and re-learning serial numbers as his unit's armament had been adjusted. It was all that the medical corps privates could keep up with to take 'em away, pull the magazine, clear the chamber by pointing towards a sandy spot and pulling the trigger, and pile them in a jumble on the ground).They felt in pockets for overlooked ammunition, grenades or detonators, and, finally, wiped some of the grime from his hands and face. He was in great pain, but able to raise his head and look around in the gloom broken by several lanterns fastened to the tent's poles, and realized that he was probably the least severely injured guy that he could spot. He had no clue what portent that observation held.

Sometime in the night they started moving guys out, each knot of medicos and stretcher bearers consulting the tablets to see if more pain medication could be administered, apologizing if it could not be, then up and out into the ambulances which growled down the track to the beach in jack-low. He was coming and going and couldn't make any more sense of what was happening around him until he realized that his litter was in the middle rack of one of the moving ambulances, the fabric of another bloody litter above him, someone moaning in the rack beneath.

The moments that he was aware of on the ship were much the same although the sense of movement was less abrupt, an awareness of the rack above him, of the sounds of his fellow wounded, and in the more confined space, the smells; bunker oil and smoke from the boilers, the sweat, dirt and cordite of the remnants of their uniforms (once onboard the orderlies had removed what excess they could, finally taking away everyone's steel pot),and more pungent, the smell of burned flesh and the acrid overtones of antiseptics as bandages were necessarily attended to even before the ship got underway.

10. PATCHED UP IN ENGLAND

Raymond couldn't keep track of the passage across the Channel. He was coming and going and just did recall the ships movement before the hubbub of docking and disembarkation roused him. The leaving of the ship and transport to an actual tent hospital, set up weeks before as part of the preparation for the invasion, was quicker than their embarkation. The medical staff was rested and efficient and he heard a mix of both American and British accents. As before, each team checked the boards on the men's chests, sorting and routing them accordingly throughout the rows of tents and duckboard walks. A couple of orderlies rolled his litter to his designated spot, removed the placard from his neck and hung it on a hooked pole at the end of a cot, helped him out of what clothing they could and cut off the remnants of the rest before transferring him to the clean sheets and, as best they could without interfering with his wounds, finished the washing begun on shipboard. Except for the dog tags around his neck he was naked between the sheets and under the blanket, which were rolled back away from his bandages. The transfer had been exhausting, and he had no idea what time it was, as his watch had been removed and put with his other personal belongings into the drawer of a small stand to his right.

The ward, if that's what you called it, gradually filled with such arrivals, and then men began to be taken away on sheeted gurneys on what seemed to be a more deliberate schedule. He looked left and right, hoping to at least make eye contact with his companions, but they lay silent, looking upwards. The main smell was newness, the clean sheets and blankets and the linseed oil odor of new tenting that hadn't yet taken much rain. Raymond, too, lay silent until he was aroused by two more orderlies who, apologizing that they were going to do this as easy as they could, moved him up and onto a gurney, grabbing his clipboard from its hook and returning it to his chest as they wheeled him off.

A short distance down the canvas corridor the front orderly backed open the double doors of what Raymond knew was an operating room, lots of masked people, men and women, a couple of whom took his clipboard, and bent over it in conversation as he was wheeled beneath the enormously bright overhead light, the Brobdignian cousin of some draftsman's drawing lamp. A couple of the faces mumbled introductions that he didn't catch except for the final comment "I think that we can fix you up." The gloved hands on either side of another mask and stocking cap brought a black cup down over his nose and mouth, and after a couple of breaths the lights went out.

11. HOSPITAL IN ENGLAND

Raymond awoke back on what he assumed was the same cot. Dim bare electric lights burned on a line along the top of the tent, there seemed to be a general murmur and bustle going on, and the canvas smell was now battling the odor of antiseptic. He felt down along his right thigh and realized that there was plaster from hip to knee with a long groove on the outside packed with gauze taped into place.

After a while one of the doctors came to his area and pulled up a stool. "Mate, we've got you as good as we can here. Your thigh bone is shattered, we lined up the bits the best we could, and opened up the path of the bullet to clean out the rubbish it carried in with it, including the remnants of the tracer round's pyrotechnics -- that's why the long incision. No going back to your unit. Another day and we should have you up on crutches, and then we're shipping you back to the states to let their orthopedic boys have another go at the bone. They'll undo whatever knitting it does while you're getting there and try to make you less of a long-term gimp. Congratulations!"

He was going home! A possibility that he hadn't considered, coming and going from the narcotics, a possibility that turned dark as he remembered the maimed veterans of his childhood, those from the first World War, and a couple from the Civil War, spending sunny days sitting on the benches at the courthouse beneath the marble Confederate soldier, eternally at order arms. What would he do? All he knew was heavy work, farming and some carpentry he'd picked up from his dad, building plank fence, building farm gates and helping to repair barns and chicken coops. He went out again after thinking that much through, not even sure that he'd thanked the doc for coming to talk with him.

He was in the same position as in the triage tent. Then he'd thought himself the least injured of those likely to survive without immediate intervention; now he was the best of the worst, as his new cohort included the survivors of the group that had been worse off than him and received field surgery. He could see, he could hear, though less well than before. He could get around on crutches, feed himself, and through the miraculous foresight of whoever had handled the plaster, he was able to use the latrine on his own!

Grateful for what he could do, for as long as his morphine-addled mind would allow, he played Red-Cross girl for the rest of the men, listening to their stories and summoning orderlies with an authority far beyond his rank of corporal when someone else was in distress. The medical staff found him at times amusing, at times helpful given the steady flow of new cases, and at other times distressing, ushering him back to his own cot when they feared for his physical stability or it became obvious that he was about to be overtaken by the burden of his own pain. It was a tent full of severely wounded men, where time was measured by the endless, cot by cot sequences of medication and dressing changes. As the time for the administration of morphine approached, any ambulatory men invariably found themselves headed back to their own areas so as to not miss a dose and then have to endure the returning pain as they waited to be caught on the makeup roster of those who'd been absent. This was a largely silent migration, as each man's previous dose was wearing thinner as his tolerance for the opiate increased and he was preoccupied with his personal way of coping, although there was always some grim laughter around the occasional soldier whose style involved a wry joke or mildly obscene reference to the approaching nurses. All that the grievously injured could do was moan as their morphia began to break. Forget the wisecracks; the lady with the morphine was everyone's favorite lady in the whole wide world!

Dressing changes were another matter. Medical doctrine required that their wounds be opened beyond their original size for cleaning, and then packed with antiseptic-laced gauze to heal from the inside out so as to leave no lingering pockets of infection. At least daily that packing had to be removed, the progress of healing noted on the clipboard hanging from the pole on the corner of the cot, any corrective measures taken, and the whole thing repacked and secured by bandages. Fast-healing tissue invariably adhered to the gauze, tearing painfully as it was removed. "Proud flesh" that wouldn't mend didn't stick nearly so badly to its covering, but it stank as it was removed, and even gentle cleaning with antiseptic-soaked wadding was agonizing. Dressing rounds were accompanied by those two competing smells, rot and remedy, and as the medical staff worked steadily down the row, they were preceded by a heightened sense of anxiety as they got within a cot or two of each man and followed by complete exhaustion, the last attendant of the team to leave wiping the sweat from the brows of those enduring what their recovery required.

There was a steady inflow of casualties and a similar movement to surgery and the post-operative ward. Those destined to recover sufficiently to return to combat were moved to tents in another row of the hospital's duckboard sidewalk maze to heal; those such as Raymond who would require advanced treatment were assigned to holding wards until a hospital ship was ready to leave for the States.

There were no other Rangers who'd made the assault in his particular medical holding company. In fact, no other Rangers from any battalion. His companions, pretty beaten up, were from all the beaches, some of the latecomers tankers from the beginning of the drive inland, where, until the GIs modified their tanks with forward-facing prongs made from remnants of the beach obstacles, the ancient hedgerows angled them skyward as they tried to nose through or over, exposing their vulnerable bellies to the cone-shaped German shoulder-fired rockets with an impossibly long name, made by stringing several shorter words together, all of which spelt bad news for those first companies of tankers unequipped to dig in and push through. Raymond did the daily drill, keeping his thoughts to himself, unsure whether they were waiting for a ship or the accumulation of enough wounded to fill it.

12. HOSPITAL SHIP HOME

Finally both of those conditions were met. At quayside were a group of ordinary-looking Kaiser-steel built liberty ship transports, modified as best they could be to accommodate the wounded rather than the hale, vastly fewer men per ship, and set up with rudimentary medical facilities and quarters for the medical personnel. The big, bright-red crosses on the sides made him glad that the submarine wolf packs of early in the war had, both reportedly and in fact, proven by the large number of fully -equipped American troops over here, been subdued. A couple of destroyers could be seen outside of the harbor, ready for convoy duty.

A reverse of the many ambulance-parades that had brought them here took them to their ship, the Harrison, presumably named after the president who got wet speaking at his own inaugural, took to his bed and died shortly thereafter. Hardly good medical precedent, but at least she'd made it over here and he, no sailor, assumed she'd pretty good nautical and military chances of getting home. Like the fruit on a banana boat, the wounded were the last aboard the transports, supplies and caregivers having loaded before them. Once all were on board they headed out to sea. Each man, still accompanied by the now-fuller clipboard which marked his sleeping place, adapted his hospital skills to their second long visit with the rolling sea. Medication rounds, dressing rounds, they continued just as they had on land. A few emergency surgeries, a number of new injuries from falls in rough weather, a couple of deaths, and they found themselves in Hampton Roads, just off Norfolk, Virginia, heading into the gargantuan naval base there to disembark.

13. HEADING FOR A STATESIDE HOSPITAL

No lines of ambulances at this point. They had spurs for the trains laid right on the pier, and the clerk at the bottom of the gangway verified their destinations and directed the litter-bearers or chairmen to the correct train, further breaking up the holding company, ending many of the friendships that had enabled men with tangible, visible, limitations as well as those limitations we all have to deal with to cope with their situation. The start of a new round. How many changes of buddies had there been? Raymond tried to remember. From farm boy onto the bus; from the induction center to basic; from basic to Ranger school; from there to his Battalion; from those who descended the cargo nets to those who survived the beach; the climbers from those on the beach; those who got to the top and those who didn't; the wounded in the three partitioned areas of the triage station; those within sight or earshot on the evacuation ship and the first days on post-op; those who could or would engage in conversation as he became mobile on post-op, in the medical holding company and aboard the ship. Easily a dozen, and now a new series of acquaintances had to begin, back in the states and far removed from forces that had previously aided their formation. Friendship was the right word for a few of them, mutually advantageous association in an effort to survive the circumstances a better term for most. The safety of being stateside took away one of the catalysts, and Raymond stayed more within himself, interacting with others only as much as was necessary to follow the drill, leaving behind much of his country-boy, hound-friendly approach to whatever circumstances presented themselves and beginning to relive those few hours on a June morning in France over and over in his mind.

Before he disembarked, the orderly told him that he was being sent to one of the newest hospitals, Woodrow Wilson, in Virginia's Shenandoah Valley, which specialized in orthopedics and head injuries, both of which generally required long periods of rehabilitation. He'd heard Grandfather talk about Stonewall Jackson's uncanny feats keeping the Yankees on the run in the Valley during the War, but had never even been to Virginia. There was an offshore wind as he was being transferred, a fresh substitution of sea air for the combination of shipboard and clinical smells that he'd become accustomed to. It brought to mind the instant that the drop of the landing boat's ramp had cleared the funk of fifty men crammed into its well, all too soon to be replaced by the sharp cordite smell of battle. What little he could see of the Navy base, endless ships of all sizes and states of repair seemed a diorama of the invasion fleet, frozen in position, no pitching and bucking, and any visible cargo nets strangely bare of soldiers.

The medical trains were short and got priority routing. He was on the Norfolk and Western line, constantly passing sidetracked coal trains headed for the Navy piers. They slowed only for the coaling towers and water tanks in Richmond and Charlottesville. The only patients (they were called that, now, rather than soldiers) who got there quicker were the critical cases, flown on Dakotas from the Naval Air Station to the airfield just north of Stanton, then ambulanced fifteen miles to the hospital at Fishersville, farm kids waving from barn bridges at the pilots, from the fields at the ambulance drivers, thrilled to get a responsive wiggle of the wings from the departing, empty planes or a honk from the driver's horn. It was maybe five hours on the train to Fishersville Station, an upgraded whistle-stop about a mile from the hospital. They'd left Norfolk late in the afternoon. East of the Blue Ridge Raymond could see and smell the piney woods, which were like home, but it was a night train tunneling through the mountain, a long stretch of smoke and real darkness, relieved by a clean farm smell once they entered the Valley.

A line of busses and new ambulances awaited them at the platform, full headlights burning rather than the blackout lights on everything back in England and France. They'd hardly settled onto their seats or into their litters before it was time to dismount.

Sorted, as always, by the clipboards around their necks or on their chests, they were escorted to the wards of the new hospital. The first thing that Raymond noticed was that the rooms were painted! Every military building he'd been in up to this point had walls showing the bare wood of the studs and diagonal sheathing and grey Linoleum floors. The cots were already made up with clean sheets and a blanket, a towel on the bed stand -- no need to deal with a supply clerk before falling in. Orderlies brought late hot chow; they ate, arranged themselves in the unaccustomed luxury, were given the evening allocation of pain relievers and fell asleep.

14. WOODROW WILSON HOSPITAL

Raymond awoke early the next morning, roused by the beginnings of hospital days that he'd become accustomed to, and got another surprise when he looked out of the window. This place was built to the same pattern as every other base hospital he'd marched by, but all of the buildings were brick veneer rather than regular-issue clapboard! He later got the word that the County's politicians had worked that maneuver, counting on a permanent postwar base or at least a re-usable, substantial group of buildings, when they negotiated with the Army, which was anxious to locate the hospital in a temperate climate with excellent rail connections with Norfolk and Walter Reed Hospital in Washington, D.C. This was the orthopedic section of the hospital, wards linked to their own surgical, administrative, and mess areas by long enclosed hallways. The head injury and rehabilitative portions of the place sprawled out elsewhere in the same fashion. There was a standard motor pool for the vehicles, but proof that they were now patients, not soldiers, no parade ground!

Probably because the chart said that his treatment would involve re-breaking the parts of his femur that had been knitting in the last month, Raymond was visited by one of the first surgical teams to hit the ward, x-rayed and scheduled for what they anticipated would be his only operation on the next morning. They didn't want the oddly positioned joins to become any stronger before they went in. His surgeon, a Dr. Hill, a Virginian from Wise County, way down near where the tail end of Virginia met Tennessee, was serious when he explained the plan, but otherwise jovial in his bedside manner. The word from the orderlies was that his Grandfather had ridden with Mosby, and that he was sorely disappointed to have been assigned to even a new stateside hospital rather than having been given the chance to prove himself as a front-line combat surgeon. Odd, Raymond thought, what some people want. In fact, Dr. Hill's heartfelt disappointment was that he'd been born in the wrong generation, unable to ride with Mosby.

It was a long day, as they'd forbidden him any solid food so that he would be at less risk of throwing up and choking when they put him under. He introduced himself to the two adjacent men, both infantrymen caught in the crossfire on the beach, both of whom were fighting deep infections that needed clearing up, or at least stabilizing before their bones could be worked on. He made one circuit of the ward in an unsuccessful search for another Ranger to talk to and then just lay on his cot re-living the morning of the invasion and the last month in his head. He remembered his Granddaddy's tales of how the Confederate surgeons had run low on ether, and considered himself blessed that this Army hadn't. He slept fitfully that night, dreaming of chains of golden bees, the men on the cliffs, and chains of orange Ranger badges. They came and got him at six the next morning, two orderlies, one white, one Colored, helping him onto the gurney, putting a strap across his chest and giving him his clipboard to hold. Headfirst, they maneuvered quietly through the ward's doors so as not to disturb the sleepers. Once they started rumbling down the hall's rougher, plain plank floor, the orderlies started talking, telling him about the weather, rainy, and giving him their opinion that his cutter, Dr. Hill, was the best in the place. "Good luck, man," said the Colored orderly as he backed into the OR doors and stepped away, relinquishing control to the gowned crew within.

More alert, rested, and determined to satisfy his curiosity than he had been before his surgery in England, he was able to roll his head from side to side and see more of the operating room than he had before. He recognized Dr. Hill's deep voice in conversation with another man, seated near some compressed gas cylinders and a console of valves that he assumed was the anestesthiologist, the big, overhead lamp, and a couple of nurses lining up the conventional surgical instruments and a number of others which looked, surprisingly like carpentry tools. He was rolled under the big light, Dr. Hill said good morning and asked how he felt, the masked man beside the gas cylinders said something unintelligible and put the black rubber breathing bag over his face, secured it with a strap, and the last thing that he remembered was seeing the gloved hand on the gas valve.

15. SURGICAL RECOVERY

Raymond awoke, exhausted, in a sweat, and in serious pain. When they'd worked on him at the aid station he'd still had the advantage of adrenalin and the two massive hits of morphine that the medics had given him. At the time of his surgery in England, he'd still had the tough body and reserves of a combat soldier and his tolerance to morphine had not yet increased significantly. The month of hospital life had softened him, and the standard morphine dose no longer did what it did for him just weeks before. He was exhausted, so weak that he could hardly move his head and his right thigh throbbed form hip to knee. A catheter led to a jug on the floor, and some clear fluid dripped from a bottle on the ubiquitous pole into his left arm.

Listening and eyeballing what he could of the room rather than actually moving his head to look around, he realized that he was not on the same ward from which he had come. He was in an iron hospital bed rather than on a cot, and there was some sort of a cuff around his calf and ankle connected to a cord passing over what looked like the coulter wheel of a John Deere plow, apparently fastened to a sandbag whose weight was calculated to keep his leg fully extended. It was peculiar, feeling one leg stretched tight and the other free to move about; it was peculiar feeling his urethra stretched by the catheter line, periodically feeling the flow of urine without any corresponding contraction of his bladder. That whole deal, he decided, was like being on a short rein with a ten-penny nail in an eight-penny hole! In addition to the pain, he felt hung over. Not the aching, nauseous hangover from too much liquor, but a kind of fuzzy disorientation and a real dry mouth.

Just then a nurse arrived with part of what he needed, a glass of ice water with a bent glass straw. He had a long drink, holding it in his mouth, savoring its comfort, and was about to speak when Dr. Hill appeared behind her. "Well, Raymond," he said, "You're bolted together now. While you were out we measured the length and angle of your left leg, then re-worked the way things had begun healing on the right so that when you mend you'll be in balance, 'cept for the weight of the wire, plates, and screws we put in you -- my advice would be to avoid boy scouts doing junk-metal drives for a while!" "Thanks, Doc," he replied. "What's the deal on this thing?" he asked, nodding towards the wheel on the footboard of the bed. "Just a rig to keep things lined up for a while 'till those bones knit a bit. You'd be too likely to shift them out of line if we let you gimp around in plaster the way you came in. Two weeks. Maybe four. There're some pretty significant gaps that have to fill in from chips and bits missing from the puzzle box." Four weeks flat on his back! Even as lousy as he felt that wasn't a pleasant prospect. It scared him to think of how weak he would be when he was finally allowed up. "You'll make it," the doc grinned, "lots of pretty nurses around here and top-notch rehabilitation guys once you reach that point." This particular pretty nurse, dark hair, brown eyes, wasn't saying much as she checked his bottles and bandages after the doc had gone, which suited him ok, as he was not feeling real conversational. He did learn from her that because most contamination had been dealt with earlier this place didn't subscribe so fully to the "heal from the inside out" philosophy as the hospital in England had, that they'd done a lot more internal stitching, matching muscle to muscle, layer to layer, and that his dressings included a number of little rubber tubes, drains for whatever wanted to leak out rather than having the liquid cause swelling that would impede his circulation and, in turn, his healing. She left, and he dozed off, thinking of what it had been like on the ladder.

After a couple of days he felt stronger and life on his back wasn't quite as bad as the prospect had seemed. The catheter had disappeared soon after he'd cleared from the anesthetic and his coordination was good enough to handle urinal, and his upper body strength was still good enough to assist the staff by pulling on a sort of trapeze bar above his head when a bedpan was in order. His bed was next to the hall door, usually open, and there was a window at just the right angle in the corridor that he could look out and tell that it was spring. A few days more and the drains stopped oozing, the vessels too small for the surgeon's cautery having sealed themselves off and his lymph system having re-routed itself through invisible channels. The nurses eased the tubes out, carefully but not painlessly. Throughout his entire ordeal he'd been surprised at his apparently high pain threshold. That was, he figured, relative, a matter of comparing each procedure with the immediate aftermath of getting shot.

He and a couple of others with wheels and ropes were the long-termers on the post-operative ward. The amputees were there either because the surgeons went into an arm or leg and found things to be beyond reconstruction and had to lop them off, or to have the oddly-shaped ends formed by battle wounds crafted into a form more likely to accept prosthesis. They tended to stay only a few days before being wheel chaired off to a ward of their own. He was, he realized, one of the prettier patients, not a mark on him that wasn't covered by the sheets. Many of the men had, in addition to the bone injuries that brought them to Woodrow Wilson, suffered severe disfigurement. The worst were the tankers, marvelous survivors of the explosive demise of their machines, but sad evidence of the little that Walter Reed could do to erase the damage done by the flames. Whenever he met one of them moving by his bed he always looked him full in the face during the conversation, but thanked his lucky stars as the other fellow moved out of sight.

16. OBSERVATIONS ON BEING IN A STATESIDE HOSPITAL

Probably the best thing about being in the states, in Virginia, was the regular mail -- delivery had been sporadic overseas. Even though given some priority as a morale booster, it still fell behind ammunition, medical supplies and food in transport allocation. There, too, had been the censors, a bottleneck on the progress of letters home and a frequent source of puzzlement to their recipients. Raymond couldn't imagine that officers assigned the duty enjoyed it, suspected, that it was often a game of puzzle creation played to make the time pass more quickly, and had no doubt that it was accompanied by the consumption of considerable amounts of alcohol. The men at the hospital were so far removed from knowledge of current troop movements and objectives that the command structure ignored regulations that were still on the books and didn't bother to cut up the mail. Letters back and forth from North Carolina only took a few days, and thanks to the Red Cross volunteers who made the rounds to help those who couldn't write or provide stationery for those who could, he wrote and received many letters. The news form back home was that although there were shortages and fuel rationing, the war had pushed farm prices up so that the family was doing well. They'd even gotten some unheard of price for the three lard firkins of rendered beeswax that had accumulated through the years! It was being used by the munitions industry as part of the compound made to waterproof cartridges and keep the brass half of packaged artillery rounds from turning green. As small farmers who'd made it through the depression, they were used to getting by with a minimum of store-bought goods, and compared to city people they ate like kings. There was nothing, too, keeping them from filling the Ford with gas from the un-rationed farm tank if they needed it for something important, like going to a distant funeral. His Grandfather had died while he was overseas, and his Father was slowing down badly enough that the draft board had deferred both of his younger brothers to farm. The bees had dwindled -- when Grandfather had passed his Dad either hadn't remembered or was too modern-minded to go rap on each hive and tell the bees that their keeper had died and that they needed to change their allegiance.

His weeks of traction passed pretty quickly and he was returned to the relative independence of crutches and a less intensively supervised ward. The x-ray films that were held up to the light for him definitely showed that the gaps connecting the hardware were filling, and now it was a question of building enough bone mass for walking without the support of the cement shell. He felt the effort of walking and the physical challenge of most any kind of movement. He'd lost his soldiers' strength before the surgery, and the long period in bed had sapped the upper body strength that had enabled him to crutch around the hospital in England, manage on shipboard, and circulate through his first ward in Woodrow Wilson. It took a few days of standing up beside his bed, sweating and straining for a few steps, then turning, and struggling back to collapse into a heap, over and over, all day, to get the strength back into his arms and shoulders. He knew, intuitively (unlike some of the patients), that the secret of crutch walking was in bearing his weight on the handles rather than letting his shoulders sag onto the padded tops. He soon got so that he could support all of his weight on the good left leg as he made the pivot, and considered himself independent when he was able to make it to the latrine and back without having to be rescued by an aide who noticed him leaning on a wall or collapsed, breathing hard on some vacant bed along the way. After weeks of the enforced intimacy and dependence of bedpans and urinal jars, it was a relief to return to participating in the arcane protocols of sharing a GI toilet; six stools three feet apart on the opposite side of the room from six corresponding sinks, a shower alcove with three heads at the end, and no partitions. It took a delicate combination of greeting, vulgar commiseration, timed eye contact, and studied ignoring of the other fellow, all learned in the first days of basic training, to make a visit that accomplished the job without discomfort on anyone's part.

Soon he was back to circulating around the ward, then wandering the long, enclosed corridors that connected them with the treatment and administrative areas. He was able to start taking his meals in the mess hall. Raymond was cordial with everyone, but still felt alone. Everyone had their story of what deadly or unlucky circumstance had brought them there, but none of them seemed to truly relate to what it had been like going up the cliff. He thought about it a lot, and dreamt of it every night, long, detailed dreams with falling buddies reaching out for him and the endless concussion of near-miss grenades causing him to writhe and hold onto his twisted pillow and blankets, just as he'd hung on and pulled himself from one rope rung to the next. Amazingly, though, the dream always resolved itself peacefully. Gradually all he could see was the twirling dull orange of the Ranger tab on each man's uniform, which transmogrified into a chain of bees and he was back home with his Grandfather, peeking into the hive, and able to sleep peacefully for the rest of the night.

Some of the other men were like him, obviously quietly staring off into their memories, but most of their accounts were of weeks and months on the line while he had only that one morning to deal with. It seemed like plenty enough for him, but at the same time made him feel a little guilty, like he hadn't made the same sort of sacrifice, and it for sure made it difficult to be the second or third man in a group telling his story. His constant inquiries turned up a couple of other Rangers, from other battalions, wounded as the fight had pushed inland and finally met the organized resistance at which the Germans were so capable, but none from the cliffs. As a result, while cordial with everyone, he was a bit reticent and at times felt very much alone.

He realized that there was something wrong with his hearing, which he had not noticed in the hub-bub of getting to Woodrow Wilson and when it did crop up he attributed it to the morphine, failing to consider that his proximity to so many grenade blasts probably equaled the cumulative effect of a lifetime on a tractor with a straight-pipe exhaust a few feet away and right at ear-level. His Father's years of noise compressed into an hour. He often had to ask people to repeat things, didn't catch comments made off to the side, and had episodes of ringing and headaches. At least he still had his ears; thinking grimly of some of the burned tankers. Those guys, he thought, were going to have a pretty tough row to hoe once they got home.

17. FREED FROM PLASTER AND MEASURED

At last the plaster came off. Doc Hill was there for the unveiling, and pronounced a success, slapping him on the back as he sat in the sawyer's stool, covered in dust. Grossly atrophied and scarred, his leg was clearly straight, with the right set so that his foot hung at just the same angle as the left. Hill whipped out a tape measure from the endless collection of medical bits in the pockets of his long white lab coat, pulled each leg out in a particular direction, measured and proclaimed them equal. The long laboratory coats, freshly laundered and starched to start each day were the distinguishing feature of the physicians -- lower beings, technical people and Medical Corps administrative types -- only had short white lab coats, and the docs seemed oblivious to their resemblance to Groucho in one of the Marx Brothers shorts.

The next step was physical therapy, twice-daily visits to a gym where the trainers put him flat on his back or on a stool and pulled his leg through prescribed motions so that the scar tissue didn't take over and limit his range of motion. They had him put his foot in a sling and pull against ever-increasing weights slung over a pulley, and took his crutches away and had him walk endlessly back and forth between parallel railings, constantly correcting him if he put his right foot down different from his left or used his back to throw any disproportionate weight onto his left side. It was hard work, painful, and difficult to keep a good attitude about the endless corrections and towards the men whose job it was to make them. After each session it was all that he could manage to get back to his area, collapse, rest, get chow and report for the next round.

Twenty, was, he thought, the wrong age to be learning to walk, and he rebelled against taking incessant orders from civilians, some of whom had come to their deferred calling even as their induction notices were in the mail. Again, the only thing that made it tolerable was the egalitarianism of injury and recovery. Just as at Ranger school, there was no rank insignia on the collar of hospital whites, and the captains, majors, and aviators were subject to the same, necessary, harassment as the privates, corporals, and sergeants.

18. READY FOR DISCHARGE AND LEAVIING THE HOSPITAL

With this regimen, Raymond improved with remarkable speed. Within a month he was scheduled for a discharge or reassignment physical. Few of the soldiers in bad enough shape to end up at Woodrow Wilson were found fit enough to return to duty except as training officers like his Captain in basic training, or those in arcane specialties like intelligence where a man with limited physical abilities could still do valuable service. There wasn't much call for busted-up riflemen, Ranger or otherwise, and Raymond got his final orders, the issue of a new khaki uniform with authorized insignia, his Purple Heart, and an award of the "ruptured duck" discharge pin, and a voucher allowing him to report to the finance section and draw a travel allowance sufficient to get him home to North Carolina. Frustratingly, General Bradley's new Combat Infantryman's Badge, was not authorized, as his first fight had been his last. An injustice, he felt, as lots of guys were walking around with them, unscathed, simply because they'd taken and returned fire from behind a farmhouse or barn on three different dates, although he didn't begrudge the award to the guys who'd had to fight in

North Africa, then moved on to France and Germany or Italy. His Battalion had been awarded the Presidential Unit Citation, a great honor, but only men currently assigned to the Battalion were authorized to pin it on.

The train schedules were posted at the Hospital, so that he was able to put together a route through Richmond and Danville to Greensboro, where he'd catch a bus out into the country and pull the cord to stop at the crossroads where he knew he could catch a ride -- figured it'd be more fun to just show up at the farm than to call ahead and raise a big fuss, interrupting a couple of day's work. After calling the stationmaster in Fishersville to make sure that the evening train was still scheduled and get an educated guess that there'd be a seat available, he went back to the ward and put his few belongings into the barracks bag he'd been issued when he picked up his new uniform. There wasn't much; the fatigue shirt he'd been wearing on the morning of the fight, a bundle of letters, a couple of books he'd kept because he thought the family might enjoy them, and a few British coins, his only real souvenirs of having been out of the states. The Brits were so short of materials that they hadn't minted any new coins since the war started, and the big copper pennies were worn almost paper thin, with just the vague silhouette of some old king or another.

He shouldered his bag, said "so long" to a couple of the men on the ward, and, ignoring a paramount rule of the hospital turned left down the corridor towards the surgery. Reaching the big double doors unchallenged, he brazenly tapped on the porthole window until Dr. Hill cursed and looked up from what he was doing to someone's left leg. Raymond saw the irritation vanish from the visible portion of Hill's face when he

recognized him, and once that connection was established, he braced his shoulders back and popped a salute, which Hill acknowledged with a nod, turning immediately back to his work. Raymond relaxed and
headed off for the Hospital's main entrance, where one
of the waiting drivers would give him a lift in an olive-
drab Army Ford equipped with, considering that they
were in Fishersville, Virginia, ridiculous-looking, unused blackout lights.

19. THE TRIP HOME TO CAROLINA

The Norfolk and Western combination, mostly
freight but with a few coaches, was on schedule, took
him through the Blue Ridge via Crozet's tunnel and to
Charlottesville on time. The benches at the Charlottesville station waiting room were pretty comfortable, and he dozed for a while. When the whistle of his
approaching train woke him, he made his way outside
onto the concourse. The porter put the step in place,
and gimping a bit at the unaccustomed and irregular
interval of platform, box, and car stairs, he boarded,
using the round-handled hospital cane to keep his balance. He, found a seat, pushed his bag up onto the shelf,
and showed his ticket to the conductor, who tore off the
stub for Greensboro, tucking it into the gap of the trim
on the edge of the shelf above Raymond's head so that
he would see it as he went through the car hours later,
insuring that Raymond wouldn't miss his stop if he
were asleep when they arrived.

There wouldn't be any siding stops, uncoupling
and dropping or picking up cars. The Southern Railroad's Piedmont was a regularly scheduled passenger
train, Pullman sleepers, coaches, like his, mail, bag-
gage, and dining cars, and a caboose -- no freight, alt-

hough it might pick up a private car for railroad, government, or military bigwigs on the run from Washington, D.C. to Atlanta and back. He was hungry, and as soon as they'd left the station he made his way back to the dining car between the coaches and Pullmans. Because it was late, there weren't many folks there and the Colored waiter led him to a table. Raymond couldn't remember having his feet under a table with a linen cloth since his last family dinner before leaving for Ranger School, and, amazingly, even though there was a war on, there were a few cut flowers in a vase in the center of the table. Even though he was still in uniform, he sure felt like a civilian! The roast beef was tender and affordable, and after a piece of pie he folded his napkin, settled his bill and headed back though the other two coaches to his seat, where a very welcome pillow awaited him. With nobody in the adjoining seat, he could stretch out diagonally, head cushioned against the window frame and his feet almost in the aisle.

As he had hoped, he slept through the night most of the way to Greensboro, aware when the train pulled quickly through a coaling tower, but not really awakened. The sunlight woke him just a few miles outside of the station, not enough time for a railroad breakfast, which was just as well as a diner near the depot or the lunch counter at the bus station would be cheaper. He looked around the car, noticing that it had become much fuller during the night's stops, and nodded good morning to those, who like him, had awakened. He grinned to himself at the strange postures, expressions, and noises of the remaining sleepers. The passengers were a mix of people, a few in uniform had battle ribbons and the ruptured duck, mustered out just like him, and others, mostly officers, without combat branch insignia, were probably between postings or on government business, likely procurement at the fabric mills, shipyards or arsenals further south. One grizzled Calvary Captain, Sam Browne belt and jodhpurs, had a set of saddlebags with a briefcase handle attached at the arch, bulging with papers -- old Army! -- God knows where he was going or what he was about.

Some of the folks looked pretty ordinary, cardboard suitcases on the shelf above their seats and greasy paper evidence of chicken or biscuits brought from home for their travelling meals. They, he reckoned, were headed for new jobs, new opportunities and probably different lives working in some defense plant or another. The one thing that struck him was that there were some women his age but not many men. The draft had gotten most of those, these fellows must have been the ones with flat feet, or who like his friend back home who'd been hit in the eye with a rock and had drawn the bad eye in his first look at the eye chart during his physical. He'd heard, though, that as the war had progressed that induction physicals were less thorough, the joke was that if the doc held his hand against your chest and discerned that it was warm and had even a quivering heartbeat that you were in! He, however, was now out. The train stopped and he got up, retrieved his barracks bag from above, and carrying rather than using the cane that occasionally was necessary to keep him upright and moving, he made his way to the vestibule at the end of the car. "Welcome home, son," said the conductor as he turned to the stairs, "Welcome home, suh," said the porter offering a steadying hand from beside the box step on the platform in case he needed it. "Thanks, Sir," was his response to both men. He made his way through the mostly empty station to the street, looked to his right down the block, saw the running dog sign of the bus station, and headed that way.

No diner between the depot and bus station on his side of the street, but once in the station the smells from the lunch counter were pretty compelling -- that roast beef had been a good may hours back. A quick glance at the chalkboard showed that he had plenty of time for breakfast before his local headed out beyond Guilford. He paid the stationmaster, got his ticket, and then turned deep into the coolness of the station. There was no one at the counter, he picked a stool about two-thirds down from the cash register, where the waitress was stacking a mornings worth of coffee mugs from the dishwashers carrying tub onto the back bar, stashed his barracks bag and stick at his feet, pulled off his over-seas cap and laid it across the stool before he sat down and swiveled around. Red-haired, young, and pretty, she swung around, put one of the still-hot mugs down in front of him and filled it from a pot she'd picked up from somewhere with the other hand.

"Milk and sugar?" she asked, smiling.

"Just black, thanks." A quick turn to return the pot to its hotplate, and she was back.

"I'm Sue. What'll you have?"

"Grits, toast, two eggs kinda hard, and some ham, if you've got it."

"No problem," she called over her shoulder, go-ing to the window to give his order to the cook, drop-ping two slices of bread from an already open bag into the toaster and pushing the handle down as she passed.

Back in front of him, her elbows on the counter,

chin cupped in her hands, she asked "what's the deal? -- home on leave?"

"More than that," he replied, tapping the duck in his buttonhole, "discharged. I got beat up at Normandy," chucking ,"and they said I could go home and join the old guys on the benches in front of the Courthouse," referring to the universal meeting place of gimpy veterans ever since the War.

"You're too cute for that," she responded, "and besides, you don't have the scraggly white whiskers!"

Not yet. Not yet, he said softly, mostly to himself, as she responded to the cook's bell and brought his food.

The food was good, the ham especially, sugar-cured, sliced thin, and fried, the first real ham he'd seen in years -- Army and hospital ham was from a can, boiled, sliced thick and never in its life anywhere close to salt, pepper, saltpeter, and brown sugar. As hungry as he was, it didn't take long to finish.

"Where's home?" Sue refilled his coffee for the second time.

"Out past Guilford." He got up, dug in his pocket for her tip, gathered his gear and moved on down to the register to settle up.

"Good luck with the home folks," she wished him well as she handed him his change.

"Thanks." he smoothed on his cap and headed outside to the white bench to wait for the bus. The early morning sun felt and he leaned back, one arm slung up on the back of the bench and watched the traffic go by, people going to work. No new cars, lots of bald tires, gas-rationing stickers on the windshields, and a good many people walking, both white and colored. He was still the only person on the benches when the bus rolled in, brakes complaining as it stopped. Several rumpled-looking folks got off, having slept on the bus in somewhat less comfort than he had on the train. The driver, forty-mission bus-company garrison cap jammed to his ears, climbed down, set a couple of suitcases and parcels out onto the platform from the mostly empty compartment beneath the side of the bus, walked around and smacked each tire with a billy club which he threw up onto his seat before disappearing into the station, probably to the toilet. He reappeared in a few minutes, hat now pushed way back on his head of grey hair, and stretched, steam coming off of the mug of coffee he'd brought with him. Looking at the empty benches, he shook his head and said to nobody in particular, "Company ain't makin' no money off this town this mornin'." He gulped the last of the coffee, handed the empty mug to the stationmaster who'd come out to stand beside him, looked at Raymond and said "come on, soldier, let's go."

Raymond climbed onto the bus, looked down the aisle, and realized that except for an old Colored man asleep in the back he was the only passenger. "I reckon," he thought as he settled into the front seat closest to the door, bag and stick beside him, "that the war still has more people leaving here than coming home." Heading out of town, he had a sideways conversation with the driver, pretty much a repeat of the one he'd had with the waitress. Before leaving the hospital he'd gotten those few lines together to explain himself, especially to people that he really didn't want to talk to, a group that included most everyone. About forty-five minutes out they passed the Post Office general store and Courthouse that was Guilford, and a few minutes later the battlefield itself, where Cornwallis and his mix of regulars and Tories had run off the American militia, still trying to fight like Europeans. Nathaniel Greene hadn't, apparently, learned much from the North Carolina Scotts' success at King's Mountain, and handed the British their last, pyrrhic, victory in the south in '81. A mile or two later he leaned over and told the driver "next crossroad's mine."

He thanked the driver as he got down; standing at the side of the road in the shade of the bus' silver flanks as it pulled off, then hit simultaneously with the morning sun's glare and the smoke cloud of badly worn piston rings, another indication of wartime shortages in the civilian world. Before shouldering his bag, he put on his overseas cap and tried, unsuccessfully, to use it to shield his eyes from the glare. Adopted, he assumed, because they provided enough protection from the sun for the top of the head to keep troops from falling out from the heat in long formations, and because, unlike billed garrison caps, couldn't be damaged when stuffed in barracks bags piled ten-high in a two-ton truck. They were, as Raymond had just demonstrated, completely useless for shielding the eyes, and were for that reason universally loathed by the common soldier. Commanders standing in review beside visiting brass disliked headgear that looked like what a soda jerk or hot-dog vendor would wear and whenever possible paraded the troops with rifle and helmet. Commanders disliked the look and disliked the inevitable audible curse and murmur from the ranks when circumstances or carelessness led to a formation called facing into the sun. The murmur was always obscene. "Cunt caps," was the barracks term. Any uncovered soldier who'd folded his cap in half and stowed it in his pocket crown first was subject to the ribald comments and intrusive finger-wiggling of the first passing jokester.

Squinting , he swung the bag over his right shoulder, gripped the strap like rifle sling, and set off down the dirt road straight towards home, holding the cane in his left hand like a British major's swagger stick, since it was too early the day for his   leg to be bothering him enough to use it. The mailbox and lane to the farm were about a mile and a half down the road.

Because of the glare he heard, rather than really saw the approaching vehicle, recognizing their pickup only as it slid to halt beside him in a cloud of dust and he heard his brother Charlie's voice hollering "Raymond, that you?!" Charlie flung the door open, engine running, jumped out and ran over and gave Raymond a bear hug. "Welcome home! c'mon!" He grabbed Raymond's bag, threw it in the truck bed, practically threw Raymond into the passenger side, ran around to get back behind the wheel, and twisted the truck into a gravel-slinging u-turn on the narrow road back to the farm. "The load of feed I was after will just have to wait. You on leave or out for good?"

"Discharged," Raymond replied, arm on the window ledge watching the familiar landscape go by. "They did the best they could, but I ended up too gimpy for them, no room for dogface soldiers with weak legs." Charlie turned into the lane and commenced laying on the horn, with the desired effect. When they pulled up into the yard, their parents and sister Mary were on the front porch, looking their way and William and Reba were hurrying from the machine shed towards the house, wondering what had prompted Charlie's wild, early return from an errand that he usually managed to stretch out until dinnertime, missing whatever work the others were engaged in.

20. ARRIVAL HOME

As soon as they got a glimpse of kakhi, Raymond's mother and sister flew off of the porch, yanked the door of the pickup open before it had really stopped, grabbed him, hugged him, their cheeks wet with tears. His father, moving like a worn-out machine, which he was, a worn-out farming machine, got there moments later, thrusting his calloused hand into the melee, "Welcome home, son." By then Reba had added her arms to the continuing embrace, and Will, slapping him on the back, kept repeating, "Good to see you, brother, good to see you!" The ferocity of his family's welcome stressed Raymond to the point that rather than carrying his stick, he had to use it on the way to the house.

After years in Army camps and hospitals, the house, fairly substantial by local standards, looked small. They went in, passing through the hall, ignoring the parlor, reserved for Sunday afternoons, visits from distant relatives, preachers, and for laying out the dead, and gathered, as had always been their habit, around the big walnut kitchen table. Raymond leaned back in the oak split-bottomed chair, sighed, and went slack all over. He was finally, firmly, home. His war, he thought, was now over. Little did he know that the far larger undertaking, living with his war, was just beginning. One of the girls put a big glass of ice water in front of him, he took a big gulp, and the questions began.

21. A FEW QUESTIONS AND A HOMECOMING LOOK AT THE FARM

"How's the leg doing?" was the first.

"Pretty well, all things considered. Lots of screws and a couple of other pieces of metal to hold things together. I had a good surgeon, y'all would have liked him, his Daddy rode with Mosby!"

"Your Granddaddy would've liked that," Father said, "He was right proud of your soldiering, especially the Ranger part."

"What I want to know," Reba chimed in, "is why you didn't bring one of those nurses home with you! Weren't any of them pretty enough?"

"I did fall in love with most of them," Raymond chuckled, although the images that came to mind were of the toughest of them, who looked like a couple of lady 'rasslers from the sideshows, "I guess that I just couldn't make up my mind." He didn't think that this was the time to try to explain the military caste system to his sister, how nurses were officers and didn't fraternize with corporals; that their caps were set for the doctors, not farm boys; how nearly impossible a connection with any of the English girls would have been; how doped-up and preoccupied with pain he'd been; and how even the nurses who kept up a friendly, flirtatious banter while doing their jobs had seen so many casualties, such grievous wounds, and so many bedside deaths that there was a barrier of self-protection just beyond their chat. Sometimes there'd been a spark between nurse and patient that burned through these barriers to romance, but it hadn't happened to him. "Don't worry though," he assured her, "I'll find someone here in the pines, sand, and red clay."

Charlie and William wanted to know about the battle. He gave them lots of detail about the ships, less about the beach, and just told them that he'd climbed like everyone else, the way they'd trained to do in the North Georgia Mountains.

"Well, did you kill any Germans?" they persisted.

"Not that I saw drop in my sights," he replied, trying to explain the tactics of suppressive fire and maneuver. "I'm afraid I only gave 'em about three bursts before they got me, gave the rest of my ammo to the other guys moving up. Enough of this," he forced a smile and rose from the table. "I'd like to get out of this uniform and see the farm. He headed for the stairs and the room he'd grown up in, William following with his bag. The working clothes in the closet still fit, smelling pleasantly of the house after their long sojourn in there, and his broken-in brogans, a bit stiff and dry at first, were old friends by the time he'd gone down to get his hat from the row of twisted-wire pegs screwed into a board nailed over the plaster inside the back door.

The shade from the broad straw brim felt good as they started towards the barn. He glanced over towards the lone beehive at the side of the lot, making a mental note to come back in along that fence. Charlie, William, and Reba, the farmers, were with him. Mary, who had gravitated towards running the house, helping their mother to keep everyone fed and tending to the canning, cleaning, and planning involved in running a farm household, had stayed behind. Their first stop was the machine shed, where he saw a second tractor, a worn but respectable McCormick-Deering on steel lugs rather than rubber tires, which used to belong to a neighbor, old man Elby Baker, who'd died last year.

"We've still got all three mules," Reba laughed, "love 'em too much to let them go, but we're not using them so much anymore, just for cultivating corn and such."

"Elby's boy Quentin come into quite a pile when the old man passed on," Charlie told Raymond what he'd already figured. "Been modernizing and updating all over." Raymond knew exactly what his brother meant. The Bakers, pretty substantial farmers in the area, had all been tighter'n the bark on a tree, and for the last several generations there'd been fewer and fewer children, concentrating the family's holdings on Elby, who did just that, holding them, but they'd been busted loose, now that Quentin had inherited.

"The old lugger's a pretty smart buy," Raymond observed. "Even though you have an extra gas ration for the farm, I doubt that the three of you could talk anybody out of new tires for the International," their only tractor when he'd left. "If you wore them down or hit a stump crazy you'd have to find somebody who'd rolled one over on a hill and broke both axles to get another tire!" The next spot in the shed had a new (to their place) hay baler -- another Baker purchase. It was a little Ford with its own Tecumseh single-cylinder engine with a heavy red flywheel sitting on top. That meant that it could be used with the old McCormack-Deering, which lacked the rear transmission power take-off shaft that powered more modern, powerful balers right off of the tractor.

"That Quentin's gonna save us some work, too," added William. "He got a new corn-picker and says he's gonna hire himself out to anyone who's interested." Raymond knew that they'd all be glad to be spared the hours of backbreaking labor involved in traditional corn harvesting; cutting each stalk with one of the ancient, forged, sword-like corn knives; building the accumulated stalks into large, free standing shocks, like Indian teepees in a row or the stacked arms of a British Colonial regiment; letting them dry in the fields; muscling the shocks onto the wagon, hauling them to the barn, pulling the ears and putting the fodder into the mow, and finally, in the evening or in bad weather, shucking the corn, so that it could either be fed to the hogs on the cob or cranked through the counter-rotating burrs of the sheller to make it ready for feed for the chickens and other livestock or be bagged for market. You drove a pickup parallel to a machine like Quentin's, catching the shelled corn as it poured from an offset chute. The chewed-up stalks, husks, and cobs were spit out the back and either plowed under to build the soil for next season, or you could scavenge most of it, running the baler real slow to give it a chance to pick up the stubble, care that didn't need to be taken with a nice, neat windrow of hay. Baled fodder was a lot easier to handle and feed, too -- like hay, the bales separated into six-inch sections, each the result of one stroke of the baler's ram, once the strings were cut. No more dragging cornstalks through the feeding room and shortening them with the guillotine-like blade of the chopping box before throwing them across the low wall into the mangers.

Raymond noticed a couple of other updates in equipment that he knew hadn't come from Baker's, a disc harrow, more efficient at breaking up the turned soil after plowing than the old drop-or spring-toothed styles adapted from horse and mule farming, and a PTO driven sickle-bar mower to fit the International Harvester, which had a lot more cutting power and a longer bar than the heavy old wheel-driven mower, pulled behind a plain drawbar tractor or a team. Leaving the shed, Charlie laughed "Old Quentin ain't a hunnerd percent for buying efficiency, though. He bought himself that last, slick-looking Studebaker pickup on the lot after the war started to drive around in!" Raymond made a mental note of that, as it meant that old man Elby's last purchase, a '38 Ford Barrel-Nosed pickup, might be bought. He still had all the Army pay he'd sent home to their mother to be banked, and two pickups would make the new style of corn harvesting easier. That, and the fact that he'd like to have a vehicle of his own, to go out and about as he wanted without having to ask permission or leave the others without theirs.

The barn and farm sheds looked about like he remembered them, just a couple of years more weathered, a piece of roofing tin here and there that had obviously been nailed back after blowing loose in a storm. The livestock looked well, the herds a little bigger because of the strong wartime markets. Sleek polled Hereford cattle, bred without horns, sparing them the struggling, sawing, and jetting blood of dehorning, and capable of producing twin calves which thrived on their good pastures and corn-finishing regimen just before market. Berkshire hogs, black with upturned snouts -- Grandfather always joked that you couldn't leave a good Berkshire boar in a lot without a shed 'cause he'd drown if it came up a good rain! Unlike some of their neighbors, the McCleary's didn't believe in the old adage "as happy as a pig in shit," and kept their hogs on good pasture, rather than in small, filthy, pens. The field had a shallow pond that they could use as a wallow to stay cool and discourage parasites, and true to their nature, they had selected a small area far from their feeding spot that they used as a communal latrine. True, the ground around the feed troughs and water tank was cut up by their hooves and muddy, but it wasn't a shit hole, and the health and productivity of the herd reflected that care.

On the way back to the house Raymond again found himself using the stick rather than swinging it. They went by the lone beehive, one of the white-painted ones from Dadant, and they seemed to be working pretty good, a steady stream flying out towards whatever patch of flowers was blooming, and a steady stream coming back, each arrival met by one of the guard bees, checking their bona fides as proved by the odor of the colony about them. Raymond knew that it wasn't as exclusive a club as it appeared to be. When there had been a row of hives, the one on the end nearest the fields always out produced the others as tired worker bees took advantage of the first opportunity to land and drop off their load, knowing the guard's tendency to be less selective when the arrival had full, golden pollen baskets on each leg! "You and Granddaddy were the ones who had the touch with the bees. Dad never has had it, and me and these boys," Reba gestured towards Charlie and William, "we just don't care to mess with them."

"I did clean those empty boxes and put them in the shed!" Charlie sounded a little defensive.

"Good that you did," Raymond replied. "Boxes don't seem to hold up outside when they're empty, which is kinda funny, since all of the wax and water-proofing is on the inside. Maybe I'll come out and look inside this one as soon as it warms up in the morning."

As they came back through the yard gate, Mary appeared on the back porch. "Dinner's ready. Get cleaned up." Charley turned the handle on the tin cistern pump on the porch for the others, who soaped their hands up over the metal sink beneath the spout, mostly used for washing vegetables. "GEM" was the trade-name spelled out in holes drilled on both sides of the hood of the pump that you could pull off to check the chain or peer down into the darkness to try to check the water level. Charlie was cranking slow, so as not to waste the rainwater, and the cool water came out in spurts as each rubber ring along the chain brought its little load up the tin pipe to flood into the box behind the spout. Dropping his hat and stick to the floor, Raymond cupped his hands and splashed his face, turned and groped, successfully, for the clean flour-sack towel that he knew would be on a nail halfway up the wall behind him. "Your turn," he said, pushing Charlie's hand off the moving handle and slinging the towel over his shoulder.

The kitchen smelled of fresh biscuits and boiled kale, and there was a big platter of sliced ham in the center of the plate settings laid out for them. They clattered into their places, sat still for a moment as their father mumbled the famously short grace that Grandfather had always used, and began filling their plates, passing biscuits and butter, pouring themselves cold, sweet tea and spearing slices of ham as Mary moved around behind them forking greens from the pot over their shoulders. It had been a long time since Raymond had sat for a meal where a prayer was offered, and he silently thanked God that his Father had adopted his Grandfather's brevity, rather than blossoming into one of those damned long-winded head of the table preachers that some families had to endure.

"You can't know," Raymond proclaimed his mouth half full, "how much I've missed real ham. By and large Army chow was pretty good, but what they called ham was some kind of pink boiled pork from a can without a hint of salt." Even a thin slice of it had to be cut apart with the side of a fork or a case-knife rather than easing apart along the gain of the muscle the way a slice of properly cured and prepared ham did.

"An excellent dinner, Mary!" Everyone joined with William, adding their assent.

"It sure has been easier on me since Mary gave up farming!" Mother leaned over and gave her a hug.

"Well," said Reba, putting down her napkin. "I reckon Will and I better get to the fencing we were gettin' ready to start on this morning when you showed up, and if Daddy goes with Charlie, they'll get back with that truckload of feed before supper. I doubt Charlie'd get done that quick if he went by himself," she laughed, "although he can be right particular about making it home for mealtimes! You've gotta be tired from travelling, so why don't you just take it easy this afternoon." Will and Charlie were working the farm, but it was clear who was running it.

Reba was right, he, was exhausted. He didn't want to go to bed so he settled into a rocker on the front porch, dozing in the shade. No idea how long he'd been asleep, he awoke to find his mother rocking in one of the other chairs beside him. "I'd made myself hope that you'd make it home, but the lists in the papers were so long that I'd also steeled myself to dealing with it if you didn't. Glad it worked out this way, just sorry that your leg's torn up, but we've been luckier than a lot of families."

"You're right." They sat without saying anything more for a long time.

"You're only twenty, but you're having to start out an old man, stick and all," she said, slowly shaking her head. "I doubt you're going to be able to farm any more than your Daddy does, and took him forty years to wear out."

"I know what you mean, Momma, I've lain for hours, days thinking on it, and what I've seen here just today tells me that although it's home and you all love me I'm not going to be able to fit in. the way the others have become accustomed to working, and I don't want to be a drag on them. The good times the war's brought for farmers won't last much longer, and while this has place supported a family of five kids through some hard times, it's never gonna support five families, and I don't think I'm gonna be up to the struggle to expand it enough that it could."

"Humph. Hell of a note. You're twenty. Not old enough to vote or buy government liquor, but you've been to war, shot, sent home crippled out of the Army, and decided after being home for six and a half hours that you can't do the only thing you know. One hell of a note," she said again, more softly, and in a thoughtful rather than an angry tone.

They rocked silently for a while longer, and Raymond dozed off again to be awakened by the sound of the pickup coming in the rough gravel lane. His mother was gone, and Reba's prediction had come true, Charlie and their father had returned just in time for supper, although Raymond figured that had as much to do with the old man's love of talking with whoever he ran into as Charlie's tendency to go slow on any solo job. He remembered the trips to town before he was old enough to be sent on errands on his own, when his father, seeing a neighbor plowing or mowing hay, would stop along the road and wait until the team or tractor completed the turns of the field, his father's friends pulling up to exchange news, lies, and complaints. Beyond a greeting, the men always talked as though he wasn't there, and keeping his ears open, he'd learned a lot about the community, farming, and how life got on. His Daddy always told him, "Boy, you got two ears and one mouth for a reason," advice that had served him well in the strange world of the Army, with its unknown customs and polyglot population.

Supper was a lot like dinner, but with roast chicken and dumplings -- Mary had taken a plump young hen behind the woodpile early in the afternoon. Reba and Will reported on the weak bits of fence that had been strengthened and those that remained, often described in connection with the escape techniques or proclivity to wandering or curiosity of specific animals. They all had a good laugh about one cow they'd had years ago who was an exceptional fence-jumper -- sort of like deer, except for her full udder rolling from side to side as she built speed for the jump across however many lines they contrived to put between her and her just-weaned calves. Grandfather had finally solved the problem; suspending an old singletree from her neck

with a milking-stanchion chain each year for the week
it took for the calves to stop bawling and for her to forget them. She couldn't quite get up a full head of steam
with a two-and a half foot piece of lumber suspended
from its central ring clattering against her knees!

After supper Raymond stayed in the kitchen,
helping his mother and Mary clean up and lay out what
they could in preparation for the next morning's breakfast. "This is," he grinned, "the first time I've washed
dishes since pulling KP," a regular duty in basic training and during the months his unit had waited in England for the fight to start. "All of those hospitals were
like living in hotels."

Their work finished, the three of them joined the
others on the broad front porch, Will and Charlie jumping up and resettling on the top step, leaning against a
post, so that all three of the kitchen crew could have a
rocker. Saturday night on the front porch, Raymond
thought but didn't say out loud. Some of his Army buddies would have ridiculed it as boring, some would
have equated it with hanging out on the stoop in their
city neighborhoods, and others knew exactly what it
was like because it was what they did at home, all
evening if they had nothing else planned, at least for a
few minutes if they did. It was where girls were picked
up for dates and guys looked over and rated by prospec-
tive in-laws, and the best porches had a swing for when
you took your girl home.

It was the last week of August, and everyone
was watching and talking about the hummingbirds.
Mary had gotten a feeder, a big red tin ring with four or
five tiny holes marked with yellow. You screwed it onto a pint canning jar filled with sugar water, turned it

upside down, clipped a wire frame on and hung it up for the birds -- the biggest damn trumpet-vine flower around! It worked like the waverers they used in the brooder house for chicks each spring, which looked like round glass cigar ashtrays which you held over a half-gallon mason jar and then turned over real quick, keeping them level as you set them on the floor. Water rose to the edge of the rim, and the vacuum created in the jar kept the water from running out but replenished the bowl as the chicks drank. The hummingbird feeder managed the same principle with its four tiny holes. Mary had hung it from a hook originally put under the edge of the roof for a hanging plant and it had been a great success all summer. Now, in the weeks before the birds migrated south to Mexico and the Caribbean, they were a circus! No sooner would one hummer settle on a perch for a couple of sips than another would zoom in, rousing the first for a three-dimensional contest of dominance to determine who could drink.

"Bunch of damn fools," Daddy observed. "If one just sat on each side, all four of 'em could eat, but no, everybody's got to show who's top dog -- lotta people like that, too, unfortunately." The birds seemed oblivious to the watchers, flashing within inches of their faces as each new arrival used his momentum to startle the eater and pull rank.

"Good thing we don't have to farm humming-birds," Will laughed as he got up from the step. "The day's long enough without having to keep track of stock that mobile! It's a bath and bed for me." It had grown dark enough to slow the show, and Mother followed Will inside.

"Guess I'll slip out by the barn lot and check the

gates," Charlie mumbled as he got up and shambled across the yard, leaving Raymond, Reba, and their father in the gathering darkness as the stars came out.

22. DARKNESS ALLOWS FOR STRAIGHT TALKING

"You did a pretty good job of sidestepping the boys, yesterday, when they asked you what it was like."

"Yup," their Father agreed with Reba. "I certainly remember what the more honest old men said about the War."

"Yeah, I guess I did," Raymond admitted. "It's hard to think about, to remember, much less talk about, but I'll tell you two what I can until it gets rough enough that I have to wait 'till later."

"Fair enough."

"Once they taught you how to march, necessary to move the heard around, almost all the training was focused on killing, one way or another. The Ranger course was killing up close and personal, but at least it had some element of doing what was necessary to survive and complete the mission. Nobody ever talked about what came next. When I climbed down the net onto the landing boat, I just figured that I was a walking dead man and would just do my job and look out for my buddies. Wading ashore was like super slow motion, because of the water resistance on your clothes and all of the extra equipment. As a climber, I was loaded relatively light, a rope coiled behind my shoulders which probably would have given me a little more buoyancy if

I'd hit a deep hole. A hole, unseen under the water, and the poor son of a bitch in a regular infantry unit on the main beaches with a mortar baseplate on his back was gone." Raymond paused a minute. "I thought being a country boy, used to butchering, that blood wouldn't bother me. But it's different sprayed all over you from the next man, the man hanging on a ladder next to you, who could 'a been you, hit halfway up. It's not like sticking a hog and then jumping away, not like scrubbing down the trestle boards from cutting meat after killing hogs when you're fighting to hold onto the rope to climb and it's slick and wet and still bright red." He paused again. "The climb was the worst, physically tough after the surf and the beach, and you were like ants in a row going up a branch for a peach, no, more like cattle in a chute, the guy above moving too slow, the guy below cussing and pushing your ass. Once the Germans realized what we were up to, they started tossing grenades over the cliff. If you weren't blown off by the metal, your head was ringing from the concussions so that you could hardly think. Those bastards up top had to have been pulling the pins and then counting the seconds, 'cause the grenades didn't fall far before they blew. One, I know, went off right at my level, but just at that instant somebody fell between, catching the frags rather than me. If he wasn't dead when he lost his grip, he sure was when he hit bottom. As soon as a few guys got up top, the grenades stopped, but the Germans were hustling to try and move their machine guns up to the lip of the pits, which wasn't flat and had a corner they had to clear to get us into the line of fire. Those guys were fighting, getting right out of their concrete and sandbag coveralls to try and stop us. We were moving up on them when they got off the burst that hit me, one of our guys got them with a satchel charge bfore they got off another. That was pretty much my war. The next two guys along bandaged me up and I gave all but one magazine and all my grenades to others as they moved up. Eventually a medic showed up; tightened the bandages; told me that since I'd lived that long, the round had missed the artery; and gave me a big shot of morphine, putting an "M" on my forehead with his bloody finger. Before the morphine hit I remember thinking "I've been marked with the blood of the lamb, death pass me over." After that all I remember is bits and pieces, even from the hospitals." Reba got up gave him a hug and a kiss on the cheek -- he could feel the tears on hers. His father reached over silently and firmly grasped his hand.

"Funny thing," he mused, "when I'm going to sleep or when I dream, it's either about the ladder on the cliff, or about the hanging chains of bees that Grand-daddy showed me as a kid, one hanging off the other making wax for the combs. 'Golden chains', he called them." Raymond got up and headed inside, thinking but not speaking, I hope it's the bees tonight.

Raymond went down the hall and to the left to the bathroom; a surprisingly large room built into the crotch of the "L" of the house when toilets came in-doors and bathtubs grew claw-and-ball feet and left the kitchen. He'd dug his Dopp kit out of his barracks bag and stashed it there earlier in the day when he'd wanted his hairbrush. Their bathroom arrangement was much more convenient than most folks, who'd sacrificed a pantry opening onto their back porches, fine in the summertime, but reminiscent of the old days in the depth of winter, making the frigid transit from the kitchen door, past the cistern head, to the oil-heater comfort of the cramped but comfortable conversion. He dug out his GI toothbrush and scrubbed away looking past his own reflection around the room. A country bathroom, but sure fancier than what he'd been used to in the Army. White wainscoting chest high around the walls, claw foot tub, nickel plated brass towel rods, a glass shelf under the mirror with a German-silvered glass holder at each end and a toilet roll holder that reminded him of a show horse's bridle and bit, curvy sides and round cheek plates at each side of the roll. Finished, he put out the light and headed back down the hall and up the creaking stairs to his room. Shutting the door to the hall behind him, he stripped down to his skivvies, hanging his pants and shirt on the bottom bedpost, shoes and socks at the ready beneath. Switching off the overhead light by the door, he went over to the window and gazed at the stars, dominated by the bright swirl of the Milky Way, then turned, pulled the covers down and slipped between the sheets.

It'd been a long time since he'd slept in a room by himself! The smell of the house and bedclothes became increasingly familiar, and despite the afternoon naps he drifted off to sleep quickly, reassured by the creaking of the cooling tin roof and framing. He was lucky. Tonight it was the bees.

23. CHURCH FOR MOTHER

Sunday came bright, with the sounds of the livestock coming through the open window and the smell of brewing coffee coming up the stairs and under the door, which got him up, dressed, and down the kitchen in pretty good order. Everyone else was at the table, the few Sunday morning farm chores done, some still eating, others just sitting there, elbows on the table, savoring their coffee. "Raymond," Mother said, "I want you to wear your uniform to church this morning." He'd figured that was coming, and had resigned himself to both going and putting on the uniform one more time before, stripped of its patches and insignia, the shirt became a shirt, the khaki pants something better than overalls to wear to town, and the brown shoes, well, just another pair of brown shoes. He realized that the request was due more to his mother's desire to show him off to the church ladies than her concerns about the salvation of his immortal soul. Mother was a practical woman who'd uncomplainingly accepted his father's gradual rejection of religion and church-going, except for funerals, generally got Will and Charlie to accompany her -- they went more to jaw with their friends as folks milled about after the service -- and had no difficulty getting the girls to go, since they liked the opportunity to dress up a bit and socialize. She, very much like he himself, wasn't fully sure where he now stood on religion, although from his letters suspected that he was headed into his father's corner.

Breakfast over and things cleaned up, they bustled around getting ready to leave on time. He didn't protest when she insisted that he go back upstairs and pin on his actual Purple Heart in place of the small horizontal ribbon that correctly identified him as combat wounded on any but the most formal occasions in a dress uniform that he did not possess. By that time the ladies all had their hats in hand, ready to pin on as they neared the church, and Charlie had bought the Ford from the shed, where they kept it under a sheet to protect it from the marks of chickens, guineas, and pigeons.

They all crowded into the old sedan, boys in the front, Raymond by the passenger door in deference to his leg, and Mother between the girls in back, one foot on either side of the driveshaft hump, not very ladylike, but completely unobservable. Charlie kept his speed down, minimizing dust and bumps but going fast enough past the farming fields and woodlots that a cooling breeze filled the car, especially when they happened to be in a dark tunnel of shadow when there were tall pines on both sides of the road. After about twenty minutes they arrived at the white clapboard crossroads church, with its protective grove of trees and cemetery surrounded by a cast-iron fence that had thus far survived the patriotic fervor of the constant scrap metal drives -- country people are particular about how their dead are kept. Even the scattered small family plots of long-extinguished families were cleaned by the land's current owners on Decoration Day and kept fenced from the cattle. Some of the Colored people had their own style of grave decoration, with dishes and other talisman. Most of the graveyards had daffodils, periwinkle, 'cemetery plant', and the odd rosebush. Anyone, White or Colored unfortunate enough to have to bury on low ground covered each grave with a carefully arched concrete slab so that there'd be no 'floaters' when a hurricane's rain supersaturated the ground and allowed a box to rise. None of them could either foresee or imagine the widespread desecration of the small plots that would occur with the coming of big-field, big-tractor farming in the next decades.

Charlie, carefully gauging the sun's path for the next hour and a half parked among the trees in a spot that guaranteed them a cool car as they started home. They got out, the ladies fixing their hats for each other and Will and Charlie each tanking a turn stooping down to the driver's outside mirror to straighten their ties and slick their hair. Raymond took a turn, too, out of uniform without an overseas cap.

From Raymond's point of view, the car had been plenty crowded enough, six people sitting on top of each other. Looking over at the people milling around outside the front of the church as they approached, he knew it was going to get a lot worse, sensing individuals and small knots of people who'd seen them drive in or looked up and spotted him starting to move in their direction. Maybe three dozen people or so, but it was a crowd to Raymond. Everyone was nice, solicitous as to his condition and saying "welcome home!", but they all crowded close, pumping his hand, touching his shoulder or slapping him on the back. Will, Charlie, Reba, and Mary got pushed away, and only Mother's grip on his left arm kept her nearby. He was embarrassed by all of the attention, by his awkward gait and awkward responses to the welcoming jabber. All of it was taking him, unpleasantly, back to the hours waiting on the crowded landing ship, making it that much more difficult to smile and respond appropriately. He was sweaty and tense, looking for an escape. Fortunately, the bell in the steeple began to ring. Those on the outskirts of the crowd closest to the church turned and headed in, and the rest stepped back, clearing a path for mother and son, followed by sisters and brothers.

Things got easier as they went in. Mother paused, pointedly, and removed the small, red-edged banner with blue star in the center signifying his service, from a line of banners, one on each coat hook along a good portion of the wall. A couple of them, he noted sadly, had gold stars rather than blue, indicating a son's death. Spread out in the church, the crowd didn't seem as bad. They had most of a pew to themselves, lots of wiggle and stretch room. The service started like usual, got about halfway through the first prayer and, sonofabitch, the preacher let loose with "We thank thee, oh Lord, for the safe return of our son, Raymond McCleary from his heroic action in France and his long recovery from the wounds he suffered there for our behalf," then took a breath and went on to praying about something else. Raymond felt himself blushing from his forehead to his toes, thankful that at least most of the adults would be following the rules, head bent, hands in their laps, with only the children sure to be staring at him. He didn't catch the preacher's message that morning, his mind wandering as he looked up at the angles of the varnished car-siding ceiling that acted as a sounding-board, mellowing the congregation's singing. He noted the patch where, one Sunday, just as people were starting to file in, the bell's clapper had come loose and crashed down, leaving a perfectly round hole above and a deep, hemispherical dent in the rail at the end of one of the pews. He, like most everyone else, was dealing with the heat by slowly flapping one of the funeral-parlor cardboard fans stuck in the hymnal racks on the back of the pews, picture of a blond, blue-eyed Jesus praying in the wilderness on the smooth front side, and the business particulars of the undertakers split in half by the thin wooden handle stapled to the back. He got to thinking how and when he'd heard God mentioned in the last few years. His amazement at the continual and endlessly creative blasphemy of the Drill Instructors, contrasted with the patriotic platitudes and exhortations of the militant chaplains during the formations prior to the invasion; the murmured prayers of the soldiers on the landing craft; the screams of the wounded on the battlefield; the cries of men in the aid stations and hospitals; and the exhausted compassion of the combat and hospital chaplains trying to ease the dying and reconcile the survivors with their new reality. The preacher hadn't a prayer of pulling Raymond from those thoughts into his North Carolina sermon, no matter how well prepared and rehearsed.

The service over and benediction said, people shuffled slowly out into the vestibule, out the one open door into the sunlight and down the steps to shake the preacher's hand and socialize a bit before heading home to dinner. He couldn't remember the other door, the one closest to the narrow steps leading up to the small gallery, ever being opened, as none of the Colored people of the community, for whom the door and galley had been included in the church, which was built right before the War, ever attended services other than an occasional funeral or wedding, when they sat in the back pew. People came over to speak briefly with Raymond and his mother tactfully guided him to the gold-star parents so that he could pay his respects. Will and Charlie, along with their friends were busily chatting up some of the younger girls, but Raymond stayed with his mother while Mary and Reba flitted through those who weren't rushing home for dinner. Raymond might have joined in his brothers pursuit of the ladies, but during breakfast and while getting ready for church, his sisters had given him the low-down on all of his old classmates and the girls a year or so older or younger; who was married to, engaged to or waiting for a soldier; what advantageous matches had been made among the more prosperous farming families; who'd moved up or down in society due to an unexpected wedding followed by a kid with "hot feet"; and who was simply gone, away at college or gone to the city following the lure of defense work and the broader horizons that offered. There weren't many desirable choices left for him on the local scene, and he couldn't spot any of them on the lawn or under the trees. The couple of years after graduation always thinned the field, but it seemed like the war had accelerated the process.

Charlie took a different route home, going by the Baker place. Prominent at the mailbox was a sign with Quentin's name and the trademark of the biggest manufacturer of modern milking equipment -- his big wager in the success of the expanded dairy herd. The new milkers helped; there was no doubt about it. You could milk a lot more cows if you just had to wash udders and rinse teat cups as you moved down the line, but you still had to collect the containers when they filled and empty them into cans, then when the can was full haul it to the cooler, wrenching your back out as you hoisted it over the edge and into the pool of chilled water!

Raymond saw the nose of old man Elby's pickup behind a half-closed shed door and enough vegetation to know that it hadn't been out since the Studebaker came home from the lot. He was going to have to stop in at milking time and admire Quentin's new setup. When they got home Mother, accurately surmising that this would be the last time she saw Raymond in uniform, dug the Kodak out of a cupboard and posed a series of shots on the front steps, each taken by a different family member so that there'd be sure to be a photo of him with everyone. That accomplished, it didn't take long for all them to get out of their Sunday clothes and into easier everyday duds, although they did a little better than the most worn, just in case someone came visiting during the afternoon. When cold chicken salad appeared on the table, it became apparent that Mary had done in more than one hen the day before. It was a good dinner, ready just a short time after they got home, and light enough that they didn't feel stuffed, as they'd not been working all morning. After the dinner things were cleared away, they drifted apart, each finding a good spot to nap, read, or like Father, just sit on the porch and rock, enjoying looking out over the farm, seeing the landscape that each of them could walk without stumbling, even on a night with no moon, but didn't consider as a whole when focused on everyday tasks. Raymond ended up on the porch near his father. "Our people haven't had this place too long," his father observed, "but I reckon there's been a heap of people live and die here since the earliest times. Those two even rows of cedars there," he gestured towards the pasture, "they've gotta be where there was a road or a lane, although I'm damned I know when, or where the house was, a cabin, most probably"

"Yep, there's a lot of things we'll never know," Raymond replied, thinking to himself not about the rows of cedars, but of who got killed on the beach instead of him, and his Ranger buddies, no doubt pushed on into the next fight a day or so after the beachhead was established, and wondering who was still alive.

24. SEEING THE MODERN WAY AND BUYING A TRUCK

Raymond, had, upon joining the Army, authorized an allotment of twenty-five dollars a month from his thirty-eight dollars pay to be sent to his mother. When he was sent overseas, the government matched that amount. When he made corporal, his pay went up a few dollars and he increased the amount. Realizing his complete incompetence at cards, he, unlike, many of his companions, didn't enrich the barracks sharps, and although he enjoyed an occasional beer in the Enlisted Club's tent, especially when in England, and followed the expected young man's rites of passage, he never was

much for drinking and whoring -- not that many opportunities had presented themselves. He'd only had a few
passes to the parts of town outside the stateside bases
which catered to soldiers' wants and needs, and once in
England found his unit strictly sequestered, first training endlessly on the closest match the Brits could find
of their objective cliffs, then the cargo nets and dry land
mockups of the landing craft, then practicing transfer
from ship to boat and eventually wading ashore on
some deserted English beach. Those practices were only days before the invasion, and everyone, even the officers, were confined to the Battalion area lest word get
out into the civilian world, risking a tip-off though
some pub companion to the Germans. Once wounded,
his need for cash was even less, and he sent all but a
few dollars home to North Carolina, writing to his
mother to use it as she saw fit. She did spend a few dollars here and there when cash-money emergencies such
as a tractor part or refrigerator came up before a crop
came in, but mostly she'd banked it for him, ignoring
the posters urging the purchase of war bonds, and he
came home to an accumulation of something over a
thousand dollars. The next time someone went to town,
he went along, stopped at the bank, and got some cash.
The next morning, abut nine-o'clock he drove over to
Quentin Baker's, figuring that he would have finished
milking by then. He'd figured right. As he pulled in the
lot between the house and barn, Quentin was just coming out of the dairy shed, drying his wet hands on his
pants.

"Hey, Quentin!" Raymond hollered as he got out
of the pickup, "looks like you just finished cleaning
up."

"Yup. Come on in here and let me show you this

setup." They stepped into the milk house end of the shed, the clean part, separated from the cattle by a railing and drop-off in the level of the concrete, which sloped away from the door so that it could be hosed down. Raymond recognized the air pump and lines provided the power that squeezed the rubber business ends of the milkers; there were six stalls for the cattle, a feed bunk in front of each; and every two stalls were divided by an alley way, slightly elevated from where the cows walked, with a few steps and a rail coming up to a gap in the milk room rail. Each alleyway had a sink with hot and cold water just the right size for disinfecting the milker heads and teat cups between cows. The milker set each new cow up with a pail as her opposite, across the alley was finishing, stepped up towards the milk room floor and emptied the milker's bottom pail from the first cow into the waiting can. The man who kept things moving up top rolled the full cans on their bottom rims over to the water-bath cooler, slipped double hooks under the handles, and was able, with a chain hoist rolling along a pivoting steel beam, to lift the forty-gallon cans over the belly-high rim of the cooler with one arm. The alleys had warm water in counterweighted hoses that the milker could reach up and pull down to wash udders and tits, and clean, dry wiping towels draped on one side if the milk room railing and a tub to thrown the used ones into behind the rail on the other side of the steps. No milking stools, no buckets. A big sink in the milk room for cleaning milker cans -- no trips to the kitchen up at the house -- an overhead hot water hose for flushing out cans back from the dairy, just in case those guys had done a sloppy job on one before it was returned, and a narrow porch with an old aluminum-tubbed wringer washer and several clotheslines for tending the towels. Just off the milk-room, there was even a lavatory with a flush toilet!

Quentin explained that the floor of the milk room was calculated to match the height of the big truck from the dairy next to the tracks in Greensboro, so that unloading the cooler was more of those one-arm zips with the chain hoist and rim rolling onto the truck rather than the gut-wrenching heaving and hauling of an old-fashioned hand milking operation run out of whatever combination of sheds and stables happened to be in place on a farm. There was an odor of disinfectant lingering from Quentin's just finished work. "I'm milking thirty-six head with two other men," he said proudly. "Ought to have a couple more coming fresh next week and all of it without breaking my back. The truck comes every two days to empty the cooler tank."

"Right good setup," Raymond said as they went back outside.

"Good to see you home." Quentin launched into the pretty much set list of questions about his injury and the war that Raymond had become accustomed to whenever he had first ran into someone he knew after getting home, and he gave his standard set of answers, enough to settle people's curiosity, but not enough to touch the most painful memories and set him brooding over them for the rest of the day. By and large, people sensed his reticence and were decent enough not to press him further.

"I wanted to see you and your new equipment," Raymond took over the conversation as they stood in the comfortable morning sun," but I also wanted to see if you'd be willing to part with your Daddy's old pickup -- it'd be a help to everybody over at our place if I had my own vehicle."

"I reckon I'd let it go," Quentin replied, laughing, "You can see from those weeds in front that I ain't been using it much." As they walked over to the shed Quentin told Raymond that his father had paid right around six hundred for it, new, in '39, a '38 left on the lot when the new models came in. When they got to the shed to look at the odometer and see how many miles were on it, it was apparent that when he'd backed it in, Quentin had forgotten to close the window, that his rooster had taken to sleeping on the steering wheel, and that the driver's seat was full of chicken shit. Chicken shit was a powerful offset against low miles. Quentin was kind of embarrassed to dicker, standing there looking at it, and they agreed on a price a good bit lower than Raymond had expected. Raymond counted out the cash on the hood while Quentin leaned on it with both hands, wrote out a bill of sale good enough for Raymond to prove ownership and get the tag transferred on a page of a fertilizer company notebook he had in his pocket, tearing the page out real slow and careful so that it didn't rip and he wouldn't have to write it over again. "I'll get Will or Charlie to bring me over later to get it," Raymond folded the paper into his wallet as Quentin re-counted the bills into his.

"Fine, if I'm not around no need to find me, just drive it off, I don't think you'll have any trouble getting her started." They shook hands again, and Raymond headed on home for dinner laughing to himself. Chicken shit!

His account of the morning had everyone around the table at dinner laughing. "I gotta see this," Reba insisted, "before you move the mountain. I'll take you back over there soon as we finish!" Prepared with a couple of old feed sacks to improve the seating, they did just that. Reba laughed 'till the tears rolled down her cheeks as Raymond used one sack to break the great pyramid apart and slide it out onto the dirt, then folded the second over the residue. They'd seen Quentin up in the field and waved as they came in, but he didn't come down. "Quentin," observed Reba, "knows he's gonna be hearing about chicken shit for weeks!" Raymond knew his brothers, and that he was going to hear about it for the rest of his life.

Raymond pulled up the side of the hood, found the dipstick and confirmed that he truck had enough oil. He climbed in onto the feed sack seat cover, and a couple of grunts after pulling out the choke, the engine caught. Easing off on the choke until it idled smoothly, he slipped it into gear and out of the shed, leaving the rooster to ponder his other choices come evening. Reba turned left at Quentin's mailbox, headed back home, and Raymond turned right and headed towards Guilford. The truck, he thought, was a pretty good deal, a V-8, no crumpled fenders, and a four-speed gearbox, shifter on the floor, with the jack-low first gear that farmers love, good for pulling stumps and getting an inevitably overloaded truck up a long grade. Pickups were designated as three-quarter ton trucks, but the usual practice was to load them down until the springs were fully compressed with the frame sitting on the axle -- far more than 1500 lbs.

This Ford, he figured, had been Elby Baker's indulgence after one of the last of his family passed on, leaving him as sole heir. Before that, ever since Raymond could remember, he'd driven an ancient cut-down Dodge Bothers car with a flat-plank wall behind the seat and a home-made box bed. It'd worked fine for him. The Ford, like the old Dodge, and in fact all of the

Baker farm's equipment had always been shed-kept, never felt the dew, or for that matter the heat of the noonday sun unless there'd been work to do. It had, however never been washed -- there were limits to old man Elby's attitude towards machinery, figuring, probably, that dry dust and birdshit had never rusted anything out bad enough to limit its usefulness, or made it hard to start first thing in the morning.

Raymond got to Guilford, parked in front of the Courthouse, took his stick, and made his way to one of the smaller buildings behind it where taxes were paid to get the tag transferred into his name. The Courthouse followed the pattern common in the old days, built of brick because of fear of fire, the large building contained little beyond the actual courtroom. Smaller, surrounding buildings, also brick housed separate functions and groups of records so that the destruction or damage of one would not put all governmental functions at risk, and would, hopefully, allow for successful bucket-brigade firefighting. He filled out the form, showed his bill of sale, paid his dollar, and they matched his name with the old tag number. Before the war the clerk would have given him a shiny new one from a stack behind the counter interleaved with glassine tissue to keep them from sticking together from the combination of new paint and heat -- had to keep those men at the Penitentiary busy! With the wartime metal shortages they reassigned any tag that was readable, giving out thick painted pasteboard ones if there had to be a new issue.

Finished out back, Raymond followed the sandy path around to the front of the Courthouse, passing the ever-vigilant stone Rebel soldier that graced the forecourt in all but the poorest counties in the South. Crossing the hot street he was glad to hit the shade of the deep, drive-through overhang behind the tall, glass-tanked pumps of the Texaco station. The Colored pump attendant, who he knew by sight but not by name, was on a bench at the back of the shade, resting comfortably against the wall. "Welcome home, Mister Soldier!" he said, nodding Raymond's way. Word sure gets around, Raymond thought, as he thanked the man and opened the screen door to the dimmer and marginally cooler store part of the station where a dusty overhead fan slushed the air around the humming, water-filled coke cooler and the several shelves of groceries, smokes, car accessories, and the unpredictable odd items that cropped up in little country stores, testimony to the salesmanship or last-ditch discount of the wholesale man on his rounds. Russell Glover, the owner and mechanic, appeared from the garage-side door wiping his hands on a greasy rag, having heard the screen door slam shut on its spring.

"Welcome back, Raymond," he said, thrusting out his right hand for a shake. "Damn sorry about your leg, though," he added, frowning, but his smile came back as he came out with "What can I do for you?" Russell was just old enough that the draft had missed him, and grateful to have been left with his family and business. Gas rationing and the shortage of tires, belts and hoses hurt him, but he had lots of repair work, patching folks' vehicles and tractors together. There wasn't much that he couldn't improvise, if necessary, relying on the junk pile out back, the 'hot wrench' attached to the welding tanks and his encyclopedic knowledge of the whereabouts of just about every derelict car in the County's ditches and woodlots and what usable bits remained on each.

"I just bought old man Elby's Barrelnose pickup off of Quentin and I'm looking for some polish to clean it up." Russell walked along behind the counter, and peering around, reached up, and came back with two flat, dusty cans, one wax, and the other polishing compound.

"I 'spect you're gonna' need that, too, if you're looking to do your work right."

"Probably so," Raymond agreed. "Gimme a slice of that cheese to eat on the way home, too, please." Russell swung the door of the screen box on the bottom shelf up and held it with his left hand and walked the knife away from the edge of the gap in the wheel of sharp cheddar until Raymond said "That's it", cut the wedge, flopping it onto a piece of waxed paper and then onto the scale, letting the little door slam down behind him. Raymond dug his wallet out, paid, gathered up the cans and cheese in his free hand and headed for the door. "Thanks," he called over his shoulder on his way out. "There ain't," he grinned, "nothing better than the thin edge off good old fresh-cut rat cheese!"

Back at the truck he tossed the polish cans and the stick over onto the passenger seat and savored the delicate cut of warm cheese and ownership of his first vehicle. A farm truck, but as nicely finished inside as most automobiles, and it had Ford's renowned V-8, subject of Clyde Barrow's letter to Henry Ford, "with your V-8 I can make any other car eat my dust!" Didn't do him and Bonnie any good when an acquaintance set them up for an ambush, though, feigning a need for help with a bad tire.

25. A BIT OF REALITY

Raymond found that the leg wound was more of an impediment than he'd hoped. There was a vast difference between walking the level floor of the Hospital with empty hands and doing 'most anything once he'd got home. He was at least carrying the walking stick all of the time and fully relying on it much more than he'd been led to believe he would. Disliking the feel of the slender, arched-handled factory cane he'd been issued he went to the brush pile where they cut firewood and looked around until he found a stick with a branch that came out at an angle that fit his hand. Unexpectedly it had a twist that kicked the end on the ground out away from his left foot, and unconsciously he'd selected something to take home and clean up by whittling that was more than twice the diameter of the cane. It took twice the diameter on the handle to fit his grip, and the main limb that the branch had forked off of was downright hefty.

He'd done what he could for the one remaining box of bees, unstacking the supers and brood boxes to scrape the inside of the bottom board clean, replaced the black, overused comb in the bottom brood box that they didn't like to use with fresh sheets of foundation so that they could draw out new comb. He'd kept that box on the top of the colony for a week and a half, rather than putting it in its proper place at the bottom so that he could put on a veil every afternoon when the bees were flying and the colony calm, about its business, and relive his childhood joy, pulling out the frame holding the comb that they were building to watch the golden chain of wax makers.

He'd been able to help his father a bit with some carpentry work, they'd put up sawhorses in one end of the machine shed and built a few gates, and gone around the place patching loose or broken boards wherever they could find them. He understood, though, what his position was in the farming operation run by Reba, Charlie and William. At just a little over twenty, he was an extra, unneeded old man, fit for the puttering jobs and the occasional trip into town for some small item, but unreliable for steady work.

He enjoyed being with his family, but much of the time he felt very much alone, reliving the experiences of the last year, mostly the few hours of the landing, the cliffs, and his brief time in the fight. Some nights he dreamed of golden chains of bees, others of chains of Rangers on the ladders, which often wakened him, once to find Charlie at the foot of his bed, who told him that he'd been shouting in his sleep.

26. BARRELNOSE CLEANUP

The dirty pickup was a welcome project, both for him and for Reba, who was running out of suggestions for farm jobs that he could do. He parked it in the shade of one of the big trees near the house, where he was close to hand if anyone at the house needed his help, and close to the cistern pump to refill his bucket when he needed clean water. The first challenge was the chicken shit on the seat. He worked loose what he could with his fingers (having sat on the deposits as he had ridden into Guilford and back had opened up a lot of cracks and freed some clumps completely), then soaked the sacks he'd been riding on and left them in place overnight. The next morning he was able to scrape down to the grain of the leather, working with a piece of soft pine like a drawknife, holding each end and repeatedly pulling a thin layer of manure towards the end of the seat where it dropped onto the doorsill and fell out onto the ground, dampening things as each dry layer appeared. The result was a generally dirty brown seat with a large greyish area beneath the lower rim of the steering wheel. He went out to the barn, dug around in the dusty tack-room until he found the red, white, and blue can of Blue Ribbon (right there on the top, a picture of it tied into a prize rosette) saddle soap, came back and worked over the grey spot and rinsed it, then worked over the whole seat, both bench and back. Standing up and stretching, he surveyed the result. All of the back and most of the seat looked real good, but the chemicals that made up chicken shit had left an irregular yellowish cast on the driver's seat. The shape made him think of a high-school textbook map showing the outline of the Ottoman Empire before its collapse, a casualty of the last World War. A small price, he thought, to pay for the good deal the rooster had negotiated for him on the truck! With soap, water, and a small scrub brush, he attacked the ribbed rubber floor mats, freeing the smooth oval in the center on each side with the 'Ford" script and each parallel groove and ridge on the rest of the floor from the cement of boot-borne manure, sand, and red clay.

With the occasional interruption of a call to help someone else with what they were doing, it had taken him the better part of two days in the cab. Starting on the bodywork, he gave the truck a good soap and water deal from front to back, sitting on an upended five-gallon paint bucket to do the low parts and balancing on top of it on his good leg to get the center of the roof that he couldn't reach from the ground. Shaking from that exertion, he realized that if he'd just climbed into the bed of the truck he could have reached the entire roof while standing on two feet. Like Granddaddy always said, "Boy, if you don't think with your head, you're gonna think with your back!"

All of the surface dirt cleared, the real work began. Starting at the right side of the half-barrel grill, he slid a small, damp rag over the cutting compound in the can and began cleaning the tight-gripping grime and oxidized paint down to the factory's deep forest green. The dullness of the paint meant that he had to make small circular strokes over about a square foot area, rinse the rag in clean water, wait for the spot to completely dry, and then buff the dull, greenish-grey film off with a clean dry rag. It was a seemingly endless process that gave him lots of time to think. Mostly he thought about what he might do when the truck was ready and he left the farm. He didn't want to go back to school. He wasn't afraid to try college, not that anyone in his family had been to college, but he couldn't envision any future developing from that except becoming a teacher, which would mean spending the rest of his life inside dusty red-brick buildings, looking out the windows over his student's heads and wishing he was outdoors. It wasn't that he hadn't done OK in high school, or that he'd disliked his teachers or didn't respect their calling, it was just that he couldn't conceive of making his life there. That, and the fact that getting qualified would mean four expensive years of being a student himself. He knew that just after D-day Roosevelt and the American Legion had talked about legislation for veteran's education, but if anything had been passed by Congress, the mechanics of how it would work wasn't in place or the word wasn't being put out at hospital ward level while he'd been around.

Preaching, he thought for just a few moments, would be a good racket for a gimpy guy, but he'd already moved quite comfortably into his Father and Grandfather's corner of the porch when it came to religion. Good for those with whom it 'took,' God bless 'em, at best a tiresome community expectation for those with whom it didn't, and something of no consequence at all for those that by virtue of age, experience or some other definition of self-worth didn't give a damn about meeting other's expectations. In any respectable denomination, it, too, would require returning to the classroom for years of study. He laughed out loud when he considered the hypocrisy of avoiding that by proclaiming himself saved and setting himself up as a holly roller preacher in some abandoned shack with a crudely lettered sign and, if the place had electricity, a cross outlined on the wall with bare light bulbs! It would be great if he could keep a straight face long enough at the supper table to lay out that plan for the family's digestion, but he knew that even though he was a consummate jokester, he hadn't a prayer of pulling that one off.

The work was boring, repetitive and required a certain degree of concentration to achieve a uniform cut into the paint -- he didn't want to be heavy-handed where the factory painters hadn't wanted to bend and twist, resulting in a skimpy spot, and he didn't want to skimp himself, and leave a dull spot that would show when he put the polish on. After standing for a long time doing the headlight, top of the left fender and half of the hood his leg was tired. He hooked the bucket around to where he was with his left foot to get to work on the low parts, but as he pivoted to sit down his bad leg grabbed him, hard. If he hadn't been in the act of sitting down on the bucket he would have fallen rather than just scrabbling on the fender to regain his balance. "Shit," he said out loud to himself as he caught his breath and waited for the pain to subside. Doc Hill h, assured him that they'd gotten the bone right, but there was sure as hell something wrong with how the soft parts they'd cut through during the two surgeries had fallen into line as they'd healed. After a little bit he went back to work, leaning as far to each side as he could before scooting the bucket along. Unbeknownst to him, Mary had seen the whole thing as she happened to look up from her work and out the kitchen window to gauge how the weather was going for everyone working outdoors.

Raymond's mood changed pretty swiftly from planning to try the preacher joke at the supper table to brooding about being a twenty year old cripple. What in the hell am I going to do with my life? He thought. A month away from the hospital, spent among the able bodied in a community that valued hard physical labor had changed his perspective, led him to, at least in some of his brooding moments, to forget those other guys at Woodrow Wilson, the ones hurt worse than him. In other brooding moments he could think of no one else. That memory added a load of guilt to the burden of his increasing frustration with his own physical limitations. Back at work on the truck he resumed making tight little circles, but when he rinsed the rag, releasing a stream of discoloration into the water, he thought about gut-shot soldiers, dead on their way onto the beach.

"How you doin?" Mary caused Raymond to look up from his work -- he was now back past the runningboad, sitting and cutting on the left side of the box and the rear fender. "It looks lots better," she continued without waiting for his answer. Raymond stood up, stretching his back and reaching for his stick to step back beside her, looking for the first time at his entire ternoon's labor.

"Yep," he wiped his brow, "it sure does. Who'd a thought that nice green was under there!"

"Just thought I'd come see before ringing the bell for supper. Why don't you come on in, wash up, and ring it for me?"

"OK." He pushed the piece of damp rag he'd been using into the now partly empty compound can and snapped the lid on tight. He dumped the bucket of cloudy water in the grass and started towards the house with her. He liked being around Mary, her cheerful nature always seemed to rub off onto him whenever they were together, and it did this time, too. By the time they'd reached the porch, the black memories he'd dwelt on half of the afternoon disappeared back into his head. "I've been studying on my work prospects some ... you might be surprised!" he grinned. "You'll have to wait 'till supper though." He wondered how far he could get into the preacher story with a straight face. Giving the cistern handle a couple of turns he caught a double handful of water and splashed it on his face over the low tin sink, reached behind him for the flour-sack towel to dry off, enjoying its feel on the back of his neck and up in the vee of his jaw behind his bottom front teeth. Clean and refreshed he went over by the kitchen door, took the loop of line off of its high nail on the pantry wall (the nail got raised when they were little kids, after the men came in from the field one too many times as a result of their fun) and gave the bell on the post in the yard three or four good licks before opening the screen door and going into the kitchen. Judging by the smell, supper was pot roast, and a good one. "Hey, Mother," he said, spotting her in her comfortable chair, pulling off her silver thimble, just fixing to put the half-finished jumble in her lap back into the mending basket. "How're you feeling?"

"Like an old lady," she replied with a wink. "Letting my daughter do all of the work!"

It was evident that the boys, Reba, and their Father, hungry and tired, had put up their tools ("Don't never leave a plow in the fields"! Grandfather had burned into their minds and their backsides for as long as they could remember) and started for the house before they'd heard the bell. Washing was quick, crowding in at the table and Father's perfunctory grace was quicker, and they all fell to eating.

After a few moments, Mary said "Alright now, Raymond, what was it you said I'd have to wait 'till supper to hear?" He demurred, trying to ignore her, wishing he hadn't felt so giddy with her mood earlier and put himself in a position of having to try what he doubted he could accomplish. "Something about your prospects, I think you said," she kept on. Everyone at the table fell silent, except for chewing and swallowing, and turned their eyes on him.

"Well," he started, "y'all know what Roosevelt said about education benefits a couple of weeks after I got hurt. I started polishing on that truck with cutting cream, remembered that and thought I'd try to figure what I might do from here on before I finished the job." He let that idea sink in and then tried to strengthen his precarious position, "I'm through in the cab..."

"Chckenshit!" Charlie murmured and poked at Will, grinning with gravy on his chin.

"And down to the tail-light on the driver's side..."

"Well," Reba was becoming impatient, "I reckon that entitles you to about half an idea -what is it?"

"It seems to me," Raymond started laying the groundwork, "that more schoolin', although based on how I did as a kid I could probably handle it ok, would lead to a teaching job, the rest of my life inside of a brick building dealing primarily with guys like Charlie and Will, who view the frequent use of the word 'Chckenshit' as an accomplishment. I don't think that's what I want 'till I die!" He got a couple of chuckles out of that, which gave him some confidence for the next move. "The next thing that came to mind was being a pastor. At least visiting the sick and going to annual conference would be an excuse to get out and drive around some..."

"And know the low-down on everybody's problems better'n they do on the dock at the feed store!" Mary interrupted.

"...the problem there, though, aside from my views on religion in general (he winked at his Dad, who was leaning back on the legs of his chair, eyes half closed and the beginnings of a smile on his lips), is that'd it would mean more school, seminary, and learning how to be both patient and sanctimonious. I ain't sure that I could handle both!" A few more chuckles, he was still doin' alright. "By the time I got back to the mud flap," he paused, savoring the lucky opportunity that description of his progress around the truck was giving him to manage his timing, "I figured out how to beat the schoolin', sanctimony, and patience. I'm gon-na' rent Miller's old store over at the crossroads, build some plank benches inside, make up a sign with light bulbs outlining a cross, take granny's old egg basket for gettin' up the collection, wire a roof speaker and micro-phone to the truck radio, get a slick suit and some loud shoes, and set myself up as a preacher-man!" There was just the right pause before they all broke out laugh-ing, even Mother, who didn't take kindly to religious-based humor. They'd started to get it when he men-tioned the electric sign, and the ridiculous image had built with each item he added after that.

"I can hear him now, Brother Ray, preaching the parable of the pickup and the rooster! Good things come from vile circumstances, Amen and pass that bas-ket!" Will hooted.

"Preacher-man," Charlie howled back, "Come on down, brothers and sisters, come to Jesus, come to Brother Raymond and fill that basket like Granny's hens so's we can keep on ministerin' to the human pickup shittin' roosters of this world. Amen!"

The vocational episode was funny, and a great relief to the family, who had missed Raymond in his pre-war role as a jokester. They laughed maybe a little too long, readjusting their own feelings about how their son and brother was doing. Mary didn't tell anyone about what she'd seen that afternoon, and Raymond kept the guts in the bucket to himself. He went to sleep easy that evening, grinning to himself about his joke, but the men on the ladders came back with a vengeance about three o'clock in the morning, and he lay awake until dawn.

27. MORE SERIOUS THOUGHT UNDER & AROUND THE BARRELNOSE

The truck project resumed the next morning, both in terms of career planning and paint reconditioning. Clean water in the bucket, the memory of breakfast, and the warm morning sun made the trauma of the pre-dawn hours disappear and Raymond made good progress on both fronts. Working around the tail-light and across the tailgate (another embossed Ford signature) and around the license plate and the other stop and signal lamp, he concluded that driving was what he had enjoyed the most since leaving the Army -- the question now was driving what, what and where. Being a cabbie was out, since that meant the city, or at least a big enough town to have people who used cabs, like a Navy ship's home port, or a military base, like Cherry Point Air Station or one of the small burgs outside the gates of Camp Lejeune. Somehow earning a living dealing with drunken servicemen or carloads of brass hats was not real appealing. Not appealing at all. Too many people, too many people he'd no desire to associate with, and he suspected that depending on conditions in the town, a cabbie's income was petty sporadic. He liked driving on the farm, tractor work and the pickups, but he couldn't imagine who'd hire him to drive a pickup. The closest thing he could think of to running errands for the farm was being a milkman, but that had the disadvantage of being a city or at least big-town job and he had doubts about climbing in an out and going up icy porch steps with his gimpy leg. The idea of figuring how to shift gears smoothly in a stubby cab-over-engine truck where the gearshift came out of the floor behind the driver was, he had to admit, though, intriguing. Driving a freight truck was just a worse version of being a milkman or Railway Express driver, because he'd have to load everything that went on the truck at the company warehouse dock, and manhandle it off and into whatever establishment the goods were to go. Driving without freight handling; driving in the country rather than in the city; and driving with minimal contact with people at each end and in the middle -- that's what appealed to him, but where to find such a job?

He had just come back from the pump with a clean bucket of water when it came to him. Fuel! Oil and gasoline, were loaded and unloaded by gravity, like the water flowing out the spout from the pump's top chamber into his bucket! No freight to hoist and carry being careful not to damage anything, just some hoses to drag and 'rassle, nothing too fragile there. It helped, too, that despite his state of origin and all the "smoke 'em if you got 'em" cries of the NCO's in an infantry company, he was not a dedicated smoker, much prefer-ring the anonymous comfort of a quid of chew or, if it was available, a dip of finely chopped Copenhagen snuff. He could at least pursue this option without daily suicidality as a drawback. He skidded the five-gallon can around to work on the passenger door, reviewing what he knew about fuel-driving. First of all, there were the big tractor semi-trailer haulers, "suicide jock-eys" the other truckers called them, while coveting their somewhat higher pay and realizing that most of their driving records would keep them from even applying for the job. Raymond had never driven a tractor-trailer rig, just two-ton straight trucks when helping neighbors who had them hauling cattle or grain, and had once or twice surreptitiously handled a deuce-and-a-half or a five-ton six-by-six in the straight line of an Army con-voy for an hour when the driver needed a nap, swap-ping off seats on the roll and unobserved, hardly ever even changing gears. Not, he thought, rubbing along in

small circles, much big-truck experience. The big trac-
tor-trailers supplied high-volume outlets and filled the
gaps in rail and pipeline coverage, but there had to be,
he figured, demand for smaller tanker service to supply
the country stores with the gasoline and kerosene tanks
that people who dealt at the crossroads post offices relied upon. Around home, those trucks came out from oil
companies in Greensboro which were supplied by railroad tanker cars.

Working his way onto the front fender, and just
about out of compound, Raymond considered the wis-
dom of going into town and looking for a local job. It
would be inexpensive living at home, even if he paid
room and board, at which he knew the others would, at
least outwardly, balk. As a local, he could probably sell
himself pretty good, knowing the roads and communi-
ties, both White and Black. Rubbing around the fat tor-
pedo of the headlight housing he realized that it was
probably best for the family that he leave the farm. The
equilibrium among his siblings and balance of authority
between them and his parents was precarious enough
without adding an outside-wage earning brother who
contributed little to the farming operation. He'd seen the
complications before, growing up, when one member of
a family took work off of the place. Unless the farm in
question had been particularly productive and the parents involved perceptive enough and willing to loosen
the purse strings, jealousies had developed between the
siblings who had to wait for a crop to come in and then
manage their share of the resources, assuming the elders were willing to share them out (and often they
weren't, protective of the surplus that meant survival in
a bad season) and the wage worker, who always seemed
to have some cash, enjoyed the wider social connections of his job, and didn't have to scrape manure off of

his boots before coming in to supper. Necessarily better informed about the world's happenings, the wage man could easily slip onto a high horse, and, disastrously, began to be granted some deference by the parents, consulted for his opinion on matters influencing the operation of the farm, overstepping his siblings' territory.

Raymond had, from his first day back home, recognized how Reba's intelligence and good humor, backed by their Father's authority guided the strength of his two brothers. Mary had, without complaint, taken over much of their aging Mother's role. The whole setup was doomed as soon as the younger players developed romantic attachments, even if they were the fortuitous kind that held promise of additional land or capitol. In-laws and out-laws could have pretty much the same effect on a family as a wage-worker sibling. He couldn't see making the inevitable balancing game harder by staying on but working off of the farm.

Better to leave, but where to go? Rural fuel delivery seemed like it would fit his abilities, but he'd still have to deal with customers and employers, and he'd still walk badly, especially when he was tired. That would lead to repetition of the series of questions that he was becoming increasingly tired of to the extent that he found himself avoiding situations in which they might arise. He rubbed more small circles, aware that he was dwelling on the negative side of things, and tried to shift his thinking.

On the positive side, he reasoned that he'd served with and under men from all over the nation and been exposed to some British and rural Virginian civilians during his hospitalizations. That, and facing the German machine-gunner who'd done his best to kill him had to count for something towards his ability to find and hold a job away from where he grew up. That was being positive, but then the downside crept in. What if those same experiences had changed him in a way that kept him from dealing with people? He was already aware that he stood back and took stock of people more than he used to before opening up to them -- that was how you made sure that you fell in with the right bunch in a new unit. He realized that while still in the hospital he'd thought through the notion that since he couldn't run with a bad leg and because his stick telegraphed that fact, he had to be on his guard in unknown situations, not that he'd encountered any since his trip home.

If he'd thought deeply about it, or had a talking relationship with another vet, he'd have realized how, after just his few hours on the line, the wounded, dead and dying were an enormous part of his otherwise limited experience of the world. Civilians generally met death and dying at expected times with expected rituals, old soldiers probably did, too, but he was rank and raw, the hours burned into him, even if he wasn't aware or conversant with anyone about it. Sitting with his Father, rocking without talking late at night on the porch, he'd thought about the look that had sometimes crossed Grandfather's face, a look that was never accompanied by words. He remembered the stories of some of the old men, and the history of how that generation of men, and some women, had come to terms with the remnants of their war, working a team all day with one arm, women successfully farming without menfolk until the next generation prematurely assumed the role. The peculiar roughness adopted by some fathers, the overly-protective demeanor of others, those that turned to liquor or the church, the stories of those who hanged themselves in barn or mill, and those who simply walked away, incapable of living in a normal society. Raymond's father knew that Raymond was aware of some of those accounts, and wondered how they affected him, but as one who had never been to war felt inadequate to raise the topic, especially since Raymond seemed to him to be getting along pretty well, all things considered.

The Valley of Virginia seemed the best bet -- at least he'd been there and knew it was a lot more comfortable than the Carolinas in the summer, and not too bad in the colder months, or at least hadn't been when Uncle Sam was paying the coal bill. He was confident that he could find a room in Saunton and he'd just have to make his case to the oil distributors, no case, really, except in being a wounded
Vet and willing to work in a wartime economy where most of the able-bodied not in the service were tied up in war work. He wasn't so anxious when Mary rang the supper bell as he had been when planning the preacher-man talk, and once they sat down and he explained his ideas the family all seemed to think that his view of the self-handling characteristics of oil as opposed to other freight was sound. They also thought that the Shenandoah Valley location was probably good, since it was close to the hospital if his leg kicked up in the traces. Raymond kept his other reasons for being anxious to leave, the precariousness of their farming alliance, to himself, figuring that it was something they'd be forced by circumstance to face soon enough, without his bringing it up now.

An oil change, a couple of coats of wax, and bolting an old carpenter's chest with a padlock hasp to

the truck's bed just behind the cab to provide a little secure storage for a few tools, and he'd be ready to head
north. Old man Baker hadn't put much wear on the
pickup's tires, and keeping it in the shed, sometimes
nosed in, sometimes backed in, when he'd wanted to
feel his skill or was anxious to be ready to go the next
morning, had kept the sun from baking them hard. The
spare'd never touched the ground, and as hard as tires
were to come by, Raymond figured he'd better run a
chain with a padlock through the hole and up around
the frame to make sure that he was the first to use it
when misfortune struck. Easy enough to happen, he
knew, with a hundred years' worth of horseshoe nails
lying in wait in the ruts of every dirt road in the country. Most of his way, though, was going to be on paved
Route 29, what the Brits called tarmac, one step up
from the Scott McAdam's "metaled road" system of
layers of successively smaller crushed stones rolled
hard and smooth. He dreamt of the bees that evening,
after having nearly rocked himself to sleep on the
porch, just sitting with the family, nobody talking
much. That, he thought, was a frequent blessing of the
summer months.

28. FINAL WORK ON THE TRUCK

The final preparations that he had thought and
talked through didn't take but a few days. As he expected, it didn't take much labor to really make the
paint on the pickup gleam after he'd cut the rough stuff
off. Two coats of wax, buffed with many clean rags,
and the deep green body and black fenders of the Barrelnose probably looked better than they had when
Baker'd driven it home to the farm in '39! He'd rolled
under on the dusty dirt floor of the machine shed, using
the old pan that they always caught used oil in for trans-

fer to the storage barrel, wiped the sludge off of the plug, tightened it in and added a couple of quarts from the farm's big five-gallon can (another example of the farmer's privileged status under rationing) then starting the engine and running it a bit to fill the oil galleries before stopping it, letting things settle before trusting the dipstick indicator to top it off properly. He grabbed the grease gun off of the nail above the cluttered workbench, put it in the bed, and drove back to the shade of the tree to do the grease job. The cool green grass stopped the itch on his neck and cleaned the shed's dirt from his clothes as he slid as purposefully as a hunting snake underneath the vehicle. Leading joints on the steering gear; back joints; kingpins behind the front wheels; brake rod ends; clutch throw-out pivot; front universal on the driveshaft; hanger in the middle, then the back joint; ends of the rear brake rods and the cable sheath for the handbrake, pushing that grease out onto his fingertip and circling it around, because the cable and a lot of other points requiring attention didn't have the Zerk to fit the grasp of the gun's head. Some of the necessary, 'official', lubrication points, laked the fitting or even the grease cup of a common machine shaft. Back up the other side, a dab on each hood latch and that was done. He unscrewed the wingnut on the top of the air filter removed the entire thing and balanced it with one hand while he plugged the resulting hole with a rag -- he didn't need any curious bugs making their way into the carburetor. He made his way back to the workbench in the machine shed, walking carefully so as not to slosh the oil out of the bottom half of the bowl. He elbowed enough space clear that he could set the top part, the part filled with what looked like oily, shredded wire cloth, and the gasket from between the bottom bowl and the breather box down. Another step and he poured the inch of oil in the bowl into the waste barrel, and then turned the bowl sideways towards the light. His bet with himself had been a winner -- there was about an inch of incredibly fine grit caked into the bottom of the air cleaner bowl, where it had been concealed, if it had ever been checked during casual servicing, by the smooth skim of oil that floated above. He doubted that old man Baker or Quentin had cleaned and refilled the bottom bowl as he was doing. They'd probably just topped it to the line and rinsed the wire-tangle contents of the top half in kerosene, which he would do as soon as he finished gouging the goo out of the bottom with his finger and a small stick. The oil-bath filters worked real good if you kept the bowl clean and full so that the oil could slosh up onto the filament wires, trap the grit and then rinse it into the bowl's sump. He rejoined the parts of the filter, carried them back out to the pickup and, after pulling the rag out, returned them to their rightful place. No more miles than the truck had on it, he wasn't worried about the grease on the front wheel bearings or the oil in the rear axle or differential--there hadn't been any indication of failed seals when he'd been snaking around below

He was, however, concerned about what might be in the gas tank. Back in the machine shed he hunted around the post braces and nails in the walls 'till he found the old, five-foot piece of garden hose that they used to scrounge fuel from one machine for another when the big tank was getting low. He took the hose and a dusty gallon glass jug from the back of the workbench out to the truck, glancing around for his brothers and glad that he didn't see 'em. Everyone had his own trick for siphoning gas, few of them were foolproof, and all of the boys, himself, included, loved ridiculing the unfortunate who ended up with a mouth full of gasoline while starting the flow. He knocked the odd bit of mud-dauber stuff out of the jug, blew it reasonably free of dust and set it on the ground beneath the filler cap for the gas tank, just behind the driver's window -- the tank was a thin rectangle stood on edge between the back wall of the cab and the seatback springs. Down on his knees facing the jug, he unscrewed the shiny chromed filler cap, threw it in onto the seat, blew through the hose to make sure the mud-dauber wasps hadn't plugged it, then slowly slid one end down into the tank until it hit bottom. Raymond's personal siphoning theory involved paying close attention to the amount of suction necessary to get gas to the peak of the hose, pulling for just an instant more as the pressure changed when the liquid crossed the divide to get things going good then jerking the hose from his lips the inch or so to the jug (this was opposed to the blow-and-bounce method espoused by Will, and Charlie's simple and reliable but usually catastrophic approach of "just suck on the bastard until you just begin to taste gas." Charlie would probably be the most reliable gas thief in the family.) Able to approach things calmly, without the usual two hecklers, his method worked, first try, with only the taste of rubber hose on his lips and a steady golden flow into the jug. There was an occasional swirl of dark particles in the flow before he pulled the hose when the jug filled -- rust from all the years the tank had set half-full, daytime humidity condensing on the steel walls in the cool of night. He lay back in the grass and let mixture in the jug settle. Before long he could see the thin white line of a layer of water in the bottom of the jug. Wrapping a rag over the mouth of the jug to catch the rust specs and moving easy so as not to break the stratification of the fluids, he poured as much of the gallon as he could back into the tank without pouring water, then threw the rest away in an arc that caught the light like bees coursing to and from a hive. Several lazy repetitions of this process, with plenty of time for disturbed water and crud to settle back to the hose's inlet finally produced a perfectly clear jug, and Raymond figured that he'd done all he could to spare himself a sputtering engine on his drive north.

29. THE TRIP NORTH

Leaving home was pretty much like arriving in reverse. It was a different vehicle, and this time as the driver, but it was the same cluster of relatives doing pretty much the same things, pictures, shaking hands, slapping his shoulder, hugging, and some crying. Mary made sure that he had some meat and biscuits to eat on the road, mother fixed him up with a pillow and comforter in case he needed, ever, to make a camp bedroll in the truck, and in case the linens in whatever room he found were insufficient. His brothers had gathered up every odd duplicate tool on the place and filled a good portion of his box in the bed with useful things, including a couple of cans with nails, nuts, and bolts, as well as a hank of bailing wire and a ball of binder twine. They'd also come up with a moderately risqué photo from last-year's calendar and glued it onto the inside of the lid. The owner of the garage that gave them out as advertising got two boxes of calendars in December, and gave each customer their choice -- the girl or the pastoral scene. Many families had one in the kitchen, the other in the barn feeding room or toolshed. All had a chart beneath the picture with a few notes about the gestation periods of common farm animals, and a series if lines marked '"dam", "sire", "service date", and "due".

Reba surprised him, handing him a large manila

envelope as she hugged him and gave him a goodbye peck. "Don't forget to stay in touch. When you find a place, let me know where I can phone a message even if you don't have a line yourself." The envelope wasn't sealed, so he glanced inside and saw that it was filled with pencils, paper, envelopes, and a sheet of stamps clipped to one of the damp-proof glassine separating sheets that she'd talked out of the postmaster, who preferred to keep them for his own drawer. He could see and hear her, leaning over the counter, playing the wounded veteran brother card to get what she wanted.

Raymond threw his barracks bag into the cab, over on the rider's side -- it was the only luggage he had, and he'd folded his church clothes carefully, the way he'd learned to keep a Class 'A' uniform presentable, and put them in with everything else. His hardest-worn overalls went into the tool box, along with his old farm brogans. He wore his brown uniform shoes, khaki trousers, and a colorful civilian shirt for travelling clothes, and he had a new, striped-ticking engineer's cap with a still-stiff bill on the seat beside him to pull on later in the day when the sun would be low in his eyes. He rolled the window down, stuck his left arm out and waved to everyone as he reached up high on the floorboards with his left foot, pushed the round starter pedal down and the engine caught. Just kissing the jack-low first gear as he started, he immediately shifted into second and eased out the gravel drive. He came to an uncharacteristic full stop when he got to the end of the lane, just to look around one last time, pasture and a lone cedar at the corner of the ditch on the left; corn ground on the right, and the big tin mailbox with their name on the side across the road. The way it had been for as long as he could remember. Turning left, he headed out their secondary road towards the main road which would carry him into Greensboro, where he'd catch route 29 north. Right at the edge of Greensboro he stopped at a station and filled up on gas -- the farm ration sticker and a North Carolina plate didn't give rise to any questions -- he didn't know what the deal would be next time he stopped, in Virginia, but he figured he could talk his way through to another full tank when he needed it.

Heading north towards Reidsville, he hit a little crossroads town at each intersection. Rockingham County, North Carolina. Not much different from home except that being on twenty-nine, which intersected with fifty-eight in Danville, about forty miles away, the east-west road leading to the shipyards and all of their related war work in Norfolk, Rockingham County was positioned to get in on the lesser-known but indubitably profitable war industry of providing untaxed whisky to all those thirsty shipyard hands who were jammed into any available sort of housing on either side of Hampton Rhoads, many of whom had brought their fondness for white lightning with them to their back porches, kitchen tables, or if the wife was either disapproving or looking for a little good time herself, the honky-tonks that had sprung up in the kinds of structure he'd described in his preacher-man stunt (not discounting the fact that the actual preacher-men probably kept the market competitive and the disapproving-type landlords happy). The Virginia counties and towns on fifty-eight were big in the market, too, Hillsville, Galax, and South Boston, all part of the market flowing from the farms and warehouses of Carroll, Patrick, Floyd, Henry, Pittsylvania, and Halifax Counties. The war had taken a local craft tradition which had always had the not inconsequential pleasure of screwing the Yankee government out of its liquor tax money and made it into a significant cash-money business. The papers were full of stories about fast late-night automobile chases, arrests, crashes, and remarkably ingenious methods of concealing stills that were once (and doubtless continued to flourish there) up in the hollows than in unexpected places more convenient to the highway. He'd even read about one funeral-parlor outfit that had plenty of solitude, room in the coffin warehouse for building inventory from the smaller producers (careful and regular payers of respect at just about every visitation viewing) and a number of vehicles that could travel the countryside without question and visit the coffin wholesalers in Norfolk as needed. With the war on, manpower was a problem for the Revenue force, which often got less than full cooperation from the shorthanded (and sometimes complicit) county sheriffs. Enough talented mechanics and skilled drivers were either under-or over-age for the draft that there was no lack of horsepower available for the game, and truth be known, a lot of the talent in production, transport, political intervention, and marketing was likely female. Raymond could only imagine the tricks that his two sisters could pull if they were in the trade!

The Ford purred along like a kitten, and the traffic wasn't bad in even the big towns, as the highway just went straight through them, usually right up Main Street past the Courthouse and Confederate soldier. He went through Danville, with its cotton mills, and passed near where the 'Old 97' lost its air and leapt from the tracks (later on he'd pass the yards of Monroe, where both the song and the ill-fated journey began). Blairs, Chatham, Gretna, Hurt, Alavista -- he found a shady spot near a station there, got a cold drink , enjoyed the food his sister'd packed for him, filled up on gas and checked his oil and water, both where they should be on the by-then cooled engine. He liked driving the Ford, and thanks to his work of the previous week, he hadn't passed any better-looking vehicle.

On up through Campbell County, west of Appomattox, where Lee had surrendered to Grant, his contemporary but not friend from the Mexican War, but who'd refused Lee's sword, provided rations for his hungry men, and set terms that led Lee to make it known that the fight was over and not to be taken to the swamps and the mountains, which had been a very real possibility for the Rebels not in his surrounded and hungry Army of Northern Virginia.

Next came Lynchburg, a real city whose immense armory, stone and brick banks and warehouses, grand homes, and Federal Courthouse reminded him that Danville, after all, was just a big mill town. He was sure that the stone Confederate was somewhere around the city, probably at a County courthouse, but next to the enormous post office on Main Street, the citizens of Lynchburg were urged forward by a bronze doughboy soldier from the last war, rifle held high in one hand, urging his fellows over the top.

As he slowed on the high, narrow bridge at the north end of the city, he could look to his right and see the complex path of railroad tracks with their switch-towers jammed into the floodplain between the James and the tall warehouses lining the entire bluff; if he looked left he was staring down into the long, low, sheds of the Lynchburg Foundry, another maze of tracks and cars mixed in with stacks belching smoke and steam and where he could see the hellish glow of the furnaces even in the afternoon light. He had to downshift to third to pull the sharp left-hand grade from the bridge up into Madison Heights on the east side of the river. At the top he passed a big roadhouse that he'd bet was jammed when each shift let off at the foundry, and jumpin' come Friday and Saturday! A little further and back through the trees to the right he just could see the big brick buildings of what everyone called "the colony", the state institution for idiots and the hopelessly retarded -- he'd never heard its formal name which was no doubt painted carefully on a State-issue sign board once you came down the side-street to the grounds. He bet that the grandees and bankers of Lynchburg had played the legislature like a fiddle to keep those unfortunate folks on the other side of the river, but have that government payroll money make its way into their businesses and deposit accounts. "Pig town," the Lynchburg folks talked down Madison Heights, which actually loomed, a mile away, over much of their city! Raymond would've noticed the railroad and foundry on his own, figured that the Yankees had focused their 'reconstruction' on the richest place around, but would have passed through Madison heights completely uninformed if he hadn't picked up a skinny kid thumbing a lift just as he came into the bridge.

The kid, maybe fifteen, was headed to his Grandparents' place up twenty-nine in Amherst, the next town after Monroe. Curious about the stick and why Raymond wasn't in the Army, he soon had his story. After sitting quietly for a minute, he volunteered that his uncle, his mom's brother, had joined the Air Corps, but had been killed two years before in a training accident. The youngest in a large family, they'd called him "Cricket." Raymond dropped the kid off at the bottom of a lane leading to the right just as things started changing from country to town. He just could see a tall, old brick house set back in the trees where the boy was headed.

Half a mile further and he experienced one of the Department of Transportation's big experiments, a traffic circle. Intended to speed the crossing at the intersection of twenty-nine and sixty, it mostly just slowed things down as people tried to figure out what to do, but the youngsters loved it, go in and drive your girl around a few times honking the horn before going out! He simply had to go in, do a half circle, and go straight out the other side, which brought him to the center of town, a bank, a couple of stores, some of stone, the Courthouse and jail. Instinctively applying the test he knew from the rest of the South, he gauged that Amherst was not a very prosperous county--it didn't have a Confederate Soldier at the Courthouse path, only a marble memorial slab. A few more houses, the cemetery on the left, and he was back in the country.

The countryside was changing as he continued on towards Lovingson, Nelson County. Fewer pine forests and more prosperous-looking small farms with cattle in the fields. He was clearly in the foothills of the Blue Ridge, now, and the little Rockfish River (how they could call it a river after the size of the James he didn't know, but he supposed that everything was relative, and that creeks must be a pissy affair where they came down out of the ridges) sparkled to his left along much of the way. About ten miles north of Lovingston (prosperous place, Confederate Soldier), he turned left and headed straight for the mountain on Route six. Climbing up six, he noted a change in the roadside, or perhaps better said, pole and guy-wire vegetation. He'd passed the elevation where it got too cold for kudzu to thrive! The Department of Agriculture's golem from the '30's, kudzu had been imported from, he thought, Japan, and touted as a miracle forage plant. It would grow anywhere, stop erosion, and provide high-nutrient forage for cattle. It could, and did, grow anywhere, anywhere and everywhere, up telephone poles, into electrical substations until it got burned, over junked cars, unused houses, barns and silos. When they put the plant in the right place, it did hold the soil and where stock could get to it, they loved it and kept it from taking over, but it was king of the roadside and brushy woodlot throughout the South below this elevation in Virginia. The forage crop end just hadn't worked out -- the tough, woody stems were too much for a ground-driven sickle bar mower, and by the time power take-off mowers, which might have had enough grunt to cut the stuff, started coming to the farms, its foul reputation had been established, the Department of Agriculture had stopped printing optimistic pamphlets, and the highway boards and utility companies were busy concocting poisons to keep it off of the signs, poles, and wires. If the stuff had been good in Japan, he thought, they must have an awfully different way of pasturing their stock and gathering forage. From what he heard about the size and fanaticism of the Japanese army, they probably had one guy leading each cow or goat along the road and up the path, eating its fill, and hundreds of ladies with baskets and bamboo ladders plucking off each leaf that the critters missed!

The real mountain started at Avon, where he had to shift down into third and hug the right-hand gravels in turn after turn where it was impossible to tell if anyone was coming downhill, perhaps taking their half of the road in the middle. It wasn't much further to Afton, store and post office on the right, a little humpbacked bridge over the Norfolk and Western followed immediately by the gravel lane down to the station in a little flat. About half a mile up the line the trains hit the second, larger, tunnel though the Blue Ridge. He membered someone -- a fellow passenger to or from the hospital, or maybe a conductor, explaining that the first tunnel, eighty years earlier had been further south; post office up the line, Crozet, named for the tunnel's French engineer. The road in the village of Afton had front porches right on the shoulder, and you couldn't go in or out of the garage's service bay without blocking traffic. Just past the garage Raymond came into the sharpest series of rising hairpin turns that he'd ever seen -- curves like that only came up in his part of North Carolina when the first road-surveying milk cow had gone around a barn some fool had left in the way and the county road gang just kept on replowing the ditches as they lay. At least in Carolina, though, a curve like that was flat. These pulled him down into second gear, and if he'd wanted time to look at the stonework in the wall on the high side, he'd have to have gone to first. The curves ended as abruptly as they'd started in a T-bone intersection with Route two-fifty that had the left end of his dashboard riding about ten inches higher than the right as he stopped to check for oncoming traffic before making his left turn. This was a place where he made the turn in groundhog low, and then left it there a while once on the straight to gain some momentum before shifting up. Afton Mountain, the Rockfish gap about two miles up, he'd cut the long grade about in half by slipping up though the steep village road, a luxury that the truckers in front of and behind him couldn't enjoy because of the size and weight of their rigs. Watching them grinding upwards, Raymond thought it curious that he'd never heard who invented the tractor and trailer truck combination. He remembered seeing an article in an ancient stack of Popular Mechanics at a friend's house that Glenn Curtiss and Ransom Olds had teamed up to make fancy camping trailers that were pulled by either a Model A with an airplane wheel hub mounted in the rumble-seat well to fit the connecting pin that pulled the trailer and allowed it to be pulled at even a right angle to make a tight turn, or by a custom Olds tractor/sedan. As might be expected, Curtiss' creations were light and structured like Jenny aircraft components. Old's tractors, however, were enormous, sleek, metal-skinned paeans to speed, power, and luxury. Raymond had seen neither in person, but he had shared the road with lots of Ransom E. Olds' REO Speedwagon straight trucks and tractor- trailer outfits.

At the top of the ridge there was a sharp curve to the right, and in the short level stretch before the western downgrade began, traffic passed under the laid-stone arch where the Skyline Drive, the WPA project in Shenandoah National Park, crossed over route two-fifty, then started the long, curving grade down the Waynesboro side of the mountain. The few diesel trucks blew smoke as their drivers, shifted into a lower gear, and the gassers like Raymond worked the brakes and shifted down, too. The brakes on the Barrelnose were manual -- leg muscles, pedal, rods, cams and curved shoes expanding inside a steel drum on each wheel, better than the constricting bands on the hubs of much older vehicles, but not nearly as good as the hydraulic brakes Ford put on the later, last Barrelnose in '39. Raymond understood hydraulic advantage because of the rams that pumped water on farms that had streams with the slight drop needed to power them, less than it took for a wheel or tub turbine, and because of a demonstration one of his high school science teachers had done. Mr. Frame had filled a gallon vinegar jug completely full of water, put a rubber plug in the neck just far enough to hold it in place without any air underneath, and exploded the jug by rapping the plug with the heel of his hand. The force per square inch of the small master cylinder exerted on the greater area of the wheel cylinders had made one hell of a difference on car brakes! The first long curve to the right was about three-quarters of a mile long, and kinked left at a bungalow in the woods painted orange and black -- a Halloween house. After that, the curves were short and steep, back and forth, smelling of hot brakes the whole way (he hoped not his own, and reasoned, reassuringly, that the smell blew back from the big rig in front of him, and that if his were overheated the guy behind him would get the stink, and he'd be feeling his grip fade, which he wasn't) until he reached the town of Waynesboro in the flat at the bottom of the mountain.

Waynesboro was a town of clearly-posted speed limits, 35 right after passing under the Norfolk and Western at the end of the last curve, even though it didn't look like anything to require it in the next flat mile except some tourist cabins and several billboards that looked like the perfect lair of the traffic cop and, judging from the tire ruts he caught out of the corner of his eye, were put to just that use. Waynesboro was an industrial town, situated, because of its early need for water power, a little too close to the uppermost usable bit of the south fork of the Shenandoah River. As the street curved left and side streets with a good many small houses began to give things more of a town feel, he passed a big brick factory building with saw tooth roof that let sunlight in everywhere. "Virginia Metalcrafters" said the big sign on the wall. There was an old cannon on a wooden gun carriage by the main door, which he recognized as a 'French' seventy-five from the 1918 war. A French innovation, a light field piece with what amounted to a king-sized shock absorber underneath and parallel to the barrel which, along with a spade on the end of the trail, kept the recoil of firing from pushing the gun backwards, 'out of battery', preserving the precise position that aided in the effectiveness of these weapons, and saving the cannoneers work, increasing their rate of fire. Many of the 'French" howitzers had been made in the States -- he guessed some of them right there that factory. He had no idea what they were producing for this war, but the curb and lot beside it were filled with worker's old cars, the smokestacks were pouring smoke, and enough heat was coming from some of the open skylights to make the tops of the trees behind the building look wavy. A few blocks more and he passed DuPont Avenue, and could see steam and smoke coming from acres of plant buildings. There was a mountain of coal next to the railroad, with roofed conveyor belts moving it to the various boilers, and pipes going everywhere from building to building. Lots of chemical tank cars on some of the compound's internal tracks, and boxcars waiting to be loaded near the biggest building. He knew from hearing about it while he'd been in the hospital that this wasn't one of DuPont's explosives factories, but was instead vastly more sophisticated, a plant where they spun fine, spidery, nylon yarn which substituted for silk in parachutes and insulation for wiring in delicate electrical gear. He knew that there were other factories closer to the river, a fabric mill, but he'd never heard what else.

The street got steeper and he had to downshift as he got into the business district, banks, stores, the Post Office, and at the far end the Wayne movie theatre and the General Wayne Hotel. Uncharacteristically for the south, especially this far in from the coast, the name of the town and its establishments celebrated a general from the American Revolution --"Mad" Anthony Wayne -- rather than a Confederate general from the late unpleasantness. The groups of people on the sidewalks were peppered with boys in the grey uniform of the military academy, Fishburne, on the rising ground south of Main Street's last busy block. It was getting on towards supper time, time to find a place for the night. The General Wayne had looked mighty appealing, but by looks Raymond knew that it was priced for officers, businessmen and chemical engineers, not gimpy ex-corporals, no matter how shiny a vehicle they could pull under the port du cohere covering the front doors to the lobby. He drove on west, out of town and about halfway to Fishersville and the hospital, and found a reasonably priced room at a camp of tourist cabins. The bed didn't look too saggy, and it had a private toilet and tin shower stall, obviously added onto the back as an improvement, 'cause the washbasin was still on the wall of the bedroom. Good thing it wasn't cold yet, as he saw no sign of a heat source, central or otherwise. He half-dragged his barracks bag in, shut the door, and stretched out for a nap before supper, the hum of passing traffic like the hum of bees in a hive as he fell asleep.

By the time he woke up, washed his face, and, combed his hair it was late enough that the traffic on two-fifty had eased off, enabling him to make a quick left-hand turn into the westbound lane. There was a little roadhouse just beyond the Hospital gates where he thought he'd enjoy eating, just a couple of tables where everyone ate together, no matter how they'd come in (if you had a girlfriend, she could end up sitting between you and some jerk, if you were by yourself, well, there was the adventure of sitting with whoever showed up) low prices, pretty good food, and in the winter, a huge stone fireplace that took up one end of the room. He'd been there a couple of times on pass from the hospital. Cresting the hill it looked like he was in luck -- the lights were on and there were a couple of parking places on the gravel that covered the pre-war front yard. Wiping his shoes on the mat as he went in, he caught the approving glance of the proprietress, a woman whose husband was gone to the war and who had come back to her home community to weather the duration. He'd been such an infrequent customer while at the hospital that he doubted that she membered him and chalked her glance up to a comment on his good raisin', wipin' his feet! She had thick blonde hair starting to go to a streak or two of grey. He didn't know quite what the story was, whether her man was still in the service, had been an early fatal casualty, or if he was just working in a shipyard or oilfield someplace that she wouldn't tolerate. The younger, brunette, waitress came over and took his order, steak and a beer, Black Label, from down in Baltimore. An older guy dressed in workmen's clothes but with nothing showing about him that could identify his line of work came in and took the seat beside Raymond. The waitress came with Raymond's beer and took the man's order -- just the same as Raymond's -- the specialty of the house due to the availability of beef from the surrounding countryside, they'd probably get few complaints if they just bought beer and food out as customers came in!

"Bob," the man turned, extended his hand, and introduced himself. Raymond said his name while shaking the proffered hand, returning the courtesy. "Early discharge?" Bob asked, nodding towards Raymond's stick on the floor beside his chair.

"Yes, sir. Got hit just at the top of the cliffs at Normandy, got sent from there to the hospital here, and now I'm back from home in North Carolina, looking for work."

"Well, with the war on," Bob said as his beer and both their steaks appeared, "there's work for those who want to do some, and jobs for right many that don't." Bob grinned, chewed, and looked a bit thoughtful. After a sip of beer he said "the war economy and the lack of men gives a new meaning to my Mother's expression, learned at her father's knee during reconstruction days, 'you just can't get no good help since the War.' They both had a good laugh over that and ate some more. "What you reckon on doing with that bad leg?"

"I thought that though pretty hard while I was cleaning up my tuck to come up here," Raymond mopped up some gravy with a torn-off piece of bread. "I like mechanics and engines, but figured hard floors and crawling around under things were out, which left driving. I can't move fright, but when I thought it through I realized that there was one kind of freight that loaded and unloaded itself -- fuel. Turn that valve to fill up, drag a hose a little ways, it can't be but so long, and turn the other valve to unload!" Both of them worked on their steaks. Raymond continued "I like being outside and I'm gonna look for a run going around to all of the country stores."

"I might," Bob wiped his mouth with his napkin and pulled on his beer. "Be able to help you. I work out of Richmond, weights and measures, I'm the guy who comes around with the calibrated copper cans to check station pump delivery, and I know most of the gas and oil guys up and down the Valley." The guy did, Raymond thought, smell a little like gasoline, and his hand had felt pretty smooth, consistent with the job he described. "You'd be wanting to talk to distributors, not station owners, even the guys that own big ones. Gulf is out of Charlottesville, Esso out of Harrisonburg, and Shell and Texaco in Staunton. If you want to be driving around the country, you ought to talk to Bill Riley, the Texaco guy, because his family's had the franchise longer than the Shell people, and for that reason has most of the country places. Hell, the Riley's weren't anything but a big country store themselves when they started selling gasoline, sold it in big square cans off of boxcars with a wire handle on top and a screw cap in the corner, just like lamp oil -- people used it for cleaning fluid and for asbestos-mantle lamps. Riley's store just happened to adjoin the Norfolk and Western side track leading from the station in Staunton to the engine turntable, so that when cars came in and they started shipping oil and gas in drums and tank cars, they were a natural, built a little spur for those cars on their back lot, then almost immediately set it up for tank cars. Bill still calls it "the store" and even though the building looks like one and I reckon that's how every invoice is printed, I doubt you could buy much more'n a cigar there that don't stink of oil!" Bob went for the last of his steak and beer. "Funniest thing, though," he continued," they don't have a retail pump to check so I never go there. Now the Wheelers, they've got the Shell business, out on the Valley Pike, Route eleven north of town, they have a couple of pumps along with their office that I have to stop in and check. Just about all of their business is in supplying stations with big underground tanks, none of those square steel ones on the front porch or on four rocks next to the front steps that you see at the old places that Riley services. Wheelers pump their gas into a big tank on their little lot next to the Baltimore and Ohio line, I don't think that their siding's big enough to hold but two cars. Riley's got enough room for more. Riley's got straight trucks, a flatbed that they deliver drum and boxed stuff to their customers with, and another with frame-mounted tanks for gas, kerosene, and bulk lubricating oil."

"Wow!," said Raymond, finishing his steak, too but with a couple of sips of beer left since Bob'd been dry from doing most of the talking. "Lucky for me you wanted steak instead of chicken tonight! Sounds like Bill Riley's the man I need to go see in the morning. I understand where Wheelers are, how do I find Riley's?"

"Take two-fifty on into Staunton, when you pass the lunatic asylum and see the B &O Station, turn right through the arch under the N&W tracks, then left on Johnson Street. Two blocks up turn left at the Courthouse and jail, and that street runs into Middlebrook road. You'll pass the place that buys ginseng, hides, and scrap metal on the right, a lumberyard and coal yard on the left, and just after you go under the N&W line and spur you'll see Riley's on the right, set back some from the road, everything but the Texaco sign painted battleship grey."

They got up and took their tickets over to the counter to pay for their supper. "Thanks, and good to meet you," Raymond said from behind as Bob paid, pulled a toothpick out of the holder on the counter and turned towards the kitchen, intent on talking with the blond-haired woman.

"Glad to help, Good Luck!"

Raymond stepped up to the counter and paid. "Thanks ma'am it was real good" The waitress who took his money looked as though she might have enjoyed talking a bit, too, but Raymond's mind was on the next day. He went out into the circle of light from the bulb over the door, and then stepped into the darkness to make his way around to the driver's door of his truck. He could see the copper measures with riveted iron-hoop mouths and bottom rims in the back of Bob's state-licensed pickup. They didn't look very official -- more like a bunch of old milk- and cream-cans with most of the green paint knocked off.

Back up the road at the cabins, Raymond took a quick pass through the tin shower stall, which, surprisingly, had plenty of hot water, and fell into bed. He dreamt of the frustration of trying to use Bob's single-handle copper cans in Quentin Baker's new dairy setup.

The morning was bright and clear, and he caught breakfast, eggs, bacon, and pancakes, at the same place he'd eaten the night before. No point in wasting time searching out another, when he knew he could get fed well there. He cranked the truck, and headed west towards Staunton, the county seat and intersection of the B& O and N&W. Route two-fifty paralleled the N&W main line. He passed a whistle stop called Brand, where the creek bottom was wide enough that there was a second track, a spur long enough to hold an entire coal train while priority traffic passed, and little else that he could see. About a mile later there was one of those cast-metal plaques that the state tourism people had put up proclaiming that there were 'Settlers Graves' nearby, although he couldn't see what was so interesting about that. Houses were beginning to crowd in a little, and he passed a cemetery with a fancy wall and custodian's house, surrounded by what he could see was a Colored community. Going down the last grade into town, he saw Western State Lunatic Asylum on his left, enormous brick antebellum buildings surrounded by an iron picket fence about ten feet tall. The big porticoes at the ends of a couple of the buildings were screened with heavy wire grids, and he could see some of the inmates, hanging by their fingers, watching the traffic go by. Just as the B&O station came into sight directly in front of him the Asylum grounds opened out into a park with a stream and willow trees, still surrounded by the tall fence. At some point, the road had crossed the N&W railroad, which was now on his right, flanked by the big boiler-house for the Asylum's heat and its private coalyard, a spur elevated on concrete pylons so that the cars could dump their loads.

He followed Bob's directions, made a right through the arch under the tracks, then an immediate left, spotting the Courthouse dome with the lady justice on top above a couple of medium sized hotels and a damn big flour mill. He turned left just after the Courthouse (no Confederate soldier, he'd learn later that Staunton had put theirs at the top of the hill in the town's rather grand Thornrose Cemetery), went by the N&W passenger station and a long line of freight warehouses followed by the spout for the engine water tank on the hill across the track from the station, curved left under the two tracks Bob had talked about, and there it was, a battleship grey country store with a couple of red Texaco trucks parked out front and some tank cars lined up in the back.

30. BILL RILEY AND MRS. RUSS

Raymond pulled onto the lot, killed the Ford, adjusted his engineer's cap to exactly the right angle, grabbed his stick, climbed out and walked over to the steps leading to the store's broad porch, where there was an older man sitting in a battered captain's chair leaning back on the rear two legs, his shoulders easy against the wall. "Mornin'," Raymond said as he got to the bottom of the steps.

"Mornin'," the man said back.

"I'm Raymond McCleary, lookin' for Mr. Bill Riley."

"You found him," the man replied in a less than encouraging tone. "What you want?"

"I want you to hire me to run your tank deliveries." Riley rocked forward onto all four legs of the chair. Raymond stayed where he was at the bottom of the steps, his head at about the level of Riley's knees, supplicant before his thane, but still a free man of the clan, standing his ground, such as it was, and standing it tall.

"Let me get this straight. You roll in here from Carolina bright one mornin'; I don't know you from Adam; I don't know nothin' about you except you're wearing army shoes and britches, got a bad leg and seem pretty good at shinin' up old pickups; and you want me to hire you and trust you to drive my truck when I ain't even thought about askin' around for a driver?"

"Yes, Sir. I reckon that's a pretty fair assessment. Let me fill it out a bit for you. I got shot at the top of a cliff at Normandy. I got patched up at the hospital over in Fishersville and decided I kinda' liked it around here. Discharged back to the farm in North Carolina where my younger brothers and sister were doin' just fine without a gimpy hand I realized that after the war was over the place wasn't big enough to hardly make a living for two of them. I bought the old Ford from a neighbor who'd inherited right smart money and had sold my brothers 'bout half of his old equipment as he replaced it with modern stuff, and had bought the last fancy Studebaker pickup on the lot before war production started. I polished on the Ford 'till I figured out what I could do. I'm a good driver, so I figured I could haul freight, but with my leg I can't load. Studyin' on it I realized that tank trucks load with the turn of a valve, and unload the same way after a little hose draggin', which I can do, although my moves might not be real elegant. I know your name 'cause I was lucky enough to be eating a steak last night next to the State weights and measures guy, Bob, who told me about your operation. I know that the last draft call got into the married men, the old men, didn't leave hardly anyone who wasn't a sissy or blind. I'm betting that you can use somebody who came up on a farm, knows a day's work, and yeah, for what it's worth, can make a dull old truck shine!"

"Come on up here, boy." Riley reached over and draggd another ancient chair over next to his.

"I don't know," Riley said kinda slow, "what thinkin' or talkin' have to do with driving a tank truck, but I kinda' like the way you do both. What kind of pay you lookin' for?"

Raymond knew this question would be coming, wherever he went, so he'd already worked out an answer. "No disrespect to them, or you either, Sir, but I gotta have something better than soldier's pay, having to feed myself and find someplace to live". Like Riley he, too, was talking a little slower, the exchange becoming more of a conversation and less of a contest.

"And what was that, what'd you muster out as?

"As a Corporal, sir, and once I was back here at the hospital I got a little over $74 a month."

"For starters, then, why don't we double that -- I'll give you $35 a week, and you fill your pickup at the same tap we fill our trucks. That's not war-plant pay, but driving a truck around the countryside gabbing with old geezers like me at every stop ain't exactly production-line work."

"Fair enough -- for starters." Raymond stuck out his hand to shake on it. "Once I know the route and the people, I'll probably be worth a little more to you."

"Mebbe so," Riley grumbled with a grin, "but remember, the profit on petroleum ain't but pennies a gallon, and the tanks on the front of those stores ain't gonna grow just because you're on the truck!"

Riley pulled out a pocket notebook and the stub of a pencil, scribbled on a page, tore it out and handed it to Raymond. "Here's the name and address of a lady up on West Beverley Street across from the cemetery who usually has a room or two to let -- too much house and too little family. Go on over there and see what you can work out with her, then get back here. Go back the way you came on Middlebrook, turn left at the rag and bone place on Lewis, then go up two blocks and turn left on Beverley. I'd suggest walking around back and knocking at the kitchen porch."

"Thanks," Raymond said, and headed for the pickup. Kicked the starter, backed up, and glanced at the paper before he turned out onto the road. 'Mrs. Marie Russ, 1206 West Beverley Street,' was written over Riley's signature by way of introduction. Turning at Klotz's apparently prosperous three-story salvage warehouse -- maybe the horseshoe set in concrete over the door really had brought luck, he went up the hill past Trinity Church (Episcopal, another one of those cast-metal tourist signs in front explained that it was the original Augusta Parish, and that the Legislature had met there after fleeing the British during the Revolution), turned onto Beverley, the town's main street, and headed west, away from the business district, past brick and frame houses which mostly looked like they dated from the 1890's until he saw the stone walls of the cemetery on his right and started counting house numbers until he found the right one, an enormous place with a curved steamboat porch that wrapped just about around all three sides of the house visible from the street, a high gable in front, and a red tin roof. He parked along the curb out front, adjusted the engineer's cap to exactly the right angle, stepped out of the cab and rubbed the toe of each shoe against the back of the opposite trouser leg, circled his waist with his hands to make sure that his shirttail was in, and stick in one hand and Riley's notebook page in the other headed up the two-track cement driveway towards the car shed that looked like it would take him by the kitchen.

His first step onto the porch scared up a cat that

had been sitting just inside the screen door, so that he didn't even need to knock to make his presence known. A brown-haired woman a bit younger looking than his mother, wearing an apron, appeared in the cat's patch of floor. When he realized someone was coming, he quickly pulled off his hat and slicked his hair down. "Mrs. Russ?" The woman nodded. "Good mornin', I'm Raymond McCleary, Bill Riley just hired me and said you might have a room to rent."

"Did he now?" she said, not so much asking a question as making a moment to look him over. "Army pants and shoes, more of a southern voice than I usually hear around Staunton, and a bad leg." she said, shaking her head, "Has Bill taken to hiring right off the discharge ward in Fishersville, where he's safe that nobody's ever heard anything about him?" Fortunately, she was smiling when she said that last part.

"Close," Raymond replied with a grin," I was back home on the farm in North Carolina for just about a month."

"Well, come on in and sit down at the table," she said, opening the door and stepping aside, "let's talk a bit while I decide if I can take you on." Remembering to shuffle his already clean feet on the outside mat, Raymond stepped in and took the proffered chair, wondering what direction this introduction was going to take.

"I've known Bill Riley most of my life, longer than since I inherited this pile of a place from my aunties. He's usually pretty shrewd about people. What's the deal with you?" Raymond gave her a somewhat more conversational version of the account he'd given

Riley. "OK," she said. "My situation: I'm widowed and have to take in boarders to keep this place going. I've got two kids, Lee, my daughter, who teaches school down the street at Thomas Jefferson Elementary, right across from Trinity Church, and Earl, who's away in the Air Corps. He says he's ground crew with the bombers and safe, but I know him; every time some waist-gunner has a bad cold, I'm sure he's taken the guy's place, happy as hell to be off of the ground. I really despair of his making it through the war to come home. Bill was right, I do have a room. The one on the left up over the kitchen," she gestured towards the sloped notch in the ceiling where the back stairs went up. There's a bathroom up there that you can share with the other boarder, David, that's like the one in most of these old houses, carved out of part of the sleeping porch. You're welcome to use the back sitting room through there," she indicated another door off of the kitchen," there's a radio in there; and the icebox if you mark what's yours. Please leave the front of the house for me and Lee. Ten dollars a week, and if you let me know what time you have to go out I'll fix you a little some-thing for breakfast. If your work schedule is such that you want other meals, we'll negotiate. If it turns out I don't like you, or you don't like me, we give each other a week's notice."

"Sounds fair enough," replied Raymond, as he fished in his pocket for his rapidly slimming wallet and pulled out ten dollars for the first week. He went out to the truck and got his barracks bag, took it upstairs and parked it just inside the door, and left, heading back to Riley's.

Riley had the left hand hood folded open on the big International tank truck, checking the oil and radiator when Raymond pulled back on the lot. The tanks were low and oval, Raymond noted, beneath the cab's back window so that he would at least be able to see directly behind him if he were backing into a telephone pole. Parked cars, he though ruefully, would be another matter, subject to side mirrors and blind spots.

"C'mon over here!" Riley beckoned with his left arm while shaking oil off of the dipstick onto the gravels with his right. As soon as Raymond was within conversational earshot Riley began: "Same rules your Daddy had, run it as far as you want without gasoline, but damn you if you run it without water or oil! She's a '36 and burns a bit, and steams some on the mountains, so you gotta check them a couple times a day." He put that side of the hood down, walked around, and raised the other. "Your bad leg'll be glad to know that '36 was the first year for hydraulic brakes on International. Here's the fluid reservoir, top it up every morning. We keep a can under the seat, there's a case to work from in the store. Battery's over on this side two, again, don't let it get low or you'll be finding someone with a tractor and chain to get you started." Riley closed that hood flap and walked back along the driver's side of the truck.

"The big tank's gasoline, the smaller one's kerosene and the others two weights of motor oil. You were half right about unloading. If the store's tank is lower'n the truck, hook the hose on the valve piped to the bottom of the tank and gravity'll do the work. If it's higher, hook it to the monkey-pump on the side. Somebody actually thought those through when they made 'em. Delivery is on the down stroke when the weight of your arm helps with the pull, on the up stroke you're just coasting, leathers flapped open as the cylinders fill.

Each pull on the pump is about a pint; lots of customers have the tin spouts off of their collection of retail oil jars and fill them while you work the pump. Keep your receipt book in your back pocket and write the amounts down as you finish with each tank -- storekeepers talk too much for you to remember all the numbers. All the valves and pump outlets have bronze caps, and there's a brass wrench on a light chain in the drip tray, don't want no sparks around gasoline fumes! Keep some sand in the tray to absorb the drips. No matter how cruddy with other vehicles' drippings and tobacco spit when you stop, any drop of oil in front of the store when you've just pulled out will be your fault and talked about for the rest of the day, not very good advertising.

"There's two hoses, black for both grades of engine oil, and red for gasoline and kerosene. Valves right behind the couplers and right behind the spouts. Gravity flow, turn the valve off at the spout before you turn the truck valve on -- that way you can work the spout valve as you fill. Working by either gravity or pump you can either stop shy of the customer's mark and drain the hose into their tank, or fill to their mark and drain the hose back into the truck tank. You're probably going to want to drain the hose into their tank, 'cause if you drain it back into the truck, you have to unhitch the hose from the tank and climb up and stick the end in the filler hatch -- I doubt your leg's gonna like that very often. Most of the customers know where you have to stop to have things come out right once you empty the hose if they're getting the tank filled, and will help you out 'till you learn. It only gets tricky if they just want part of a tank, which happens sometimes if their business has been slow. My guess is that the hose holds about seven gallons." Riley took a wiping rag out of a box on the running board and cleaned off his hands after handling the ends of the hoses and valves. Raymond noticed that there was a pair of oil-soaked leather gloves in the box for the driver's use.

"Every customer's tank is like a model T Ford's -- it's got a dipstick that tells you how many gallons are in there. Check it before you fill, write it on the slip, check it after you fill, write it on the slip and do your subtraction right there to arrive at the number of gallons that goes on the bottom line. They sign the slip and keep a copy; we calculate the price and tax and mail them a bill each month. No arguments. Sometimes, though, there ain't no stick, or there's a new, penciled one that ain't been used before. Lots of reasons for that; kids run off with it, it fell through the cracks in the floor or irretrievably behind the tank, or if it's a special delivery to a farm, they maybe never had one. There's a stick marked in inches behind the seat in the cab, got a hinge in the middle to unfold it and split it in two if you need more length, and this," he unbuttoned his shirt pocket and pulled out a well-thumbed little booklet, "there's one in the glove box in the dash. PETROLEUM DEALERS GUIDE TO TANK DEMENSIONS AND VOLUME was embossed on a cover that made some attempt, foiled by long usage, at being oil-resistant.

The booklet had four tabbed sections, one each for rectangular/square, round, oval and half-round end cross-section tanks. The top of the first page of each showed a line drawing of the type of tank covered by that set of tables with an indication of where to take the necessary measurements and, to add absolute credibility to the work, in bold print, the algebraic equation needed to work out the volume of fluid in each when the variable factor was the distance in inches measured from the bottom of the tank. The tables were exhaustive. If a tank could be positioned in more than one way, set on end, on its side, or laid on its belly, there was a drawing and table to match. Sizes went from a gallon can up to tanks big enough that Raymond would have to tie an extension onto the brass-tipped stick in the truck to reach the bottom -- the book was obviously prepared for the entire industry! From long use, the book naturally tended to fall open to the pages that matched the containers of their customer base, and it was thin enough that you could jam it into your back pocket along with the carbon-papered receipt pad while you were dragging hose and turning valves.

"Alright," Riley sort of half-barked. "Time for driving and loading lessons. Take the truck over alongside that closest tank car, the one by the shed. Raymond crawled up into the red truck's cab, deposited his stick on the right-hand side of the seat, and adjusted his engineer's cap to exactly the right angle. Right foot solidly on the brake, he threw in the clutch with the left and jiggled the gearshift around until he was confident it was out of reverse, in which the truck had been parked, and wiggling reassuringly in neutral. It had been years since he'd driven anything larger than the pickup -- Army life had consisted of incessant travelling in the backs of tucks driven by men who understood that moving forward for ten or fifteen feet, then slamming on the brakes would pack the soldiers tighter than familiarity called for on the long parallel benches, allowing loading of the final few men or bags of equipment. He pushed the small knob on the side of the stick down checking that the cable-controlled two-speed rear axle was in low; pulled the choke button out from the flyspecked flat red steel of the dash; and turned on the ignition, the key encapsulated in one of those leather folders with a metal snap on the side, designed to keep the key from poking you in the leg while it was in your pocket, and to provide a tactile cue when you wanted to retrieve it, but which draped down from the switch like a rotting maple leaf on a rock at the edge of a trout stream, because the key had never been removed from the switch since the tuck was delivered eight years before and the leather had absorbed the dirt and oil from every hand that turned the switch on or off. He pumped the accelerator a few times to prime the carb and tromped down on the starter. A couple of grunts and the engine fired. A few moments of pedal fanning and sliding the choke in and out and all six cylinders were running smoothly. He grabbed the hand-brake handle, holding the button on top down with his thumb so that it would clear the locking ratchet as he released its hold on the driveshaft just behind the transmission, and he was ready to go, having paid a lot more attention to the process than to Bill Riley, who had his hat pushed back on his head and was patiently chewing a toothpick. The track ballast made the grade of the spur high enough that the cars could be unloaded without resort to a pump. Riley had built a long shed next to the spur with a dock at the far end with the right elevation to transfer drums and box goods to the flat-bed, and counterweighted hoses and valves for three cars, one gas, one oil, and one kerosene at the near end. The shed doubled as a cover for the trucks. A long pole, as deep as a tank-car, marked in inches, hung from wire brackets along the trackside eave.

Raymond triple-clutched the clash-box transmission, pulled the gearshift into second in order to line things up to ease silently into first, crawled the truck into the spot Riley had indicated, killed the engine, left it in gear, pulled the brake ratchet on tight, and got out leaving his stick behind, as he figured the next step was gonna involve climbing up onto the tanks. "Good," Riley called out as he sidled over into the shade. "Get on up there and undog the gas tank." Raymond clambered from the back edge of the running-board onto the drip-pan where the hoses lay, higher up on the freight fame of the truck, and used the welded-on handholds to pull himself up top. The oval shape of the tanks made an easy place to stand, and he was surprised to see that each tank had a nautical looking opening and cover with a brass rim and bronze dogs much larger than the hose, nozzle, and valve required. He shuddered when he realized that, like some of the oval deck-plates he'd been told covered various tanks on shipboard, they were just man-sized. Man sized for the youngest, slimmest guy in the crew. He hoped that tank-cleaning wasn't part of the job. "Open her up and pull the red end down," called Riley. "I'll save you some climbing and open the car valve when you tell me that yours up there's closed. You need turn it on gradual to understand how it pushes against the rim. When you're by yourself turn off the valve at the truck tank end, set its lip against the lip of the open tank, and scramble down to open the car before going back up to top off. I know that sounds like an extra trip up and down, but you have to be sure that the filler line isn't hanging up in the rafters with the valve open before you crack open the car valve." Unlike the smaller hoses that were used to unload the truck, the hose with the brass nozzle and gate valve hanging above the truck was a good four inches in diameter -- Raymond could see what a loss would result from a mistake. He put the nozzle, with a hook that kept it from slipping backwards off of the edge of the tank in place, opened the gate valve in two or three turns and watched the level rise in the tank. "We don't," Riley continued, "generally stick the car tank unless it looks like a short load. We have to crawl up there when we start on a car and loosen the dogs a bit to have good air flow in as we drain out, and always check the level then if it looks lower'n it should. The refinery people have an in-line flow meter that they read when they send us our invoices, matched by car number. The tank on the truck filled surprisingly quickly. Raymond closed the valve and pushed the filler head back into the rafters, pulled and held there by a greasy steel cable through a pulley attached to an apparently carefully measured Texaco grease bucket full of sand as a counterweight. Raymond could imagine the day that they were installed, Riley on top of the truck with each hose full from an open car valve, instructing his helper to add or remove sand until the balance was just right for the variations in weight of each valve, hose, cable clamp and differing liquid content. That had probably been a long afternoon! The buckets had their lids crimped back on to keep the sand dry and their weight constant. "Come on down. The gasoline tank was the only one that was low enough to worry about." Raymond closed the lid, tightened the dogs, worked his way down to the ground and wiped his hands on the cleanest rag in the running-board box. "Better wear the gloves next time," his boss directed.

"'Bout noon," Riley said, putting his pocket watch, which hung from a leather thong in the button-hole of the flap of the adjacent pocket that held his pencil and notebook, back into the central, side-opening pocket of his overalls. "Let's get some dinner, take my vehicle." Raymond grabbed his stick out of the cab and fell into step, headed towards the front lot of the store.

Bill Riley's pickup couldn't have been more un-like Raymond's. Although a Ford, it was about ten years older, hadn't an undented panel on its body and bore liberal evidence of the bit of subsistence farming with which Bill smoothed over any rough spots in his income from the oil business. A couple of hogs, a milk cow, a couple of elderly brood cows to provide an annual steer, and a mess of chickens. They drove to the nearest restaurant, on the corner of Beverley and Lewis, where rather than parking on the street, they pulled into the back lot and a place by the kitchen door. Riley got out and grabbed a forty-gallon steel garbage can from the bed and swapped it for the two-thirds full one by the door. "For the hogs", he explained. He wiped his hands on his overall legs and led the way in through the back door.

"Vames's Lunch and Candyland" read the name painted at the top of the chalkboard menu behind the counter that ran down one side of the narrow restaurant, the outside wall next to Lewis Street, with small tables tight against the common wall of the adjacent building, just enough room left in between for customers and waitresses to maneuver. Riley settled onto a worn stool and Raymond fell into place beside him.

"Hey, Bill," the waitress said as she plunked some silverware and paper napkins down in front of them. "Who's this?" she asked, nodding in Raymond's direction.

"My new tank truck driver. Sally, meet Raymond, Raymond McCleary. Raymond, Sally Snyder."

"Howdy," Raymond said. "Pleased to meet you."

"You, too."

"A beer and a hotdog, coleslaw and chili, I'm buyin' for both of us" Bill preempted any further conversation.

"If that's the case, I reckon I'll have the same," Raymond responded to her questioning look in his direction.

Sally reached down and pulled to dripping, cold beers from the cooler under the counter, popped the tops off in the Coke opener on the counter's edge, set them down in front of her customers, turned and hollered (no other word described her vocalization) to the cook on the other side of the pass-through window, "two dogs with it all!" Raymond looked around as he sipped his beer and concluded that "Candyland" was no tearoom. He and Bill Riley fit right in, in fact were two of the neater customers, most of whom were men.

"Curious thing," Bill commented. "There's two Vames' restaurants on Beverley Street. Everybody calls this 'un "Upper Vames' ", and, the other, down a few blocks on the same side of the street, just before you get to New Street, is "Lower Vames' ". I reckon this is the older of the two, since it has another kitchen upstairs with molds for making chocolate Easter rabbits and Santas. Damned if I see any other differences between them. Maybe a generational distinction or disagreement, since the oldest man in the family is the one that does the candy each season."

Their hotdogs, slathered high with chili, onions, and coleslaw, which just about cancelled each other out so far as taste was concerned, arrived, and Bill finished his off in about three big bites. "C'mon," Bill said, wiping his mouth on the back of his hand and depositing a big pile of change on the counter in payment, since Sally was busy elsewhere, "we got deliveries to make!" Raymond crammed what he had left of roll, dog, chili, and slaw down, turned up the last of his beer and followed Bill out the back door, where he was already in the truck and starting it up. "This afternoon," he announced, I'll show you most of the Valley run."

31. THE VALLEY RUN

Back at the store, they changed over to the tanker. Raymond started it up, looked Bill's way as he headed around to the street, "which way, Boss?"

"Left here on Middlebrook, then up Lewis." They were heading out along the flats of Lewis creek's floodplain, so that Raymond could get up through the first three years without having to knock the axle down into low, then double-clutched and pulled back to second to go around the sharp bend onto Lewis at Klotz's. "I'll tell you what burned old man Klotz up last winter," Bill grinned. "He was boxing up the season's ginseng to ship off to his buyer, kinda flexing some of the nicer roots as he packed them, and they seemed a little too resilient, none of that slight cracking feel you'd expect inside a dried root. Broke one open and each stem had a piece of bailing-wire inside! He'd told all his people to watch out for the old nail trick and flex the fresh-dug roots before they weighed them as they came in, but some slick old digger, he'd figured that half of the extra weight was better'n nothin' and switched to balin' wire. Klotz had to break every damn root he suspected of not feeling right, even though his buyer preferred them whole. I'll bet there won't be but one man weighing 'sang when it's brought in next season! Turn right here on Beverley, go to the top of the hill and turn left, Coalter Street, we're going to the stores off of the Valley Pike north of town." Traffic lights and the last long hill on Beverly kept them in the low gears, and the sharp, s-shaped curve in the grade past the edge of Mary Baldwin College and King's Daughter's Hospital got them down to first until they crested the hill at Cabel, just down from Staunton Military Academy, and hit the downgrade past the school's football field that gave them the momentum to get partway up the hill on Coalter to the edge of town before a noisy downshift. Riley knew the old International's transmission, and made no comment on the sound, content with Raymond's efforts, doubtless noticing that he was double- and triple clutching each gear change in an effort to achieve a next to impossible smoothness.

Bob the Standards Department guy had been right about the Riley's getting in on the ground floor of the petroleum business and how the other distributors operated. Just north of town they passed the Shell distributor's place, two tall tanks filled from the cars by pump, and a tractor-trailer to make the deliveries. All of the modern, tank-in-ground service stations that they passed were supplied by Shell, or by Standard out of Harrisonburg, the next town of any size to the north. They, however, stopped at every mom-and-pop store along the highway. There was one stop in Verona, about four miles out of town. Folks said the village was named by or for Italian laborers whose camp was there when the Valley Railroad was put through in 1870. It was the location of the Staunton airport, and they could hear the drone of C-47 Dakotas coming and going. They passed a steady stream of Army ambulances headed from there to the hospital in Fishersville. Sadly for all of the oil dealers, the Army had its own trucks and hauled from cars on the Fishersville siding to the cavernous tanks underneath the hospital motor pool. Beyond Verona, they passed the Willowspout, a pipe grown into the side of a tree at the public horse-trough left over from turnpike days, the grim barracks of the Augusta Military Academy, and the Old Stone Church, turning right in Fort Defiance. Originally known as Bell's Crossing, because of the most influential local family near the road's intersection with the railroad, the obstreperous old Colonel who ran the Academy, the son of its Confederate veteran founder, lobbied for years, finally successfully, to have a post office established there with a name befitting his school – 'Fort Defiance', based on the Church's history of serving as a refuge during the Indian wars. Looked damn good, competitive, in the ads for military schools in the back pages of the National Geographic. The road east to New Hope was a real cow path, following tight against the bluff of a creek bottom, nice and cool in the summer, but icy and shaded from the sun all afternoon in the winter. Halfway there was Grove's Mill on the Middle River, one of the three uppermost tributaries of the South Fork of the Shenandoah, from which the Valley took its name. Grove kept a 1x4x4 gasoline tank just inside the truck-shed. Raymond found the measuring stick on a nail above it, filled the tank and the ticket and interrupted Riley's jawing with Grove and the loafers just long enough to get a signature on the ticket and give Grove his copy. Because the valley streams generally lacked the head or vertical distance between dam pond and millrace necessary to operate an overshot wheel, most of the operating mills were tub turbine mills. Grove's had three, two to power the rollers that crushed the grain and powered the chain and tin-bucket conveyors that moved grain and flour between the silos and bins, and a third at the end of the millrace that didn't require as much torque and generated electric power.

The dam had something Raymond had to ask about as they pulled off. He'd never seen a dam with the series of small, water-filled terraces rising like steps off of the end away from the mill. Riley explained that it was called a fish-ladder, that the suckers and eels and catfish and bass used it to go upstream to spawn and back downstream as they liked, flopping from one level to the next. Bill preached a little bit about the elvers, the baby eels, going all the way to the ocean, to the big wad of seaweed called the Sargasso Sea, to mature returning in a year or so when it was time for them to spawn. Raymond figured he'd just keep his mouth shut and drive rather than respond to that whopper.

"Take a left when you get to the village," Bill interrupted himself as they went past red bank barns, German influence there, and down the last hill into New Hope. Wilbergers, the only store still open there, was one of their biggest and oldest customers, an eight by four by four tank just outside the door, which when he sticked it, Raymond found to be almost completely empty. On the other side of the double screen doors was the kerosene tank, half as big, but not nearly as empty -- fewer people used lamps than when it was put in. Bill found a good audience to entertain while Raymond did the tanks and the receipt. Old man Wilberger didn't look like the kind of fellow who'd take math errors with much forgiveness, but Raymond got it right and Wilberger said "Thank you, young feller," as he took his copy of the ticket. They slipped around the corner of the next road to Harner's Garage, a repair shop, which didn't need much gas, but was just about out of summer-weight oil. Mr. Harner asked them to send out a barrel of ninety- weight gear oil and a tub of grease the next time the flatbed truck came that way. Looking around just inside the door, Raymond noticed that for at least one year in the last decade, Harner had gone highbrow in his annual calendar selection. Even though out-of-date, there was a fly-specked calendar from some years back with all but December torn off and a picture of a sad, beautiful woman leaning against the beached end of a big, flat-bottomed boat with the word "Evangeline" beneath it. When asked about it later Bill, explained that Harner, as a young feller, was taken by a long poem by that title, Longfellow, he thought, taught in his senior year at New Hope High School by a good-looking English teacher with whom he was even more, impossibly, smitten. Man never got over it and couldn't bear to take the calendar down, just hung the new ones beneath it.

Backtracking to Fort Defiance, Bill filled Raymond in on Wilberger, who also ran New Hope's undertaking establishment and farmed about like Bill did. "People dying kind of kept him with a steady income in the worst of the depression, but nobody thought that the store would make it. Every time he ordered, he'd double up on things he really didn't need but knew would eventually sell if he could stay in business, overalls, work shoes, fence staples. Sometimes the drummers caught his fancy with crazy stuff they couldn't move, ladies hats, a new fishing lure. He'd tell his supplier's he'd take a dozen of the things he knew had lasting value if they'd give him another dozen at cut price, and their orders were slow enough that they'd do it to make their sales quotas, throwing in the oddities at even steeper discounts. Mr. Wilberger picked up the crates at the (now) Fort Defiance railroad station on his old solid-rubber tired Olds truck and packed the stuff in the back and upstairs of the big store building. Damned if the war didn't come along with rationing and some things that you just couldn't get, and he started unpacking all his stuff and selling it for a better price than what he'd paid. It didn't make any difference what the style of the clothing was or what damned country the barbed wire had come from!" By the time the lowdown on the storekeeper/undertaker was over, they'd clattered across the loose, noisy boards of the high, steel-frame bridge just downriver from the Grove's mill power plant and a cluster of two or three good size frame houses. A bit further the road practically met itself curving around an ancient brick house facing east, one field from the river. A pickup was raising a cloud of dust as it came up the lane through the field straight for the house. Bill waved good afternoon to the driver of the pickup, Raymond did the same to the old man on the porch of the house on his side of the truck. Bill didn't have to teach him that you always speak to folks, even if it's just raising your index finger from the wheel as you pass at a narrow place.

"Stop here at this station, then we'll go on right," Bill directed as soon as they got back to the crossroads at the Valley pike. This station was Bellwood, that family name which had been so pesky for the Colonel, purpose-built as a service station with underground gas tanks filled by the Shell distributor, but a one by four by four kerosene tank by the door that they filled -- the Shell distributor didn't fool with kerosene, tried to make their money on volume gas. "Next stop is Mrs. Petrie's in Mount Sidney." Bill said and they drove in unexpected silence for maybe half a mile. "Don't let anybody fill you with a lot of crap about the names of the towns on the Pike. Mt. Sidney, Mt. Crawford, Mt.Jackson. Some fool will try to talk to you about the hills in the road or behind it, somebody else will tell a

tale about a Confederate patrol and who got on his
horse first after each tavern stop. The real deal is that
each of the towns is twelve miles from the next, the distance a team could pull a coach or wagon in the early
1800's before being worn out. They were re-mount stations where horses were kept in livery and switched out,
and the name got shortened to include just the word
"mount" and the name of hostler who ran the stables
when the whole system first developed. The names got
adopted as post office names, and didn't change when a
different hostler took over the stable. Same thing with
names like "Steele's Tavern" up near Lexington, or
"Cross Keys, east of Harrisonburg, where there was a
Civil War battle. t The tavern sign there had crossed
keys painted on it, early on letters were left with the
keeper to be picked up, and when the formal postal system was established, there was your place name." Explanation, given, they were crossing the first hill in the
village, Colored Methodist church on the right, elementary and high school down an alley to the west grandly
marked as "Bolivar Street," then Lutherans and Meth-
odists on opposite sides of the road, and the old town
hall on the right, the upstairs previously shared by the
Sons of Temperance and the older, failing, Guilt-Edged
Order of Junior Mechanics on different meeting nights
during the week, but now chopped up into four apartments, the proscenium arch of the auditorium protruding from opposite sides of two sitting rooms. Mrs. Petrie's store was on the left at the north edge of the village, just past where the counterweighed turnpike pole
had been raised and lowered as tolls were collected. It
was a tank as big as the one at Wilbergers in New
Hope, but a monkey-pump job. Highway improvements
by the Works Progress Administration before the war
had significantly widened and cut down the road, carving away dooryards and shade trees and putting retain-

ing walls along the edges of the road. Mrs. Pete's store was on the uphill side, so that the expansion took the pull off from the front of her lot and left uncomfortably steep concrete steps up to her store porch and the neighboring houses had a chest-high retaining wall breached here and there for their driveways. Raymond sticked the tank, made his first note on the pad, rigged the hose and started pumping. Bill stood in the doorway, one eye on the rising level in the tank and most of his concentration on a conversation with Mrs. Petrie inside, behind the counter. She and her husband had rented the store after the owners moved on to a more ambitious grouping of several more modern markets; her old man died, and she kept on as she had before, living in the back, and seldom leaving her station behind the counter where its support in the front and the limitless handholds of the shelving and shallower counter behind enabled her to work despite crippling arthritis. There weren't many loafers in her store since there wasn't a man around to trade ribald stories with, and anyway, loafers couldn't be counted on to stoke a stove on a cold night. When the arthritis had gotten bad, she'd had the store's stove made over to burn kerosene, a setup with an oil tank the size of a breadbox on one side with a teapot-lid filler cap. Her plumber had rigged a monkey-pump on the side of that tank tied into the kerosene tank on the porch of the store so that she could lift the lid to check the level, and replenish the fuel without any assistance. As Raymond worked the route by himself, he would come to realize that despite appearances she was shrewd with the suppliers and did as well as any of the small storekeepers, maybe a little bit better, people wanting to help out a crippled widow lady -- he could relate to the last part of that. The dead stock that filled eighty percent of the store's shelves dated from her husband's time, and about the only reason anyone ever went beyond the stove in the middle of the store was to show some newcomer the two-headed calf that the landowner's son had stuffed and put above the hardware counter when his family still ran the place. It was a bit dusty and mangy in places, but its faces were white and its back and flanks still red. The boy'd been killed with a barnstormer up at the Staunton airport back in the late twenties -- a wing had come off the Curtis Jenny at the top of a loop, and, well, that was it. "Easy, now," Bill called out. "Two more pumps." Raymond pulled twice more, then locked the handle down, reached up and took the hose from Bill's outstretched arm and gave him the ticket book to take inside and finish filling out. Closing the valves at both ends of the hose, he stretched it, full of gasoline, along the inside of the drip tray. Unless Bill told him different, he'd seen right away the inefficiency of climbing up top to drain the hose when it was likely the next customer would be gas, too, and the full hose would be ok for either gravity or pump delivery. It was spring and they weren't unloading much kerosene. Bill came out and gave him the book back, and made no comment on the hose arrangement if he noticed it. Hose looked the same in the tray, both valves closed like they were supposed to be even if it had been empty.

"On down the Pike to Burketown." Bill went around and climbed into the passenger side, slamming the door.

Raymond started the International up, craned his neck around to check for traffic coming from the south, quickly confirmed that nothing was headed towards him in the lane he was using and gunned the big truck across. They were at a level spot and he could pull though the first three gears in quick succession, using first to break the inertia of parking, second to take advantage of some high revs to cross the lane, and third to start moving up towards highway speed, which would gradually be achieved in forth, letting the power of the heavy six-cylinder pull them ever faster, despite the longish grade and right-hand curve just north of the last houses. The tanks didn't have baffles and were now low enough that he could feel the load shift and then rebound as he straightened up in his lane. As that happened he could feel the stress on the truck's suspension, opposite springs relaxing and compressing, and a difference in the bite of his steering. There was a big peach orchard covering the ridge to the left, a low packing shed with a loading dock down by the highway. Peaches weren't in yet, not on this side of the Blue Ridge, anyway. The next little place was Burketown, just a collection of houses and an old (once Burke's) mill. Bill didn't think that it had ever been a post office, even in pre-RFD days. The little store there took about twenty gallons of gas, and five of kerosene, and Bill directed him west on a dirt road down by the mill, "man hanged himself in there a couple of years back," Bill observed as they passed. When you thought about it, a mill was a right good place if a man was of a mind to hang himself. If he was dramatic, there was the beam protruding from the ridgepole above the doors in the eaves over the drive; if he was more private-minded, there were plenty of exposed structural timbers to tie off onto and endless stairs and ladders to step off from. If he had a taste for the bizarre, and knew which lever to throw, he could start something turning and take the long, slow ride up until rope winding around a shaft jammed it or a carefully calculated length of line tied around his waist and to the control mechanism brought things to a halt with nothing but air for him to stand on. "This road," Bill continued, takes us over to Route Forty-Two, the road that runs north and south on the west side of the valley -- on the east you got Route 340, the Eastside Highway, put through by the WPA, and we just got off of Route Eleven, the Valley Pike. Before that called the Great Philadelphia Wagon Road, and before that, well I haven't any idea what the Indians called their trail." Raymond was amazed, not at the long history of the road that ran the length and center of the Valley, but that there was something, anything, that Bill Riley would freely and completely admit that he knew nothing about. You had to admire Bill's way, though 'cause he would hedge his position, saying "I don't know about that, but in my opinion," and continue, treating his opinion as a solid factual base for the rest of the conversation.

Their road came out just south of the North River dam and the town of Bridgewater. They turned left, 'cause the Store's territory was Augusta County and Highland County to the west, and Bridgewater marked the beginning of Rockingham County. The first stop was a crossroads called, improbably, Moscow. Little towns in North Carolina no doubt had this same variety of names and stories, but Raymond had never paid much attention to them, just names he grew up with that were as familiar as every acre of the farm. It was different when you were holding a folded roadmap you'd never seen before and learning all of the places was part of your job. They topped the store's tanks without seeing anything so unusual as a three-legged dog. There was a store at Stover's Shop, once a wheelwright's shop, but now a little car repair place and general store. They took plenty of gas and a good bit of motor oil, but didn't have a kerosene tank. One farmer, a Shifflett, "two f's, two t's" Bill had explained, had called saying he needed gas, so they poked up another side road to his place.

        As was usually the case with farmers, Shifflett
had no stick for his tank, and Raymond got some practice with the stick from behind the seat and the
smudged book of tables. Fortunately Shifflett was the
trusting, if observant, type and passed the time with Riley while Raymond took what he knew was probably
more than double the usual amount of time to produce
the ticket for signature. "Dead on!" Shifflett comple-
mented him. "It always takes that much when it's low
enough that I can see my face, collar, and first shirt button in the reflection when I pull the bung and check it.
Sure as hell don't want to run out," he observed in parting as they backed around and pulled out.

        "Parnassus is next. Didn't know we had Greek
Gods here in the Valley did ya?" Bill grinned. "Some
of those early settlers thought big when they had to
come up with a name for a place where there was absolutely nothin', not even a cow crossing the road. Have
to admit, it made a mighty fine soundin' Post Office"
Fifty gallons of gas, ten of kerosene. For some reason
Bill didn't have much to say to the proprietress, so the
stop didn't take long. A few miles down the road they
stopped at an obvious competitor (or perhaps predecessor) a crossroads with the grand name, 'Roman'. "Come
on inside when you finish," Bill said, "there's something
behind the counter you've gotta see." Raymond topped
off the tanks, they didn't take much, wrote the ticket,
came in to the dim interior of the store, put the pad on
the counter for signature and looked up. There, with the
shelves built around it to give it pride of place was a
large, maybe 12"x 24" framed and glassed sepia photograph of some dozen or so men of all ages, dressed in
uniforms that at once evoked the proprietary spirit of

some lodge, the fun of the circus, and the somber sense of purpose of uniformed veterans of the War he'd seen in childhood. All but three had valved brass instruments of various sizes with bells pointing upward past their capped heads; the other three were in front, two at one side, sticks poised above the heads of their snare drums, and the third, turned sideways so that the photographer had a clear view of ROMAN VIRGINIA SAXHORN BAND painted on the business side of the bass drum. The storekeeper followed Raymond's upward gaze while Bill stood by, silent but with a proprietary air.

The storekeeper responded to Raymond's inquiring glance. "'fore my time, think it was back in the '90's. They'd broke up before I was born to hear 'em play."

Raymond ground through the gears, and a mile or so later they got to Churchville - no mystery in that name, judging from the old look of the stones in the cemetery. "Keep east on two-fifty back to town," Bill directed. No point wearing you out your first day, now that you've had some practice with the tanks and ciphering." Inexplicably the twelve miles or so into town was without so much as a shack selling gasoline at a crossroads. Smooth running with the now much lighter truck in fourth, the axle cable pulled up into high. Close to town Bill had more instructions. "Watch out for this grade we're starting down, One Mile Hill. It'll overload your brakes before you realize it, even without much of a load, and overload your ass when you go around that big easy curve at the edge of the City limits and there's a cop waiting for speeders!" Raymond heeded the advice, and they took it easy going into town, admiring the ducks on the pond at the side of the park, with their Victorian folly of a duck-house on their island and the keeper's flat-bottomed boat upside down on the bank, chained to the iron fence to discourage pranksters. Amazingly, the hundreds of feet of elegant iron fence forming the enclosure had survived the patriotic scrap-metal drives of two of the three wars that had claimed most of the town's forged gates. The Confederates had been desperate for cannon; the Boy Scouts for the glory of dragging in two fifty-pound gates they'd sweet-talked and browbeat some widow out of. The patriotic little plunderers probably carried hacksaws with them to take down gates that had been properly hung so that they couldn't just be lifted off, the top hinge pin set so that it pointed downward, clamping the gate in place. As usual, there were people, old and young, single and together, casting bread upon the waters. "Goddam fat ducks!" Bill let loose. "Fed better'n half the people in this town"-- but then he laughed and ginned. "They make a lot of people happy, and a lot of lonely people feel better, all pretty cheap for a handful of chicken scratch or a slice of bread!"

Once around the park they took the left fork at the old pumping station house, an imposing brick building that held the pumps that pushed water from the park's many springs up into the open-topped tank, more of a cement-lined pond, really, on top of reservoir hill. A few blocks more and they turned right on Lewis Street towards the store. A few minute's wait for traffic when they crossed Beverley Street, rumbling over the old streetcar tracks which used to run to the cemetery, park, and fairgrounds, down the hill to a tight right-hand turn onto Middlebrook road at Klotz's and they were back home in the railroad flats along Lewis Creek, where the store lot backed up on the turntable and work sheds, which were, across at the other side, pushed close by the covered cattle pens, scales, and small sawdust auction arena of the livestock yards. Across the road where the stock was trucked in from the farms for sale, the far boundary of the flats was the siding where the work cars were more or less permanently pulled in, moved out onto the line only in the case of some spectacular incident requiring lots of labor for more than a day. Ancient, wooden boxcars with house windows and doors cut into them, they served as mobile dormitories during the work-week for the section crews that maintained the track and sleepers. Beyond, the town's houses ascended the steep hillside, garnished with bigger porches and more gingerbread the higher one got above the flats. "Just pull her in under the shed," Bill said in a voice that indicated he wanted to get his can of lunchtime scraps on home to the pigs. "See you in the mornin'," he added as he climbed out where Raymond had paused on the lot next to the pickups. Raymond ground the old International into first and pulled it into the shed, shut it down, set the handbrake and threw the key under the seat as his own, uninstructed, security measure. The last thing he needed was some fourteen year old stealing the truck his first evening after work, although one could still play hell with the valves and oil if he took a notion! Since Riley hadn't given him any instructions about locking up the building, he assumed that he'd come to a decidedly law-abiding town. Those sorts of things had probably improved in the last couple of years, "prison or the Army" being the watchword of many of America's judges and destruction and reformation of the individual being the method and delight of all of the country's D.I.s!

Grabbing his stick, he went over to the Ford, started it and headed to Beverley Street, Main Street, to see what he could find in the way of restaurants other than Vamse's. He parked in the middle of town, and just walked up and down, finally settling on a place that had a chalkboard on the sidewalk advertising pot roast as the night's special. He was hungry and it was good. Coffee and pie for dessert, and afterward he took the Ford around the block on a side street to get going in the right direction headed out to Mrs. Russ's house -- his new home. That morning he had noticed a graveled piece of ground adjacent her garage, so he followed her two concrete tire tracks of a drive back behind the house and parked there, out of her way if she needed to go out. The ground didn't look like anyone parked there regularly -- no oil drips or tire depressions, so he figured he wasn't claim-jumping on either the other boarder, David, or the daughter, Lee. He said good evening to Mrs. Russ, who was at the sink when he came through the kitchen, acknowledging and affirming her "I'll see you at breakfast," and headed up the stairs.

Past the newness of the entire day, about half-way up the stairs he realized how tired he was, how his leg dragged and he had to pull on the railing to make each step, and how much he stank of petroleum. Different from the smells of the country, more like the smells of the Army, cattle trucks with benches and the hours of confinement on the transport, waiting to get onto the nets for the landing craft. He wanted a hot bath. Fortunately, the other back hall resident wasn't in evidence, so he untied his shoes and put them beside the bed, grabbed a clean pair of pants and a shirt, and headed for the bathroom. Cut off of the corner of a screened sleeping porch, it had the basics, tub, toilet, sink, each apparently salvaged from a different source and so updateable to the period of the house's construction and providing no real clue as to when taking in boarders became part of the household routine. He soaked and soaped and scrubbed--plenty of hot water, a window for summer and, he noted, a curious big round radiator plumbed into the house's boiler for the winter. The hot water felt good on his leg and he reached down and massaged the knotted, unfeeling but always felt scars. Assuming that the towel racks and washstands on either side of the sink were allocated to the two of them on the back hall, he appropriated the towels stacked on the one with no toothbrush in the glass. He'd bring his personal gear in and put it in the drawers later

Finished with his bath, bathroom washstand loaded with his shaving gear, hairbrush, toothbrush and soap, he went back to his room and hung his work clothes on the back of a straight chair by the open window to air out. The smell of petroleum, he thought, was just something he was going to have to become accustomed to, like tobacco farmer and the reek of nicotine. Beyond that, he mused, there was a strong parallel between the dealership rights that Bill Riley held from Texaco and the acreage allotments passed from one generation of tobacco growers to the next, or sold by the sonless widow for vastly more than the land itself was worth His family would understand it if he explained it that way. He thought, too, with a smile, of a conversation he'd had once with a neighbor, Mr. Patterson, who was mucking out his pig shed after shipping a load of hogs that morning. "Mr. William," he'd said, full of cheer, "smells a lot like money 'round here this mornin' doesn't it?" "You got that wrong, boy," Mr. William replied, kinda tired-like, leaning on his manure fork. "You'll learn, boy. Money smells like shit."

Money wasn't what was on his mind -- he wanted to get a letter off to the family. He'd noted the house number on his way in after work, 1026 West Beverley

Street, so he was ready to go. He pulled out the big envelope that his sister had given him, took a new, already sharpened (Reba, she was good) pencil, and started at the top center of the pad "Russ House, 1026 West Beverley Street, Staunton, Virginia, May 6, 1945."Down a bit at to the left, he put the inclusive salutation "Dear Reba (and everyone else)," And started telling the tale of the last two days; the smooth trip up into the Valley, his luck in having met the weights and measures guy, the fact that the employment pitches he'd practiced with his family had worked, that his boss had fixed him up with a good place to stay, and that in his first afternoon of work he'd seen the stuffed remains of a two-headed Hereford calf, been to Moscow, seen the portrait pose of the Rome Saxhorn Band, and managed not to embarrass himself driving an unfamiliar heavy truck under his boss' close observation over some right twisty roads and within hose-length of all of the customers' tanks. He ended the letter saying that it was clearly going to be different from farming, but that he was optimistic about the job, the town, and his ability to get along. Sent everybody his love in the closing, spaced just like they'd made him do it in composition class in high school, addressed an envelope, filled it, licked it shut, put on a stamp and lay it on the corner of the small table so that he'd remember to take it down to breakfast so that Mrs. Russ could put it out with her mail. He hadn't, as his sister had asked, thought to find out the telephone number, but that could go into their next letter.

By the time he'd finished the letter it was dark. He set his little hospital alarm clock for six, brushed his teeth, and crawled into bed and fell to sleep laughing to himself about the pretentious names of the crossroads towns.

32. DAVID, WOULD-BE ENGINEER

He was jolted awake in the dark by pounding on his door and an unfamiliar voice shouting "Raymond, Raymond, you alright?" He jumped out of bed, pulled on the beltless pair of pants he'd left on the bottom bedpost, responding "yeah, yeah, I'm OK," and opening the door to have David, the boarder across the stair landing almost fall onto him as he'd begun another onslaught of pounding. David regained his balance and stepped back into the landing, where the light was on, and Raymond, glancing down, could see Mrs. Russ peering up from below.

"Buddy," David said shaking his head, "you was screamin'. Not just no bad dream and wake up, but over and over, like you was fightin' for your life!" He reached over and put his hand on Raymond's shoulder. "You sure you're alright?"

"Yeah, I'm ok," Raymond replied, noticing that Mrs. Russ had withdrawn without comment. "It just happens sometimes..."

David dropped his hand. "Let's go down and sit in the kitchen for a bit -- Mrs. Russ always leaves the cold coffee from supper in the pot in case I want some. They went down barefoot to the kitchen, found a couple of cups without turning on a light, and Raymond followed David, who was silently gesturing with a pack of Luckies in his other hand out onto the back porch where they settled on the edge of the worn, grey-painted floor with their feet on the cool top cement step. They both sipped their coffee; David set his cup down beside him, lit one cigarette and handed it to Raymond then shook out another, lit it for himself off of the same match and picked the cup up again. They sat there like a couple of kids, elbows on their knees. Raymond chewed, didn't habitually smoke, but had shared enough butts in the Army and the hospital along with the occasional late-night smoke with his father or one of his brothers on the front porch that he was comfortable in the ritual and to tell the truth, comforted, distracted from what had just happened by the expected burn of the smoke in his lungs and rush of nicotine to his head.

"How'd you stay out of the war?" Raymond asked David, figuring that he was about the same age and didn't appear to have any obvious 4-F characteristics.

"The railroad. Ever since I was a kid I loved trains, wanted to be an engineer. Back before things got hot, I signed on. So country-simple I didn't realize that to get into the train-driving end of things you needed more than 'want to', but needed to know somebody, which I didn't. Bein' a White boy with a section gang wasn't gonna work out, so I did what nobody else wanted to and learned about the insides of the switch towers and boxes, how they worked, and what runs the signals. I trouble shoot and supervise maintenance. Since I'm helping by showin' them how to do something rather than just bossin' them, I got no problems with section men ten, fifteen years oldern' me, either color. I'm assigned to the Mountain Division, here to Clifton Forge, come and go as I'm needed, and if there's no problem I ride in either the cab or caboose and keep my eye out for what might develop. I'm good at solving problems -- seems like I'm more patient than most in looking for the link that's dragging cause its warped or something's under it, and have an eye for the discoloration of a corroded wire even when it looks solid under the insulation just beyond the terminal. I haven't given up on engineer yet -- hopin' I get hooked up with those right people.

"What got you into the war? Drafted?"

"No, I joined up before they could do that, although I suppose it wouldn't have been long if I'd waited. Graduated high school, six or eight of us pallin' around, had never left the farm, and went over to town to talk to them, next thing we knew we were on a bus to Charlotte for a physical. First guy had been hit in the eye with a rock when he was a kid came out and told us all what he could see with one eye and not the other. Somebody else with the same problem, playing the dumb-ass high-school buddy game memorized what the first fellow'd said, and we all sniggered when he fooled the tester. Wonder where each of 'em is tonight, and if he still thinks telling or knowing the first line of that chart by heart was a good thing. Answering your question, though, I really don't know what led us down there, maybe deep down we knew we were goin' an figured, in our dumbness, to have one more cut up together. When I went home after the hospital I saw some gold-star banners in the church vestibule along with the blue, but to tell you the truth, except when it was real obvious by the way people acted or what they said, I didn't try to find out all of the names, where they were, alive or dead." They just sat, sipped their coffee and drew more calmly on what was now their second smoke. Raymond, thinking down a rabbit trail away from their previous conversation, realized that he needed to go by city hall and sign up for a ration book -- he could then repay his neighbor for the smokes and have some for himself if the mood struck him. Back in the moment, David's polite silence seemed to elicit further explanation with more insistence than a direct question would have. "After basic training I got selected for Ranger School, finished that, got shipped to England and spent months practicing climbing what seemed like every cliff on every deserted beach around the whole damn island. D-day we climbed the cliff at Pointe du Hoc, between the beaches, and I got hit about ten minutes later. War over"

"Plenty rough," David replied, picking up their butts, walking over to the gravel drive and stripping them. "Glad that you made it home. Let's go on in and try for a couple more hours of sleep." As quietly as they could, they went in, rinsed their cups and put them on the drain board, and went back upstairs to their rooms.

The conversation, coffee, and cigarettes had, Raymond thought, calmed whatever had set him off screaming -- he had no recollection of anything between laughing to himself about place names and David's beating on the door. They weren't, however, conducive to getting back to sleep. That, and his leg was playing a neat little trick it had learned. During the weeks he'd been in traction in the hospital, he'd had to tense his leg muscles kept the weight from pulling at anything painful. If he let them slack off it was only a short time until something -- nerve, muscle, bone, he didn't know what -- registered pain and threw the leg into a spasm of correction that made everything go off, leaving him drenched in sweat. The interval had usually been just enough time do doze off, so that he spent his nights going through the cycle of exhaustion, dozing off, and being jerked awake. The cycle had persisted until the hour for the nurse with the morphine to make her rounds. The lady with the morphine, his favorite lady in the whole world. Momma didn't come close. The nasty trick he was left with, was that now, just as he started to fall asleep, he sensed the leg relaxing, and the patterned message from deep in his mind "OK Boys, here it comes!" would tense the muscles of his leg and wake him. It could happen six or eight times before the rest of his mind convinced that little bit playing the trick that it didn't have to warn him anymore. He was able to get some rest until six, time to get up, but never really went back to sleep. Mrs. Russ greeted him cheerily at breakfast, made no mention of the night before, and promised to put his letter out under the clothespin on the side of the box before the postman came.

"I'm glad you're keeping up with your people," she said as he thanked her for breakfast. David was nowhere to be seen -- Raymond assumed that his work with the railroad had carried him off early.

33. THOUGHTS ON DEATH ON THE WAY TO WORK.

Raymond went out to the Ford, started it, and took a moment while it was warming up and he was easing in the choke to look at himself in the rearview mirror to get the angle of his engineer's hat just right. He looked tired, even to himself, as he killed the last of the choke, turned by backing around over the double cement lines of the drive, and pulled out to the street, headed to work. The house was directly across the street from the entrance to the town's principal cemetery, acres of ground surrounded by limestone walls with crenelated towers at the corners, a castle of an entry gate, an even larger stone folly at the crest of the first hill and a high street of death, fancy mausoleums paralleling the public street. 'Thornrose' it was called, and it predated the War. Staunton's marble Confederate was up the winding lanes at the crest of the second hill, commanding a full battalion of unknowns gathered from the county's battlefields and unmapped skirmish sites. Mrs. Russ had told him when he asked about it that probably the most important person buried there was Jedidiah Hotchkiss, Stonewall Jackson's mapmaker during the War. She told Raymond to remember that prior to the War, West Virginia was part of Virginia; in fact, Jackson's boyhood had been spent in that region. Hotchkiss was an astute individual who, as he mapped unexpected routes for the Stonewall Brigade from one watershed to the next noted the location of actual and likely coal deposits. The men of the Stonewall Brigade were Infantry troops, but they called them Jackson's 'foot cavalry' because of their seemingly impossible speed of march, unexpected appearance, and willing-ness to fight immediately, without rest, when they achieved surprise. After the War, Hotchkiss' geology notes proved invaluable to Staunton's investors -- his mansion, The Oaks, was on the other side of the busi-ness district, up Gospel Hill and out near the east end of East Beverley street. There were three other cemeteries in Staunton -- Staunton National Cemetery, known universally as the 'Yankee cemetery' east of town on Richmond Road, surrounded by the little Colored community known as Uniontown, platted out after the War, the big, unkempt crazy quilt of the Colored ceme-tery just north of town, and slightly further out, the tiny Hebrew cemetery. Queer, Raymond thought, how that much evidence of death could flash through your mind while waiting for one car to pass so that you could turn right and go to work! Making his turn and heading down the street a few blocks, he passed Trinity Church and realized that he'd left the old graves surrounding the church off of his list. A forth cemetery. He hadn't been in town long enough to know that there were two others on the grounds of the Lunatic Asylum. A couple of turns later he parked the Ford beside Riley's at the front of the store, didn't even bother going in, grabbed his stick and headed back through the gravel to the tank truck, threw his stick into the cab and began climbing onto the tanks and undogging the covers in preparation for the hose-and-valve drill that Riley had shown him for getting the tanks filled in preparation for the day's deliveries.

Still thinking about what he'd seen on the way to work, the enormous, elaborate cemetery, he thought about death back home. Crazy as it might sound to say, death was an important part of life back in North Carolina. The ritual of funerals that everyone attended was sort of reassuring, reminded folks of the ties of kinship, and more importantly, but never discussed, made it clear to all the generational changes in power and authority and the re-organization of economic capability throughout the community. He hadn't been to a funeral, though, since he enlisted. Even though he'd seen the gold star banners in the church vestibule when he was staying at the farm, he hadn't inquired who they represented, although changes in family circles and people's comments sometimes made him aware. A young soldier's death usually just meant that there'd be one less hand come the end of the fighting, although it could cause some changes if he were an only child or only son, spreading the eventual ownership of land out among family members or concentrating it in a daughter who might be looked at very differently when she came of age because of her potential holdings. Raymond's concept of death was no longer that it was one of life's expected passages. For him, now, death was luck on the ladders when you'd kept your head down or raised it, or which Higgins boat someone ordered you onto. It was the marker of blood in the water or on the sand, or blood on the rope telling you to curse the man in front to climb faster. There hadn't been any message of orderly progression accompanying the death that he'd come to know, only the morbid hope that the body of the man falling beside you would pass at the precise instant necessary to protect you from the next grenade blast.

34. V.E. DAY & THE HIGHLAND RUN.

"Raymond! Raymond! Get up here!" he heard Riley hollering to him from the back door of the store. Careful to close the valve he was working with, he slipped down onto the drip tray, then onto the ground, got his stick and started to hustle back across the lot. All of a sudden he heard car horns honking, lots of them, and then a moment later the church bells began ringing, one by one, all over town. "They've quit!" Riley shouted as he got closer. "The president was just on the radio, the Germans have quit! Come in here and listen to what they've got to say! He got inside, grabbed a chair and turned it around to lean on the back with his crossed arms in front of him, joining Riley, staring at the beat-up old radio. A news announcer so excited that he forgot to sound pompous was repeating that at nine o'clock the President had called the reporters in and made a short speech, saying that the Germans had surrendered, that American and Soviet troops were in Berlin, and that it was believed that Adolph Hitler was dead. The war in Europe was over! Raymond was glad for all the guys over there, but didn't know what else to say. The army seemed so removed from his current circumstances, his war had been so short, but was still with him when he clenched his teeth with every step that he took, and with him more nights than he cared to think about. Riley, too, wasn't saying much. "Now," Riley said quietly, "we've still got to deal with the Japs." You had to admit that for a guy running an old fashioned oil business that relied on a stick and a greasy little book to make the accounts come out straight and took garbage cans of restaurant refuse home to his pigs each day, Bill Riley had a pretty good grasp of the size and shape of the world, and of the trouble to took to raise armies and shift the focus of a campaign. "Come on," Bill said," I'll help you load, it's quicker 'n easier with two, and I know every stop that we make today's gonna be full of talk.

Nobody came by while they were finishing with the truck, so that loading went pretty fast. Riley shut the doors to the store and they started out, this time headed west on Beverley Street, past where Raymond was living. It wasn't far from Mrs. Russ' house to the official edge of town. Riley said that everything past the episcopal churchyard, no matter how old, was called "Newtown" because it went beyond the way the streets were originally laid out, which explained the immediate change from a grid to a series of gradual curves in either direction. Past the Cemetery there were a couple of little nondescript corner stores that took a few gallons of fuel or kerosene. Their next stop was a short turn off of what was, after leaving town, known as Route 254, the Parkersburg Pike. About a mile down the Cedar Green road was the Cedar Green store, and next to it, the Cedar Green School, the school for Colored in that part of the County. The store was a busy one, and it and the school were the core of the little community. "Well, Mr. Bill," said Ed Smith, the storekeeper while they filled a gas tank as big and old as the one at Wilberger's store in New Hope the day before, "who's this new man you got with you?"

"This man," Riley replied "survived climbing the cliffs at Normandy, got shot up in his first fight up top and migrated to us by way of England, the Fishersville Hospital, and Guilford Court House, North Carolina. He owns what is probably the shiniest Ford Barrelnose in existence, and stays with Mrs. Russ. I expect some of your friends helped him get well." Raymond's jaw dropped. He'd told Riley he'd been with a Ranger unit and had been hit the first day but never any details beyond being in Woodrow Wilson Hospital. The rest of the introduction he recognized as giving Mr. Smith the basis for trusting him on the route and identifying him for the Colored in that part of the County by what he drove, that he was trusted by a 'quality' landlady, and that there might be some small North Carolina connection for somebody in the neighborhood -- a bit of real information if that somebody took the trouble to write to a sister or cousin near to Guilford. Smith's store took a good bit of lamp oil, too.

As to the war, Smith's only comment was "'thank God this part's over, but we're likely gonna have to hold on hard to finish the rest. Look forward to seeing you next time, Mr. Raymond," Smith said as they climbed back into the truck and turned left, back towards the Parkersburg pike.

Once on the main road Raymond had hardly run up through the gears when Riley spoke up. "Next stop's just after this third house, on the right, Westview Store. The day's news had circulated enough by then that a new, full-sized American flag; probably last used to cover someone's coffin, fluttered from the gallery of the storekeepers quarters upstairs.

"A great day!" she greeted them. "We'll all remember the first words we had with anyone after we heard the radio!" As Bill continued the conversation, Raymond pulled on his gloves, sticked the store's gasoline tank, and started working the hose and valves. First ticket for the gasoline done and reaching for the kerosene stick on its nail beside the window casing, he glanced over and realized that all of the advertising cards had been removed from the lower sash, the glass was freshly cleaned, and a gold-star banner hung from the latch. He'd been right about the source of the flag fluttering above the Texaco truck. He put his gloves into the box on the drip board, finished writing the second ticket, and followed Riley and the store keeper inside to get her signatures on the originals before he tore out her carbons. He stepped inside, removing his hat as he entered the shade, his eyes taking a moment to adjust.

"Raymond, this is Sarah Thompson." With her broad-brimmed hat off so that he could see her more clearly than he had when he'd glanced her way outside, he realized that she was much closer to his age than most of the storekeepers.

"Pleased to meet you, " Raymond said, laying the receipt book out on the counter for signature, holding the cover that wanted to curl closed flat with on hand and steadying the signing side with the other. " I saw the golden star -- I'm sorry."

"Thanks. John joined up in the Air Corps soon after we'd inherited this place from his mother, figuring

I'd worked here enough that I could handle it by myself -- I don't think that he intend this. He wanted to do his part, and he'd been crazy to fly since he was a kid. He was killed on a training flight that crashed down south right after he'd had leave before being shipped out, probably for North Africa, although of course he couldn't say." Raymond remembered that there'd been a set of pilot's wings clipped onto the banner. She signed the tickets and he tore off her copies and handed them to her. "Bill tells me that you were hurt at Normandy and came to us after your stay in the new hospital. That must be an awesome morning to remember."

"Don't hear it much except from preachers readin' the Old Testament, but awesome is probably the right word. I didn't think it was possible to get so many men, ships, and planes together offshore and then onto the beaches, especially the way the weather looked the night before."

"Well, c'mon boy" Riley said. "We're done here and have a long day ahead going out to Highland County. Raymond and Bill climbed into the truck, checked for traffic and pulled out onto the road, headed west towards Buffalo Gap, the break in the mountains just short of where the road began following the Little Calfpasture River on towards Bath County and West Virginia. The little store at the Gap didn't need anything -- unusual Bill said -- but everyone has a slow week now and then, and they may have just had a slow week in payment of their accounts and figured they could wait a bit longer before filling the tanks. They headed north on Route forty-two, which paralleled the mountains towards Churchville. This was an odd stretch of road in that it was about five miles with only two crossroads and no stores. They'd already tended to the businesses in Churchville the day before, so they turned left onto Route two-fifty. Their first stop was just a few miles out into flat, open farm country, Lone Fountain. The store and garage combination there needed about thirty gallons of gas and their motor oil tank filled, forty gallons, said that they were sucking air when they cranked the handle on the pump to fill their last jars.

A few miles more and Raymond found himself pushing the big six harder and harder -- they were starting into Jennings gap, the beginning of the Appalachians on the west side of the valley, but it pulled the grade without downshifting. They stopped at White's Store, at the top of the gap between Crawford Mountain and Hankey Mountain. Following the same drill as earlier in the morning, Raymond did the unloading, then went inside and was introduced to Mrs. White, who was ecstatic about the war news, glad for the whole community, as she had no kinsmen in the service. The store was really more of a bakery and restaurant than a store, with four tables, one selection on the day's menu, and fresh bread and pies on the counter, all carried from the kitchen in her house a few yards away, the meal kept warm in a couple of those rectangular enameled cookers with the aluminum tops and milk-can handles that he'd seen at the end of yards of plugged-together extension cords at every reunion and church picnic of his life. Good as the pies smelled, Raymond's attention was above the counter. Mr. White was a beekeeper (lots of honey in that baking!), and had built an observation hive on the wall away from the windows, a half-dozen glass panels in a shallow cabinet, with a big brood-box frame behind each hinged door with its twist latch, and a long inch-and-a-half piece of galvanized plumbing pipe reaching across the room to the back wall and the outdoors, allowing the field bees to come and go. When he asked Mrs. White about it, she said that her husband worked them at night, with the lights off, relying on moonlight and his familiarity with the setup to avoid creating a disturbance that would fill the room with bees. He'd put a piece of queen-excluder, wire grid that the workers could pass, but the bigger queen could not, used in full sheets by some beekeepers to keep brood out of their comb honey supers, over the end of the pipe to keep the demonstration queen inside, and swapped out frames with another hive just outside as soon as they became full. He'd changed one frame the night before, and the bees were busy making wax to draw out the foundation for honey cells. Raymond smiled when he saw the dangling threads of bees, the golden chains his Granddaddy had shown him what seemed so long ago. Riley joined him at the counter.

"Pretty interesting, huh? I have to admit, bees are something I don't know anything about -- I'm scared of them 'bout as much as I am of snakes."

"Reckon I got you, then. I grew up working them on the farm in Carolina." He went on to explain to Bill what he was watching, Mrs. White standing by with her arms crossed, pleased to have someone visit who had some understanding and more interesting comments than the inevitable story about being stung as a child and being 'allergic.' Lesson over, they made their manners to Mrs. White and were back in the truck making the easy run down the other side of the gap through the forest to the narrow valley to West Augusta, a store and post office in the valley where the Calfpasture river started, flowing southwest parallel to the Little Calfpasture but on the other side of Great North Mountain. Headed downhill on the curving road, Raymond became aware for the first time that day of the shifting of the load in the baffle-less tanks, gravity wanting to keep it to one side as he moved the chassis of the truck to the other, the otherwise almost immobile springs of the truck compressing on one side, stretching up on the other. Right smart different from driving a farm pickup pressed flat down onto the axle with an overload of feed or fence wire!

West Augusta Store did a good trade in kerosene -- a lot of their customers were off of the power lines, either because they lived off of the main road, where the lines were, or because they couldn't afford to wire their houses. As you got into the mountains, prosperity was pretty much limited to the few farms in the narrow river bottoms. Everyone else got by the best they could, doing some logging, cutting some firewood from the tops and downed trees, or if they were lucky, driving into town or over to Augusta Springs to the Clearwater fabric mill, or to the cement plant at Fordwick for work.

After West Augusta the road took a sweeping curve to the right, hugging the bluff side of the valley. Out of the driver's window Raymond looked out across the unexpectedly broad and beautiful bottom to his left. Riley followed his gaze. "Pretty, ain't it? One of old man Hunter's holdings. He's the President of the Valley National Bank down on Beverley Street across from Langs Jewelry -- probably the biggest landowner in the county, farms scattered everywhere."

"I don't know that gentleman's story. If he's a bank man, his people probably built up their holdin's over a few generations, maybe less if the family started big and got small but held onto their land." Raymond was thinking of Quentin Baker's father. "There were a couple of families like that back home in Guilford County. There were also a couple of others who had money when things were hard, came to every farm auction, bought what equipment and stock they wanted cheap, and at the end of the afternoon, the land for less than the county assessment. Folks didn't like that second bunch much, except for the suck-ups who wanted to associate with the big dogs, and who seldom came from people with any background of their own. Just liked the smell, thought that if they rubbed up against money they were big dogs, too."

"Yup, that's right. Funny thing is that two, three generations, after everybody who knows or has been told what's what has died, the land-grabbers whose children and grandchildren haven't drunk or womanized everything away are turned into pillars of the community. I'm told it was that way right after the War and again after a big railroad speculation bust in '79. The respected ancestors get memorialized in the little engraved plaques beneath church window panels."

The road changed abruptly. It narrowed, got snaky, back and forth like a rider in the backcountry following the easiest path around rock outcroppings and trees. It generally followed the nearby stream, Jennings Run, which they glimpsed from time to time where the vegetation allowed. As they entered Ramsey's draft, the wedge in the ridges of Shenandoah Mountain that led to the crossing gap, the stream and road straightened out, and the grade steadily increased as they proceed through the flatwoods. The engine was pulling hard, but Raymond didn't have to downshift until they reached the foot of the mountain, where the road simultaneously veered right a full ninety degrees and the full height of the International's windshield was filled with the narrow strip of pavement and gravel shoulders of a sudden change of grade that defied working down through the gears, forcing him to come to a dead stop and begin working up from low first. The view from the driver's side window was a sheer rock wall, as high as he could see without sticking his head out and twisting it to search for the sky. Bill's initial side view was nothing but tree trunks. Winding through low and into high first changed it to lower limbs on the closely-spaced oaks. Low second brought high limbs, full second the treetops. At that point there was no more road in the windshield, just trees and a little bit of sky as Raymond started downshifting to preserve their little bit of momentum as he shouldered the wheel into a left hairpin turn.

Once around the turn, the view from the side windows reversed, Raymond had treetops and sky, Bill a rock face just a few feet away. The progression of road, trees, and sky filling the windshield repeated itself, and Raymond shifted back down to nothing to crank the wheel through a right turn as tight as the last, left one, and he could feel the chassis come up off of the suspension on the right side and bear down on the left as the oil and gas shifted, inertia persuading the liquids to try to stay in the same place as the truck turned under them. Baffled tanks, Raymond thought again, would be a great improvement. He'd have to remember in bad weather and when meeting another vehicle and heading for the shoulder that he was essentially steering with one front wheel and he'd best keep that wheel on whatever available portion of the road gave the best purchase. Definitely not like crop field and feed mill driving back home in Carolina! After five or six of the switchbacks he saw less mountain above him, and Bill said "next one's the top--stop there." Pulling out of the curve onto the shoulder at the only level spot, Raymond killed the engine, put the transmission into reverse, and set the emergency brake, relieved to release his grip on the wheel and let his shoulders slump back onto the top of the seat.

"Whew! What a ride!"

"You ain't seen it all yet. We've still got to go down this mountain and then across two more, Bull-pasture Mountain and Jack Mountain, before we get to Monterey. Once we're down in that valley, it's pretty much like going around back home, just fewer people and lots prettier."

They sat in silence for a few minutes, letting the engine cool after the hard pull rather than chance boiling over. Riley gestured with his head out of his window and up a little ridge. "That's where the Confederates had a little fort, just breastworks, really, to control the pass. Nothing much happened up here, but there was a pretty good fight along the way to where we're going at the bottom, at McDowell. Stopped the Yankee's flanking movements, even after they dragged some cannon up onto a ridge, Stonewall Brigade held the line, fight was probably what you'd call the start of Jackson's Valley Campaign, tyin' up a world of men the Yankees'd rather have marching on Richmond." Riley was sounding more and more like Raymond's grandfather, but Raymond couldn't tell if his people had actually been in the War or if he just knew all of the local stories and liked to tell them, either out of interest or to fit in with the community. Either way, Raymond was learning a lot of local history, which along with his southern accent would probably make him more acceptable than some in gaining the storekeepers' confidence.

"Let's head on down. Keep it in high first, you'll see why in just a minute." Raymond stared up, pulled out and made a moderate turn to the left, passed a sign announcing Highland County, felt a bump where there had been a miss-match between the paving done by the Augusta and Highland County road gangs and found himself facing down a steep grade that had to be half a mile long with nothing visible at the far end except a wall of rock -- the first hairpin turn on the west side of the mountain. He kept his foot solid into the brake the whole way, grateful that they were hydraulic, multiplying the pressure he put on the pedal and the narrow master cylinder when the fluid hit the somewhat broader wheel cylinders with their shorter stroke. Foot off of the throttle, he let the engine wail, its dragging compression doing more than his braking to keep the truck's speed down to where they could safely make the turn at the bottom. Once around, there were a couple of flat miles of nothing. Nothing except the stream along the road, before they came up against Bullpasture Mountain and he had to resume grinding gears and shouldering through the switchbacks. Not so many up as there'd been on Shenandoah Mountain, but just as blind, steep and tight, and, like the first mountain fewer on the downward slope -- each successive valley floor was at a higher elevation. It wasn't but a mile or so past a couple of naked crossroads in the flatwoods till they hit a flat with some open fields, a stream, about three houses and the Headwaters store.

The small stream was the top end of the Cowpasture River, draining south into the New River watershed. The store building was impressive, as big or bigger than Wilbergers back in New Hope, but as they pulled in, Raymond could see from the curtains on the windows the flowers in the yard and the stretch of farm buildings behind that two-thirds of it was the storekeeper's home, rather than a warehouse, the center of what, from appearances, was a substantial and productive farm extending up the bottom side of the stream. The bluff side, not two hundred yards beyond the store, was the beginnings of Bullpasture Mountain, the second they'd have to cross. Their roles now defined by practice, Riley climbed down and headed into the store and Raymond went to work sticking and filling the tanks and penciling the tally into the delivery receipt pad. The biggest tank was, as usual, gasoline; the smaller kerosene; and for the first time at a store not connected with a garage, two slim forty-gallon tanks for the two weights of motor oil that they carried in the smallest divisions of the International's compartments. The store was just about out of both gas and kerosene, but didn't need but a couple of gallons of lubricating oil.

Shucking off his gloves and putting them in the box on the hose tray, Raymond straightened his cap to exactly the right angle, got his stick, pulled the filled-out pad out of his back pocket and headed inside. As he pushed the door open he could hear an electric bell begin to ring back in the residential part of the building. The ringing stopped when he got inside and closed the door, and glancing up as he took his hand off of the knob he could see the switch at the top of the door-frame, with two wires with woven, red-and-white waxed thread insulation going up to and across the ceiling, then down to the top of another doorframe where they disappeared. He guessed that the bell and a couple of tall, dry-cell telephone batteries were on a shelf above the far side of that door. A setup that no doubt brought someone from the household to tend the store if the owner was doing farm work, or maybe just more comfortable, reading the paper in his favorite chair. Riley was leaning against the counter, which was a surprisingly short distance into the room, but went the full distance across the front of the building, with the Post Office window and boxes making an "L" across one end, talking with a white-haired man in the same posture on the opposite side -- they could have been setting up to arm-wrestle, he laughed to himself. With the counter that far into the front door's side of the room, the place just wasn't set up for socializing, just business and mail.

"Raymond," Riley gestured towards the man, "Charles Miller."

"Pleased to meet you, Sir," Raymond put the book down on the counter and reached his right hand across to the one Miller was extending in greeting. "Got 'em all four topped off," he finished, pulling back the cover and used pages of the receipt book and turning it around for Miller's review and signature.

"Pleased to meet you," Miller said as he looked over the figures, signed, and handed the book back to Raymond, who tore out the carbon pages and gave them to him. "And pleased to know that one more of our men is safe, back here in Virginia, even though I understand that you had to bring that stick back as a souvenir."

"Thanks, Sir. I'm glad to be back and glad to have this job with Mr. Riley -- there wasn't a place for me on the farm back in Carolina with a bum leg, and I think that this work's gonna suit me real well."

"Suits both of us," Riley interjected. "I needed a good man and the Army had most all of them 'till this fellow came along, talked plain to me about what he could do, and got himself hired."

"How big a place your people got in Carolina?" Miller inquired.

"About eighty acres, Guilford County, that's straight south of Danville. Daddy's getting old enough he can't do too much, and my sister and two brothers run the place and my other sister and Mother take care of the rest of them. With the war prices for stock and corn, they're doing all right; I'm not so sure how they'll get on when things get back to normal."

"I know what you're sayin' about farming -- right now I could afford to live without running a store, but I know it'll change once the war's over, stock prices'll drop and I'll be glad to be answering that bell and maybe my boy'll be back to help with the farm -- right now he's doin' war work, factory job building bombers with Martin down in Baltimore, and I'm like your dad, maybe workin' harder than I want to."

"I reckon we better be gettin' on over to Monterey. See you later, Charlie -- come on, Raymond, you got one more mountain to learn."

"Right," Raymond picked his hat and stick up off the counter. "Good to meet you Mr. Miller, I'll be seeing you in a week or so."

"Be good to see both of you whenever you're through here next. I'm sure those tanks'll empty out by then."

Back out in the sunlight, Raymond pulled his cap down against the glare, checked to make sure that the hoses were secure in the tray, and that he'd closed the lid on the box where the gloves, wrenches, and odd extra bits of valve assembly -- some new, some with just enough use left in them to get by in a pinch -- lived as he walked around the truck and climbed in. He started up, turned right, and just after they crossed the bridge over the small stream, Shaws Fork, and found himself facing another sheer rock wall, where he had to downshift, turn left, and start the grade. "Miller's alright," Riley observed, "not as sociable as the next you'll meet, Peterson, but that's understandable the way he's set up. A damned sight more comfortable to wait for customers in his favorite chair with the radio or newspaper than to provide entertainment for a whole town of loafers!"

Raymond lost count of the turns going upward, but as they came down he could see two more turns and they hit the village of McDowell at the bottom of the second downward grade, crossing the stream they'd followed from the last curve where it passed through the race of a towering old mill jammed up against the right side of the road, a mill where there was enough head for an overshot wheel. They passed a few houses and a church, and then Raymond followed Bill's silent gesture and pulled off on the right into the gravel in front of the store and post office.

Bill rolled out of the cab in perfect synchronicity with the owner's movement through the front door. They met halfway, shook right hands while resting lefts on each other's right shoulder and both talking at once said "how are you, you old sonofabitch?" Raymond thought the whole thing looked like some kind of lodge ritual. "Raymond," Bill hollered, get over here! I want you to meet Mr. John Peterson, Postmaster, store-keeper, and chief businessman of this town." Raymond pulled his cap to exactly the right angle, grabbed his stick and beat it around the front of the International as fast as he could. "My new man Raymond McCleary," Riley announced as he reached them and took Peterson's proffered hand. "He's young, but he's good, and I 'spect you'll be seeing more of him than me this summer."

"Oh, don't break my heart," Peterson replied, winking over Riley's shoulder at Raymond. He slapped Riley on the back as they turned to go inside. "You know how much I'll miss your accurate accounts of everything between here and Staunton, word of every out-of-state car and every dead skunk in the road!"

Raymond knew and followed the drill. While Bill was inside bullshitting with his buddy, he measured the gas and kerosene tanks with the sticks hanging where they should be, on a nail just behind them, walked back and forth with the hoses, turned the valves on and off, draining the hose into the tank when he judged its contents would pretty much bring things to the top without running over. Fortunately, he'd developed a quick eye for that call and hadn't yet run anything out onto the ground anywhere. The sticks were marked at the top with the number stamped beside the filler hole, so he knew that they'd come with the tanks and he could rely on them to compute the gallons to fill out on the pad without gauging the dimensions of the tanks and consulting the green book in his pocket.

Everything done, he stepped into the store, taking off his hat and letting his eyes adjust to the dimmer light. John and Bill were reared back in a couple of chairs against the front of the counter, away from the cold stove in the center of the room, both still talking at once, this time apparently about various women they had known. He'd come to realize that almost every little business they served had its own touchstone -- the Roman Saxhorn photograph, Mrs. Petrie's two-headed calf, or Wilberger's sheer quantity, and illogic of inventory -- and looked around to try and figure out what made Peterson's in McDowell different besides the regulation sign over the Post Office counter's window. The deer's head mounted on the wall exhibited normal anatomy, and while the sugaring buckets and spouts were new to Raymond, he knew that they had to be in every store in this maple-sugar producing region. He was struck, though, by the amount of floor space, the polished stove and its surrounding circle of chairs -- real, comfortable, although unupholstered, armchairs like you would find on the customers' side of the desks in a bank lobby, thoughtfully interspersed with coffee cans half full of sand for butts and tobacco juice. Peterson himself was the distinction, his love of conversation and his providing plenty of good chairs rather than the usual packing crates and three-and-one-half legged or partially-seated castoffs made his store the center of conversation and comradeship during the long, hard winters that Highland County's elevation imposed. Raymond went over to where the two older men were talking, and saying nothing to interrupt their conversation, held the ticket book and his pencil out to Peterson.

"Bring you a chair over here, McCleary," Peterson said as he took the book. "It ain't all business, sit a spell. Looks alright to me," Peterson said as he tore out his copy and handed the book back to Raymond as soon as he got back with a chair and sat down opposite him, putting his stick flat on the floor to his left -- he'd learned that trying to hang it from or prop it against anything usually resulted in its falling with a clatter that led to an uncomfortable silence, a break in the conversation, and an explanation he'd just as soon avoid. "Bill, here, says I won't need to check the figures with you, that you always get them right. Don't agree with him. I've always figured that checking while the man's still here means you never have to puzzle something out later on your own." There was more than one reason that Peterson's store was a success.

"Riley says you were at Normandy," Peterson said as soon as he'd handed the book back and Raymond had gotten settled. Raymond groaned inwardly and felt his gut tighten up. He could appreciate that people were understandably curious for a firsthand account of the battle, and generally genuinely solicitous in wanting to understand his wound and recovery, but telling the story of the landing and ascent with any accuracy left him on the one hand feeling ghoulish and drained, and on the other hand, much candor about his long recovery made him look on himself as weak, a whiner. No matter what account he gave, he thought of little else in any private moments during the rest of the day, and knew that his sleep that night would be broken by nightmares of the ladders. Because it was just the three of them, because Riley and Peterson were obviously old confidants, and primarily because although he knew Bill must have been curious since the day they'd met, he'd been polite enough not to demand a war story, he gave them a reasonably accurate account. He ended by talking about their schoolboy visit to the recruiter, making a joke about the respective fates of the two bad eyes, pointing out that the first, who couldn't read the eye chart ended up with years in a community full of lonely young women, and the guy who memorized the chart, well, if he'd been lucky he'd stayed on KP in the European Theater, and was probably just now hoping for equally good luck in Asia.

Tom and Bill chuckled at that, then Bill, pretty somber, said "Thanks, Raymond, for telling us just how it was. I'd been wanting to know since I first took you on, but figured you'd tell me when it suited."

Not realizing the truth of what he said Tom added "I hope my curiosity didn't force you into anything unpleasant -- I expect you've had to tell the tale a few more times than you've cared to already."

More than you can imagine, Raymond thought as he said "I'll be ok."

"I can't fathom having the guts to do what you guys did," Peterson went on. "You got a Purple Heart because of your wound, but to my mind you and all of your buddies on that cliff deserve a damned sight more!"

"Thanks," Raymond replied, blushing and feeling kind of confused inside -- after all, he was still, for some unfathomable reason, alive, while lot of the others were gone. Dead, both above and below him on the ladder, order of march had nothing to do with survival; there was no reasoning it out, no comfortable explanation in either the telling or thinking alone, in the dark every night. That, and what made him feel even more down on himself, the way it ate at him that some men who never got a scratch but 'exchanged ball ammunition with the enemy on three separate occasions' by shooting around the corner of stone farmhouses, prompting inaccurate suppressive return fire at an absurd range, qualified for General Marshall's new Combat Infantry Award, while he didn't. He'd heard that the Second Ranger Battalion had been awarded a Presidential Unit Citation, a real honor, but not a ribbon he'd been authorized to wear on discharge, since he was no longer a member of the unit, having been assigned to a medical holding group.

Riley looked over at the clock beside the Post Office window. "Raymond," he said, we better be goin', one more mountain and a whole bunch of stops waitin' for us." They made their manners to Peterson, climbed back into the truck and ground out onto the road, climbing through the gears as they passed the couple of churches and maybe twenty houses that made up the rest of the village. The ground and road as they headed west was remarkably flat for about four or five miles, broad crop-fields and pastures full of good-looking cattle and sheep. They met few cars, mostly farmers hauling whatever needed moving in pickups, all of whom gave a friendly wave, either an arm out the window or an index finger raised from the wheel. Raymond was enjoying looking around at the farms and stock, getting kind of used to relaxed driving in high gear on a straight road when Bam!, they came up against Jack Mountain and he had to resume grinding gears and shouldering through the switchbacks. Not so many up as there'd been on Shenandoah or Bullpasture Mountain, but just as blind, steep and tight, and, like the second mountain fewer on the downward slope -- each successive valley floor was at a higher elevation.

Jack Mountain didn't have as many switchbacks;

instead, it was a series of long grades, each of which reduced them after a hundred yards or so to toiling along in first gear. Comfortable amount of wind coming in the windows, and plenty of time to look out across the little valley. They bore left at the top of the ridge, and rode the brakes all the way down the other side. After one switchback, they could see Monterey, the south end of the Bluegrass Valley, at the bottom. Just after the peak they passed a quarry and small yard where the county kept its road equipment, and it wasn't long till they got to the bottom -- the floor of the Bluegrass Valley was considerably above McDowell

Bill had told Raymond that Highland County and its neighbor to the south, Bath County, which held Warm Springs and the grand Homestead resort, were the two least-populated counties in Virginia. Despite that fact, it turned out that Monterey, the county seat, was a bronze Confederate soldier town. The business section was made up of the opposite side of the road from the front of the jail and courthouse, making an 'L' to include the side across from the court's west front. A restaurant with a large, leaping painted tin trout picked out in red neon on its roof, above a couple of apartments, corner to the Courthouse, marked the beginning of one of the stubby residential streets, just a few houses with pastures and hayfields behind. The county produced more wool than any other in the state, but its unusual business was a trout hatchery and a couple of trout farms, which took advantage of channelizing the best springs and streams through a series of incremental rectangular cement ponds where the fry got fat and were either trucked to market or trucked to stock ponds and streams in several states. He could imagine what it was like driving out of those mountains with a sloshing,

un-baffled tank full of live trout listening to the constant bark and wheeze of the small engine and compres-
sor on top of the cab that made sure there was enough
air going through the water to keep the fish supplied
with oxygen!

"Pull up there at the trout," Bill directed, "We'll
get some dinner, then drive around on these little
tanks." Raymond followed Bill inside just in time to
hear the proprietress call out "Hey, Bill, we got some of
that lemon moo-rang pie you like today!" "Well, bring
us some, with two trout plates and coffee, he hollered
back," pulling a chair out from one of the little square,
checked-cloth tables for Raymond, then the other for
himself. So much for looking at a menu, thought Raymond, but then, looking around, realized that there
probably weren't any. People from away who came
here came for trout, and regulars, who might like the
pie but never want to look another trout in the eye knew
from long experience what else could be had. Anyone
in between those categories, like him if he'd come in
without Bill, well, they just had to ask. Their coffee
and a checked-napkin lined basket cornbread arrived as
they waited. Raymond was actually as much interested
as he was hungry -- he'd had plenty of catfish, bluegill,
and bass, pinfish out of farm ponds and the sluggish
streams back home, but he'd never, before today's drive,
seen a stream fast and cold enough to harbor trout, and
he'd never eaten one. When they arrived, with side
bowls of beans and applesauce, he was kind of surprised that they were flayed out, backbones and ribs
removed, sides spread wide on the smallish plates, and
that they still had their heads on, two dead white dots
looking up at him from the center of the eyes. Bill
looked over at him and sensed his hesitation. "Don't be
put off, boy. Flip 'em over on their back and you don't

have to look 'em in the eye; then just kinda flake the meat off the skin real easy with your fork. Mm mm....," he continued, shifting from instruction to demonstration. Raymond fell to it, liked the trout, and it didn't take the two of them long to finish the fish, bread, and vegetables and get into the pie. The young girl waiting tables brought them more coffee, and after they'd finished that, Bill got up, Raymond following, went over to the counter to settle up, saying "Annie, that sure is good pie! This is Raymond McCleary, my new route man, I'm teaching him the stops and where to eat so's he don't get poisoned."

"Well, I reckon he's safe here." She handed him his change and nodding with a smile to Raymond. "Nice to meet you."

"Thank you, Ma'am. I'm sure I'll be back."

The rest of the afternoon went pretty much like all of their rounds, crossroads stores and more difficult to locate farm tanks. Although most farmers had a legible name on their mailbox if they didn't still go to the store for it -- mail was too important a break in their day to take a chance on missing it, either RFD or down at the store. The gasoline man, Raymond realized, especially Bill Riley, was considered pretty fair entertainment as well. As a consequence farmers who had called Staunton or left word at the nearest store on the route usually found some job of work to do in the vicinity of the tank on delivery day. Some were either so straightforward in their desire for conversation with someone other than their wives and dogs that they and the dog were waiting in the pickup pulled into the shade nearby, or so trifling that they waited with a tractor rigged for the day's work, talk first, work later. Riley never disappointed. For those who wanted to talk war, he was ready with war; politics, he could do either side convincingly; theology, he could usually bring the largely Presbyterian and Baptist listener around to a point where he could be suitably impressed by Bill's knowledge of Anabaptist theology and history, which was surprising, given that Bill was Catholic. Raymond asked him about that and learned that Bill had once been the junior man on a job where his boss spoke of nothing else and it was more amusing to learn it all and try to catch him out in his recitals than to pose opposite positions which the other fellow, being, according to his beliefs, right, wouldn't or couldn't argue in a very interesting way. Bill's favorite farmers were the ones without interest in any particular topic. They found themselves regaled with Bill's current favorite topic, which might be news on a cargo cult sprung up on a remote Pacific archipelago, as reported to Bill by some Seabee acquaintance, or the recitation of peculiar facts and historic occurrences that he had garnered by many a day spent with various almanacs while tending the store in Stunton, starting back when he was a kid helping his dad and it really was a general store rather than the ghost of one selling oil products.

Bill was, Raymond decided, an impossible man to imitate, and he resolved to use his lifelong credo, learned from his father and grandfather, 'boy, you got two ears and one mouth for a reason,' to ease in with the customers. He understood that many of the farmers would enjoy his listing ear, and that most would consider him fair company if he only gave them one or two comments that made it clear that he could pay attention to a conversation and retain his ability to simultaneously calculate the volume drained or pumped into their usually non-standard tanks (more than one transaction began "bet you can't tell me where that tank come from" but Bill was pretty consistent on clueing him in so that he knew which chart to use in the little book). The farmers did have peculiar sources of tankage, mostly having to do with some cousin or brother-in-law's employment -- ship fitting (Norfolk and Baltimore were in about the same proximity), railroading, mining, and the distillation or processing of various substances (often the previous generation's home variety, and DuPont had a big plant over in Waynesboro). Crossroad mechanics and farmers' sons who learned to weld a seam in FFA and had access to the equipment could approximate a tank out of the damndest, odd, flat stuff, as no rolled steel plate found itself anywhere close the civilian market, even the relatively protected farm market. Blown down or out-of-date advertising signs were right good material, having the advantage of never having held gasoline, as was any body panel at least two feet square from any car, truck, farm machine or industrial fabrication unlikely to be used during the duration. Piped-together stacks or rows of car tanks worked pretty well if you had some extra fittings, the muscle to scrape the joints clean and the balls to drop molten solder in place from a copper heated over a blowtorch behind you the moment before to make a tight cold-solder joint. The lucky fellows were the handy but untidy sort that had let a rocky, hidden corner of their farm grow into a community junkyard before the war, usually unbeknownst to their wives. Homemade tanks were all gravity fed -- again, the war-industries had all of the monkey-pumps. Up on a rack just higher than the tank on a tractor with a little shed roof to keep the sun from spiriting the gasoline away, and filled through a screw-cap that used to live on the crimped-on top of a five-gallon paint can, all required Raymond to stick the truck's tank to figure deliveries. At least he knew which page in the <u>Guide</u> to consult. Bill Riley said that they'd have damned fewer of these customers if they lived back in Queen Elizabeth's time when everything the Crown owned was stamped with three small lines, a stylized broad head arrow, and discovery of that stamp on any part of a private device meant that the sheriff got out his hangin' rope with no questions asked and no lawyers arguin'.

They spent the entire afternoon going up and down both sides of the 'Devils Backbone', a ridge with exposed rock on top where you could dangle a foot on either side, which divided the Bluegrass Valley. They filled the tanks at all of the stores there and stopped again, in Monterey before heading home, to stick the truck gas tank and empty it into the underground tank at the town's one large garage, whose owner bought whatever was left after each run as a favor to Bill, minimizing the load shift on the way home.

They'd taken care to check the radiator and engine oil and fill the International's own tank before dumping the last of the gasoline load -- the kerosene and motor oil would just have to shift around, but they didn't have as much room to cause trouble, because the tanks were smaller. The drive home, late in the afternoon was an express trip -- no stops along the way. Raymond was tired from driving and climbing up and down off of the truck, and Bill was tired from talking with his friends, playing the route salesman game with those he didn't have such positive feelings for, watching and advising Raymond, and, as he put it, "being ridden by the International, rather than the other way 'round." The truck was, after all, sprung for a two-ton load rather than running what amounted to a full day of errands. Mentally ciphering whether or not the full tanks exceeded that rating would be a good pastime for a day when he was alone. Bill wasn't saying much, and in fact, Raymond caught him out of the corner of his eye, dozing, when they were in stretches where turns weren't bouncing him off of the doorframe and seat.

Across all three mountains, Raymond now had a fair idea of how the switchbacks went and didn't have to devote so much of his time to the truck in each turn. He approached the turn, saw the rock in front of him, started shouldering the wheel, and as the expanse of stone slid across his vision in the turn, something unconscious in him looked for foot and hand holds, looked for those cracks in each ledge where a bayonet would hold firm. He was aware that the cliffs reminded him of his training, North Georgia and then all of those isolated coves in England and of the cliffs a Port Du Hoc.

Bill stirred and grunted, "Boy, you're a good driver, smooth....I kinda nodded off there for a while. For a man to be tired enough to sleep in this re-plumbed monster -- he grinned and kicked the big cast-iron radiator under the dash -- you gotta be beat."

"I'll be glad to see Staunton."

Bill pushed his cap back, scratched his head and turned towards Raymond. "I reckon you'll feel it for a couple days, until you get used to horsin' that wheel and straining your neck to see up out of the corner of the windshield into every turn even though there's probably nobody there and your reflexes haven't absorbed the fact that there's no point in trying to look 'cause you can't see nothing anyhow." Bill looked ahead. "Got a proposition for you that'll maybe cut you a little slack. My last man painted the store and loading shed, bit by bit, on the days when he was wore out from this run." He looked over at Raymond and grinned, "I see that look about your eye, you don't need to bother asking me where I got battleship gray paint for him to use. My proposition is that you take this old International, which the sun has faded to Texaco pink back to its original Texaco Red. I know from your hognose Ford that you can do it without any problem, it'll just take time 'cause its lot bigger. Nothing unusual about the job... "Bill paused and tried to strike a dignified air, "except that unlike your Ford, which has that godawful stain on the seat, the cause of which I have been and remain too discreet to require or expect an explanation, the interior isn't an issue."

"Sounds good," Raymond replied, thinking to himself that spending as much of tomorrow as wasn't tied up in calls to fill empty local tanks puttering about by himself in the shade of the loading shed sounded better than good. "I suppose," Raymond tried to match Bill's feigned hauteur, "I suppose that I'll have to use Texaco products on the job."

"Correct." Bill replied. "They," he paused for emphasis and spat out the window, "will have my ass if I don't get rid of those dusty boxes of compound and polish and order some more!" They pulled into the lot a good bit later than their usual quitting time and Bill scrambled off towards his pickup. "Gotta fill these cans 'fore I go home; see you in the mornin'," he called and pulled out, turning left towards the restaurant rather than right towards home.

Raymond dragged his feet as he walked from

the loading shed here he'd parked the International. Leaning heavily on his stick, he made it to the Ford and collapsed into the driver's seat, throwing stick and cap over on the other side. He was glad that Riley had been anxious to get the restaurant scraps for his hogs and had left the lot first and in a hurry. Glad that Riley hadn't seen him walking to his pickup. Riley was a good employer, and doubtless knew how physical the Highland route was from doing it himself, in a truck without a modern transmission or a comfortable seat; that's why he'd made the proposition about polishing the tanker. Raymond, though, was frightened of Bill realizing how severe his limitations were, afraid that the good job he'd lucked into might disappear just as quickly. He backed the pickup around just far enough to be able to make the turn for the gate, turned left on Middlebrook, left on Lewis, then right on Beverley Street, headed for a little restaurant over on the Coalter Street hill with a neon sign on the top of the roof proclaiming "Eats". He liked the food and the Colored couple who ran the place, Mr. and Mrs. Tate, and the prices were the best in town for cooking exactly like he was used to at home.

The prospect of supper and sitting in the booth with a cup of black coffee made him feel a good bit less tired, as did the meal, which came pretty quick, but when he got up to pay his tab, his leg was still giving him hell and he had to ride the stick right heavy, moving with an obviously abnormal gait to the counter by the door to pay for his meal. "Hard day?" Mr. Tate asked.

"Yes, Sir. My first day driving the tanker over to Monterey, since it was all mountain, jamming my bad leg on the brake a full half of the time."

"I know it ain't easy, but it'll come. You'll get stronger and you'll start to trust that transmission to do more of the braking -- I done my time haulin', too." Mr. Tate advised as he handed Raymond his change.

"Thanks. Probably see you tomorrow evening," he continued as he put his cap on at exactly the right angle and headed outside.

There was a phone booth on the far side of the restaurant lot. Aspirin hadn't been doing him much good, and he'd been thinking about calling Colonel Hill out at the hospital, but had always, until now, found some excuse to put it off. He knew that Hill would be unlikely to be in surgery this late, given the ungodly early hour that he always started, and also knew that unless he had changed his habits, Colonel Hill would be in his office doing paperwork rather than socializing at the golf club bar or the Hotel Stonewall Jackson, both heavily patronized by the command's officers. He put his nickel in the phone, heard it fall, and the operator came on the line, "how may I help you?"

"Woodrow Wilson Hospital, please."

The switchboard operator at the hospital answered, "Woodrow Wilson."

"Orthopedic Surgery, please."

The extension rang four or five times, but, as he had anticipated, "Colonel Hill," was the greeting he received.

"Good evening, Sir, This is one of your old patients, Raymond McCleary." He hesitated, unsure where to go next.

"Of course I remember you. It hasn't been that long, and I reckon its *Mister* McCleary now, right? What can I do for you?"

"Well, Sir, I don't mean to complain, but there wasn't much future for me on the farm down home so I came back up here to Staunton and talked my way into a job driving a gasoline and oil delivery truck -- crossroads store accounts, if you know what I mean. I just got back from Highland County this evening, and my leg is killing me. I've been taking aspirin, but it doesn't touch the problem, and I haven't dared ask the druggist to let me sign for anything stronger, 'cause I'm not sure he has it, what with the war, partly out of pride, and because and I'm scared of trying to drive as loopy as I was in the hospital."

"I just happen to have time for a telephone consultation -- you're not the first. Put in another three or four nickels if you have 'em" Hill directed. Raymond put in the coins and he and the operator, who he knew had stayed on the line, watching the clock, since it was a pay phone, both heard them drop. "When you have pain, do you feel anything shifting, things grating against each other?"

"No, Sir,"

"More like constant aching, worse when you use it a lot like you did today?"

"Yes, Sir. It got worse as the day progressed, this evening it feels like my muscles are trying to pull themselves off my bones every step I take."

"Good. Sounds like the bone & metal's holding tight, but you've got to remember that you've been shot, dragged off of a battlefield, and had two extensive surgeries -- things just can't be lined up normal in there, and there's so much scar tissue that no muscle gets a straight pull. It's always across another one or some nerve that it would usually slide alongside of. Keep you from going to sleep or wake you up at night? Feel decent enough in the morning most days?" Hill piled on the questions.

"Mornings and most days I can manage. Right as I start to go to sleep, as I start to relax, it's like something in my head says "here it comes boy", and my leg goes nuts, starts to relax, then tightens up and grabs hold of me. That series of spasms takes a long time to stop so that I can go to sleep, and yes, I do wake up with it in the night." Raymond didn't tell the doc what else went through his mind that made it difficult to go to sleep, or that when he woke up he was screaming, and not just from the pain in his leg.

"Now what to do about it." Hill mused. "The pharmacy'd probably let you sign for Librium or morphine tablets, but with the tolerance you developed in the hospital, your effective dose would increase so fast that they'd get scared to give you enough to do any good, that, and, as you say, driving loopy doesn't work real well. Family history time. I don't mean to be insulting, but is your daddy a drunk?"

"No, Sir."

"Uncles or grandfather on either side drunks?"

"No, Sir."

"You or your brothers or your cousins?"

"Nothin' more than the usual stupid growin' up stuff, Sir."

"Good" Hill replied. "My daddy was a country doctor down in Wise, and he always said that ninety percent of his patients could be made comfortable with either aspirin or alcohol. Me being a surgeon, I add ether and morphine to the list, and recognize that lots of 'em wouldn't make it if it weren't for penicillin. You've tried all but one of those. My suggestion is that you take a good, strong drink of whisky right before bed. Not a sip, not a jigger, but a good strong drink. It should let you get to sleep and rest, and from what you tell me, your leg isn't so bad if you're rested. Don't drink beer, because to get enough in you to have the desired effect, you'd just have to wake up again to piss. You won't have the problem of being drugged at work, or get gossiped about as an addict, and if you're telling me the truth about your family, I don't think that my advice is going to turn you into a drunk."

"I'm bein' straight with you, Doc. Thanks for talking with me, thanks for the advice."

"Glad to know that you've recovered enough to find a job. Take care of yourself, McCleary." Doctor Hill broke the connection.

Raymond went back to the truck and got in, just sitting there with his hands on the wheel's rim thinking. Doc Hill seemed to understand how he felt, and gave a logical explanation for it, along with some reassurance about his bones. He'd given him a practical solution, but one, unfortunately, that wasn't available at this hour of the evening. After prohibition ended, Virginia had kept a State monopoly on liquor sales, and their store hours were over long ago. He guessed he just go home, have a bath and grit his teeth until tomorrow.

Parking in his usual place beside Mrs. Russ' garage, he noticed that David's beat up railroad sedan was there, too -- all signals in the Mountain Division must be working this evening, he thought to himself. He cranked up the window, grabbed his stick with one hand, cap with the other, not bothering to put it on, as it was nearly dark. He could see Mrs. Russ, her daughter, Lee, and David sitting at the table, the coffee pot in the center on a potholder to protect the oilcloth from melting. They'd arranged themselves, the cream and the sugar around the table to suit their tastes; Lee could reach the pot and nothing else, David the pot and the sugar, and Mrs. Guss was in the chair with her favorite cushion, in easy reach of the sugar, cream, and kitchen extension telephone, confident that neither of the others would let her cup get dry and ready to relay whatever news came through the TUxedo exchange.

There, as Bill would say, was a thinker. The City's society folks and those who looked upon themselves as society folks -- not to go down a rabbit trail, who fell into that second group, which was another thinker -- always emphasized the word, *tuxedo*, dragging it out when they gave a number to the operator or some new acquaintance. The thinking centered on why that word, out-of-place for even a snobbish southern town, had been selected. You couldn't deny that Staunton had its share of people who knew that superiority was their birthright, and loved the sound of the name of the exchange, evocative of the high life in <u>The Great Gatsby</u>. Bill was quick to point out that the TUxedo designation was geographic, common to all in the City of Staunton, and that a prostitute successful enough to rent a house on one of the streets on Sear's hill, across the footbridge over the tracks between the station and the swinging water tower arm, was able use to the same word, with the same delight in the sound and the delicious the irony arising from knowledge of the blind self-satisfaction of those who felt that it had been selected for and because of them and their position in society. Raymond figured it had something to do with long-distance calling, that they'd just got on in the alphabet as they got further and further from the central switchboard, and had gone through the first letter "T" and come down to "U" in the second letters. "Tummy," "tumbleweed," "turnip," "turnstile," or "turtle" just hadn't met the 'phone fellows need to sound good, and they'd paged back and forth in the dictionary until they hit on "tuxedo." The one thing he was sure of, no Southerner had selected the word.

As Raymond dragged himself across the double-tracked drive and little dooryard behind the back porch, he noticed that Mrs. Guss, or maybe Lee at her request, had gotten one of those big tin cans that the restaurants bought food in, painted it red, and half-filled it with sand for him and David to use, rather than field-stripping their late-night butts into the gravel beside the garage. From whatever source, those two ladies had accurate inside knowledge of how a barracks was set up and run!

When he put his foot on the porch, he tried to pull himself together a bit. Put his cap on at exactly the right angle so that he could take it off normally as he entered, wiped his feet on the mat, and gritted his teeth as he opened the screen door and swung his right leg in with his best approximation of his normal gait, pulling his cap off as he eased the door shut, not letting the spring slam.

"VE Day!" Dave called out. "We've been sitting up talking about it and wondering if you were out celebrating or if old Bill Riley just worked you late -- pull up a chair and join us."

"My vote's for Bill Riley," Mrs. Guss responded for Raymond. "His looks confirm it."

"Agreed." said Lee, pouring him a cup of coffee. "He moves work tired, not happy tired, and I remember him mentioning at breakfast that they were going to Highland County today."

Raymond sat down, slid his stick under the table and put his hat on the tabletop beside his cup. "Just can't fool you-all. You see all, know all, and guess the rest," and with a wink at Mrs. Russ, "the accuracy of your guessing probably improved by a phone call with Bill while I was at super."

"It's tiresome that I'm so predictable," she winked back. "Must be because I'm getting old."

"No, Mother, it's not age, it's experience -- you know the sources and the timing," Lee spoke the truth but also didn't want her mother to start burying herself before she was dead with the 'I'm old' talk, as she was sometimes inclined.

"What do you think of the news?" David demanded.

"I'm glad to hear it, for everybody, not just our guys. The civilians in all of Europe have been takin' a beatin', and the ordinary German soldier has to be glad to see the end. I guess some guys'll be lucky and get to stay in Germany for guard duty, and the rest will get shipped home for a few days then sent to the Pacific. Right out of one war and into another, another that we've been going slow on, and against people that I don't think that we understand."

"One hell of a boat ride," David commented.

"Bill's got an interesting take on that," Raymond picked up. "He says that the Russians have one line, the Trans-Siberian, that could move troops to the east, but that our Army would have to build its own railroad through the territories that the Germans and Russians fought through and tore everything up. His next point was that since we strafed the hell out of every German train that we could find and they no doubt did the same for the Soviets, there's probably not enough rolling stock in all of Europe to move our armies east. His final comment was that if Soviet trains were like Soviet everything else, we'd get our tracks and our phantom railcars to the western terminus of the Trans-Siberian, which is probably now just a bunch of twisted rails on a battlefield, only to find that the distance between Russian rails is about two inches greater than ours, since they've always announced such big plans! All that supports a ride on some of Mr. Kaiser's boats across the Atlantic, enough home leave to let the brass have time to figure out what they're gonna' do next and move the rest of the Navy to the Pacific, then give the troops a fast train ride across the US, and put them on another batch of Liberty Ships to get to Japan. *I* think that they're gonna' have to keep a good many Liberties in the Atlantic to keep taking food the Brits and everyone else, and that any real movement will depend on how fast the welders in the shipyards on the west coast can work. The Russians will probably just start marching east, and get to Japan when they do, no matter who or what is in the way."

Mrs. Russ invoked her matriarchal and property owner's prerogative to change the subject. "Enough about the war, Raymond, let's get back to what we were talking about, your day across the mountains. What was the driving like, who did you meet and what did you think of them? "

Raymond, mindful of the close connection between his landlord and his boss, emphasized the differences between driving the mountains and the Valley or North Carolina, praised the International's wide choice of gears and hydraulic brakes, and minimized how tired it had made him. Of all of the storekeepers, he allowed as he liked Sarah Thompson at Westview Store the best."

"Good choice," Lee observed. "You might have a pretty good chance!" making the others chuckle and Raymond blush as he realized that despite everything else that had happened that day, he'd unconsciously filled the time in between events calculating his chances.

David rose from his chair. "Thanks for the coffee, Mrs. Russ," he said as he rinsed his cup and put it upside down in the wire rack on the drain board. "Raymond, I'll tap on your door to see if you're awake if I get up for a smoke -- you don't need to be waking me up again! He headed upstairs.

"Lessons to prepare, Mother," Lee got up, rinsed her cup and went towards the front of the house, where Raymond figured she had either a desk or table set aside for her schoolwork.

"Now, boy, I'll tell you what I know and I expect you to do the same," said Mrs. Russ in a serious voice, turning to lean her elbow on the table facing Raymond. "Bill Riley said that you got on perfectly with all of the storekeepers, handled the truck like you grew up driving it, and that he made up an excuse to get the hell off of the store lot before you walked from the loading shed to your pickup, because he knew that you were whipped pretty bad and he didn't know what to do or say if he saw you fall down on the way. I think that he wants to keep you on, but he's avoiding the issue of your leg." She turned her chair sideways and leaned back, arms crossed in front of her chest, attentive to Raymond. "Now it's your turn."

"I'm pleased that Bill says what he does about the stores and the truck, and I noticed that he was hot to get out of there without saying a word. He's right -- if you were to go over there now with a flashlight and looked at the gravel, you could see I didn't fall down, but you'd also see that I dragged my foot every step to the pickup. I think that I'll get stronger with each delivery run, and eventually be OK if he can see his way to giving me the chance." He grinned. "At least Bill didn't wake up from any of his little naps and catch me trying to poke my stick onto the brake! I have to admit that the idea crossed my mind, but I realized that for it to have a chance of working, I'd have to wire it to the left side of the pedal ahead of time so that I could still use my right foot when I needed to. I couldn't have finished the day if the truck hadn't had hydraulic brakes."

"Well, at least you and Bill have stories that match, so I reckon you're both telling me the truth. What'd you do the rest of the evening?" '

He told her about how supper at the Tate's restaurant helped, and about his conversation with Colonel Hill, omitting the pissing part. "I came in here planning to talk to you about the Doc's suggestion -- I know that you have pretty high standards for this place."

"I do expect folks to behave, but I'm not heartless." She got up, went over to a door in the cupboards he'd never seen opened before and returned with a water tumbler three-quarters full of whisky and put it on the table in front of him. "I've got standards, but I'm not heartless. My Daddy and Husband would have given you the same advice if they were alive and here to talk with you this evening. Careful you don't spill this on your way upstairs. Leave it on your bed stand while you take your bath, and, mind you, put something under it so that it doesn't leave a ring on the wood. Follow Hill's advice and no more, and you and I and you and Bill Riley will continue to get along just fine. I'll be glad, too, if the whole house isn't waked up the way we were the other night. Don't worry about your coffee cup; I'll get it with mine."

Raymond could hardly believe his eyes and ears. "Thanks Mrs. Russ, thanks for a lot of things," he said, getting up, getting a good grip on cane, cap and glass before heading upstairs, thinking to himself that his father and grandfather had told him right -- speak the truth even when it's hard, 'cause that's right, and because it's a whole heap easier than trying to keep two stories straight.

Raymond had finished his bath, pulled on a clean pair of pants to be decent during the interval before he crawled into bed, and was just putting his petroleum-scented work clothes over the backs of two chairs next to the window when he heard a soft knock at his door. David, he figured, and discovered that he was right when he opened it while pulling on a shirt against the mosquitoes and saw and heard David say "join me in a smoke?" Barefoot, they made their way to the back porch stoop and lit up, sending out plumes that gradually dispersed into the calm night air.

"What's new with the railroad? I see that they've given you a car to use."

"Yeah. When I'm checking local gear they figured putting me on the road saved man-hours and kept the line open longer than if we went by handcar, work-train, or one of their road vehicles rigged with retractable rail wheels. I can usually park next to a crossing and walk where I need to go along the tracks rather than bushwhacking through the blackberries, locust pointers, barbed wire and ditches. If they know something's not working they send a work-train with enough men and material to rebuild the whole switch, although most of the time I can figure the problem out short of that. Rebuilding's usually for gear that's just worn out from use, rather than being troublesome for the brakemen or jammed. Mostly I can figure out and fix troublesome or jammed by myself. When they do send an engine, I always get to ride in the cab and have gotten to know the yard engineers pretty well, them and some of the line drivers. I'm still hoping they'll get me out of this switch and signal slot and into engineer training. A word from those guys might help." Raymond thought, but didn't say, that David was making himself entirely too useful to the railroad in his present job to have a prayer of train-driving unless he managed to marry the right man's daughter, and it was pretty clear that he hadn't an idea who she was.

"How're you doin'?" You looked done for when you came in this evening."

"This was my first time driving over to Highland County and back -- Bill had told me that there were three mountains to cross, and I thought they'd be like Afton Mountain that I crossed coming up here from Carolina. They weren't. The roads are a lot worse, and I hadn't thought much about the difference between a two-ton and a pickup. My pickup only has manual brakes, but I didn't have any problem with it on Afton, but even though the International's got hydraulics, the truck and the load kept me standing on them, hard, on every downgrade. Takes a lot more muscle to turn those front wheels going slow in the switchbacks than I'd imagined. You can't see a blessed thing that's coming when you start into them and you've gotta stay slow in the turns to keep traction on both front wheels -- no baffles in the tanks to steady the load, and all the weight shifts to one side. If that's the side in loose gravel, your steering's not as quick, even though the wheels are angled. I never got out of second gear on either side of any of the mountains, spent most of my time in jack-low and low range on the back axle. After the driving, climbing up and down off of the truck didn't come so easy as usual and finished the job of wearing me out."

"How you gonna deal with it?"

"Well, I guess it's like army physical training or any other hard work, the more you do the easier it gets, so long as you don't get hurt along the way."

"You," David observed, looking carefully out into the darkness rather than in Raymond's direction, "are starting this thing hurt."

"No shit." replied Raymond, also avoiding eye contact and lighting another Lucky. "I called my doctor out at the hospital after supper this evening. He quizzed me pretty good and told me he thought the patches on the bone were sound, but that the muscles and leaders and nerves are all crossed up from the surgeries so that, for example, walking muscles pinch each other or nerves where they should lie beside each other and work together. He says that scar tissue from the healing pushes things around even though the doctors do their best to keep them straight, they can't predict what the scar tissue will do and I'm sure that there's also lot of little stuff that they can't begin to keep in line. Under the skin I reckon I'm kinda like a tomcat who likes to fight but ain't no good at it. You can't clip the fur off of the whole damn cat looking for the bites. The surgeons reach a point where they have to stop looking and patching. Colonel Hill said that the best thing was rest, and told me to drink a glass of whisky just before bedtime every night -- I was just about to do that when you knocked. I didn't know how Mrs. Russ would react, but she agreed and even gave me a glassful for to tonight, since I hadn't had an opportunity to go to the store."

"Sounds like a plan. *I'll* like it if you don't start

screaming again. You gotta watch that drinking and work, though. The railroad has real strict rules about it, which most of the old-timers grin and ignore to a limited degree, but let some young guy step across the line, and bingo, where is he? On a line gang if he's working at all."

"Yeah. A lot of that in the Army, too. OK for privates to make fools of themselves on pass, but it was the Drill Instructors you smelled it on at morning formation in the middle of the week. Well, let's see if it works." he reached over to stub out his butt in the red can and stood up to return to his room. "We need to remember to empty the can she put out for us every day or so."

"Right," David replied, still smoking, "see you at breakfast". Raymond went upstairs, stripped down to his skivvies for bed and drank the whisky is three long swallows. The fumes in his nose made him stop for breath in between, and every drop burned, all the way down. Clueless that the burn was going to become as potent a precursor to relief in his life as the lady with the morphine's needle had been when he was in the hospital or the medic's rough jab had been on the battlefield, he went to sleep easily and dreamt of nothing until the alarm woke him the next morning.

35. BIG TRUCK POLISHING BY A HARD MAN

When he got to work he parked the Barrelnose, put his cap on at exactly the right angle, and went into the store -- Bill was already there. He had organized a three-foot stepladder for reaching the high spots, had brought a pile of rags from home, had found a five-gallon paint bucket (battleship grey) that had had an easy enough life since the painting that it could still hold water, and had brought out a case of Texaco polishing compound and a case of Texaco polish, both of which were unopened and thick with dust. The district salesman who had left them years ago had been new and hadn't understood that the store's clientele had more sedans cut down to carry homemade truck bodies than Packards or LaSalles. "Looks like you got it all. Thanks for hunting it down for me." He opened the cardboard cases and slipped out a shiny old-stock can of each product, put them in the bucket with the rags and headed for the loading shed, where, in addition to the hoses from the tank cars there was a water pipe. The ladder was just the right height for sitting · while working on the fenders, so he started with the left front. Damp cloth, put the compound on a ridiculously small area for so large a truck, but an area that could be buffed out with a dry rag before it became so hard that it became part of the pink encrustation. Move a few inches and repeat, until the entire panel was done. Then and only then put polish on the whole area, smoothing out the minor differences in sheen caused by the direction of the cutting cloth, and again, polish before the haze got so hard that it felt like you were pulling it off rather than buffing. He knew the drill. A few days of this, he thought, and he was going to feel like he was driving a city fire truck through the country! He was busy and productive and it felt good to be off of his leg and using different muscles than those he'd worked the day before.

Mid-morning he heard the telephone ring a couple of times -- there was an outside bell up at the store. After the second call, Bill came down and said that they needed to take a tub of grease out to Harner's Garage in New Hope, and that Wilberger was running a little low on both gas and kerosene. "That's flatland driving and might help work the soreness out of your shoulders," Bill said, then observed "I reckon there's not much difference between me and a tub of grease, so you can just leave me home and carry it out on the passenger side. Take it easy, if you have any errands to run, you can do them on your way back." They both knew that he had to go to the liquor store before it closed at just before five that evening.

Raymond got to a quitting place with his polishing, filled the tanker, went to the back dock of the store where they usually loaded boxed goods onto the flatbed truck for delivery, rolled the heavy tub of grease on its lower rim across the warehouse to the edge of the dock adjacent to where he had parked the truck with the passenger door open, stood between the truck and the dock and pulled the tub off of the edge, flipping it over into the seat as it fell -- a nice, easy move if he did say so himself! He enjoyed the drive out to New Hope, jawed a while with Mr. Harner at the garage, then went over to the store and filled Mr. Wilberger's tanks. Realizing that it was dinnertime, he bought himself a soda and some cheese and crackers and found a more or less complete chair near the cold stove where he could sit and eat. Looking around, he realized that this might be a good opportunity to do some shopping -- his old farm shoes were starting to come apart from all of the climbing and he wanted a pail to try and start carrying his dinner, which he figured would save some money and allow him to eat better. Wandering to the back of the store as he finished his soda, he found the solution to his shoe needs. Most improbably, since New Hope was in the center of hundreds of acres of cultivated land and only had a part-time sawmill where one farmer had a sideline of cutting boards for his neighbors out of trees from their woodlots, he saw a pair of high-topped loggers' boots displayed atop a pile of boxes marked in various sizes, the kind of boots with speed-lacing tabs instead of the top four lace holes, a pronounced heel and a little fringed flap just beneath the bottom lace, to shake water off so that it didn't soak through the tongue of the shoe onto your foot. Arguably like a frontiersman's fringed buckskin coat, he suspected that the real reason for the tab's existence was the fact that loggers, even though there were none in New Hope, liked the look. He figured that they were just what he needed for continual climbing on and off the truck -- and he kinda liked the look, too. He found a box labeled with his size, tried them on, and decided to wear them out of the store, tying the laces of his farm brogans together and throwing them over his shoulder.

The next item he was looking for was a pail to carry his midday meal in. Farmers eat breakfast, dinner, and supper. They come back to the house at noon to eat dinner and cool off before returning to the field. Miners carry a dinner bucket with them down the shaft to the coal seam. Factory workers sufficiently removed from the farm adopt the urban designations of breakfast, luncheon, and dinner, and carry lunch pails or boxes with them as they clock in each morning. Raymond found what he was looking for, labeled as a lunch box, its light-weight cardboard carton faded and dusty. Wilberger had doubtless bought his stock before the war, as no steel had been allocated for this use since the need for thousands of mess kits had arisen. Stocking the lunch boxes wasn't as strange as stocking the logging boots, though, as there were DuPont and a number of smaller factories in nearby Waynesboro, where many New Hope area residents and small landholders worked, doing their farming in the off shift, on the weekends, and giving as much of the work to their wives and adolescent children as they could. The box, rectangular with an arched top that held a Thermos, was exactly what Raymond was looking for. He paid at the counter, climbed into and cranked the International, and headed back to town. Riley, he thought, had made his usual profit on the tub of grease, but he suspected that the truck had used as many gallons of gasoline, at cost, as he had unloaded with the wholesaler's markup.

Before going back to Riley's Texaco he stopped at Staunton's Virginia Department of Alcoholic Beverage Control store -- at the end of prohibition, Virginia had imposed a state monopoly on liquor sales. The ABC store, most people called it, although it was known by some wags as the Green-front supermarket because of the Bedford County greenstone that sheathed the lower portion of the wall outside the door where serious customers leaning against the wall with one foot propped up, waiting for opening time, would've left scuff marks on the paint (Circuit Courthouses had little signs on the lower window casings in the hall outside the courtroom reading 'please keep feet off of walls'). The stores were stark, long, and narrow, exactly the same, inside and out in every town. The control board's architect had, no doubt, hit on the use of Bedford stone in order to organize political support for the approval of an exterior that would have delighted Benito Mussolini, sharp lines and stylized faschi incorporated into both the concrete and the light fixtures. The stores, although supposedly aimed at maximizing tax revenue from liquor, were set up and their procedures organized for the maximum intimidation of all but hardened drinkers. The walls were white, the floor highly polished black linoleum, and every piece of metal except the brass door locks painted army olive drab.

The setup was kind of like Miller's store in Headwaters, with the counter only a couple yards from the door, but the stock-shelves, instead of facing the customer to display the merchandise as in a country store, ran parallel with each other the seemingly endless length of the building behind the clerks, an arrangement that left only their plain steel ends facing the customer, who could see neither the goods nor their price. A newcomer approaching a clerk to ask what was available or the price was churlishly referred to a broadsheet price list in miniscule type displayed on an olive-drab lectern opposite the counter to make their choice, then come back and tell the clerk. If the clerk didn't happen to know where that particular bottle was on the shelves, he was apparently trained to ask the customer for the stock number in a voice calculated to convey the message "you fool why didn't you bring me the number to begin with". The lectern was equipped with neither pencil nor notepaper.

Raymond parked the oil truck at a right angle across several spaces in the middle of the mostly empty lot -- he figured that the few cars present probably belonged to the men who worked there. He grabbed his stick, glanced in the rearview mirror to make sure that his cap was at exactly the right angle, and walked over to the door. He went in, shut the door behind him, and was about to automatically remove his cap, as he'd been taught was good manners indoors, when he glanced at the clerk and immediately had the feeling of an Army recruit facing a drill sergeant for the first time. He left the cap on, at just the right angle, locked his face into the hardest look he'd had to master as a soldier, walked over to the clerk and said " 'afternoon. I need a bottle of whisky, please." He could see the clerk looking him up and down, preparing to start the "are you twenty-one years of age" game, and was instantly determined that he was God-damned if he was going to let some civilian clerk play with him. Raymond took a step closer to the counter, lay his stick across it, supporting himself with both hands on the edge, and without changing his facial expression or tone of voice asked "what are your best sellers and how much do they cost?"

The clerk got the message and answered, but still managed an attempt to put part of his customer relations training to use. "That depends on what size you want," he said with just a hint of a smirk, but when Raymond said nothing, he didn't refer him to the lectern to learn which brands came in which sizes. "Folks who want pints generally buy Four Roses -- that's the cheapest we have. Our best sellers in fifths are Granddad and Rebel Yell," he went on, naming their prices.

"One of each, please." Raymond had done some mental arithmetic and realized that a nightly drink of the size he'd had last night was likely to take more than a fifth a week, and he didn't want to run out after one o'clock on a Saturday, closing time for the store. At that point the clerk, realizing that Raymond wasn't going to be any fun, turned obsequious as he made change and carefully slid each bottle into the right-sized bag (Granddad was tall and slim, Yell sort of squat like an antique wine bottle) and then the two into another paper sack that just fit the combination. How many sizes of bag does that guy have under the counter? Raymond wondered to himself, still not changing a muscle of his expression. As he slid the bag across the counter, the clerk whipped out one of the broadsheets, expertly folded it twice and slipped it between the bagged bottles. "Here's a price list for you to check if you like. Thanks for coming in."

"Thank you," Raymond said with a victor's grace. "I'm sure that I'll be in again." He took the bag in the crook of his right arm, his stick in his left hand, and did the best approximation of an about face that he could as he left the store. Back in the truck he silently shook his head at the two roles acted in the little scene he'd just been part of and at the fact that, for the first time in his life, he'd played the hard man card.

Back at the store he parked the tanker under the loading shed then walked up to the store to put his dinner bucket, liquor, and old shoes in his truck, putting the liquor under the seat so that some passing bum didn't help himself. There was no breeze today, and he could hear Bill listening to the radio inside, where he had a big old fan going, so Raymond went inside to find out if there had been any more delivery calls or if he could resume cleaning the truck. Bill must have heard a new sound as Raymond crossed the room, his eyes adjusting to the dim light -- Bill had been sitting there for hours and could see anything in the room, or about Raymond, clearly.

"Whoooeee!" Bill hollered, "lookit them boots!"

Raymond blushed, but by now knew how to respond. "That's exactly what I thought when I saw them at Wilberger's! Why wear shit-kicking brogans when you can drive a tank truck with the same style as those guys who haul logs. Just wait till the girls see these little fringes go flipety-flap when I'm up top sticking the tank!" By this point Raymond had ceased to blush and was rather enjoying himself. Bill looked a bit crestfallen, his thunder stolen.

"Did you get a good price on 'em?" Bill asked, in a more serious tone.

"Yup," Raymond replied, naming the figure and continuing, "My old farm shoes weren't in the best of shape before I went in the Army, and the truck-climbing business was pulling them apart. These babies are about the same weight as army boots, so that's not a problem; they ought to last; and they might keep me from having a sprained ankle when my foot hits a slick spot -- we do, after all, sell nothing but slick spots, albeit in a concentrated form." Raymond leaned on the counter, and made his voice serious-sounding. "The only drawback I can see with these boots is that my boss wants a pair so bad he can feel 'em on his feet already, and that's gonna bust my advantage with the ladies!"

"How," Bill roared, standing up and throwing his arms wide, "in hell, did you learn to do that so fast? It takes most guys at least six months to get the idea and another six months to build up the brass to talk back to me like that. Some of 'em never figure it out. You took about two weeks!"

"Just lucky, I guess. What you can tell me is how in hell these boots ended up in New Hope, where there isn't a tree big enough that you couldn't cut it down with a dull axe."

"It's like I tried to explain to you on the first day we went out there, but you must have been concentrating on something else, like maybe driving the truck.

Back in the depression years Wilberger had a little more money than most storekeepers because of his farmin', undertakin' and inheritin'. When a drummer from a shoe company, or any company for that matter, came around, Wilberger squeezed him good. He wouldn't argue price on the basic, necessary order, so the salesman looked good to *his* boss, but Wilberger would always demand a discount for doubling the order, or would offer to take something that wasn't moving, like those boots, off of the salesman's hands and out of the company's inventory for ten cents on the dollar. Filled that enormous warehouse that makes up the back and upstairs of the store, and now that production's focused on the Army, he's selling it out, no matter how strange some of it might seem. He was better backed than me, but it was good business sense, just like my takin' care of the little stores nobody else wants to fool with has added up to a living." Bill sat back down with his fan and radio. Raymond was tempted to tease him about the living including cans of restaurant garbage to be picked up each day, but realized that he was too new to twist Riley's tail again so soon. Instead he got back to business.

"Any more delivery calls or anything on the regular schedule?"

"Nope," Riley replied. "Guess you're still in the truck polishin' business -- do a good enough job and I'll consider hirin' you out to City sanitation!"

Raymond was glad to head back to the loading shed and his bucket of rags. He liked Bill Riley, but it was kind of fatiguing to be around him too long, you had to keep reading him and respond according to his moods. He hoped he hadn't pushed it too far about the boots, but finally figured that they had been taken as words in self defense. Mentioning the garbage, though, would have been crossing the line. He was glad that he'd had the instinct to stop. Funny stuff, instinct, he thought as he polished. Most of his came from his up-bringing, and little things like always wiping his feet on the doormat even when he knew they weren't muddy had always served him well. In Army training his instinct had always been to be a bit reserved, observe what was going on before jumping in, and to be slow to make alliances, which he knew could, like in high school, put you in a position of having to do something stupid or dangerous just to continue to fit in. He polished some more, cap pushed back on his head at what was definitely not the right angle. Was it instinct, he wondered, that had made him move out fighting as soon as he topped the cliff, instinct that told him to pause was to die, and instinct that made him throw his lot in with the infantrymen and sappers who didn't know each other's names but were coordinating their move on the machine gunner? Polishing some more, his thoughts moved forward to his experience in the liquor store that afternoon. Was it instinct that made him able to realize that he was about to be played the fool, one instinct that cancelled another, ignoring his upbringing that said to remove headgear when indoors, instinct that made him do something he'd never done before except in jest -- the preacher man stunt at supper back home -- present a false impression of what kind of man he was? Cutting and polishing on, he asked himself if the hard man persona was really an act. Thinking back on it, he'd not stepped forward and laid his stick on the counter as a piece of theatre. He'd done it in preparation for grab-bing the clerk by his collar with both hands and drag-ging him across the counter had he asked a smarmy question about his age. A hard man. Maybe that's what

he was inside, now, and every day was carefully orchestrated theatre allowing him to assume the persona
of a Raymond Lewis McCleary who had not gone to
war, had not killed and wiped death off of his face with
his sleeve, had not been shot and given over to the medics and surgeons. He polished some more, changing the
water in the bucket which had become as pink and thick
as the drench that they used on the farm to worm sheep.
If that last thought was true, his instinct told him that he
had a damn hard row to hoe, as every step he took gave
the lie to what he was trying to do. His instinct told him
that he'd go crazy trying figure it all out, so he stuffed
all of those questions down inside, and concentrated on
making each set of circles on the truck as red as the last.

Raymond had the left fender, left half of the
hood, and the left door done by evening. "Bill." he said
as he brought his bucket and ladder back into the store,
"I'm gonna need some more rags tomorrow -- tear up
another of your old lady's dresses for me!"

"Righto. I'll sneak it out to the woodshed so's
she won't hear me committing the dirty deed." He got
up, walked over to the door and looked down at the
loading shed to check Raymond's progress. "I was
wrong, boy," he let out a whistle, "you might enjoy
those sanitation trucks, but it looks like the money's
gonna be in rentin' you out to the fire department! They
could get old Jumbo out of Mr. Taliaferro's barn, and
you could make it shine for a parade, although I guess
that they might be a bit embarrassed having to push it
along with another truck -- I 'spect it's been a good fifteen years since they've had him running."

"Let's just get this one finished before we make
plans. See you in the morning."

"Yup, you, too," Bill bid him farewell for the evening. Raymond needed supplies to break in the dinner bucket, so he stopped on Johnson Street at the big Piggly Wiggly grocery on the corner opposite the Courthouse and jail and bought bread, cheese, mustard and baloney for sandwiches, a packet of waxed-paper bags to wrap them in, and a few apples because he knew if his mother or sister were with him they'd tell him to get some fruit in his diet. He also handed over his ration coupon and got some Luckies and a pouch of Red Man. That accomplished, he continued on Johnson Street to the gasworks, made a left onto Coalter Street and pulled in at the Tate's restaurant. He ordered their special, meatloaf with gravy, off of the chalkboard before sitting down, and when Mr. Tate brought him his coffee, he nodded his head approvingly.

"You're looking a little better this evening. Did you take the truck out today?"

"Yes, Sir. But I didn't do any mountains, just out to New Hope and back."

"Wise move," Tate replied, smiling. "Limber those shoulders up a bit but not to strain 'em. I'll have your special right out." Even after a relatively easy day it felt good to lean back in the booth and sip his coffee. Physically, he knew he was gonna make it, it would just take time to build up what muscles he could and to acclimate himself to whatever level of pain remained. He'd never known a farmer that hadn't grown old working hurt, and he figured that was just life. As to the instinct stuff he'd spent the afternoon thinking about, maybe that was just word games with himself. He'd never spoken with anyone trying to untie such knots, no matter what kind of curve balls life had thrown them, and just resolved to try to focus on other things. He finished supper, paid his ticket, made his manners to Mr. and Mrs. Tate, and headed home to West Beverley Street. Mrs. Russ was cleaning up the dishes and cookware from the supper she'd made for Lee and herself, and when he asked, showed him a spot in the refrigerator to put his food.

"You'd better wash that bucket and Thermos out with soap and hot water. God only knows where it's been and whose hands have been on it, even if it is new." He took her advice, using part of her dishwater, and left them on the drain board to dry. "There's a letter there for you," Mrs. Russ said as he turned to go upstairs.

"Thanks," he said, picking it up from where she'd leaned it against the salt shaker on the kitchen table. "Have a good evening if I don't see you before bedtime."

"Same to you, Raymond, same to you."

36. NEWS FROM NORTH CAROLINA

Looking at the envelope, he was not surprised to see that the letter was from Reba -- nobody else except Bill, the ration office and the car license people had his address. He hadn't even worked long enough for Bill's bookkeeper to have sent his name in to the Internal Revenue Service. Once upstairs, he pulled off his boots and wiggled his toes, unbuttoned his shirt and sat on one of the straight chairs, feet up on the windowsill, catching the breeze across his chest and belly. Reba reported on everything. Her work force, Charlie and

William, were still cooperative; they'd been getting enough rain; there'd been no significant equipment breakdowns during the small grain season and first cutting of hay; and that Father was doing less and less of the regular farm work and, surprisingly, taking an interest in the bees. When the first hot weather came in May, he'd gotten dressed up in Grandfathers veil, fired the smoker, and sorted through the one remaining hive, looking for swarm cells. He'd cleaned up a couple of other boxes, and when he found two frames with the cells that would produce new queens, causing the old queen to swarm away with half of the colony, he put one of those frames in each clean box along with a frame of bees, a frame of leftover honey, and a frame of sealed-over worker grubs about ready to hatch. He then filled each box by adding three frames with thin foundation wax on each side of those with the bees and put frames with sheets of foundation in the vacant spots in the old colony. 'Making splits' is what Grandfather had called that process; it weakened the donor colony some, but not nearly as bad as if it had swarmed. With the swarm cells gone, and presented with eight new sheets of foundation stamped with just the faintest outline of hexagonal cells, the bees quickly draped themselves in chains, each individual adding their crumb of wax to the ball that was passed along to the builder at the end of the chain, who formed the new cells with her forelegs and head. The queen particularly liked new cells, and would immediately start laying in them to rebuild the population that had been removed. The splits were unlikely to produce more honey than they needed to get through their first winter that season, but next year should be good producers. Reba said that Father was being careful to check the main hive every week or so since, cutting out any other swarm cells that he might find to keep the colony strong for making honey as all of the different plants on the farm began to flower. Reba said that Father was quick to say that he knew tending the chickens was the old man's job, but now that he was there, he understood his father's preference for the bees, which had always puzzled him -- working with bees rewarded slow movement, and they smelled a damn sight better than the chickens! Reba told who Mary, Charlie and William had been seeing, but opined that nobody was, as yet, serious about anyone. The lack of comment on her own social life was notable. There was some community news, who'd received a telegram telling them of a death of a son somewhere in the world, and accounts of a few others who, like him, had made it home patched up and were trying to figure where they fit in. She closed by asking for particulars about his work, what arrangements he was making to take care of himself insofar as he'd never kept house, and asking if he'd met any of the Staunton ladies.

As usual, he hung his work clothes in front of the window to air them out overnight, poked his head out in the hall to see if the bath was free -- it was -- and had a good scrub. After his bath, he pulled on a clean pair of pants and sat down to answer Reba's letter. As the first sergeant had preached, 'you gotta write 'em to get 'em.' He told Reba about driving the mountains; about his fun with Bill Riley over his new boots; that immediately after closing the letter he was headed downstairs to make sandwiches for tomorrow's dinner at work; and finished by reminding her that although he hadn't ever kept house, he had been a soldier, and that the Army was pretty good a teaching a fellow to tend to getting his basic needs met. He didn't tell her how wretched he'd been the evening before, and he didn't tell her about the remedy that Dr. Hill had prescribed.

Addressing and stamping the envelope, he took it downstairs and leaned it against the salt shaker -- that was where Mrs., Russ had told him to put outgoing mail.

Sandwich making was the next order of business. It didn't take long and David came in just as he was finishing, putting the materials and two waxed-paper packets in the fridge.

"Hey, Dave."

"Hey," David replied, sounding tired.

"I'm starting to pack my own dinner to take to work. Mrs. Russ told me to keep my stuff over to the right on the second shelf."

David came over and got his favorite cold-coffee cup out of the cupboard. "Want some?" he asked, and when Raymond nodded he pulled out a second cup before closing the door. They filled their cups from the cold pot on the stove, headed to their usual perch on the edge of the back porch and lit up off of the same match.

"Not too much risk being second man on a match," Raymond said, "it's the third man's dead."

"What?"

"Old army saying from the first war, you don't want to be the third man to get a light off of the same match. Sniper on the other side has his attention caught by the first flare of light in the darkness -- you'd be surprised how much a match shows in a blackout -- lines up his sights the second time the hands protecting the flame from the wind unfold, and pulls the trigger the third time. "Spot you, range you, death angel snatch" is the way the Jody call goes."

"You Army guys," David took a deep drag and then watched the plume as he exhaled, "are full of some weird shit."

"Ha!" Raymond snorted. "We're absolutely pure straight-arrows compared to the Navy and especially the Marines. Marines. Now *there's* a group that has institutionalized bad habits and practices! He hoped he could avoid talking about anything serious by joking about another branch of the service, and he didn't think it likely that Dave'd turn back to the Army. He'd mentioned the Rangers to David when he told him his story the first night they'd sat on the porch, but it was obvious that he didn't know anything about what they did other than climb the occasional cliff, and probably didn't care. A bone-tired railroad man was not, Raymond thought, relying on his instinct to hold back from involvement with others, the guy to talk with about his afternoon of thinking confusing thoughts. Instead, he decided to screw with him, maybe cheer *him* up a little. "What about your beloved train engineers? They've got a union that makes secret fraternal orders look like a Sunday-school picnic, and talk about killers! It's not question of if they're going to kill at grade crossings and in crashes, but a question of when, how often and how many!"

"Fair comment. That first nut's the one I'm trying to figure how to crack, and as to the second, maybe that's why they hang so tight and act so independent, like each train is theirs, personal. I know that some of the yard engineers used to be line drivers and either asked or got told that they were changing to a position that didn't call for much nerve. I'm hoping that the shift of troops to the west coast to head for Japan is going to make the railroads need so many more drivers that things'll open up for me."

"Maybe you ought to marry the stationmaster's daughter," Raymond giggled. "She and her father would see it as a step up. Better not try the engineer's little gal, though. His old lady knows what she's been through and wouldn't wish it on anyone, especially not her baby!"

"Romantic and career advice from a gimpy oil-truck driver," David replied with a laugh of his own, "no wonder I'm getting ahead." Laughter having improved both of their moods, David complained of equipment unnecessarily replaced because crews failed to take the effort -- or were averse to the risk of getting their overalls dirty -- to take a pail and paddle out of the switch shack and lubricate essential points in the mechanisms, which then worked hard, didn't fully close and wore out as thousands of wheels pounded across them when they were not in total alignment. Raymond told David about his truck polishing assignment, new boots, and letter from home. David knew nothing about bee-keeping, so that it took Raymond a good while to explain what his father was doing, making splits. Explanation finished, they rinsed out their cups, turned out the kitchen light and headed upstairs, David to the bath, Raymond to bed. He poured and drank his whisky. The fumes from the glass filled his nose and head, again causing him to finish the glass in several big swallows, feeling the burn of every drop as it went down. He went to sleep quickly and rested well. In the early hours of the morning he began to dream that he, not his father was working the bees, a happy dream until he got to the part where he put new frames and foundations into the hive and the bees began making golden chains. The movement of the chains turned to the writhing of the rope ladders on the cliff-face, and he was among the climbers, the fallers, and the bursting grenades. If he'd called out, everyone else in the house was either far enough away or too soundly asleep to hear him. He awoke suddenly, completely drenched with sweat, tangled in his bedclothes, and, for a moment, completely unaware of where he was. When he did recognize his surroundings, he realized that it was only about fifteen minutes until his alarm clock would have gone off, anyway, concluded he'd gotten a pretty good night's sleep despite the dream , got dressed, and went on down to the kitchen.

37. SARAH

Work fell into a pretty steady routine. He alternated polishing sessions on the truck with local fueling runs, spending more time on the road each day as the week progressed. He noticed that even though the store didn't have a Post Office and didn't sell crackers and cheese, that a steady flow of folks dropped by all day to talk to Bill, parked by the radio and fan. He had been right in thinking that there was a real similarity between Bill Riley and Tom Peterson over in McDowell. He talked with Bill about scheduling, and Bill agreed to let him put Cedar Green and Westview on another day, so that when the Highland run came around again, Raymond topped off the tanks the evening before and , without Bill, got an early start the next morning. He headed directly west out Churchville Avenue by the park to Route 250 rather than making any local stops.

The mountains were a little easier because he now knew what to expect; his leg was getting a little stronger; and, as Mr. Tate had suggested, he had now come to trust the engine and transmission's braking ability in situations where he'd been jumping on the brakes before. He was cordial with the storekeepers, but without Bill each stop was a lot shorter, and even taking it easy on the return trip he was able to park the International in the loading shed before his usual quitting time. Up at the store Bill thumbed through the receipt book and confirmed that Raymond hadn't missed anyone on that day's Highland list. "Boy," Bill said with a grin, "get on out of here before I think of something for you to do during the next hour." Raymond didn't have to be told twice. He'd learned in the Army that 'when you ain't got nothin' to do, don't do it here,' was a good workplace rule, else the boss'd get around to finding something else, usually somethin' triflin', to fill the time!

It was a nice afternoon and the Barrelnose felt like a sports car after a day in the two-ton International. Raymond started home, but as he neared the house decided to keep going, to go out West Beverly Street beyond the city to the Westview Store to see Sarah Thompson. He'd never had a chance to speak with her outside of Bill Riley's company, and he figured that it might be a pleasant way to use his unexpected free time, as she was almost sure to be at the store at this hour, tending the customers who stopped for this or that or their rationed dribble of gasoline on their way home from work in Staunton. Staunton didn't have any big employers other than the Western State Hospital lunatic asylum, but it did have Mary Baldwin College, Staunton Military Academy, and its fair share of small businesses such as machine shops and cabinetmakers who had war contracts for small items that by themselves were almost unrecognizable as part of the war effort, like the plain but exacting wooden box which stored the artilleryman's transit or the simple, two-holed toggles used to tighten the ropes on all manner of tents. The farms of Augusta, Highland and Rockingham counties were by far the most important defense industries around, and lots of those folks chose to stop by Sarah's store in the late afternoon to pick up a few needed items and the kind of local news that wouldn't be reported on the radio, might or might not make the next day's newspaper, and would be completely stale by the time the next church service rolled around.

Raymond pulled in and parked at the corner of the store, ran his fingers through his hair and set his cap at exactly the right angle before getting out. Sarah met him just outside the door. "Pretty pickup," she observed. "No wonder Bill put you to work on his tanker, even though," she laughed, "at this stage of your efforts it looks like an old patchwork quilt that's seen too much sun, some squares bright, others faded to nothing."

"Yeah, I reckon you're right about that, but I'm takin' things slow 'cause Bill's threatened to rent me out to clean the city's garbage trucks, he thinks I'm so good at polishing."

Sarah laughed again "Dear old Bill!" she said, "he is, I think, what people call 'a piece of work'."

"Well, I didn't come out here to analyze my boss -- I came to see you! How're you doin'?".

"Not gettin' rich like Bill Riley," she answered with a twinkle in her eye, "but the store's gettin' by.

Can't get enough of a lot of things my customers like because of the war, but everyone with good health and any gumption is working and has a little money to spend. Personally," she said, her expression saddening, "I don't know what to say -- some days it's like my world's over because John's dead; some days it's like he's just overseas like everybody else's fellow and is coming back; and some days I'm at peace with it and just kinda daydream what's next in my life , like any other girl my age." By that point she looked more thoughtful than sad. "Is it like that for you, the change in your life because of your wounds?"

Before Raymond could even start to think through an answer, a couple of cars pulled onto the lot and Sarah turned and headed back towards the door. "Business calls! Come on in a have a seat, we can visit some more once I'm through," she called over her shoulder. Raymond did as she suggested and followed her into the store where he snaked a cold, wet Coca-Cola through the galvanized metal labyrinth that suspended them in the chilled water of the cooler by the ring of glass just below the familiar metal cap reproduced in three dimensions on the most prominent advertising signs. He wiped the bottle dry with the dish towel hanging from a homemade wire hook added to the screw at corner of the red box's chrome opener and used cap catcher -- Coke's designers hadn't thought of everything -- and popped the cap off, taking the first, freezing carbonated gulp as he looked around for a seat. There were two split-bottomed rockers next to the cold and dusty stove, away from the grocery counter where Sarah was busy reaching items down from the shelves as they were called for. He sat in one, taking off his cap and leaning his stick against his leg, and reached over to scratch the head of the black cat who occupied the other. Rocking and relaxing against the easy flex of the chair's back and sipping at his drink, he decided that watching Sarah do her grocer's dance and catching the music of her chatter with the shoppers was the most pleasant experience of recent weeks, far superior to sitting and smoking with David, relaxing as that might be. Having come to that realization, Raymond was savoring the moment, but was cut short by the recollection of Sarah's question about the changes in his life because of his wound. Trying to parse an answer, which he knew would be called for if not when these particular customers left, then after the store closed for the evening, he came to the conclusion that he'd largely avoided the issue, even with himself, ever since his simultaneous discharge from the hospital and the Army. His only real thoughts on the subject had been in the context of whether or not to leave the farm, which he'd studied through as he'd cleaned the pickup.

He was grateful to be alive, and thankful not to have been facially or manually disfigured like a number of the men he'd seen in the hospitals, and having those two advantages, had spared himself consideration of his own condition, thinking to himself that he didn't like complainers and that he ought to be content to count his blessings. Sarah's question made him appraise things beyond that point. To begin with, he lived with pain. No matter how accustomed he was to the sensation, no matter that he seldom let it show on his face, he clenched his teeth with every step, stopping the nerves and muscles in his neck and throat from releasing any sound as the nerves in his leg sent the message up 'get ready boys, here it comes'. Whether or not anything more than this warning order welled up from the scars along his leg depended on how tired he was, how he was standing, and, to a surprising extent how he was feeling emotionally -- what was going on, both around him or in his head. Grandmother had always said as an explanation of folks idiosyncratic complaints that whatever was troubling a person always showed up in their weakest place. If the wrong stars were in line, and most particularly if he'd stood in a particular posture -- leaning over as if to check someone's schoolwork spread out on a table, or the order of the parts of a rifle field-stripped onto the blanket of a bunk for inspection -- and then stood erect and tried to take a step, everything in his leg let him know. Pain severe enough that it cut short any words he was saying, and but for his stick or whatever surface he could grab onto, dropped his right leg out from under him.

It was becoming obvious, both to him and those around him, that he both lived and slept in the horrors that he had experienced during his few short hours of actual war and relived during the longer hours of altered consciousness as he recovered from each step of his treatment. His housemate, David, his landlord, and her daughter Lee, had all witnessed his night terrors, so common among the soldiers at Woodrow Wilson Hospital that they hardly merited the two-word description being charted at the morning, change-of-shift nursing report unless they'd caused a wound to be torn open or someone got choked or slugged by the sleeper. Bill Riley, mindful of Raymond's privacy and therefore interrupting with neither comment nor query, noticed how he could abandon what Bill considered fascinating subjects in mid-sentence, driving with perfect safety, but with his mind obviously far away. He seldom had a pleasant look on his face when he fell silent, and Bill noticed the behavior more and more frequently when he went on the Highland County run with Raymond, usually coming over him during those first few seconds of a hairpin turn when a wall of rock loomed before them.

Another small change, one that Raymond had noticed and kind of laughed to himself about, was that even though he was a peaceable sort of fellow -- he'd gotten through his whole time in the Army without participating in a barracks or bar fight other than by helping to break one up before the authorities got called -- he now sized up every situation in terms of combat or evasion. He knew that if presented with a bad situation, he no longer had the option of running because of his bad leg, so that he more or less automatically scanned his surroundings for potential trouble, and if he identified it, planned how to ease away if it looked bad; talk it away if got too close for that to work; and decided how, if it came to it, he was going to fight and win. The primary talk line, which he'd practiced many times in his head but never actually had to use, he planned to couple with the show of either adjusting his cap or taking it off and carefully putting it down while looking the room over, was "Well, seein' as I can't run, I guess we're just gonna have to have some fun. No point in wastin' time, lets us get started." The cap business added a little drama, gave the other guy a minute to reconsider, and gave him a second look at the situation, which may have changed after he'd concluded things allowed him no exit.

So far he'd been lucky and hadn't needed to implement his plan. On the one occasion that might have led to trouble, he'd pretended to ignore the couple of guys he'd heard saying "gimp" to each other, looking his way without coming any closer, and after an interval just long enough to covey that he wasn't really reacting to the taunt, he'd slipped out. Thinking on it, he figured that it could be that the hard man from the ABC store showed without his realizing it when he was thinking of getting ready to state the cold, hard facts of the situation, and had been noticed by either the drunks or their buddies, all of whom had then piped down. Considering the consequences of the application of his daydreamed plan, he hoped he would never have the misfortune of a dispute with anyone who shared his sure, simple assessment of a situation.

Part of his scan of the situation pertained to the first rule he'd learned in the Army, 'face your front but never ignore your flanks or rear.' Even going into places he knew and liked, like Tate's Restaurant, he sat where he could see who came in and where nobody could come up behind him, and was always conscious of what was within his and anyone else's reach. Rule two had been 'never hit anyone with your fist if you can hit him with something else,' expanded for him to 'never consider hitting anyone with your stick in a way that might break it or you might lose it.' An otherwise welcome and acceptable lull in the fun would be useless if he hadn't the mobility to take advantage of it. The stick could be used to deflect a blow, swinging with the impact so as to be undamaged. If it was to deliver force, he knew that he had to have both hands on its shaft to get his full weight behind a blow extended beyond his reach by its length and delivered in line with the shaft by just the tip so that there was no chance of the leverage breaking it. Raymond had sort of found it amusing that he consciously went through some of these calculations, but in thinking of how to respond to Sarah's question, realized that he'd have to admit that he saw people and situations in ways that he'd never looked at them before, and that no matter how automatic or practiced he became, it took enough time while he was making his evaluations for him to be perceived differently than he would have been a couple of years before. Because perception was entirely in the other man's head, what that perception was of the time Raymond took, shy, aloof, slow, distracted, stupid, or rude depended on how that other person's day was going, and didn't necessarily give rise to cues that Raymond could use to get past the awkwardness. He was improving there, though. If he sensed any awkwardness, he'd learned to stretch and yawn like he was real tired; grin at the person and wink; or, especially if he was with Bill, start into something completely outside of the ballpark like lamenting still being unable to remember the punch line to the joke he'd tried to tell before lunch or loudly and enthusiastically calling out a woman's name, "Helen! Helen! That's the name I've been trying to tell you, she's the blonde waitress at that restaurant in Winchester!"

The other, every day thing that he noticed was that he was slow. Although he levered along on his stick to compensate for it, often to an extent that the able-bodied with him complained, telling him to slow down, when he moved naturally, it was at old man's pace. Keeping up normal or better pace came at a price -- he was exhausted every evening when he left work.

Sarah saw the last customers out, and in one pirouette put up the closed sign, pulled the shade down and locked the front door. She came over to Raymond's spot by the summertime-cold stove, transferred the contented cat from the chair to her lap as she took his place in the other rocker, rubbing his ears. "I think that I'll be a bad storekeeper tonight. Since you're here I'm gonna wait and total things up and check them against the cash drawer when I open tomorrow instead of doing it now."

"Suit yourself. Mr. Cat and I have both gotten

comfortable here and can wait as long as you need us to."

"I'm used to Oscar coming and sitting in the middle of my evening paperwork," Sarah laughed. "It's you, just sitting over here perfectly quiet that's the decider. I don't think I can ignore you as well as I can him."

"Having some experience of the persistence of cats' interference with the reading of newspapers, I'll take that as a compliment," Raymond responded, adding his fingers to hers working on Oscar's ears and neck.

The three of them just sat and rocked for a little bit, until Sarah shifted Oscar around to a different position, claiming his head for herself and leaving Raymond with an idly twitching tail. "You've had lots of time to think about it -- what do you have to say to my question about your injuries affecting your life?" Raymond had been right in thinking that she would recall precisely where their conversation had been interrupted and would take it up again at the first opportunity.

"Well, I think that John's death any my getting wounded changed both of our options in life. My first thought was "limited" our options, but I edited that word out because it made us sound like a couple of quitters, that we're just sitting around waiting for something good to happen in our lives, and holding onto an excuse if nothing does. Not meaning to be disrespectful or unkind, what's happened to us has, morbidly, given us both more freedom. Since I'm too busted up to do the work, I'm relieved from any responsibility I may have believed I had to stay on the farm; since you're widowed, you're relieved from any responsibility that you may have felt to subordinate your dreams to John's -- that is, if they were any different, and I know they may not have been. For a few months, even his options had been opened up -- he was flying, what he'd always wanted to do, rather than keeping store, which I suspect he got into out of a feeling of responsibility to help his parents before they died and hadn't yet figured a way to leave. The second thing that comes to mind about myself is that my injuries and the surgeries -- let's face it the effects of the cure have been about as bad as the cause, once they got me past the possibility of bleeding to death -- have slowed me down physically. I get tired more easily, and another part, which I never would have expected, is that it's made me what they probably call a little paranoid. Since I know I'm physically limited, everywhere I go I find myself checking things out, trying to figure how I'd handle some guy if he got wise, either handle him or how I'd get away. The choice of getting away is the wisest solution for anyone, and I'm probably fortunate to have the realization come upon me through the process of reflection rather than the consequences of doing something young, dumb, and stupid. That feeling is mixed up with the realization that there will be situations where I can't leave, literally can't run, and will have to be more of a stand-up guy than I ever was before. I won't say that makes me feel tougher than before." He laughed, "Not being able to run is one strange way to gain self-confidence! Maybe I ought to put Raymond McCleary ads on how to change yourself in the back of comic books!"

"Interesting," Sarah replied, still working her cat. "Options, slowed down, and tough. I guess that you're right about more options being open to both of us, even though we surely didn't ask for them. Like you,

I'm tougher than I once was because I have to be, no choice, other than to give up and claim that excuse you mentioned, but I don't think it'd be pleasant riding that horse, even a short distance. Slowed down – "more deliberate" is a higher-sounding way of saying it. I'm deliberate about making choices because it would be so easy for me to make the wrong one and ruin the rest of my life. I don't know what label they put on that kind of thinking over at Western State Hospital, but I'm sure they've got one to match your "paranoid!" You think things through pretty good for an oil-truck driver, Raymond McCleary. I like that. How 'bout you come on up and have some supper with me?" She stood up, deposited Oscar in the chair, offered Raymond a hand up, and then turned behind the counter to the door which led to an obviously boxed-in staircase. "Oscar," she said over her shoulder, "Oscar, you'll have to use your own four feet to tell me if you'd rather be a house cat or a store cat, come or go, whatever you like."

As she started up the stairway she continued talking over her shoulder, this time to Raymond. "This was John's place before it was ours," she explained. His parents were a little unusual in that when he finished high school, they moved him out here, on his own except for supper at their house up the lot each evening. The arrangement sure got him away from the apron-strings, he had to eat two more meals every day so he got a job pretty quick, and it got him out from under his old man's thumb but still close enough under his eye that he wouldn't do anything *real* stupid. From the perspective of what might charitably be called the "greater community" it made little sense to frequent the store lot after hours with a nineteen- year-old and a rabbit-ear twelve-gauge upstairs. John got to both take some responsibility and sow his wild oats in a somewhat protected situation." She turned to face Raymond at the top of the stairs while he was still two steps down and their eyes were on the same level. "I reckon," Sarah gave a wicked grin, "I reckon that I was the last crop. His folks didn't seem to see it that way, though; they treated me like a lady and a daughter from the day that we met."

As Raymond's head got above the box surrounding the stairwell, he looked around. The door to the back porch and the outside stairway was right beside them, at the head of the inside stair, glass panes down to waist level. Opposite were the doors to the gallery above the store's front, where he'd seen the flag on VE day, glass panes down to your toes; to the right was as small kitchen and table; the center of the room was a seating area surrounding the chimney, with the Warm Morning oil heater directly above the big woodstove downstairs, the apartment gaining the advantage of the heat that rose through a floor/ceiling register. To the left the bed, covered with a bright quilt, was tight against a car-siding partition (the other walls were plastered) and a windowless door with a clothes hook which he assumed led to a bathroom. The gap between the end of the partition and the front wall had a partially-drawn curtain which revealed a full closet with rods made of galvanized water pipe, not, he thought, likely to sag under any load!

"Nice place!" Raymond exclaimed, genuinely impressed by the layout and workmanship of the visible carpentry. "Someone took some trouble with their work."

"John's father built this place when his folks were still living in the old house and there was enough ground left to be called a farm , the good economic times for farmers during and right after the first war made construction affordable, put them in the notion that a store could be profitable, and to tell you the truth, I think that John's grandfather envisioned himself as a grocer in his old age rather than his son, but the times got hard, farm prices dropped, land had to be sold and John's dad found himself a storekeeper in order to support the family. After John was born there was some moving back and forth to adjust accommodations -- John grew up in the big house, his grandparents grew old and died up here -- and then the place sat, furnished and dusty, until his parents offered to let him move in after he graduated. We liked it up here, and never got around to moving to the big house after John's folks passed -- now it's the one full off dusty furniture!" Sarah gave him a friendly sideways hug. "Make yourself at home," she said with a broad gesture, "while I get some chicken into the skillet."

Raymond walked over and fingered back the curtain on the doors' windows to look out across the front gallery and the road. Open countryside. Turning and heading for a chair at the table near where Sarah was working he glanced down to find a convenient place to park his cap and realized that he was being trailed by Oscar, no doubt hoping for a soft lap and suppertime handout. Sitting down and leaning forward with his chin on his palms and his elbows on the table, Raymond presented no lap and Oscar resorted to repeated ankle-rubbing in order to maintain contact and a presence in Raymond's consciousness until the chicken was served up. "Things," Raymond observed, "seem to have been complicated in John's family. Back home we all just lived and died in the same house, kept on farming the same ground, 'cept for some who married out. I reckon that Granddaddy and I were the only two men in

the family who ever even had the *chance* of dyin' any-
wheres else, him up here in Virginia, me in France."

   "I'm not starting game of 'I'll show you mine,
you show me yours,' talkin' about family. Eternal home
place or not, I'm sure that there's some complications
in the McCleary clan, but we'll not explore them now.
Supper's ready." Raymond got up and helped with
moving dishes and food onto the table, and then they
both sat down and tucked into it, chicken, green beans,
yellow squash and cold lemonade from the icebox. A
workday supper, nothing that required much preparation by a tired storekeeper after hours, they finished it
off with some coffee and the last slices of a pie that
she'd been nibbling at all week. Oscar got his accustomed 'last bites' from the crumbs on the plates -- Sarah laughed and laughed, describing the discomfort of a
customer down below one evening who thought the
call she heard from above was "last rites, last rites
c'mon Oscar, time for your last rites !" It didn't take
them long to clean up -- she washed and he dried. When
they finished Raymond started towards a comfortable-
looking couch, but when he turned to look back towards
Sarah, he was surprised to see her opening the door to
the outside stairway, his cap in her hand. "I've decided
that I like you, Raymond McCleary," she smiled.
"Come back about six tomorrow evening and we'll help
Oscar finish the chicken. Don't," she winked, "plan on
going home 'till Sunday." A bit dumbstruck, first at being ushered out so early in the evening, then at being so
confidently propositioned, Raymond kissed her lightly
on the cheek that she offered, took his cap, put it on at
exactly the right angle, and headed outdoors and down
the stairs.

The ride back into town was the smoothest he'd ever had in the pickup. Hell, it was probably the smoothest in any vehicle or on foot since his short trip in the Powerwagon ambulance after he got hit, except this time he knew he had a shit-eatin' grin on his face instead of the medics' bloody 'm's', the mark of the lamb, the saved, on his forehead. As he pulled into the drive at the house on West Beverley Street, he could see the kitchen light on and the whole household gathered around the table, talking with a good deal of animation. He parked the truck, and before he reached the porch he'd caught enough of the excitement to know that David had gotten his transfer to engineers' school. Before he got his hand on the screen door he realized just how lucky he was, that anyone would assume that his unusually broad grin was for his buddy and that he was not going to have to explain that Sarah was the cause. Wiping his feet and pulling off his cap he went through the screen door into the kitchen. "Congratulations, buddy, I could hear the good news from outside!"

"Thanks. It was a long time coming." Everyone nodded or murmured their agreement.

"What I want to know," Raymond continued, looking over his audience just as he'd always looked over the family at the table back home before springing a good line, "is who's ugly daughter did you have to propose to marry to get in? You still have a way out of that if you can't face it -- learn to engineer, then join the Army. Railroad Daddy ain't gonna let the weddin' happen unless she's outta his house with union-rate wages to spend, and some recruiting sergeant'll get promoted when he produces a real, live, civilian-trained railroad driver who coulda' had a deferment!" Everyone howled, including Dave, who'd heard it all before and was just glad that Raymond had left out the part about train-drivers being sicker in the head than Rangers, 'cause they knew they were bound to kill and that the victims would be random innocents rather than other soldiers trying to kill them.

"I didn't believe the preacher man when he said "all things come to those who wait"," David replied, "but I reckon he was right." That, he thought but didn't say, and the fact that the manager of the Mountain Division was getting tired of bi-monthly carbon copies of his request for admission to a trainee class, each of which resulted in a request for comment by the selection panel. The railroad had filled part of the wartime demand for engineers by allowing those willing to keep working after the permissible retirement age to do so, and they had doubled the number of qualifying classes and kept them full. Raymond's joke about the recruiter had been closer to the mark than he realized. The military railroads were expanding fast, not only in Europe, but with improbably short short-run lines on the Pacific islands and more frequent small, high-security military trains running from the East to the Southwest. The railroad men approaching seniority were holding their breath, hoping that the Army didn't start up its own train engineer school which would, after the war, flood the market with union-busting veterans. Accordingly, they praised anyone who pulled a stunt such as Raymond proposed as a patriot rather than blackballing them, and worked their expanded schedules without complaint. "Well, thank you all for your good wishes, but I'd better be getting my gear together. I got a train to catch tomorrow if I want a chance of snagging a good room on the railroad's floor of the hotel, rather than waiting 'till Sunday and having to settle for what's left." He disappeared up the stairs.

"That man," Lee observed, sipping the last of her coffee, "has got things figured out!"

"Sure does," Raymond agreed, "as long as he's been trying for that school, he's talked to a lot of old timers and learned how to behave -- the things he should and shouldn't do to keep the railroad and the guys with seniority happy, and how to look out for himself, like the hotel room stuff he mentioned ."

"That's right," Mrs. Russ agreed. "Ain't no flies on that boy. Just like you, Raymond!"

"Thanks," he replied, thinking to himself that he had plenty of weak spots, but pleased that Mrs. Russ, a pretty astute observer, didn't seem to think them significant. Raymond feigned a yawn. "I reckon I'll head up, too -- it's been a long week," and followed David up the stairs. He couldn't prevent Mrs. Russ and her daughter from turning their conversation to their remaining boarder after he left, but he could keep it from being a question and answer session.

He was right, of course, about the direction talk took as soon as he hit the stairs. "That boy," Mrs. Russ observed to Lee, "carries more harm from the war than he knows. As a child I listened to old people talk about men who were never quite 'right' after the War. Some of them knew it right away and took off for the West, Mexico, or Brazil, and others had to come into it gradual, on their own -- becoming mean when they used to be kind, reclusive when they used to love to come to town, drunks when they had been sober. It came on them gradual; they and everyone else blamed incompatible spouses, a stretch of poor weather and worse crops; or

the seldom-mentioned black sheep of previous generations somehow passing it on. Wasn't until the Old People, the survivors, looked back that they realized how
long the sadness of the War had lingered on, living
among them, voiceless. I fear that's waiting for Raymond, him and a lot of others, and there's not a blessed
thing anyone can do about it."

"Oh, Mother, don't be so gloomy. It's not surprising that Raymond has some bad nights, with all he's
been through, but I think that'll settle down once his life
gets more regular and the past has had time to become
less immediate."

"Maybe so, girl. Maybe so. I hope you're
right." the older woman shook her head as they rinsed
their cups, put them on the drain board , clicked off
the light, and disappeared into their part of the house.

Raymond slept until the sun was high enough to
wake him at the back of the house. He had a painful
number of hours to wait before he could decently show
up for his supper invitation and set about filling the
time with every chore he could think of. Having done
those, he cleaned and put polish on his boots, then set
them aside to harden before buffing them; he took a
bath and washed his hair, returning to sit in his skivvies
and finish his work with the buffing brush and flannel;
he found his old but still good-looking pair of Army
khakis and a shirt that hadn't absorbed the odor of his
work, and got dressed. Three o'clock -- still too early!
The only other thing he could think of to do was to
catch up on his letter writing, so he pulled the envelope
of stationery that his sister had sent him off with out of
the drawer and began:

Dear All,

It's a beautiful summer day here in Staunton. I've been doing my Saturday chores; washing clothes, the truck, and myself. I even went downtown and got a civilian-style haircut. The barber, an interesting guy who sidelines as a magician, says that he's responsible for that part of my rehabilitation.

Delivering oil, I've discovered is a bit like farming in that it has its own pervasive odor. I have to try to keep some of my clothes set aside for the rest of my time. This is an old house, so I've got the same shallow closet as at home, but that's plenty big enough for me. Every evening I put my work duds over a chair by the window to air out, and never wash them in the same tub as the others -- the Maytag gets 'em clean but still with a whiff of petroleum.

The back yard here is full of blight-proof oriental chestnut trees that Mrs. Guss' husband planted, but she hates them, says that only her sentimental nature saves them from the wood-pile. She loves the color of the nuts, but won't eat them and despises having to find someone to clean up the prickly hulls. I've worked a deal with her to trade the nuts for cleaning up the hulls -- I figure that all of the storekeepers I see will want a few. You-all've always said I was nuts....so I'm going into my real field of exper-tise, less to study up on than if I followed through on the preacher idea.

Speaking of storekeepers, one of them, Sarah Thompson, who has the first store west of town, has asked me to supper tonight -- the second time. She's a couple of years older than me, blond, and I think pretty good-looking. Her husband was a pilot, killed early in the war in a training accident before he got shipped out. She's been running the little store that he'd inherited from his parents since he enlisted. I'll see if she has s camera so that I can send you a picture -- if she doesn't, I just have to buy one so that I can.

How's the season coming on the farm? Is Father still working the bees, or are they just flying around thinking they're their own masters? How has Quentin Baker's dairy operation worked out? Is he getting the return he expected on his investment or still living off of family money?

There's really nothing new going on with me other than Sarah. The only other boarder at Mrs. Russ' moved out -- he got his lifelong wish, the railroad pulled him off of switch maintenance work and sent him to engineers' school. He wouldn't 'fess up to whose ugly daughter he agreed to marry to pull that off.

I'm getting pretty good at being a gimpy guy -- a fellow down at the barbershop who got crippled up years ago when a tree he was cutting jumped the stump tells me it comes natural if you remember to tell yourself that you can do anything except run, you can figure a way around for 'most everything else. Worked for him, I guess it'll work for me, given enough time. I know I've worked out ways of climbing around the truck without much problem, and can pretty consistently remember that I'm not in the pickup and have to double-clutch back through neutral for every gear change, not just when going down into jackass low like on the Barrelnose. Jack low on the two-ton requires coming back through neutral, then into second to line things up before it can be eased into first without grinding coffee. If I forget there's plenty of noise under the floorboards to remind me! Bill Riley has turned out to be a pretty good guy to work for -- if I finish the route early and have finished loading for the next day he always says "boy, if you ain't got nothin' to do, don't do it here," and sends me home without changing my pay. Mrs. Russ is a good landlady, not nosey, although she's so tight with Riley and everybody else in town that if she's interested she can learn my every move without my even knowing it! Nice lady, though, I feel sure that she'd slip me the word if I was takin' up with anyone better avoided, although there's a clear , unspoken message that her daughter, Lee, a teacher, is off limits to back-stairs boarders. I don't know what her background is -- certainly some money years ago to have built this top-deck of a steamboat place, and since, to have maintained it in such perfect condition. Not so much left now, though, since she's taking in boarders. If I ask Bill I know that he'll tell me the financial stuff and maybe even if there's anybody behind the woodpile!

Time for me to go. My love to all.

Raymond

He addressed the letter with both his parents'
names, grabbed his new, non-oily engineer's cap, wondering as he picked it up how David would feel about
his continued incursion into sacred territory. Downstairs he propped the letter against the sugar bowl on
the table, confident that Mrs. Russ would send it out
Monday morning.

The Barrelnose caught on the first crank, and he
headed out to Beverley Street, being careful to keep his
tires off of the grass and on the two lines of concrete
put in as a drive when the house's occupants, whatever
their names, had brought home their first Ford. Maybe
it wasn't a Ford, he thought to himself. Given the age
and size of the house, it may have been something more
exotic, a Pierce-Arrow, or maybe a boxy Baker electric.
Again, he thought, Bill could tell him, as every family's
early automobile purchases had to be part of the community lore.

Turning left on Beverley Street it, was just a
moment until the stone wall of Thornrose Cemetery
turned away at turret just big enough for a couple of
folks to stand in to follow Thornrose Avenue north. The
turret was pretty much the edge of town, although a
couple of more sparse blocks with the occasional house
or business breaking the pastures and brushy woods in
between were, technically, within the city limits. He
passed Frogpond Road, which he'd cut through many
times with the tanker from Route 250, which entered
town on the far side on Churchville Avenue by the park
in order to avoid the speed-trap at the bottom of one-
mile hill, stay out in the country a little longer and get

back to the store, as Riley called it, true to the browning documents that established his franchise with Texas Oil for Augusta and Highland Counties. Funny thing, though, he'd never spotted a pond on the length of the road. Not a big one, not a small one, not even a marshy place where one could have been drained. Maybe, he thought, the road, as an obvious shortcut from one side of the town to the other, had gotten the name because it was the first turn off of the Parkersburg pike or the Churchville Road for the route giggers headed to some other wetland. He swung around the left-hand curve that separated Mr. Moore's store on the right and his house on the left; up a down a couple more hills and he could make out Sarah's place, the first of any size in Westview, as he got closer.

Pulling off of the road onto the corner of the store lot, he could see that the shop shutters were shut and the closed sign was on the screen doors. Sarah had the doors open onto the gallery above, the curtains fluttering out into the breeze. Kinda, like me, flutterin' inside, Raymond thought. He took the pickup around behind the shop, to the bottom of the stairs, but having acknowledged the fluttering, it vanished as he shut off the engine and set the handbrake, pocketing the key. He looked in the mirror to run his hand through his hair; set his cap at exactly the right angle; rolled up the driver's side window; grabbed his stick; got out, shutting the door firm but quiet; and started up the stairs as smart as he could go. Raymond got about halfway up when Sarah, Oscar circling her feet, came out on the landing to greet him. "Hey, you! I figured you'd be out here before supper time," she called down. He'd reached the landing and they embraced as she mumbled "Welcome back," as best she could as they squeezed the breath out of each other and looked at the changing scenery over each other's shoulders as they moved to keep their collective balance and avoid stepping on Oscar, who was close around their ankles. Raymond realized that Sarah's joy at seeing him arrive was real and deep -- he could see it in her face. Sarah could see the same joy in Raymond, both her reflection and something breaking loose from within him. "I think," she said as she led him inside, taking his cap and putting it on the empty nail beside the door and leaning his stick against the wall so that he had to depend on contact with her and an occasional hand on the furniture, "That you've just given the lie to your usually well-timed and delivered statement that your favorite lady in the world has always been the lady with the morphine."

"You're right," Raymond replied, with a grin and a kiss on Sarah's lips. "She wouldn't be welcome right here and now."

They had ended up, by Sarah's guidance, in neither the kitchen nor the sitting area, but by the bed. On the way she said "It's really too early for dinner, so I figured we could play a while first. Get your appetite up for leftovers and fresh pie!" Raymond was speechless at how easy, how normal, Sarah was making the encounter for him. She kicked off her shoes, undid the combs that held her long blond hair, shook it out to far below her shoulders, and started undoing buttons. He had to perch on the edge of the bed and fumble with his bootlaces before he could follow suit. She was naked before he'd hardly got his shirt and socks off and gave him a good slow look, front and back, as she pulled the coverlet aside off of the pillows, slid beneath it and held it up with one arm for him to join her, her other arm and palm supporting her from the waist up as she waited. "Don't get flustered and rush," she said softly, "I like seeing packages unwrapped." "Besides," she added with a giggle, "I cheated by not wearing as many clothes as you." Raymond grinned at her joke and as he turned from hanging his pants on the footboard post he palmed a couple of rather crumpled GI condoms from his pocket only to notice when he deposited the khaki squares that had lived their whole lives pushed into a corner of his Dopp kit onto the bedside table that Sarah had left the drawer ajar and that it contained, along with other sundries, a box of their pristinely-wrapped civilian brethren. He dropped his shorts and purposefully turned left for a moment before settling into the bed to give her time to visually inspect his scarred leg. As soon as he was beside her she'd dropped the coverlet and they were embraced in a wet, rolling, exploratory kiss, lips locked for the most part, but with hands and the occasional tongue branching out in exploration. Exploration led to arousal, which led to action and their discovery that they fit wonderfully well together in a number of ways. They fell asleep in each other's arms.

When all the rolling about stopped, Oscar found a comfortable place for his nap low on the coverlet, his back against intertwined feet. Sometime later, rested and wanting his supper, he made his way to the head of the bed, plopped down on the pillows between Sarah and Raymond's faces and set about the work of purring his cook and serving staff awake. Sarah was the first to hear him, reached out and scratched behind his ears, and smiling broadly looked around at the disheveled bed, abandoned clothes, and Raymond's sleeping form. A moment or two later Oscar got through to Raymond. He reached over and rubbed the cat's head, then nudged him out of the way. "Hey," he said to Sarah, giving her a hug and a kiss before she could reply.

"Hey, yourself," she responded, pulling free, tossing her hair back and reaching around to fasten it into the simplest sort of ponytail. "Oscar says it's time to eat."

"I reckon he's right," Raymond replied, reaching for the breasts being held up before his face and getting two hands full before they both collapsed in laughter and then got up, each collecting the minimal amount of clothing necessary to be comfortable at the range and table.

It didn't take long to get the leftover chicken sizzling in the skillet. As soon as that was started, Sarah put Raymond to work shredding some fresh kale off of its thick stems and into a pot with just enough water to boil into steam to turn the dull bluish leaves a dark but bright green, kinda like the transformation that had occurred when Raymond had buffed out the paint on the Barrelnose. Oscar supervised, secure in his knowledge that 'last bites'' would be forthcoming as soon as his people had eaten, and took a position on the side of the table where there weren't any plates, forks, glasses and napkins set out. Sarah turned the chicken in the pan and pulled Raymond's pot of greens onto the adjacent burner, turning it up and watching for it to reach a boil. Raymond sat at the table, chin cupped in his hands, looking across Oscar at Sarah's back for the remaining couple of minutes it took to warm the chicken and cook the greens, thinking how different, how much better his life had become in the last hour and a half, a friendship now cemented by intimacy. It could, he realized, have had the opposite result, a friendship blasted by irrepressible memories or physical revulsion. His odds, he figured, had been greatly sweetened by the fact that he brought no significant memories or expectations when he came up the stairs, and the fact that Sarah had spent some time doing her mourning and wanted to be alive again. Sarah's odds had been sweetened, too, by her late in-laws open ways about her early relationship with John and the acceptance shown by Mrs. Russ and Bill Riley as they caught sight of two damaged young people starting to rebuild their war-shattered lives. There was, he felt, even some unspoken leeway as to 'decorum' allowed by folks in the community, less involved or understanding than his boss and landlady, for the widowed and wounded.

The food was ready, and they ate with gusto, talking and gesturing with chicken-greasy fingers, chewing and sucking at the ends of bones with thoroughness that paid respect to the chicken's well-lived life by wasting nothing. They each piled a few 'naughty bits' as well as an occasional prime morsel on the edge of their plates, saving them for Oscar, who kept track of the accumulation but made no move to cross the table. "Don't bother saving him any greens, he won't eat them." She brought out the promised apple pie that she'd baked in the morning, putting a largish slice on a clean plate for each of them, leaving the remainder within easy reach. "Cooked apples and pastry, though, they're acceptable. We'll have a mighty disappointed cat if we don't make a little allowance there." Last bites were duly saved from second helpings of pie, then scraped onto one plate placed on Oscar's side of the table. As they cleared their dishes into the sink, Oscar tucked in. Used to the routine from growing up, Raymond grabbed the dish towel from the nail above the drain board and dried as Sarah washed, putting the dried dishes with their fellows on the shelf. Sarah paused, both hands in the dishpan, and looked into Raymond's eyes. "You, Raymond McCleary, you're a right useful feller," she told him, winking as she turned her gaze away, looking in the pan for the last fork. "Yep. Right useful in all sorts of ways!" They both laughed. Raymond went over to let Oscar, mewing at the door, outside onto the stair landing. Sarah pulled the curtains out of the way and went out onto the gallery overlooking the road and the open farmland to the south. Raymond followed and joined Sarah in one of the miss-matched chairs on either side of a little table holding the morning's newspaper, a couple of magazines, a pack of Chesterfields, matches and an ashtray. "Want one?" she asked, shaking the pack out towards Raymond.

"Thanks." Raymond accepted the proffered cigarette, then struck a match, holding it first for her, then himself. They leaned back, put their bare feet up against the railing and enjoyed the first long drag of tobacco.

"Second man, I reckon maybe you'll have a chance to stick around." Looking at him, then looking out over the evening fields with their lengthening shadows she began softly singing the rhyme from the trenches of the nineteen-eighteen war, 'Third man on a match -- spot you, range you, Death Angel snatch!'

"It happened before. Got to hang around a bit longer, I mean."

"Glad you did," she said, reaching her left hand over to cover his, resting on the table. Funny, Raymond thought to himself as they held hands and smoked, I'm hopelessly right-handed with everything else, but once a smoke hits my lips I manage it with my left. Guess that's because I need to keep the right free. It grew darker, they started noticing bats catching bugs and the orange embers glowed as they drew down the last of their cigarettes. "Close the curtains as you come in, please," Sarah said as she stood up. "I'm going to call Oscar."

Raymond stood at the railing, taking one last look around the countryside before following Sarah in. There wasn't much moon in evidence, just a few stars. He saw some headlights swing skyward as a car came from town, but never heard its engine, only saw the wild change in the beams' bearing and elevation as the car pulled off on the south side of the road and became invisible as it moved away down a farm lane. Lucky, he thought to himself, hardly described how things were going in his life. He headed back inside, pulling the curtains closed as Sarah had asked. He could hear her behind the closed bathroom door as he got some water from the kitchen tap. Oscar was stretched out at the bottom of the bed intent on some detail of his right forepaw. Sarah came out into the lamplight wearing just a man's shirt -- one of John's, no doubt -- its tails sliding around her thighs as she walked to the bed, sat down, lifted her legs up onto the covers, and tried to get Oscar's attention with her right big toe. "Your turn in there," she told Raymond, indicating the bathroom without taking her eyes off of her toe and Oscar's as yet sheathed claws. He didn't take long, relieving himself, having a bit of a quick wash and brushing his teeth with the new brush conspicuous in the glass with Sarah's. Carrying his clothes rather than putting them on, he turned out the bathroom light and went over by the bed to fold them across the back and seat of the chair beside which he'd left his boots.

"What," Sarah, gently traced the intricacies of the scars she could reach as he stood naked by the bed. "Is that leg really like?"

"Well, for starters, I can only feel about half of what you're touching. Nerve damage from the round and the surgeries. That's worse in the cold, when the scars go numb pretty quick -- they don't have the blood connections of regular skin. As you've seen, I walk kinda goofy. That's for two reasons; first, when they set the bones there were bits that had gotten shattered and contaminated by the bullet and were cleaned out in England to stop infection. Doc Hill at Wilson hospital didn't have a full deck to play from when he reorganized things to match the other leg, and growing ends back together there's a limit to how far you can stretch each piece; second, every time a muscle got cut, either by the bullet, a bit of displaced bone or by surgery, it healed back in a slightly different line. Groups of fibers mixed up with interior scars that behave like the ones you're tickling. Put those together and the geometry's off -- different ropes, pulleys and poles in each leg. Right leg gets tired quicker, probably because no matter how much they're used and exercised the buggered up muscles can't match their cousins on the left, and as they start to tire, the imbalance increases. I don't have much pain anymore when I get started in the morning, but it builds during the day. The more I do, especially the more I stand, the worse it gets. Going to sleep at night takes a long time as the knots around the scars unwind, and there's some sort of weird subconscious memory if that happens right as I'm going to sleep, I guess from lying there after I got shot or from having muscle spasms when I was in traction and unknit bones ground against each other, that says 'watch out, boy, here it comes', that slaps me back awake quicker than you could. Enough of an answer?"

"I think so. I just needed to have it explained rather than imagining. Making up stories for yourself about what's in other people's heads can be a dangerous pastime. There are plenty of real reasons for misunderstanding other folks, and I try to avoid creating my own. Oscar," she turned away from Raymond and looked towards the cat who had sprawled in a big stretch across the foot of the bed facing in the other direction when he realized that Sarah was paying attention to talking with Raymond instead of the toe-and-paw game, "Oscar, you move over and make room for this man!" At the same time she reached out and pulled Raymond towards the bed -- it didn't take much effort as he was right willing to come. As they had in the afternoon, they fit together -- perfectly. When Raymond fell asleep, arm around Sarah, he didn't dream of the war, he didn't dream of the bees and their golden chains. He didn't need to dream at all.

38. A-BOMB

The weekend a pleasant haze behind him, Raymond was back in the fueling shed, on top of the International's tanks, patiently going through the series of valves and hoses necessary to fill the load without a spill, and watching his footing as he climbed about so that he didn't fall and bust his ass -- there'd been a couple of times he'd miss stepped to find himself flat on his back in the gravel, the wind knocked out of him. Fortunately those had been times when either hoses stayed in place by themselves or valves hadn't been opened, sparing him the indignity of both an oil bath and an explanation of his ineptitude. Working steadily but slowly, just the way he'd been shown, he was surprised to hear his boss holler at him. "Raymond! RAYMOND! Get up here -- NOW!" He made sure that the valve under his hand was off, climbed down, grabbed his stick, and took off up towards the store. It wouldn't have taken a Navajo tracker to follow him -- when he got in a hurry his leg bothered him the most. Not knowing if Bill was hurt or what was going on -- Riley, despite all his bluster hardly ever yelled at anyone -- Raymond gritted his teeth and moved as fast as he could. Getting closer to the store he could hear the radio going much louder than usual. As soon as he got up the steps and inside, Riley started talking louder than the announcer. "Boy, they just hit the Japs with some kind of new block-buster! None of that sneak-in-and prove they're not invincible stuff like Dolittle back in '42; none of the keep 'em awake all night firebomb raids like the last year; it was just one plane, one devil's firecracker of a bomb, and this whole city, Hiroshima, wherever that is, was gone, up in a big mushroom cloud of smoke and fire!" He stopped to catch his breath, and Raymond was able to catch a solemn yet excited voice say ''again, the War Department announces that this morning, Monday, August sixth, 1945, the Japanese city of Hiroshima was destroyed by the blast of a single Atomic bomb dropped from an Army Air Corps bomber.." "A-tomic bomb," Riley drawled. "Whatever that is, it's sure some Jap-killer!"

"Know anything about the town? Was it next to an army base or a harbor?"

"Don't know myself. Radio fellows not sayin'. I don't reckon after what was bombed in England and

Germany and what's gone on in the last year with Tok-ee-yo, that whoever plans things much cares if its soldiers or your granny gets killed."

"I reckon that's so. "One bomb", those radio fellows keep saying." They listened to the mostly repetitious broadcast interspersed with cigarette advertisements. Given the diminution in the availability of most consumer goods in favor of war production, the Virginia and North Carolina tobacco companies had the airwaves largely to themselves, and at damned good prices, too. "How in hell can one bomb take out a town, much less what they call a city? I'll wait for pictures from the tail gunner to come out in the paper, and even then I'm not so sure I'll believe what they print if they keep saying "one plane, one bomb"."

"I dunno," Bill replied. "If you were listening instead of listening *and* talking, you'd hear they're saying that this "atomic" deal is new, that they only tested one, out in the desert, before putting the one that they used on a fast cruiser to whichever was the closest island airfield when the ship hit the far Pacific. *That* tells me that whatever an atomic bomb looks like, nothing flying from a carrier can load it!'

"Maybe so." Raymond rose from his chair, leaning on his stick and pulling his hat brim just right. "Call me if there's anything new, please. I've gotta finish loading -- I expect there'll be lots of talking everywhere today and that the route's gonna be a long time gettin' done."

"Prob'ly right, boy. Prob'ly right. I'll come down and tell you if there's anything new before you pull out."

Raymond dragged back through the loose gravel between the back door of the store and the loading shed. He didn't have but the last compartment to fill, gasoline, which didn't take long. He checked the International's engine oil, it was good, didn't need any added, and filled *its* gas tank, which was easy to forget. The time he'd done that he'd been lucky, nobody came along to see him stalled in the middle of the road, out of gas, crawling around with the hose and twisting valves to get a snort out of the load. He'd had enough left to get back to town, but that gas came from so low in the big oval tank that it had to have been part of the first load Riley had ever hauled. It might have come from the guy who owned the truck when it was new! He started the International and as soon as he could began easing the choke off, let it crawl across the gravel lot to the front of the store in low gear. The idle was enough to pull it over level ground, and the shifting of stone under the dual rear wheels was about as loud as the engine. When he got to the little porch at the front of the store he pulled the stick out of gear and back to neutral, the torque load so low that he didn't need to throw in the clutch, pushed the choke button all the way in to the dash, set the handbrake, a shoe on the driveshaft just behind the transmission, and got out to check with Riley before starting out.

"Nothing new on the radio," Riley greeted him as he stood in the doorway. "Announcer has to work pretty hard to keep any urgency in his voice! Wonder how the radio preacher at 9:30's gonna cope, that is if they let him go on. I 'spect they will, though -- station makes those boys pay cash money up front, no bill in the mail subject to the frailties of either the collection plate or the hollerin' man's flesh between broadcast time and the thirty-first!"

And I coulda been one of them! Raymond laughed to himself, remembering his suppertime prank back home. "Anything special on the route today, Bill? Any box goods for the passenger seat (Raymond often carried small quantities of things usually delivered by flatbed if folks phoned Bill and said they needed them.)?"

"Not a thing. Once you get past that blond-headed woman at Westview store, you kin pick up all the pretty hitch-hikeresses that you can fit in the cab!"

Raymond grinned, thinking of Sarah, then responded. "Times have changed since you ran the route, Mr. Bill! Those women you wore out that seat with have all done got old and their daughters are all either ugly or driving Buicks!" He turned out of the doorway as the sound of Riley's laughter mixed with the Radio, got in the truck and headed right as he left the lot and just a few minutes later, the City.

He passed a weed-choked quarry on his left, the source of most of the town's curb and foundation stones, distinguished by the deteriorating advertising signs for Staunton Caverns, a tourist attraction set up by the owners in an effort to shift gears after the depression stopped construction. Sadly, it stopped tourism as well, and all that remained of the operation was a rusty iron door moved from the quarry's empty powder magazine to secure the cave entrance and parallel rows of blue glass power line insulators going up the grey rock face towards a single pole standing against the sky at the quarry's rim, all that remained of the electrical arrangements.

A quarter mile further he pulled into a little store at the edge of a Colored neighborhood -- "Dave's" everybody called it, after its proprietor, Mr. David Jones. Jones came outdoors as soon as Raymond cut the engine. "Mornin' Mr. Raymond," he called before Raymond had even gotten out.

"Good mornin' to you, Mr. Jones," Raymond replied out of the open window.

"I don't need a thing today, but thanks for stopping," Jones continued business talk over. "Does this mean the war's gonna' be over soon, Mr. Raymond?"

"I hope so, but you'd better get an opinion from someone smarter'n me -- I'm just a dogface soldier who got shot in my first fight. Maybe Mr. Tate down at the restaurant, Mr. Smith out at Cedar Green, or my boss, Bill Riley."

"Yeah, I reckon so, " Dave concluded. They both waved as the International ground through the gravel, off the lot and onto the pavement.

A couple of miles more and he pulled into the store at Cedar Green. He could see Mr. Smith inside, busy with several customers, so he went ahead pulled on his gloves and sticked the tanks. The kerosene was lower than the gas, but both were at about half, so he started getting the hose down and hooked to the correct valve. The customers came out and drove off, and Mr.

Smith joined him beside the tanks. "Some bomb, huh, Mr. Raymond,"

"Yes, Sir. Hard to believe, though. One plane, one bomb, one city. Doesn't match up with what I saw -- they bombed the shit out of the Germans at Normandy, all the air they had, all the naval, and those guys were still home when we came callin'. New they say, must be so. Kinda' hard to believe that they'd lose all those aircrews over Germany if they had the one-bomb deal."

"Maybe. I'm an old man, been watching a long time, and can't shake the notion that somebody counts Asia people same as Colored, and didn't care that it was a whole town, not just an airplane factory or oil refinery. Even so, if it ends things quick, that'll be overlooked, just like a lot of other stuff over the years."

Raymond kept his eyes on the kerosene level, intent on not running the tank over but his mind was doing some hunting around trying to absorb what he'd just been told. He'd been brought up in a community with Colored people, been taught to treat them with courtesy and respect despite their marginal economic status, but had never been spoken to so forthrightly by a Black man. Most conversations were sort of scripted on both sides, calculated to tend to business and calculated not to offend. Really, he suddenly realized, no matter how friendly the relationship, he'd never been exposed to a Colored man's view on race issues, although he'd listened to plenty of whites rail about the 'niggers' or talk them down as slow or ignorant. His Father and Grandfather had taught him by example to refrain from joining in affirmation of such conversation and, insofar as possible in society, to treat Colored people the same as everyone else, "Mr." and "Yes, sir" to his elders, no first names unless the man offered the privilege of using them. Mr. Smith was taking things further, speaking his views to Raymond as though he was part of the Cedar Green community.

"I can't say if that's in it or not, but I am glad that you speak to me so plain -- it's a way of looking at it that I never would have thought of. Going one step further, I wonder what it feels like for guys in that Japanese-American outfit that fought up through Italy?"

"Now you've got me looking at it a way I never figured. Thinking on these things you can count on what an old man told me, once. He said that no matter who, White, Black, Red or Yellow, there a situation where every man was somebody's nigger. Figure out how that was, he claimed, good way or bad, 'cause there's two sides to the nickel, and you know your man."

"Never heard it put quite that way, but it sounds right. Each of us has his master, money, sometimes another man, sometimes a job, sometimes, " he said, thinking to himself about how often he woke up in the night screaming, and the pain he'd grown used to at every step, "it can be a man's past." By that time he had the hose back in its tray, his gloves back in the box, and was penciling it the ticket, which he held out in the book and Mr. Smith laid on the corner of the kerosene tank as he signed, then tore off his copy before handing it back to Raymond. "Thanks for the business." Raymond swung up into the truck. Bill Riley had told him in no uncertain terms that the phrase or its equivalent *would* be part of the conversation at each stop. The two men waved as he departed, headed out towards the Parkersburg turnpike, about a mile up the road, where he'd hang a left and head for Westview and Sarah's store.

Sarah was busy with customers, so he started sticking the tanks without talking to her, although they did exchange a wave through the window. Gas and kerosene were both just about empty -- more business here on the main road, that and a larger group of customers than at the last stop, as Cedar Green's store was pretty much limited to the surrounding Colored community. The shoppers left, arms full of paper sacks, nodding to acknowledge Raymond's presence, but quick to transit the cloud of petroleum fumes that encircled him. A couple of minutes later Sarah slipped out of the double screen doors, their waist-high protective plates advertising the local bakery. "Hi, Love," she said, running her hand across his shoulders. "How's your morning going?"

Raymond turned his head and grinned at her, keeping one eye and his ear focused on the filling tank. "Good so far," he replied. "How 'bout yours?"

"Busy. Busy and full of bomb talk. Everyone has a theory or opinion, and Oscar and I have to listen to all of them. At least he gets to close his eyes. I have to be the good storekeeper and act like I'm fascinated even if I've heard it three times or think that it's completely looney!"

"Know what you mean -- I feel about the same after Bill Riley and two stops. It's gonna be a long day for the old ears!" More customers came and Sarah disappeared inside with them as he finished his work.

Hose stowed and gloves in the box, he penciled in a new page in the book and took it inside for Sarah's signature.

"Those Japs just ain't human," a portly man, wife by his side and a full order of groceries bagged on the counter in front of him was sayin'. "They ain't no better'n crazy killer monkeys and rats and deserve everything we can do to 'em" He'd obviously got the message of the graphics of the war bond posters.

Sarah kept her head down, focusing on making change from the drawer for most of his rant, and brought her gaze up with a smile as she handed him his change. "Maybe so, Mr. Persinger, maybe so. Thanks for the business, have a good day Mrs. Persinger," she said by way of dismissal. After she was sure that their car had pulled off she turned towards Raymond. "Here I stand, saying "have a good day" while wondering how on earth Mrs. P. could ever have a good day havin' to listen to her old man carry on so. Maybe when he goes out to the barn, but I'd bet the cows have to listen then. It's a wonder they can let down their milk, the tone of his voice!"

"I know what you mean," Raymond replied, "but I'd bet he couldn't get 'em to stand still if he sang a lullaby. I'm sure he talked just as nice about something or somebody else every minute before the war. We don't change as we get older -- we just get to be more like ourselves."

"I'll let you explain him, Raymond, but you'll not excuse him! It amazes me how those who have the least in this war, the ones who have lost nothing, and are even prospering because of its needs, are the ones who have the most to say!"

"I reckon it's just their way of trying to act patriotic," Raymond replied, handing her the receipt book and pencil. Sarah signed, tore off her copy and put it in the cash drawer as she handed them back to Raymond.

" Which route you doin' today?" She sounded a little friendlier.

"Monterey, Hightown -- the long one. I'm gonna be tired of talkin' and sure to get back late."

"Well, love, I guess I'd better send you along," she smiled, came around the counter so that they could enjoy a kiss and a long hug. "Drive safe," she admonished, "and I'll do my best to keep silence or a civil tongue."

"O.K." He put his cap on at exactly the right angle and headed out to the truck.

The rest of the day was what he and Sarah had expected. More talk than usual, most of it like what he'd heard at her store, which in its own way gave credibility to the view from Cedar Green. A few people, most of them folks who had someone at risk, or had suffered losses like he and Sarah had, expressed sorrow and sympathy for the bomb's victims. It was, he realized, largely a question of one's experience, that, and partly the result of the amount of flag-waving jingoism that came in the same box with the war. Even with the talking, it was a good day for business and he didn't have many gallons of gasoline to offload in the Monterey station's big tank. It was getting dark when he started back over the mountain, and he was going slow, both because he was tired and hurting, and because it was the time of day that the deer were coming out of their daytime cover and prone to cross the road and he didn't want to hit them. By this point he'd driven the route often enough that he remembered the sequence of curves and was rarely surprised by them unless there was another driver, frightened by either the rocks or the edge, approaching in the center of the road or completely over in the wrong lane. This evening, paying more attention than usual to the roadside, he realized that in between the places where deer could leap out of the forest he was scanning the cliff faces for hand- and foot-holds. If he couldn't spot either of those, he found himself straining to locate cracks or layers in the stone where a bayonet could be slipped in as a handle or step. Braking and downshifting more than the road required, he concentrated more and more on the rock faces. He was a climber again, anxious to find the best route up before he became a target. Clearing the last of the rocky switchbacks and gaining speed on the long, straight grade past the bottom of Ramsey's draft he suddenly became aware of the chill of the wind on his sweat-soaked shirt and his white-knuckled grip on the wheel. He didn't remember a thing about his trip over the mountains. Glancing up into the mirror, he saw that his hat was askew. He adjusted it to just the right angle and eased without considering it into his usual driving position, left elbow out the window sill, a couple of fingers on that hand steadying the wheel and his right hand loosely at the opposite meeting of spoke and rim, ready to slip down to shift or move the back-axle speed knob. The rest of the trip into town was uneventful. He put the truck under the shed, and, since it was late, headed home to Mrs. Russ' for a sandwich rather than going to a restaurant. Nobody was in the back of the house when he came in, but they'd left the kitchen light on for him. He snagged his cap on the right knob of his chair, fished a cup out of the carefully stacked dish drainer, filled it with lukewarm coffee and went about making his sandwich.

"You sure had a long day!" Mrs. Russ exclaimed as she appeared from the front of the house.

"Yes'm", he replied, glancing up at her, then back to his half-completed sandwich. "More talk than fuel, I'm afraid."

"I imagine so, imagine so. Haven't heard this much talk since D-day, maybe it, along with the destruction in Japan, is a sign of the beginning of the end of this thing."

"Let's hope so," Raymond backed up against the refrigerator door to close it as he headed to the table.

"I don't," Mrs. Russ said, sitting down across from Raymond, "see how even the Japanese can endure what they have with the last year of fire-bombing and now this! What would our abilities and resolve be if we'd had anything like that on the same scale in this country?"

"Hard to say," Raymond replied, working on his sandwich. "All you hear is how crazy devoted to their Emperor they were in the island battles. Hard to imagine anything less if we actually have to invade their home." He finished the sandwich and got some more coffee, asking her if she cared for any, which she didn't. Sitting back down Raymond sipped the bitter, lukewarm stuff for a minute, thinking. "As for us, if we were bombed and burned and then invaded, I think that we'd lose a lot of ground and people, maybe even the government, but that there'd still be those who'd take the fight to the mountains. That's what my Granddaddy said the South would've done if Lee hadn't told them not to after Appomattox. Can't think that the Japanese'd behave any different. Let's hope that the end *is* coming, for the sake of all the GI's coming back from Europe and facing getting shipped to the Pacific. Once they get there it sounds as though each man moving forward is gonna have to have another walking backwards behind him for protection!" He said that last bit with a laugh, although he really thought that there might be some truth in it if it came to an invasion. He got up to take his dishes to the sink, no longer hungry, but still plenty tired.

"Well, I'm glad you've gotten something to eat. Hope you sleep well," Mrs. Russ got up and returned to the front of the house.

39. A GOOD NIGHT AND EASY RUN IN THE MORNING

Raymond retrieved his cap, turned out the light and started up the stairs. Halfway up he remembered climbing the stairs to the second floor of the wooden barracks where is Ranger school squad had been billeted. He felt the same fatigue, had the mental picture of the unpainted interior of the ubiquitous, standard-issue building, and the smell of its newly constructed pine boards in his nose before he reached the top landing, where a bright oval rag rug on the floor brought him back to Staunton, Virginia. His leg ached and his foot drug on the floor as he crossed the room, taking off his shirt and hanging it over the back of a chair next to the window so that as much of the oil smell as could would air out before morning. He got a rag out of the box beside the desk where he kept his shoe shine kit, went to the bathroom, dampened it, came back, sat down by the desk to take his boots off to clean them. As he bent over, the bottle of whisky and drinking glass at the back of the desktop caught his eye. It wasn't, as Doc Hill had prescribed, bedtime, but he didn't consider those instructions as he poured a full glass before continuing with his boots. He anticipated the burn of the first mouthful in his throat, and that anticipation, foreknowledge of the state of relaxation soon to come, made him sit easier even before it hit his throat and stomach. Returning his attention to his boots, he pulled them off and carefully wiped away the days dust, taking care to note any scuffs into the bare leather that would require extra polish, and to clean under the little fringed flaps beneath the laces. 'Kilties,' he laughed to himself as he took another full swallow. That's what one of the old loafers in one of the stores who'd worn himself down to being a store loafer by a lifetime of logging had told him the woodsmen called them. Raymond took considerable pleasure and pride in those boots. They, and his railroad hat, pulled down 'just right' were what he felt set him apart from every other Joe on the street. Although he'd never considered it after leaving the farm and planning to find his present job, decisions where it was a big consideration, he didn't consider himself handicapped because he walked with a stick and leaned on the fenders, doorframes and store-counters when he left it in the truck while he was doing things with both hands. He didn't consider that anyone might think that how he got around might be more distinguishing than how he looked and carried himself. He thought of himself and his way of doing things   normal and laughed at himself when he saw someone walking along the street and silently wondered where their stick was.

The whisky was doing its job and he didn't feel as tired as he rubbed the polish into the leather, and then set the boots aside to dry while he took a bath. He ran the claw foot tub full and steaming, scrubbed himself clean and soaked until the water started to noticeably cool. Dried off, he pulled on a clean pair of pants, drank the last swallow in the glass and buffed his boots, first with a horsehair brush, then a soft cloth. Satisfied that they looked good, he set them in front of the dresser, got out his clean underwear, socks and bandana handkerchief for the next day, laying them on top, wound and turned on his alarm clock, which he kept on the dresser, away from the bed because he had a tendency to switch it off before it sounded if he kept it nearby. Dousing the overhead light, he paused at the desk and poured his prescribed, bedtime, whisky before settling under the covers to look over the paper that Mrs. Russ had left in the kitchen for him, moving it around in the little circle of light from the bedside lamp as he went from page to page. He'd been in Staunton and listened to Bill, Lee, and Mrs. Russ talking enough that at least the family names if not the individuals mentioned in the Society Column and the Police Blotter had begun to mean something to him. There was often some piece, either tragic or comical about the goings on at Western State Hospital, the ancient -- before the War-- and enormous public lunatic asylum that was the City's largest employer. Today it was a few lines about a dozen or so conscientious objectors brought in because of the staff shortage caused by the draft. Those guys, he chuckled, didn't know how close their experience would be to the real thing, given the nut-case ways of the Army! As always, the comics were his favorites, Lil' Abner and Snuffy Smith so far back in the sticks that nothing from Europe or the Pacific touched them other than the revenuers' pleasing lack of manpower and gasoline or Barney Google blaming Spark Plug's lack of success on a 4-F jockey with a badly crossed eye and feet so flat that he couldn't keep them in the stirrups for a whole race. Not too far off from a few of the customers at a couple stores where he made deliveries, he thought, shaking his head from side to side. It wasn't just war casualties that had to deal with impairment. Finished with both paper and drink, he put out the light, stretched and twisted his pillow to a comfortable spot, thinking about Sarah and the fact that he had an easy day coming up tomorrow, the run out to Wilberger's, which would give him time to stop at the ABC store before it closed at 4:45, a maddeningly calculated hour that screwed with a working man, driving him into the arms of the bootleggers and back-porch re-sellers of pints. He'd asked about the closing time, and had been told it was set to give the employees time to check the register tape and secure the building in time to leave at five. The difference, on a couple of levels, he figured, between storekeeping and a state monopoly.

He woke up before the alarm, got breakfast, and headed to the store. This early in the morning, before the tin roof had a chance to bake up hot, the shed was a nice, cool place to work, which made all the climbing around changing to the right valves and hoses less tiring. After getting the load on, he checked the truck -- its oil was okay, but after yesterday's run he did have to pull out the delivery hose and gas it up.

The drive out north of town on the Valley Pike was pleasant, not much traffic and he could satisfy his

curiosity, looking over the Fairway Inn and the surrounding golf course, built to serve the clientele of the
Stonewall Jackson Hotel back in '29, neglected while
the economy was bad, and enjoying wartime prosperity
as the de facto Officer's Club for the doctors and administrators at the hospital. He'd heard frequent mention of it when he was there, the context of which he
had trouble imagining as he'd never seen the building
and any knowledge of golf was well outside his raising.
Part of the place was home to diplomats and families
from Axis countries in Europe, waiting for or perhaps
dreading, repatriation.

He passed through Verona, with its long line of
fir trees along the highway and regularly saw Army
ambulances in the oncoming lane transporting soldiers
from their gooney bird ride to the Staunton airport to
the Fishersville hospital. He always waved or popped a
salute to the drivers, who waved or saluted back. The
Bellwood Store, just past Augusta Military Academy
and the Old Stone Presbyterian church needed a few
gallons of kerosene. Finished there he backed around
on their lot and turned onto the snake of a road that followed tight against the bluff side of a creek bottom almost to Middle River, headed to New Hope. The twists
in and out of the contours of the bluff shaded much of
the road from the morning sun and so long as it ran with
the bluff, its height completely shaded the road in the
afternoon. It would be, he thought to himself, one icy
son-of-a-bitch come winter. The bluff ended at the
flood plain of the river, where the road made a three-
quarter turn around the front yard of an old brick house
just above the bottom fields. Nice old place, it had a
blue porch ceiling and a swing. Finishing that curve left
him maybe half a mile more, pretty straight, to the iron
bridge from which he could see the dam and millpond

for Grove's mill, the halfway point between the B&O at Bell's Crossing and New Hope. Raymond liked to stop on the bridge for as long as traffic allowed to study the dam because it had a fish ladder, a staircase with a small pool at each step and water flowing down it that allowed fish to cross the dam in either direction. Being lucky enough to see the silver flash of a climber was something special. Bill Riley had pointed the ladder out to him and explained how it worked, saying that he stopped to watch every chance he got. Raymond took that statement as both instruction and permission, concluding that Bill didn't consider his stop there to be goofing off.

Once he'd seen a couple of fish jump, Raymond eased the truck into gear -- by now its ways were as familiar to him as those of the Barrelnose (or Hognose, Bill called it when he wanted to try and twist his tail) -- and enjoyed the view of the Blue Ridge mountains as he headed east, the last mile-and-a half into the village. There were no cars in his way when he pulled onto the store lot so he pulled up next to the square, monkey-pump tanks, looked in the mirror and got down. Mr. Wilberger saw him through the screen doors and waved from behind the counter; Raymond waved back and began sticking the tanks. He heard a car come up on the other side of the truck, glanced up when heard its door slam, saw the back of a tall, skinny guy disappearing into the store, and went back to filling the tanks, both of which were pretty low. There was a garage in town, Mr. Harman's, that had a reputation for good repair work, but no gas pump, and since there were no service stations closer than Bellwood to the west and none at all for several more miles on the surrounding farm roads until they hit Route 340, the Eastside Highway, a WPA project that followed the edge of the flatwoods along the base of the mountains into Waynesboro, Wilbergers did pretty good business in gasoline for a country store. He finished the tanks, put the hose back in the tray and ciphered up the ticket, which was easy because the store had good, clear measuring sticks and he didn't have to figure things from the tank book. Wilberger had come out, helping the skinny customer with his groceries, and he could hear them talking on the off side of the tanker. Receipt book in hand, he grabbed his stick off the seat and headed around the front to get Mr. Wilberger's signature. As soon as he got around to them, Wilberger took the book, signed it, tore off his copy, and said "Raymond, I'd like you to meet this man. This is Fritz Stout."

"Pleased to meet you," Raymond stepped forward and held out his hand, Stout unfolding himself from a comfortable lean on the old Chevy's fender to stand, stepped forward and took it, saying "Me, too," before resuming his position m against the car. Stout was tall and slender, surprisingly deliberate in his manner, moved smoother than most folks, who were always fussing about no matter what they were up to. He didn't lean on the car like an ordinary general-store loafer; he reclined against it like the world was his oyster. He was smooth-faced and paler than most ruddy farmers, Raymond reckoned that he was the kind of fellow with enough sense to wear a broad-brimmed straw hat when he had to work in the sun. If you'd dressed him in a double-breasted jacket and an ascot and put him against a more appropriate backdrop, he could have passed for the Duke of Windsor, if you ignored the fact that, judging from his pictures, the Duke was a good head shorter.

"Fritz farms a little over at Pine Top,'' Wilberger went on. "The last draft call got a little too close for the small producers, so Fritz got himself a job up at Martin aircraft in Baltimore, saves his days off until he gets enough to come down here for a week to catch up on whatever his neighbors haven't got done to help him and his Mother."

When Fritz had stood up, Raymond had registered in the corner of his eye that something was odd about the car he'd been resting against, and shifted to be able to look beyond the other man. Stout caught his move, stood aside so as to not block Raymond's view, and grinned as though he'd been through this before. "Like my tires, do you?" Raymond was taken aback with what he saw. All four of the old sedan's tires stood outside of the fender wells, and the edges of the openings of the front fenders had neatly torched gaps long enough to allow the outboard tires to clear the fender as the driver made a turn. There was a gaping hole in the center of each wheel mounted with a tire through which he could glimpse the lugnuts of a naked rim spacing each one out from its axle hub. "Mother needed tires for this old thing last year and we'd already used our ration to have safe tires on the newer car to drive back and forth from Baltimore, so I went looking at the junkyard. The only wreck that they had with good tires was a big Packard, but they hadn't had any buyers because they wouldn't fit anything else. I got 'em cheap, brought 'em home and used the hot wrench to make 'em fit. Ain't much the hot wrench can't deal with! They're okay for around here, but I have to admit they're rough as hell over thirty-five 'cause I was too triflin' to balance them. Mother was pleased to have good tires -- and she never drives that fast."

"Well," Raymond responded, "I reckon I like 'em okay, it's just that they're a little...surprising'."

Fritz laughed. "Suprisin' ... that's the most polite thing anybody's called 'em yet! The war rationing pushed me to it, but I can't remember what's given me as much fun looking at people's reactions since I was dating my wife Mary and one night she said that the light sparkled on the glass reflector in a highway post by a little bridge like a diamond, so I just stopped, chained it up to the bumper and dragged it out for her. Poor girl, she'd been engaged to a preacher before she took up with me, I had to teach her what fun was."

This guy, Raymond thought to himself, is okay, both of my brothers rolled into one. "I know what you mean about gettin' people goin' just to watch 'em," he replied, and told the story about his suppertime announcement that he planned to take up preachin', describing each family member's look as he'd unfolded the plan. Fritz, rolling a cigarette from a pouch, grinned and nodded in agreement at each stage of the account.

"That's good," he said as he lit up, offering his makings to Raymond, who declined.

"My problem is I can't keep a straight face that long, I have to do things like smoke next to a gasoline truck to get people going."

"Yeah, " Raymond agreed conspiratorially, "but I bet you checked that you were upwind, and I don't see you dangling that smoke down low along the tank, where the fumes flow."

"Righto, my friend, righto." Fritz folded himself into the driver's seat and cranking the Chevy, which caught sooner than Raymond would have expected, given its looks. "See you gentlemen later," Fritz called out to Raymond and the storekeeper as he backed off the lot.

"Quite the joker, Fritz is," Wilberger shook his head. "But there ain't much that he can't fix or build. His older brothers were real generous in deeding the home place to him, along with the care of their mother, the mortgage, and his invalid sister. Some nice bottom land, the farm at Rife's ford, but not enough of it to let him buy any new or even decent equipment. He had to make himself into a magician with a welding torch instead of a magic wand and a junk pile instead of a top hat. He can pull those rabbits out, but damned if some of 'em aren't strange built!"

"I know of a couple of fellows in that boat back home, place not big enough or land not good enough to really keep them going. Sad thing for them that they don't have Fritz's skill or imagination, and have to live a pretty hard life -- both money-wise, and always being beholden to the folks that help them. You can tell that their pride takes a beating, and its hard on a man, hard on a family to live like that, year in, year out."

Raymond climbed into the cab and shut the door. Before he could crank the engine, the usually serious Wilberger (his other line was, after all, undertaking), emboldened by having listened to Raymond and Fritz bantering, came over, put his hand up over the door's rolled down window, and with a twinkle in his eye asked "How're you likin' those pretty boots you bought from me?"

"Love 'em," Raymond replied. "They're perfect for climbin' up and down off this truck without slipping. Funny, when I was in the Army I swore I'd never shine another boot, that any boots I had once I got out would be rubbed with neat's-foot when they got dry and that would be it -- but these, I clean and shine 'em every night!"

"'Good for you," Wilberger replied, then went on. "I figure they stayed in the store so long 'cause the farmers around here were afraid their friends would tease them about those fancy little doodads beneath the laces!"

"Kilties. Kilties", that's what they call 'em," Raymond replied as he eased the truck into gear and moved off, sliding Wilberger's hand from the windowsill and leaving him to ponder the word. Driving back through the village, he shook his head and laughed, imagining Fritz's persistent questioning of a farming boot-wearer about the comparative utility of the little frills while haying, milking, and mucking out manure. "How're those things for hayin', do the little flippers toss the chiggers away from you? " "How 'bout milkin'? Bet you can't hardly keep the bucket under the tits for the barn cats chasing those flippy things!" "I can see how those high heels are a help when you're cleanin' out a stable, keep you above it all. Do you have to grease those fringes special to keep your pants cuffs clean?" Raymond was comfortable with what the old logger had told him about kilties. He'd have been confused if he'd realized that the men he passed swinging their clubs at golf balls along his way home had the same arrangement below the laces of their expensive, low-quarter, cleated golfing shoes.

The drive back to town was uneventful. He stopped the tanker at the upper side of the lot to check and see if any orders had been phoned in. "Nothing new," Bill called out as soon as he got in the door. "Slow afternoon -- if you got nothing to do after topping off the truck, I suggest you don't do it here,"   He was glad that there was just the gasoline tank to fill because by this time of day the shade under the loading shed was hot. The corrugated roof creaked, each piece expanding, bellying down or bulging up, pushing noisily along the rusty length of nail that it had loosened from the sheathing. No wind stirred and the shed stank, of petroleum, creosoted crossties, and hot, dusty tin and wood. Funny, Raymond thought as he went about finishing his work, the late-morning still heat and combination of smells in the shed was, other than fatigue, the only unpleasant association he had from working with Bill Riley. He turned the valve shut at the filler-pipe wedged under the truck tank's lid; climbed over to the tank-car, and closed its valve; climbed back onto the truck and opened the filler-pipe valve, drained the hose; shut the valve and let the counter-weight pull hose and filler-pipe up into their stowed position, clear of the truck but within reach. The gas and kerosene lines dripped clean, but you had to put an oil-can and baling-wire feedbag on the oil fillers to keep the spots off of your cap. He dogged down the cover on the International's biggest tank and his work was done. Raymond climbed down, put his gloves in the box on the hose tray with the odd valve bits he'd not yet been called upon to use, got his stick out of the cab, pulled his sweaty cap to exactly the right angle and headed up the lot to the back stoop of the store, even though the Barrelnose was around front. He stepped inside and Riley, realizing that Raymond was passing through just in case something had come up, said "Man, you just keep on walkin'. Have a good evenin'," all without looking up from his paper, held at precisely the right distance and angle from his torso that it remained unruffled and readable, despite the oversized fan on the side of the desk cooling his back. "Regards to Miz Russ, Lee, and Sarah," he called after Raymond just as he was clearing the front door.

"Yessir!" he heard Raymond reply. Funny, Riley thought to himself, momentarily distracted from his paper. Hot days seemed to have a lot to do with droppin' the letter "g", runnin' words together and butcherin' formal pronunciation. Ready to lay into or philoso- phize the next of his cronies, depending on which op- portunity presented itself, he went back to the paper, reading all of the ads for *everything* -- that's how a businessman kept on top of what was going on in town.

40. A MOVIE DATE

Raymond took the Barrelnose on a path it was beginning to learn as an after-work alternative to going straight to the barn at Mrs. Russ' -- to the liquor store. The stark counters and shelves no longer bothered Raymond, and since he now knew the clerks, they were no longer aloof, and he was no longer defensive. Just a couple of minutes and he and a week's supply were headed home, out Beverley street, west across town. At Mrs. Russ' he came into the kitchen, parked his cap and bags from the state store on the bottom step heading up to his room, and turned through the passage to the back sitting room, which could be used by boarders, and which had the accessible telephone. "Hey, Mrs. Russ!" he called towards the front of the house. "Bill cut me loose early today," he added, explaining his odd schedule. Plopping down in the old overstuffed chair, he picked up the handset and dialed 'O' -- no cranking on the Staunton, automated, TUxedo exchange. When the operator came up on the line, Raymond said, "Good afternoon, can you patch me though to Westview Store, please, Swoope 47 F11. "

"Sure, honey, she replied," setting it to ringing.

"Liable to take a while, it's a one- woman show out there, what with John's death," Raymond told the operator. The telephone at the store rang for a long time with no answer.

"If you have the time to wait, Sir, our lines don't have much of a load at this moment and I can just leave you connected," the operator spoke over the drone of the ring.

"Thanks, " Raymond responded, "but why the switch from "honey'" to "sir"?"

The operator laughed. "I reckoned there wasn't any future in fishin' with "honey" bait when I realized that you knew how things are out at the store. Tell Sarah that Debbie down at the switchboard says "Hi!" "Debbie went to another caller just as Sarah answered.

"Hey, Sarah, Debbie at the switchboard says "Hi!"."

"Figures that it was the two of you, the phone ringing forever as I finished pulling down an order. Oscar even woke up! What's Debbie up to? -- I didn't realize that you two knew each other."

"I've just now met her on the 'phone," Raymond answered. She said she'd been fishin' with "honey" as bait but gave it up when she realized that I knew you and started callin' me "sir"."

"Debbie getting dates with callers," Sarah laughed. "She'll get canned if the old-style operator who's her supervisor catches on. She's found some good ones and some losers. Says she's got the ear, that she's gonna nab a rich, handsome fellow -- I tell her that the way this world works he'll be rich and handsome, but also married and an axe-murderer looking for his next, sweet victim. 'nuff about Debbie though, why're you callin' instead of haulin'?"

"Bill hollered out that if I had nothin' to do after getting the load on for tomorrow that I better not do it there, so I took off, ran an errand and then called you. Any chance of closing the store in time for supper and the early movie? *Arsenic And Old Lace* -- Cary Grant -- finally made it to the Visulite.

"I'd rather not miss the trade I get from people going home after work, but once they're safely around the supper table I can close and make the show. Shall I drive in and meet you?"

"Nah," Raymond replied." You need to save your gas. Some rationing inspector can come closer to making a case of personal diversion against you and your monkey-pump than me and Texas Oil's tank cars." Besides, he thought to himself, the likely invitation up to Sarah's place afterward was a better prospect than any he could offer in town.

"If there's anyone justifying their job by digging small potatoes, you're probably right about the tanks. I also agree with what you're thinking but not saying -- coming back to my place after is more fun! Pick me up at six-thirty and we'll be there on time. Bye!" She hung up before he could say a word.

Raymond shook his head, grinning, as he got up and replaced the phone on its cradle. There was certainly nothing wrong with having a girlfriend confident enough to be forward in these matters. He had a couple of hours before having to leave to pick up Sarah, so he decided to relax with the paper, a bath, a nap, and a sandwich in his room as an early supper. He fixed the sandwich, caught the paper from the table and collected his cap and bag from the first step as he made his way up the stairs to his room. Putting all three on the desk, he pulled out his pocketknife and holding his thumb against the opposite side circled the blade around the cork of one of the bottles just above the glass of the neck, neatly severing the paper label and tax stamp that covered the cork. Folding the knife closed against his leg with his left hand, he poured a generous glass of whisky with his right, then, still standing, took a long satisfying drink, savoring the burn as it started down. Sitting in the desk chair, he looked over his boots and decided that all they needed was a wipe with the cleaning rag and good brushing, not a full polishing job. He unlaced them far enough to pull them off, just down through the brass speed tabs, not into the eyelets and fell to wiping, sipping, and buffing, a comforting routine. The horsehair buffing brush had enough wax hidden inside that if you pressed it a little harder on every other stroke it didn't take long to cover the day's scuffs and abrasions. Finished, he put the rag and brush back in their box and went through the routine of putting his work clothes over the chair to air out, stripped off his socks and skivvies, tossing them into the laundry box. He grabbed a clean set out of the dresser and headed to the bath, pausing for just a moment to drain his glass. Being the only roomer on the back stairs, he could parade around as immodestly as if he were back in a barracks, and without having to field a single wise-ass comment from anyone relaxing on a bunk or footlocker. As always, Mrs. Russ' boiler provided an immediate, satisfying tub of hot water. Soaking in the afternoon was an unaccustomed pleasure, and he indulged until the water began to cool before soaping up with Mrs. Russ' gentle Castile which served as both soap and shampoo. Probably would be tolerable as toothpaste, too, but he'd as yet not been tempted to try it. He rinsed, ducking his head under, got out, toweled off and pulled on the fresh skivvies and socks. Moving over to the sink he squeezed an inch of shaving cream out of the tube from the Dopp kit into his palm, then rubbed his hands together to raise the lather. After moving the lather to his face, he snaked the medicine cabinet door open with his cleanest fingertip, got his razor and commenced scraping away the foam. His beard wasn't particularly heavy -- he could go a couple of days before looking rough and routinely shaved at bedtime so as not to have to fool with it in the mornings. This shave was a courtesy to Sarah, more an indication that he was willing to take the trouble than a necessity. Finished, he rinsed the razor and returning it to the glass shelf in the cabinet. As always, he noticed the slot in the back of the metal cabinet with its decal 'used blades' and laughed, wondering if anywhere, even a hotel room, had ever had enough blades deposited to fill the wall cavity behind, piling up from the sill plate like the chicken shit on the seat of his Barrelnose until an obsessively neat shaver couldn't force one more King Gillette into the crypt!

Clean and shaven, he got a glass of water from the tap to drink with his sandwich. Back in the bedroom, he finished getting dressed and spread the paper out so that he could check the front page as he ate. Nothing but vaguely-worded war news, stale after listening to the radio earlier in the day; local casualties, one killed, four wounded; a car wreck "apparently occasioned by an evening at a roadhouse"; and the agenda of an upcoming County Supervisor's meeting. As a farming area, the County's tax revenue had remained about the same during the war, but manpower and materials shortages made the supervisors' principal jobs of dealing with roads, bridges and school busses considerably harder. He finished the sandwich, gulped the last of the water and half-filled his glass with whisky before settling back, feet up, holding the paper in front of him to study the more interesting letters to the editor, classifieds and comics. People were writing about the bomb's promise for the end of the war and about the poor performance of the dog-catcher -- not a young man, thanks to the draft calls, and apparently someone who'd failed to learn the wily ways of canines as he'd aged. The classifieds leaned towards consumer goods in short supply -- washing machines, pickups ('runs good'), and forgotten but unused spare tires being pulled out and tapped for cash. Today the thing he could relate to the most in the comics was one of Dagwood Bumstead's long soaks.

Raymond looked at his watch -- four-fifty. No need for an alarm clock in order to head out at six, he figured, and stretched out diagonally on the bed, on his back, boots dangling away from the coverlet. There was a good breeze through the window and he dozed off without contemplation. Opening his eyes and sitting up, he checked his watch again -- five forty. Good shape.

He splashed some water on his face, brushed his teeth, and headed out, pausing for a moment to tell Mrs. Russ and Lee, who were eating their supper, that he was taking Sarah to a show. "Have a good time!" they said, Mrs. Russ giving him a wink. The Ford purred as they headed out of town, and when he got to Westview he pulled around behind the store and parked at the bottom of the stairs. Sarah came out as soon as he pulled up and met him at the second step, giving him a 'head higher than you' hug and bending down for a kiss.

"Mmm," she said, laughing and licking her lips. "You either relied on Doc Hill's sleep prescription for your nap or you started the party without me!"

"I'd never do that," he lied. "Doc Hill's infalli-ble." He lied again, automatically and without guilt or hesitation, Fact was he'd come home feeling like a couple of drinks and had arranged his supper plans -- a sandwich in his room -- to make it convenient.   They made it back into town with plenty of time to buy their tickets and choose their seats. Mid-week and the film had been showing since last weekend, so that finding good seats was easy. The Visulite was boxy, the newest theatre in town, it was purpose-built for showing films and had no vestiges of a vaudeville or 'opera' stage. The projector was *behind* the gauze-like screen so that there was no flickering, overhead, cone of light to at-tract the moths. Candle-flies, he thought to himself and commented to Sarah after explaining the rabbit-trail that had gotten him to the words. "Candle-flies," he

said, "that's what the old people always called them."
He went for popcorn and drinks for them both, aided in
locating his seat while returning by the carvings of the
signs of the zodiac spaced in front of the low, indirect
lighting along the theater's walls. The newsreel, comfortably, dealt with war production rather than commentary on combat footage.

The cartoon was an old Popeye that they'd both
seen before, with Bluto as the heavy, one that was made
before the stage of the war when someone in the government decided, and got the studio to agree that the
sailor man was the fellow best able to demonize the
Japanese -- as if they weren't doing a good enough job
on their own. He whispered the notion to Sarah.

"It might," Sarah observed dryly," work the other way 'round. The studio, looking for an edge in getting good war footage for newsreels or getting other
military film work may have convinced some Colonel
that the way to win the war was to make ten-year-olds
hate Japs and proposed that they were in the best position to deliver."

"You could be right," Raymond responded just
as the resplendent film company opening began, "it
probably wouldn't work using Goofy or Elmer Fudd."

Arsenic and Old Lace was great. Raymond and
Sarah nudged each other every time a new character
appeared; whispering who it reminded them of in one
of their families or the community, either Staunton or
back in Guilford. The only ones they couldn't match
were Cary Grant's and the nephew who ran up and
down the stairs pretending to be Teddy Roosevelt. Neither of them knew anyone as unflappably smooth as

Grant or as harmlessly but demonstratively insane as the nephew.

The moon was up when they got out, and the ride home to Sarah's was a nice snuggle, and she didn't say a word about the inconvenience of having to adjust her calves and skirt around the gearshift once he had it in high. "Come on up for a nightcap," Sarah invited as they pulled onto the store lot. "Tomorrow's a work day so it's too late for serious fun, but" she teased "we may as well finish the party you started this afternoon."

"I'm crushed," Raymond kidded as they climbed the stairs, turned on the light and were greeted by a big yawn from Oscar who'd been sleeping on the newspaper Sarah'd left on the table. Sarah go a couple of drinking glasses out of the cupboard, a choice which Raymond liked; filled a small pitcher with good well water from the tap, a woman's gesture; and fussed about getting a few ice-cubes out of the tray in the Frigidaire's little freezer compartment and putting them in a bowl, which he thought completely unnecessary. She put the whole business on the table on a tray between Raymond and Oscar. She reached into the lower cabinet, pulled out a bottle, uncorked it, and poured a drink into each glass -- one finger. Raymond's heart sank, and it must have really shown.

"Just had to know, Lover Boy, had to know," she laughed as she added a couple more fingers to the glasses and Raymond relaxed. "I'm no stranger to the bottle and knew you weren't either, but figured that little game'd let me see how good'a friends you were. It did, and for your information, Id've, reacted about the same." She handed him his glass and he took the sip he'd been waiting for as she added water and ice to hers. "No need to be coy," she said, taking a long swallow and smiling. "Drink it the way you're used to and pour as much as you like -- I've got more." Raymond rested back in his chair feeling both relief and surprise. He was also full of admiration of Sarah based in his own pride in developing full awareness of every new situation he encountered, wondering if he would have been as savvy as she had their roles been reversed. They finished their drinks, just the one round, and after a final embrace at the top of the stairs he headed for his truck, then back into town. As he drove he thought it through again and figured that Sarah had revealed as much information about herself as she had learned from him.

When he got back to his room he hurried through his usual bedtime routine, and fell asleep about eleven-thirty. About two he woke himself up wrestling and grasping at the covers. He was shaking and sweaty, and knew that he'd been dreaming of the ladders or the fight above -- he couldn't be sure which. A glass of whisky and a couple of smokes sitting in the cool by the window and he calmed down enough to crawl back between the sheets and lulled himself asleep by focusing on the good things in his life, good memories and Sarah. He awoke before the alarm went off, a little tired and fuzzy, but was himself again after some cold water on his face and a glass of it to swish around and swallow.

41. ANOTHER BOMB & VJ DAY

Wednesday was going to be just another hot August day. He'd loaded the afternoon before, so that he didn't stay in the shed by the siding long enough for the sun to start the roof creaking. Bill sent him on the mountain run and he got back late enough that he put off reloading the truck until the next morning. Thursday morning seemed pretty much like the day before, except that he was still loading when the roof was beginning to creak as the sun hit it strong and the air got warm enough to fill with the mixed smells of gasoline, kerosene, motor oil, and the creosote of the railroad ties. He was closing a valve when he heard Bill hollering. "Raymond! Raymond!, Get up here!" He made sure the valve was fully closed, grabbed his stick, and hustled across the gravel to the store, stepping smartly at first, but with his leg dragging more and more, slowing as he got closer to the door. As he grabbed the rails, pulling up the few steps of the office stoop, he could tell that Bill was playing the radio loud, loud enough that a rattle from a little tear in the speaker's paper resonating cone intermittently cut into what was being said. Bill didn't give him a chance to listen. "They done it again, Raymond," he talked over the broadcast. "Dropped another a-tomic bomb on Japan, wiped out a place called Nagasaki. War can't last much longer if they keep this up. Wonder how many of those things we have, anyhow. At this rate seems like we can just keep at it until the whole damn place is done for." The news announcer kept on in pretty much the same style as with the first bomb, talking in a self-important tone without giving any real additional information. Raymond leaned on the counter a while, listening just to make sure his first impression had been correct.

"Well, Bill," he finally said, straightening up, "that's exciting news, but I doubt there's gonna be anything more revealing said unless there's a surrender. If that happens, you or somebody else is gonna holler loud enough that I'll hear no matter where I am. I better get back to work."

"Suppose you're right." Bill turned down the radio and headed around his desk to his chair and account papers as Raymond headed for the door. "Makes it damn hard to concentrate, though, wondering what's going on. A good day for you to just concentrate on not wrecking my truck and not going crazy, having to listen to the same gab at every little store." His tone brightened. "Be a good day to work on your W.C.Fields, "Go away boy, you bother me." Raymond laughed and headed back to the truck. Bill always gave him an out -- this time he could tell the gabbers that he'd heard it before and that his boss's instructions were to practice the line. He could recite it, tapping ash from an imaginary cigar, and the loafers would laugh, then leave him to do his work. W.C. Fields, hell! Bill Riley was coaching him on how to do a good Bill Riley!

Bill's ploy worked just fine that day, Thursday; he hardly needed it in order to get through Friday; and by Monday, after the weekend, folks were back to their usual topics of discussion, some fascinating, some tiresome, but at least varied. Raymond marveled at the ways in dealing with people that Bill had developed in his years of filling tanks and carrying the gossip from one little village to the next and realized that he'd been as much a student of those ways as of the greasy little book that guided him as he filled out a ticket for a customer with an odd tank.

Tuesday morning he was at work loading the truck when, for the third time, he heard Bill bellowing his name. This time Bill was running down the lot with his old-man gait, meeting him halfway from the store. "They quit! Surrender!" Bill huffed, grabbing Raymond in a bear hug. "It was just on the radio," he said in a more normal tone as he caught his breath. "It's over, finished!" Raymond could see the wetness of tears on Bill's grizzled, stubbly cheeks. Raymond hugged him back, and as they held each other at arm's length, felt his own eyes welling up.

"That's great!" he responded, and Bill, still huffing a little gestured towards a couple of empty, upended five-gallon grease buckets at the edge of the loading shed's shade. They walked over and sat down, elbows on their knees, and just sat, neither saying anything as they thought over what they had just learned.

"Well," Bill broke the silence, "two things; first, probably the biggest thing in your lifetime has both started and ended, and second, things are gonna be changing, all those fellows leavin' the Army and lookin' for jobs."

"I reckon you're partly right on the first, and dead on with the second. The biggest thing in my lifetime was part of the war, the battle and what happened to my leg, but they're not over yet. I've thought about them more than I've liked, and know that they're gonna stay alive in every step I take until I die and in my head some part of every day and night until the morning I don't wake up. I'm glad the war's over for the country and the fellows coming home, but it's scary, knowing that it'll never end for me, or for a lot of them. I'm in luck though, on your second part. I've got a job that I can do, a comfortable place to live and a great girl -- it'll take a long time for the fellows starting home soon to pull those together!" They sat, silently for a few more minutes.

"I see what you mean about its never being over, " Bill said softly. "Never really thought that one through, figured that if people got over loosing loved ones, they got over wounds and battles, but never having been hurt bad myself, it didn't occur to me how things are constantly brought back. I can see how difficult it must be to keep physical pain from bringing back snatches of memories when you'd rather stay with where you are, what you're doing." Bill paused to spit some tobacco, and then replenish his chew, offering some to Raymond, who accepted. "As to what happens when you're asleep, hell, none of us are the masters of our dreams. I know how bad mine can be when all I've had to endure was my teachers in school demanding proper behavior, running this business, my wife and children, and being responsible for a few head of livestock. I can't begin to imagine what the Devil gets up to when you and the other men who survived the fighting or any of the folks who took care of you if you got hurt lay your head on the pillow and close your eyes." They sat silently for a few more minutes, listening to long blasts of far more car horns than Staunton traffic could require and the eventual peal of church bells.

"Thanks. Thanks for understanding rather than thinking I was just complaining." Raymond stood up, leaned more heavily on his stick than usual after being hunkered down on the low bucket, and stretched. "Reckon I better finish loading and get out of here, see how all the storekeepers are celebratin'." They could hear Bill's phone ringing.

"Yeah, I reckon so, too," Bill replied and grunted up from his bucket, headed for the telephone and his fan. Raymond set his cap at exactly the right angle and went back to work.

42. MEN COME HOME AND LIFE GOES ON

The hot, humid, days of August drug into September, and Raymond realized that a four-o'clock thundershower was just about as predictable in the Shenandoah Valley as in the pinewoods of North Carolina. The runs to the cooler altitude of Highland County once or twice a week were welcome and Raymond enjoyed noting each landmark at which he experienced increased relief from the engine heat radiating back through the International's firewall. Opening the slats of the winter front on the radiator shell kept the engine at proper operating temperature pulling the long grades, but the speed in low gear cut the airflow through the windows, and the cab could get stifling even though he had been careful to shut the valve under the hood that led to the cast-iron radiator spilling out from the lower edge of the right-hand dash back in the spring. The tank in the back for the customers' cars and the truck's crankcase had been carrying forty-weight oil since the beginning of June to stand up under the heat. "Summer's no problem," Bill had said from in front of his carefully adjusted fan. 'Just stay in the shade and walk slow. Watch an old tomcat go up the Beverley Street hill to Coalter -- he'll be hugging the last inch of shade under the stone wall at noon! Winter, now there's the bitch, ain't no natural way to get warm."

Demobilized men started coming home. There was a big parade and welcome for Staunton's National Guard unit, called up with others from North and South to form the 29th Infantry Division -- they'd been at

Normandy. The little town of Bedford, southwest of Staunton, had lost the better part of a generation of its young men then. Calling up the guard units kept them all together and the community suffered the same sort of mass losses that had come from the British continuation of the practice of locally-raised regiments in the last war. Staunton's guardsmen had the particular honor of being called the Stonewall Brigade, successors of the Confederate militia that had stood with Thomas Jonathan Jackson at first Manassas, earning him the sobriquet 'Stonewall' (The northern illustrated newspaper, *Harpers*, characterized him somewhat differently, as a "lemon-sucking, maniacal, blue-eyed killer"). The brigade's brass band stayed together after the War, and it really sounded good to have the guardsman members back on the bandstand with the civilians who'd done their best to keep summer Friday evenings pleasant. It seemed as though everyone with a ruptured duck pin called Mrs. Russ hoping for lodging. Two men were sharing the big room that David used to have and what Raymond had come to consider his private bath and stairway. They were nice enough fellows, but only one had served overseas, and he had not been in combat or had much of a close look at its consequences. Raymond didn't drink or smoke with them and held only polite conversation at the breakfast table. Most of what they talked about either didn't interest him or involved people that he didn't know -- they were both enrolled at the Dunsmore Business College, a big brick building on the south side of the street as you walked from Mrs. Russ' downtown. He'd asked her about the school when he first noticed it, she'd said that they taught a good enough course of study, but that the practical advantage of graduating from there was that their diploma was the biggest of any school in the state, looked quite impressive on an office wall.

Sarah's first invitation to Raymond to stay out at Westview became a standing invitation. After a couple of months of that, she asked him if he'd like to move in with her. Didn't take him long to decide that one, and when he gave Mrs. Russ his notice, she congratulated him on his relationship with Sarah, said she would miss him, and then laughed, telling him that she had about eight names on her waiting list and figured that she could convince two of them to share his room. After shifting some furniture from the attic to make the room a double, her breakfast table would be completely filled. Out at Westview Sarah had cleared John's things from part of the curtained pipe which had served as a clothes closet for him, and Raymond didn't own any furniture, unless the tool box he'd unbolted from the bed of the truck and used as a low table and footstool counted. It was harder to carry up the stairs than to find a place where it added to the apartment. Oscar accepted his sudden full-time residence with an equanimity that blossomed into outright demonstrative affection.

Raymond made good on his promise to Mrs. Russ to gather the chestnuts and dispose of the hulls. Out on his route one day he noticed a couple of steel cans that rail bolts or spikes had been shipped in where the section crew had left them at a grade crossing, scrounged them (his good Army training and farm-boy raisin' kicked in), and got one of the men at Staunton Machine Works on Greenville Avenue to cut and weld them into a brazier and a couple of roasting pans. The welder thought that Raymond was a whacko when he explained his project, and only charged seventy-five cents for the work, laughing that he figured that covered the gas and rod and that he'd have enough fun with the story to make up the rest of his time. For as long as the

nuts kept falling, he and Sarah put the brazier in Mrs.
Russ' iron wheelbarrow on Friday and Saturday evenings, fired it up with kindling and husks (as Mrs. Russ
had predicted, the fire had to be going right good before
they'd burn!), and walked it downtown to a sidewalk
spot central to all four movie houses to set up shop.
Raymond tended the fire and cut the crosses through
the shell on the flat side of the nuts that were necssary
to keep them from exploding with steam as they roasted
and Sarah chatted up the customers, some leaving the
first show, others coming to the second, folded paper
cones out of newspaper, and served up the savory nuts,
a nickel a brimming tin cupful. They always sold out,
and since Sarah knew almost everyone who stopped,
she said it was like a street-party, more fun than if they
were going to a show themselves. At first Raymond
was overwhelmed by the number of introductions, but
found that he remembered most folks when he saw
them again and even had to introduce Sarah to some of
the people he knew from the wide loop off his route.
During the second show, if their stock lasted that long,
Sarah gave him the lowdown on everyone he'd met --
both what she already knew and what she'd picked up
that evening. If they ran out, she told him on the ride
home.   The chestnut harvest spread out over about
three weeks. Raymond had to gather them as they fell,
morning and evening, to keep the squirrels and ground-
hogs (neither Mrs. Russ nor her neighbors had a dog
patrolling the area) from taking more than their fair
share. He'd been right about the irresistible color and
feel of the nuts in a small box or basket on a store counter. On the days that they didn't have a roasting
planned he carried a box of nuts with him in the International and seldom brought it home anything but empty. A few extra dollars for him, and Mrs. Russ had the
satisfaction of having her lot kept clean and seeing the

fruit of her husband's hobby put to use rather than raked into a pile, doused with kerosene and burned.

43. A TRIIP TO NORTH CAROLINA

At Sarah's suggestion they decided to take a trip to North Carolina to visit Raymond's family. When he telephoned to find out when they'd be welcome, his sister, with some justification, accused him of having abandoned them because he hadn't written to them for such a long time. After he confessed, she said that he was forgiven, and that his forgetfulness was "probably (giggle) due to his new living arrangement" which she had managed to discover during the first couple of sentences of the conversation. It was Mary on the phone, but she'd changed in his absence, become much more direct in her way of speaking, almost sounding like their sister, Reba. What, Raymond wondered, would Reba have become during his absence? "Sarah's especially welcome, and on her terms -- Reba 'n I'll deal with any old biddy who even starts to shape her lips to say "Whore of Babylon!" Raymond could see them in action in his mind's eye, almost hoped he'd be able to see it for real! A date was agreed upon two weeks away, and they said "goodnight" and hung up.

Sarah decided to just close the store for the few days that they'd be gone, taking the precaution of arranging for a neighbor's son to sleep nights so that any would-be thieves would know that someone was upstairs with a shotgun. If they were careful thieves, they'd be observant enough to notice that it was a testosterone-loaded, trigger-happy adolescent, just as it had been back in John's day! Bill, as Raymond had expected, had no problem with him taking a Friday and the following Monday off, and even told him he'd have his full pay both weeks "cause you're gonna be making up the work the other four days, same as when the railroad or the great Texas Oil Company foul up and leave us with an empty tank-car." Raymond thought that was a good enough deal. He changed the pickup's oil, greased everything, and cleaned the air filter, being careful to get the fine, invisible if you just glanced down inside, sediment from the bottom of the black bowl. That telltale finger-smear of that sediment had provided many a motor-sergeant a beer in the evening after motor-stables! He took the wooden toolbox from the apartment and bolted it back into the bed, made it a point to stop at the liquor store when he was out one afternoon, and filled one corner of it with a case. Sarah, more like Reba than Mary and his mother, didn't spend any more time than he did planning what clothes to take -- they both just made sure that enough got done on laundry day to last. Mother and Mary, he thought, would have actually packed three times and unpacked twice, missing the third undoing and fourth rearrangement only because it was time to load the car and leave.

They took the same route south that he'd followed north. Not surprisingly, Sarah's rating of the prosperity of each of the little towns that they passed through was based on their store rather than on their Confederate monument. One or two old brick stores still in use, and especially if there was a similar bank showed a long history of prosperity, probably diversified agriculture and railroad based; relatively new brick stores with modern windows and a block of sidewalk on that side of the street meant that a mill had probably moved south just in time to catch profitable wartime contracts, but that things could be dicey pretty soon, depending on how things were, postwar. Sarah's opinion was that it would take six months or a year for factories to shift over to making civilian goods, but that the last five years of folks doing without would lead to a pretty good spell for shopkeepers. Raymond's response was that a lot would depend on how quickly the demobilized men got back to work -- if it didn't happen in that same six months, any pay sent home and saved would run out and there'd be some hard times. As they went along, the amount of paint on the exterior of the little crossroads stores seemed a pretty good indicator as to whether the surrounding countryside was productive or if it had been farmed out or logged over. Sarah was fascinated to learn that isolated clumps of trees in the middle of a farming field in this clay and sandy-soiled country always meant either a disused family cemetery or the ruins of an old home, rather than, as it usually did in the limestone of the Valley, the existence of a plow point-breaking ledge.

The drive seemed a lot shorter with company. They turned into the farm lane just before suppertime. Everyone was in from the afternoon's work and poured off of the front porch and around the side of the house when they heard Raymond's pickup. Will and Charlie practically pulled Raymond from the driver's side of the cab with handshakes and back-slapping; Reba and Mary did the same with Sarah on the other side, hugging the breath out of her in greeting; Mother and Father stood close by, arms around each other's waists, waiting for the tumult to pass and for Raymond to come over and introduce Sarah, which he did. "Welcome," they said, with Father adding "If Raymond's taken the trouble to bring you down here, you can consider yourself one of ours." He continued with a wink, "just don't ask around too close exactly what that might involve. "

Will and Charlie dropped their suitcase at the bottom of the stairs and everyone headed back to the kitchen to the smells of ham, sweet potatoes and biscuits. They took turns pulling on the shallow-draw pitcher pump by the sink that brought rainwater from the cistern under the back porch until hands were washed, then filled every chair around the table. "Father, thank you for this food, bless it to our use and to thy service amen," Father dutifully intoned. Grandfather's brevity in saying grace had carried on after his passing, and Father had, perhaps inadvertently, trimmed it a bit further, omitting the "us" between "and" and "to" and the full stop between "service" and "amen" that would, if properly written out, call for at least a comma and probably deserved a period. Sarah was relieved to find herself in the midst of the sort of stoic, laconic religion that she favored. Grace was just that, no listing of names, no drawn-out account of lessons and blessings derived from an ordinary day of dirty farm work, and best of all no singling out of the newcomer, herself, for praise, thanks or other special Godly consideration. Knowing Raymond and what he'd told her about the whore of Babylon, she hadn't particularly feared a kitchen-table preacher, but you never know -- sometimes one generation's attitude in such things was a reaction to the plentitude of another's.

As dishes were passed, Reba spoke up. "I guess I'll go first in trying to catch you up on what's going on here. The farm's done pretty well the last couple of years, strong prices for cattle and hogs and we logged about five acres of pines that were big enough for saw timber -- you wouldn't believe the market the war made for timber that would hardly have paid for its own cutting before! We traded some for sawing and got some nice, clear, boards to patch a lot of things that needed it, fences where you couldn't find a place at the post end of a loose board to nail it back up without scabbing a scrap on and such. We were able to find a couple of good pieces of used equipment like the small combine we bought from Charlie Smith when he doubled the small grain he put out and went to a self-propelled one, and a good three-row corn-picker from another farm which got something better. I've been seein' a good bit of old Charley...."

"And not necessarily about farmin', either!" Chimed in Will.

"You and your brothers aren't the only ones entitled to a social life!" Reba retorted.

"Tell me who, Will," Sarah followed up." I don't know which girls around here have crossed eyes or double first cousins, so I can't be judgmental."

"Fair 'nuff. "I've been after Molly Wilkerson, and Brother Charles, he's chasin' 'Lizbeth Poteat." None of them, thought Raymond, were spending time with anyone but solid farmer's sons and daughters.

"Don't forget Mary, dear." mother said. "She doesn't spend all of her time in the kitchen, although I can't say if she's after Quentin Baker or if he's after her!"

"Tell one, tell all," Father added. " I'm still for that young thing I always was, 'gesturing across the table at Mother, who blushed.

This, "Sarah proclaimed, "Is more than I asked for. This isn't Raymond's coming home dinner -- it sounds more like the closing scene from one of Shakespeare's less bloody plays, the name of which I forgot as soon as the test was over, where everyone gets together with the right person at the end."

"You're right, Sarah," Raymond said, taking her hand. "We're the first couple come up in this discussion, and except for my gimp, there haven't been any potential in-laws with deformities or imbecility mentioned. Except," he laughed, "for Charlie and Will, who come pretty close to the definition, but the younger Wilkins and Poteats are blinded by love, and the old ones, I reckon they're just gettin' on and don't see too good." Both Charlie and Will made their best idiot faces and the whole table howled with laughter. Reba winked at Sarah, as good as saying "you handled that slick, sister." Sarah winked back at her, acknowledging the compliment.

The most pressing subject of discussion and curiosity having been addressed, the family fell to eating, most subsequent comments being about the quality of the food and, please, what needed to be passed to the hungry diner. As they finished, Sarah blended into the cleanup routine with the other ladies, and Father, trailed by his three sons, headed for the row of rocking chairs on the front porch and the gathering dusk. It was cool out there in the evening this time of year, but still pleasant enough to sit, look at the cattle in the pasture and try to guess who went along the road while they visited. "Sit there," Father said to Raymond, gesturing to the chair that Grandfather had favored before he'd passed. "He was right proud of you, you know."

"Yes, sir. Thanks," Raymond replied, settling into the chair and starting it moving. Will and Sam settled into two other chairs -- the porch was full of them for summer evening visitors, not yet pulled to the back of the porch, out of the weather, turned upside down against the wall so that winter winds couldn't set them to rocking, shifting position and eventually falling off onto the ground. Their house was too old -- its chimneys were built outside of the exterior walls -- and too plain to have a railing around the porch. The Old People knew that there was no saving a house if the flue caught fire in an interior chimney, and no later generation had tried to modernize by aping the band-sawn gingerbread trim and porch railings of the houses built after that became the style.

After a few minutes of stetting, rocking, and successfully identifying the rapid passage of Quentin Baker's Studebaker headed back towards his place, Father cleared his throat. "Raymond, we know you've got that oil-driver job you figured you could do, but not much else. Tell us how it all came together." By this time the ladies had come out and the row of chairs was adjusted to accommodate them, Raymond still next to his father, Sarah on his left, and Mother next to father on his right.

Raymond, asked, told the whole story, beginning with his chance encounter with the weights-and-measures examiner at the roadhouse, his first encounter with Bill Riley, at which Father smiled, nodded his head and said "Well spoken, boy." Raymond went on to explain how Bill's call to Mrs. Russ had fixed him up with lodging that same day, gave an account of the arrangements there, and marveled at how association with his boss and landlady seemed to let people accept him as though he'd lived in Staunton all of his life.

"Their high opinion was good enough for me! " Sarah added, reaching over to give him a smile and pat his hand on the arm of the chair. He left out the drudgery of his job, keeping everyone in stitches with his accounts of Bills methods of dealing with people, stories about different customers, and the pretentious names of some of the barely-surviving stores.

Charlie allowed as names that didn't fit weren't unique to the Valley, naming a few in their part of the country, also to general laughter. "We mustn't be too hard on them, though," Sarah said as she was still giggling at the last. "Most of them used to be Post Offices back before Rural Free Delivery. The new postmasters, mostly storekeepers like me, got to pick the names, which had to be different from any other in the state. Some of 'em never were anything but nonsense or a person liking the sound of a word, but I'd bet that if the stories could be told they'd be made up of ambition and high hopes, pride and history, dreams that couldn't possibly be fulfilled out of a crossroads, and loves that couldn't be spoken." Everyone had to sit and rock a minute on that, then, one by one, each came up with a believable story for one of either Charlie's or Raymond's examples.

"Mine's the simplest," Sarah said. "My little village is called 'Westview', no doubt because after leaving Staunton heading west on the Parkersburg turnpike it's the first place with a clear view of the mountains. It once had a Post Office, and there's just that one word on the sign John's folks put up when they opened the store. Their hopes, and I guess my future, came about because automobiles made it easier for more folks from the country to work jobs in town, and even with competition from the chain stores they seem to buy more than just what they forgot in town. They like a place to meet and gossip, and they like my cat, Oscar." Her face clouded over and she grew quitter. "I won't discount the possibility, too, that they're just trying to help out the village widow," but brightening, "I like to think that's not too large a percentage of things."

"I'd like to think not, too, dear," Mother replied. "But folks do like to help folks. Some of us grow too old before we learn that being on the accepting end carries no shame and completes a circle that began when we were the helpers. She continued, kindly, but in exactly the way that she would have expected from Raymond and had observed in Sarah for the better part of an evening. "I could tell from your face when you lowered your voice just now that you'd cut pretty close to the bone. We'd like to know your story and it might be easier for you, rocking and talking into the twilight, now that you've come close to part of it."

"Thank you. It is easier talking into the dusk. Just a shame it's too late in the year for fireflies." Raymond reached over and put his hand over hers as she began. Sarah more or less worked forward from her introduction to Raymond the first time he and Bill came in; their second, longer meeting on VE Day, when she'd just come downstairs from hanging the flag from John's funeral from the balcony; the reports she got from her friend, Marie Russ about Raymond's ways and boardinghouse behavior; and her conscious decision to encourage his visits to the store on his way home from his route, which let her see for herself how he got on with Oscar and how much he picked up on her customers' personalities while appearing to be loafing with a black cat and a soda. The continued reports and observation led to more interaction and then to their present arrangement. She told them about John's death, which had left her with personal demons akin to Raymond's, about his parents and their approval of her and John being together in the months prior to their marriage, their deaths and the newlyweds becoming storekeepers without having planned to. She spoke of her ancestry, Scotts-Irish on one side, Dunkard on the other, but said no more about her childhood and parents than she had to Raymond, which was practically nothing beyond mention of a farm upbringing. Mother, Father, Reba and Mary said nothing, asked no questions, but each noted to themselves that Sarah probably coped with more than John's loss. Perhaps an earlier, as yet unexplained loss of connection with her people. She had more than the one demon. Not focusing as clearly looking amongst their own, they thought that Raymond hadn't any beyond his bad leg.

A little more silent sitting and rocking, a few comments about its almost being time and cool enough to go in, prompting Father to allow as he'd sit and visit 't'll dawn if he liked, and that he didn't care for a quilt over his knees, not just yet. The family laughed, remembering all of the nights that they'd dozed off in their chairs, then roused themselves enough to slip off to bed without interrupting Father and Grandfather as they talked on. Nobody knew if they had ever actually kept at it until sunrise. If asked the next morning, Father had always just grinned, saying nothing, and waited for Grandfather to answer, with a wink, that he couldn't really remember, but that he was an old man, and that the family would have to not begrudge his making the wisest use of his remaining few hours, even if it meant that his son couldn't go as hard with the next morning's work. Making up the difference, he always concluded in one way or another, was the only good reason for keeping grandsons on the farm rather than sending them off to sea, to a turpentine plantation, or the mines at Birmingham, all situations where they'd have room and board and he'd have their wages.

William broke the next little silence. "Raymond, how's your leg doin'? You told us all of the funny stuff about what you do, but didn't talk about the real work."

Raymond had hoped to avoid the subject, but was honest about it. "Don't like being a complainer," he replied, thinking of the burned tankers in their row of beds, "but it bothers me all the time. I use my stick when I walk, or use the side of the truck or something else to keep my balance. When I'm pulling around a fuel hose, its steady weight and resistance works. Climbing on the truck is a shoulder-strength deal, jumping down, well, that has to be real careful"

"Are you," Mary asked, "in pain?"

Raymond was really unhappy about answering that one. "Well, we're all like the old folks. We put up with what we have to. I'd be lying if I didn't admit that every step doesn't start tightening the muscles in my neck that clench my back teeth, but I'm so used to that so that I don't really pay it any attention."

"You are talking around my question, not answering it. When are you in pain rather than successfully ignoring it?"

Caught, Raymond thought. " If I forget and jump out of the cab or off of the hose trays alongside the tanks; anytime I put a hustle on instead of walking;

every day when I get off from work, and every night when I go to sleep. I'll stretch out and relax, and just as I start to doze off some little misplaced nerve will twitch. I'll think 'okay, boys, here it comes,' and it always does, one misaligned muscle spasming against another or a nerve or some scarring 'till I can't even tell 'em apart."

"I'm sorry, " Mary replied, her voice so soft as to be barely audible.

"What," Reba asked, can you do to deal with it?"

"Accept it as much as I can, try not to think about it. If I do, I remember all the fellows hurt worse than me, and figure I'd better be grateful that I'm not one of them. I talked to Doc Hill, the Colonel who worked on me at Woodrow Wilson Hospital, he was still there when I got to Staunton, about it. We agreed that going down to the pharmacy and signing the morphine ledger every week wasn't a long-term solution. He said that at the dosages I was used to I had such tolerance that I'd have to take so much that there'd be no way I could drive. After that he quizzed me if anyone in the three generations of the family that I knew was a drunk, and when I told him "no," he suggested a good, stiff drink at bedtime to help with things. It felt strange at first, but really has helped."

"Interesting, " Reba replied. "That Colonel didn't much mince words if he actually said 'drunk'. Don't think that I ever thought of evaluating our people that way."

"He speaks right plain. That's probably why I liked him so well. He always told me plain and clear what he was doing and what I could expect. No big words, and he talked man-too-man, didn't let either the white coat or the birds on his collar get in the way."

A little more rocking, and it was Raymond who broke the silence. "Speaking of all that, I could use that drink now. Do any of you care to join me?"

"We'd all be proud to, a celebration of what sounds like your success, and a celebration of Sarah!" Father replied. "Will, how 'bout you and Charlie bringing out some glasses and a little water." Sarah was already heading out to the pickup for the liquor, two bottles, she thought, with that many people. By the time she was back to the porch, Mary and Reba had pulled over a small table to where Mother, Father, and Raymond sat, gathering the other's chairs around it, and the boys were back with a small pitcher and the right number of glasses, not on a tray, but carried man-style, suspended in clusters, fingers down inside pressing the sides together.

Raymond leaned over on one leg to reach into his pants pocket and get his pocketknife. He cut the paper seal that went around and the long red tax stamps that went across the cork, loosened it from the neck of the bottle, which he handed to Father to pour. Father put three fingers in each glass. He and Raymond let theirs stand neat and he others added varying amounts of water. When everyone had their glass in hand, Father raised his in salute, saying "I made the speech when I accepted Raymond's offer to join him." The others raised their glasses in response to his gesture, then began sipping, rocking and talking. Raymond felt the usual sense of relief as the first sip of whisky burned his throat, relaxing and forgetting his pain before the heat grew, then dissipated in his stomach. He could taste the second without the burn, and by the third the first was in his blood, going to the muscles in his leg and starting to untie the knots. His father hadn't been talking with the others as he drank, but had instead been watching Raymond's face. "Better now, Boy?" he asked quietly.

"Yes, Sir," Raymond replied in the same tone.

The two sat silently as the others became more talkative. In a bit, Father, facing out into the darkness, said "Good. I'm glad it helps you."

When he'd finished his glass (Raymond had been nursing his in deference to the others) Father picked up the bottle and asked, generally, "More?"

"Lands, no," Mother replied. "We've got to show Sarah where things are so that they can get situated." Mary rose with her and they hustled Sarah, who paused to smile and wink at Raymond, into the house, reclaiming the suitcase that his brothers had abandoned in the hall before supper and heading upstairs. Reba, Will, and Charlie put their glasses on the table with Father and Raymond's for another round, which required opening the second bottle.

As they finished, Reba stood, saying "come on boys, help me get these things to the kitchen and wash them up. We'll just leave these two silent old men out here by themselves."

As they left, Father put his glass on the table and splashed in another finger. He looked questioningly at Raymond, who he could see in the light from the hall that came through the screen door. Raymond nodded, put his glass on the table and was given the same. After they'd both turned back to face the darkness, Father spoke again. "I know it was hard for you to leave, but you were right to go -- you'd have never had a chance, faming. Sounds like you've got something now that you just can do, and storekeeping with Sarah to do when you can't and while you figure what might be better -- kind of like the week you spent polishing that Ford." Father stood up, tossed back the rest of his drink and headed into the house. Raymond did the same, parking the bottle on the bottom step as he passed it on their way to the kitchen. "We've really missed you, Boy," Father said without turning as he rinsed their glasses and put them onto the wire draining rack. "Hell of it, too," he said to Raymond's back as they went back through the hall and started up the stairs, "none of us has the touch with the bees like you and Grandfather."

Raymond awoke drenched in sweat, with Sarah cradling him into her long blond hair against the bosom of her nightdress, stroking his hair and whispering "take it easy, Love. Everything's all right. You're safe, you're safe." The room was dark except for a little moonlight at the widow and there was no crack of light under the door to indicate that anyone else was up and about. He didn't need her to tell him what had happened. He'd awakened her and probably everyone else in the household with his screams before he, himself, fully awakened under the touch of her hand. He was weak, totally drained, and as he gained an awareness of where he was and who was holding him he wondered which it had been, the ropes, the fight at the top of the cliffs, or the hospitals. He knew from the reports of his former back-stair boarding companions that it was usually one of the three. He'd told Sarah about the incidents, but

Sarah had never experienced any of his nightmares before, and he could feel her shaking and her tears even as she tried to comfort him.

Once he was awake and recovering his own composure their roles reversed. Somehow, without any conscious movement, they had exchanged physical positions and Raymond was holding her close to his chest, stroking her hair and neck, whispering the same words that she had been using back to her. When they had both stopped shaking, were able to steady each other at arm's length, and look into each other's faces Sarah, eyes red, her hair matted from her tears, was just able to whisper "I thought I knew about battle, but had no idea of the horror. You poor, poor man!" She gathered him back close to her and held him gently, rocking the both of them. Raymond now had at least part of the answer of what his nightmare had been about, but didn't press for details. Sarah, still crying some, and not loosening her hold on Raymond, let out what was, unmistakably a small laugh. "You, Raymond McCleary," she continued, half laughing, half crying, "had better be glad of the thick walls of this old house and hope that your parents sleep with the door closed. They had to have heard you, but I hope your momma couldn't make out the words! What you were yelling, apparently to the men above and below you, and the names you were calling the Germans trying to kill you would clear out a bar full of sailors!" She gave another sobbing giggle. "You just might go down to breakfast and find a hunk of lye soap on your plate!"

Raymond laughed, too, as much out of relief that Sarah wasn't asking any questions as at her joke that he might have his mouth washed out. "You reckon?" he replied, pulling the both of them back into a more comfortable position, but being careful not to weaken the embrace that he knew he still needed, giving him the time to gather himself so as to hang on, just like the embrace more than one nurse in the hospitals had given him as he waited for the just-injected morphine to act. "Hang on, Buddy, hang on. It'll hit, Buddy, it'll hit," they'd whispered in the dim light of the ward. The nurses, he suspected, had been ordered, against their natural inclination but for the protection of their own sanity, to limit their words of endearment in such circumstances to that soldier's word, "buddy".

"Your bothers," Sarah said, finally able to sniff away her tears, "are going to get you out behind the barn and make you repeat the words they didn't hear clear -- I know they're big on that kind o' learnin'!"

"Maybe so," Raymond replied, sincerely hoping that it didn't come to that, or if it did, that they simply asked for a class in Army cussin', without reference to what they'd heard in the night.

As they grew more relaxed and shifted into a comfortable sleeping embrace, Sarah spoke slowly and with little emotion. "I used to dream, an imagined dream. There was a big plane flying at night, you could only see the dark silhouette against the stars. A glow would grow on one wing until it was obvious an engine was afire. At the instant that became obvious, the entire aircraft erupted into a fireball. That's when I'd wake up. I guess that's the story I made up about John's death. As soon as there was a problem big enough to see, just less than a second, John's mind was probably filled with starting the emergency steps he and his crew had been taught, then oblivion. All over before he'd had time to register fear, just adrenalin making him move and give orders without emotion in the instant before he died. Sometimes I'd cry, sometimes I screamed in warning, sometimes I'd have to sit on the balcony, smoke and drink liquor for a while, looking at the stars, before I could get back to sleep. Gradually, by about the time you showed up, I'd stopped screaming a warning, just watched and woke up. I'd even begun to go back to sleep without crying or boozing by making myself think of John and smiling. I don't know where I'll be now."

Raymond stroked her face and gave her a gentle kiss. "Same place, love, same good place," he tried to reassure her. "You've found peace, no reason for it to leave you now," he bluffed. "Thanks said, she kissed him back and fell asleep. "Finding peace," he thought. 'Will it ever happen to me? What will my dreams do to her?" He couldn't answer his own questions, didn't expect to. Exhausted, he, too, fell asleep, both of them resting well until daylight; the sounds of roosters, the kitchen and the smell of breakfast awakened them.

Questions of "how did you sleep?" were asked of no one. Talk was of the day's plan, a ride around the area with the young people for Sarah to see the sights and meet everyone's sweetheart. Reba, Father and the boys had been up at their usual hour and finished the feeding and milking before breakfast, so that all that remained to be done before they started was for Mary and Reba to change from their usual Saturday morning clothes into some glad rags for their beaux. Will and Charlie's work clothes were presentable enough, and dropping in on folks on a Saturday morning, there was no telling what they might get asked to turn a hand to. Dressed as they were, Raymond chuckled to himself, they likely wouldn't be asked to do much. If they got duded up, though, each of the four farmers they planned to visit would take advantage of the opportunity for some fun, coaxing them into helping with some bit of work wildly inappropriate for their dress.

Sarah had wordlessly shooed Mary out of the kitchen and helped Mother clear things up in the kitchen. When she finished she dried her hands and joined Raymond who was leaning against a post on the back porch, looking out towards the barn. "Show me the bees?" she asked, taking his hand.

"Sure. They're just outside the yard, around behind the smokehouse."

As soon as they were out of the yard and behind the building, out of sight and out of earshot, she stepped in front of him, turned to look him full in the face, taking both his hands. "Are you all right?" she asked, intent on the muscles of his jaw and his eyes "after last night, I mean."

"I'm the one that oughta' be askin' you about that," he replied. "I've had enough of those that they don't mean much once I'm awake and calmed down." Sarah could tell from his voice that he was genuinely concerned about her reaction, but she could see his jaw tighten just like it did if he tried to walk too fast, could feel the sudden rigidity of his arm muscles with her hands, and saw something in his eyes, not exactly fear, more of a haunted look. He was true in asking about her, but he was lying about being over last night. She knew that her question had, for a few seconds, returned him to the night before, maybe even to the climbing.

"I'm okay," she said, letting go of his arms, stepping back to his side, and taking his hand to resume their walk. "It was just a little startling, waking up like that," she lied, hoping that being out of Raymond's direct gaze and only touching his hand protected him from noticing. Inside she was still shaken by the horror of his cries, disturbed by the realization of how much more remained for her to hear on other nights, and frightened that the experience may have cost her the mastery of her own dreams.

"There they are," Raymond changed the subject and gestured towards three faded white beehives lined up along the fence in front of some tall pines" Used to be a couple more, but they've been pretty much on their own since Grandfather died and I'm not around." The deep boxes at the bottom of the stacks are for the brood nest and winter food and the shallower boxes on top are called supers, they're the ones you harvest honey from. Even in the cool of the morning, Sarah could see a few bees moving around on the boards projecting from the narrow slot beneath the each stack that was the bees' entrance. Getting closer, guided by Raymond to the side of the leftmost hive, she could make out two lines of bees in addition to the handful on the landing board. She could follow a row of three or four headed out in the same direction before the specks became invisible, and by looking where they disappeared see more dark specks transformed into a row of discernable bees returning from the same direction. Both lines moved steadily at about the same pace and interval, with only occasional pairs arriving or departing with closer timing.

"Amazing!" she exclaimed. "I've seen bee boxes before, but always at a distance. Like most folks," she said, putting her arm around Raymond's waist and grinning, "they're more interesting if you somehow get the courage to sidle up to them. Thanks for making me brave."

"You're welcome," he replied, remembering how many weeks of sitting in the store with Oscar in his lap it had taken him to sidle up to her.

They could hear discussion from the porch and heard William backing the Ford out of the car-shed, where they kept a tarp thrown over it to protect it from pigeons and independent-minded hens and roosters who avoided the crowd on the coop's roosts. Raymond and Sarah made it to the front of the house just as the car did. They piled into the back seat with Reba on the off side, Will and Charlie in front, with Mary in the middle. Quentin Baker's place was closest, so that's where they went first. As they pulled into the drive, Quentin was just coming out of the dairy, wiping his hands dry on the butt and thighs of his overalls, having just finished the morning wash-down of the place and equipment. Coming out into the bright sunlight, he squinted at them with the look of any farmer towards a carload of strangers coming to his land, but on recognizing the McCleary sedan his look softened, and when he saw Mary through the windshield, he burst into a grin, threw up his arms in greeting, and hollering " 'mornin' " hustled over to where they were stopped. Charlie had the door open, starting to get out, but Quentin just leaned in over him and gave Mary, who had moved as close to Charlie and the door as she could a big kiss. 'A special good 'mornin' -- to all of you!" he said, winking at Mary as she and Charlie finally made it out of the car. "I know that feller in the back," he said, nodding towards Raymond, "but tell me why there's a good-lookin' woman sittin' with him!"

"We think," Mary replied, "that he caught her up in Virginia and made her come visiting."

"'Or the other way 'round," said Reba. 'Sarah, this is Quentin Baker, one of Raymond's old classmates turned progressive dairyman"

"Pleased to meet you," Quentin said, receiving the same from Sarah, who was by now out of the car and coming around with Raymond to shake hands.

"Progressive dairyman and former owner of the pickup with the rooster seat! " Will made sure the introduction was complete. "Sarah, you owe this man more than you realize -- if he hadn't sold Raymond that truck, he'dve never left Guilford, would probably have turned preacher-man by now! They all laughed, including Quentin, although he didn't know the story of Raymond's prank that fuelled Will's joke for the others.

"Come on up and sit a spell," Quentin invited, so they all settled onto the front porch, arranged about like the McCleary's, a pleasant, shady spot out of the gathering morning heat. Raymond couldn't follow lot of the talk because, although he knew most of the names, he didn't know anyone's current associations, and more importantly, hadn't a clue where they'd been or what they'd done since he'd left for the Army. After about twenty minutes or so, Quentin, still under Mary's enchanted gaze, stood up, saying "I reckon you boys are in luck this mornin' -- I ain't got one lick of heavy liftin' to do." All of the McCleary brothers waited for what might come next -- it was a coin toss as to whether they would be dismissed or pressed to "light work" such as climbing onto the roof to grease the weathervanes atop each gable's lightning rod. "I'm just gonna have to run you-all off," Baker continued. "Saturday's my laundry and housekeepin' time, and if I don't get started soon I won't be finished in time to relax and listen to my favorite shows this evenin'. I've gotta' keep the pressure on Mary here to make up her mind to come take care of me!" He hugged her and laughed. The others laughed, too, as they got up to leave, but for all except Mary the laughter was a bit ragged because what Quentin had said was a little too close to the truth for her liking.

They piled back into the car, Will asking "Where to next?" as he backed up and turned around. "I guess Charlie's place is next down the road," Reba answered, referring, of course, to the Smith home farm rather than any property just acquired by her younger brother.

"Okay," Will responded, turning the wheels to the right and moving through the gears once they got onto the road, the expected cloud of dust rising behind them, marking their progress for anyone looking up from their work or out of a window.

"Charlie and his Dad," Reba said to no one in particular, but for Raymond and Sarah's benefit, since everyone else knew anyway, "have been renting more land each year, they're farming probably four times the acreage they had with just the family place." That increase in production, Raymond thought to himself, had been more than enough to make Charlie's labor classified as essential to the war effort and exempted him from the draft, so he at least knew what he'd been up to for the duration -- working his ass off. Old man Smith was a worker, didn't tolerate anyone who wasn't for help, and Raymond knew that whatever fortune may have been spent on upgraded equipment, whatever favors might have been called in or deals cut to make the scarce available, there'd been a heap of work to do, and Charlie had done his share. In fairness to both of them though, the older man would've worked beside him, hour for hour, and Charlie would have insisted on the going rate of pay, either in cash or percentage and received it without complaint. If it had been the latter Raymond knew he would have assumed his share of responsibility and his father would have proudly made him into a joint decision-maker. None of the old 'work for me 'till I'm gone, boy, and it's all yours' only to find out after the funeral that the cash'd gone to the church the old man had left lifetime rights to your stepmother and the remainder interest to both you *and* your sister. *"All yours,"* he'd said. Sharecropping for a few years for the old lady wasn't too bad, she'd been good about taking care of your dad, but after that, a de facto partnership with your triflin' brother-in-law. 'Unevenly yoked, unevenly yoked," folks would repeat the scriptural fragment and shake their heads. The savvy would do this in private amongst themselves after the next term of court, when the will came open for public inspection. The likes of the brother-in-law would see who was doing what jobs of work and talk among themselves at the feed store, just as brother-in-law started his engine and pulled off.

The farmyard between the Smith house and the first of the farm buildings was crowded -- old machinery that had been displaced in the sheds by better, and several old tractors and trucks serving as parts mines to keep their working counterparts in operation. Similar to a battalion motor pool in that respect. Hearing them turn off of the road, Charlie poked his head around the corner of the closed side of a machine shed, and recognizing them, then ducked back in before emerging, working the grease off of his hands and arms onto a 'first use' rag -- part of an old striped bath towel. "Howdy," he called as they got out, giving Reba a kiss and a sort of stand-offish hug because of the dirt on his clothes. "How're y'all doin'?" he continued," 'specially you, Raymond," hustling over to shake his hand.

"Gettin' by."

"Well, if you're gettin' by after all your troubles, I'd say you're doin' as good as any of us!"

"Charlie," Reba said taking Sarah by the hand and guiding her around to face him, "this's Sarah, Raymond's girl from up in Virginia. She's a storekeeper 'bout like Mr. Williams over on Greensboro Road, and took a few days to come down and meet us."

"Pleased to meet you," said Charlie, touching the brim of his farm-machine greasy cap.

"Me, too. What are you workin' on in there this mornin?"

"Tryin'," he grinned, "to get the corn-picker set up. When it was put on last year the implement fellows did it -- big difference me figuring it out the first time! Looks like you just roll the tractor into the notch in the middle jack 'er up and bolt 'er up -- that's all it looked like those fellers did, but it's not as easy for me."

"Let's see," Will offered. He'd heard from Reba about the eight-row picker, but had never had a chance to look at one to see how they were set up.

"Sure," Charlie replied, and they all trooped around to the open side of the shed, the men and Reba edging in alongside the tractor and picker, Mary and Sarah content to stay out front in the sun, talking between themselves rather than joining in the fragments of mechanical comments coming from around the two machines.

"They look and sound," Mary whispered, giggling, to Sarah, "like the story of the five blind men examining and describing an elephant!" Sarah laughed out loud and Mary joined in. The others looked up for a moment without any notion that they were the subject of the women's laughter, then returned to their poking and advising.

The eight-row picker, unlike its smaller predecessors, worked cornrows on both sides of the tractor. It had lots of smooth, flowing sheet metal surrounding the machinery that twisted the ears off each stalk, husked them, and threw them into a box-wagon behind the almost-hidden tractor. The smooth sides were necessary to slip by and avoid knocking down stalks in adjacent, unpicked rows, and the low beak in front, sweeping up alongside the front end of the tractor, separated the two rows on either side of the path of the tractor's tricycle front axle, guiding the cornstalks into the pickers collecting rollers. Smaller beaks that hit on either side of the three rows on the left and right of the tractor guided those stalks to their collectors, all ending up among the group of specialized rollers on each side that wrenched the ears from the stalks, rubbed the shucks from the ears, hurled the ears into the wagon, and let the mangled stalks and shredded leaves and husks fall into a rough windrow below. If it had been a poor season for hay, folks'd bale the fodder to feed to the cattle that winter. More often they just plowed it back into the field the next time they worked ground.

The Smiths figured that their best tractor could handle the eight-row picker, taking into consideration its age and the drawbar horsepower claimed by the manufacturer's engineers and the power requirements specified by the harvester maker's men, subject, respectively, to over-and understatement and the fact that they used both ear and shelled corn for feeding and sale. Corn pickers could be had with or without an internal sheller, and they figured that if they got a machine without a shelling train, there wouldn't be any difficulty with power.

Shelling what corn they needed wouldn't present a problem. They'd bolted two old hand-cranked shellers, the kind with two protruding turned wooden handles sticking out of each end of the wooden case so that they could be carried by two men, like a short-coupled corpsman's stretcher, to the barn floor between the wagon drives; had a bigish electric motor that they'd scrounged somewhere long ago knowing that it'd eventually be of use; pulled the cranks off of both shellers, moved the flywheel on one to the opposite, outside end of the shaft; bolted a pillow-block mandrel to the floor parallel to the shafts of the shellers; and did considerable calculatin' to arrive at the right sizes for the six pulley-wheels belted together to have enough torque that the thing wouldn't stall out. Made a hinged chute that'd lay level with any wagon bed so that the man up there was scoopin' ears not lifting them up and throwin' 'em in; and they had rigged a foot-operated kill switch for the man on the bagging end so that he could stop the whole deal to change sacks. Couldn't scoop enough corn into it to fast enough to drag the speed down more'n about a quarter and they both grinned like Cheshire cats when they used it.

"I think we've got it," Sarah and Mary heard Charlie Smith call out. They moved into the shade of the shed and saw one person standing at each of the four attachment points, a screw jack blocked underneath each one. "Reach around through the frame and slip the bolts through, I want the nuts and washers on the outside where I can get to 'em. Twist 'em on finger tight, please, I'll pull them down after I get the drive belt over the pulley." All of the workers came out into the sun, squinting, dusting their hands together, and taking turns wiping smudges of grease off with the old towel.

"Charlie," Reba announced, "was just being himself, trying to do everything by himself. When he went from jack to jack making adjustments, the other three just shifted off. When we brought 'em all up together, well it was smooth!"

"I'm guilty, " Charlie replied, continuing, "those two fellows from the implement place must've done it so often that they could each work one to a side, lining up two plates." He walked a few steps, hitched himself up onto the bed of an empty hay-wagon, patted it with his hand. "Come on over here and sit a spell," he said, and then concentrated on pulling out a bright bandana handkerchief, first to polish his eyeglasses, then to wipe his brow and finally, blow his nose. The others followed him over, and just as he had backed up against the wagon, pushed down with the heel of their palms to hoist themselves up, then scooted back until the steel-rimmed edging plank was comfortably behind their knees, their weight on the smooth wagon-bed. "I'll make it easy on everybody and be nosy," Charlie said, handkerchief safely back in his pocket. " What's your story, Sister Sarah, how'd you get mixed up with Raymond? Smith wasn't a churchman, but sometimes his Dunkard ancestors' form of address surfaced in his conversation. Sarah told the tale, used to doing so by now, assisted by the fact that Reba had, at some point, explained Raymond's reasoning in looking for an oil-delivery job to Charley. She didn't go into the part of her story that dealt with her marriage and John's death, and none of the others mentioned it. So far as Charles Smith knew, she and Oscar had simply dropped from the heavens into the rocking chair and behind the counter of the Westview store.

"'It is," she finished up, "more pleasant being a storekeeper now that the war's over. You don't have to listen to an awfulized version of the news you heard on the radio at breakfast every time the little bell over the door tinkles and someone new comes in. That, and the ignorant haters, especially the ones with no dog in the fight -- no family in risk of danger -- who'd come in ranting about the damn Japs or the worthless French. Now," she laughed, " they're reduced to complaining about the weather as though they have fields of crops in, when in fact they're too triflin' to set out a row of onions -- I know 'cause they buy big ones from me!"

"I met a few of that kind, too," Reba's Charlie said. "Them, and a few with boys in the service," he took off his glasses and studied them as he continued," they didn't like me bein' at home instead o' the Army. Got called everything but a gentleman more than once by both kinds. What you call the haters, I'd say to them 'I'm feedin' folks, what the hell do you do except blow wind?' and walk off. The others, I'd say "yes, mam," or

"yes, sir", tell 'em polite that I could respect their feelin's, ask about their sons, and explain about growin'
food. Most of the time we'd end the conversation
friendly, although there were a couple of times when
someone'd just gotten a telegram when that just
couldn't happen. I still feel bad about those."

"You don't have anything to apologize for,"
Raymond said quietly, but loud enough for everyone to
hear. "Nothin' except havin' good sense. When I went
down to sign up there was a bunch of us joking and
shoving, like after a ball game. Some damn joke. There
was even a guy with a bad eye, been hit with a rock
when he was a kid. He got someone further up the line
to tell him the passing row of letters on the eye chart,
then rattled 'em right off when it was his turn, acted like
he'd got one by the principal back in school -- I don't
want to know what happened to him."

"Grandfather, " Will replied, "said after you
left that the same young-buck craziness happens with
every war, that when one got started a young man was
better off if he was overworked and back in the sticks,
that then he'd have the counsel of old men and plenty of
time when he was working tired to consider things.
Grandfather laughed then, and allowed that what he'd
been saying didn't really protect a young man at all, because old men have remained silent about the truth of
war for so long that they are incapable of expressing the
horrors they may have experienced. The young men
remember the stories that had been easily told and admired and if those bits of glory were in a young man's
mind, especially if he and the mule are both tired and
there's a third of the field left, the easy stories are all he
knows and pretty quickly soldiering gets seen as the

easier thing. After that, it don't take long for the easy to become right, patriotic, and Christian, and he's gone."

"Never heard that one," Raymond said. "As always, Grandfather didn't talk unless he knew what he was talking about." As he'd been listening to his brother, Raymond had been thinking how true the 'lifetime of silence' was. There just weren't words to convey the images, feelings, smells, and states of mind running through his head. The old men had kept silent all their lives because no words came forth with the memories, and for the lucky ones, the memories faded. Nothing, he thought, was fading for him. If anything, each dream built on the last. Like a spasm in his leg, he'd get a sense of what was coming, recognized it when it hit, and was left, weakened, with the trigger set, a background sensitivity for the next thought , dream, or 'okay boys, here it comes' over which he had no control.

All that thinking on Raymond's part took no more than an instant. As he was finishing, Mary was saying "Come on y'all. Off the wagon and into the car -- we've got more places that Sarah has to be shown off." Being only a dirt tractor-path and wire-fence from the barnyard, no front porch or yard gate to pass, and no older folks being around, their leave taking, while genuinely friendly, was much shorter than most in the South.

"My turn," Charlie announced as they settled into their seats and Will backed around. "On to introduce Sarah to Liz Poteat!"

"Poteat?", Raymond half-said, half-asked. "That sure ain't no Scotts name."

Mary was quick to needle Charlie, speaking right away, "Well, you know they got their indentured servants from most ANYWHERE back in colonial times."

Will didn't let up the pressure, "Nothin wrong with havin' 'dentured servitude, in your background. There was that time they say that the McLeod on Skye got behind on keepin' up the island and sold a boatload of low grade McLeod's, McCrimmons, and McCaskils to North Carolina. I'd bet that those Poteats, their people got away from Oglethorpe down in Georgia and ran north!"

"Oh," Charlie moaned, shaking his head like a schoolmaster with a room full of dunces. You all know that there's Poteats all over both Carolinas, descendants of French Huguenot dissenters who wanted religious freedom."

"We accept your explanation about four generations of interbreeding with the rest of us rough lot spreading them around, Charlie," Reba said in her best, even, mock-serious tone. "But I want to hear you, Miss Elizabeth, or either of her parents explain one point of disputed theology that I can verify in the Encyclopedia Britannica over at the library. Do that and I'll say ' 'nuff'. Otherwise I'm with those who hold that not many of our ancestors bought a boat ticket over here!"

"I'll see what we can do, sister, see what we can do." Charlie turned to look out the window, effectively ending a line of conversation that wasn't going his way.

By that time they were at the Poteat farm. It was almost noon, dinnertime, Sarah thought to herself.

Showing up unexpectedly at this hour would certainly be rude, so she figured there'd been more scheduling behind this outing than it had seemed when they'd left. As they pulled up to the white picket fence surrounding the small dooryard, she saw a tall brunette that she assumed was Elizabeth, followed by a couple of youngsters, come out of the front door, across the porch and out to the gate, which they unlatched by lifting off what was either an old maul-ring or the end of a wagon-hub draped over the point of one picket of the fence and one of the gate. Heavy and unstable enough that only a barnyard master could nose it off! Charlie was at the gate, appropriately affectionate, when Elizabeth made it through behind the youngsters. "So you did get the whole day off!" she said as soon as she was released enough to resume normal breathing.

"Yep. Daddy said that there wasn't time enough to do introductions at four farms without a holiday. "Nothin', he said, that couldn't wait 'till Monday 'cept milkin' and feedin'", which we'd do on each weekend anyway."

"Hello!" said Sarah, who somehow found herself next in line behind Charlie. "I'm Raymond's girl, from up in Virginia." She looked around, a little nervously, for Raymond. Somehow he was at the back of the line instead of with her.

"Hey, 'Lizabeth," he called, craning his neck around his brothers and sisters and waving his cap.

"Good to meet you, Sarah," responded Elizabeth, waving, at the same time to Raymond, then continuing "good to see you all! Come on in, the table's already set for dinner." They followed through the gate and up the path to enter the house, trailed by the children, the smallest and slowest of which was last and stretched tall to hook the gate with the heavy ring. You learned young, on a farm, to close gates and to latch 'em.

Inside things were set up and done a bit different from at the McCleary's. There was dining room with a long table set for them off of the kitchen, with a smaller table in a bay jutting out into the screen porch for the children, who found their places without interrupting their constant stream of jokes and teasing. Mr. Poteat, a man with a smaller build than most farmers, but looking like he was all gristle, rose from his seat at the head of the table where he'd been reading the newspaper. Folding the paper and putting it behind him on the seat of his chair as he stood, he spread his arms wide, looked over his glasses, slid down on his nose for the small print of the classifieds, and said, very loudly, 'Welcome, welcome!"

Mrs. Poteat, nearly a head taller and a handsome woman, was in the doorway to the kitchen, aproned, with her hair up. "Yes, welcome!" she echoed, "find seat, dinner's ready." Elisabeth slipped into the kitchen after her mother and each emerged with a steaming dish in hand. Two trips and they were finished and found their places. At that point silence fell and Mr. Poteat delivered a prayer only slightly longer than Mr. McCleary's. He, apparently, was either more particular or had a memory that focused on religious matters and had not made Raymond's father's abbreviations to the previous generation's standard. Looking up, he gave everyone a wicked wink and asked Charlie to please sort out who wanted iced tea, who wanted water, and provide it from the pitchers on the sideboard. Dinner was cold roast beef, cornbread, mashed sweet potatoes and sauerkraut. French Huguenots, Raymond thought to himself, ate right much like Scotts highlanders and German Drunkards after five or six generations in the South. The first round of conversation was the same telling of Raymond and Sarah's stories, demanded wherever they went, going a little easier now as the other family members took on the telling of one bit or another, so that the two of them felt less like they were having to give testimony for either the court or the congregation. After a spell of eating, the second round of talk was complementing Mrs. Poteat on how good the food was, especially the cold sliced roast beef, eaten with a generous amount of home-ground horseradish "So much easier than when I was a girl," Mrs. P. responded, continuing, "electric deep-freezers let you plan and fix what you want rather than needing to eat what you have. Back then unless you had family of biblical proportions on both sides within riding distance, ready to share a beef when butchered, you had to belong to a 'beef company', a group of farmers large enough to use a whole cow divided up among them before the meat spoiled. Each farm took their turn slaughtering about once a month, with some of the others helping with the work, all according to the rotation someone had worked out. The only way we had to keep fresh meat cool was to cover it in buckets and lower them down into the well, and we ate beef three meals a day to get through it before it spoiled. A few people had ice-boxes like folks in town used, but since you couldn't get ice delivered if you weren't near the railroad, prosperous folks had to burn oil lamps with one end of those chemical-filled Crosley IceyBall coolers in their metal chimneys, the other end stuck into the ice side of the box, with rags stuffed around the pipe connecting the two balls to keep the cold in through the notch that had to be cut in order to close the door. Easier than hauling buckets up from the bottom of the well, but they still had to eat about as fast as we did."

"Good thing I rescued you from back in the sticks, dear," Mr. P replied, "we were able to keep our buckets cool in the trough in the springhouse," the last delivered with another wink.

"I," Elizabeth said, "am just glad that you got electrify before you got me!" Everyone had a good laugh on that one, and continued eating.

The springhouse that Mr. Poteat mentioned, now greatly supplemented by a second, larger building with a much deeper trough was central to the success of the farm because the water was so cold and steady flowing that the tough provided a milk cooler every bit as good as Quentin Baker's, just not as convenient or as easy on a man's back. Elizabeth's brothers, the fathers of the children at the table, were the third generation to manage the Poteats' successful dairy operation, but it was all old-fashioned, father and sons milking by hand twice a day, carting the cans to the milk house below the spring and lugging them to the truck that picked up every other day. They had improved things to the extent of cutting and gravelling a narrow extension of the lane to the milk house, so that they didn't have to cart the cans a second time, just grunt them onto the truck once it edged in. The truck driver didn't like getting slapped in the back of the head by low hanging limbs and shrubbery while straining to check his mirrors as he backed in, and had learned to make sure that his wheels were dead straight when he stopped at a memorized spot so that he could just ease back blind until he felt his wheels leave the new gravel and hit the edge of the concrete slab that kept the ground outside the door from turning into a mud -hole. That wasn't going to work when the dairy marketing co-operative got a bigger truck. A lot of things were going to have to change in order to make the farm successful for a fourth generation, and change if Charlie McCleary was going to join in and keep Elizabeth in her extended family.

The children, not spending as much of their time talking as the grown-ups, finished eating first, asked to be excused from the table and were. It was quieter in the room after they left. "Raymond," Mr. Poteat began, and Raymond knew exactly where he was headed, "how's that leg of yours doin'?"

"I'm gettin' by. Good days and bad days, but there were a lot of men hurt worse'n me -- he thought about the burned tankers -- and a lot of guys who didn't make it, so I don't complain." Raymond then went on to explain how he'd set his sights on a job where the truck loaded and unloaded itself, and gave a brief account of how things had fallen into place up in Virginia. "A real run of luck," he concluded, "topped off with finding Sarah." He reached down to the edge of the tablecloth and gave her hand a squeeze, the two of them smiling and looking into each other's eyes.

"Sounds like you made the plan work," Mr. Poteat observed. A bit of a pause and he went on, "Let's hope that you can hold up 'till you drive enough miles in the mountains to think a way through to something lighter."

"Maybe assistant clerk in a country store," someone chimed in, bringing on general laughter. "We," someone else piped up "know where you might get hired!" Raymond blushed and looked down as the laughter gave way to Will's beginning efforts at getting the group up from the table and headed off to the Rogers place.

Mr. Poteat had paid him a complement for thinking through the oil-delivery job, but Raymond also took the caution in his suggestion that he use his driving time to think out the next move. Raymond had seen lots of men growing up who worked hurt. His father and Mr. Poteat had no doubt worn their bodies out to the point that every task was done with some degree of pain to which they had become accustomed, denied, or stoically accepted and forced out of their consciousness. Reminded again that at twenty he was an old man, worn to the point of having to watch out for himself, but in other respects perhaps a bit wiser.

The Rogers' place wasn't too far off, a couple of miles through the pine woods that, like the McCleary place, opened onto broad pastures and a small amount of cropland. Most of Mr. Rogers' living, and a good deal of his passion was in polled Herefords, light red beef cattle with white faces, a little white on the belly and legs, a white bush on the swishing end of the tail and most importantly, not a trace of horn. Easy-tempered and productive, the breed was the darling of the cattle-men over at the North Carolina State Agricultural and Technical College and Rogers probably made more from the sale of brood stock and young bulls than he did on steers and culled heifers that he fed out for beef.

The house at the Rogers place was small and old, but had an unusual feel of elegance. It was set on brick foundation piers, no cellar underneath -- a dog after a cat could run clear under. The front porch was hardly big enough for four chairs, and the exterior chimneys were stepped out towards the flue, free from the house as they went above the smoke-shelves of the upstairs fireplaces, a bricked gable in them and the wall shedding the rain, then stepped out again half a brick's width one course at the top so that any rainwater hitting the top bricks dripped free rather than running down through the mortar joints. The eaves were decorated with what folks called 'dental work', little blocks of wood spaced like equally gapped teeth all around the house, just where the soffit-board met the wall. The shade in the yard was beneath several enormous magnolias and the lane was mostly lined with ancient crepe-myrtles, with younger cedars having been set to fill the gaps. There was a well with a pulley, rope and bucket out back, but when you looked in to see the reflection of your face against the sky, the picture had a dark line poking slightly into the edge -- the ell of the pipe that led deep to the brass-screened foot-valve that supplied the pressure system for the kitchen, bath, and stock-tank. The electric pump was covered by a chest-like box on the back porch to keep its noise outside and the tall cylinder of the pressure tank and smaller electric water heater took up a good bit of the old pantry that had been turned into the bathroom. Given that the power did go out sometimes there were still hand pumps by the well and in the kitchen, the one at the well with a diverter valve that shut off the spout and sent water into the stock-tank line, the other with a valve and line to fill the reservoir of the wood range rather than emptying into the kitchen sink.

The Rogers' family story always came around to the War. *Their* Major Rogers had been wounded badly enough in the first of the fight at Chancellorsville that he was invalided back home, but his real distinction was that he was mentioned in dispatches to Richmond as having volunteered to give up his place in one of the few proper ambulances leaving the field when word passed from the line that General Stonewall Jackson was being brought in, wounded. Not many could top that, especially when casually and humbly dropped in amongst accounts of his and other ancestors' experiences in the fighting and wartime privations on the farm.

This time everyone gathered in the parlor, the right-hand downstairs room of the two-over-two house. Mr. and Mrs. Rogers settled into their accustomed overstuffed chairs on either side of the radio, each flanked by a small table overflowing with preferred reading material and set up with a bright floor lamp. The others filled up the remaining seats of the modern, plush, suite of furniture then drew rush bottomed, plank bottomed and split-bottomed chairs from the edges of room to complete the circle. Depending on a person's build and the maker's design the dragged-out chairs afforded varying degrees of comfort, and there were a few surreptitious exchanges as everyone got settled. Mixed as all the furniture in the room was, it was clear that all but the newest was craftsman made and equally certain that the assembled legs and feet had never touched the floor of another dwelling.

Mrs. Rogers made the expected offer of refreshment, and Will and Molly were sent back to the kitchen. As they were coming back Mr. Rogers rose, allowing that it was right early in the day, but since it was Raymond's homecoming and his Sarah's debut, that the offer extended to drink of liquor if anyone cared for some. He opened a breakfront cupboard and passed around liberal portions when requested, some of which were sipped neat, others weakened with careful transfers from the small water pitcher brought in with the glasses. Raymond was enormously grateful and noted that the door to the cabinet was left open, the bottle on the breakfront's ledge. "To Sarah and Raymond!" Mr. Rogers proposed, and all raised their glasses and responded, then drank. With the burn in his throat, the pain in Raymond's leg and the sense of unease that had been growing all day began to subside.

Starting out, someone got Raymond to tell his story, as he had seemingly countless times over the last few days. Sarah's story was next, then Will and Mollie's, told for Raymond and Sarah's benefit. Mrs. Rogers skillfully wove the Rogers history in with the other stories, although given the context of battle wounds and keeping a general store stocked during rationing it wasn't a very hard task. Sarah noticed that although the stories dealt with the Rogers clan, Mr. Rogers hardly said a word. Did some nodding in agreement and gave a couple of misplaced details, but didn't say much else. Mrs. Rogers was the spokeswoman, but of her husband's family history. What, Sarah wondered, of her side of the house, if all she spoke of was his as if it were her own?

Raymond had always known that Mr. Rogers did a bit of surveying, but was intrigued to learn that Will had become his rod and chain man -- Will hadn't mentioned it.

Mr. Rogers got up, motioning to Raymond to follow. "The surveying, now that's something about the family that's more than stories. Each generation since the boundaries of this place were first staked out, one of the men has done it. If he sticks around, Will'll either have to change his name or get Mollie interested enough to crawl through the brush! This," he pulled a tripod topped with a wooden instrument, both dark with age and scarred from usage. "was my grandfather's.' " It was a simple transit, two columns with sighting slots on either side of a rotating ring above a compass with a black-and-white card noting a mariner's eight points. "The old people," he explained ," worked by making calls according to a natural feature such as a stream or tree and a cardinal or quarter direction, some achieving a higher order of accuracy with the addition of a sailor's 'by north' or 'by south' to the call." Well made for its time, the compass had a lever to lock the needle, with leathers on both the inside and outside of the case to keep the dirt out, still supple -- a good seal. A hand-forged chain hung from a hook on the wall, many of its hundred long, hand-forged, pencil-thin links worn and repaired. "My learnin' started with pullin' and pinnin' that chain as soon as I was big enough !" he laughed and recited," twenty-five links to a rod or pole -- that's sixteen and a half feet -- four rods to a chain, eighty chains to a mile. By the book that works out to 7.92 inches for each odd link I counted and called for Granddaddy, but I'm sure you'd not find much of a per-centage forged and worn to prcisely that length if you brought a sewing tape over here and checked 'em." He and Raymond paused to refresh their glasses as they returned to their chairs.

"All of Daddy's talk of links and chains," Mollie told the others, " always makes me think of Morley's ghost visiting Ebenezer Scrooge on Christmas Eve. It's more pleasant to go to sleep after an evening when he has had a victim to lecture about Herefords."

"Don't get him started!" her mother replied, everyone, including Mr. Rogers having a laugh.

"Guilty, guilty," he admitted. Spying Sarah's empty glass he said "y'all help yourselves" and gestured towards the breakfront's ledge.

As people shuffled around and passed glasses Will spoke up. "I'm not put off by the idea of chains like Molly. I enjoy the work, but if I had to pull an actual chain all day, I'd dream that I was one of those poor fellows on the road crew from the county farm, under the gun of a fat, tobacco dribblin', unsympathetic deputy, shackled to the long chain! I'll stick to the hundred-foot Stanley tape and the scale-bench, thank you. All I dream about then is Mollie." More laughter and a happy blush on Mollie's cheeks.

"I know what a steel tape is," Raymond said, "but what's a scale bench?"

"It's an old flat-bottomed kitchen chair with the back cut off," Will answered pausing a bit to see if he could get a response from Raymond, but Raymond didn't rise to the bait. "Really," he continued, "that's what we use, although I guess you could pay a heap for one with an instrument maker's name stamped on top. Mr. Rogers sets his transit over the last working stake   with the plumb bob, and I walk out following his directions unrolling tape as I go. He hollers for me to stop and hold the target rod vertical according to the level vials on two sides, and I slide the target to where he reads it clear to get his bearing. The bench has a three-or- four inch hole in the center that he can see the stake and use the plumb bob. The bench lets us get better line measurement than a chain or the tape by itself. He sets the legs steady and puts a foot on the back rung for me to pull against, then hooks one end of a good-quality spring scale on the right nail head to place its other hook between the plumb-bob and stake, then hooks the end of the tape on that hook and calls for me to draw up some slack to hold it there. Next, he uses a short tape to measure down from his line-of-sight to the hook and calls that number to me so that I know how many inches down from the target to hold my tape against the pole and increase the tension while he reads the spring-scale. The tension to level depends on how many feet of tape are out, he's got a table copied out in India ink and shellacked over on the bench, and tells me when to stop pulling. I call the distance I read to him. There's a ruler under a couple of easy stops screwed to the bench that he slides up to measure how far the scale hook has pulled out from the plumb- bob weight. He adds what the ruler tells him to the tape length I call, and writes the length of our horizontal line in his notes. While I'm still holding tension, he re-checks his plumb with the stake and his image with the target. If they're still on point he calls "clear." I ease off so that he can unhook and roll up the tape through a clean cloth and set and number the next stake as he marks down the stake number and heading in his notebook and moves forward. It's the same all the way around, all day!" Will grinned at Mr. Rogers with the last bit.

"All day, hot or cold, but not in the rain," Mr. Rogers agreed with a chuckle, "Good explanation, William, good explanation."

Charlie stood up thrusting his left arm out so that his watch was evident beyond his cuff. "I hate to break things up, but it's gettin' on towards chore time." There was murmured agreement, drinks were finished, someone spirited the glasses back to the kitchen, and Will, having taken the opportunity to linger a moment in the hall with Mollie, was the last back to the car, where Reba had taken his place behind the wheel. As they pulled onto the road heading home Raymond expressed his admiration for what William was learning.

"I'm getting the simple stuff, and if I'm lucky enough to stay on, I'll eventually get the complicated things. What I'm not sure about ever getting that special sense that Mr. Rogers has. He can tell which grown tree was the 'pointer' in an old survey call and have the lines close. He can look at the scattered stones near a corner and tell where the 'rock pile' in the call is when all I see is piles of rocks!"

"You'll get it," Raymond reassured him. "Just like we all bent a lot of nails 'fore we got so that we could drive 'em."

Reba pulled in at the house long enough to let everyone out, then drove the car out to the shed. While she was doing that the others changed whatever clothes they needed to, then headed to the kitchen or the barn.

"Come on," Raymond said to Sarah," you can help me do the old man work -- gathering the eggs and throwing down some scratch to tempt the hens in so we can shut them up, safe from any fox easin' by." They went out the kitchen door and Raymond pulled his cap down at exactly the right angle as he grabbed the egg basket from its nail up by the eaves. Bigger than a picnic basket but not as large as a peck, it was made of welded steel rod with gaps just below egg size (you had to use a tin pail for a while after the chicks turned white and you were getting tiny pullet eggs), all but the swinging handle dipped in what must have been a nasty vat of liquid red rubber which left a cushion on each rod to protect the eggs, which worked even if the basket was full, given that eggs are designed to be piled and pushed against each other under a brooding hen. They went out past the smokehouse to the coop, which was actually a pretty fair purpose-built structure. Broad eaves on a shed roof with the high side and its windows aimed southwest to catch the heat from the afternoon winter sun and as varmint tight as could be accomplished by repeated patching with old license plates when a rat-hole appeared down low. The hens knew the drill and hustled in the main door around Raymond and Sarah's feet or ran up the plank ramp to their usual entrance, anxious to get their share of the several handfuls of grain that he scooped from the covered barrel just inside the door and flung across the floor. "How 'bout stepping outside shooing in any stragglers and dropping their door, please," Raymond instructed Sarah. She had already turned and started to tend to the task -- it wasn't as though she'd never been in a chicken house before! Raymond had to give her bee tutorials, but she was about as knowledgeable as he in other farm matters. One row at a time they unlatched and folded down the shutter covering the front of the nest boxes -- the hens jumped in and out through the half-side at the rear of the box under the floor of the roosts. The sound of thrown scratch had brought all but one or two hens off of their nests, so that the egg gathering went quickly, with only a minimum of cajoling and feeling under hens to see if they really had laid an egg or were just getting in the mood to.

"Whatcha' think of today's parade?" Raymond asked as he pointed to the rooster in his spring-through fall preferred evening spot on an odd beam at the top of

the corncrib. A few more weeks and he'd be marching
up the ramp to share in the communal warmth of the
coop's roost.

"Didn't much like Quentin Baker -- I hope
Mary sees what a taker he is and decides to wait for a
better man. Reba's found someone willing to accept her
on her terms. The boys, perhaps wisely, seem to be
looking as much for families as wives. Lord knows the
hours I've been caught behind the store-counter listening to complaints about triflin' in-laws!" She giggled,
"it'd be a hoot to line up the three or four I've heard described as the laziest men, white or black, in Augusta
County and pick the winner! What do you reckon the
prize would be?"

"Oh, that's easy to figure. The winner would be
awarded the stepladder he borrowed from his brother-
in-law six months back, and the other contestants would
be given the consolation of a chew from someone else's
plug and a pull from yet another man's bottle!" He
latched the coop door, glanced over to confirm that the
hens' door was shut tight, picked up the basket of eggs
and they headed back to the house. As he had noted before, Raymond was reminded that a principal disadvantage of walking with a stick was the inability to hold
your girl's hand if you were carrying anything. Sarah
was pretty consistent in compensating by resting her
hand on the small of his back, as she was doing now.
Not quite an arm around the waist, but that was an im-
possibility given the distance imposed by the stick's
path on one side and the load on the other. It was suppertime when they reached the kitchen, so they put the
eggs in the pantry to be washed after the dishes were
cleared away, washed their hands and joined the others
around the table.

Raymond added what positive things as he could about Quentin Baker to the flow of conversation out of deference to Mary's feelings and was genuine in his praise of his brothers' and sister's current choices, and made sure that his parents understood his admiration for the strides William was making as a budding surveyor. Their interest proved his suspicion that Will hadn't told them much about it, and he could tell that they were pleased. Charlie, of course, had to make sure that Sarah knew exactly what condition the Barrelnose had been in when Raymond had bargained with Quentin and brought it home. Raymond had already told the tale on himself in order to explain the bright spot on the seat, but Sarah played along and laughed as if she'd not heard a word of it before. Mother announced that she wanted to show them off to the church folks next morning, suggesting whose extra shirt, tie, and jacket he could borrow if he hadn't brought church clothes, which he, intentionally, had not, in hopes of avoiding the occasion. Mary and Reba told Sarah to come with them once supper was cleared away and they'd get her sorted out.

"Don't y'all worry," Will said with wink at Raymond and Sarah, "I'll be driving and'll lay around the curve 'till I hear the first peal of the bell, then park close to the door like I ought to for a fellow with a bad leg so's to get away quick after you shake the preachers hand at the door and lie to him -- you'll have to -- about how good the sermon was." Everyone laughed, including Father, who they all knew would not be participating, as he would spend the hour in his favorite chair or tinkering with something or other about the place.

"If you get surrounded and can't make it from the preacher to the car," Charlie's voice betrayed his growing enthusiasm, "I'll rescue you. I'll rush up, worried-like and remind you that just when we'd passed the pastures on the way to church we'd seen that the dairy bull'd gotten through the fence into the section next to the stock bull, that they'd seen each other and started some bellerin' and pawin' and that we'd trusted the Lord for an hour and forty minutes, but there were limits to trust and that we needed to get home and keep 'em from tearing up a second fence!"

"Give'em your best tired-farmer look instead of a worried look," Father added his view of what was likely to be most effective. "Worried look might not make 'em believers, what with young fellers always bein' worked up about one thing or another. Give 'em a face that lets 'em know that you've had a cold dinner and missed your nap before 'cause of those bulls and don't want it to happen again today"

"We can help you, Charlie," Reba added, "without lyin', if we all point out as we leave that it's true, that you do prefer a nap to associatin' with good Christian folks!" Mary rose to start clearing the table, and the rest joined her, all, including Mother, laughing at the plans for Sunday morning. Sarah retrieved the eggs and the market carrier, a wire and wood-slat openwork box with layers of slat trays to steady each layer of eggs, and she and Raymond sat at the table with damp cloths and wiped and packed the basket of eggs that they had gathered.

As his sisters carried Sarah off to hunt for a dress and his brothers and Mother settled around the radio in the sitting room, Raymond rinsed out his egg-cloth, re-dampened it to use it to clean his boots and stuck a couple of drinking glasses, budging, in either side pocket. He went upstairs, got his bottle of whisky, came down and ducked into the low closet beneath the stairs and retrieved the shoe-shine box from where it had lived for as long as he could remember, and joined Father, sitting in the dusk on the front porch. He set the box down, pulled one glass out, and half filling it handed it to him, receiving a wordless nod in acknowledgement. Sitting down in chair just on the other side of the small table he poured his glass and took a drink before putting both his glass and the bottle down on the table, bottle within his father's reach.

Raymond leaned forward, unlaced his boots and pulled them off to clean and polish them for church. As he expected, he'd hardly stated wiping the dust off when his father, with courtesy but evident amusement said "those're some right fancy boots you got there boy." He paused to see if Raymond was going to take the bait, but when he didn't, said "reckon you better tell me the story that goes with 'em, then." Raymond explained how he'd gotten the loggers boots cheap because none of the local farmers would buy them because of the ribbing they'd have to take from their buddies. They could've dealt with the gruff that high tops and slightly higher heels would bring, but none of them could face up to what they'd have to endure because of the kilties.

"Kilties." Father repeated thoughtfully after Raymond had finished the story but was still buffing with a rag. "What a strange little word for such a rough bunch of men to use!"

"I was surprised to learn it from an old man at one of the stores out in Highland who'd spent most of his life logging." Raymond replied, "Thought I was in for it the day he asked me if I knew the word for the fringes beneath the laces on my boots, but he just told me straight-up after I'd answered "No sir." The old man was real nice, and said that I'd stumbled onto just the right boots to protect my feet and ankles, climbing all over the tank truck and hose trays all day." "Just think," Raymond laughed "what those Augusta County farmers could have done to one of their own with that word!"

"About like your brothers would here, given a victim, "Father chuckled. "Think how long they've hung onto that pickup seat full of rooster-shit!"

Raymond wiped his hands on the damp cloth, folded the others into their box with the cans and took them stocking-footed back into the house, coming back out with his stick, which he'd abandoned earlier at the hallway cupboard after filling his hands and maneuvering out to the porch by gritting his teeth and leaning against the bannister's descending pickets and the front doorframe. Back out on the porch he raised the bottle towards his father, who held his glass out for a refill. He then filled his own, put the cork back halfway into its rim and sat down. They could hear snatches of the radio actor's voices interspersed with the rest of the family's laughter through the hallway, but sat contentedly, sipping and sharing silent company, looking out at the few stars becoming visible as the dusk deepened. In a bit Mr. McCleary spoke: "Raymond, you know that story you're fond of telling about when you were a little boy and you Grandfather showed you the bees in golden chains making wax for new cells?"

"Yes, sir," Raymond replied."

"I remember him telling me one time about
something similar but unsettling. I didn't see it, 'cause
as you know the bees have never gotten along as well
with me as they did with him, and I didn't work them
with him unless he knew there'd be a lot of heavy lifting. No need of lifting on that day -- it had been warm
in early spring, then it got cool and the clover was slow
in coming out, a couple of weeks after the locust bloom
fell, so that they only had little patches of this and that
to work, nothing you could call a honey flow. The clover came out, but then it got so dry that the clover ended before the thistles came into bloom. The bees were
hungry, and Grandfather was feeding them sugar-water
from those feeders made from upside-down tin-topped
jars with a couple of pinholes punched into the top fitted into wooden blocks that partially covered the hive
entrance so that only the bees from one hive could get
into the feeder -- the guard bees on the landing board
kept strangers from edging in from the side. Don't remember but three or four times in my life that the season'd been poor enough that he'd had to pull them down
from the top shelf in the shed except at the end of winter. He checked inside each stand as he refilled the
feeders, and told me that inside the strongest colony he
found a frame with a dozen supersedure cells -- queen
cells like swarm cells that you find every year on the
bottom of the frames and cut out to prevent swarming
or save to split a hive and get new stock -- spread high
across the face of the comb. They were, he said, draped
in two arcs like two strands of a necklace on the velvet
cushion in a jeweler's case. Strangest thing. It was the
strongest colony with the best-laying queen but the
stress of that season made the workers keep her crowded away from that comb so that she couldn't kill any

new queen that might emerge, and the undecipherable mind of the hive kept pushing them to build those cells, forced by their instinct to survive, to ignore the powerful scent of their own queen and try the only remedy they knew. Of course he had to cut them all out, and the thistle started to bloom before the bees rebuilt them. I guess it was just an example of how anything pushed too hard goes haywire -- automobiles, livestock, crops and trees, even men."

"Interesting, interesting and strange," Raymond replied, shuddering a bit inside because of those last two words, "even men". He was observant enough to recognize that he was more than a bit haywire, the way he woke up screaming, the way he looked at a room and the people in it, and the way he broke into a sweat and let the truck slow to a crawl if his mind wandered and he got to looking up at the rock faces as he drove through the mountains. "Never heard of bees acting like that."

"Well," Father responded, "'your Grandfather only saw it once, and he messed with 'em for a lotta years." They sat and rocked in silence a bit longer. The radio had been turned off and Raymond caught only the tone, not the word, of an occasional exclamation from the inside conversation, along with frequent peals of laughter. His family wasn't given to profound discussion, politics, religion, and such. In fact, one of their favorite topics consisted of wry examination of the otherwise unacknowledged antics of those who did. "Raymond," Father said unusually softly, "the only thing that your Grandfather ever compared those bees to were a few men he knew, or knew of, who couldn't find no peace after the War. He came home thankful to be home uninjured and focused on that until the Yankees left and the scallywags and carpetbaggers got voted out, then took up his normal place in the community. Those men who couldn't find peace within themselves weren't capable of that. A year after coming home one of them took off for Texas, hungry for the border fighting there -- nobody ever heard anything more from him. The second waited a couple winters before hanging himself in the barn. The third spent the rest of his life avoiding people and drinking himself to death. You seem to have been pretty successful in fitting into your community and don't seem to have problems dealing with folks, but you have nightmares and pain. Pain don't get easier as you get older. You drink right smart for that, but I don't see you mean or stupid. I'm frightened, Raymond, that you might end up like those men. Frightened and angry that I don't have any advice to help you."

"I remember hearing about those men, but never heard them described as 'unable to find peace after the war.' That's a good description of how I feel the day after a lot of nights and after some wool-gathering moments in a day. Frightens me too."

Raymond slept peacefully Saturday night, but it was Sarah's turn to dream, of a bomber, flying low, navigation lights blacked out, shutters over the waist gunners doors for a stateside transport run The gunners were probably asleep however they could jam their parachutes into a comfortable resting spot rather than looking out of the small window at the port wing. She could see a small reddish-yellow glow mid-outboard of the number two nacelle, invisible to the pilot, had he twisted around in that direction rather than staying focused forward. The glow intensified into flames extending back along the outboard side of the engine and started to trickle downward across the wing, like some weird leak both pushed and channeled by the wind. She had to watch the fire for an interminable length of time as the plane flew on, in her dream always remaining clearly in sight as though she were a powerless but entranced angel compelled to follow, knowing from the beginning what was to happen at the end, all the while understanding from the unwavering course of the aircraft that the crew was unaware of the fire. Eventually the flames reached the fabric-covered control surfaces along the back edge of the wing and flared up until they were consumed. Now aware, the pilot killed the engine and feathered the prop, struggling to maintain control with the remaining engines and only half of his ailerons. The fire now had the entire engine, melted through the wing, the fuel tanks exploded, a fireball burst from wing root to tip that illuminated the profile of the bomber's tall tail. The ship fell off, tumbling as the burning wing stopped producing lift; there was a second fireball from mid-fuselage; and a third when the starboard tanks went; after that it took only moments for the last, glowing fragments to drop from the sky, leaving only the stars. Sarah woke up shaking, terrified, but silent, not awakening Raymond. Her panic was heightened because she initially had no idea where she was -- a strange room, none of the familiar, mingled, odors of home above the store, and no dark shape of Oscar curled anywhere on the covers. She caught her breath, calmed down, eased one arm under Raymond's head and, rolled towards him, embracing him with the other. Comforted by his warmth and regular breathing she was soon able to go back to sleep, but not without shaking her head a bit and trying to laugh inside. "Helluva' note," she thought, "if it ain't him it's me."

Down in the kitchen next morning before break-fast Raymond had gotten his cap on at exactly the right angle and was halfway through the door to the porch starting to reach for the egg basket when he heard his father. "Hold on there, Raymond," he said, hurriedly standing up from the table, pushing his chair away with the back of his knees, gulping the last swallow of a cup of coffee, and wiping his chin on the back of his hand. "I'll steal the eggs from those old birds this mornin' -- you gotta save that shoe shine for the Christians.

"Thanks," Raymond replied, laughing. "Would-n't want them thinkin' less of the family."

"Yup," Father replied, "those old ladies have two lists, the 'good name' and 'bad name' lists that include everybody in the county, and I'd hate to have us go from head noddin' to head shakin' whenever we get mentioned." He got his hat and headed out to the chick-en coop.

Charlie and Will came down and disappeared to do the milking and minimum of feeding, looking over the stock in the pastures as they went to and fro, making sure that all was well there, nobody missing, limping, or just looking puny. Charlie's planned bull-pasture ruse had plenty of basis in day-to-day, hour-to-hour animal care.

The women had gotten half fixed for church when they first dressed and were therefore more fully aproned than usual as they got breakfast together before the men came in -- father had fixed the big pot of coffee when he'd gotten up at his usual, unspeakably early hour. He always said he figured he got a few extra hours outta' his life that way, and besides, the first cup of coffee tasted better than what was left when he came in from the barn. Eggs, bacon, and cornbread were ready by the time the men came in. Father said his usual grace -- no Sunday embellishment or reverent change in cadence -- and reports of the condition of hens, cattle, hogs, fences, and buildings were shared as they ate, mixed in with a discussion of who was planning to wear what and speculation over who was likely to be at church based on the week's worth of knowledge about who'd gone visiting and who'd been under the weather a short or long enough time that they might be staying home. That last bit was tricky, since some folks were known to drag themselves to meeting in hopes of divine intervention and a cure; some were known to milk an illness for sympathy, for which they'd have to show up to fully enjoy; some were willing to exchange indirect sympathy for either the convenience of staying home or an aggrandizement of their plight, 'so bad off she couldn't even make it to church two Sundays straight'; and those who'd only been sick for a day or two had to decide if they'd gotten well or were on a downhill slope, which, of course, made them run the risk of being branded as backsliders if they showed up, hale and hearty when the mail was put up at the Post Office on Monday morning. Mother truly enjoyed this convoluted set of weekly, wicked calculations. Mary and Reba found a superior sort of amusement in watching it unfold, usually laughing and pointing out the winners and the losers on the way home. Will and Charlie really didn't give a damn, used their time before and after services to joke with their buddies and sidle up to their girlfriends. Raymond and Father found the whole business tiresome -- another brick in the wall between his private beliefs and organized religion.

It didn't take long to clear the table and do the dishes. Everyone had plenty of time to get ready before Will brought the car around. Raymond, who had been talking with Will on the porch and had kept his seat turned his head towards the footsteps that he heard from the hall, and stood up as the screened door opened and the procession of churchgoers filed onto the porch. He turned towards them, removed his cap and waved it towards them in as much of a sweeping bow as could be managed by a man standing with the help of a cane. "My, my. You ladies do look fine!" Amid the murmured thanks he continued, "Charlie, you look pretty good, too, downright civilized!' Charlie gave an orangutan grunt and scratched under his left armpit.

"Drivin' that train to church?" he asked Raymond, pointing at his cap.

"A gentleman," Raymond replied, adjusting the cap to exactly the right angle, "never goes out without a hat."

Will, good to his word, lay back around the last curve before the church until the bell commenced pealing, then drove on, and pulled up in a spot near the door. As they got out, Raymond, with a wink and a grin at Charlie, pulled off his cap and tossed it onto the car seat. They fell into line behind the last few people waiting to go in, and were led to 'their' pew, the row where the family had habitually sat since anyone could remember, although there were neither pew-rents nor assignment in their denomination. They squirmed into as much comfort as the unpadded benches allowed, then after the preacher strode in, adjusted his papers on the top of the pulpit, rose for his opening prayer and the first hymn, identified for the congregation guided by the worn white-on black numbers on the cards displayed in ornate wooden frames above each front exit, this week's three hymns just above the tally of last week's offering.

There was a certain amount of rubbernecking going on, surreptitious efforts to get a look at Sarah, both by those who had heard of her visit and those taken aback by the number of people in the McCleary pew, usually populated by just Mother and one of the three children at home. Raymond responded to a good many slight nods of recognition and welcome before the congregation was seated, heads bowed for prayer. Probably because the preacher wasn't sure of Sarah's name, they didn't get prayed over, just greeted as "Raymond McCleary and his young lady" in the week's announcements, for which Raymond was thankful.

The day's scripture and sermon dealt with the story of Job. Raymond listened with polite attention, more than could be said for some of the dozing congregation and choir, but couldn't help but think back over having heard sermons on the topic before and his inability to come around to the preachers' conclusions that it explained how and why bad things happened to good people and joyful acceptance of whatever came along. Hard, he reasoned, to reconcile the New Testament's mostly loving and forgiving God from previous sermons with this Old Testament God who seemed to be pretty casual in attitude towards the suffering imposed and endured in the course of a barracks wager with Satan over Job's behavior. Coupled with this was the basic theological viewpoint that the Devil was not trustworthy, leading to the conclusion that there'd turn out to be a catch involved with the good things he offered in exchange for one curse. About all he came away with was a continued appreciation of the soldiers' profane stoicism, the farmers' eternal hope for a change in the weather, and the conclusion that no matter what happened, you could, if it gave you cold comfort, tell yourself that whatever happened was God's will. Raymond's final condensation of the whole deal was that a man had to bear whatever hardships presented themselves, curse as much as he needed to getting through them, but be careful to draw the line short of cursing God. He'd not compared himself with Job during the last couple of years, maybe because he'd started out as a dogface recruit rather than a fellow with wives, herds, riches and the leisure to look them over from the shade of his gourd tree. Caught up by green enthusiasm into something incomprehensibly beyond his control, he'd thanked his New testament God for the luck of making it onto the beach, up the cliff, the deflection of bullet and bone away from the artery in his leg, the appearance of the corpsman and the skill of every medical procedure after the first bloody "M" on his forehead. He for sure thanked him for Bill and Sarah.

The benediction was pronounced and everyone filed to the rear to pump the preacher's hand. He seemed genuinely pleased to see Raymond and meet Sarah. Once down the stairs, Mary, Reba, Molly and Liz crowded around them, making introductions and giving Sarah bits of information about folks. One of the fiercest of the matrons pushed her way in and announced "I'm Katherine Margaret Killian. Pleased to see that Raymond has a young lady."

"Sarah Thompson,'' Sarah replied. "Pleased to meet you. Such a lovely church you have here. Is your farm close by?"

"Yes, it *IS* a nice old church," Mrs. Killian replied. "I'm not a farmer," she continued, "I live in Guilford. My late husband, George, was president of the bank there, but we always stayed with this congregation, the one he grew up with, even after he sold his home-place to the neighbor, Mr. Baker. I understand that you and Raymond live up in the Valley of Virginia, where so many of those horrible battles were fought. Do you-all live near any of those places? "

Raymond and Sarah both winced inwardly at Mrs. Killian's ignorance. There had been famous battles in the Valley, New Market, Cedar Creek, and the countless small fights of Jackson's Valley Campaign, but nothing like the horrors of Sharpsburg, Gettysburg or the Wilderness. "We both live west of Staunton, in Augusta County, there wasn't heavy fighting there because both armies wanted to preserve the junction of the two railroads for their own advantage."

"Oh, I see," said Mrs. Killian, who drifted off to a knot of her own kind, frustrated that she could give no definitive report of the scandal of co-habitation. The young women continued visiting among themselves and Raymond excused himself to go and talk to Will, who had stationed himself behind the open driver's door of the car, looking anxious to leave. Raymond retrieved his cap from the seat and pulled it on at exactly the right angle, enjoying its relief from the noonday glare. He pulled out his smokes, offered one to Will, who declined, then lit up and leaned back against the front fender, looking over the gradually dispersing congregation. The older folks looked much older than he remembered them looking; his recognition of the identity of anyone under eighteen was at best an educated guess based on red hair or who they were standing with; and although he recognized former classmates here and there, he didn't feel like hiking around to shake their hands and meet their girls. No doubt some of them had been to war, but they stood so easy, looking relaxed and confident. Their engaging with others without any sign of vigilance gave him enough evidence that he knew that their wars had not been like his. He didn't want to repeat his story as he would be asked to in the course of each conversation, and knew that his return to work with Bill Riley, infused with the smell of petroleum, would be easier if he couldn't mull over the successes of contemporaries who'd sidestepped the war or had a 'good' one.

Before long Raymond saw Charlie approach the ladies, ready to tell his bull pasture story, and heard his laughter as he was told that it was unnecessary. The group then headed towards the car, Will holding the rear door open in his most deferential style when they approached. Everyone got in and seated with the decorum that he inspired, but as soon as they pulled onto the road Mary and Reba collapsed into rolling, tearful laughter. "The old biddies," Mary began, and started laughing again,

"Sent their champion." Reba completed her sister's sentence and then went on, "the formidable Widow Killian. 'Put Sarah in her place right now,' I'll bet that's what they thought. Not a chance in hell that they hadn't already figured out or been told that you two live in sin. Their game was to get an admission in order to stage a pubic denouncement to which the whole molting flock could shake their heads and cackle their agreement."

"Sarah, you were magnificent!" Mary had recovered her composure." Mrs. Killian was put seriously off balance when you implied that she was a mere farmer's wife -- hadn't you looked at her clothes and seen her polished Cadillac? Then you exposed her ignorance of the War, a subject she carefully avoids because she, like her late, banker husband, thinks it backward and not commercially important."

Reba took over again. "The sterling piece, Sarah, was your beautiful response "Raymond and I both live a little west of Staunton". It didn't give her the 'we live' that she wanted, and unlike some of the plain spoken farm wives she holds herself above she didn't have the courage to ask straight up if you two live together and took off to make what she could of your truthful answer. What a hoot! Now the rest of the birds will cackle behind her back about her failure to corner you."

"I can hear 'em," Mary speculated. "Old Killian sure didn't pick her for her brains," followed by a wink and "I'da just flat out asked her!" " Everybody was still laughing, even mother, whose fellow churchwomen were the butt of the joke as they passed the bull pastures, fences intact with the old fellows peacefully on either side of a big tree in the line. "Shame Charlie didn't get to tell his story," Raymond said, looking out the window. "Won't be wasted," Will replied. "I'll remind him how much he knows about bulls the next time we get a call that one of 'em's out, remind him as I'm handin' him the hammer, pliers and staple bucket." Everyone but Charlie laughed. As they headed in the lane he allowed as he could hammer staples and stretch barbed wire, but that if the weather was bad, he'd need a surveyor to show him the line. William winced but didn't bother to keep things going with a reply.

"I know," Mother said, "that if those fellows get to bullin' that both of you and your father will all be tending to it."

Will stopped at the house to let the others out, then drove the car out to the shed, parked it and pulled the tarp over. Quite a design, he thought to himself as he looked at the pigeon and rooster stains on its outer side. He grinned, sill thinking, but now that Raymond could certainly appreciate their work!

Back at the house everyone scattered to change into everyday clothes. Father, of course, was already, and remained, in his Sunday best, a newish pair of bib overalls ("overhalls" was how he said it) unstained and without tears from sharp bits of equipment, protruding nails or barbed wire, and his newest shirt -- presently red plaid flannel. "How'd it go?" he asked as the others filtered into the kitchen and adjacent sitting room.

"You should've come to see it." Mary answered. "Sarah was toe-to-toe with Mrs. Killian, and Katherine Margaret Killian was the one to back down. Turned absolutely speechless and fled to cover without having the grit to ask Sarah the question that brought her over to 'introduce herself ', whether or not Sarah and Raymond live together."

"Miz Killian speechless or even talking about something other than Miz Killian would be a sight to see", Father agreed. "What I don't go for is the whole bunch of 'em bein' so inquisitive about what a respectable war widow and a hard-workin' wounded veteran do of an evenin' two hunnerd and fifty miles away. Besides," he laughed, "all their children are grown up past danger of corruption by seein' two certified sinners who might visit twice a year. I think that they're jealous, and just look for evidence of young people bein' together because their imaginations are so dried up that they can't get the pleasure of wishin' it was them without the image of their victims in their heads."

"My!" Mary replied with a laugh. "I knew you didn't think much of that group of ladies, but had no idea you had it worked out so particular!"

"Did it this mornin'," Father beamed back at her. "Since the fightin' stopped, there ain't much on the radio on Sunday, 'cept radio preachers and they stop bein' amusement after just a few minutes."

The rest of the day was slow after the pace of the visit and the morning. Raymond and Sarah did just enough laundry to have clean clothes for their drive on Monday. Visiting all afternoon, with faces in the sitting room and kitchen changing as family members left and then reappeared after their Sunday afternoon naps.

Will and Charlie, emboldened by the passage of time and Raymond's success as a civilian became much more forward in asking him about his war experiences than they had been during the weeks he'd been at home before -- Father had probably warned them off , then -- and he tried to answer their questions as briefly as possible. He understood their curiosity, but it was not his favorite topic because he had to filter things as he put them into words. The questions about Army life and training were easy enough, but the questions about the battle his wounding, and the hospitals made him struggle to skirt around the things he usually tried not to think about. In one respect that wasn't so difficult, because what he usually tried not to remember was a feeling or an image, something visceral, not something he usually put into worded thought. If he listened closely to the question he could word the answer to answer it exactly, and then tag some sort of joke or bit of irony onto the end to ease away from the likelihood of a more difficult follow-on question. They wanted to know what the landing craft were like, and he was able to tell them that most, the Higgins boats, were plywood and vulnerable -- one reason silencing the cliff top guns was so important. He explained that the Commanders of the British SAS , Special Air Service, their equivalent of our Rangers, had prevailed upon their navy command, 'The Admiralty,' they called it, to provide steel landing craft for the Rangers, providing a bit more protection to keep their courage up on the way in.

His brothers wanted to know what sort of weapon he'd carried. He explained that as a climber he'd been given a choice of weapons, a standard Garand, a shorter, lighter carbine, or the even shorter Thompson. He'd chosen the Thompson figuring that it, and its vest of flat magazines, would be less trouble on the way up, and that it was unlikely that the Germans would be standing back, courteous-like, at distances requiring a rifle once he reached the top. He didn't explain that he knew that the grenades bulging in the baggy leg pockets of his combat trousers were likely to be the real deciders up there, and that if he needed a rifle, there'd be plenty to pick up from fellows who'd run out of luck. He got away from that subject by joking about how he'd been cross-eyed from basic training until they left for the beach from having to tell the arms-room sergeant the serial number of whatever weapon he'd been assigned, and how morphine-funny he'd found the behavior of the first guy at the aid station, who'd grabbed each soldier's weapon from his hands or stretcher; shucked out the magazine to throw in one pile; worked the action to jack the chambered round in a more widely defined direction; clear any unejected round by pointing in the direction of a sand-hill and pulling the trigger; and then toss the weapon into the heap behind him with his left hand while using his right to either grab the next or help the litter bearers pull grenades from pockets. So much for weapons accountability! They had, Raymond chuckled as he explained, a heavy wooden crate for the grenades, close enough to drop them in after checking that the ring was tight up against the spoon's hinge. They were working fast, but they weren't stupid. He couldn't help his brother's much with their curiosity about getting shot or having surgeries. Those things felt like what they were and nothing else. He did tell them of the brief instant before the extent of his wound registered in his mind, probably, he said, because of the excitement of the fight and the confusion of falling. A very brief instant, he revised as he explained. He could describe the hit of a shot of morphine, the wet finger of the medic on his forehead, and the descent of the anesthesiologist's mask onto his face.

"Like the mark of the Lamb," William said quietly. "You were passed over." Raymond was relieved when the conversation was ended by Father's coming through the room saying "Time for the chores, boys, Sunday evening's like any other for the stock."

Sarah came with Raymond to tend the chickens and gather the eggs. "You doin' alright?" she asked once they left the house. "I was listening from the other room, ready to come and make a diversion if I heard you getting quiet or philosophical."

"Thanks. They're my brothers and have more right than most to be told. They're my brothers, they would have understood if I'd told them I needed to change the subject." Sarah knew to scare the last couple of birds in and shut the flap as Raymond was throwing down the evening's scratch. On the way back to the house after gathering the eggs he said "step over a couple of steps and I'll show you how I used to get mother all stirred up ... if she happens to be looking out of the window now, she'll be shaking her head that I'm showing off for you!" Sarah moved away a bit, and Raymond stood in one place but started turning in circles, faster and faster. As he turned, he gradually raised his arm until the egg basket was swinging horizontally around him, centrifugal force keeping the eggs tight against the bottom of the out-turned basket. When he reached that speed, he gradually changed the angle of his swing until the basket was twirling vertically, the eggs visible against the sky, tight against the bottom of the basket as it flew from knee-height above his head. After a few turns, he began circling again, reversed the process and gradually returned the basket to its proper place hanging down from his hand as he stopped turning and stood still

"Your mother'd be right!" Sarah laughed, clapping her hands. "You are showing off for me."

"Aw, that's nothing. I used to be able to do it while I was walking, but a fellow has to learn to accept his limitations."

"Where'd you pick that trick up? From a clown at the circus?"

"Closer to home. Watching Father and Grandfather doing it with the milk pails. When mother caught me doing it with the egg basket, I got scolded that if I spun a full basket, I'd crack all the eggs in the bottom." Raymond winked and gave Sarah a wicked grin. "I can tell you though, she was wrong. Many times!" Either nobody had been looking or they'd paused just out of sight, because no one said anything as they came into the kitchen. It had been a one-man, one-woman show.

Raymond's generosity in satisfying his brothers' curiosity had the result that Sarah feared and had silently predicted to herself when she'd passed by and overheard their topic of conversation. About one thirty in the morning he started shifting around abruptly in bed speaking loudly and distinctly but not yelling with so full voice as to awaken the rest of the household or himself. As on other occasions, he was back on the cliff in his mind, giving voice to what had been his unspoken realizations at the time, to his direct encouragement to the men around him, and to his invective directed at their unseen enemy above, an expression of his fear and frustration at the slow, irregular ascent in a form that also helped his fellow climbers to hang on and move up. Rather than awakening Raymond, Sarah held him, gently stroking his hair and forehead. Better," she reasoned," to let his mind empty itself since it was doing so without alarming the household." Maybe the purge would ease things for him for a few days.

She listened to predictable cries of anger coupling every curse word she knew as an adjective with the nouns Nazis, krauts, or Germans. The same for every vulgar noun she'd ever heard coupled with the same three words in their adjective form. With nothing to do but listen and rock back and forth she had to laugh at herself, thinking about how the words were put together. Although none of the utterances were in any order, by listening carefully, she was able to piece together how the climb had gone. Early on there were exhortations to keep moving. There were verbalized thoughts, ''poor bastard", "God help 'im" and the like that she took as references to wounded or dead soldiers falling alongside. "Pull your bayonet!" she took as word being passed downward to get ready to claw past a weak step, rope cut by shrapnel from a grenade or chafed by the stone. "Grenade right!" or "Grenade left!" passed down as Raymond's mind re-entered the zone at which the explosives dropped from above were detonating, warnings to turn your shoulders and press your face into the stone. "He saved me!" the thought from when a falling soldier's body took a blast so close that it would have killed him. "One man up!" passed back down the ladders, then "two", "three", "four", and eventually "secure above" as the number of grenades slowed markedly, all but the best German arms pushed beyond their capacity. "Look for your men," " where's some cover", "Run! Run! Run like hell!", all indicative of the start of the fight up top. Sarah had pieced this sequence together from a good forty-five minutes of mumbling and seemingly unrelated words, often out of sequence with her imagined progression of the assault. Raymond was asleep in her arms -- he'd never awakened. Exhausted, she fell asleep propped up high against the pillows and headboard, thinking as she fell asleep that she now understood at least a portion of what, when pressed, Raymond described by saying "We did our job. Rocketed the hooks up, rigged the ladders and climbed them. Had a hot fight up top, and I caught it early on. It was hard and we lost good men, a lot of good men."

By dawn he'd rolled out of her arms and they'd migrated into their normal sleeping positions, and awoke yawing, stretching, and rubbing their eyes. Packing for the drive home and getting dressed took place at the same time and they took their suitcase downstairs to the front hall as they went to breakfast. The meal was quiet. Everyone thinking of their imminent departure, there wasn't much motivation for joking. The family mostly discussed things that they hadn't got round to doing and asked for or put forward bits of information about family history and the people and places that had filled the visit. Farewells were the reverse of their welcome, Mother and Father close to the porch and quiet, brothers and sisters crowding around the doors of the pickup, all talking at once. When they were finally in with the doors shut, Sarah straightened her hair out of her eyes. Raymond checked the rearview mirror to insure that his cap was at exactly the right angle, felt beside himself for reassurance that he had his stick, switched on the ignition, pulled the choke knob halfway out from the dash and tromped down on the starter with his left foot. The barrel-nose caught on the first try. As the oil pressure needle started to rise and the cylinder heads warmed he eased off the choke until the V-8 was idling without an occasional goosing of the accelerator. Satisfied he leaned over and gave Sarah a kiss on the cheek, waved to the family and eased out the drive. He stopped at the road to check for traffic, first turning around for a last look at the home place through the back window and over the tailgate. Raymond pulled out as smoothly as a chauffeur driving a rich man's Packard; a foot and a half in groundhog; maybe fifteen in second; fifty yards in third; and a final, equally undetectable shift into fourth, where he got them up to travelling speed. "I like your people," Sarah said, covering his hand on the wheel. "They're smart, they're fun, and they look out for each other."

"That's good," Raymond replied, glancing over at her. "I like 'em too. A shame," he continued in a more serious tone, "that I couldn't figure something to do down here with them -- but," more cheerfully, "if I hadn't come up to the Valley I wouldn't be keeping company with you!"

"Me and Oscar. I've missed him these few days." She then nodded off to sleep, her head bobbing up and down with each dip of the road. The pace of the visit and disruption of their sleep by both sets of nightmares had them pretty worn down. There wasn't much talking on the way home. Now that Sarah knew the route, she drove when Raymond needed to doze. She did a lot of thinking as she drove; of what a wonderful man Raymond was and how much she liked being with him; of his clever brothers and sisters, dear mother, droll father and how they had incorporated her into the fabric of their world within minutes of her arrival; and, without enthusiasm, of the mutual nightmares that had so robbed them of rest that today they were acting like a team of long-haul truckers rather than lovers returning to their nest. She thought, too, of Raymond sitting and drinking with his father to lay the pain before bed, just as he did at home. She'd shuddered inside when his father had pronounced Raymond neither sloppy nor mean after the amount he needed because in a walled-off part of her life she'd experienced both. Would Raymond's sweet disposition protect her as his pain continued and his tolerance for whisky grew? Would her nightmares draw her into the downward spiral of drinking? Raymond was asleep. She eased his cap off to use against the late afternoon glare, adjusted it to exactly the right angle, and drove on.

With Raymond driving and Sarah awake, having snatched enough rest to have been awake and making conversation since Lovingston, they'd made pretty good time and got home just at nightfall. They hadn't run into any fog on Afton Mountain, and had enjoyed the same good laugh that they had at the beginning of the trip over the way the road twisted and almost met itself twice on the edge of the village of Afton. The uphill road was a world different from the railway grade patiently defining the lower edge of the village, nudged just enough out of parallel with the line of the mountain that each mile rose up the side at a gradient that the train engines could manage.

Oscar recognized the sound of the truck as they pulled around the store and met them as they got out at the bottom of the stairs, coming down from his usual evening vantage point on the upper landing's railing. "Hey, sweetie!" Sarah swept him up into her arms. "Miss us while we were gone?" Oscar replied by stretching up, claws lightly in the arm and shoulder of her sweater to nuzzle and purr into her ear.

"I reckon that's a "yes," Raymond said as he pulled the suitcase out of the bed and came up beside them. "I could hear his motor going from the other side of the truck as you stooped to pick him up!"

Their own place smelled just right as they came in. They had peanut butter and jelly sandwiches and went through the accumulated mail and newspapers that their watchman had left on the table for them before unpacking, cleaning up and going to bed. Stretching out

on their own bed felt good after so much driving and
the strange (at least to Sarah) bed at the farm which
had felt vaguely reassuring to Raymond, but not entirely like the real article insofar as he'd never shared it
with a woman before. Their pent-up travelling yearn-
ings and the stimulation of the road's vibration brought
them together in a sexual embrace despite their fatigue.
The fatigue fell away and it was good and it was long,
and they went into a deep sleep, Raymond dreaming of
the golden chains of bees, Sarah of the delightfully inconsequential routine of shop keeping with John
Thompson before the war.

44. BACK TO WORK

As usual, they awoke before dawn without need
of an alarm and with plenty of time to start the day -- it
was just their week that was off, Tuesday morning
'stead of Monday. They both pulled on their work duds,
and Sarah fixed bacon and eggs while Raymond filled
his lunch box with sandwiches made of last week's leftover bread and baloney that smelled a lot better after
the first cut. He was careful to spread lots of mustard on
the bread next to the gray side of the first slice, cheese
against the fresh, pink side. Pig lips, he thought to himself. Lips and cheeks and sides too thin for good bacon,
along with the same leavin's from the beeves, that's
what they pressure-cooked and ground and squeezed
through pipes to make his lunch. Ugh! Amazing, he
thought, what we eat for convenience, the same leavin's
we'd eat, if we had to, for survival. At least it wasn't
suspicious little tins of 'potted meat'. He figured that
highly-processed and spiced product had to be made of
what the Brits called 'the naughty bits,' open shoat's
snouts, ears, boars' tits, and worse. Spam, on the other

hand was pretty reliable either in Army rations or from rationing coupons. It clearly economized by mixing cheaper cuts of meat, but Chicago's Hormel Meat Packers knew that anatomical indiscretions would be spotted and publicized. It had the right proportion of fat to fry or grill without gagging a fellow if he had to slice it cold. It had plenty of salt and a good blend of other spices, ground coarse before being cooked and compressed into the gently tapering bricks that slipped so easily from the tin (even in hospital and full of narcotics his mind had picked up and retained some of the English manner of expression!). You had opened it by snapping off the clock-key soldered to the bottom, fitting the slot of the key onto the tab exposed at the corner of the label and winding off the three-sixteenths inch band of metal between two scored lines precisely weakening the can's wall just beside the crimp of the larger end, leaving what really did look like a greasy, broken clock spring hug on the corner of the lid as it came away. The war had changed his eating habits. Before enlisting home-ground sausage, cured hams, shoulders and bacon sides had been the only processed meats that Raymond had ever eaten. The making of sauerkraut and sausages was undertaken in many Lutheran and Dunkard households, but their German had left them so many generations before that "*wurst*" had no meaning and sausage was, well, just sausage, without any further description.

Before the war 'All-beef' bologna and cans of sardines had been the only things next to the crackers in Thomas' Store, but the distribution of foodstuffs under rationing had brought some strangely-named sausages to the small stores in the countryside, where few Italian foodstuffs other than spaghetti boiled almost to a paste on Monday evening before being hit with halved mason-jar tomatoes and the leavings of whatever had been roasted for Sunday dinner -- beef, pork, or chicken -- were known. Folks bought 'em and liked 'em, even if the names reflected the ancestral geography of an immigrant culture unknown in their part of the State

Raymond and Sarah met crossing the room, gave each other a hug and kiss, wished each other a good day, and disappeared down different staircases on their way to work. Raymond felt the morning chill as he stepped out on the landing and started down the steps. It was a more subtle change for Oscar and Sarah as they descended the open inside stairwell, ending smack against the door that opened into the store from the last stair-tread without landing or threshold. The store, unheated in their absence, was root-cellar cold. Sarah crumpled some papers, took a handful of kindling from the box and a match from the tin match-safe, and started a fire in the stove. "A handful and hot," Sarah explained to Oscar." That's what gives the draft enough pull to catch the bigger stuff when you put it on." She gauged the temperature of the flue pipe with her hand up as high as she could reach without stretching, decided that the chimney was now drawing warm smoke up from the kindling rather than letting the cool air settle, which would make the just-lit fire smother itself, and added some heavier kindling, then some real firewood to warm the place up. Oscar settled into the worn cushion of the rocker he'd shared while Raymond was working at catching Sarah's attention. Sarah went about the routine of opening for business, pulling the long iron bars from the forged staples that protruded indoors from the closed shutters through drafty groves in the window framing, their narrow legs clenched over into the oak of the outside face of the shutters, themselves protected from loosening or tampering by a cross-brace whose nails were clinched and set on the inner side of the shutter. After opening the shutters for the first few times, she'd laughed to John that the whole arrangement began to smack of the Red Queen's logic from *ALICE*. How many times must the small, sharp ends of forged staples and nails be toenailed, set, and hidden under another plank before security is sufficient? However many the Queen proclaims! Sarah pulled open the twin inside screen doors, protected from the worst wear by the regional baker's metal advertising signs that caught the eye wherever one pushed, pulled, kicked or looked, the message even painted onto the screen at what must have been calculated as average purchaser's eye level. On the other side of the screens were the outer doors, secured like the shutters but easier to open because the bars were right within reach and lacked the heavy length built into the shutter bars. She undid them by reaching rather than stretching for the irons.

The fresh air smelled good as Sarah opened the outer door. The route man had already left their bundle of ten morning papers on the bench, and Anna Williams, who balanced her ledger page at the store by bringing daily deliveries of brown eggs and seasonal things, like amazingly beautiful windfall apples from what remained of her grandmother's orchard, and butchering-time ponhoss and liver pudding, which, if you'd killed a few hogs at once, accumulated at an alarming rate, far exceeding the appetites of family and help alike for such tasty but soon-overwhelming frugalities. The look of the eggs, the ancient, odd, shapes of the apples and the flavor of frugalities all appealed to Sarah's customers who still lived in the County but drove to work in town. Anna Williams didn't need much cash money to settle up at the end of the month. As folks would say, "she got by."

Raymond turned towards town, into the morning sun, good reason for his cap to be at 'exactly the right angle.' Past the cemetery and Mrs. Russ', he turned right on Lewis Street and threaded his way out to the store at the beginning of the Middlebrook road, just past the railroad flats, with the covered stock pens and the junkyard adjacent to and threatening to encroach the engine turntable that had been outgrown and seldom used once the big coal trains and longer- route freight took over from local railroading, dropping off a couple of cars at the siding, then picking them up on return rather than running a smaller, more regional train. A yard-engine used it occasionally, but that was about it. He could both hear and smell the cattle as his wheels crunched onto Riley's graveled lot. His nose hadn't yet got full of petroleum! When he went in, Bill was on the phone, back towards the door, reared back against the springs of his swivel chair, feet up on the desk, laughing uproariously. He turned a bit when he heard the door, ended the conversation, then pulled his heels from amongst the mail he'd picked up at the Post Office, and squeaked around on the chair's pivot to greet Raymond. Tears in his eyes, he'd been laughing so hard, he called out "Mornin' Raymond! I 'poligize for not explainin' what's got me laughing so, but it'd take too long, what with family histories an' all. Let's just say 'lo how the mighty have fallen,' but in such a way that nobody got hurt except for the scrapin' away at some excess pride. How'd your trip go? Your people have enough good sense to appreciate Sarah?"

"I'm not insulted to miss your joke -- must've been good to make you cry -- 'cause you're right, there's not enough time for me to absorb a sufficient amount of your rogue's encyclopedia at this hour. The drive was a pleasure with Sarah along, and yes, my people showed good sense. Did the oil peddling business hold up without me around?"

"'Course it did!" Bill replied, sounding hurt. "These people love me, it was a treat for them to see the boss instead of the gimp dogface underling,'' Bill responded with a grin.

"I'm sure that it *was* a treat, " Raymond replied, joining Riley in the chair catty-cornered across the cluttered desk. "Watching you huff and puff and drag the hose down!"

"Yeah, yeah, yeah!" Bill replied without losing his smile. "You better get out there and load the truck I emptied while you were gone. Gotta keep those lamps lit and those flivvers flyin'."

"Yessir, yessir! " Raymond replied, adjusting his hat at exactly the right angle, picking his stick off of the mixture of magazines and invoices on his corner of the desk and heading out the back door.

The International was in the loading shed. Raymond made sure that it was in gear and the brake set before climbing up onto the tray and tank. Groaning a little to himself, he was surprised to have the sound overwhelmed by the noise of a smallish engine nosing another tank car onto their siding As Raymond went about his work, he could hear the railroad man going about his. There was a gradual whoosh as pressure was gradually dropped from the boiler; a vicious hiss as the engine's air bakes set; the clatter of the engineer's boots down the cab's short ladder, crunching along the ballast forward along the front of the engine;

and clattering up the taller ladder of the tank car. As
Raymond squinted into the open oval port to see if the
gasoline tank was full enough that he had to back off on
the valve, he could hear the squeal of a brake wheel being set. It had to be done the old way, turning the horizontal wheel above mechanically setting a brake shoe,
to leave the car movable on the siding, airbrakes off.
Raymond turned valves, shifted downpipes, and began
filling the kerosene tank. He heard the trainman clatter
down and shuffle around on the ballast and sleepers. A
slight hiss let him know that the valves isolating the air
in the engine and car brakes had been set and the connecting hose released The clink of chain and protesting
groan of a dry link being dragged open told him that the
car was uncoupled, ready for the engine to steam up
and reverse to the main line switches to rejoin the line
of cars that had been split to break out the lone triplex
tanker with big red Texaco stars on its flanks.

To Raymond's surprise, the sound of footsteps
on ballast got closer rather than retreating to the waiting
engine. He stopped the flow of kerosene from the valve
he was watching, straightened up and balanced his way
back along the top of the truck's tanks to be able to peer
around the side of the shed and see who was coming.
Before he got to look he heard the voice of his old partner from Mrs. Russ' back stairwell and porch stoop.
"Hey, Raymond, that you up on top the truck?"

"Hey, yourself, Dave!" Raymond responded,
reversing course to climb down, drop his oily gloves in
the box and grab his stick from the cab before heading
out into the sunshine. Habitually, he adjusted his cap to
exactly the right angle as he walked. They met for a
handshake and backslap, then Raymond asked "got time
for a smoke?" gesturing towards the two upended

buckets Bill had put at the edge of the trees a safe distance from the loading shed for just that purpose.

"Yeah, reckon so, 'Dave replied, and they
walked over, got comfortable, leaned back against two
of the less brushy trees growing in and through the
fence, and lit up.

"How is it," Raymond asked, "that you're back
in here dropping cars for yourself? Never heard of an
engine-man doing that."

"My men ran into a couple of their buddies
back at the main switch and I told 'em to take a break,
that I could deal with one car. Frowned on by the Railroad and the Union, of course, but me and my men get
along because we selectively decide which chicken-shit
regulations to ignore when nobody's around. Not likely
that there'd be a company man lurking down here behind the stockyards, and the fellows up at the switch'll
stay outta' sight. Glad I came -- I was hoping for a
chance to catch up with you. What's new?"

Raymond told him about moving out to Sarah's
and that they were serious enough that they'd taken the
trip to North Carolina. Dave explained that as soon as
the war had ended most of the engineers who'd stayed
on past retirement out of patriotism (and the double pay
that they could draw) had gone home and that everyone
his age was being shuffled around and that he'd been
offered this division because of the knowledge he'd
gained during his years of tending switches and signals.
"I was glad to take it, like it up here. Just got in this
morning. Gotta' call Mrs. Russ 'n see if she as a room --
I'm tired of railroad hotels and liked staying there."

"I don't know how she's fixed right now, but I'll tell Bill that you're here and I'll bet she'd go so far as to open a room on the front stairs to get you back! She'll say that now you're an engineer that you're a professional man and that would result in no impropriety."

"How's the leg doing?"

"Bout the same." Raymond lied.

"How 'bout the nighttime stuff?"

"Not a problem." Raymond lied again.

"I better get movin' " Dave said as they stood and field-stripped their butts, crumbling the remains into the gravel as they walked. "I'm not above stoking a little, if I have to, but I'd just as soon get back to the main line with the steam I've got. How do you and Riley switch cars between your sidings when you empty one?"

"The hard way. Bill's too cheap to call an engine out. We've got 'bout a five and a half foot crowbar he picked up somewhere when it got dropped and after a corner chipped off. Takes us the better part of a day, switching off between working the bar and climbing up and down to turn the brake wheel."

"Come on back to the engine with me then," Dave said, "I'll leave you something to make your work easier."

He must have a longer bar, Raymond thought to himself. They reached the engine, Dave climbed up, disappeared into the tender, and when he reappeared started lowering the strangest tool Raymond had ever seen down to him. It had a wooden handle thicker and heavier than a logger's peavey, with about forty pounds of loosely- jointed steel at the end being lowered to him. The forgings wiggled so much that Raymond couldn't get a grip until he got both hands on the wood of the handle. "Appleton Car Mover." Dave explained. "Uses compound leverage to just slide 'em along. I picked up a dozen poking around in the back room of a closed military rail compound in the Norfolk yards. Whoever scavenged that place'd done a complete job -- you could tell by the dirt marks where the clock, fire bell and pencil sharpener had been unscrewed from the wall. There were twelve new Appletons in an open crate in the back room. Those fellows couldn't have been rail men to leave 'em behind, probably figured they weren't worth dragging off since the end of war production has dropped scrap prices to hell. Took me six trips to lug 'em to the boot of my car. That's where the other ten still are. I keep two in the tender so my crew don't have to work as hard as others. Nice green paint on 'em shows they were Army, not Railroad, so no company-book man can fuss at us for having yard-crew tools in the tender."

"Thanks. This'll be peachy."

"I'd better get." Dave leaned out from the cab to check behind the engine. "If I stay any longer, the boys'll have made up a tale about me having a girlfriend so ugly she has to live by the stock-pens. I'd hear 'bout it for months!"

"Know what you mean!" Raymond called as Dave eased the engine back to negotiate the couple of longer spurs to where his crew waited at the main switch. Raymond put the unwieldy tool into the cab with his stick, pulled on his gloves and got on with loading the truck.

Dave's crew appeared from out of nowhere as soon as he approached the mainline spur's switch, which his brakeman opened without his having to stop. The fireman swung aboard and by the time he'd shoveled enough to make the boiler pressure gauge start easing up, the brakeman had walked back to the other cars that they'd left on the spur and was giving the signal to reverse and pick them up. Raymond, Dave thought to himself, was lying to me. In their boarding-house days he'd seen through the glib 'loads and unloads itself' explanation and knew how climbing on and off the truck and dragging hose all day pushed Raymond to his absolute physical limits. God knows what the days they switched cars between their two sidings did to him. 'No problem' about the night horrors had been too quick an answer, too. Dave felt the cars couple and watched for the brakeman to swing wide from the caboose rail before easing forward. Remembering the nights he'd been awakened by Raymond's screams and cursing, he shuddered. What, he thought to himself, would the railroad do with an engineer in Raymond's condition? They'd have to get him off the line, maybe a switching job at the shops at full-duty pay. If he couldn't handle that, they'd probably find some sort of desk job in operations or stores. If he wouldn't accept a job off of an engine Dave figured they'd retire him early at full pay so that he could drink himself to death quicker than he would have switching or sitting behind a desk. He shuddered again, and then gave his full attention to driving. His fireman had jumped down to open the switch on the main line, and he saw the brakeman's wave, swinging out wide from his ladder after the switch had been closed and locked. The fireman joined him at the cab's other window. They were on an old portion of the line between where they'd come on and off the freight spur just west of Staunton's elegantly curved passenger concourse where they had to both leave and retrieve cars. As an old part of the line in a middling commercial area filled with wood yards, coal yards, and warehouses, active and inactive, the Railroad had not yet organized things with a branching side spur like the one where they had just left Raymond, built because of the traffic from the stockyards, and it seemed like he and the fireman were checking the position of a rusted switch on one side or the other every couple of rail-lengths.

Raymond finished loading and pulled the truck up at the back door of the store to check with Bill before heading out on his route. Pulling the car-mover out of the cab along with his stick he had to choke up on the handle deep into where it had disappeared into the ferrule to be able to achieve the balance needed to carry it one-handed. "Hey, Bill," he called as he came up the stairs an in the door. "Engineer Dave brought our full car and stopped to visit. Gave us a gift, too."

"Whoa!" Bill exclaimed. "Glad to hear your buddy's back in town, I can even imagine him bringing you some goofball present, but I'll be damned if I can guess what he'd be bringin' to both of us together."

"I don't think he planned it. While we were talking he just realized that he had extra of something we could use." Raymond held the tool upright in front of him for Bill's inspection.

"Whooee," Bill gave voice to his surprise and enthusiasm. "My back feels better already! I been keepin' an eye out for one 'a those things for years!" As Raymond laid the tool down on the corner of the desk, its levers worked apart and they could see the words "Appleton Car Mover ptd" on the flat of the inner lever. Raymond told Bill how Dave had come into his hoard. When he finished, Bill said "Let's look at this thing a little bit -- I've never seen one up close, just watched fellows working with them a ways off. One fellow, one car, and him not walking like his back was broke. Dual leverage, that's what does it."

"Compound leverage, I think that's the official name for it."

"That'd be right. Dual means two, and this thing has more pieces than that. Gotta remember, too, that the last throw is the wheel, straight in from the tire to the center of the axle." They puzzled a bit and finally agreed that they didn't know which of the shorter sections were powerful levers and which were merely connecting links. Bill stood, held the tool in its working position on the already-scarred desk, slightly working the action. "Looks bit like a lady's slipper, from the top, dunnit?" He moved the handle to raise the next lever a bit. "There, look at the top of her foot strain as she gets up on tiptoe!"

"Lay her down and let's look at the part that grips the rail," Raymond replied, without any further female simile. He ran three fingers along the sole. "Look here where it drops down on both sides along the rail to keep from losing energy slipping sideways."

"One 'a those slips is prob'ly what took the corner off our crowbar."

Raymond continued slipping his joined fingers along 'till they slid across a slightly raised crosspiece. "Curved to the exact crown of the rail," he pointed out. "Stops the little bit of wiggle the sides don't."

"Replaceable and adjustable," Bill noted, fingering the adjacent, recessed nut. "I'll bet that little bit is hardened steel, the exact spot where the force presses on the rail."

"And this," Raymond fingered a bump in the center of the slipper's toe, "looks like a chick's egg tooth. Goes all the way through, bet it's steel fitted in a hole in the casting, then peened over. Has to make the final stroke, putting force dead-center on the tire against the rim-to-axle last arm of the lever."

"Think you're right,'" Bill confirmed Raymond's figuring. "Makes you want to go out and move some tank cars!" he laughed, walking .over to the door to spit and check the weather.

"Next week'll come soon enough, " Raymond grabbed his stick and walked over to join Bill at the door, adjusting his cap at exactly the right angle before heading to the truck. "I'm sure things'll be easier, but we still won't be playing baby buggies," he said as he passed.

45. WAR STORIES

The week progressed normally, Raymond and Sarah falling quickly back into their routines of the fuel route and the store. The talk was different now that the war was over, and Raymond was meeting people he'd only heard about, those who'd been mustered out of the service, those who'd come home from wartime jobs in Washington, D.C., Baltimore and Norfolk, and even couple of men who'd been conscientious objectors, one of whom had spent the war fighting forest fires out west and another that'd been working at the Western State Lunatic Asylum right there in Staunton but might as well have been away across the country, no more time away from his duties than he'd been allowed. Apparently the superintendent there'd liked the Selective Service's offer of free help and had worked 'em all like privates on fatigue duty. Nobody, it seemed, ever made corporal or buck sergeant in that outfit.

Raymond held true to his belief that you got two ears and one mouth for a reason, and stood back listening to the talk around the stores. He realized something that was logical but which in light of his own experience he'd never considered -- that fighting a war on two fronts on opposite sides of the globe put as many, if not more, soldiers along the far-flung supply and communication lines as it had into battle. Most of the war stories he overheard as he leaned against the store counters were just that, stories repeated by 'clerks and jerks", usually honestly prefaced or followed by "this one guy told me," "I was lucky not to have been there," or "thank God they found out I could type with two fingers and put me on a teletype machine rather than an aircrew!" Other times he would recognize the marks of first-hand experience in just a few words. When he sensed bravado and enthusiasm on the part of the teller, he always hung around for the end of the story, waiting for one or the other, admission that it was a second-hand story, or some feeling that the guy'd been there.

For most of those animated talkers he was either an anonymous addition to their audience, just the young oil-truck guy, whose appearance was an inconsequential, momentary break in the narrative when the storekeeper's attention was distracted by the out-thrust receipt book. If there was no acknowledgement that the story was hearsay, he'd always sidle up to the teller on his way back to the truck, look him in the face and shake his hand, saying something like "good to meet you, your people must be right proud of you if they know that." Sometimes he couldn't be sure who was real or not until just that moment, when he could sense either the silent affirmation of the teller that *he* knew why Raymond understood, or fear, like that of a bluffer's cards being called, from the blowhards. He never lingered or said anything else. They didn't know him, didn't know his story, but he knew that as soon as the slam of the cab door signaled his departure, the storekeeper or one of the regulars would tell them. He took some perverse satisfaction in the liars' inevitable moments of panic and relief that he hadn't exposed them. He knew that the fellows who were real had already sensed that he was a brother and appreciated that he was gentleman enough to stay quiet and let them savor their moment. He could understand the motivation of a small man exaggerating his experiences to an audience unlikely to catch the lie that raised his status. The ones he couldn't understand, and who frightened him a bit, were the few who were both real and pleased to be re-telling the tale. He was careful not to linger, unwilling to face answering questions from the garrulous combat veteran or his audience. Everyone, he thought to himself, is different in how they see themselves. He just couldn't understand how person could take to presenting an identity based on the worst that they understood war to offer.

These encounters lay in the back of Raymond's mind. He found himself going over and over them as he drove, sticked tanks, and filled them. Because he realized how troubling the preoccupation was, he talked about the braggarts with Bill and Sarah, but having the war constantly in mind, the dreams came every night, leaving him exhausted every morning. Sometimes their discussions through the evening brought Sarah's dream, too. Hers was guaranteed before morning if he awakened her by struggling with the bedclothes or crying out. Sarah awoke exhausted every morning. They were so worn down that going to sleep wasn't a problem -- Raymond was so tired that he didn't even need that last, extra, glass of liquor to help get past the pain. Making an effort to talk about other subjects after supper and before bed, the only antidote that they could think of, didn't provide any relief. During lulls in business at the store Sarah sat with Oscar in her lap, mulling over the same things she'd studied on the week before, driving while Raymond slept. At night, after she'd rocked Raymond back to sleep and awakened from her own horrors, she lay awake, unable to think of anything except Raymond's Father's account of Grandfather saying that some men had come home from the War unable to find peace and had either hung themselves, drunk themselves to death, or gone west, never to be heard from again. In the small hours of Saturday morning she decided that she couldn't deal with Raymond becoming one of them and in the process turning her into a woman who couldn't find peace because of because a war she hadn't even witnessed, the single horror invented by her mind enmeshed with those he had experienced and haunting practically every moment of their life not absorbed in purposeful activity. They slept in late that Saturday morning, catching up on the sleep that they'd missed during the week. Raymond awoke first, rousing Sarah as he returned to the comfort of the sunlit bed. They snuggled together, kissed, exchanged affectionate pleasantries and chuckled over Oscar's changes in position, luxuriating in the sunbeams.

46. THE BREAKUP

Sarah fluffed her pillow and leaned against the headboard, pulling Raymond's face into her bosom and stroking his hair. "Love," she said softly, "it just isn't working. We're both going to go mad. You'll have to leave." She was frightened as to what might happen next, had no idea what Raymond's reaction would be. He surprised her by not moving other than bringing his arms up to hug her, then totally relaxing, seemingly relieved.

"I know, Raymond replied softly," I've known for a good while but just couldn't bring myself to say so. I'll pack up and go this morning." Mutually relieved of their burden, they fell asleep again, and when Oscar, bored with the sun and looking for breakfast, woke them by batting their cheeks with his paw, they got up and silently went about their Saturday morning routine. After breakfast, while Sarah was finishing up in the kitchen, Raymond packed his few things into the toolbox that they'd been using as a low table and walking without his stick used both arms to half-carry, half-slide it down the railings of the outside staircase and put it into the back of the truck, not bothering to bolt it down. He went back upstairs and met Sarah, now ready to go down and open the store. They embraced, both tearful.

"I tried, Raymond, I really did," Sarah whispered.

"I know," Raymond whispered, still holding fast but attempting to comfort her by patting her back. "Maybe we can make it work later," he said, completely doubting the proposition.

"Yeah, let's hope so,'' she replied, sincerely, but without a shred of hope in her heart. They kissed, held each other at arm's length, exchanging teary smiles, letting go when Oscar gave a questioning mew from the top of the stairs leading down to the store. "Gotta open up." Sarah turned and moved towards the cat and her staircase.

"Yeah, that time of morning. I've got to get going and see how to get situated," Raymond replied, picking up his stick, stepping out the door and closing it gently behind him. He paused on the landing to adjust his cap to exactly the right angle, went down *his* stairs, pulled the Barrelnose's choke out about half, threw his foot up to the starter and as soon as it caught headed into town, working through the gears without waiting for the oil to warm up.

Raymond ran through the pickup's gears without thinking, and pushed the choke knob back to the dash only after the engine began to stumble at the top of the first hill, warm enough that it didn't want a rich mixture. When he left Sarah's place he didn't know where he was going, but as he got closer to town he decided to go by work and either call Bill or talk to him if he was there, reading the paper and waiting to visit with any of his buddies who might drop by, anxious to expand the time they spent running errands and minimize the hours of the day left for domestic chores they hoped to avoid. No rooms there, he said to himself as he followed the elegant stone wall of Thornrose Cemetery past Mrs. Russ' house. Dave had telephoned a day or so before to tell him that Raymond had figured it right, that the rooms off of the back stairs were full but that Mrs. Russ *had* considered him to be a satisfactory front-stair man.

Bill's truck wasn't on the lot when Raymond pulled in. He had a key to the store and let himself in, leaving the door open to let the morning sun in -- the stove hadn't been banked up the night before so that it was about as cool inside as out. He sat in Bill's chair, hunched over the desk as he dialed Bill's number out on Smokey Row. Bill answered on the fourth ring, sounding kind of harried, as his last cup of breakfast coffee had been served up with his wife's views on what needed doing around the place rather than loafing at the store, but more cheerful when he recognized Raymond's voice."

"'Mornin'. What's up m' boy?"

"I'm down here at the store, but don't worry, everything's O.K. here," Raymond said, pausing for a minute to gather his thoughts.

"Well, what is it?" Bill replied, the cheerfulness slipping away from his voice. This was the first time Raymond had ever called him at home, and he figured it couldn't be good news after that opening.

"I had to leave Sarah's place and wondered if I could camp here for a day or two until I get situated somewhere else." Raymond couldn't think of any easier way to say it.

"Umm," Bill paused, then figured he might as well ask straight out. "Nightmares get too much for her?" Bill knew they'd been bad, because he'd asked why Raymond showed up at work half asleep. What he didn't know was that Sarah had them, too.

"Yeah, that's it." Bill's inclination was to tell Raymond to come out to the farm and stay, but remembering his wife, Mary's reaction to his mention of why Raymond was behind on his sleep, he knew that he couldn't make the offer without consulting her.

"Yeah, I reckon that's O.K.," he responded, feeling like he wasn't doing Raymond right. "Just don't burn the place down!" he continued in as much of a joking tone as he could muster.

"Thanks, I'll be careful an' less trouble than the mean watchdog you're always threatening to get."

"I'm not coming in this mornin'," Bill announced. "Too much to do here on the place."

"I know what you mean. See you Monday morning." Raymond hung up.

Even with comin' from a farm and with all his troubles, he don't know, Bill thought to himself as he headed back to the kitchen. He at least didn't have to sit here and listen to the chin-music that came with last that cup of coffee.

"Who was that callin'?" Mary asked as he came back into the kitchen.

"Raymond," Bill drained the last dregs of coffee into his cup and sat back down at the table. "Askin' permission to sleep down at the store -- apparently Sarah couldn't take his waking up screaming anymore. Felt kinda' bad leaving him there, not asking him out here to stay, but figured I better speak to you about it first. What you think?"

"I think," Mary replied with some deliberation, "that anybody so crazy from the war that he scares Sarah Thompson, scares me and I don't want him in our house."

"Didn't say that he scared her, just that he kept the both of them awake." Bill took another sip of the tepid coffee. "We sleep downstairs, these old brick walls are two foot thick, put him in the far upstairs bedroom, we'd never hear him even if he shot himself!"

"That's exactly why I don't want him here," Mary replied, sitting down across from him and looking straight into his eyes. "What if he takes to sleepwalking and dreams that we're Germans in a bunker? He could kill us in our bed without any of us having to wake up! Bad enough that you have him driving your big old truck through the mountains half asleep without him living here too " Bill knew there was no changing Mary's mind that morning, so he gulped the last of the coffee, grabbed his coat from back of the door and headed out to tighten the netting around the chicken yard. Maybe after dinner he could convince Mary to ride with him over to Sarah's store, buy what they needed in the way of groceries, and hear the full story if Sarah would tell it.

Raymond put the phone down gently and let out a sigh, looking around at his dismal surroundings. Bill called it 'the store' because it had been the busiest general store just west of the city limits when his predecessors had negotiated the exclusive local rights with Texas Oil. Biggest part of the petroleum line back then had been square gallon cans of gasoline for Aladdin mantle lamps and lanterns and square cans of highly refined kerosene, better than the stuff that they shipped now, for wicked chimney lamps. The walls were shelves all the way to the ceiling, with odd remnants of unsold merchandise here and there, covered with dust and cobwebs. The counters and lower shelves were stacked with boxed petroleum products, most of which were relatively dust-free. He pulled a piece of newspaper and a handful of kindling out of the box and arranged it in the cold stove with the amount of coal that it could handle, leaving the scuttle close by for the real stoking. Straightening up, he fingered a match from the faded tin match safe nailed to the chimney advertising flour from a mill with a name he didn't recognize from his route -- either flooded out or burned down before my time, he thought to himself. He struck the match on the cast-iron side of the stove as he crouched to light the twisted paper. Rising back up watching the flame move quickly from paper to kindling, then much more slowly from kindling to coal he smiled, remembering Grandfather. 'Barn burners' was his name for strike-anywhere kitchen matches. "Boys,'' he was fond of saying,'' if you got serious work that you're about, don't be fumbling around with them safety matches, 'specially the fold-up paper matchbook kind. Get you a good pocket-full o' good old barn burners!" As the first lumps of coal got to going good, Raymond emptied the rest of the scuttle into the stove and shut the door, fingering the perforated discs of the dampers to make sure that they were open to give the fire plenty of air. He stepped outside to the coal-pile, dry against the foundation beneath the building's deep eaves and refilled the scuttle. Coming back in, he decided to run some errands, get supplies for the next few days, while the place warmed up.

First of all, Raymond figured he'd need something to do over the weekend. He headed over to the public library, an old house willed to the city which was literally in the middle of the block bounded by Market Street, East Beverly, Coalter, and Kalorama, the street with the big, turreted brownstone that everyone called 'the castle.' The library building had probably included that entire street frontage in its original grounds but was now only accessible by a narrow, steep alley going by the south end of the house from Market to Coalter. The library and its remaining grounds were so overgrown with ivy that you could, if distracted by something, drive straight through and come out the far side, still looking for the library! Raymond, however, knew where to ease off into one of the obscure parking places. On entering the library he said good morning to the lady at the desk and headed for the waist-high cabinet of small drawers holding the card catalog. 'B' was easy enough to find, 'bee' wasn't very productive. Children's books with supposedly adorable titles. There was even an oddly-indexed card for a book about the Granville brothers' deadly short-fuselage Gee Bee air racer. Somebody, he thought to himself, either hadn't been doing their homework, or large allowances had to be made for the library volunteers' narrow frame of reference. He imagined some little old lady figuring that the book was another cute title involving a draft horse command and bees, represented on the cover by the closest cross that she (or in fact, the Granvilles, who had no formal aeronautical training) could imagine between an airplane and a bee. Eventually he hit the card saying 'see: Honeybee, bee-keeper, bee-farming.' Going to that drawer, he took down one of the cut-up sheets of paper with one unused side that were in a tray on top of the cabinet, and using one of the pencil-stubs from the same tray that were way too short to be held properly to do cursive writing drills, scribbled down a couple of names and reference numbers to search for on the shelves. After a bit of wandering to orient himself, he found the right shelf numbers and then the books themselves: <u>The Hive and the Honeybee</u>, by L.L.Langstroth, <u>The ABC and XYZ of beekeeping,</u> by Elijah Root, and two novels, one called <u>The Beekeeper</u>, by a woman whose name he'd never heard of before, and another, curiously without the word 'bee" in its title, <u>The Oak Openings</u>, by James Fennimore Cooper, a name he did recognize. He took them over to the desk and laid them in front of the librarian, put his stick and cap down beside them, and leaning his left hip against the counter's edge fished his wallet out of his pocket and got his library card out of its slot. "Two weeks," the librarian said, copying his name and number on the charge slips, hardly looking up No point, he thought, 'in telling her of two address changes since West Beverley Street, the last of which was to a defunct general store used as an oil dump. Raymond thanked her, put his cap on exactly the right angle, and headed out to the truck, books under his right arm.

The primary item that Raymond had to supply himself with was whisky -- he knew that he'd need it come nightfall and afterward, and he'd not carried any away from Sarah's place. Looking at his watch he saw that it was only 9:30 -- he'd been alone with the librarian, probably the first customer of the day. The ABC store didn't open until 10:00, so he decided to ride out to the little store at the far end of Brand's Flat, almost to the Hospital at Fishersville to get bread, cheese, and whatever caught his eye to fix for sandwiches. If he wanted ice cream he'd have to buy it in town and eat it as soon as he got home, but a dusted-off shelf in the store as far away from the stove as possible would be plenty cool enough to keep sandwich fixin's. Keep 'em for me and the mice! He chuckled to himself. He took his time shopping, chatting with Mr. & Mrs. Roadcap who were both there already there dealing with the morning customers. If they wondered why he was shopping there when he lived with a storekeeper on the far side of town they were polite enough not to raise an eyebrow or ask while other people were around.

He took his parcel out to the truck, laid it on the seat, and headed back to town, just kinda' dawdlin' along, looking at things. As he passed the iron bridge over Christian's Creek, which ran between the road and the railroad, he could see under the tracks to the first house beyond. He always liked looking through there, because the stonework arch under the railroad framed an ancient steam tractor, not painted up fancy to show off at the fair, but obviously well cared for, a galvanized washtub with a big rock on top covering the smokestack to keep the firebox dry during the months of the year when it wasn't rumbling from farm to farm towing a threshing machine during wheat and barley harvesting season. The tub had a couple of slats under it so that some air could pull through the firebox and boiler tubes. Raymond figured the man had the firebox door shut to keep the mice out and had cracked the dogs on the smoke chest to give a bigger edge for the air to ease in around. There were still enough small farms with small, hilly fields where a combine harvester couldn't work very well, or folks couldn't afford a combine harvester and a tractor powerful enough to drive it, and they gathered their small grain with a binder, the final evolution of McCormick's reaper, then had the steam-powered threshing engine come and separate the grain from the straw and chaff.

The binder, pulled by horses or a gasoline tractor, cut the grain with a sickle-bar, teeth that moved back and forth against each other, like a hay mower, pulled the cut grain and straw into the maw of the machine with a reel as wide as the cutting bar, kind of like a light-weight steamboat-wheel suspended at just the right height, to be raked to the side, each crossways sweep of the collector arm gathering the right amount of still-stemmed grain heads to be bound into a sheave tied, with twine and then moved on a broad, cleated, canvas belt to a holding platform. When the platform was filled the pressure of the following sheaves against a bar triggered a release to dump the four or five that had gathered on the platform to the ground in a clump. There was a step there, too, so that a man could stand at the edge, riding, watch the flow of twine, spot any trouble with the knotter, pick out what weeds he could as the reel and belt did their work, and by stacking sheaves on top of each other increase the number in each pile released, minimizing the number of later truck-or-wagon stops. The grounded sheaves were either forked onto a following wagon or pickup by a man on foot, or gathered by a group of workers after the entire field had been cut. Raymond was glad that his life didn't depended on explaining how gears and steel fingers could tie a knot in twine on either a binder or a baler -- Reba'd be the one who could explain that.

The threshing machine, a box bigger than any wagon, filled with flails to knock the grain from the stalks, screens to separate the wheat from the chaff, an endless chain bucket conveyor to carry the clean grain to the top of its discharge chute and an enormously powerful fan pulling wind through the whole business, capable of sending a plume of straw and chaff high through the air through a directable spout, would be pulled to the farm by the steam tractor, moving at a crawl, both on cleated metal wheels, clattering on the pavement, digging in where the road was dirt. They'd put the threshing machine on a level spot near the live-stock yard outside of the barn's manger and stalls, scotch all four wheels, and drop the tongue to dig into the ground and brace against the tractor's pull. The tractor didn't need any bracing after it was stopped about thirty feet away. An enormous leather belt, its shorter component sections stitched together by staples looped around a heavy steel wire, every other one clinched well back into alternating sections of belting, (Raymond interrupted his recollection of threshing work to laugh to himself, imagining how big an old bull would have to be to yield a hide from which a sixty-foot, nine-inch wide belt that didn't need even the one splice to form a loop. Even Paul Bunyan's blue ox, Babe wouldn't be big enough! It'd probably have to be Tarus the bull, pulled down from the heavens as shown on the page in the *Hagerstown Almanac* just before the section advising which sign each crop or vegetable should be planted under after you'd found your region number by running your finger through the table of miles north or south and east or west from the town of publication.) was run around the five-foot drive pulley on the engine's side and the ten-inch pulley head-high on the side of the thresher, then the tractor was eased back to take up enough slack for the belt to clear the dirt by a couple of feet. The tremendous torque of the steam tractor entered the thresher at high rpm and was adjusted to the different speeds required in threshing, winnowing, and moving the grain, chaff, and straw by an internal system of cogs and slack-link chain that made enough noise by itself to justify the insult that a fellow's loose-fender, knock-valve split-muffler pickup 'sounded like a thrashing machine.' As the strings were cut and the sheaves were thrown into the hopper feeding the flails the thresher added a different, full-stop note to the din with each step of the process, all held together by the roar of the fan that threw an arc of chaff and straw high from the opposite end. The men regularly adjusted that flow onto a rough, temporary timber frame loosely roofed with planks of slab wood erected in the middle of the barnyard. The resulting straw-rick had an enormously thick thatch roof slipping off into and joining with piles walling off three sides of the frame with the fourth left open. Any cattle confined to the yard in summer and early fall could shelter inside from the sun and rain, and for most of the winter as straw was pulled down for bedding or blew down with the wind.

Raymond's reverie, started by his glimpse of the steam tractor, had carried him past the Colored church, the rest of the Brands flat siding, to the outskirts of Staunton, where he could see the tall, white columned building of DeJarnette's Sanatorium to his left, outlined against the two wooded hills, Betsy Bell and Mary Grey, named by the early settlers from an old Scotts story. The place was called De Jarnetts, he'd been told, even though it had some other official name, because it had, at one time, shared the same director, Dr. DeJarnette, head of the Western State Lunatic Asylum, a century-old landmark and one of the City's biggest employers, which, with its farm, lay against the far slope of the hills.

Raymond passed the Highway Department's tourism plaque announcing the location of "First Settler's Graves" at the top and explaining, if you took the trouble to stop and read the smaller cast text, that they were approximately one and a half miles north, but failed to explain that there was neither another, corresponding marker on the parallel County road nor a gate or path through the farmer's pasture to the actual site. State wants 'em to rest in peace, I reckon, Raymond thought to himself. He glanced up on the ridge ahead to the right where there was, for the wartime years, an unexpectedly new and good-looking poultry house, sited so that its windows could take advantage of the low winter sun in the southwest, and so that the prevailing winter winds from the west hit nothing but a solid wall. It had two low wings, half dug into the hillside, and a two-story center section. Raymond figured the lower was the feed and egg room and the upper was living space for a hired man. The place had caught his attention before the war was over because the finish and material seemed identical to every frame building he'd ever seen on an Army base (identical in materials to the buildings of every other military hospital in the country, other than the one just east at Fishersville. Woodrow Wilson Hospital's frame walls were faced with brick veneer rather than clapboard, the result, he'd been told, of hard bargaining by state and local politicians calculating that an apparently more durable hospital might become a permanent military post, or failing that, would be cheaper to maintain if put to some other public use). Coming up to the gate at the dirt lane that followed the curve of the hill down to the highway, he saw a freshly painted sign, "EGG MAN WANTED" with a telephone number at the bottom. Thinking of Bill's habit of matching people up in a variety of ways, he pulled over at the gate and jotted down the number to give to him, first of the week.

By the time he passed the Asylum, with its chain-link fencing covered porches filled with patients and made the hard right turn in front of the B & O station to go under the C & O tracks (the two lines intersected there in Staunton) to go downtown it was after ten-o'clock and the State liquor store was open. He pulled into the lot, parked, and adjusted his cap to exactly the right angle before going in. No longer intimidated by the surly clerks and recognized by them as a regular customer, he ordered a case of his favorite. Cash, he thought to himself, remembering the round tobacco tin of savings at the bottom of his toolbox back at the store, was not a problem, at least not this morning. His task this morning was to make sure that he had plenty to eat, plenty to read, and adequate whiskey to lay the pain in his leg. He wasn't allowing himself to own up to the pain in his heart, having busied himself with practical matters all morning, pushing it back as 'one of those things.' He drove back to the store, now nice and warm, took his books and purchases in, added a bit more coal to the stove, and settled down behind Bill's desk to make a sandwich to go with a Coke from the case that Bill kept just in reach beneath the left-hand set of drawers.

Having fixed the henhouse fence, tended the few head of stock that he had, eaten a Saturday dinner of the last week's leftovers, and taken a nap, Bill Riley proposed to Mary that they take a little ride over to Westview and get a few things they needed at the

Thompson store. Mary, as curious as Bill, though she'd never admit it, agreed. "We can make our list on the way," she said, getting her everyday hat and coat from behind the kitchen sink before Bill could even reach for his, and snatching up a shopping basket.

"Reckon there's a scrap of something to scribble on in the truck, and there's always a couple of pencil stubs in my work coat pockets," he replied as he reached for that garment, the one he wore every day to the store, denim on the cuffs frayed enough that you could see the blanket lining. To preserve what little he cared about appearance, he had to constantly cut dangling threads with his pocketknife, rather than let things degenerate to the level of the absolute tatter that he wore for chores. Mary found an old envelope pushed half between the cushions on her side as she got in, Bill fished in his pocket and handed her a whittled pencil about half the length of his thumb as he reached over to pull the choke and stomped on the starter. "There you go, woman, commence a listin'!" Without any indication or comment that her actions were in any way connected to his command, Mary laid her purse buckle-side on her lap, smoothed the envelope against its top surface and began talking to herself and writing, scrawling, really, given Bill's tendency to get to looking at something, allowing the truck to stray a bit and sometimes require sudden corrective steering.

"Baking powder, flour, salt fish if she's got 'em in yet." A pause as Mary's eye was caught by something along the road. "Any kind of fruit she has, if not, some prunes for stewing."

"A good ball of string. Couldn't find one when I was hanging poultry wire this mornin', had to eyeball things. That and a box of twelve-gauge buck in case Raymond comes lookin' to kill us in our sleep tonight."

"I'll put the string down," Mary replied, thinking to herself that during the many years they'd been together she'd never known Bill Riley to be more than 'eyeball' particular about anything. "As for the shells," she continued after a bit, " I know we've got a drawer with at least half a box for every gun on the place and some for guns I've never even seen -- maybe you've got your own extras down at the store (she was right about that) and I don't appreciate you joking about my concerns about our safety!" Bill grunted and wheeled onto the gravel in front of the   store. Good, he thought to himself when he realized that there were no more customers' cars on the lot. We're the only ones here.

As they came into the store, Sarah was sitting in the rocker by the stove with Oscar in her lap. She got up, carefully putting Oscar down on the cushion. "Hey Mary, Hey Bill," she greeted them as she crossed to the counter, where she and Mary dealt with the transparent excuse of a shopping list. Bill wandered around for a few steps, looking at whatever bit of merchandise caught his eye and then settled onto one of the missmatched, orphaned straight chairs near Oscar's rocker and leaned over, scratching gently behind the cat's ears. "Come on over and sit 'till I get busy," Bill heard Sarah invite Mary as she put her change into her purse. Sarah lifted the folding section of the counter and led the way over to the stove. Scooping Oscar up into her lap and settling into the rocker Sarah sighed. "Raymond and Oscar spent hours sitting here before we took up with each other. He'd stop in at the end of his route when it'd come out this way, and I suspect sometimes when it hadn't, 'cause lots of times he'd have the pickup rather than the big oil truck, buy a bottle of pop and sit here loving Oscar and nursing his drink. Never said much except "hello" and "thanks", just watching and listening as people came and went, back here by the stove no matter whether the season had it red hot or stone cold. When he finished his drink, he'd thump over on his stick, put the bottle into a space in the crate of empties by the door, nod in my direction as he adjusted his cap to just the right angle, and leave." She held Oscar up against her cheek. "Raymond's a good man, kind. I've got Oscar to witness to that on all those evenings. He may be a black cat, but he won't tolerate anyone who's evil." Bill and Mary murmured their assent and a few comments about animal sense.

"How," Mary reached over and touched Sarah's knee, "are you?"

"Numb and hollow and scared inside but putting on my best businesswoman face," Sarah replied, dropping that mask enough that Bill and Mary could see it in her eyes, but keeping her voice controlled so as to be able to resume her role in an instant should the door or sound of tires on gravel signal the arrival of customers. "I really appreciate y'all making up that list of unnecessaries in order to check on me."

"Told you to include those shells!" Bill winked at Mary. "That would have completed the list."

Sarah was too preoccupied to even hear the little husband-and-wife joke, much less follow the conversational rabbit trail that it promised. "As you know, in addition to living in pain, Raymond has nightmares, sometimes about getting shot, sometimes re-living some painful hospital experience, but mostly about the ladders going up the cliffs."' Sarah smiled and let out a little tear at the same time. "Trying to explain in as nice a way as possible, Raymond told me that the ladders and men climbing them were as closely spaced as the golden chains of honeybees dangling down the face of the honeycomb making wax. Said he even thought of his Grandfather showing him that for an instant as he grabbed hold of the ladder and started up, but quickly realized that the golden chains of bees, however fragile they looked as they dangled there had immediately been returned to the safety of the hive, while he and his companions climbed into worse and worse danger. If a chain of bees grew heavy, it merely split and continued work. As the Rangers climbed the cliff, every man was needed, every rung was filed and the danger grew greater for all until the top was secured. Even then a lucky German shot or grenade could cut a line. That's why more grapnels and new lines were started up with the men as the first sound of American weapons above reached the beach. Raymond relives that climb almost every night, sweating, clutching the bedclothes or my arm and either calling out or muttering to the others. I'm a pretty light sleeper and was getting good at recognizing his early signs, pulling him close to gently wake him and rock us both into a deep sleep, thankful that I was dealing with a man who didn't have horrors of hand-to-hand combat among his memories so that I was not at risk of being slugged or strangled." Sarah paused for a bit and Bill and Mary, thankful that it was the time of day when folks were deep into whatever task they'd chosen, putting their visit to the store off as after-work socializing said nothing and let Sarah gather her thoughts.

"Bill," Sarah begin again, "Raymond's grateful to have work with you, you've been good to him, and having run those routes yourself, you know the hard work of climbing up and down from the tanker and don't fall for his palaver of the ease of working a truck that 'loads and unloads itself.' What you may not know is the pain he works in every moment of the day. I'm astounded at the extent to which he accepts it. "My normal" he says, but it wears on him. Working the truck he moves enough that he trades one hurt for another. The worst is standing still, like when filling a really empty tank at a store where he has to be in one position to have the light just right to check the level as it rises. Standing just so lets that moment's particular pain grow and grow as he clenches his teeth and doesn't talk 'cause he's 'paying attention to the level.' The release of the pent-up pain and shift to the next is so disorienting that he makes jokes about how clumsy he is with the hose when he stumbles. Working around the truck, he's always leaning against it and using those powerful arms to move smoothly. Most bizarre, he says, is what happens when he comes into the store and leans on the counter handing the receipt book over for signature. You'd be right to think that taking his weight on his elbows and shoulders would stop the pain in his legs, but when he stands up, all of the surrounding scar tissue resists the reloaded muscles and damn near knocks him down. Putting the book back into his pocket and making his manners before straightening up is more than casual style. He has to get a death-grip on the stick in his left hand. The silent pause to set his cap 'exactly right' that folks notice and laugh about is a clenched-jawed moment to gain control for the first step."

"He's explained a little to me," Bill responded softly, "but I didn't know it all."

"When you put it all together, it's easy to understand how he found sitting with Oscar preferable to standing around joking with the loafers on their way home from work. You can imagine what he's like when he gets home, pulls himself upstairs by the handrails, and takes off the day's mask as he hangs his cap up inside the door. Soon after Raymond moved up here, he asked his surgeon out at Woodrow Wilson how to deal with pain so that he could sleep. After quizzing him about his family's drinking history, Doc Hill told him to take some whisky before bed. As you can imagine, he needs it as soon as he comes in the door. Needs it for pain and needs it especially bad if he's had one of those days when he sees men climbing the rock faces along the road from Highland, slowing to a crawl and freezing his ears leaning out of the cab in winter looking for enemy soldiers above the ice flows he takes for ladders of climbers. I take a drink with him and talk, getting back to reality and onto pleasant subjects, such as Oscar, who is real calming for Raymond, and knows when he's needed most."

"You-all were talking about animal intelligence a while ago. I reckon I've got a little of that, that's why I know deep down however much I love Raymond that the two of us are eventually headed towards drinkin' away all that's good in our lives. What's even worse is that I've started having dreams where I helplessly watch John's plane burn and explode. They always start about the time I've gotten Raymond back to sleep, and then I'm awake until dawn, grieving for all three of us, holding Raymond close for comfort, frightened because my animal sense tells me I can't survive this way much longer. Raymond and I've talked about all of this many times. This morning we decided that it couldn't go on."

Neither Mary nor Bill said anything, Mary stood up beside Sarah's chair, letting her rest her head against her side as she ran the fingers of one hand gently over the younger woman's hair. After a bit Bill shifted in his seat and cleared his throat. "I reckon,'" he said slowly and as easy as he could, as though he were following Sarah's analogy, talking to a tired and frightened animal, "that the two of you did the right thing, the hard thing, and the only thing that gives you, girl, a chance to save yourself. I know that your love could do a good bit to make Raymond's pain more bearable, maybe even quiet his mind a little, but from what you describe, you'll destroy your own and then neither of you could make it. You've got the loss of your husband to deal with, Raymond has his troubles. You're both strong people, and if anybody can make it on their own long enough to find a way of playin' the cards you've been dealt, it's you two."

"Thanks," Sara whispered at just the same moment that the sound of tires crunching on gravel, the sudden silence of an engine being killed, and the slightly out-of-step sounds of two car doors slamming shut announced the arrival of customers "Back to work," Sarah said in her storekeeper voice, easing Oscar down into the warm hollow of the seat. "I guess that it'll be my salvation, busy all day, tired in the evening, like it was before I took up with Raymond." Mary and Bill collected their groceries and notions as Sarah busied themselves with the folks who'd come in and left.

"Well,'" Mary looked straight ahead but addressed Bill on their way home. "What you gonna' do now?"

"Nothin'."

"Wahtta' you mean "nothing"?"

"Nothin'." Bill said it a second time, his voice just as flat as before. "We went and satisfied our curiosity, which Sarah, fortunately, took as a supportive visit instead of an intrusion into her private affairs; I told her the truth about their decision being hard and her only chance of survival; and I told her the optimistic lies that she wanted to hear about Raymond and herself. There's nothing more to do."

"But what about Raymond?" Mary asked, overlooking her earlier fears for their personal safety if they became more involved with him. "Can't you do something more to help him?"

"Nope."

"Whatta' you mean, 'nope'?"

'Nothin,'" Bill replied, the flatness of his voice beginning to sound almost normal. "The man called me stone cold sober and asked for his choice of a warm place to stay, which I agreed to. He knows how to get in touch with me, his old landlady, Sarah, his train-driver buddy, and his people if he wants talk or company or anything else before Monday. When I go in to the store Monday mornin' he'll be ready for work, drunk, or hangin' dead from a rafter. Nothin' I can do will change how he handles this. I ain't lookin' forward to goin' into town Monday, and I ain't happy 'bout the effort I'll be puttin' in between now and then to steel myself not to be surprised at whichever of the three I do find when I go."

Raymond sat at Bill's desk, his library books on end in a row before him, deciding where to start. He picked up Langstroth's The Hive and the Honeybee, but lacked the determination to start at the beginning and work his way through, and instead started thumbing through, backwards and forwards, until something caught his eye, reading a bit and then thumbing some more. The first was an illustration and explanation of harvesting liquid honey from the combs by using a heated knife to cut the caps off of the honey cells, then placing the frames into a centrifugal extracting machine to drain the honey out -- putting the principle and force of his old milk-bucket and egg-basket trick to work. Depending on the number of frames they held at once, the machines were either cranked like an ice-cream freezer or electrically driven by a motor and belt with an idler pulley acting as a clutch and speed control. Start too fast and the weight of the combs could break them, too slow at the end and it took forever to get the last bit out. He'd understood that liquid honey was ta-ble-ready, but had never considered the idea that bees produced more honey when you were able to give them last year's combs back to repair and use again rather than having to draw out new ones each year when har-vesting like they did back home, cutting the combs from a frame over a meat platter to catch the liquid from the cells that were broken. The system required some management though. You couldn't just stack up the boxes of empty combs and throw a sheet over them to keep the dust out over the winter. If you did that and the bees had raised brood anywhere in the combs, as they invariably did, wax moths would run their filthy tunnels through the combs, looking to eat the discarded skins of the pupae from which the young bees had once emerged and subsequently layered into the cell walls. The remedy was for the beekeeper to build racks under the eaves of his shed where the supers could be stored, loosely spaced and on their sides, allowing light and circulating air to penetrate, effectively discouraging the moths and their worms. The centrifugal machine was invented by a German fellow in 1865-66, although it appeared that other fellows were working along the same lines at the same time.

The next thing that caught his eye was the chapter dealing with bee space, the distance that the bees left open for free passage which allowed the frames of a hive to remain free and removable rather than glued in with propolis or surrounded by burr comb. He remembered Grandfather explaining the idea, but, if Grandfather had told him, he had forgotten that the precise measurement was three-eighths of an inch -- probably a good number to commit to memory, to know if he ever got to messing with bees again. The historical information was interesting, too, that Langstroth, an Episcopal preacher, had figured it out in 1851, designed and built a successful movable-frame hive, and had everybody and their brother steal his idea. Hardly made a buck from it, probably got a little something in royalties from his book before he died, but had to keep on preaching for a living 'till then.

Subsequent chapters talked about the invention of sheets of wax pressed with a continuous pattern of hexagons -- Grandfather'd shown him that, too -- which made the movable frames consistently usable because they came close to compelling the bees to follow the desired pattern.

He got up, poked at the fire a bit, added some coal, grabbed his stick and stepped outside to stretch and relieve himself in some weeds along the foundation just beyond the coal pile and out of view of the road. No point in hiking to the privy at the back side of the lot 'less you have to, he thought as he buttoned up his fly. Back inside he figured that the afternoon had progressed far enough and that he ached enough to pour himself a solid drink of whisky to go with one of the novels, figuring the book would fill his time for the rest of the day.

Moving Bill's desk chair over closer to the stove and arranging one box to prop his feet up and another to keep his glass at hand, he took up The Oak Openings, primarily because he recognized the author of The Last of the Mohicans, one of the books he'd read in school. They'd had a whole box of them, some with broken backs, most with many years of student doodles and initials in the margins and inside the covers on the yellowing wood pulp paper of the cheap edition, but enough of them that any senior class at a school like Guilford's could all be assigned to read it during the same term. Enough blood to satisfy the boys, enough romance and chivalry to keep the girls involved. Old Mr. Cooper'd known his business. Oak Openings had a foreword of a few pages informing him that although written in 1848, the story was set in 1812, in the northern central part of the country, peopled by Indians, both local and those squeezed west by settlement, French trappers, and a few British soldiers wanting control of the area drained by the Detroit, Erie, and the Ohio. Oak openings, he learned, was the frontier term for the last, scattered remnants of the great Appalachian forests found when settlement moved into what is now Ohio and Indiana below the reaches of the Northern coniferous forest. The storm-blasted hollow trees of these small forests were the westernmost available nesting places for the descendants of the swarms that had escaped from the eastern colonies.

Ben Buzz was what the settlers called the solitary honey-hunter who ranged between their most outlying farms and the rivers. *Le Bourdon*, the drone, was what the French trappers called him, and the Indians, watching from a prudent distance as he broke into the homes of hordes of stinging insects, admired his courage as well as thinking him a bit mad.

Ben Buzz's technique was like bee-lining, capturing feeding bees, then following their direction of flight from two widely spaced locations. You followed the two lines to their intersection and started looking and listening for the bee tree. Unlike Grandfather, who had used a pocket Prince Albert or Velvet can to catch his bees, Buzz used a glass tumbler and a small piece of perfectly flat board. Ben's technique was superior, too, in that he used a bit of comb with a few drops of honey in it to make sure that his guide bees were full up and would fly straight home -- some of Grandfather's would just fly to the next clover patch. "Part of the game, part of the game," he'd say, patiently recapturing them to try a second or third time. Buzz didn't try to fight the bees. He just knew and followed their ways. He'd drop a bee tree and sit back, safe, for however long it took the colony to decide that they didn't like living sideways where everything had been vertical or living in the jumble of broken comb following the fall. Sooner or later most of them would come out and ball into a swarm on a nearby branch, then leave after their scouts had located a new home. After that it was safe for Ben to move in, split the tree if it hadn't split as it fell, and harvest the remaining honey. The swarm's combined bellies were never enough to carry it all off, and while the hundreds of bees left behind looked and sounded fierce, they were just as loaded down with honey as those who had been in the departing swarm and intent on figuring out where to go rather than attacking Ben Buzz unless he was clumsy and hurt any of them.

Raymond leaned back, took a satisfying pull at his drink, which was near finished enough to have begun suppressing the pain in his leg and the discomfort in his mind that he'd been refusing to acknowledge existed. Book in one hand, glass in the other, he gimped the couple of steps over to Bill's desk to refill his glass without his stick, rolling like a sailor matching the swell and only halfway clenching his teeth. Replenished and back in his chair he sat and sipped, thinking about what the foreword glossed over while explaining about bees. It simply stated that he made kegs to transport the honey, and Raymond was turning over and over in his mind the woodcraft knowledge the man would have to possess in order to make tight enough containers to transport honey with only knife, hatchet, and axe. He concluded that it couldn't have been any conventional cooperage but was most likely sections of hollow trunk or limb, taken, if the man was lucky, from the felled bee tree, if not, with as much labor from another. Knowing that once the bees were established in new home and their order restored they would come coursing back to empty the combs that they left behind, Ben Buzz would have to work like fury to cut his sections fill them and set them aside, probably with a thick layer of green leaves carefully laid in as temporary tops and bottoms. Whatever honey leaked out from broken comb was cleaned up by the scavenging bees and the leaves kept them out of the rounds so that they couldn't rip open any sealed cells and steal his load. Thousands of scavenging bees would fly around him from dawn to dusk and Buzz could peacefully keep on with his work, secure in his understanding that they wanted honey, not a fight. Any watchers, White or Red, lacked this understanding, kept their distance, and continued to think him brave, crazy, and perhaps the beneficiary of some gift from the gods. If a bear showed up, well, Buzz had to back off to where he had set his rifle, and hope that the got the bear before the bear got him.

Raymond imagined Buzz's camp life in the following days. He'd have made things as comfortable as possible, probably brush lean-to in case of rain and to catch some heat from the fire if it was cool, and a line over a branch away from the camp itself to cache a bit of game. His working area, within sight, would provide a choice between sun and shade for the slow, careful preparation of the comb-laden sections for transport. The first step would be sealing the rounds into rudimentary, if immensely heavy kegs. It was easy to reave small, straight grained boards from an empty circle of hollow trunk with axe and hatchet, as good as if they'd been quarter-sawn at a mill. Pressing each board's ends between a slab of bark at his knee and the most convenient solid place at hand for a carving-horse, he'd use his great knife to draw the sides down as straight as possible. As soon as he'd finished enough boards to cover the end of a honeycomb section, he'd try their edges together for fit, carving a bit here and there for adjustment. After laying his boards on the ground in good order, he'd use the point of his knife to scribe a diagonal across the lot so that he could easily reestablish correctly-paired edges if he scuffed them about as he rim-rolled one of the full sections into the right working position. Having exposed a layer of honey-wet leaves, he would be joined by enough scavenging bees to keep his reputation going. Next he'd use knife and hatchet to clear the hollow's rot back to clean wood, making the best grove he could all around to receive the head-boards. By eye and mark he'd use axe head on hatchet to trim them to fit, remove chips and leaves from above the combs and hammer the head boards home into the groove. Given that it was camp work with only woods-man's tools, there were always gaps to be tamped full with smooth strips of inner bark. Glad to stand up and stretch, Buzz would the walk to the felled tree, select a double handful of empty, beeless combs from the wreckage, melt the wax in his skillet and serve his joints like a sailor on deck with his pitch-pot serving a weakened seam.

The head complete and sealed, Buzz would reverse the round, making the head into a bottom, and repeat the process to finish sealing the round. Turning the headed comb sections into transportable form involved removal of the bark and excess wood of the walls to approximate the thickness of a cooper's stave. The bark could be knocked off easily enough, and Raymond figured that Buzz could be pretty precise in how much wood he removed in each pass from top to bottom by using the same trick the old people used in facing logs or squaring beams with a broad-axe. Ben could strike groves across the grain to a uniform depth every few inches with his hatchet, then quickly split the chips in between out from top to bottom, using his knife held horizontal, tapped with hatchet head, which would give him as much control as a man reeving shingles from a block with a froe and club. The finishing work, removing the last bit of weight from the rounds he would have to pack out in stages using his own legs and back if he had no horse with him, he'd have to do like he'd done truing the edges of the head boards, his great knife skimmed back towards him with both arms like a draw-knife, bark against his knee as a carving horse. "What an impossible amount of work!" he thought as he went to refill his drink, this time taking his stick and returning with both glass and bottle. "Not really, though," he decided after sitting back down and considering the question for a few sips. Bees stay in our hives because they seem like home, about the size of a tree hollow. Old Buzz's have to be pretty lucky to find and fell a bee tree that yielded him as much as two or three two-foot sections. Thinking back on it, he could only remember a few years when Grandfather'd stacked bee boxes six or eight feet tall. Old Buzz more likely only had to do a single keg at each tree.

Raymond set to reading in earnest. The first chapter gave the lie to his carefully-imagined technique of keg-making in that it took the reader to the honey-hunter's cabin and stated, Raymond thought, without adequate explanation, that he made his kegs in the conventional way and had a good supply of staves that he had prepared. It did not, Raymond noted, tell of him taking any kegs with him when he went out, stating that he carried only a small wooden bucket with his tools-- axe, knife, rifle and spyglass. With what Raymond knew of colonial-era cooperage and its specialized tools, he still thought his imagined approach to packing backwoods honey more likely than Cooper's, but didn't find fault. After all, the man was an author of frontier adventure stories, not overly concerned with such details, which wouldn't add any excitement, and it was amazing that he'd put forth a honey-hunter as a main character, especially given that Raymond never knew such men existed.

The opening scenes had him, improbably, encountering a reprobate white man, a lone Indian warrior and an Indian runner or messenger who then accompanied him while he was locating what turned out to be an uncommonly rich bee-which they felled and found to contain several hundred pounds of honey. The real action then began with the killing and scalping of the warrior, left propped up against a tree, rifle in his lap, but powder horn and shot-bag emptied. It seemed that Bourdon and his whisky-loving new associate had enjoyed the misfortune of taking up with   the two most unpopular Red men in the region, so that without time to keg up that afternoon's three hundred pounds, they had to load the season's honey and bearskins (the logic was that insofar as bears liked honey, honey-hunters got to kill and skin more than what would be an ordinary man's share) and beat it down the Detroit river ahead of the pursuing Indians to rescue his new friend's wife and daughter on their way to lake Erie and the safety of New York state settlements. Raymond, having been educated in rural North Carolina, knew that there had been a War of 1812 -- the Star Spangled Banner, burning of the White House, and all -- but it had sorta' been squeezed in between the local Revolutionary War battle of Guilford Court House (a British victory, but at a cost that ended their Southern strategy and led to their unfortunate encampment at Yorktown) and the many battles of the War, mostly in Virginia. His knowledge of the historical complexities framing Cooper's narrative was slim and he had to accept the book's references to the geography of the Detroit River with blind faith. Ignorance didn't make the tale any less exciting, though, and it filled the afternoon. He did notice the repetition of a prisoner's escape from torture but not death by the long rifle shot of a lone disappearing Indian. This time the poor devil avoided being suspended stretched and eventually snatched in two as two bent trees tied to hands and feet straightened as opposed to spit-roasting, the planned fate of the British officer in Mohicans.

Finished with his book, Raymond stretched, took his stick and went outside for a walk around the building to clear his nose of the store's ever-present odors of petroleum and coal-fired stove. He wondered how many years of boots tracking in minute quantities of oil it had taken to overcome the diverse and subtle smells established during its era of general merchandising. Refreshed, he went back inside and ate another sandwich, supper, at Bill's desk. Now two of Bill's stash of Coca-Colas were gone. During supper he leafed through one of the beekeeping manuals, picking up a new fact or technique every page or so. Finished, he decided to tackle the second novel, The Keeper of the Bees. It had gotten dark outside as he ate, so he turned on the couple of dangling overhead bulbs and rigged Bill's gooseneck desk lamp on a shelf so that it shone over his shoulder, added a bit of coal to the fire, and settled back down to read.

Raymond could really relate to the opening of this book, in which a veteran of the last war, shunted from hospital to hospital with a shrapnel wound in his chest, stopped to rest on a bench in a restricted area under the camp commander's office window after an overly ambitious walk down and back along the steep, winding drive of a posh resort turned into a hospital. His service, wound, long convalescence, and exhaustion sufficed as justification for ignoring what he thought was a chicken-shit restriction against sitting there, probably put in place to keep up appearances for visiting politicians and brass hats. As he rested and caught his breath he realized that there might be more behind the restriction than mere appearances -- he could hear every word being spoken in the office behind him through the open window over his head. Relaxing and without really paying attention, he was aware that medical officers in the office were discussing the proposed transfer of patients to other hospitals. He sat bolt upright and listened for sure when he heard his own name mentioned. The chief medical officer cited his records, saying that his chest wound had not improved in the several months that he'd been there, which was true, and proposed shipping him out to a camp that he knew housed tuberculosis patients. He heard his own doctor raise his voice, protesting that the fellow had a bad chest wound with 'proud flesh' that wouldn't heal, not TB, and that sending him to the other camp in his weakened state amounted to a death sentence. The ranking officer responded that they needed his bed here for someone who might benefit from it, and that the transfer order stood.

Right off the fellow decided to go AWOL, no big problem since the resort wasn't up to a normal camp's security -- no guard details, just a couple of MPs drinking coffee all night with the officer of the day, their jeep with special paint and an electric siren parked outside. Even in daylight nobody had commented on him wandering away from his assigned area down the long drive to the highway and back. As soon as it got dark he followed the drive down again, rested, walked a ways from the entrance, hoping to avoid the rare military vehicle that might come in at that hour, and raised his thumb for any passing vehicle. He didn't care which direction, he just wanted some miles between him and the Army before next morning's roll call.

Raymond's leg was starting to ache pretty bad even though he had his feet propped up, so he reached for his stick, went over and brought the bottle and glass from the desk, where he'd left them after eating sandwich. The lady who wrote the book had been around soldiers, either guessed or knew that the way to keep your head straight wherever you ended up in the service was to pick one chicken-shit rule that you were gonna' ignore in order to be able to stomach the rest of 'em. She had it right, too, about security at civilian places turned hospital -- the MPs stood by wherever headquarters had been set up, waiting to be called out to any disturbance beyond the tolerance of the owners of any local night spot or manager of an on-base club. There wasn't much security at a stateside Army hospital 'cause there weren't any weapons other than the MP's and the soldiers were likely to be in too bad a shape to raise hell with each other, even those sent to finish their recovery at some requisitioned resort. A regular Army hospital would, though, have a perimeter road allowing the MPs to take advantage of a cooling breeze by riding it all night in hot weather. It'd be a little harder to go AWOL there, but not much more so. The MPs were, of course, busy ignoring *their* selected chicken shit rules, which often meant turning a blind eye to the coming and going of the more able patients who hadn't established reputations of being both wounded and nut cases. Sipping often enough that the whisky no longer burned on the way down and his leg began to feel better, Raymond wondered when the book was going to hit enough bees to justify its title.

The fellow in the book got a good lift pretty quick because he was in uniform, had some adventures, found out how slow rides were after he got into rough mufti and ended up most dead from fatigue and his wound at the beekeeper's house only to hear that gentleman calling for help. He responded, and called the doctor who sent an ambulance, leaving him alone and in charge of two acres of hives by the Pacific shore when he could hardly stand and knew nothing about bees. But than a twelve-year-old tomboy girl who'd tagged after the beekeeper was introduced, and she showed him as they went along. The whole time he was trying to get well, relying on sun, salt-water and good meals provided by a neighbor. The book was a good enough mystery and filled Raymond's evening in trying to identify purposely unnamed characters but really didn't say much about bees other than using the bee-yard as a location to carry the plot along.

The book did, however, talk about a wounded vet's darkest thoughts, fears, and memories. Whenever those came up, Raymond couldn't help but compare them with his own. This fellow started out pretty bad, thinking that he wouldn't last a year that he would either die from his wound or drown himself in the sea. His people were all dead, he hadn't even a book from his preacher father's library to remember them by, only his Scotts name and ways. Again, Raymond had been through some rough days and hours himself, though he'd always had the family back on the farm to draw strength from. Maybe that's the reason that he'd never gotten suicidal, that and the fact that his had been a case of being patched together into a reasonably functional gimpy guy as opposed to growing weaker and weaker from an infected wound that wouldn't heal. The fellow in the book was different from him, though, in that he really hated Germans, bristled when he heard Black German bees called by their name. Raymond figured that a German dogface soldier was about like one of ours, doing what he had to do. Sure he'd cussed them something horrible on the day of the landing and in most of his dreams since, but that was because they'd been trying to kill him and his buddies, not out of hatred for the people of a nation. He figured that the German soldiers up top on the cliff had been just as rude towards him and his companions for the same reasons, fear and either army's constant in-house publicity efforts to boost combat effectiveness by dehumanizing the enemy. You ain't got much of a soldier if he pauses to think about the other rifleman's kinfolk! The fellow in the book certainly had his personal reasons to dislike Germans, his time fightin' and his wound, but things went deeper for him. The author made it plain the he was a first-generation American citizen that both his parents had been born in Scotland. He made reference to the German treatment of a Scotts regiment early in the war, something that folks who'd been in the First War must've all known about but Raymond didn't. He did, however, know of the reputation that the British Colonel Banastre Tarleton earned in the South during the American Revolution.

'Tarleton's quarter,' the slaughter of wounded and surrendering men, was a Revolutionary War phrase that survived the lore of the intervening and preoccupying War between the North and the Confederate States, and Raymond figured that Jamie MacPherson's ill will must have stemmed from a similar event.

The book was a good enough mystery about who was who, had a pleasant ending, and got Raymond through the evening hours. Finished reading and thinking about sleep, Raymond figured that he'd be more comfortable on the beat-up old sofa that Bill kept for summer afternoon naps than on the floor so he shoved and drug it over nearer to the fire. That took several stages because he could only manage one overstuffed end at a time. He'd brought the pillow from Sarah's in from the truck and he shook out the comforter from home as he unfolded it from the tool box. He stoked the fire, adjusting the damper to keep it going slow for as long as possible, refilled his glass and set it alongside the couch within reach of the pillow, turned out the lights and carefully made his way back towards the orange glow from the crack around the stove's door and the fainter light from between the damper's almost closed row of overlapping shutters. He sat down on the couch and put his cap and stick down just by his glass. He paused for a minute, considering, before swinging his booted feet up onto the couch, not bothered when he'd reflected on how Bill did the same; threw the comforter down his legs, pulled a bit of it back up to his shoulders and settled on his back, head and shoulders propped up by the sofa's cushioned armrest and his pillow.

Reaching down for his glass, retrieving it and sipping, he realized how thoroughly and unconsciously he'd orchestrated his day, one thing to do after another, books to read, and no time to think about more than what came next. Grateful for the whisky's effect on the pain that returned to his leg as he'd lurched the sofa across the floor, he realized that he had to start thinking things through beyond Sunday's three sandwiches.

He was lonely for Sarah, but sad rather than angry about their separation. She'd said the word to leave, but they'd talked about their combined terrors and he'd agreed to go if they started tearing her down. She had, he thought, probably let him stay long after the tearing down began, and only this morning had to lay awake herself and realize how bad things were becoming. A good woman, he thought, sipping again. He didn't blame her for his being on Bill's old office couch, and was grateful to Bill as a friend who'd let him hole up for the weekend rather than having to search for a room the day he'd left Sarah's place. The day full of settling in where he was in familiar surroundings had, he thought, kept him calm enough to think straight now that he was faced with it. Sarah had been right, he figured, in their discussions about the job with Bill being more strenuous than he ought to be doing. Right, too, in saying that climbing all over the truck made his pain worse, that pain made his sleep worse, that lying half asleep, hurting got him to thinking back over the war so that when he did drop off his dreams took him straight back to the worst of it, and that hurting and not sleeping kept him drinking more and more as his tolerance grew. It really wasn't any different than if he'd gotten onto the morphine book at the pharmacy, just easier to ignore. He didn't know, he reflected, how much longer he had before he'd need to drink before work, then during the day. It already made Saturday and Sunday easier if he got started in the morning. Hell, it made it easier to get up from the chair at breakfast if he topped off the last, cold, half-cup of coffee. Thinking on that, he lay there looking at the light around the stove door without being aware that at the same time he'd sipped another mouthful from his glass and was letting it ease down his throat, bit by bit. The light around the door was, he thought, like the first hint of the engine fire that Sarah described in her dream.

47   DECIDING TO BECOME AN EGG MAN

Shifting his weight to fit his aches into the lumps of the sofa, he continued to study on the subject of working for Bill. Sarah was right about the physical part, but he'd never explained more than he had to about the extent to which thoughts and visions of cliffs and ladders preoccupied him while on the mountain road. He'd acknowledged the problem to her on days when he'd come home especially tired or visibly shaken, but it had, in fact, become a regular feature of that route, and it frightened him that the diversion of his attention from the road, especially in cold weather when seeps of ice draping the stone made his imaginings more real and at the same time made the driving trickier. It probably was, he concluded, time to move on. Change jobs before he physically or emotionally broke down, before it got to where Bill could no longer tolerate his drinking, and before the accident with the big International that was just waiting to happen. He mouthed another sip, musing the question of what job, and suddenly remembered the 'egg man wanted' sign and the telephone number scrawled on a scrap of paper in his jacket pocket. Working with poultry hadn't been a high point of his years on the farm, but he had no doubts about his ability to do the job. Throwing out scratch and gathering eggs were, after all, the last real farm work that an old man could do before settling in to wait by the fire and on the front porch. Sunday or not, he resolved to call the number at one o'clock the next afternoon. Facing life without Sarah's understanding and comfort was still too much for him to allow himself to think about, and he really wasn't sure where they stood with each other than no longer living together. Confining himself to practical steps, he figured he'd done right by her in leaving; he figured he was doing right by Bill by planning to stop driving the tanker before circumstances demanded it; and figured that he was doing right by himself, he concluded while savoring another swallow of whisky, in getting away from places and things that made his mind wander and his leg throb. Doing right by himself even if it meant dealing with chickens. The Army, he chuckled to himself, had at least prepared him to face chicken shit.

Thinking back over the day's reading he wished that he could hope to become a bee-man, but he knew that unlike Quentin Baker's modernized milk house, there was no modern way to avoid lifting, carrying, loading and unloading heavy hive bodies and supers and if he ran enough bees to as much as supplement Sarah's income he couldn't handle it. Feelin' no pain and getting sleepy, he reviewed what he'd learned about beekeeping that day as he emptied his glass and set it on the floor. Grandfather, he smiled as he thought it, easing back into his pillow, would be pleased, knowing that the boy was still, at heart, a bee-man, and still learning. Raymond drifted off to sleep, dreaming of the golden chains of bees as the old man held them up for him to see.

Raymond woke up on Sunday morning feeling pretty good. Having thought through a plan before going to sleep rather than lying half asleep reliving his break with Sarah and listing everything he couldn't do because of his wound he'd had a good night's sleep. If someone like Bill were there to ask him, he'd admit that sooner or later there'd come an evening of whisky and self-pity, but no one *was* there to ask the question, so the idea never crossed his mind. Deal with what presents itself, that's what growing up among farmers had taught him. Deal with it with bailing-wire and sheer determination if that's all you have at hand, and don't bellyache about it. Ranger training had been a lot like that, marching for miles in rough country, going on nothing but sheer force of will, with those that bellyached washing out, their names not even called at the next barracks roll-call after the field, sent back in the night to wherever they'd come from. He was, as best he could tell, taking the available steps to keep going with what he had left.

Breakfast was another sandwich and boiled coffee from Bill's pot. Bill's pot could likely produce boiled coffee even if you didn't put any grounds in with the water, since it had never been cleaned beyond swishing the last leavings around and throwing them out the door. Anxious to be doing something but unable to call the number from the sign until the man he had to talk to had finished his dinner, he went out to the loading shed and took his time filling the tanks on the International for the next day's deliveries. He hooked up a hose and sprayed the dust from the barrel-nose, wiping the drops of water with one of his undershirts since he didn't have a chamois -- despite all the work he'd done when he first bought the truck, he'd never been so car-proud as to think of buying one. Wiping with the shirt, he happened to think that he ought to get a big one, chamois that is, not undershirt, which he could tuck between the back and seat cushions and drape it across the width of the driver's seat, completely hiding the chicken-shit stain.

Finished with both trucks, he still had a good bit of the morning left. He went inside, stoked the fire up and got a drink to make his leg ease off from climbing around in the loading shed and working around the Ford without his stick, strategizing that if he was careful to have no more, the number of hours left and his noon sandwich would keep most the smell off of him if he was lucky enough to get a chance to meet the chicken man later in the day. He got a rag, his shoe-polish and brush from the five-pound sugar sack he had them wrapped in to keep his other things in the oak box clean and took his time erasing the morning's scuffing from his boots, carefully working the stain into each wound that showed the color of cut leather, then working back around to level the polish off even on the entire surface. By then his leg had stopped aching, so he stretched out on the sofa, cap pulled down over his eyes for a nap while the polish dried. He wasn't really tired, but still had the soldier's habit of catching a few winks when he could -- 'never stand when you can lean on something or sit; never sit when you can lie down; never lie down without napping unless there's a need to remain alert' -- those were the rules of coping with the 'hurry up and wait' inertia of day-to-day Army life.

He dozed without dreams and awoke thirty or forty minutes later, alert and close to pain free. A couple of minutes with brush and polishing rag and his boots looked good enough for a job interview. He'd have to be careful of scuffing them sideways on the pedals as he drove, and chuckled to himself, considering whether kilties might be a plus or minus. Could be that he man he hoped to talk to was the kind that paid attention to hats and food on shirt-fronts, but it wasn't smart to assume he wouldn't look down. Another sandwich for lunch, eaten with enough care to make sure that he did not decorate his shirt with stains from coffee left over from breakfast, and Raymond was ready to dial the phone. Problem was, though, that it was only twelve-thirty. If the chicken house owner was a church man, and his preacher had the common decency to let people loose by noon, he was probably just getting home. He decided to make himself wait until twenty after one to make the call. If the fellow was a fast eater, he'd be done by then, dawdling with his last half-cup of coffee, not yet committed to start some sort of project or a one-thirty radio program. If he was a slow eater, he'd have to 'fess up to it, and Raymond could make his manners, apologize profusely, and have his conversation before the guy hit the couch for his regular, one-thirty Sunday after dinner nap. People, he'd observed, were funny that way, matching life's little rituals to even fifteen minute starting times like mariners steering by points on the binnacle's card. Twenty after was good, and he'd gotten through a good ten minutes of waiting musing over it! He picked up his coat and dusted it over with the other hand, making sure that there weren't any grossly stained spots and brushing away the light ones. Did the same for his hat. Couldn't remember when he'd last put gas in the pickup, so he grabbed his stick and went out in his shirtsleeves to check the gauge -- it was plenty full. Going outside without a coat chilled him enough that it was easy enough to finish the wait until one-twenty sitting by the stove, thumbing through one of the beekeeping books.

At one-twenty he went over to the desk, sat in Bill's chair, laid his stick on the desktop by the phone, leaned forward, picked up the receiver and when the operator came onto the line said "TUxedo 6-0661, please. Tuxedo exchange, he thought as he waited to be connected, concluding that the chicken farmer lived here in town. After a couple of rings, a man who sounded maybe eight or ten years older than himself answered in a tone of voice that gave no indication of irritation over interruption of either dinner or nap. "Good afternoon, sir," Raymond replied. "My name is Raymond McCleary, and I'm calling about the egg man job you have a sign out for. I apologize for callin' about business on Sunday afternoon, but a chance at the job's right important to me."

"No need to," the man chuckled. "My name's Frank Hess. Just put that sign up after gatherin' eggs yesterday morning, so I guess your callin' today gave you the jump on any other fellows who might be interested. I've been tending those birds three days now, since I discovered my last man'd quit when the cook out at the hospital callled Thursday evening wantin' his eggs for Friday morning. I don't see talkin' to you about the job on Sunday afternoon's any more of a sin than gatherin' eggs and puttin' out feed was early this mornin."

"Thanks."

"Are you working anywhere now?"

"Yes, sir. I've been driving an oil truck for Bill Riley since last spring. I like Bill and I like the job, but I got gimped up in the war, and climbing up and down from the tanker's gettin' a little hard for me to handle by the end of the week."

"I know Bill, good man," Hess said, neither statement a surprise to Raymond. "Don't want to be stealin' his people. You set on leaving there?"

"Yes, sir, soon as I can find something that won't fire my leg up so bad."

"Told Bill that yet?"

"No, sir. Just figured out last night myself that I have to change. I plan to tell him first thing in the morning."

"I need someone willing to live there with the birds, not fancy. You willin' to do that?"

"Yes, sir."

"How 'bout your leg? Can you work out whatever notice Bill needs?"

"Yes, sir, it's not so bad that I can't stay on as long as he asks."

"Can you meet me out at the farm in an hour?"

"Yes, sir."

"Good, see you there."

Mr. Hess, obviously, had to change clothes before coming to 'the farm'. Raymond figured that if a man lived in town, likely had a town job, and owned ten or fifteen acres with a producing poultry operation just beyond the boundry of the town, he was entitled to use the term, however strange it sounded for land with no house and no barn. Sounded better than 'can you meet me at the chicken house in an hour?', and might indicate a sense of humor, taking up a phrase that his wife or friends used to tease him. He knew that if he got the job, Dave's first greeting afterward would be something like 'Those feathers on your boots? Thought you were a big oil-man.' Raymond figured it would take him at most ten minutes to get out to Hess' place, so he sat down to thumb through a bee book some more, unable to concentrate, just looking at pictures and their captions.

He'd been right, it didn't take ten minutes to drive east on Richmond road to the farm gate, which was open. He followed up the lane and parked beside what he assumed was Hess' car, one of those 'businessmen's coupes', two seats and an elongated boot, good for salesmen with sample cases to carry and deliveries to make. Not new, black, clean but not polished. He pulled his hat down to exactly the right angle, grabbed his stick and walked around the back of the pickup towards Hess, who was just getting out himself. Hess was a small, neatly dressed man wearing old but impeccably clean real farmer's clothes and well-polished brogans.

"Hello," he said, holding out his hand." Frank Hess."

"Raymond McCleary. Pleased to meet you." Raymond shook his hand.

"Likewise. You're here on a pretty good recommendation since you work for Mr. Riley. Let me show you what has to be dealt with if you come here." Hess opened the ground-floor of the two-story central portion of the south-facing building from which the single-story henhouses stretched out to the east and west. There was enough light from the door and windows to make out that it was a granary with several feed-barrels, buckets upturned on their covers, but when Hess reached the center of the room and pulled the light-cord, Raymond realized that it was a workroom and bare-bones kitchen as well. There was tin sink with one tap under a closed cupboard with a couple of dishpans upside down on the drain board; a kitchen range with a hot-water tank on the end, flour-sack dishtowels drying on an overhead wire nearby; and a plank table with a couple of chairs and a tall stool. Half of the concrete back wall (the back of the first-floor room and henhouses was dug into the slope of the hill), on the other side of the chimney from the stove and sink, was recessed into the cool earth and stacked floor-to-ceiling with square wire-and-wood slat egg carriers with 'HESS' stenciled in white on the sides. Pivoting around, Raymond saw a door leading into each henhouse, and narrow, open stairs leading to the room above. His eyes followed them up to the ceiling, across to a black heat-register grate, then across and down to a double rabbit-ear shotgun on pegs above the door they'd just come thigh. "Have a seat," Hess invited. Turning back towards him, Raymond noticed that the table held a ledger, a glass with a couple of pencils, an aluminum egg-grading scale and a home-made coffee can egg candle.

Raymond pulled out a chair and sat down, laying his cap and stick on the tabletop alongside the candle. Made of a coffee can, it had four small carriage bolts for legs and feet and shaded vents in each end to let the heat of the bulb out. Rather than just a hole to let the light out to shadow the egg, there was a lip cut from the rim of a smaller can soldered into exactly the shape of an egg held small end up and necked out far enough from the hot can that you wouldn't brush your hand against it and be burnt. "Your work?" Raymond asked, tapping the candle. "Nice."

"Yep, no point in buyin' what you can make."

"Nice," he repeated, sitting back to listen to what Hess might have to say.

"I've been taking care of the birds for the last few days. My last man didn't give me but a day's notice. Kinda inconsiderate, but I really can't get mad at him. He'd been seein' a real nice lady, and she asked him to move in with her. My wife's a big church woman and thinks it's a scandal, but I know that a fellow doesn't get asked that question twice and can't fault him for sayin' yes and goin'." Raymond wondered if Hess had any idea how well *he* understood that situation. "I have the contract to supply eggs to the hospital over in Fishersville. Need a man to live here, tend to the birds, wash the eggs, and deliver twice a week. When the weather's good enough to let the birds out I expect him to be reared back in a chair outside the door with the old Nitro Hunter in his lap, ready for hawks, foxes, and stray dogs. So long as those things are done, the rest of his time's his own. If you want time off, you've got to get somebody to take your place. I've got a list of a few fellows you can call. Sound like something you can handle?"

"Yes, sir."

"Tell me what you know about takin' care of chickens." It was Hess' turn to sit back and listen, Raymond leaned towards him, forearms and hands flat on the table as he answered.

"Feed 'em and make sure that they have plenty of clean water, mornin' and evening. Pick up any dead birds soon as you see them, make sure that the oyster-shell box stays full. If the weather's too bad to let 'em out throw some scratch in the straw mornin' and noon to give 'em something to work at. Check the boxes and count the setting hens before you throw out scratch or put out feed and start counting birds at the door so that you get an accurate count. Carry one of the little note-books that the fertilizer man gives away and a stub of a pencil so that you can jot your numbers down with the date. Clean the floor and under the roosts before you have to -- keeps the birds healthy and saves your back by keepin' the work light. Don't try to cut the corner by throwing clean straw over a dirty floor. Gather eggs morning and evening, wash 'em with plain cold water and a rag and put them in the crates to dry, separating them by grade and whether or not they've got double yolks or blood spots in 'em."

"What if there's hard manure that your rag can't get off?"

"'Don't use soap or hot water. Just work it off with your thumbnail or one of those rough scrubber-cloths that you use on pots and pans."

"What do you do if somebody gets pecked on?"

'Pour on a little pine-tar. It stops the bleeding and tastes bad to the next pecker.'

"I do believe," Hess leaned forward the same way Raymond was, "That you and I graduated the same chicken-school! There's a rake, scraper, scoop, and wheelbarrow in both sides; a hatch in back on both sides to throw straw in from the shed; and a can of tar over each door jamb. No point in walkin' and carryin' when you don't need to. Your leg gonna let you do all that?"

'Yes, sir. I think so since there's plenty of things to lean on and I can rest a bit when I need to."

"Good. I wouldn't want to hire a man and work him back to the hospital."

"If you don't mind my askin', how'd you get the hospital order?" Raymond inquired.

"When I saw work start on the hospital, I went out there and asked about twenty men who was in charge of buyin for the kitchen. Seventeen of them didn't know and sent me on to someone else who didn't know, but numbers eighteen and nineteen got me to the local procurement officer, a Captain who was just setting up in a new office. Asked him if he had eggs yet, he said no, and that I should write him up a bid. I took a few days to get one together, and within a week had a letter accepting it and a list of people, mostly lieutenants and sergeants who I was to call whenever I needed things.'" Hess laughed. "There's no way he could have asked for or considered other bids, he got back to me so quick. Probably glad to have something checked off of his list before he'd decided where to put his wife's picture on his new desk. Probably liked the sound of the bid, too, how it would read to whoever inspected his work. I'd proposed to supply him with clean, fresh eggs from healthy birds managed by Department of Agriculture standards in a new, disease-free house built to their latest design, which I'd gotten mailed to me along with a full pile of poultry pamphlets as soon as I got the notion to go out there. I'd read through them as I wrote the bid and was ready to talk government language if I had to, plans under my arm ready to roll out on the table, but I never got the chance. Bid required the Army to supply the materials, easy enough when they were getting trainloads to build a hospital, and me to provide the carpenters and land. Also got a letter from some general giving me priority at any hatchery that had chicks."

Warming to his story, Hess leaned back, chuckling. "My carpenters, two country fellows way too old for the draft, were quite a combination working with the Army folks. They're barn carpenters who've always got along by arguing with each other over any measurement or decision that has to be made. One's a heathen, the other washed in the blood of the lamb, so that when they work it's a steady stream of cussin' and prayers, cussin' and prayers. They split up once, but got back together after a couple of jobs because they both made mistakes, working with a helper who accepted all of their measurements and calculations. First days on the job it sounded strange because they complained in unison about building this chicken-house different from what they'd done all their lives. That stopped, though, when I explained how the bid'd gotten them into the Army lumber yard. Every board that came in, they inspected for warps and knots, hauling the rejects home at night on their pickup. They were like kids when they discovered that the Army's unit of issue for nails was 'keg, one each' which the clerk wrote, the supply sergeant approved, and the truckers delivered. I was amazed, watching the variety of kinds and sizes of nails necessary to go from cement forms to roof, to the trim and to the slider-guides for the window screens of the room upstairs as they came in with each truckload of materials. I teased the boys about being so much neater than I'd ever seen them be before -- no pile of scrap and rejected boards -- they acted hurt and told me that they'd just been lookin' out for me, since there were sure to be Yankee guvmn't snoops looking at an Army contract job. I thanked 'em and asked them to keep up the good work." Both men had a good laugh.

"I have split firewood delivered, stacked in the shed out back, and I'm sure that the feed man will accommodate us by bringing the bags in and giving the barrels all they'll hold, limiting your lifting to half-sacks or less. There's a phone upstairs, you'd have to settle with me for long distance. I was paying my last man..." Hess stated a figure half again what Raymond was earning at Bill's. "Could you work for that? It includes room, of sorts, but I realize that a man gets tired of what he can fry up on the range and sandwiches, you'd better figure on eating out most evenings."

Throughout their conversation Raymond had been trying to sort Hess out. His farm clothes and knowledge of poultry were real, but didn't fit his model of automobile, even if it wasn't polished. Raymond could see a bit of himself in the man in the shined brogans and the fact that he, too, had a physical impairment. When they'd shaken hands, Raymond had noticed a tremor just as Hess started to put some force against his grip. He'd seen it again when Hess had opened the door and when he positioned his chair at the table. Hess obviously understood people and didn't appear to be judgmental, giving the view of the fellow who left to be with his girl as much respect as his wife's opinion that it was a scandal. He knew and respected Bill Riley; had maintained a longstanding working relationship with a couple of argumentative barn carpenters; and could see the opportunity for a government contract, plan how to make his bid both attractive to the Army and to his business advantage. Raymond didn't have time to puzzle on it any longer. The man had asked him for an answer.

"Yes, sir, Mr. Hess. I'm willing to take it on if you'll have me.'"

"Good." Hess extended his hand across the table to seal the deal. Raymond watched Hess pull exactly the kind of notebook he'd described moments earlier from his pocket, pencil something on a page, tear it out and hand it to him. "That's my number at work. Give me a call after you talk to Bill and find out how much notice he needs, please, so that I can get temporary help lined up and not be over here twice a day myself."

"Yes, sir. I'll do that. And thanks for taking me on!"

"You're welcome," Hess stood up. "I hope that putting egg crates on a pickup is easier on your leg than crawling around on that big old International." Raymond understood that Hess' doing him the courtesy of standing signaled the end of the interview. He took up his stick, put his cap on at exactly the right angle and let himself out, leaving Hess to tend to his evening chores. Sonofabitch! he thought to himself as he pulled the Barrelnose out of the gate and onto the road leading back into town. The man even paid enough attention to what passed him on the road to know what kind of truck he'd been driving for all of these months!

It didn't take any longer to get back to the store than it'd taken to go to the chicken farm. Since he'd already loaded the oil truck that morning, about all he could think of to do outside was to top off the gas in the pickup, a matter of only a couple of gallons, and walk the lot, policing up any trash that had blown in. Not much of that because the fencerows were right brushy and stopped blown paper on the other side unless there was a whirling wind to lift it up and over. He opened the back door, got the coal scuttle and filled it before going in and taking off his coat and hat. The fire had died down; he stoked it with another shovel of coal and adjusted the damper as it began to catch. Time, he figured, as he walked around and pulled the dangling strings to turn on the lights, to sit and think. He got both of the bee books, put them within reach of the rocker next to the stove, and since his leg was starting up, got a glass of whisky to sip on while he sat next to the fire. Sipping, he considered his situation. He missed Sarah, the cheery comfort of her place, and Oscar in his lap. Not having her to talk to was about as bad as not feeling her frequent, passing touch. Having had to break off their living arrangement, he didn't have a great deal of confidence in their ability to successfully continue in a less intimate relationship. He felt bad about having decided to stop working for Bill, but was, at the same time excited about his chance with Hess. Neither job had any real prospect for advancement other than from the other people he might meet in the community. He wasn't going to work his way up to foreman when he was the only employee. Bill was a pretty shrewd fellow and while Raymond had learned a lot from watching him deal with people and listening to his stories, he sensed that there were some well-defined limits to his range, the world of chain-store and pump-service threatened general stores. He doubted that they'd completely die out, but could see their need of a kerosene and gasoline wholesaler dropping. He mused over the daylight dreams he'd had while driving the mountain road and couldn't imagine anything about being a chicken-man that would start that process going. He'd have to be at the hospital twice a week, but only at the kitchen door, not on the wards, and he seldom had nightmares about his hospital experiences, usually just dreams that he understood when he awoke, tangled in the covers. He figured that he could manage the egg crates -- they were small enough to handle with his right arm while supporting himself on his stick with his left, and was confident that once he'd made friends with the kitchen staff they'd help him unload. The ancient, rabbit-eared Nitro Hunter was so unlike a military weapon that he figured it would take his mind hunting back home rather than back to the war.

Having thought through what the new job required, he remembered what his father had said, that the men who couldn't find peace had hung themselves in the barn, gone West and never been heard from again, or drunk themselves to death. Considering his own situation, he figured that having to leave Sarah and his job, both at once, was enough trouble that if he was the kind to cut and run he'd be on the road right now, rather than rocking by the stove trying to understand himself. If he was the hanging kind, he'd been alone around plenty of strong beams with a clear drop in both the store and the loading shed and hadn't given them a thought until just now, as part of his review of things. Looking at the nearly empty glass in his hand, neat whisky, and feeling his leg beginning to throb from sitting too long, he knew which of the three was going to get him if he didn't find peace, whatever that was. He reckoned, taking another sip, savoring the now diminished burn and calculating how soon the liquor would sooth his leg, that peace would be a freedom from his involuntary bouts of memory of the ladders and his nightmares, freedom from his calculating evaluation of every encounter with people and places, making a barracks assessment as to how he, as a gimp, could deal with any trouble that might come up, and although he doubted it possible, freedom from the pain of his now healed wound.

Finishing the last sip, he got up, leaning more heavily than usual on his stick, and moved around a bit to try and ease things in his leg. He collected sandwich fixings from cold storage on the shelf at the far end of the room and fixed supper. It'll be nice, he thought, to have the range at the henhouse and be able to fry up some meat and bloodspot eggs rather than living on baloney and cheese when he didn't want to go out. He ate, brushed the crumbs off of Bill's desk and put the leftover food away. Facing the rest of the evening, he considered writing to his family or even calling down to Guilford, but decided to put both off until he had more news of his job change. He settled back down beside the fire and was starting to thumb through one of the bee books but was startled by the sound of wheels crunching in the gravel, an engine being killed, and his buddy Dave calling as he let himself in. "Raymond, what you doin' down here? I was driving home; saw the lights and your truck, so I pulled in. What are you doing down here at the store on a Sunday evening?" He looked around. "Camping out by the looks of it." Dave came all the way in and stood with his back to the stove, hands behind him, warming his fingers as he waited for Raymond's reply.

"It's a long story. Get you a drink, freshen mine up, pull over a chair, and I'll tell you."

Dave did as he was asked, lighting one cigarette on the way, then another off of the one between his lips, which he handed to Raymond along with his glass. "Kinda like the old days on Mrs. Russ' back porch."

"I remember those evenings as so easy that they hardly seem to have been real," Raymond replied, launching into the full explanation as to why he was no longer at Sarah's and putting all of his previous hours' thinking into words. That, interspersed with Dave's comments and questions, took the rest of the evening. After David left, Raymond lay down on the sofa, which after one night felt like his own. Talking in such detail with his friend must have cleared his mind. When he awoke in the morning he didn't remember having dreamt of anything.

First thing in the morning Raymond stoked the stove and put some grounds to boil in Bill's coffeepot. He pulled the sofa back to its usual spot and put his box of gear back into the barrel nose's bed. He was working on putting his breakfast sandwich together when he heard the sound of Bill's truck pulling in, unusually early. He'd figured that he would have been finished with breakfast and the desk swept free of crumbs by the time his boss arrived.

"Caught you!" Bill practically bellowed. "Eatin' on company time and drinkin' my coffee. Gimme a cup!" Raymond had no idea of the fears that Bill had carried with him to work that morning, the alternative possibilities as to Raymond's condition when he arrived that he had outlined for his wife two days before. Bill had been pretty sure Raymond was alive when he'd first seen smoke from the chimney -- not likely, he'd thought, that a feller'd wake up, stoke the fire, and then decide to end it all. At that point he'd figured fifty-fifty whether or not Raymond'd be drunk, and although he was mighty pleased that he wasn't, wouldn't have been disturbed if he had been. He'd known good men who stayed drunk for more'n two days after losing a woman. Raymond handed him his coffee and Bill pulled over a chair, leaned back, put his feet up on the edge of the desk opposite Raymond and sipped his coffee, studying his cup as he did so, determined that he would not speak before Raymond. Raymond finished making his sandwich and proceeded to eat it, slowly, determined not to start a conversation until he had finished, cleaned up and put away his fixin's. The place was awful quiet except for the slurping of coffee and the creaking of the stove and stovepipe as a change in the wind or a sweet or sour spot in the coal made the fire change intensity. Raymond finished up, refilled his own cup and Bill's, put the pot back onto the stove, returned to his seat and assumed Bill's posture, a mirror image, studying deep into his black coffee on the other side of the desk.

Finally Raymond broke the silence. '"Bill, I just don't think that I can do your work on the truck any longer. Back home I figured that oil trucks loaded and unloaded themselves, but I didn't know enough to understand that a man had to climb up and down all day to make that happen. My leg can't keep up with it, and I can't keep up with my leg without drinkin'. Petroleum smell's right strong, but it can only cover up but so much whisky smell. I figure that if I don't quit, it's not gonna' be long before you have to ask me to go." Bill didn't say anything for a long time, just sipped his coffee, thinking about the problems that Raymond had in addition to pain.

"Reckon you're right. It'd be a hard day, tellin' you to go, but you're right. Those storekeepers have good noses, and it would only be a matter of time 'till I got a couple of calls. If you had enough in you that you wrecked the truck, even if nobody was hurt that'd pretty much put me out of business. Every pump station goes in cuts back on what the stores sell, and that's our franchise market. I'm countin' on that old tanker to last me until I'm ready to quit or the business just dies." This time Bill got up, got the near-empty pot, and refilled their cups. "You got any idea where you'll go from here?"

"Yes, sir. I called the number on a sign at the gate of the chicken house that sits north of the Richmond Road just as you leave town wanting an egg man. Met with a Mr. Frank Hess out there yesterday afternoon and he offered me the job, subject to my working out whatever notice you wanted." Bill pushed is hat back, rubbed his face with his hands, and when he took his hands down he was grinning.

"Boy, 'cept for maybe me, and I'm not real sure about that, you couldn't find a better man in the County to work for. I'll tell you to git right now, so you have a good start with him, and considering that you haven't had a raise since you got here, I pay you this week's wage so you got a little extra to tide you over to your first check from him. I'll load up and surprise everybody on today's route that it's me and not you comin through the door."

"Thanks." Raymond leaned across the desk and shook Bill's hand. You've been awfully good to me, starting with just giving me a chance to work. By the way, you don't have to load, I did that yesterday."

"Good man. Now let me tell you about Hess."

They both leaned back and put their feet up again, Bill's favored posture for less serious talk than hiring, firing, or quitting. "Hess is a farm boy from Centerville, over past Mt. Solon. Only child, he was orphaned before he was ten, I don't know the particulars, but figure from his age that it must have been the influenza, back before 1920. Didn't have any close kin, no aunts or uncles, the neighbors, Ciracoffe, I think the name was, took him in and raised him with theirs. Farmed his farm and didn't cheat him. When he finished school they had money in the bank for him and he came to town and studied at Dunsmore Business College -- Frank always jokes that he was too embarrassed to frame his diploma and hang it on the wall because it was so big. Dunsmore advertises by making his diplomas twice as big as any university's so when you go into a successful businessman's office, you know right off where you ought to send your boy. While Frank was at Dunsmore, he roomed at Mrs. Russ' -- met his wife, Mary Frances, a school teacher, there. They have a place out on Taylor Street now, back yard runs right down to a farmin' field and they look out their kitchen door over the tops of the orchard and at the front of the old music college. He works for the bank, don't know exactly what his title is -- doesn't have enough money, land, or family connections to be a vice-president, but I do know that if anything important is going on, they've got his hand on it." Bill chuckled. "Not that you'd hear it from him. He'll tell you that his first job at the bank included filling the inkwells on the counters and emptying the spittoons, and he'll admit to picking up the Saturday mail and keeping it at home in a canvas satchel so that the drawer won't be overly full on Monday, making someone have to wait in line at the counter, but won't say a word about anything else. Try to get any inside word from him, he just smiles and quiet-like changes the subject. Express an opinion about a deal you think somebody's makin' and ask what he thinks about it, he'll say "might be, might be. Know you've got better sources 'n I have on that."

"Well, that explains why the farmer's clothes he was wearing were real, and his shined brogans, but what's the deal on his route-salesman's car?"

"He keeps a room with the family he grew up with, and 'most every weekend he goes out to his farm and either helps with whatever's bein' worked on or just piddles around, nailin' up loose boards, brings home a carrier with the week's eggs from his Rhode Island Reds. Sometimes his wife goes with him and they spend the night. They sell that automobile with the deep boot for drummers to look stylish and carry their sample cases. Frank carries his tools, just about a full farm workshop without a workbench, 'though I'm sure he's got a plank with a vise on it that he can brace one end on the bumper, weight the other end with a tool box and the spare tire and do his work just as well."

"What's the story on his shakes, has he always had 'em?"

"No, they came on after he'd been with the bank a few years, they're in his writing hand -- toting up too many ledgers. He's still a damn good shot with a rifle so long as he can brace it alongside a tree, but he has to rest it after three or four staples before he can hit a hammer good enough to finish fastening fence wire down a new post."

Bill stood up. "Reckon since you've loaded I might as well head on out." He pulled his wad from his pants pocket and counted off Raymond's week's wages, then handed it to him.

"Thanks, Bill.'" Raymond stood, leaning against the desk. He shifted the cash from his right hand to his left and held his right out towards Bill. "'Not just for the extra cash but for a lot of things." Bill shook his hand.

"Been a pleasure havin' you along. We don't need to stand here makin' speeches at each other, not like we won't be seein' each other around."

"You're right. Not like I'm leavin' home."

"Well, I'm gonna' go coax the International to life, you need to get on the telephone to Hess. We've been sittin' here talking about him long enough that he's had plenty of time to get to work, and if his ears are burnin', odds are that he's calculated that we're the cause!"

Bill left without further conversation. Raymond sat back down at the desk, fumbled the paper with Hess' work number out of his pocket and gave it to the operator as soon as she picked up. Three rings, then "Augusta Bank, Frank Hess speaking." The number either went directly to his desk or he was the first man there -- more likely the latter, considering what Bill'd told him.

"Raymond McCleary, Mr. Hess. Mr. Riley said he didn't mind my leaving without notice, so I can start today if that suits you."

"Good, good. That'll give you the day to get yourself settled in, and I'll come out after work to see how you're getting on and point out a few more things."

"Thank you, sir. I'll do that and see you this evening." Raymond hung up, heard Bill grinding through the gravel leaving the lot and looked around the store to see what he had to gather up and take with him. He'd put most everything in his box on the pickup, but was glad he'd checked, because one of the bee books had been left out on the chair by the stove. Wouldn't do to get those ladies at the library annoyed with him! Stick in one hand, cap at exactly the right angle, book and the remains of his sandwich-fixin's in the other, he went out, piled those few things on the passenger side of the seat, started the Ford and headed off for his new job and lodgings.

48. LIFE AT THE BARN

The gate off of the Richmond road was well planned, two sections of fence pulled in at an angle to traffic on either side so that even a two-ton straight truck would be safely off of the road while the driver opened and shut things, and a cattle guard made of steel pipe over a pit a foot or so deep, worn shiny where tires rubbed across it. Raymond followed the sod track up behind the building and pulled in under the shed. The side nearest to the back door of the sleeping room was stacked to the eaves with firewood, with a passage left right in front of the door. The left side, where he got out after pulling in had been double-stacked with wood at the beginning of the season, but most of the inside rank had either been burned or moved to the closer wall. There was a scuttle-door on the building down to the side of the couple of steps leading inside so that a fellow could throw wood down into the box beside the range in the workroom without having to carry it on the stairs or dirty up the sleeping room. One side of the back of the shed was a tool-cupboard with a padlock, the other the privy. The path through the opening between the two enclosures led a little ways out into the pasture where several yards of woven-wire fencing was anchored to a steel post, formed into a cylindrical incinerator for domestic refuse and dead birds. To the side there was a growing heap of burned cans that had been cleaned out of the wire, mostly sardines and Vienna sausages, judging from their shape, along with enough of a mixture of bottles and jars to prove some months of a previous bachelor's existence at the place.

It didn't take Raymond long to move in. He'd never bolted the oak box back into the truck's bed after leaving Sarah's. It was about as big as he could handle, but it went in quick. He hung his few clothes up in the wardrobe in just a couple of minutes. Mr., or perhaps Mrs. Hess, likely because of the West Beverley Street grapevine, had done him the courtesy of providing clean sheets on the bed, a towel, washrag, and soap on the washstand along with another serviceable set on the wardrobe shelf to switch out when he did his washing. He decided that the floor of the wardrobe was the best place for what remained of his case of whisky, although he set one bottle out to take downstairs with the food that he had left from camping at Bill's store. There was a radio upstairs on a small table by the head of the bed, and a good-enough lamp on top for reading.

There was an empty cardboard box in the wardrobe that he took advantage of to carry his odds and ends, including one of the bee books downstairs. He left the bee book on the table, added the cheese and baloney to the sizeable slab of side-meat that his predecessor had left in an egg crate with extra screening to discourage the mice, down against the foundation corner where it was coolest . He put his whisky in the dish cupboard, noticed that there was salt, pepper, and a few other cooking oddments there. It looked, he figured, like he could make it through supper and breakfast -- there were eggs! -- without going out to the store. Probably better make up a shopping list after thinking over it during the evening, he decided as he put another stick of wood into the range. There was a second, small stove upstairs, but it was cold when he came in. The way things were set up he could mostly rely on heat from the range and water tank rising through the floor register to keep the cold out of the bedroom.

Figuring that he might as well get to work before Hess arrived, he filled a bucket with mash from one of the barrels and went into one of the houses to check the feeders. He was surprised to find the lights, six or eight bulbs strung the length of the shed, on, but didn't look for the switch to turn them off, as he was likely to need them before he finished gathering eggs. The feeders, like the design of the building, were modern. About waist high with a wooden perch on either side of a steel trough about eight inches wide, they were topped by what looked like a perch made of three strips of steel butted together and pivoted with steel pins to the top corner of triangular braces that connected the top edges of the trough at regular intervals. Any bird that landed there got dumped off. Feeders that saved a lot of feed from being wasted. Comfortable wooden perches on the sides and the overhead bar encouraged the birds to peck their food out from the sides, rather than indulging in their natural inclination to get in a trough and scratch as they ate, kicking a lot of feed out onto the floor and heedlessly shitting in the trough behind themselves as they fed. He'd seen home-made wooden feeders with a bar on top, but they usually sat on the ground where the birds would get at least one leg in to kick, and they used the top bar for daytime, going-from-here-to-there perching, leaving manure to contaminate the feed. The spinning bar on top of these feeders stopped that, and it took a really determined bird to get a leg up and over to scratch out feed while standing on a perch low enough that she had to stretch her neck to peck from the trough. Before he was halfway down the room Raymond appreciated the fact that he didn't have to stoop over to check the feed. Being up on steel legs made the feeders less attractive, although not completely inaccessible to rats. The only design flaw that he could see was that the birds could only eat from the center, the far side was too much of a reach and the base of the near side too awkward unless the bird was really hungry and twisted her neck uncomfortably. Given, he laughed to himself, chickens' dealings with men, there was probably some inborn dislike on their part of even an uncomfortable twist to the neck! As he came along each feeder he shook mash from his bucket into the middle, where the hens had left bare metal showing, then swept his hand through to mix the leftover feed from each edge with the new. Maybe, he thought, it was the result of using a trough shape that was easier and cheaper to manufacture. Just as likely, though, the designer corrected two problems that he'd seen or been told about and the feeders went into production before they went into a henhouse where the second step for the feed man became obvious. It wasn't a big deal, though. The extra pass of the hand didn't require stooping or bending over, and the finely crushed grain flowing between his fingers actually felt kinda' good.

Raymond finished one side, went back to the workroom to refill his bucket and leaving both wooden doors to the henhouses open, screen doors behind them keeping the birds in their place, began refilling the feed troughs in the second room. The lights were on there, too, just as well because it was getting dark enough that he needed them. He'd emptied his bucket and was walking back up the row of feeders when he heard Frank Hess' car pull up. They more or less made it into the workroom at the same time and their greetings of "'Evenin' "overlapping each other.

"Gettin' started." Raymond told his new boss. "Filled the feeders and was just fixin' to start lookin' for eggs when you got here. All the lights got left on this morning -- burnin' when I first started feeding."

"No mistake about the lights, that's one of the things I needed to show you. Since we're obliged to produce on schedule, they're on timers to keep the hens workin' a full day. Look here." Hess opened tightly fitted hand-sized panel just above the light switch adjoining the door to the east hen house. When he stepped aside Raymond could see an electric clock in a heavy Bakelite case that exactly matched the dimensions of the tiny cupboard. Metal tabs just big enough to pull with your fingers were studded all around the face, a little more than half of them pulled out a quarter of an inch further than the rest. "Best coffee-pot timers I could find from a restaurant supply place. They wanted the earth for poultry-house light timers, and I figured that six bulbs down a line couldn't draw more current than a big diner coffee-pot. Cost me about a third of what the poultry boys asked, and the main difference that I could see was in the housing, so I made these little boxes real tight to keep out the dust. The brass-colored tabs are AM, the red-painted ones are PM, each one is a half-hour, turns the lights on when it's pulled out. Figurin' that they'll put their heads under their wings some at each end, I keep 'em on sixteen hour days; change the settings once a month to keep even with the season."

Spotting the bottle and glass Raymond had left on the table, Hess changed the subject. "Bill tells me that you're a drinkin' man. I'm not. He also told me that you have more of a reason for the habit than most, and I can respect that so long as the birds are tended right and the people you deliver to don't complain. Can you handle it that way?"

"Yes, Sir."

"Good. Let's gather the eggs, and I'll show you about the ledger and paperwork you'll need at the Hospital kitchen tomorrow morning before I go." He tossed Raymond a basket, took one himself and headed into the west henhouse. Raymond took the east. When they finished, Hess explained the bit of bookkeeping. Delivering eggs turned out to be a lot like delivering gasoline. Hess left, Raymond got the skillet, made himself a bacon-and-egg sandwich, turned the radio upstairs on loud enough that he could hear it, and commenced processing the day's eggs to add to the rest of the next morning's delivery.

Raymond finished his work in good order, had his nightcap, and slept well in the new bed. Better'n Bill's couch! he thought, splashing water on his face. He didn't shave, figuring that little was expected of chicken-men but that they drive, well, like they were hauling a truck full of eggs. Fried eggs, boiled coffee and bacon for breakfast. He'd have to get more bacon on the way home.

He pulled the Barrelnose around to the front, backed up to the door and let the tailgate down all the way, off of the chains, so that he could reach further into the bed. On his first trip he grit his teeth, laid his stick on the table, and gimped two egg carriers to the truck, managing to hit a chair at the table and the door-frame to keep his balance on the way. Not smart, he reflected as he went doorframe to table and chair to sit for a moment. Pulling an oil hose he'd had a predictable weight to lean against and had pretty much carried his stick as he went to have it for later use. The two egg carriers, even though they were small and light enough for his arms and shoulders, had swung in their wire and wood bail handles, magnifying and perpetuating each oddity of his gait so that even though he could manage the pain of walking, at least for that one trip, each step was a dance with the weight shifting in his hands, no step predictable. Egg men could probably get along without shaving, but he knew damn well that five or ten dozen dropped, broken or cracked eggs wouldn't do. He moved the remaining six carriers one at a time, stick in hand, pushed them forward to the front of the bed to the spot where they'd get the least jump out of a bump, put up the tailgate up and filled the remaining space in the bed with empties so that there could be no sliding. He glanced into each house, saw that the birds were busy with the scratch he'd thrown down earlier, put a stick of wood into the firebox of the range, pushed the pot with the leftover coffee to the far back corner where it'd stay tolerably warm but not boil into tar, put his cap on at exactly the right angle, and set out for the Hospital.

He'd driven the route countless times in both the pickup and oil tanker, but never taking consideration of anything except curves and speed because of his load.

As a chicken-man delivering eggs he poked along, avoiding or easing over any rough spot in the road, relieved to turn off onto the smooth lanes of the Hospital grounds. He stopped at the guardhouse stop sign, but the unarmed sentry saw the unmistakable egg crates from his stool by the window, waved him through and resumed reading his newspaper. The place is even less military, now, he thought as he headed towards the kitchen. He knew exactly where to go from his convalescent walks around the place. As he backed up to the door, a Colored man in cooks' whites emerged, directing him back and then stopping him with one hand's gestures. He got out, pulled his cap to the right angle and moved towards the back of the truck and the man already unhooking the tailgate chains. They looked at each other at the same instant, reaching to stack the empty egg crates out of the way so as to get hold of the full ones.

"Mr.Corp'l 'Cleary?"

"Sam? Sam Miller?" Raymond took a couple of steps and held out his hand to one of the orderlies who'd taken care of him during the times he couldn't do for himself. Another step closer, handshake completed, they embraced each other, then let go with a good mutual back slapping. "What're you doin' behind the kitchen?"

"More ladies back here."

"What you doin' with feathers on your boots? Last I heard you was Texas Oil Company man."

"Time for a change." They took the eggs in, Raymond was introduced to the head of the kitchen,

who signed the receipt book and they took the empties
out and loaded them so that they wouldn't bounce
around and be damaged. Raymond leaned on the back
corner of the bed, pulled out his pack of Luckies and
shook a smoke out to Sam, leaning on the raised tailgate, who took it with a nod. Raymond shook the pack
again, took one for himself, lit up from a kitchen match
which he then shielded with his hand and held over to
Sam. Sam savored and exhaled the first drag.

"This kitchen deal's a civilian job. Army's
winding things down here and didn't want no more
Black orderlies when they had extra White nurses. Discharged, I was lucky to get in here."

Raymond blew out a puff. "Turned out that un-
loadin' oil was lots harder on my leg than I figured.
Never thought about the climbing up and down all day.
Had to leave the lady I was with 'cause I have nightmares and was givin' them to her. Lucky enough to be
the first fellow to see a 'man wanted' sign Mr. Hess had
up the next day." Having both 'fessed up to the reason
for the changes in their lives they took their last drags
in silence, field stripped their butts into the gravel,
raised their hands in parting salute and wordlessly returned to the kitchen and driver's seat.

Going back with empty crates was relaxing,
regular driving. He stopped at the store at the beginning
of Brand's Flat and bought bacon and bread, told his
friends there that he'd changed jobs. He explained and
they understood about the physical part of his reason
for changing; he didn't go into the rest of it. They had,
of course, heard about his leaving Sarah's, and were
sympathetic without being nosy. Good people. Even if

they had heard bits of the private side of things, they kept quiet and didn't push for more to tell back to whoever'd gossiped to them. He went downtown to the Post Office on Fredrick Street, just up from the barber shop, and registered the battered rural free delivery box by the gate in his name and bought some stamps, wrote his new address in the corner of the envelope of the letter he'd written telling his people what he was doing now and put it in the slot. The Post Office was kind of interesting because it had WPA artwork in the lobby, relief carvings of Cyrus McCormick building and testing his reaper, the precursor of the binder he'd been daydreaming about not long ago. He looked over towards the barber shop, but decided against a haircut because he hadn't shaved and didn't feel like getting razzed by that crew about his appearance or change in jobs. Unlike the folks out at the store in Brand, he knew that none of the barber shop crew would cut him any slack, and he might end up with a cut-throat razor shave, which he'd never experienced, paid for by the loafers passing the hat so that the barber could put on a show with him as the victim.

Back to the barn, he'd decided that he'd call it that, a chicken barn, a word that sounded better and was easier to use in conversation than hen-house, chicken-house, or egg factory, because you could leave the poultry part off. Pulled up alongside the front door, unloaded the empty crates, put the receipt book on the table with the ledger, the bread in the tin breadbox, and the bacon into the rodent-proofed crate in the cool corner. Driving around to put the truck in the shed he realized that he'd been relieved to find that the breadbox, unlike many, didn't have a cheerful rooster enameled on its sides. Being a chicken-man was taking a little getting used to.

He went downstairs, stacked the cases he'd un-loaded by the door back in their proper corner, took a quick look into each house to satisfy himself that the birds were happy, and made a bite to eat. His leg ached enough from the morning's running that he finished off with a glass of whisky. Sipping, it occurred to him that his new position afforded him a luxury unviable in his old job -- a midday nap. Through with his drink he latched the front door but left the doors to the houses open so that he could hear any disturbance among the birds and went upstairs to stretch out on the bed.

Even upstairs he could hear the background flutter of the two houses through their screen doors. Steady and not evocative of any experience, good or bad, it let him slip easily asleep. He awoke just as smoothly about an hour later, ready to get on with the afternoon work, checking feed and water, throwing down some fresh sawdust bedding where it was needed and scooping up wet into the wheelbarrow in each house to be taken out when a load accumulated. He gathered eggs and made a start on washing, candling and grading before he began to get hungry. Rather than having a sandwich, he went down the road to the res-taurant near the hospital where he'd eaten his first meal in the Valley. The lady at the counter remembered him from his visits in the past, and when he came in with his cap at exactly the right angle and looked from side to side in order to see and size up who was there, she caught his eye and wordlessly directed him to a table against the wall with a view of the entrance. He got a steak and pie, a nice change from his recent days' sandwiches, ate quick, paid and headed home.

A chunk of wood into the fire, another glass of whisky, he settled down and finished the eggs, noting the production in the ledger, and finding the answer to a question that had been in the back of his mind. Even with the lights, he'd wondered how Hess managed to keep production even with demand, month in and month out. The ledger revealed that each house was managed as a separate flock. Birds being birds, they tended to return to their own roosts at night, even if they'd been outdoors mixed up in the lot, encouraged by the single rooster on each side who worked to keep his own. Raymond could see that when production on one side began to drop as the hens aged, there'd be a notation of chicks purchased and a couple of months later the expenses of hauling to a slaughterhouse and the wholesale amount received for the dressed birds, headed, no doubt, to a soup cannery. Hess apparently raised the chicks into productive poults at his real farm, where he grew up, and brought them in as soon as the emptied house was cleaned and dried out. Egg production and bird management worked out according to the numbers by a farm-boy banker! A final check of the birds and he went up to bed.

The chicken business went smoothly. Sarah came out to visit couple of times, but never overnight. On her first visit, she was scandalized that his bedroom windows had no curtains, so he bought a couple of roller shades and put them up. On her next visit the birds were out in the field and they took a couple of chairs out into the shade of the eaves, leaned back against the wall and talked while keeping watch for hawks, shotgun across Raymond's knees. Things had changed between them. He liked talking with her, but it was now like talking with one of his sisters rather than a companion, a lover. He sensed that the relationship had changed in the same way for her, too. Talking to a brother that she knew had been broken, whose raw terror she had heard and held close, feeling it as it subsided, then taking what comfort she could from his exhausted arms as her terrors returned. A peculiar intimacy that transformed common courtesies like "How're you doin' today?" into thinking-traps as to whether or not the other was going to respond fully, and if they didn't, decisions as to whether or not to ask a deeper question at the risk of bringing unnecessary trouble to the surface.

On a rainy afternoon when the birds were inside Raymond and Sarah were sharing coffee in the workroom, talking and listening to the noise of two rooms of birds hustling after the scratch they'd just thrown down. Sarah took the risk. "You know, it's been a long time since I've had that terrible airplane dream. I think of John a lot, but it's usually during the day and pleasant, like when I see something that I know would have pleased him or made him laugh. Are you still troubled at night?"

Raymond stiffened, wrapped both hands around his coffee cup, and stared into its depth rather than looking at Sarah as he answered. "Yep. Every couple of nights I'm back there again. Good thing about this job is that I can catch a nap or two the next day and not have to work exhausted. If I holler," he added with a wry laugh but still staring into the coffee, "the birds don't complain."

Sarah wordlessly reached out to touch his arm, to comfort him, but he never shifted his gaze to her or her hand. "I'm sorry," she spoke softly and stroked his arm.

"I'm glad that you can remember John from before the war. Seems like I never think of anything from then except the bees. Had the bookstore get me a copy of Langstroth so I didn't have to keep checking the library's out over and over." There was a long pause while he sipped, then started again, still looking into the cup, but speaking low. "I talk to them, the chickens. You need to talk to stock when you work them, horses and mules so they know where you are and don't get startled and kick or throw their head and hurt you, cattle to keep 'em calm while you're milking, don't want the bucket knocked over, feedstock just because it seems to help them with the routine of your bein' around, doin' what you have to do. That's what some of my chicken talk is 'move over ladies, let me put the feed out', that's how it started. Now it's like I think out loud to them and it's always about the war. Gathering eggs I'm a sergeant giving a class on hand grenades, the Army instructional method: Gentlemens, this is the hand grenade A-1-M-1; after your rifle it is your most deadly personal weapon; bursting radius is fifty-seven feet -- throw it like a lady, you'll have a chance of catching some of your own steel. Kill zone's maybe half that. Gentlemens, throw it like a baseball in the open, like you're putting a rotten egg over granny's fence while she's gardnin' if the enemy's dug in. Girls, the thing looks like a spoon is called a spoon even though the writin' boys call it a safety release lever. Pull the pin; hold the spoon next to the pineapple and you safe. Let go, count four, and the two of you better be in different places! Throw and hit the dirt, helmet towards the blast. Don't never hook them on you by the ring; carry 'em in your baggy pockets, one to a pocket so they come out easy, nothin' gettin' tangled. Don't put 'em in the pocket with your girlfriends' garters! Some

Lootenant tells you to carry a whole bunch extra, ask real polite where's the bag? They put a flour-sack satchel with pockets inside for a dozen in the bottom of each crate, but every driver in the Army wants one to stash extra rations slung behind his seat! Any questions? No? Then smoke 'em if you got 'em.'" It was impossible for Raymond to continue to stare into his cup as he warmed to the mimicry. They made eye contact halfway through and collapsed into relaxed laughter as he finished.

49. WHAT HE TOLD THE BIRDS

When they stopped laughing Sarah got up, gave him a hug and a kiss and headed out to her car. Raymond stood in the doorway, waved and watched until she turned from the gate onto the highway. Sighing, he went back inside, shut the door, filled his coffee cup with whisky and resumed sipping and staring. He'd told Sarah the funny part of talking with the birds, but not the rest. He'd taken to telling the full story to the birds, over and over. Sometimes quietly, sometimes loudly, sometimes while he was sobbing. Those closest around him knew about the ladders from his nightmares, so he had explained that and he'd told them about being shot and his hospital care because they asked about those things. He hadn't told them that of the men from his unit who made it to the top of the ladders only fifteen had survived without injury and that it had been more than two days after he was wounded before he was loaded into an ambulance. Nobody had asked for the full story of the fight. It was difficult and painful to think or talk about, and it had been easier to just let the short version created by people hearing him at night and asking their questions circulate as an explanation of his gimp and his ways. He'd started out just mentioning the two days to the birds, to get that fact said to some creature so that he felt like less of a fraud for not mentioning it to anyone, but he kept remembering more and more and had to tell them the new things that he remembered. When he wasn't focused on his specific jobs of work or occasionally diverted by reading about bees, the fight was all he thought about. He'd go to a restaurant, order supper, and then disappear into its details until roused by the noise of the plate put in front of him. Listening to the radio it was only a matter of minutes before the sound of the program was just background noise, like the scuffle and flutter of the birds going to roost. An excited sports announcer's exclamation about a hit or play might snap him back, but just as easily was heard as one of the shouts of his comrades as his thoughts raced on, raced as fast as they had during the experience itself, or crawled, slowed to the speed that time passed as they held out and morphine ran low.

The mission of Dog Company, Second Ranger Battalion had been to scale the cliffs at Pointe du Hoc halfway between the Normandy beaches code-named Utah and Omaha at dawn and take out a battery of German heavy artillery that threatened the main landings that were to about to start, men and boats moving into position even as they climbed. As they practiced on English costal cliffs for months before, wags in British Intelligence told their Colonel "three old ladies with brooms " could stop the Rangers from climbing the hundred-foot cliffs. They didn't think so, although they knew that it was going to be a rough go. The air reconnaissance flights revealed a battery of heavy artillery atop the cliffs, settled into revisions of casemates that the French had built long ago, and it was the Rangers' mission to fix the six guns before they could fire a shot.

The heavy machine guns that they'd faced once they got to the top had been dug in to rake the length of visible beach with fire -- that's why the crew Raymond and his buddies faced was fighting from a hastily taken position, their weapon dragged halfway out of its pit and away from its aiming stakes after an alert sentry heard the rockets sending up the grappling hooks and the hooks' scraping as the men below pulled to set them hard enough to hold a man on a line, then a ladder. Quite a surprise for the machine gun crews, who had no perimeter of riflemen and wire and had to leave their primary weapon and rush to the edge of the cliff to fight as the Rangers started to appear, then fall back to their re-positioned guns. That was the part of the fight where he'd been wounded. His first recollection after going down was of one of the other men moving forward saying "hang on, buddy" as he stooped to pull two extra magazines from Raymond's vest. The sergeants and the one Lieutenant who'd made it up, George Kirchner -- they called him "Lootenant K" when no brass was around and he loved it -- organized the men still standing, some of them more than a bit bloodied, and headed for where the photos showed the gun positions. When they got there, there were six dug-in but empty positions and one wrecked gun. Apparently one of the random, harassing bombs or shells that the Air Corps and Navy laid down along the coast each night had made a lucky hit and the Battery commander, thinking that his position had been targeted, had moved his remaining two and a half sections a couple of hundred yards away. It was easy enough to follow the trail of the heavy guns and their tractors but the delay and noise of dealing with the machine gunners put the artillery fellows on notice of what was happening. Raymond heard sharp outbursts of fighting as the tiny groups of Rangers located the five scattered cannon, approached from whatever direction was best, drove the gunners back just long enough to rush up, shove a thermite grenade into the cannon's breech, slam it shut, and pull back before the Germans could regroup. The presence of the Americans was confusing even though the cannoneers had heard gunfire from the cliffs – they all figured that it was impossible for anyone to have climbed up, and no forces screened the battery after its hasty move. The machine-gunners they'd fought were apparently detached from another unit, and hadn't moved with the artillery – partly because they didn't view their mission as protecting the guns, but putting fire on the sea approaches to the beach and using their cliff's-edge perch to direct artillery fire if communication between the battery and its forward observers broke down. The other part of the reason that they weren't inclined to move was they hadn't had the bad luck of damage to *their* position and weren't going to move and break their backs digging in along the cliff closer to the battery unless they were ordered to. One or two gun crews fought hard for their beloved pieces, but the Rangers got the job done.

The patrols drew back and a defensive line was formed along the cliff side of the supply road leading to the fortifications, taking advantage, where possible, of roadside bomb craters and earth thrown up from the flat-trajectory naval shelling, digging fighting holes where they had to. Across the road there was a strip of well-grazed sheep pasture, level for a pretty good distance , but not beyond accurate small arms fire before it dropped down enough to give the Germans, be they the enraged gun crews or whatever security patrol they could summon to assist them, cover and concealment. Things had by then started with the main landings, and the remaining Rangers, taking fire from the Artillerymen who'd pursued them hoped that *they'd* have trouble calling up assistance.

The Rangers on the cliff top were having additional problems. The first machine gun emplacement that they'd silenced on their move inland inexplicably came back to life, manned by gunners either wounded or recovered from the concussion of the charges thrown among them. They kept a good number of wounded, including the Colonel and the last men up, including the Lieutenant with the heliograph, cut off, and pinned down near the cliff's edge.

Raymond had fallen inland from that line of fire from the resurrected machine gun and was brought forward, fortunately not a long distance, by being dragged backward between the craters, a man's arm under each of his, his right boot temporarily tied above his left ankle, skidding on his left calf and heel, teeth clenched and weapon clutched to his chest. Of the 225 men who'd started out from sea, only fifteen remained unwounded in the forward position, and they needed every man capable of firing a weapon, wounded or not, to fill a spot on their line. The three armored British landing craft were the only ones who'd made it to the beach. They'd lost the bet that they wouldn't attract much fire on the way in, had lost one landing craft and their supply boats and had massive numbers of casualties on other landing craft and on the beach before hitting the tiny protected defilade right at the base of the cliff. The amphibious DKWs sent with them simply couldn't deal with the steep, slippery shingle and had to withdraw, further limiting the manpower and equipment on hand.

Quick two-man scrounging details sent to the former gun emplacements and dead machine-gun emplacement were successful on their run, returning with a couple of cans of water, a couple of medical bags, some rations, and a couple of rifles with a good bit of ammunition.

Raymond had been lucky in that the round that shattered his thigh had entered on the front and exited on the side, missing and pushing the bone fragments away from the artery. Their sole medic tied things up tight to minimize the bleeding, gave him some morphine, and moved on to the next man. Despite the morphine and wound, he was conscious and able to use his arms and did what he could to arrange himself to return fire when the inevitable attack began.

All hell was breaking loose along the coast, which probably helped them. The German force that had them backed up against the cliff was beginning to hit them with increasing small arms fire, but they were the gunners and their cooks and truck-drivers, not trained infantry, and while murderously intent on any shot they took, were ill-trained to form an organized assault. They'd no doubt called for assistance, but so had everyone else along the front. Any mobile reserves were being sent to the main landing points, their commanders no doubt mindful of what would befall them if they abandoned their assigned defensive positions to help mop up the survivors of a suicide mission. The Rangers were outnumbered, pinned down, but it could have been worse -- the rest of the German Army didn't seem too concerned with helping *their* Germans in the cliff top fight. At least not at first.

Nobody had to pass the word. All the Rangers knew that their survival depended on economy of fire from enough different positions to belie their small number. Kirchner and the sergeants kept moving from hole to hole, drawing fire every time they moved, but enabling even Raymond's spot to appear to shelter a couple of capable soldiers. He concentrated all of his effort on looking for the one good shot that might present itself -- he had the skill to touch a Thompson's trigger sharply enough to fire one round rather than a burst. Never in his life had he been so grateful for sheep, the sheep that had kept the ground across the road grazed low, free of brush or weedy spots. They were on the high ground, used for pasture and clear to their front for seventy-five or eighty yards inland before the wind-twisted bushes and trees that had screened the artillery positions began. The Germans on the other side of the road, realizing that there was a major invasion underway, were not terribly interested in dying in a sheep-pasture charging a group of pretty capable commandos that they had pinned down at the edge of a cliff ready to be wiped out as soon as the rest of their army found the time to give them some mortar or artillery support. They waited, not realizing how busy the rest of their army was and how inconsequential their request seemed to those directing battles against entire American divisions. Being German, however, they didn't slack off but kept things hot for the Rangers, firing on the slightest target and constantly moving snipers among the few gnarled trees that offered concealment and a marginally better firing position. The scrounged German rifles came in handy dealing with them because most of the climbers had carried Thompsons, good in a close fight but without much range.

The Rangers were waiting even more anxiously than the Germans, who, correctly, surmised that the Rangers lacked the strength for a break-out and nowhere to go except deeper into German territory if they did try and were successful. The Rangers didn't have a radio -- too heavy for the climb -- but they did have a red-hot Colonel commanding their battalion who had the ear of the generals who'd wanted the battery silenced. Their Colonel had argued with the general who wanted him to stay behind, and disobeyed his order by dropping into the third armored boat, not, probably, to that officer's surprise. Rangers were paid to be aggressive, and a colonel less loyal to his men would have been a disappointment. When the landing ships reported that they weren't taking fire from *Pointe du Hoc* the general knew that some of his men had survived the trip and the climb and was pushing hard to keep a relief column a command priority.

Raymond was in a hole edged into the side of what had been a rough, partially sunken lane which, fortunately, turned a sharp right angle and came to the level of the field a couple of yards further down, protecting him and his buddy, Vernon, pretty well on their front. They'd made such efforts as they were able at digging a fighting bench, helped by one of the other men who slipped in with a handful of food and a full canteen of water to trade for one of their empties. The bench was really just a sloping ledge, dug with their knives to suit the way that they had to lie because of their injuries but allowing them to get up onto their elbows far enough to put fire on their front. The fellow who brought the water and helped dig explained to them how the other men were positioned and with what weapons, and slowly easing his head high enough to look out of the top half of his eyes, pointed out the spots where he'd seen German fire coming from across their front. There were a couple of fully capable men, one with a rifle, in the hole to their left, closest to the cliff edge, ready to stop any attempt to flank the defense. He said that the medic would be through eventually, that he'd started his rounds on the far end of things, and then headed to the next position with food and water for the day for those guys. His movement drew a couple of shots from the Germans, which missed, and they heard a response from down the line and the hole he was headed for.

"Well, Vern, sun's pretty high so I reckon it's dinnertime.'" "Yup" was the only response he got. They each took a couple of nibbles of food and a sip of water. Water, they knew, had to be conserved. Both of them were dehydrated from loss of blood and wanted more, but neither of them was bleeding much now that they'd settled in and tightened their bandages, and held to the water discipline that everyone faced. Vern was scared to drink much more than to wet his mouth because one of his wounds was deep into his belly and he didn't want to flush his guts into himself. The morphine that they'd been given early in the morning had long since worn off, and with the distraction of digging in over they struggled to focus on their front instead of their pain. "Let's keep a lookout so's we can make one o' them bastards hurt as bad as us" was Vern's plan. Raymond just tried to follow it, using every grind of bone on bone when he shifted to keep from going numb or to relieve the pressure of some stone as a reminder of his business. He couldn't believe that a pebble under some other part of his motionless body could trump the pain of his leg. Choosing his words carefully and adding just the right amount of vulgarity to sound like a soldier rather than someone's granny, he explained to Vern that he now understood the story of the princess and the pea. Vern's response was a grin and sort of a moaning chuckle. Even with the occasional gunshot and return fire, the afternoon was endless, or maybe timeless was a better description, because every minute was about the same for both men; more pain than either had ever experienced, fatigue beyond patrol training when they'd marched more asleep than awake, and the overwhelming necessity of watching their front. Raymond fired a couple of shots, hours apart, once at what he believed to be the top of a man's helmet rising up from the dirt dug out around a foxhole, the second time at a hint of movement that Vern pointed out. At least they'd let the Germans know someone was watching and had enough ammunition to try an impossibly long Thompson shot. They could see the columns of smoke and hear sounds of battle some distance up and down the coast, and wondered which units might be headed their way.

Late in the afternoon the medic scuttled up to the rear of their position. As promised, he was working the line. "Hey, Doc!"

"Y'all know my name's Bill." They knew that, and that he hated being called anything else, but they couldn't resist, since their situation left them nothing else to joke about.

"You're the closest we got to one, glad to see you!" was Vern's less-than-hale response.

"Better get on with it then, although you guys are waaay too early for an appointment. What I have for you is half a load of good German morphine. Vintage, pre-war stuff from the date on the label." He pulled Vern's collar over as far as it would go towards his injured shoulder, spit on a spot and rubbed it clean with the outside of a bandage. "There along your collarbone's about the cleanest spot you got on your body. Sorry about the spit, but I'd better use my water twice. I'm putting this stuff into a blister under your skin, and I doubt you'll pop it there like you might on your forearm. Hits slower this way, but lasts longer than if I give it to you in a muscle." He busied himself checking Vern's bandages, feeling for bleeding or seepage and retying those that had shifted. He pushed Vern's helmet back and held the back of his hand to his forehead for a moment. "Bit warm. I'm afraid that you're getting infected inside, but at least it's not gone far enough to start soaking through. You must be following my instructions to go easy on the water."

Bill turned to Raymond and gave him the same kind of injection on the left, after confirming that he shot right-handed. "Clotted up good, I see." He was giving Raymond's bandages the same feel and adjustment that he'd given Vern's. "Hospitals change bandages, I just look for leaks and add more." He reached around and got two slats from a crate that he'd brought with him stuck in the back of his belt and put a rough splint on Raymond's thigh, careful to arrange them so that they didn't press on or conceal the bandages directly above the wounds at the entry and exit spots. "That should help minimize the pain when you shift around. Locked knee isn't gonna' make you walk slower'n you do now." As he bandaged, he'd wordlessly pulled the few grenades that they had out of hard or impossible to reach pockets and placed them in easily reached spots that didn't interfere with the small amount of shifting for comfort that the hole and their strength allowed. They talked for a few minutes, watching their front rather than each other as Bill gave them the word on who was hurt and how bad. "Lootenant K's on the job. You'll probably have a visit from him before morning.

It ain't that I don't enjoy your company, but I got a couple more house calls. Nobody hurt real bad, but they're the ones that tear things loose and start bleedin' again." The medic pulled the strap of his German aid-bag over his head to free both hands, pushed its bulk around to behind the small of his back and crept off to their rear.

Raymond and Vern lay with the upper halves of their bodies pulled up onto the shelf where they had some visibility, concealment, and some cover if they dropped their heads down a bit. Neither of them spoke, but they were thinking the same thing -- Bill'd said this kind of shot was slower to kick in, how much longer 'till it does? As evening approached they began to feel it. The effect of the morphine and their pain was immediately overcome by a jolt of adrenalin as the entire German line opened up, firing to keep the Americans down, providing cover for their soldiers racing for the closest point in the American line. The Rangers with rifles returned fire from all along the line, those at the narrow point at the attackers, those away from the targeted sector at the exposed supporting riflemen. The Thompson gunners in front of the attack held their fire until the Germans were well within effective range, then let loose, each man timing his three-round bursts. That stopped it. The attackers fell back, dragging their wounded, and the Americans left them to it, conserving their ammunition. Two or three rounds to a burst saved ammo, and kept the muzzle from climbing beyond a man's ability to concentrate on keeping things accurate. Raymond didn't fire a shot. He saw no target that he was sure of hitting. The Germans had worked all day at keeping Kirchner's men at the alert and unrested, but hadn't considered the effectiveness of heavy close-in automatic firing in defense. Runners immediately began moving between holes, shifting ammunition to those who'd been firing the most. Raymond had two unfired Thompson magazines, one of which got passed down the line along with Vern's two spare pistol magazines, leaving him with just the one extra and the one in his .45. Raymond pulled the magazine out of his Thompson, replaced it with the full spare, then shucked the shells out of his pistol magazine to replenish the two rounds he'd fired during the day and the couple of bursts he'd fired before getting hit in the other, leaving him with two full twenty-round Thompson sticks and one round under the half-cock hammer of his pistol. Vern still had eight rounds, one under the hammer and seven in his pistol's magazine.

Darkness brought a little respite. Doc Bill had been right, the morphine under the skin had lasted longer, and the two of them could still sense an edge being taken off of their pain even after the German attack. Having been bloodied themselves, the Germans weren't as vigilant as they had been all day, unless someone did something stupid, like lighting up a smoke anywhere but in the depths of hole. The rangers were too well-trained for the old 'third man on a match' rule to endanger anyone, but it was dark enough that the flare of an unshielded match low on a fighting bench would draw a couple of harassing rounds. Ammo redistribution complete, runners again distributed small amounts of rations and water. The men who had been able to resume control of their bodily functions after the gut-stopping adrenalin and exertion of the climb, fight for the guns, and the enemy's first run at the line eased away from their holes to relieve themselves. Those who hadn't, resigned themselves to their filth, and like everyone else took turns with their buddies to stand down for a few moments of rest. The reality of a full day of fighting and holding a defensive position in shallow holes was far different from their training days when, on a long march the sergeants growled 'keep moving, shake it out' at those who hadn't completed things at that morning's latrine call. Raymond and Vern were equally foul, having been unable to even loosen their trousers and roll to an edge of their hole. Vern insisted that Raymond rest while he kept watch, and Raymond didn't argue. He didn't even say a word before dropping his helmeted head to the ground, weapon still at hand.

Vernon stayed alert until a while after twilight passed into full darkness. "Raymond! Raymond!, he hissed and Raymond snapped back awake as quickly as he'd fallen asleep, a bit disoriented for a second or two, then realizing where he was and what was up. "Called you 'cause I can't stay awake no more," Vern mumbled as he saw Raymond's head come up, and let his own drop in response to exhaustion and fever.

Shortly after Vern collapsed Lieutenant Kerchner eased into place beside Raymond. A quiet "Let him rest" was his greeting, indicating Vern with the tilt of his head. "How you doin' with the leg?" Raymond liked the Baltimore-bred officer. He'd been the first man off of the boat, leading from neck-deep water, reminding the men to keep moving for the beach, that returning small-arms fire from the water was pointless against dug-in machine guns at the far reach of a rifleman's range. He found the Lootenant's habit of wearing his .45 scabbard on the left, grip facing forward, like a horse cavalryman, an appealing visual reminder of stories of the War, and did the same when given the opportunity -- the absence of brass overly concerned with a corporal's adherence to regulation appearance of weapons on a parade-ground.

"I'm gettin' by, Sir. Vern, there's a lot worse off 'n me." At that point they both heard the low growl of trucks coming up behind the German lines. Two engines coughed to a stop, two tailgates fell, and they sensed as much as heard the muffled noise of men dismounting and filtering forward into the lines.

"Company's arriving." Kerchner observed. "Probably two platoons. Nightfall finally broke some troops loose to help our cooks and cannon-cockers. More of 'em, but other than the truck ride I doubt that they're any more rested than anybody else up here, been a busy day for the German Army."

"Yup." Neither of them said anything, but both of them were hoping that the absence of a third truck indicted that the reinforcements had no heavy-weapons support, no mortars. Vern woke up, moaning, but forced himself to stifle when he saw Kerchner, who asked how he was doing.

His response to the officer's question was "Ok, I got Raymond here lookin' after me. How're the other fellows doin'?"

"Some a little worse'n you; some about the same as you two; and most dancin' as pretty as me." The Lieutenant didn't mention that they and Easy Company, on their flank, were down to less than half their number as fully-able fighters. "Hang on men,' were his words as he moved on down the line.

The new arrivals on the German side were obviously experienced infantry, with noise and light discipline as good as the Rangers'. It was still possible, though, to understand that the German line was being expanded to put pressure on the flanks of the Americans' position. German or American, a soldier can't scrape a fighting hole in total silence. Without resupply, firing discipline had become the Rangers' priority. One shot, one kill was the word passed along the line. If that didn't work, grenades at a closer range would have to do the job that the submachine guns had done when the attackers had closed before. Their left flank controlled access to the empty gun positions and the chewed up ground around the casemates where their injured Colonel had set up his headquarters and had limited lamp communications with the destroyer in the invasion fleet tasked with supporting them. Because the fight had ended up away from the cliff edge and line of sight signals, that support had been limited to carefully directed shellfire to silence the machine gun that had come back to life while they were in pursuit of the big guns.

Halfway through the night all hell broke loose again. German infantrymen had crept within extreme grenade rage of the holes on both flanks and started doing their best. At the same time a larger force than before tried the point where the lines were closest. The grenade attacks on the flanks were quickly recognized as diversions when no advancing troops followed the explosions. They were well executed and kept the men to their front occupied, but had little effect on the fighters in the positions that had to deal with the main attack. The Regular German infantrymen there advanced more quickly than the untrained men of the first attack, but fell back because they were taking too many casualties once they came within range of all of the Ranger's weapons, the same automatic fire that had stopped the first push. A few got damned close, but the Americans' need to make each round count was too hot for them. Raymond didn't fire a shot, although he and Vern were alert for anyone shifting down the line as they advanced. He was glad that he hadn't had to fire, because he was worn down to the point where he had doubts about his ability to fire accurately. Perhaps fifteen minutes passed between the explosion of the first grenade and the last rifle-shot at a German reentering his line. The pasture provided neither cover nor concealment. The attack had been a bet by the Germans that a larger number of better-trained men could cover the extra distance. A defensive position had minimized the Rangers' casualties and enabled their marksmanship to pay off. As before, ammunition was redistributed. Raymond and Vern were left with twenty-one rounds for the Thompson, one in the chamber and a full magazine locked into place, one round under the hammer of each of third .45s, and six grenades. Doc Bill came down the line with fewer bandages in his bag than the last time they'd seen him.

"Saved you boys a shot to share." Were words which they'd almost given up on hearing and the prospect of even half a dose raised their spirits. Dawn came with a real surprise. Two paratroopers, blown far away from their landing zone, had heard the fight, worked their way along the coast and had then been sent forward by their wounded Colonel and his companions. Two more alert fighters and their ammunition load were awfully welcome.

The second day was worse than the first. The morphine was exhausted, not that anyone had been given enough to really provide relief or enough that the medic tagged them to prevent an overdose. Those with abdominal wounds, like Vern, were well into the fever of their internal infections, unable to even serve as lookouts, using what strength and consciousness that they had left to try to remain silent in order to conceal the low number of remaining effective fighters. Those like Raymond flitted moment by moment between concentrating on their duty and the unspeakable reality of their pain. Given that constant struggle, interrupted by fear that one would overcome the other, leaving a catastrophic gap in the line, there wasn't much to distinguish one hour from another except the progression of the sun across the sky and the occasional sniper's shot, more from the German lines than their own, since their riflemen had to wait for a genuine target rather than waste a shell on a suspicion of movement. After the Navy had knocked out the pesky machine gun nest, someone had been able to salvage a couple of more jerry-cans of water from just alongside the entrance to the pile of rubble that had been their blockhouse. That helped. Somehow Doc and Lootenant K. managed to keep moving, working the line, encouraging, tightening bandages, and providing a bit of relief when they saw some way to take the weight off of a wounded arm or leg. They had to have been taking timed five-or ten-minute naps as they rotated through the strongest positions. The paratroopers had been put into the line at the point where they'd been pushed twice and men were shifted so that someone was capable of firing from every hole. Despite his fears about how he might perform, Raymond was that man in their hole. Whenever anyone came along the line they tended to their immediate business, then told him to rest. When they quietly said his name and nudged him awake so that they could leave, he had no idea how long he'd been out because he felt exactly the same as he had the moment he'd been told to stand down. Late in the afternoon the Germans tried again, far away from Raymond where their flank tied in with equally battered Easy Company. Again, accurate fire stopped the attack. The second night passed much like the first, except that having become accustomed to the routine of the defensive position Raymond's thoughts began to drift back to the morning before, the landing, and getting wounded. He listened to the sounds of the Army fighting in from the beaches and hoped that someone reached them soon, knowing that he was becoming less and less capable of responding to an attack on his part of the line.

After daybreak everyone heard sporadic firing on the German position's flank -- apparently the scouts of their long awaited relief column. No matter what its size, they had made contact, about the best news that could be had. Almost immediately the Rangers heard the two heavy trucks that had brought the German infantrymen cough to life and warm to an idle, along with a number of other vehicles that, other than one motorcycle, they couldn't identify. They judged from the sounds that each of the vehicles started moving out as soon as a load of men had climbed aboard, raising a dust cloud as they headed down the road and out of earshot. It seemed that the Germans had left, but nobody was particularly eager to rise up and provide an easy target for any snipers that might have lingered. A bit later they heard the unmistakable American holler "Hey, y'all, were here to git you! Lookit my hat comin' up!" An American helmet was raised on the bayonet of an American rifle above the rim of a hole in the middle of the German line. "We're the rest of the Battalion comin' up. Holler back!"

Raymond heard Lootenant K. respond, still down out of sight "What Battalion? What commander?"

"Second Ranger, you careful bastards. Colonel

Rudder, if he ain't been broke to private for comin' with you after the General ordered him not to!"

"Sounds good to me. Stand down, men!" The sounds of agreement could be heard along the line and American helmets began to ease upward on both lines, the men in one group relieved and optimistic, but still cautious, the men in the other both amused by and understanding of their fellows' caution. The newly arrived troops were being slow and easy themselves, lest a suddenly appearing shadow noise or silhouette be misunderstood by an exhausted defending trooper and made a target. Their first two days of combat, pushing out beyond other units to relieve the men at *Pointe du Hoc* had taught them the very real danger of making even friendly contact without coordination. The apprehension only lasted a moment before Raymond and his buddies were either heads up or standing, letting out a welcoming yell. Aside from than the few scouts sent out to watch the direction in which the Germans had gone, the men from the other two companies swarmed over them, sharing saved bits of rations, stories and smokes.

That's when a medic with plenty of morphine found Raymond and the story everyone else had heard began.

50. AFTER HE TOLD THE STORY TO THE BIRDS FOR THE LAST TIME.

Raymond got busy and finished with the afternoon's work, feeding, gathering the eggs. He set things up on the table to start cleaning, candling, grading and packing. Before getting to work, he poured another coffee-cup of whisky then sat down at the back of the table, facing the door, where he always set things up, satisfying his need to know who might be coming in, and pleasant to look out over the field to the highway if it was a nice evening. It felt good to be off of his feet. He leaned both elbows on the table, cup in his palms and relaxed, just looking at the closed door and letting his mind wander as he enjoyed the familiar burn in his throat with the first sip, the immediate warmth in his belly, and subsequent subsidence of the throbbing pain in his leg.

Frank Hess drove out to see how Raymond and the birds were doing as soon as the bank closed. Pulled up and, as he always did knocked once and called out "Frank, here," before opening the workroom door and stepping in. As he closed the door behind him he caught sight of Raymond, grader, candle, and wash pan on the table, a basket of eggs on the floor at one side, crates for three grades of eggs ready on the other. "'Evenin','" he said, mildly surprised that Raymond hadn't risen from his chair and spoken first, the usual result of his polite upbringing. Raymond didn't respond. "Raymond? You alright?" It was evident that he wasn't. He just sat there, looking off into nowhere, giving no indication that he even knew that Frank had come in. Frank leaned across the table and touched his hand. "Raymond?" No response. He stepped around and shook Raymond's shoulder pretty hard, still no response. He picked up the empty coffee cup and sniffed it -- not surprisingly, a faint odor of alcohol. Raymond didn't look like he was in a drunken stupor, he wasn't flushed, was sitting erect, nothing about him was disheveled. He looked like he just froze after turning the candle on.

Frank puzzled on what to do, and after a bit decided to call Bill Riley because he was the man in town that knew Raymond and his ways best. When Bill answered, Frank was brief. "Something's wrong with Raymond. Can you come over here?"

"Sure." Bill swallowed the last bite of his supper. "He ain't drunked up is he? That ain't his way. Is he hurt?"

"No, not those. He just won't say anything, just sits and stares."

"I'm on my way. Keep an eye on him."

"Righto." As soon as he hung up, Hess got the operator on the line again and called Mary Frances to tell her that there was a problem and that she should go ahead and eat without him. Frank heard the creak of the treads and the rattle of his stick against the risers as Raymond came wordlessly up the stairs, crossed the room and went outside. He heard the creak of the privy door opening and closing.

"Are the birds alright? came over the 'phone.

"Yes, yes, they're alright. It's Raymond. He won't talk, just sits and stares, looks like it came on him just as he started to clean eggs." The privy door creaked again and Raymond passed through on his way downstairs without any sign that he even knew that his boss was standing in his bedroom making telephone calls.

"Is he feverish?"

"Not that I can see. He's not drunk, walks like he always does, and his clothes are neat. I've called Bill

Riley to come and see if he can wake him up. It'll be a while, 'cause I'll likely have to do the eggs."

"I'll keep your supper warm. You two be easy with him, I can't imagine that he's joking with you like he might've done Bill."

Frank went back downstairs and saw that Raymond had resumed his former place. "Let me pull a chair in beside you, I'll help you get on with your work." Raymond didn't say anything or even look at Frank, but worked his chair over to the side a bit so that Frank could reposition things on the table and reach around him for the basket of eggs. Frank didn't press him to talk, just started doing the eggs, thinking that realizing that work was underway might elicit some response. He'd done about two-thirds of a dozen without success when he heard Bill's pickup pull in.

Bill came in loud and jovial. "Raymond my boy, what's up? Darn good prank you've pulled on Frank, here" he laughed. "Got him going two-hunnert percent. You'da had a harder time with me!" Raymond gave no indication that he even knew that Bill was there. "'This he was like when you got here?"

"Yup." Frank held an egg up to the candle, balanced it on the spoon of aluminum grading scale, put it into the correct crate and reached for another. "He came up and went to the privy while I was on the 'phone, then right back down here."

Bill leaned on the table with both hands directly across from Raymond and lowered his face directly into Raymond's line of sight. "You can stop funnin' now. You won. I've heard you laugh a dozen times about the shines you pulled on your family. This one's done." No response. "You try touching him like you would a sleepwalker?"

"Yes, even shook his shoulder pretty hard. No luck."

"Damn." Bill sat down outside of Raymond's gaze. "Set that basket over here and push me the pan. I'll wash and you grade." The two older men sat and worked in silence, finishing the job without any notice from Raymond. Frank carried the crates of eggs back into the corner while Bill rinsed out the rag and banged the pan around in the sink loud enough to ruin anyone's sleep. Still no response. They looked at each other over Raymond's head, shrugged their shoulders and raised their eyebrows at each other, arms half-raised, palms upward.

"Frank, you go on home -- you got a pretty young wife. I'll sit here with him tonight and see if it breaks."

"Thanks. Mary Frances will appreciate that. Call me if you need help."

"I'll do that, but I 'spect it'll be a long night of nappin' and listenin' to the radio," Bill chuckled, "strange stuff from those outlaw stations that double their power after decent folks are in bed. If Raymond don't like it, maybe he'll speak up."

After Frank pulled off, Bill went up and called *his* Mary. "Mary? Problem over here's that Raymond's mute and starin'. Enough there that he'll go to the out-house when he needs to, but Frank Hess and I sat there and cleaned the day's eggs in front of him without him sayin' a word or lookin' at us. Told Frank I'd sit the night with him so I reckon I'm here 'till mornin if he don't snap out of it."

"You're too good to both of 'em! Get comfortable if you can, maybe help yourself to a bit of Raymond's whisky to make restin' easier."

"Done thought of that," Bill laughed. "Done thought of it. I'll call you in the mornin' or if anything changes. Goodnight." Back downstairs nothing had changed. Bill took a quick look into both chicken-sheds, and satisfied that the birds were all right returned his attention to Raymond.

Rummaging around in the dish-cabinet for a couple of glasses, he also found the opened bottle of whisky that he wanted, although he'd noted the open wooden case in the cool corner with the eggs and rat-proofed pantry box in case it was necessary to start a fresh one. He sat down and put the glasses and bottle down on a corner of the table away from Raymond rather than across from him in an effort to get him to shift his gaze. "Know that leg's hurtin' you by this time of the evenin'. Pour you a drink and join you if you don't mind." He poured a good three fingers into each glass, and leaving Raymond's on the table, took the first taste of his own. Raymond didn't say a word or move a muscle. Bill slid the glass over directly in front of his friend, and in a moment Raymond took it up without lowering his eyes or making a sound, and joined Bill in the endeavor, politely taking a sip whenever Bill, within his peripheral vision, did, not rushing to finish. 'Ah! Bill thought, now we know that he's still in there, feels pain, and appreciates relief." Hoping to push Raymond to the point of going up to bed Bill said out loud "Been a long evening" and poured himself another, then poised the bottle's lip over Raymond's empty glass. No response. He poured another three fingers and Raymond drank with him as before. Bill went upstairs and turned the radio on where Raymond had left it set, WTON, the local station, loud enough to hear downstairs, went back down, and sat and listened until it signed off for the night. Popular music, hillbilly music mixed in with slick cowboy songs, news, the stock-market report -- cattle and hog prices -- and a radio preacher with enough fire and brimstone to either let you rest secure in the knowledge that you weren't going to rot in hell with all of the heathens within reach of the transmitter and tower or, if you hadn't been drinking enough to take the edge off of the message, have some truly inspired dreams.

The loud static of the open frequency hissed as Bill busied himself rinsing the glasses and put them and the nearly-empty bottle back in the cupboard. He went back to Raymond, picked his stick up, held it out to him, and put his hand on his shoulder. "Come on boy, time for bed." Raymond grabbed the stick away from Bill, twisted around to grasp Bill's wrist and stared directly into his eyes. Bill knew the look. He'd learned it as a kid. His family had an old dog and when Bill played too rough with him, he'd grab Bill's arm or leg, tight enough to hold on but not breaking the skin, then look into Bill's eyes conveying the message "I'm giving you a chance to stop. If you don't, I'm really gonna hurt you." He'd seen the same look from a bull he'd cornered trying to get him back across the fence from some open heifers and from a sow when he'd gotten between her and her piglets. He'd always been careful to avoid situations where he might get that look from a man or woman. Bill, real easy and smooth, let go the stick, removed his hand from Raymond's shoulder and stepped back. Raymond turned back to the table and whatever he was watching in his mind.

Bill went upstairs, diddled with the radio and found some station in Oklahoma. When he came back down, he took a seat on the opposite side of the table, put his head down on his folded arms and tried to rest, half listening to the radio, alert to any sound or movement from his friend on the other side. As much as he'd been around folks, as many yarns as he'd listened to about what you do when somebody ain't right, just sittin' with him was all he could see to do. Try to protect him from hurtin' himself and just be there so that whatever it was, Raymond didn't have to be fighting it alone.

After a while the Oklahoma station got their preacher goin'. He couldn't stand another round of that, so he went upstairs and went up and down the dial, found some station playing polkas, went back down and resumed his vigil. He'd kinda' dozed off when he heard Raymond's chair scrape and the bump of his stick on the floor. Didn't want to spook him by rising his head, but he opened his eyes and twisted around to see him start up the stairs -- maybe to bed! No such luck. He heard the outside door open and shut --- Raymond had again gone to relieve himself. Having thought of it earlier in the evening but unable to act, Bill jumped up, pulled the Nitro Hunter down from its nails above the door, broke it open, pulled out both shells, put them in his pocket and the shotgun back above the door, both ears on half-cock safe, as before. He'd just gotten back to his seat when Raymond came back down the stairs. "How you feelin'?" No response as Raymond sat back down and resumed staring beyond the far side of the door. The Texas station had gone off of the air and he didn't look for another, ready for another nap at the table. A bit later he stirred and saw that Raymond had put his head down too.

Sometime later Bill was jolted awake as Raymond, sitting up, staring upward, but still apparently asleep let loose a stream of unholy curses mixed with cries urging companions on or warning them of danger. Bill recognized the ladder nightmare that Sarah had described. As suddenly as it had started, it stopped. Raymond, drenched with sweat, looked around, gave no indication that he saw Bill, and put his head back down and slept until he smelled bacon in the skillet the next morning.

Awakened by the smell, Raymond, still without saying a word, went out back to relieve himself, washed his face and combed his hair at the pitcher and bowl upstairs and came down to resume sitting and staring. "Here's your's, mine'll be ready in a minute." Bill put a plate of bacon and eggs and a cup of coffee in front of Raymond without reaction. As soon as he brought his own food over and sat down, however, Raymond ate like he meant it. Being off in the head apparently didn't block some of the courtesies of Raymond's upbringin', just the ones about talkin' to folks.

The telephone rang as Bill was finishing. He wiped his lips on the back of his hand and went up to answer the call he was sure was from Frank Hess. "Mornin', Bill. Since I haven't heard from you, I figured there hasn't been any improvement."

"Nope. He won't say a word, will eat and keep himself decent. Did look at me when I laid my hand on him to try to get him to bed, but it was such a she-bear with cubs look that I didn't try again. Had a hollerin' nightmare, apparently about climbing that cliff, and didn't even wake up."

"I've called one of my backup fellows to come in and tend the birds, and Doctor Thomas from out at Greenville says he'll meet me there at seven-thirty to take a look. How're you doin?"

"Feel like I've spent the night half-awake sittin' at the table. If Raymond don't have his pain medicine out when I go downstairs, I'm gettin' it down for both of us."

"Won't mention that to Mary Frances in order to keep up your good reputation. See you in a bit."

Back downstairs Raymond had put the dishes in the pan, poured himself a coffee cup of whisky, put the bottle and cork next to Bill's cup with its teaspoonful of boiled-coffee dregs, had his boots off and was slowly cleaning and polishing them with the brushes and rags from a small box under the table. He'd polish a little, take a sip, stare off to nowhere for a bit, then repeat the process. Nothin' bein' said to him, Bill didn't try to start a conversation, but gratefully filled his cup from the bottle, sipped and watched. Old Eddie Smith, the fill-in egg man came in, exchanged greetings with Bill and got started with his work. Raymond didn't respond to Eddie's greeting, just looked through him like he wasn't in the doorway and went back to his boots. Frank had obviously told Eddie what was up -- he didn't push anything, just got out into the henhouses as soon as he could.

Frank Hess and Doctor Thomas pulled up right at seven-thirty. Hess poked his head in the door. "You want to come out here and fill in the Doc before he sees Raymond?"

"Nah, just have him come on in. I got nothing to say that I won't say in front of the man. Might do him good to hear it repeated. Frank and the doc came in and the four of them sat around the table. Bill explained what had happened in the last day, how he knew Raymond, what he knew about Raymond's wounds and Army experiences, his family, and about his relationship and split from Sarah. The tale was a long time in telling, and the doctor watched Raymond rather than Bill the whole time. Raymond finished shining his boots, put them on, put the polishing kit back in its box, toed it under the table and resumed sitting and staring. Doctor Thomas put his instrument bag on the table, pulled out his stethoscope and held it against Raymond's chest and back, more to see if he could touch him than to listen to his heart and breathing, which were normal. Either the depth of Raymond's state or his subconscious recognition of the rural practitioner's sign of authority opened beside him on the table allowed the intrusion. Doc Thomas looked quizzically at the other two men.

"That was smooth," Bill responded. "Now hand him his stick, take his shoulder and tell him he needs to go upstairs for bed-rest." The doctor did, and got the same result that Bill had the night before.

"Looks like his war's caught up with him, presenting as a catatonic state. Lord knows what's behind the mad bull look other than a lot of anger and repressed pain, which he comes by honestly, and his training to be paranoid and aggressive in order to survive. What he needs is to be away from the world for a while and, if he's lucky, sort it out internally. If he's not lucky, I reckon he'll stay like he is. Leave him here by himself he might get along 'till he runs out of food and whisky. Probably wouldn't work too well if he went out for groceries and liquor for his pain. If he was down with his people they might be able to keep him in a chair in the kitchen, but there's no predicting if he'd stay catatonic or feel that he had to act defensively. Be an interesting train ride home! I don't hear y'all sayin' that anybody up here can keep him and watch him that close. I'll stop by Western State on my way back to Greenville and talk to whoever I can catch and try to see if they can make it as easy as possible for him once you get him there. I'd suggest taking him in one of your vehicles, but getting the sheriff out here to start him moving, or maybe an officer from out at the Army hospital."

"Thanks, Doctor Thomas. We really appreciate your coming out, and from what I know about the administration out there, your stopping in will carry some weight 'cause everyone, top to bottom will know that a local doc is following the case. Bill, can you sit for a spell while I make a couple of calls?"

"Sure. I can sit a spell and then ride him over to the hospital in my pickup. Only work I got planned today is a couple of calls to people to tell 'em they won't see me 'till tomorrow 'cause I didn't sleep well last night." The doctor took his leave; Frank went upstairs; and Bill sat down.

Hess came back down the stairs saying that he had it arranged. The procurement officer that he knew, a newly-promoted captain when he'd first met him, now newly-promoted major, would come in an hour and a half, after making an attempt to scan Raymond's medical record. Sheriff Shaver would meet them at the same hour. "A major." Bill paused, "That'll be good. Raymond's used to lieutenants and captains, but a real brass hat'll catch his attention. Scrambled eggs on the brim'll do the same thing over at the Hospital. Frank went back upstairs, called his boss at the Bank, who'd just come in, explained his absence, and was told to come in after he'd taken care of his chicken man. By that time Eddie Smith had gathered the mooring's eggs, so the three of them set to work just as Frank and Bill had the night before, washing, candling, grading and packing.

As they were finishing they heard two cars pull up and their doors open and close. After the murmur of introductions and brief conversation outside Sheriff Shaver opened the door and held it for Major Jackson to enter. Jackson uncovered as he said hello and shook Frank's hand. Shaver kept his hat on and fluctuated between stern and avuncular, unsure which expression would be most helpful, but was diect in what he said.

"Raymond, Doctor Thomas said that he thought that the best thing for you was to just be away from the world for a while. These gentlemen agree and have come to make it easier for you to get into Bill's pickup and ride over to the hospital, where all four of us will see to it that you get settled in safely." Raymond didn't say anything, move or shift his gaze.

Major Jackson put his garrison cap on and extended his hand. "Come on, son. Get your stick and your cover and we'll load out. One of us will police up your gear and bring it along later today."

Raymond didn't say anything, didn't take the Major's
hand, but stood, picked up his stick, walked over and
got his cap from its nail, and put it on at exactly the
right angle, all without appearing to look at what he
was doing, apparently relying on his peripheral vision
to move among them. "Good man. Mr. Hess, will you
please get the door? Mr. Bill why don't you go get your
truck started? Sheriff, if you could please drive out first
and help us stay together at intersections, Mr. Bill and
Raymond will follow you and I'll come along after Mr.
Hess. The gate was open when I got here so I figure
there's no stock in the field. It's probably best that we
keep moving rather than your waiting for me to close
it." Bill went out and they heard his truck start. Hess
and Jackson got on either side of Raymond "Let's go,
son." "Time to go, Raymond." Raymond didn't move.
Glancing at each other and exchanging a nod, Hess and
the Major tried again, this time each putting a little
pressure on the back of an elbow. The sheriff sensed
what they were starting to do and without even thinking
let his right hand drop down along his thigh to the grip
of his slapjack in its special narrow slit sewn inside the
liner of his regular pocket. Raymond responded to their
touch and began walking rather that assuming a defensive stance. They all relaxed, which Raymond apparently sensed, walking easier as they went outside and got
into their vehicles. Bill watched Raymond out of the
corner of his eye the whole way across town, especially
when the Sheriff tapped his siren to get the right-of-
way, but Raymond just stared straight ahead. He didn't
show any reaction when they turned off of the Greenville Road through the tall black-iron fence and mean-
dered along the drive through the park-like front of the
grounds with its little stream, ancient willow trees and
gazebo, and pulled to a stop in front of the broad stairs
leading into the main building. This part of Western

State hospital was at once pleasing and impressive, a balanced grouping of large buildings in what Bill thought of as classical architecture, with walkways and copulas on top from which every part of the original hospital grounds could be watched. Staunton people compared it to Monticello and the University of Virginia, said that it had to have been some of Mr. Jefferson's former assistants supervising the work -- not an unreasonable assumption for a State government project started in 1829. Probably just as reasonable to assume that some of the same craftsmen, free and enslaved, cut and laid the limestone foundations and watercourses that, more than a century later, protected the buildings from the intrusion of surface and soil water that ate away mortar and weakened the lower courses of brick on most of Staunton's other surviving buildings from the same era.

The group of vehicles headed by a sheriff's car and ending with an Army sedan stretching along the curb from one side of the grand stairway to the other perked up anyone who happened to glance out of a window, and they all waited and watched to see who would emerge. The older man who got out of the pickup and took charge of his passenger, clearly a new patient, looked like anyone's father or uncle doing the job. It seemed odd, though, that a gimped-up but otherwise unremarkable catatonic was being brought in by the law, a businessman some of them recognized from the Bank, and an Army officer of some rank but who drove his own car. As the group ascended the stairway the watchers went back to what they were doing, confident that they'd hear the story before the day was over.

As they entered the broad hallway, a young doctor -- that's what they assumed from the white laboratory coat, tie, and dangling stethoscope, although he was wearing what were obviously his old army khaki trousers and brown low-quarter shoes -- rose from an armchair to greet them. The usual admission team, a clerk behind a battered desk with a large, worn ledger and the morning paper and a couple of colored orderlies lounging in chairs along the wall beside him hardly looked up from their reading and conversation, knowing that the doc was here to meet this new fellow and would eventually provide notes for transfer to the ledger and instructions on where to take him.

" 'Mornin', I'm Farley Witt. Doctor Thomas came by early this morning and told us to expect you, so I was called down from the wards."

"I'm Bill Riley. My friend here who needs some help is Raymond McCleary, this is his boss, Mr. Frank Hess, and Sheriff Shaver and Major Jackson came with us 'cause it took the presence of some authority to get Raymond up and over here." Handshakes all around except for Raymond who stood and stared away down the long hallway.

Witt ushered them a couple of doors down to a meeting room with a table big enough for everyone to have a seat. He pulled out chair for himslef along one side rather than at the head, leaving the others to find their places. "Put Raymond opposite me, if you can, please." That was accomplished and Bill took the lead again.

"Reckon I've known Raymond longer'n anybody in town. He talked his way into a job with me and handled it real well in spite of his wound, was honest with me about drinkin' to deal with pain and how the war messed with his head, gave him nightmares and made him break up with a fine woman." Riley then explained each of those points in detail.

"He left Bill to work for me after a year or so and the end of his romance." Hess took it up. "I have the egg contract with the hospital kitchen through Major Jackson and Raymond came to work for me maybe six months ago when my previous man left on only a couple of days' notice. He was honest with me about his pain and whisky. Bill told me about the other things, but I never asked him about them, figured it was his personal business. He was good with the birds, moved slow and talked low to them to keep 'em calm. An excellent egg man until last evening when I looked in on him and found that when he'd sat down at the work table to clean and grade eggs he'd just locked up. Starin' off into nowhere, he wouldn't answer you, even if you touched him. That's when I called Bill."

"I got there and tried to jolly him out of it, accused him of pulling one on Frank, but it didn't work. Laid my hand on his shoulder and got the look of a dangerous animal, same as Frank and Doc Thomas next mornin'. Sat up with him all night. He got up and went out to the privy when he needed to, drank some whisky with me -- I knew that he needed it for the pain and I needed it for the sittin'. Wouldn't go to bed, I fell asleep with my head on the table before he did. Later, without waking up, he had a screaming, cussing dream about fighting up the ladder, then slept until I woke him up with the smell of fryin' bacon. Ate, knew when to go piss, had pain and was willing accept a drink to ease it, but still stared ahead and wouldn't talk. We got the Sheriff and Major to come over in the hope that a display of authority and two more men might convince him to move. Lucky that worked. Even with the bad leg, I wouldn't want to be even one of four fightin' him into doin' what he won't. Climbin' up and down over my oil truck as long as he did got him over bein' soft from the hospital. More important, he's known reaches of pain that most men can't imagine and don't mind gettin' hurt a little, if that's what it takes to find the advantage in a scuffle. My Daddy taught me that the man who wins a fight is the first man to convince the other fellow that gettin' hurt don't bother him."

The doc asked some specific questions about Raymond's pain, how much he had been drinking to tamp it down, about his background, if he'd ever been suicidal or aggressive, what they knew about his war experiences, and their observations about his ways with people. Answers came from all four men. Sheriff Shaver said that he didn't know him except to throw up his hand when he'd passed the oil truck along the road. "Sorry, it's the only the folks in the County you don't want to be 'sociatin' with that I can tell you about!"

Major Jackson had never met Raymond before that morning, but was able to report that deliveries were always correct and on time, that the kitchen staff liked him and that he always lingered for a smoke with one of them who'd helped care for him as an aide when he'd been a surgical patient.

When Witt stopped asking questions Frank Hess got right to the point. "We've been doing most of the talking, Doctor. Your turn. What's wrong with him? Can you explain what caused it? What can you do for him? What are his chances?"

"Sounds like you're asking one big question with a string of little ones. I like that. That way nothing gets left out. I'd say that medically Mr. McCleary here is case of what we call catatonic schizophrenia. Catatonic is what we call folks with varying degrees of rigidity like his sitting and staring. He's not as bad as some, your display of authority and his response to his physical needs makes him different from those that can only be posed like a mannequin. Catatonia used to be included in *dementia praecox,* catchall for those that couldn't be described as imbeciles, melancholic, or senile. Schizophrenics are people with delusional beliefs that interfere with their ability to cope normally. The Hospital, sadly, is administered along practical rather than current scientific lines. We have separate wards for catatonics, whatever the cause, because they require a lot of care with eating and such, and because they're easily victimized if mixed in with physically active patients." The Doctor spared them the actual ward designations: Male Catatonic; Male Catatonic, Incontinent; Female Catatonic; and Female Catatonic, Incontinent. That same, administratively practical ward structure was extended to the violent, non-violent, senile, and escape-prone without consideration as to what might be an underlying cause of the illness. "Because Raymond was functioning normally, I diagnose him as having some all-controlling delusion, quite possibly connected with the war, leading to his mute and motionless vigilance in one direction and extreme reaction to interference with his person. From what you tell me, he had some horrific moments in the war, leading to his nightmares, but his presentation almost seems more consistent with the delusions of someone who'd manned a trench observation post in the previous war. As to whether we can help him, I don't know -- as I've said we've wards of catatonics that have shown no improvement. The fact that you acted quickly rather than his having had months or years to practice this behavior may be in his favor. Lots of folks get brought here after years or decades of dysfunction, cared for in their altered state by relatives who have died off along the way. I'll push to keep him off of a ward with the argument that the liquor or laudanum that he'll need for pain put him and others at risk there. You've said he follows things well enough to appreciate an offered dram; other patients might push for his with mighty rough results. This old building has enough single rooms from the old days that I'll find him one rather than force him to survive, fifty men to a ward in the newer buildings up the hill behind. Only time will tell if he comes out of it." He pushed his stack of papers, a fresh sheet and his uncapped pen on top across the table. "Leave me your names and numbers and I'll call you if there's a change. Otherwise, check with me in a week. Since he'll be by himself, he can have visitors anytime during the day; I can't give you any assurance of anything beyond meeting the night clerk at any later hour.

Having observed the day clerk on their way in and again as they filed out, the four men could only imagine the level of ineptitude after hours.

51. RAYMOND'S HOSPITAL STAY BEGINS

"I hear that you had breakfast already, I'll bring your dinner soon as the cook's through with it." One of the Colored aides, after a quiet conversation with Dr. Witt, had led Raymond down a narrow, twisting staircase to his room on the ground floor, two doors in on a hallway from the courtyard between the row of old buildings and the rows of harsh new dormitories ascending the hill behind. The difference between the hard, shiny, machine brick of the new wards and the soft handmade brick of the old building was clear to Raymond's gaze through the open outside door as they walked along the corridor. Those newer buildings were long, three-story brick boxes with porches on each end, covered floor to ceiling with chain-link fencing rather than fly screen. Raymond's room, while in the basement and without a window, was fairly large, the front half with several chairs like a sitting room, the back half furnished as a bedroom, bed, one straight chair, and a washstand. The pitcher, basin, slop jar, and chamber pot were all of chipped metal enamelware marked with the Hospital's initials. The two halves of the room were divided by a waist-high wooden partition topped by iron bars extending to the ceiling with a door of iron bars at one end. "Go on back to the bedroom, please, Mr. McCleary." Raymond did as he was asked, resuming his vigil seated on the straight chair opposite the foot of the bed. The orderly pulled a big ring of keys from his pocket, mostly Yale cylinder keys, but mixed in were three or four ancient warded-lock keys, one of which he used to secure the barred door before he left.

As he'd promised, the Colored man reappeared with Raymond's dinner just before a bell sounded from one of the buildings' copulas, the signal for patients with freedom of the grounds to come to their assigned eating spots, and telling those at work in the gardens, barns, chicken-house, and dairy to stop work and head for where their cold-dinner buckets had been delivered. "Hey, dinnertime!" The orderly unlocked, brought Raymond's tray in, arranged a place for it on the edge of the wash-stand, and re-locked as he left. "Be back for those dishes in a while." Raymond sat and stared until the smell of food and coffee caught his attention, then shifted his chair and the tray so that his back was to the wall as he stared and ate. "Good to see you eatin', Mr. Raymond. It is all right for me to call you that? You get 'round to talkin', my name's Bell, Rafe Bell. I'll answer to either or both. 'Rafe' is short for Raphael. Family name comes down from slave times, not all my people were field hands! Either <u>Pilgrim's Progress</u>, some learnin' 'bout foreign painters, or a mighty strange corner of the Bible that slavin' man went to for a smooth-soundin' name to have come up bein' said in the big house." Rafe took the tray, locked up and disappeared. Raymond stood, moved over and urinated in the chamber pot, replaced its cover, and resumed sitting and staring without bothering to move his chair back to the morning's spot.

52. THE BEGINNING OF TREATMENT

Mid-afternoon Dr. Witt stopped in, carrying two large coffee mugs, a Thermos, a ring too big to fit even the side pocket of his lab coat which appeared to hold the key to every door and cabinet in the place, and a clipboard filled with a jumble of roughly clamped papers, some in envelopes and file jackets, some printed or typewritten, the topmost appearing to be his own handwritten notes and reminders of the day. He unlocked Raymond's gate, swung it open, took a seat in one of the sitting room chairs away from the bars, and put the mugs and clipboard down on the small table between himself and a closer chair. "Farley Witt, Medical Doctor. You might not have caught the name this mornin'. Come out and sit a spell with me if you like. Don't feel like talkin', that's ok. Join me in a drink if you like; it's whisky in the Thermos and mugs, not Joe. Reckon your leg's hurtin' enough by now that you need it. I welcome the medical necessity of enticing you with drink. It gets me around Doctor DeJarnette's rule against drinking while on duty that has remained in effect even though He's no longer the Superintendent of the Hospital. I doubt the rule applies behind the closed door of the present man's office with his faithful secretary keepin' folks away. Learned in the Army the best way to stay sane was to pick out the most chicken-shit rule as you learned your way around a new outfit, follow all the other rules perfectly, and ignore the chicken-shit rule as often as it suited you when you could do so without being stupid. Could be that you're doin' that now with society's rule about makin' polite conversation and that whatever you're staring at in your mind's eye is important enough that the choice isn't stupid."

Raymond moved silently with his stick from one chair to the other. Didn't pick up his mug until the Doc picked up his, didn't sip until he'd sensed that the Doc had done so, relying, probably, on his peripheral vision and the Doc's little sigh of satisfaction. Witt figured he'd been right about the pain and maybe just a drinker's need, observing a slight tremble as Raymond raised the mug to his lips, and the gradual steadying of his hands as the first mouthful of whisky progressed into his system. "Army pushed my class through medical school fast, lots of work on diseases of concentrated populations, more trauma care, and doubled surgical rotations. Just a couple lectures on obstetrics, and only one that I remember on mental disorders. Got to Europe just as things were ending there, got brought home, put on a boat for Japan, and things were over with them before we were halfway there. The infectious disease work came in handy doctoring on a troopship, and there was trauma from fights and accidents, but I never scrubbed for surgery -- no appendicitis on my ships. Got home, those with time in service and time in grade that wanted to stay in the shrinking medical corps stayed and I was awarded the Ruptured Duck. Wouldn't make much of a general practitioner, given all I hadn't been taught, couldn't face going back to school to fill it in, and ended up here in this dry-land liberty ship. Lots of similarities in being a doctor for any group of people crowded together, soldiers, prisoners, or the insane. I got here and fit pretty well. I do some reading, keep my eyes open, picking up enough to do about as much psychiatry as any other doc on staff. That means that I can put appropriate labels on people. None of us do much by way of treatment because there isn't much that medicine knows to do. Keep people as well physically as circumstances allow, some improve, and most don't. Some people mellow out of the behaviors that brought them here as they age; some have symptoms that get worse." He paused for a deep sip of 'coffee'. "You heard me tell your friends what I think of your chances."

"Here's how I see things going for you. You're a bit of a celebrity here because of what we know you did in the war -- I saw those cliffs from a distance when my ship came in. You're going to get some preferential treatment because of the entourage that brought you here, an Army major that nobody knows but who caught everyone's attention both by bein' a major and because he tended to your business privately -- no soldier driving his car, and a businessman and banker known to everyone local who works here, all escorted by the Sheriff. Those things, plus the fact that you scream bloody hell at night and look as though you'll kill anyone who touches you or your stick got you isolated in this museum-piece of a room rather than put in a bunk in a dormitory with fifty other men. If that's where you'd ended up, somebody would inevitably face off with you, either because they're so impaired that they can't understand to leave you be, or because they want the liquor you'll be given pretty regular for your pain. The staff here figures that you've had some training and experience of killing people and they don't want no trouble. That's the one thing that you've got to understand about this place. They don't want no trouble. The town's watching through your friends. Even though they probably don't know you from Adam, the critics of Dr. DeJarnette in the legislature that took him down will be watching the paper, and if anything happens to you your friends they'll report it. If you do something to anyone else some staff member will talk and the paper'll be all over it. The Hospital administration still can't figure why the Army's interested. From their point of view majors don't show up on account of egg delivery guys who talk with the Colored kitchen help. They think that a major without a driver is a major who doesn't want anyone to talk, even if his brass is Medical Corps. Really worries them -- you ain't got a Medal of Honor as an explanation, unless you've been holding out on everybody."

"I see a few more days for you here in the pen, for staff to judge how bad your pain is and see what a course of aspirin, whisky, and laudanum at night does for that and your dreams. You'll get as much hand-care and feeding as some politician's anonymous kin. Everyone on medical staff, including the director, will be in to look you over, partly out of curiosity and partly so that they have a chance for claims of professional excellence if they happen to be the one talking to you if you should happen to snap out of this spontaneously." Dr. Farley Witt laughed. "I'm not excluded from that last bit, even though I stopped in 'cause you seem like a nice enough fellow and provide the perfect alibi not only for a drink, but for a drink with a patient! After a few days your door'll be unlocked during the daytime to see if the regular toilet down the hall or a chance to sit on a bench in the courtyard will lure you out. If you take to sittin' out there peaceably, probably nothing else will change until you do." By then their mugs were empty. When Witt stood, Raymond stood, and leaving the mug on the table, returned to the other side of the room. Witt wordlessly closed and locked the barred gate, silently raised his hand in farewell salute, and left with his clipboard of papers, the empty mugs dangling from his fingers.

Dr. Farley Witt was right. Four more physicians, including the Hospital director came to see him through that afternoon and during the next day. None of the others did him the courtesy of allowing him to come out and sit with them, much less bring him whisky. All of them tried to get him to speak, asking endless, usually trivial but sometimes insulting questions. All of them tried to avert his gaze, arguing that there was nothin in the space in front of him, or describing their guess of what he was focused on -- Sarah, his childhood, the death of a German soldier he'd killed in battle. The Director, a tall, unsmiling man, was the most unpleasant of all, trying to rouse Raymond through anger, using every question or statement to imply or flatly state cowardice in battle, common alcoholism, and failure as a son, employee, and lover. The final, astounding rant was that if he showed no improvement that he'd die here, a burden to the taxpayer, unable to even contribute labor to the Hospital's farm and gardens, and that he'd just as well get on with dying sooner than later. The Director did end on a positive note. "I see from your record that you've no children. We can be thankful that you've not passed whatever peculiar defect that you have on to another generation." After pausing a moment to see if his onslaught had any cumulative effect, he shook his head, frowned even more deeply, and left.

Moments later Dr. Witt appeared with the afternoon mugs of coffee. As before, he opened Raymond's door, put his mug on the table, and sat in the far chair. "I was lurking 'round the corner and heard that one -- remarkable, remarkable." Raymond eased out and joined the Doctor. "Didn't hear the others, but at mess, each of them talked about their pet theories of what would shift you. Junior man, I just kept quiet and listened. It's probably less troublesome for you that because I'm the doctor that admitted you, I'm the one who'll be checking on you regular after I deal with my wards." Another deep pull on the mugs by both men. "It's clear from your friends' account and your behavior with Rafe and me that you're able, on some level to receive, process and use information. There's something, I can't explain what, that keeps you silent and staring. Maybe something actually wrong in the meat of your brain -- I'd think that if you'd been hit in the head before coming in -- or some thing or things that you've experienced at any point in your life that have taken priority in determining your behavior. I figure that when you're able, you'll talk and look around of your own will. It is my sincere hope that until then you are in such a state that your limitations are not a torment to you, wanting to speak but unable." They had just about finished their coffee "Funny thing, all of my colleagues read the intake report which said that you talked to the chickens to calm them as you worked. When they talked over breakfast and dinner each of 'em had to count along their fingers, some halfway or more again, to remember what they'd asked you. I don't recall any of them asking you what you told the birds. I'm not going to ask you.

Figure if it's important you'll know I'm aware of the issue and tell me when you want."

53. A VISIT FROM HIS FRIENDS AND ROUTINE SETTLES IN

Bill proposed to Frank Hess that he and Sarah go out and get Raymond's truck and personal things so that he could get a new man established. She drove him out so that he could drive the barrel-nose back to storage on the oil company lot. Raymond had put the oak chest unbolted from the truck at the foot of the bed upstairs. While Sarah began filling the chest with Raymond's clothes, Bill went below to gather his coat from its nail, look around for any other gear, and return the two shells that he'd pocketed from the Nitro Hunter to its chambers for the next man's use. The only other things that he could identify as Raymond's rather than the remaining food were the half-empty bottle in the cupboard, a half-empty case of whisky back next to the pantry box, and the smaller canned-goods box under the table -- Highlander peaches, the black outline of a Scott with kilt and bagpipes embossed into the soft box-elder end boards along with the name -- where Raymond kept his shoe polish, brush and rags. Bill put the bottle into the case, the smaller box on top, slung the coat across his arm and carried them slowly up the stairs, feeling for the unaccustomed depth of tread and height of riser with his toes because the load obscured his vision. "Wasn't much down there, coat, whisky, shoeshine stuff. Raymond loved to make those boots stand out, a challenge to see if he could get a rise outta' anybody 'cause they didn't look ordinary."

"Not much up here, either. A couple of changes of clothes, his Dopp kit, and his bee-book. What do you reckon we should take to him?"

"Probably one change of clothes, his shoeshine stuff, and kit without any razor blades. If we put that on top and show that we took the blades out, show some smokes but swear there aren't any matches maybe they won't sort through the rags and polish and find the two bottles I'm gonna' put on their sides in that peach box." They laughed because their pulling such a stunt was funny, and because they both knew that Bill was really going to try it, while both of them made distracting talk. Worst that could happen would be that an orderly would feel the bottles in the rags, wink at them then take one for himself while his back was turned, setting the box down in Raymond's room. That's why Bill figured two bottles, a fifth for Raymond and an easily palmed and pocketed pint for the orderly. If they called ahead the next time they wanted to visit and said they were coming, the same man'd adjust things so that he'd be in the hall to escort them, find two bottles more rolled up in clean shirts and underwear, wink again, and things would be established. No point in Raymond hurtin' in the night.

"Help me get the big box into the boot of my car. I'll be the one tendin' to clothes. You can put the others in the floorboards of his pickup. We probably ought to take his bee-book to him too. Much as he likes 'em it might help him to snap out of things." Sarah didn't care if Bill drank some of the whisky, but she wanted to count and manage the savings in the can in the bottom of the box herself.

The next afternoon Dr. Witt was pleasantly surprised to find Raymond sitting in the outer room when he arrived, coffee mug in each hand, papers tucked under his elbow. In a more open room, a more comfortable chair, but still mute and staring. He put the papers and mugs down, produced a pack of cigarettes from a pocket, shook one out and offered it to Raymond. "Smoke?" When there was no response, he put it to his own lips, lit it with a Zippo that had medical corps insignia soldered to the case, took a deep drag and exhaled with a sigh before taking his first sip of coffee. As before, Raymond waited for him to take the first drink before taking one himself. "Good to see that your social graces still include waiting for others; your loss that they don't extend to accepting an offered smoke. Tobacco's a popular amusement here. Cigarettes -- mostly roll your own -- chew, snuff, and the occasional cigar. Cigars, they're a regular for the superintendent. Patients may have the makin's but no matches -- gotta ask staff for a light. For those who can't get anything else, the State provides 'blue bag' and papers. Rumor has it that blue bag is the floor sweepings from the factories in Richmond, bagged up and donated. Can't say that I've tried one. Some of the old timers are amazing rolling artists. Crease the paper so that one edge stands up just a bit at the heel of the left palm; shake out the tobacco, finger it if it didn't fall right; and then give it a right arm slap, straight from the shoulder, lick the edge to seal it. Hold it up for a light from the attendant who'd either been watching the whole show or heard the slap." Raymond stared straight ahead without any change from his studied, directional hyper-vigilance, unaffected by what usually passed for hospital humor. They sat and sipped. Witt, at a loss for what to talk about next, sat back and savored the whisky and breaking the rule. "Early days are the most important for catatonics.

That's when they have the best odds of snapping out of it. Can't try to force 'em, just strengthens their resolve. Have to give 'em as many opportunities as possible. You're making progress, coming to this side of the room, I'll feel better 'bout you if I come tomorrow and you're sitting on the bench just outside in the court-yard." Raymond continued to stare and sip. "I'm going to send an interesting fellow around to see you. Sam Weaver, Mennonite guy. Came here as a C.O. during the war and stuck around. God knows why. Maybe he wanted to try the job as a regular employee with days off to see the bright lights of Staunton before heading back to the farm. Finished? Thought so." Witt gathered up the mugs and his papers and left, leaving the door to the hall half ajar.

Just a few minutes after Doctor Witt left Rafe Bell stuck his head in the door. "You got company comin'. Mr. Riley called, asked when my shift got off, that he and your lady-friend were coming to bring you some things and they wanted to catch me here 'cause I look after you more'n anyone else. Don't know that I can tell 'em anything extra, 'cause you act the same with everybody but it was considerate of them to ask to talk to me. Seems like you got pretty good people here even though your family's down south. Proves what I figured from the start, you been a pretty good man since you've been around here and was probably a good man for the Army before you got shot up. A real shame that you've got this starin' tribulation after all that."

Rafe was there before breakfast and usually went home just before supper. Sometimes he lingered to bring Raymond's supper plate, but somebody else, whoever they caught and told to do the job came and got the dish when he was done. He met Sarah and Bill in the front hall, taking their box without letting the fellow at the desk look at it, put it on a chair and ran his hands through it, looking as he felt. "There's nothing here but clean clothes, Dopp kit, smokes and shoeshine stuff, George; this way folks, then down the stairs." Rafe took the box under one arm, indicating the direction with the other and giving Bill a wink as he passed by. "That George, he takes forever goin' through people's stuff lookin' for things they're not supposed to have, even though with the farm, kitchen, and shops they get access to most all of 'em anyway. Man's strange. Likes feelin' through other folks socks." Even Sarah had to duck her head a bit on the twists of the stairs. "This way, second to last door on the left." When they came in, Raymond was sitting in the front room, staring at the wall rather than out into the hallway. "Hey, Mister Raymond, I'll just put your things back by the bed." Rafe brought the third chair out through the gate so that both Sarah and Bill could sit, and then stood sideways in the hall doorway, half in, half out. Bill caught Sarah's eye, winked, then nodded slightly towards Rafe. She saw that he looked pleased, and when she looked carefully she realized that his right arm, out in the hall was crooked just enough to steady the smaller of the two bottles in the off-side pocket of his jacket. "I think Mr. Raymond's doin' good. Comes out here to the sittin' room every mornin', it takes some folks months to heal enough to do that. Doctor Witt says he oughta be moving on to the bench outside in the courtyard soon. That doctor looks after him good, visits and brings him a drink for the pain every afternoon, something extra besides what the hospital gives mornin' and night. Both his doors are unlocked all day. Night orderly locks the hall door after he brings a little glass of laudanum for pain and sleepin', leaves it on the table and Mr. Raymond has always drunk it by morning. He locks the door for protection, so nobody can wander in and mess with Mr. Raymond or his medicine."

"Thanks for filling us in on things, Mr. Bell. I know it's the end of your shift and I believe Miz Thomas and I can find our way out if you need to get home to supper. We'll let you know when we're coming again so that you can keep us current."

"Yes, Sir. Good evenin'." Raphael Bell disappeared, leaving them alone with Raymond.

Without speaking, Sarah brushed Raymond's cheek as she settled onto the nearest chair.

"Hello, my boy! That box in there has some clean duds, some of your personal things, your shoe-shine fixin's, smokes, and, thanks to Mr. Bell's unsolicited cooperation, a bottle to help you along if you've a bad time between whisky rations." Bill sat down; Raymond continued to stare straight ahead. "Got your truck parked on the lot at work, key's up on a shelf, not in the cash-box where the first fool to bust open a door would find it. Sarah's got your oak box with your clothes and stuff out at her place. She's the one insisted on putting the bee book in with what we brought you." Raymond still stared. "The evening after Sarah sorted out your clothes I called your folks down in Guilford and told them what little I knew. They wanted to know if they should come up, but I told them it would be better to wait until we knew exactly what was happening, and that I'd call again after seeing you." Raymond still stared, silent. Bill and Sarah just sat without talking as well, not even carrying on a conversation between them. They'd been in enough sick-rooms and death-rooms to understand that their presence was more important than attempts at conversation with Raymond and secure enough in that understanding that they felt no need to amuse themselves with polite talk.

A few minutes after the last word had been spoken, Raymond's cheeks began to dampen with tears. Sarah and Bill exchanged glances but said nothing. If there was to be a breakthrough it would have to come from within Raymond. They had no confidence in their ability to coax a word from him, and feared that a failed attempt would only reinforce his silence. He still stared straight ahead and made no sound as the tears welled and flowed down his face, dripping onto his shirt. Bill watched Sara hold her composure for what seemed a long time, but was in reality probably only a few moments before she, too, began weeping, first silently, then with enough sound that it would be perceptible to Raymond if he hadn't seen her out of the corner of his eye. Bill waited long enough to see if Raymond would respond, and when he didn't, rose, guiding Sarah gently by the elbow.

"We'd best be going now. We'll be back to check on you again in a few days." Sarah rose, brushing her hand on Raymond's face again, and the two of them left, closing the hall door behind them. Once down the hall, around the corner and out of earshot, Sarah collapsed against Bill, sobbing. Bill's eyes were tearing up as he held her free shoulder to steady her as they both regained their composure.

"Would it have come on him if I'd persuaded him to stay? That's what I ask myself."

"What if it had come on him while he was with you? Don't blame yourself, girl. We both know it's from the war and nothing any of us could have done would'a stopped it."

Just as Raymond was finishing his breakfast the next morning, the 'interesting fellow,' Sam Weaver, pushed the mostly open door back on its hinges, came in, introduced himself and took a seat. Raymond continued staring and eating without acknowledging Weaver's presence. "Accomplished dining technique you have there, McCleary. The usual variant we see around here is two-handed without utensils. Less common is insisting on eating out of a bowl on the floor without use of the hands like pets or livestock. You, however, rely on your peripheral vision in a way I've only heard described in connection with the 'squared meals' required of cadets being hazed in their first year at some of the military schools. It's optional here. I 'spect you'll grow tired of it soon." Raymond wiped his lips on his napkin without looking or responding.

"Farley Witt enlisted me to be one of your people. His theory is that imposed socializing with staff rather than patients has the best chance of cracking your nut. Rafe Bell has his eyes and ears open to report how you're doin', and his gentlemanly ways may touch a memory. Witt's bait, besides the institutional prestige of regular medical doctor's visits, something that you've yet to develop an appreciation of, is, of course, whisky, cigarettes and wry comment on every aspect of this place. In Witt's view I may be useful as an irritant -- you're a combat veteran and I started working here as a Conscientious Objector avoiding military service. Thinks you might not be able to stomach the association, so I'll drop in when I can to see if I can do you any good besides carrying out your breakfast dishes." Weaver left, doing just that. Raymond sat and stared until Bell brought his diner in right before the noon bell rang.

Returning and gathering up the empty dishes, Bell paused on his way out. "Mr. Raymond, why don't you come outside and sit a spell -- there's a bench against the wall just outside the door, not but a few steps when you decide to come back in." To his surprise, Raymond rose and followed him out of the room and into the courtyard. Rafe didn't let on that this was unusual or unexpected, just kept on with his normal pace and tone of voice. Mental patients, he'd learned, were right much like livestock, go easy, talk soft just enough to let them know where you were and things would usually be pretty smooth. He remembered, though, from the farm, that you couldn't listen to your own soft talk while you were within head-tossin' or kicking distance. Had to keep your eyes and ears open for anything else that might spook 'em, and for the subtle bodily tensioning that showed in the split-second before an animal or man lashed out. "Here's your seat. I'll stop back by and sit with you a bit if I can." Bell kept moving slowly so long as he was within Raymond's sight, but then hustled to drop the dishes at the kitchen and then to find Dr. Witt.

Witt and Bell looked down from a third-floor window. Raymond was on the bench in the sunshine erect and alert, hands resting, with his stick, ready, on his thighs, his back straight but taking advantage of the comfort and security of resting full against the wall. "He just followed me out when I suggested it, offhand-like."

"You ought to be the handler for more folks in this place!"

"We oughta' get more people right when they take sick, rather'n the ones that've sat on the porch and by the stove year in and year out, learnin' how to keep on actin' peculiar."

"Probably so. Probably so. Slip down and keep an eye on him please, don't let anyone stir him up. I'll go by my office and get our coffee, then come down and tell him what he's not looking at."

Bell hurried down the stairs, ambled across the courtyard at his usual pace and settled on the other half of Raymond's bench. "Just come to sit for a little while. Excuse me for not makin' conversation." Rafe leaned back with his head against the wall, posture far more relaxed than Raymond's, half closed his eyes, keeping watch that no one approached to confront Raymond, possibly driving him back indoors, smiling to himself. It'd be sweet if some supervisor or busybody came along and brought him up short for idleness. "Doctor's orders," he'd tell 'em. "Doctor Witt's orders for me to sit with this man."

Witt himself came over in a few minutes, clipboard of unruly papers pinched between elbow and ribs, a big, dark blue enameled mug in each hand. "See you later Mr. Raymond." Bell ambled off to check on someone else.

"You surprise me, McCleary. Didn't expect you out here this soon, but it's a good thing." He put one of the mugs onto the bench between them and assumed Bell's stance against the wall, but kept his eyes full open. He looked out across the yard in front of him and didn't, generally, even bother to look Raymond's way

as he spoke. "New mugs to keep our coffee lookin'
black. The white china ones would make it obvious that
our coffee was brown, like whisky, and I don't think
folks'd accept a sudden switch on our part to tea. Any
odor of alcohol that passersby might catch will no
doubt be accepted as consistent with my reputation and
not cause any closer examination." By then Raymond
had picked up his mug and was taking a long pull. Silent and hyper vigilant, he nevertheless felt the old burn
in his throat, its spread through his belly, and he relaxed
just a bit, unthinkingly aware that the aching in his
thigh would shortly ease. "What you see in front of us
is the building with kitchens and dining rooms on the
first floor for those who can come off of the wards for
meals. The rooms upstairs were originally for staff, now
they're crowded with patients. The few staff that live
here now are above you, scattered in the better bits of
the main building. The Superintendent and Medical Director have modern, that is early twentieth-century,
houses set back but facing Greenville Road, downstream a ways from the spring out front. Past the kitch-
en the two rows of barracks-looking three-tory brick
buildings at a distance up the hill are the primary wards.
'Round the corner is a building that was a book bindery
before the typewriter nixed *that* work for institutions.
Over towards your right, about halfway up to the wards
is the dairy, right behind it the dairy barn. The other
farm buildings work their way up the ridge through the
farmland. The right side of this courtyard is the carpentry shop, originally the carriage house for an omni-
bus, the superintendent's gig, and a couple of buggies
for other staff to use. The tack rooms and stalls beyond
are used as a warehouse, and the nicer staff housing,
including my rooms, is upstairs. My office, logically
and unfortunately, is a closet-like affair on one of the
wards. Not much of a refuge." Raymond never shifted

his gaze or spoke, but at some level he was both watching the line in front of his fighting hole and absorbing the information about his new surroundings -- when his condition improved later on he didn't need to be told what was what. Coffee finished, Dr. Witt made his manners and returned to his wards. After a bit Raymond rose, eased sideways to the door and backed indoors, turning only to enter his room for a nap. He left the hall door slightly ajar for the air and closed his inside barred door, arranging a chair so that there'd be some warning scrape on the floor if it were opened. Stretched out on his back, stick by his side, the side away from the door, he made sure that the heels of his boots were beyond the end of the covers, pulled his cap down to shade his eyes, and fell asleep. The whisky helped, both by itself and by taking the edge off of the pain, but sleep came easy. He was exhausted, from both his hyper-vigilance and the dreams that awakened him just a couple of hours after the laudanum let him get to sleep the night before.

Sarah and Bill kept up their schedule of visits, providing clean clothes rather than subjecting Raymond's limited wardrobe to the wear, tear, and thievery of the hospital laundry, loosely supervised and manned by patients. Bill always came with Sarah so as to be able to break things off, say "time to go" before helpless emotion broke them both. Raymond was still away in his head, passively cooperating with the visits, but intent on what was in the distance, unable to turn and look at either of them. Rafe Bell had done so many show inspections in the front hall that George just grunted and waved them on even if Rafe couldn't be there, so that Bill was always confident that Raymond had a little extra alcohol if he needed it.

Sarah kept the folks in North Carolina up-to-date. Things were changing there that didn't bode well for Raymond's going home. His parents were failing rapidly, Father unable to do much but tend an old man's share of chickens; Mother, short of breath and stove up with arthritis that made attempts at any but the lightest housework futile. The courtships that Raymond and Sarah had observed during their visit had, with the exception of Reba, progressed as predicted. Quentin Baker had, in fact, merely wanted a housekeeper instead of a wife. It was good that the Baker place was close by, allowing Mary to spend a great part of the time at home, doing what Mother used to. The brothers were happily involved with their new families, generous with their labor when they could be spared, but that was unpredictable, and the nature of farming was such that they were least available in the busiest seasons. Reba was essentially running the farm by herself, although Charlie Smith usually showed up with his men and machinery after getting in his crop if he knew Reba was still working. Despite their love for Raymond, bringing home a third person to care for just didn't fit. Three folks on the porch, one of whom had to be led by the hand, consumed vast amounts of whisky, and woke everyone up each night was just too much of a load for the kind of farm that Reba was running to carry.

Reba and her brother Charlie came up to visit Raymond when it became evident that his improvement seemed to have stalled in the courtyard. They were at once pleased and taken aback at his ancient private quarters, then totally pleased after a quick visit with Dr. Witt to a couple of the wards. They stayed with Sarah, shared some stories; retrieved the truck from Bill's lot, shared many more stories; and drove back to the farm at Guilford, feeling sad and guilty that they weren't bringing Raymond home, but reassured about at least his physical surroundings, the loyalty of his Staunton friends and the attentiveness of his caregivers. They agreed that it was frightening to discover how little medicine knew of his illness and how to treat it, circumstances that likely explained the fate of many of Grandfather's 'men who went West and were never heard from again.'

Sam Weaver knocked, and then pushed open Raymond's door late one evening to bring his laudanum and check on him before locking him off from the hall for the night. "Still up, I see." Raymond was in his accustomed chair in the outer room. Remembering Dr. Witt's instructions to raise the CO issue, he eased into the other chair. "Like I told you, I came to Western as a CO. I'm a Mennonite from down in Rockingham County. Most of the CO's around here were either Mennonite or Brethren. Reckon there must have been at least a couple that you knew back home before you went in the Army, what with the Quaker school there at Guilford. They assigned me to the Forest Service at the old CCC camp at Sherando, but a bunch of us asked to come to work here at the hospital. A bunch of guys from the Grottoes camp volunteered to be smoke-jumpers out west when they came up with that idea. The remaining forestry workers got consolidated at Grottoes and they turned Sherando into a POW camp. Even as a POW camp I'm sure it was still a damned sight better'n what Dr. DeJarnette set up for us here! Our barracks was next to the pig-pens and the water in the pipes ran rusty and nasty. Sherando had good water and the smell of pine boards and tar-paper roofing. Not sure why I stayed on here, 'cept I found the people interesting, and wanted to see what a regular shift and a day off were like. During the war we had anywhere from ten-hour shifts for the few fellows working the farming crews and usually fourteen on a ward, with four hours off in the afternoon every two weeks. Get on different shifts and you wouldn't see some of your buddies for months except when bad luck or bad food put you both on sick-call. There wasn't good supervision of the patients doing butchering or in the dairy back then -- they've corrected that now that the end of the war brought some qualified people back into the local labor market. Us COs didn't believe in fighting war 'cause of our church upbringing. It was a real eye-opener to discover that when we got on some of the wards we'd be fighting and wrestling every day, breaking things up or trying to keep things calm. Didn't take but a minute for me to realize that a man who thought I was Satan and 'must be vanquished' wasn't gonna' take time to talk theology or logic and that I had to grab his ass before he grabbed mine. I'd been told about Dorthea Dix, the founding of this place as a peaceful haven where people who suffered mental disorders could rest and possibly recover. I knew that there were a lot of patients here, but had no idea that the Hospital was instead a set of holding-pens for morons, idiots, the demented and the delusional. They have doctors here but no real treatment for those conditions -- just confinement. The doctors try to keep people from coming down with ordinary illness, patch up cuts, set broken bones, and do a little surgery, the occasional appendix and sterilizing those of the morons who show any sign of being able of breeding more of their kind. Brother Shank, our preacher, wouldn't like to be told it, but I've got more use here out of growing up around Daddy's mean Holstein bull than a lifetime of his sermons. If you're in the same pasture or pen with that bull you better not forget about him, even when you've just turned away from watching him nose into the trough or grazing real peaceful. In a snap of your fingers that old boy can turn and be on you." I learned right quick which patients required the precautions I learned 'round that bull. When you came there was some talk that you might be one of them, still might be, once you get movin'." Raymond gave no indication that he even knew that Weaver was in the room, just sat still, looking ahead. Despite the amount of energy expended in his watchfulness three full hospital meals a day rather than bachelors' bacon had him putting on weight. His muscles were constantly poised to react, but it was evident to anyone who knew him before or had seen him regularly at the Hospital could see that he was getting soft.

"It's right sad, the way some folks grow old and die here; others die too young. I reckon that what caught and keeps my interest is the fact that some people *do* get better. Nobody knows why, maybe it's just from being away from the world for a while, not having to even assume responsibility for their own day-to-day existence. That 'being away from the world' bit certainly fits in with Dix's theories, as I understand them, and matches the definition of 'asylum' when it isn't following the word 'lunatic.' Difference is the fact that while they may be away from the world, they have to cope with an environment full of crazy folks under minimal supervision. Amazing that the two don't cancel each other out, amazing that what's triggering peoples' illness is worse'n being here."

"You, there's no doubt it was the war. What your family and friends have told us seems horrible enough to land you here, but I'd bet it's what you've never told them, told anyone, that's got you jammed up. I grew up listenin' to men tellin' the cows 'bout how their wives don't understand them and how the preacher's got it all wrong, things they couldn't tell anybody, and would've been whisperin' to the cows rather than talkin' out loud if they'd known there was a ten-year-old in the barn. I bet that you got to talkin' to those hens and that what you were rememberin' was too much for you to handle. What do I know? I'm just one of those COs who hid behind the skirts and bonnets of the church rather'n doin' my duty."

When his last sentences failed to elicit any response, Weaver got up, locked the hall door as he left, and made a mental note to talk to Dr. Witt the next day.

Weaver was back the next day. While on some errand across the courtyard, he didn't see Raymond out on the bench, knew that he had to be in his room and nosed in to find him the same as the night before. Taking the previous evening's chair himself, he started up again.

"You, my friend, through some mysterious sequence of events have landed in a private room just on the outskirts of all the madness we talked about last night. Correspondingly, it appears that there has been some improvement in your condition since your arrival -- perhaps you're benefitting from the institution's original model. My advice to you is that you don't cause anyone any trouble. Don't get in fights, even if they'd not be your fault. Don't try to run off, don't decide to parade around naked, and don't ever, ever, lay a hand on staff. A curious thing about this place is that things don't change much except where there's trouble. Other than having to look at a barred partition you've got a pretty sweet deal here compared to a ward. There are a surprising number of patients in the same situation, tucked away in all the strange nooks and crannies in these old buildings. Some of 'em have been there for years. They got private quarters for all kinds of reasons, from political influence in Richmond to simple overcrowding on the wards turning a store-room residential. Half of 'em nobody even remembers the reason, folks just figure they're gettin' along so why change. The only exception to that rule of inertia is if somebody causes a problem. Don't make any trouble. If you keep quiet, the Director's office'll forget that you're around while they're dealing with whoever's trying to twist their tail from Richmond."

Raymond didn't respond, Weaver hadn't expected him to, and left. As things turned out the phrase 'if you keep quiet' must have penetrated and been remembered.

Frank Hess wheeled his three-window coupe down the hill, through the stone arch of the C&O viaduct that still had smoke-marks from the Yankees' unsuccessful explosion, passed the B&O station on his right and turned left through the gates of the tall iron fence into the Hospital's park. He knew that on nice days like this Raymond tended to pass his time in the courtyard, so he bypassed threading through the halls and stairs, pulling around the end of the building where he could park and follow a path alongside the old bindery headed towards the kitchen and the courtyard. He spotted Raymond in his usual place. As he got closer he realized that Raymond wasn't staring ahead, but had turned his head and was looking at him! Raymond's gaze was following him, either recognizing him or catching the different look of his business-suit as he crossed the courtyard among right many people in the several variations of institutional dress.

"'Mornin', Raymond." He kept his normal tone of voice and didn't let his face show any surprise at having been watched. Raymond didn't say anything and Frank couldn't honestly tell himself that there was any spark of recognition in his eyes, but without tensing up or tightening the hold on his stick he turned and watched as Frank walked in front of him to sit on the other end of the bench, then went back to gazing into the distance.

"Good to see you, son, good to see you. Sorry I haven't been by as regular as Sarah and Bill, but I reckon they've got to be on schedule since they're running laundry and resupply. Things are going reasonably well with the birds, just brought in a new bunch of pullets for one side. I've got a pretty good man there now after a couple of false starts. Pretty good, but not as good as you. Don't think your gentle ways, soft talk and vigilance with the Nitro Hunter'll ever be matched. A real shame if any of your way of working led to your being here. Saw Mrs. Russ this morning, told her that I was coming to see you. She sends her regards and expects a report. I'll be pleased to tell her that you broke your stare to watch me walk over -- I'd say that's progress, about as big as the first day you came outside."

Raymond glanced at Frank just quick enough to convey the notion that he hadn't expected Frank to be so observant, but didn't say anything and went back to staring.

Frank caught the glance but decided against commenting on it. "I know it takes time to get turned around from situations like yours. Rough being up here away from your people, but I'm not sure that just sitting on the porch at their farm, feeling useless, or being in some hospital in a different part of the state from them would be any better. Speaks well for you that the friends you've made here in the Valley do for you 'bout like your own people would. Look! There's Doctor Witt coming out and headed this way. Two mugs, must be coffee time."

Raymond did look, just for an instant to make sure that Frank was right, and the flicker of an expression of pleasure crossed his face before he went back to vacant staring. Frank slid over to the farthest bit of bench to make room for Witt and rose to his feet to greet him as he approached.

"Good morning, Doctor. I won't offer my hand to a gentleman with a mug in each of his and a clipboard of papers trying to escape his elbow." There were enough papers irregularly positioned under the scarred clamp that they gave every indication of being close to success in their attempt to escape. "The news this morning is that I spotted brother Raymond here averting his gaze to watch me cross the courtyard, then caught him giving me a quick glance telling me that I wasn't supposed to have done so when I mentioned it." Raymond showed no response.

"Really?" The Doctor sat down between them, handed one mug to Raymond, clearly perceived and accepted in the range of his peripheral vision, and lodged his board of papers between his feet, edge on the ground. "That's good." He took his first drink and Raymond followed suit.

"The other good news is that Raymond gave another quick glance, in your direction, when I said that I saw you coming."

"If I'd realized you were here, I'd have tried to manage three mugs. You're welcome to sippers from mine if you like -- I won't be shortchanged since I can always catch up when I take the mugs back to my office."

"Thank you, but no. I'm afraid that the smell of coffee on my breath would be the start of gossip once I return to the Bank."

"As you like. I always try to remember what an old man I followed around when I was a kid told me more'n once. "Live while you're livin' Farley boy, live while you're livin', 'cause you're a long time dead." I've had right many good moments by followin' that advice."

"I 'spect you have and say keep on with it. My joining you just wouldn't fit in at the bank."

"So you're lookin' around now. That's good. I know you've studied 'most everything in sight by varying the direction of your stare, probably know every person who comes through here by sight and everyone who has been addressed within earshot by name. That's good, too. Now you're getting to the point to use some of it." Witt took a deep drink of coffee and leaned back against the wall with a sigh and satisfied look. "Mr. Hess, I wish that I could tell you that I've done anything to bring on this change, but I can't. All I've done is allow tincture of time to do its work, probably aided by Raymond's relatively quiet lodgings and the rumors that flew after his unusual arrival that the Army was using us to conceal the most demented of its killers which kept people from bothering him. I will take credit for any good accomplished by regular one-sided conversation, companionship, and regular dosing with tincture of coffee, none of them therapies I've observed in regular use here. They tend more towards field, kitchen, or laundry work, cold baths, restraint in poseys if you're troublesome and irregular double-drams of whisky if the arthritis flares up for the old folks. All of it ordered for administrative convenience and economy rather than selected for possible benefit to any specific patient. As you can imagine, I am somewhat professionally offended by a medical facility run along the lines of administrative convenience. Maybe by the time Raymond recovers, some brass hats will have retired and I'll be able to ease my MD back into the Medical Corps and learn the arts of peacetime Army doctoring, which, despite that institution's hidebound ways, I suspect are both scientific and luxurious compared to here. At least Army commanders are ultimately accountable to someone. My impression is that the legislature provides for this place about like most men would a red-haired stepchild and our Director may do as he pleases without interference so long as he insures that the folks in Richmond are presented with no embarrassment."

"I'd say that's an accurate assessment. Seen similar arrangements between bank managers and directors. Sometimes it's good, usually it's not. Speakin' of banks, I'd better get back to mine. Have a good afternoon, gentlemen."

After Hess got up, Witt slid over to give them both a bit more sitting room. '"Raymond, you sure picked up a variety of friends here in town; banker, train engineer, widow store-keeper, old-style oil man, Army Major, high-class boardinghouse lady. Damn lucky that they're stickin', too. Lots of folks get sent to the hospital and people forget them real quick. Completely changing subjects, if you don't mind, since you're getting more adventurous, you might consider sitting on the bench under the tree over by the carpentry shop. That'd let you focus on what happens here as you look into the distance, get some perspective on the main building. To the extent you want to look out of the corners of your eyes, watching the carpenters is more interesting than the foot-traffic by here. A couple of the carpenters are kind of grouchy, but they tend to work back from the door so that they can avoid folks and enjoy their mutual gloom. One of them, Earl Ralston, is a pretty good fellow, likes to work in the doorway or just outside if the weather's nice. I'll tell him about you and that you know farm carpentry. Look around this place and up the height of the wall you're leaning against and you'll see why the biggest part of their work is window-sash, either broken out or rotted out. Fixing doors probably comes next, then assorted projects of furniture and cabinetry. They try to keep an assortment of coffins on hand. Earl tells me that when he came on they still custom built old-fashioned toe-pinchers, but now they just do plain boxes and try to keep one of each size ready."

Witt finished his last bit of coffee, took Raymond's mug when he'd done the same, and headed over to talk to Mr. Ralston. Raymond kept an eye on them, and as soon as Witt left for his office and Ralston became refocused on his work, moved over to the new bench.

54. UNDER THE INFLUENCE OF THE CARPENTERS

    The bench did afford a good view of the building where Raymond lived, and of which his only impression had been formed during his quick march up to and through its formal front entrance. Looking at it from the rear, he could appreciate the complexity of its protruding wings, chimneys, banks of windows, cupolas and widow's walks. The original design had not only provided many well-lit rooms but had allowed observation well up into the gardens and pastures, now blocked from view by the dismal brick warehouses, the wards that marched up the hill.

    Witt, to the extent that a physician could influence the actions of the carpenters, which was mighty little in the case of Ralston's grouchy companions who went to any length to preserve the independence of the maintenance staff and remind everyone of their seniority and exemplary skills, had made his request of Ralston. The fact that Ralston was a pretty good fellow and had been observing and approved of Witt's incessant maneuvering to do his work in a way that ignored as much as possible the long-entrenched rituals of administrators and senior medical staff meant that he'd follow the young doctor's suggestion. As soon as Raymond seemed settled in with a good fixed stare towards his old bench and the doorway leading to his room, Ralston spoke up.

    "Witt says you're a North Carolina man who don't talk much, that if I get tired of watchin' you sit and say nothin' that he encourages me to talk at you. Said I didn't have to use good grammar or be polite, that if I wanted I could be downright insulting, even say bad things about your parentage and upbringing. I think that doc wants you to talk pretty bad." He fell silent and went back to his work on the window sash on the sawhorses in front of him, chiseling out a rotted and broken mortise, the first step before cutting a patch out of a bit of scrap. He kept one eye on Raymond as he worked and it wasn't long before he caught him looking briefly his way. "Doc Witt," he said without looking up or letting on that he was aware of Raymond's furtive scrutiny, "tells me you were a farm boy before they made you into a killer with some little orange patch on your sleeve. Reckon you've nailed plenty of boards on fences 'n barns, maybe even pulled boards off a sawmill to sticker 'em for drying, but I'd bet that you never done any real carpenterin'. Carperentin' like we have to do to keep this place from fallin' in or the wind blowin' through. My dyin' thought will probably be of the next pile of window-sash that needs fixin'. They're pretty pleasant work though. No two get smashed out or rotted out exactly alike, so each one takes some lookin' and thinkin' to repair. Most of the sash in a building are close enough the same size that we can keep a few extra on hand, take the broke one out, put a good one in, and do our work here in the shop without a rush and without bein' surrounded by a tribe of idiots wantin' to steal our tools to play with or kill one another. Bet the Army didn't teach you how to kill folks with hammers an' screwdrivers. Spend a lifetime workin' with carpenters, some of 'em mean, some drunk or off their rockers, ready for this place, maybe two or all three, you'd see how. Now a hammer on top o' the head, that's Keaton 'n Chaplin stuff. Maybe a knockout. When someone says 'upside' your head, they know their business, 'cause low on the side where the level line of a fellow's spectacles goes, that's your spot. Thinner bone, head of the hammer goes in right up to the root of the claw, gotta pry it out and after you do they bleed like it was butcherin' time."

Ralston went back to his work, now measuring and marking to cut the tennon on his piece of scrap. Witt had told him to do anything he could to entice or offend Raymond into watching him and, hopefully, speaking. He'd thought that homicidal carpenters might do the trick. After marking the dimensions of the tennon, he sawed to the correct depth on all four sides of the block of wood.

"Now look here, Mr. Raymond. Here's where we start gettin' different from barn carpentry. You know how to cut off the rotten end of a board and measure and cut another piece, but I'll bet you never cut any joinery. What I'm doing here is making a replacement tennon, the rectangular piece that fits into the opening of a mortise-and-tennon joint at the corner of a sash and is then pegged and glued into place once everything checks out square." Ralston turned to the side and selected a chisel from a group of them standing in slots at one end of his toolbox. Turning back, he caught Raymond turning away from watching him.

"Like my toolbox? Painted it red to match my wagon (he'd pulled the heavy box outdoors on a large, red child's wagon). Makes me stand out a bit from those fellows back there" -- he gestured over his shoulders towards the other two carpenters at work in the gloom of the interior of the building, dark-colored toolboxes beside them on stationary stands about the same height as the wagon. "Lets me work out here where there's good light and I can enjoy the day. You decide you want to try making anything, the scrap pile's right there at the door, and you can use tools out of my red box when I'm around to keep an eye on you. Hell to pay if you pick up one of the other fellows' tools even to give it back when it's been left out at the end of the day. Touch any of the power tools and all three of us will whip your Army ass. We don't need the grief we'd catch if one of those monsters changed over from belt to electric a few years ago grabbed you, chewed you up and spit you out. In Ol' DeJarnette's day and since, I've seen a lot of patient's asses whipped for one reason or another, don't bother the administration much. Somebody gets hurt by farm machinery -- or power equipment -- that's a whole different matter. Gets into the Richmond newspaper and then the Director, *he* catches hell, which then rolls downhill, not stopping 'till it's gone in front of or behind everybody in the place, past the dishwashers and toilet-cleaners and lays there steamin' and stinkin, smoking itself out on the ground."

Timing *his* glance just right, Ralston looked out the corner of his eye and caught Raymond glancing his way with just a hint of expression on his face. Never used the phrase before, he thought, it just kinda' grew and happened on its own as I was sayin' it. A good 'un, seems to have got the man's attention. I'll have to remember it! He continued with his work.

"Once you've cleared the mortise of the broken tennon -- that's what usually gives way after a direct blow because it's the smaller piece of wood -- and decided the frame piece with the mortise is still solid, you cut the new tennon like you just saw me do, then you've got to decide how to splice the piece with the new tennon into the old sash. 'Couple of ways to do that; have to pick the one that fits the condition of the frame. This one's splintered on one face from when the joint got broken, so I'm going to strengthen it by cutting the splintered thickness away, cutting the opposite side of my repair piece off, then gluing and pegging the joint and splice together."

Ralston busied himself with the necessary marking, cutting and trimming until he was satisfied with the result, not getting much attention from Raymond, who was staring across the courtyard, re-indexing his mental encyclopedia of who went where when from the new perspective, which allowed him to include some points of origin and destinations he hadn't been able to see before. He did take a quick glance when he heard nothing from Ralston's direction, then another when he heard him return. Ralston was carrying what looked like the dirtiest, nasty gallon paint bucket he'd ever seen spliced on top of a kerosene barn-lantern whose chimney had been replaced with two overlapping, equally smeared and streaked tin cans.

"Glue pot," Ralston announced. "Know you didn't have one of *these* on the farm. He filled his pipe, lit it with a barn-burner match from a scarred metal matchbox that looked like a rough-sided shotgun shell. He'd given the cylinder of the box half a twist, folded one end to the side to shake out a match, and then struck it on the tooth double-cut side. Raised the chimney lever on the bastard lantern and the cans came up enough for him to light the wick. He shook that match out, returning the stick upside down to his matchbox, and filled his pipe from a leather pouch and lit it with another match, stowing the stick as before. "Always good to have a smoke or two while you're gettin' the glue ready, and the matchsticks are good for pushing it into where you want it without having to search around

for something else just the right size. Got to get the
glue hot and liquid but don't scorch it -- kinda like in
the kitchen. Hide glue, comes either ground up or in
blocks. Heat it with water, but don't boil it. Scums over
between times, usually just a question of heating the
liquid beneath to dissolve the scum and thin it to what
you need for the job. Supposed to thin it with water,
I've used coffee -- real coffee -- reckon you could use
piss if you didn't mind making the smell bein' even
more noticeable. Call it hide glue 'cause it's boiled-
down hooves and hides. Tough as both once it soaks in,
fills the voids in a piece of wood and cures. Ship-
wrecked sailors used to make soup outa' it, kinda rein-
forced bullion." Ralston poked at the disappearing
scum with a paint-stirring stick holding it up a foot up
in the air and letting it slide and dribble back home.
Had to do it both before and after re-charging his pipe
before he could catch Raymond glancing at the show.
As soon as the glue's consistency suited him he turned
the flame down to what would have been the faintest
glimmer if the lantern were stills a lantern, just enough
to hold the glue at the right point. Ralston clenched his
pipe tight with his teeth and worked fast with the stick,
a rag and his fingers. "Got to get a thin, even coat on all
surfaces of each piece that touch each other. Soaks into
the fibers of the wood real good while it's warm and
liquid. Push 'em together tap 'em with a hammer or mallet, throw a try square up against them and tap 'em a
little more if they need truin' up." He paused to wipe a
bit of glue off of the blued steel blade of the hand-
sized square, the short arm of which was brass-bound
ebony, as pretty as the frog on a fiddler's bow, and put
it back into its slot in the toolbox. "Now, when things
are stuck enough to stay straight but the glue's still settin' you drill the holes through for the pegs you whittled
beforehand. Dip the pegs in the glue and drive 'em in,

drawing your patch tight. Run your finger along the edges, pushing any glue that squeezed out into any gaps or irregular spots. Set her aside to dry overnight, next day saw the pegs off flush and move her to the finished row for the painters to do the glazing and touch up the paint, then we'll have one that size next time there's some excitement."

It was getting late in the day, so Ralston gathered his tools up, wiping here and there with an oily rag as he fit them back into the box and snapped on his padlock. Stacked the sawhorses one atop the other, balanced them on his right shoulder, circled the wagon and toolbox around with his left hand and disappeared into the gloom of the shop. In a moment or two he was back with a push-broom and large dustpan, the kind hinged from a long wire handle fastened just back from either side of its lip so that it wasn't necessary to stoop down to use it and with a back end like a bin that held a lot of sweepings when the lip was pulled straight up. He cleaned the bricks where he'd been working, then sat down beside Raymond, commencing to fiddle with pipe, tobacco pouch and matches, each of which had to be found in a different pocket of his clothes. "Get old, you've learned not to stoop down les' you have to. I like that long-handled dustpan as much as my wagon and sawhorses. Learned not to stand when you can sit, too, but movin' it around to fix the problem and gettin' enough purchase on your tools to shape wood, those windows are stand-up jobs. Not many sittin' jobs with carperintin'. See you got a pack of smokes there in your shirt-pocket; share a light with you if you like." Raymond didn't respond, but didn't object when he reached over, took the pack and shook one about halfway out and held it near Raymond's hand. Without looking Ralston's way, Raymond took the cigarette and allowed the older man to push the pack back into his pocket. While Ralston was fussing and drawing on his pipe, Raymond put the unpacked, shedding butt to his lips and was ready when Ralston reached over, shielding the flaring match to give a light, then shaking it out as part of the same motion before it burnt his fingers and returning the stick to its safe. After a couple of satisfactory draws on his pipe he got back to the subject of homicidal carpenters.

"I know you army fellows have bayonets and sheath knives. All us carpenters have along those lines are marking knives, pocket knives, and short awls, not nearly as long as the beat-up wife's favorite, an ice pick. What we favor instead are screwdrivers and narrow chisels. Both of 'em got good long tangs extending up into the handle, some of 'em are made extending through to the top, so's you can really get your weight behind 'em goin' after the other feller." Ralston took a couple of draws and a sideways glance at Raymond, catching him tapping some ash off, not looking at it or anything else. "Problem is, men got ribs. You know how they lay, protective-like. Unless you were a mean 'un to start with, Army had to teach you to bring your thrust up, not down from on high like play-actin' or the pictures. Get the tip of your knife under the lay of the rib and let it guide your power up and in rather than skitterin' off to the side, down and out. Problem for us carpenters is that you can't rely on the straight tip or sharp corner to catch and guide. That's why we focus on the front and side of the neck and throat, avoid the back of the neck, 'cause it's as bony as ribs. Flesh on the neck is nice and soft and kind of a roundhouse swing gets you in deep enough that as you shift your weight or your man starts to go down you can lever on either the neck bone or the jaw and rip the whole business out.

Messy as can be, but there's usually sawdust and chips on the floor. Your man won't get up if you've caught him right." Another pause to draw on the pipe and a peer at Raymond. Enough unattended ash had fallen into Raymond's lap that Ralston reckoned his accounts of woodworking assassins' methods were being heard. He'd have to report to Doctor Witt in the morning. They finished their tobacco in silence, Raymond field-stripping the butt by feel and Ralston reaching down without looking to tap out the bowl of his pipe against the side of his left shoe's heel, confident that his ankle and hand were at just the right angle.

The next morning Doctor Witt began his morning by hunting down his team of talkers, Bell, Weaver, and Ralston. He started with Ralston, the most recent addition so that he might bring the other two up to date when he talked with them.

"Jesus, Earl! You're gonna have that boy convinced that the two grouches that you work with are really here as homicidal maniacs rather than as employees."

"What if I do? Half the people here think McCleary's at the hospital because *he's* such a killer that the Army had to hide 'im. As I told you, he warmed to the topic enough when I brought it up the second time that he dropped ashes on his britches. Seems significant to me, as fastidious as you say he is about his boots and cap. Could be, too," Ralston grinned, "that he ain't never seen a carpenter with a red toolbox on a little red wagon. Maybe my ways appeal to the little boy in him."

"The red wagon caught my attention when I first met you. Keep talkin' to him please, more about what you're workin' on than inflicting grievous bodily harm, but feel free to go back to that if you can top your first two examples -- I'd kinda like to learn what's next on the progression, just in case I get a patient who's followed your line of work. See you this afternoon at coffee time if our man happens to be with you then."

Witt's next conference was with Sam Weaver. "Doc, I just been talkin' to him whenever I get a chance, sit by him on the bench or stay a few minutes when I stop by in the evenings to lock his door. He won't rise to the bait of my havin' been a CO -- guess that's just not as big a deal for him as it is some vets. I mostly just talk to him about how things work here, how if he doesn't cause trouble he's likely to stay off of a ward. Never get any response from him either way, not so much as a sideways glance."

Witt told him about Earl Ralston's shenanigans which had gotten Raymond's attention. "Probably good that you're just giving him straight talk -- he's obviously listening. Keep your ears open for anything that might be building up among our more excitable patients from the rumor that the Army sent him here to hide him, don't want somebody trying to make a reputation from jumping him."

"Always keeping cheerful thoughts in the forefront aren't you, Doc."

"Probably caused the architecture and the company. Really isn't my nature, although I tend to be pretty accurate in my observations. A hundred lunatics kept together and subject to an institutional schedule share more behaviors with the soldiers of a company of infantry than my last employer would care to hear."

"Wouldn't know about that, other than having had some experience with group conformity. Now if you want to get into a discussion of shunning....."

"Nope. Afraid that it would lead to the conclusion that all of us here are undergoing that punishment, administered by the entire population of the Commonwealth outside of the fence rather than our more pious Dunkard cousins! 'Scuse me, but I have to go find Rafe Bell and get his report on brother McCleary."

Witt headed over to the kitchen, where he figured he'd be pretty sure to find Bell, flirting with the staff cooks and enjoying any tail-ends of the morning's biscuits or cornbread. Found him, helped himself to the offered cornbread and coffee and gestured for Bell to follow him into the dining room, empty except for a couple of patient stewards finishing their work, ordering tables on the far side of the hall in preparation for dinner.

"I already heard that tales of bloodthirsty carpenters caught our gentleman's ear." Bell laughed. "Never would have dreamed that Ralston would have it in him to come up with such a thing!"

"I knew he'd come up with something, but that was a surprise. Maybe we now know the reason his tool box is painted the same color as the gun decks on a sailing man o' war! Whatever it takes." The Doc made a face. "Either not enough coffee or too much coffee in this brew. Good thing I have to stop by my office before doin' morning rounds, be able to get a real sustaining beverage. How's he coming from what you see?"

"Totally, silently, cooperative with anything that I ask. Knows everybody's routine so well that he gets down the hall to the toilet without notice. Not too many folks go through there. Don't think he bathes, just washes himself, but he's always clean, those logging boots shined. Empties his own slop jar and refills his on pitcher, though I've never seen him at it. Thought about layin' for him but decided against it, didn't want him to think I was a sneak. Since he's takin' good advantage of it I stay more regular and predictable for him than for anyone else. Some of 'em you gotta surprise now'n then, others, like him, just follow the schedule."

"I'd say you're plain' it right. A man to trust, 'specially since you're his whisky agent. Think he's gettin' enough along with the Librium to hold his pain and sleep?"

"He, as my aunty would say, 'drinks like a gentleman,' spacin' it out so it don't particularly show and always keepin' some reserve for a bad night." He grinned and winked at his co-conspirator. "You'd be knowin' the kind of gentleman she meant." They both chuckled. "I do wonder how long his friends are gonna keep up with him. They've already lasted longer'n most folk's families. Maybe that woman Sarah's still hangin' on as an unconscious way of not gettin' involved with anyone else. His old landlady may see him as 'one of her boys'. I guess he just made a hell of an impression on his employers. Understandable that he hardly hears from his people down south; his parents got feeble right about the time he got here, and his brother and sisters are in a busy time in their lives, takin' care of the old folks, new young 'uns and tied to farms without time to travel up here and too damn worn out to write letters that they don't know'll be read and are certain won't get a reply. Don't know what'll happen when it's just him and the hospital, but I can't imagine that it'll be improvement."

"I've been thinking about that, too. We've got to keep pushing while things are stacked as much in his favor as they are now. If you think he's ready, you and Weaver can stop locking his door at night to give him the chance to venture out to piss and bathe. Leave him the key to the inner gate so he can feel more secure when he needs to. Ralston has his ear at the moment, I'll speak to him about trying to pry the man off of the benches and into doing something." They took their mugs and plates back to the kitchen and thanked the cooks a second time before heading off to their morning duties.

"'Mornin' brother McCleary,'" Earl Ralston called out when he saw Raymond on the nearby bench while wheeling his wagon of tools into the sunshine. "More windows ash this mornin', never an end to 'em, but they're light work for an old man and a State paycheck. Lighter'n doors, I'll leave those to the other two fellows. They think sashes are tedious and like goin' around hangin' doors so's they can put on a travelling carpenter show. I'd just as soon not traipse around everywhere unless there's something more interesting to do. Our occasional heavy job takes all three of us and is usually enough of a puzzle to be interesting, some structural failing or another. The number of copulas and roof walks on the old buildings make for some strange framing with big timbers, all of 'em plagued with leaks where they join the roof. Have to figure out how to brace things to hold while you're working, then do what I do, the same stuff I'm doin' here with odd-angled timbers big enough it takes two men to position them while the third either fits bolts or drives pegs as thick as three fingers bunched together with a maul. I like doin' that. Know how much damage you can do a man with a good smash from a two-handed maul?" Earl looked up quick as he said that, confirming from a glance and bit of an expression that Raymond was still intrigued by the potential for murder and maiming among the modern-day practitioners of the gentle Nazarene craft he'd been told about in Sunday school.

Sharing his smoke break with Raymond on the bench as he'd been doing since that first afternoon, Ralston commented that it was looking like rain, that he'd be moving back just inside the shop doors with his work after dinner, and that Raymond was welcome to join him there rather than staying in his room alone all afternoon. The rain did begin at dinnertime, and as Ralston was getting his first piece of work for the afternoon set up, he saw Raymond coming his way through the rain. Never saw that before, he thought as he watched. Damn difficult to blend a catatonic stare with hustling to get through the rain without being soaked. Kinda' a contradiction in motion.

"Howdy. There's a couple of solid crates you can pick from there in the scrap pile for a seat." Raymond turned, shaking off the rain, and was able to pick a box and move it out of the pile while facing away from the carpenter. I wonder, Ralston thought, if he's keeping up the pretense of his stare while he's rummaging around over there. Kinda' hard to imagine that he is. Raymond got situated and turned his stare towards the wall beyond Ralston's head, his damp hat adjusted at exactly the right angle, feet flat on the floor, both hands resting on the top of his stick in front of his knees.

"More sashes – they're my stock in trade. Serious in my offer the first day we met, welcome to use my tools if you want to fool with the scrap you pulled your box outta'. Maybe you need a bookshelf, shoeshine box, maybe a nightstand -- I don't know if your room has anyplace for your personal things. Private space for anything is pretty rare around here." Raymond said nothing, but in fact, the nightstand in his room had only one medium-depth drawer. He kept most of his clean clothes folded on top of the shoeshine box his friends had brought from the chicken-barn. The Highlander Peaches box was the cheapest kind from the mill, made of box-elder wood, soft enough that the printing plate pushed the surface down as it was rolled across in the last station of the box-mill line, too prone to shatter to be used for boxes holding anything but glass jars, contents that insured careful handling.

The rain kept up steady all morning. Ralston chuckled as he watched Raymond did his catatonic-stare hurry through the rain back to his room for dinner, missing every puddle in the courtyard's worn and randomly sunken brick pavement. A wet season, he thought, would do that boy a world of good. He joined the other two carpenters as they arranged themselves comfortably on a stack of lumber with their dinner buckets, taking his turn heating his pail of coffee over the glue-pot lantern, from which they'd unsnapped the foul bucket. "No point in drinkin' cold coffee from breakfast while we're in the shop."

"You're right, there, George. Like they said back when I was in the horse-cavalry, if you don't have life's little comforts in garrison, ain't nobody's fault but your own."

"Well, three years sure burned it into your brain, as often as it comes up in your conversation," George laughed, Earl joining in.

"I reckon so," Oliver chuckled along with them. "Thought about that myself, sometimes. Maybe it's 'cause I was green 'n impressionable, but it's funny how much of that stuck. Can't imagine how close to the bone soldiering must be for those who had to fight."

George, for his own reasons, grew quiet, but Earl took it up. "Could be that those fellows don't talk soldier talk 'cause they want to forget that part of their lives. Look at this boy, Raymond, that Doc Witt has set me to tryin' to lure into carpenterin'. He won't talk at all, and you know his head must be full of horrors."

George had the last turn with the heater, blew out the wick, put the glue pot back on top and then settled with the others on the smooth, sweet-smelling pine. "Oliver, just how long were you ridin' those horses? Did you help bring Geronimo back to Fort Sill in '87?"

"Yeah, remind me I'm old," he replied through a mouth full of sandwich that required a good slurp of coffee before he could finish his answer, "but I ain't your granddaddy. I was lucky, joined up in the last six months of the 1918 war, just old enough to lie that I was of age so's the recruiting sergeant winked instead of coverin' his mouth and laughin'. By then the Army'd realized cavalry wasn't much use in the war they were fighting but they liked it too much to give up havin' any, kinda like the farmers around here who still kept their last team, harness hung up in a brooder house like hams, draped from wire hooks with tin squares on top to drop the rats off, while they run the first crankcase or two of oil through their steel-wheel McCormick-Deering. I stuck for three years, made corporal before the last parade when they cased our regiment's colors at Leavenworth. Army was shrinkin' fast then, they didn't even push for me to stay on doin' somethin' else. It was a fine life for a young, single fellow with no war goin' on. Not decent for a family man, though, 'less he was an officer."

Earl took it up again. "I agree with George. Been my observation, too, that those who had a couple of peaceful years in the Army talk more about it than those who were in the trenches, actually fightin'. Not hard on them to remember. The others, maybe they don't talk much because they have such a head full to forget, like that boy Raymond that Doc Witt has set me to luring off of the bench and into piddlin' around with whatever I can him to do. He had to have been in the thick of it, and he won't talk at all. Tryin' to get his attention, thinkin' about what to say, I realized that I can't remember more'n a few patients through the years that I've known to have been in the first war. How 'bout you-all?"

"Now that you mention it," Oliver replied, "I can't either. Men the right age are here for all sorts of reasons, drinkin', tryin' to kill themselves, but it ain't often that the subject of soldierin' comes up 'less it's somebody like your man who wakes up screamin' 'bout it and disrupts the routine of a whole ward."

"I got curious right after we heard about our son," George said quietly. "Took some time when I was workin' over in the records room one day and thumbed through the admission ledger for the first few years after the last war. Didn't find but a handful of entries that mentioned soldiers, always mixed up in the occupation line, like 'farmer, former soldier.' One made me think the most was for a woman, a nurse in '19 or '20. Line for reason for admission said 'hard duty.' Made me wonder if she'd been overseas." The three men finished eating; snapped their dinner pails closed; one of them put the glue pot back into its accustomed spot; and they got back to their work.

55. FURNITURE MAKING

Earl pulled out his pipe, filled it, and enjoyed a smoke while he turned the first sash of the afternoon, damaged in several places, over and back again on the sawhorse as he visualized what had to be done. He was peripherally aware of Raymond's third dash through the rain for the day, but taken completely by surprise when, rather than settling on his shipping crate, he came up to him, silent and trying to look another way, and handed him folded sheet of paper, dry from his pocket. Ralston unfolded it and saw a drawing of a boxy chest of drawers, one deep drawer up top, three shallow ones below. Meant to be, he assumed from his earlier comment, a nightstand for Raymond's room.

"Good drawing. Go ahead and see what you can pull out of the scrap-pile to work with, then we'll compare what you've found with your drawing and we'll see how well it'll do. Put your drawing here in the toolbox - - when you get to working, you'll have to pencil in some notes about measurements." Ralston set about the first steps of the repairs he'd decided on for the sash before re-lighting lighting his pipe, which had gone cold, careful to stand on the side of his work that allowed him to glance up and check Raymond's progress. First thing he noticed was that Raymond had pushed his engineer's cap back from his forehead, a striking change in his appearance, exposing a lock of hair and giving him more the air of a farm-boy than a soldier. For the first time he saw him moving his head and face to look around normally, pulling at the ends of lumber to see how long the piece was, shifting the overburden when something hung up or he needed to simply move what was on top to see what was underneath. He was leaning his stick against the wall when he needed two hands, then picking it up and leaning on it when he went back to studying the pile. That, Ralston thought, is the first time anyone here's seen the stick out of his grip. As Raymond selected his first bit of wood and set it aside, Earl focused on his own work, listening more than looking to keep track of Raymond's progress.

He'd finished cutting and shaping the scabs he needed, was almost ready to go set the glue-pot to melting when he glanced up and saw Raymond standing beside the red toolbox, drawing in hand, staring towards the odd collection of boards he'd propped against the wall. Earl pulled a second intact box next to the one Raymond had spent the morning on, gestured for him to take a seat, and began fumbling with his pipe and tobacco. "Have a seat. We'll have a smoke and look over what you've found." Nearly burned the match back to his fingers before the pipe took to drawing properly, then asked "want a smoke?", reaching towards the pack in Raymond's pocket. No positive response, but no telltale hardening of any muscles that he could see, so he fished out the pack, shook one out, rapped it on the cellophane to properly pack the tobacco, and held it out within Raymond's reach. Raymond took it, holding the end still dripping a crumb or two of tobacco out for a light which Earl provided after he'd put the pack back in Raymond's pocket. "Don't know what fool painted that 'no smoking' sign on the wall, been there since I came to work. Old men were smokin' then, we've been smokin' ever since. Some things people come up with you just gotta ignore to have any peace in life. It ain't like this shop was the powder room on a pirate ship. Now if they'd painted 'no smoking near open paint' or 'over sawdust and shavings' by the machinery, they mighta been listened to." They both smoked, silent and content, the noise and low conversation of the other two carpenters behind them in the depth of the shop. Earl took up the drawing. "Show me what you found for legs." Raymond leaned a piece of oak 2x2 out from the wall. "Good choice, but you're gonna need three more, the legs need to go all the way to the top, meet with some other pieces and make a frame for everything else. That looks from the nail-holes like a corner-piece from a crate, outta' be three more in the pile. Top and drawer fronts?" Raymond leaned a number of similar-looking pine boards out. "Drawer frames and rails to slide on?" Raymond indicated some less-well matched pine of about the right dimensions, some of it down-right rough. "That'll do. Places nobody sees don't have to be pretty. Your back, two sides and drawer-bottoms?" Raymond leaned about five thin plywood box sides or tops out from the wall. "That'll do, but I don't like the stuff. Moisture gets in it and it goes all to hell. Started seeing it at the end of the war, they were makin' it to conserve good timber. Face you see is ve-neer from a decent log; middle layer is pieced together from trash -- as much knotholes with the nubs still stuck in 'em as good wood; backside, 'bout all you can say good about it is that it's better bred than its middle brother. Guess that we're stuck with it from now on, though, 'cause the lumber companies learned they can squeeze a dollar outa it." He stepped over to the doorway, reached into the rain and tapped the ash from his pipe out against the doorframe. Raymond followed silently, field-stripping his long-cold butt into the palm of his hand, then tossing the crumbs around the corner of the building into a bush just off of the pavement.

"Pull those boxes together and make yourself a desk. You got some studyin' to do." Earl reached a folding carpenter's rule and a tolerably good pencil out of the red box and handed them to Raymond, who had the drawing in his hand. "Measure up your leg to how high you want your table-top, then cipher out the dimensions for everything else. Once you've done that I'll suggest a way of doing the carpentry, you'll have to decide your way, and I'll help you if you need it." Raymond pushed his hat back and started ciphering. Earl heated up the glue and went back to his sash.

Twenty minutes or so later Ralston looked up in the midst of evaluating what he had to do to the next sash and spotted Doctor Witt coming through the rain. He caught his eye and motioned towards the side of the big door away from where Raymond was working. Witt came in shaking water from his old company-grade garrison cap and the GI raincoat that he was wearing as a cape over his clipboard of papers, thermos, and coffee mugs. "Looks like you've done the trick, Earl!" Speaking as lowly as possible, trying not to make enough of a distraction to break Raymond's concentration, Ralston gave Witt the day's story. "Amazing. Took the right bait to catch his attention, the right attitude to allow some trust, and something challenging but within ability to draw him out. We don't need more docs around here, we need more carpenters with common sense!"

"Can't claim all that much credit, Doc. It was you that set the rest of us onto him, each from a different angle. Mine broke through either because he has a taste for the absurd or because he's such an insatiable killer that he was glad of the learnin' and the Army was justified in hidin' him here."

Witt folded his raincoat over one arm, shoved his hat back on his head in a way that would've made a sergeant ask him if he was a bus driver, and went over to Raymond. "Hey, buddy, coffee time. Make me a spot to sit?" Raymond moved his paper, pencil and rule to the box where he was sitting. Witt sat on the other, emptied his arms into his lap, handed Raymond a mug and poured. They sat and sipped, looking out into the rain. Witt was silent, waiting to see if anything would be said, but there wasn't a word, even as the mugs emptied and Raymond balanced his on his knee with a bit left, anticipating the usual offer of a topping up. "Glad you've taken a shine to Earl and want to do a project with him. Not complaining that you're not talking and scarcely looking at anyone." He raised his mug in salute. "Great progress my friend, great progress. Let's just enjoy our coffee and watch it rain.'

"Break's over, I'm a hard boss. Get back to your figurin' so you can get on to buildin'." Raymond did so, adding and subtracting from his pile of box-lumber as the calculations demanded. Just as he was completing the glue job on the second frame, Ralston was aware of Raymond standing beside him. Reaching first down to turn off the glue pot's flame, and then into his pocket for his pipe and tobacco, he motioned towards the boxes they'd been using as seats and Raymond moved ahead of him. Packing tobacco, finger and bowl inside the pouch, he glanced sideways and saw Raymond pulling his smokes out of his pocket, shaking one out, rapping it on the pack, then holding it, then staring into the rain while waiting for a light. Small steps, small steps, Earl thought, smiling inwardly as he struck his match and let the flame grow about a third of the way up the stick before drawing the flame down into the pipe, holding it in there with several long, steady inhalations. Didn't quite catch with one match, but after a draw on the second he cupped the flame between his hands and held them out to Raymond, who lit up before Earl's fingers got burned. "Let's see what you've got marked out there." Raymond didn't hand him the sheet, but gave no sign of objection, let go when he reached over and grasped it. They smoked in silence as the carpenter absorbed the dimensions and proposed method of assembly. Searching the pile, Raymond had found enough thin boards to join together three at a time to make the side and back panels, only resorting to the plywood for the bottoms of the drawers. "This is all right," Earl looked towards Raymond, who still looked off into the distance rather than towards him as he spoke. "You've got it all laid out with butt-joints, a rectangle to provide slides and support for each drawer spaced up the legs. Not fancy, but with a long nail straight into each of them, along with glue it'll be plenty strong for something you ain't gonna' dance on. Only thing I don't like is the way you have your sides and back lapped over the legs. You want a piece of furniture made out of old boxes rather than a crate with drawers in it! I'll show you how to cut a rabbet on the inside corners of the uprights so that your sides are inset, like proper furniture panels." Earl tapped out and refilled his pipe, Raymond stripped his butt, shook out another and they lit up for a second round.

"I have to confess, Raymond, that I've been funnin' you a little about the two fellows back there, Gorge and Oliver. Wasn't kiddin' about not messin' with their tools, but they're Ok folks. Good friends for years, they just tend to stick together and carpenter, don't have much truck with patients or the docs, that's where they're different from me. Think they're missin' the most interesting thing about workin' here, the people, but everybody looks at things different. George, he's widowed -- lost his wife last year. Oliver, well, let's just say he don't look forward to goin' home to his of an evenin' and is glad to turn in the front gate seven-thirty sharp every morning."

Earl took a few silent draws to let the information sink in. "Cuttin' those rabbets you'll have to be working at a bench near them. Probably easier on your leg, too, if you do most all of your work there. Somethin' solid to lean on."

Standing, Earl put his pipe in his pocket, ashes and all. "You bring one of your sideboards, your paper and rule, and your four uprights, I'll grab you a couple of tools, introduce you to those fellows back there. Better bring a piece of scrap, same wood as your long pieces." Earl got a hand-size block plane, a chisel and mallet from his toolbox and Raymond, paper and stick in his left hand, rule in his right, everything else under his right arm. On the way back towards the bench Earl told him, real quiet, that if either man put out his hand, it'd be a good thing if Raymond shook it rather than staring past him.

They set their load down on an unused bench and turned towards the two men working at the other. "Boys, this here's Raymond McCleary. I've been tellin' you how he's been comin' along, but you haven't had a formal introduction. Raymond, this is Oliver Freeman," Oliver turned from his work and nodded in Raymond's direction, "and George Tanner." George stood, held out his hand. "Good to meet you." Raymond reached out and shook his hand, looking past him rather than into his face. "Raymond's not talkin these days," Earl covered up the lack of a response, "but at least he's willin' to meet people." Raymond, in looking past George scanned the toolbox behind him. There was a gold-star banner half hidden by the two handsaws fitted to the inside of the lid. George hadn't only just lost his wife; he'd lost a son, too.

"Come on, Raymond, let me get you started. These iron hooks here and there in holes on the bench are bench dogs. Didn't have them doin' barn carpentry! They're good clamps. Put 'em in a hole where you want them, get your work straight underneath, then hit 'em on the top to tighten 'em, smack 'em from behind when you want them loose." Earl dropped one into a hole next to one of Raymond's boards. "Give it a try!" Raymond hit the iron a lightish blow with the mallet, tugged the board a bit, then hit the top of the dog harder, then grinned when he couldn't move the board. Grinned again when a light tap on the back of the dog let things loose. "What you need to do is to cut a rabbet -- that's what cabinet-makers call a groove that follows an edge -- same depth as your side boards along the full length and width of your frame where it meets the sides. Lemmie see you mark that off one of your scraps." Raymond slid the little brass rule out of its slot in the first leg of the folding rule, measured his board, marked the measurement onto adjacent sides of the stick of wood, and connected the marks with a ruled line. "Good. You've probably used bigger plane to edge boards on the farm, this one's sized for this job and I've set the knife real shallow since you're working hardwood. Remind you what your daddy probably told you, only an ignorant man sets a plane down on its face once the knife's set. Clamp another scrap on over your work as a guide to press the cheek of the plane against, allowin' for the gap between the knife and the side, then cut out what you've marked. Run all the way out at the top end, stay back from the spot where the side board bottoms out above the floor, cut that bit square with the chisel." Raymond practiced on the scrap; Earl was satisfied with his work. "Have at it. Don't forget that the front legs only have one corner cut."

Doc Witt came up to where Ralston was working in the doorway. "Where's our man?"

"In the back," Earl motioned with his head. "Doin' good, buildin' himself a nightstand."

"Not scared of blue-eyed, manical, killing carpenters?"

"Nah. I 'fessd up to him that I'd been makin' George and Oliver out to be a little more anti-social than they really are."

"Talking?"

"Nope, not that good yet, but he did shake hands when George offered. See how he does on his project, I think he'll do good, maybe you can put him on the books as assigned to the shop."

"I think that can be done pretty easily. Look good on the reports to Richmond; they love hearing that patients earn their keep. How's his leg holding up?"

"He's good with the stick, leans on the wall, balances on one foot, and grits his teeth a lot -- about what you'd expect for how he's been blown apart and cut on. Gettin' him educated about working at a bench, always a solid support at his hips leanin' into the work. He'll adapt pretty quick, find his own ways and be as well off as a man with pain like his can be. Better for him workin' here than sittin' down someplace."

"I believe you're right, both physically and mentally. Much more inactivity would have locked him in, wherever he was. Not talkin' yet, but I'll call him a success for this place."

Witt moved on, and before long, Raymond came to the doorway, standing silently where Earl would eventually look up and notice him, focusing his stare on the carpenter's work rather than on some un-known point. "Ready to move on?" Get the rest of your lumber moved back and I'll bring you your tools." Raymond gathered the remaining lumber from his pile and headed back to the bench. Ralston followed with a saw and a small square, blued steel blade with a Black-wood head, working edge faced in brass. "Here's my second-best crosscut saw for you to use. I'm working with my favorite. Looks like the boards you're making your panels with came from the same crate, you can even them up with your plane, won't need a rip tooth saw to cut 'em lengthwise. Once you've measured, use this try-square to run your line clear around the piece, make it easier to cut true. Get all your cuttin' done this afternoon and I'll help you glue it up and nail things in the mornin'." Raymond got to it, and finished in time to return Earl's tools as he was packing up and the sound of the bell told him he'd better get back to his room to meet either Sam or Rafe with his supper.

Raymond was at the shop the next morning before Earl had finished muscling the folds of the doors back inside along the curve of their overhead roller track. Heavy work for a man of his age, even in the carpenters' area, where the wheels were kept oiled and the bottoms of the panels painted so that they didn't swell from moisture and drag on the floor or sill. The doors on the hospital's barn sheds were a different matter, even harder to open, usually dragging some section in the dirt -- patient labor wasn't much on keeping a path dug clear or oiling, and the supervisor didn't get a whole lot of help from the carpenters or painters, who focused on ward repairs and the publicly visible buildings unless word of visitors from Richmond gave the superintendent reason to send them out to the farm buildings.

"Looks like you're ready to go!" Raymond didn't say anything, just looked towards his unfinished job back on the bench. Earl pulled a claw hammer and the try-square from the red box and selected a nail-set from among the drills and punches nestled vertically into holes drilled in the intentionally thicker side rail of a wooden tray. "Go get the glue pot, please." Earl paused by a supply shelf, picked up a couple of paper boxes with different sizes of small-headed finishing nails. Raymond set the glue pot at one side of their workplace and Earl lit it, fiddling with the wick until he was satisfied with the flame. "Cover the bench with old newspapers from the box over by the stove, then lay out the pieces for the rectangles that make your drawer slides and separate the drawer fronts. That's where we'll start. You dab some glue on the two ends of the butt joint, I'll hold 'em in place while you hit one good finishin' nail in to pull 'em together. We'll do that on all four, then you press the frame flat on the bench and check the corners with the square. Glue'll still be soft enough that you can pull things true. If they're off, pry one out as far as you need to with your pocket-knife. Once the glue's set square we can fill any gap with a chip and more glue, then cut off any change in the outside dimensions with a plane." Raymond followed instructions and was able to get each nail in without bending any -- good thing that all the parts other than the uprights were softwood while his arm was remembering how to swing a hammer. "Don't aim for the head of the nail you're holding," he membered his father telling him as a boy. "Aim for where the head of the nail will be after you've hit it a lick -- that's the way to get 'em in straight." He and Earl did the same for each of the drawers, resting their tops on the bench as they trued them up so that there'd be space on the bottom of the back and sides to nail and glue the plywood bottoms without their show-ing on the front. After that, they glued and fit the two side panels into their groves, pulling them together with nails through the uprights into the upper and lower edg-ing boards -- the back panel would have to wait to be joined to the two sides once their glue was set hard enough that they could be handled and nailed without pushing them out of square. "Turn off the burner on the pot, boy. We have to take a break until the glue sets." Earl started walking towards the doorway, rummaging for his pipe as he went, and settled onto one of the in-tact crates that they'd been using for seats. Raymond joined him, and about the time they got lit up they saw Dr. Witt crossing the yard burdened, as usual, with his clipboard of papers, a thermos and two coffee mugs. "Doc must be havin' a rough mornin' if he's bringin' you coffee before noon!" Raymond didn't respond, just stared off into the distance and drew on his cigarette. It would, Earl thought, be hard for anyone but the Doc to believe that five minutes earlier the same man had been following instructions and assisting with work that required considerable understanding and cooperation.

The doctor's face brightened a bit as he approached. "Coffee time, gentlemen!" Raymond just stared and drew slowly on the remainder of his smoke. Witt looked his way, then, questioningly towards the carpenter, who was working another charge of tobacco into his pipe.

"Things been goin' pretty good, gluin' up Raymond's furniture. Follows every instruction. You're hours early with coffee. Things alright on the wards?"

Witt pulled over another free crate, sat down, and was relieved to see that Raymond returned from the distance sufficiently to participate in their charade of a conversation. The Doc didn't know what had set him to staring at this hour. It was probably too early in the day for pain and fatigue to be a factor. Perhaps today was an important date in his life, unknown to Witt. His observation had been that anniversaries of significant events, even when a man didn't consciously remember them, colored even sane men's behavior. The best thing, he mused, would be if Raymond's total involvement in the nightstand project had him looking farther back than before, pulling up some association from before the war. "The wards are still the wards. Try to keep people clothed, peaceful and following a marginally civil toileting routine. The clerks are still penning their ledgers;

who have arrived, who's departed, who's assigned to work, and tallying how many meals for the dining room an how many dinner buckets to send 'round on the pickup. Early morning's probably the worst time for those scribblers, 'cause of changes on someone's part every day, often based on a patient's unpredictable belief or condition. That, and the cooks' demand for the earliest possible count. Afternoons are better for them, preparation of neat, single-page reports of categories for administrative consumption, none of the blots, stains and interlineation of the ward-books themselves. Raymond, you'll be pleased to know that your assignment to the carpenters' work and supervision has met with everyone's approval. The question going around, though, is what the Army will think of it. You, at least as far as the rumor mill has it, are still a soldier. Speaking personally, it seems that I actually still am. Got a letter yesterday telling me that I've been recalled into some medical reserve battalion that I hope only exists in some Pentagon file cabinet. If it turns out to be anything more, it damned well ought to be accompanied by a uniform allowance check to replace the khaki pants and shoe leather I've worn out around here. Would be a bit of fun, though, if there was a muster and I got the chance to pass my droopy-sided rain hat off as an Air Corps twenty-mission hat. Folks'd shy away from me as an Air Corps shrink crazy enough to have logged the air time penciled in on manifests and his pay record! In any event, even a paper battalion of practitioners as removed as this from the carriage trade clinics as I am would be a group to behold. Its liquor bill alone would make the top of someone's daily report." He proffered a refill and Raymond, somewhat more present, held out his mug with steady hand.

After Witt departed, Raymond and Earl returned to their work. The glue was set strong enough that they could tap the heads of the finishing nails below the surface with their nail set without pushing the pieces out of square and cut the few irregularities that showed themselves against the truest frame away with the plane. Once that was accomplished, they glued and nailed the plywood bottoms to the drawers, setting the nail heads so that they wouldn't drag on the rails. The next step called for gluing and nailing the rails and facing boards to the front legs, excess glue wiped from edges with care so that the drawers could be set in place as spacers to hold the rails in correct alignment for fastening to the back panel. Fitting the back panel involved a good deal of direction on Earl's part as he and Raymond traded off holding, gluing, and nailing. They laid what they'd assembled on its face, penciled the location and width of the rail frames on the now upward facing back legs to avoid nailing into the back of a drawer, spread glue on the back side of the rail frames, then eased the back panels into place, nailing and gluing them the same as the sides, with the addition of rows of several small nails along each rail frame. Their wrestling match completed, they stood the thing on its feet atop the bench and pulled out the drawers before any stray glue could seal them closed.

"Time," Earl announced, "for another break to let this mess of glue set. Turn the burner off on the pot again, please." Raymond did that. "Let's carry three or four broken sash up by the door for me to work on the rest of the day." Earl took one frame in each hand out of the eternal pile of damaged windows; Raymond got one with his right, changing his walk a bit as he used his shoulders to shift the extra load over to his left side so that the stick rather than his bad leg carried the weight. "Didn't skimp on size or materials when they made these old fellows." Earl pulled a sawhorse into place, hooking its leg around with his foot, and laid his two sash over the pair of them. Raymond leaned his against the end of the sawhorse Earl had just moved. "Smoke?' Earl was rummaging for his fixin's and moving towards their usual seats as he spoke. Raymond accepted a light after Earl's usual pipe-filling ritual. "Good job of work. You have a good feel for fittin' things together without forcin' them alongside one another -- not to say that like on the farm, brute force isn't sometimes the carpenter's final argument. Here's a few matches for the glue pot,' he said, reaching over and dropping them from the closed palm in which he'd been holding them as they smoked into Raymond's, turned up and open quickly enough to catch them. "I think you'll figure the top out easily on your own. Come and get me if something doesn't look right to you before you fasten it down." Earl got up, shuffled over to his own work and got started; adjusting the work on the sawhorses so that he was more or less crossways in the doorway, able to follow the daily goin's on in the courtyard and keep an eye on Raymond without being obvious about it.

Raymond had done is measuring, cutting and planning the day before. This morning he just had to lay things out and mark where he had to nail in order to clamp things down onto the glue -- easy enough to lay the top boards in place, upside down, hold 'em steady and lightly run a pencil around the stand beneath. Flip 'em over and the mark, offset a bit to allow for the thickness of things, gave him his nailing line. He cut a piece of scrap to match the overhang so that he could position things the trouble of measuring in from the edge and without getting glue on Earl's rule. It wasn't long before the smell of heating glue told the carpenter how far along Raymond was in his work. The gluing supplies included a pile of old newspapers. Raymond spread some on the bench beneath the nightstand and stretched a couple of sheets around the top drawer and slid it into place to catch any glue that might drip from the butt joints between the three top boards. He figured that he could angle the nails a bit when he put the last board on to kinda clamp the three tight before he nailed the middle one, closing the gaps as tight as possible. The glue was thick enough that he figured a second application along the top cracks as soon as the first cooled enough ceased to flow would seal things well enough that a glass of water (or whisky) spilled on top would stay out of the drawers. Precautions taken and hammer, nails and gauge laid out, he used a stick to run a bead of glue around the edge on which the top would rest. After that he used his wooden gauge to position the rearmost top board and hit a couple of nails in far enough to hold it -- he'd finish driving them later, right then his bead of glue around the rim was cooling. A quick stroke of the re-wetted glue stick along the inner edge of the nailed-down board, both edges of the middle board and the back edge of the front board, then he positioned those last two, guided in large part by the board he'd nailed down but checked with the gauge to make sure that just eyeing things hadn't allowed any drift. The trick of angling the front nails worked, drawing in the gaps and slightly bucking up the center board. When he nailed the center down flat, the gaps closed tight beneath a bead of squeezed-out glue in all but a couple spots. He drove all of his nails home to within one stroke of the surface in order to keep from leaving dimple marks from the face of the hammer, dabbed a bit more glue onto the remaining gaps to fill them, turned off the glue pot burner, and leaned on his stick, looking at his work as the glue cooled and hardened. In a bit he used the rounded tip of his pocket-knife blade to cut the still-pliable beads of glue flush with the surface of the top, then removed the drawer, tore off what paper had stuck to the drips, turned the whole business upside down and did the same on the inside surface. Changing to the shorter, heavier clip blade, he got good, strong grip and scraped any visible glue from the other outside joints, holding the blade at right angles to the surface, and rotating the piece so that he could work on the right-hand side, pulling with the full strength of his arm and shoulder to break the beads of hardened hide glue from the fibers of the wood. After another moment's rest he balled up the dirtied newspapers, disposed of them in the stove; tidied up the bench, placing his tools and nailboxes together at one side; slid the drawers into place, staggering them open like a staircase; adjusted his cap at exactly the right angle, and went over to stand where Earl would notice him.

"Ready for me to take a look?" Earl put his tools down where they wouldn't fall if something shifted, and turned into the shop. "George!, Oliver! Come on over here; let's see what this feller's got done." They all got to the bench with Raymond's work at about the same time.

George reached out and pushed against a corner. Nothing wobbled on the flat surface of the bench. "Good work, good work."

Oliver looked around at all sides, ran his fingertip over a few joints, half-frowning at first but with a smile growing as he went. "Yup. Good work. Nice touch, too, settin' those drawers out like a store-window display before getting' us back here!"

George had wandered off, but reappeared carrying a couple of pieces of half-round molding. "Here you go, Raymond. Put this around the edge of the top 'n it'll give it more the feel of a piece of furniture than a crate, go with those inset panels we heard Earl helpin' you with." The other two men agreed that the edging was a good idea.

"Put that trim on and it'll be about quittin' time. Let her sit overnight for the glue to get real hard, and you can sand and varnish tomorrow," Was Earl's final comment.

The next morning Raymond came in and after Earl showed him where the sandpaper was, got to that job. Oliver came in and stopped to inspect his progress. "Got something for you," he rummaged in his pocket and pulled out enough turned wood knobs for drawer pulls. " Found 'em at home last night, figured you'd use 'em now rather than me forgettin' I had 'em and buying more after I get old and retire." Raymond didn't say anything, but stopped sanding, started marking the center spot on each drawer by holding a straight scrap corner to corner and making a light penciled "x" where the lines met. Earl brought him a drill, screwdriver, and screws from the red toolbox, and it wasn't long before the knobs were in place and Raymond was back to sanding. Sometime later George eased over, and after Raymond noticed that he was there, ran his hand over the wood. "Good enough. Let me show you what comes next." Raymond followed him to the paint shelf where they loaded up third arms with a can of varnish, an empty tin can, a can of turpentine, rags, and old newspapers to protect the bench. "First off, take a rag damp with a little terps and wipe it down to get all of the dust out of the grain and corners. For your first coat, cut the varnish in half with terps, mix it a little as a time as you use it so that you don't have any left over. Let her dry during dinner, sand it light all over to catch what grain raises up and cut the shine, then put a full coat of varnish on. Have to let that dry overnight, then take 'er home." Raymond pulled the drawers out and stood them on their back ends so that the varnish would flow even on the fronts and went about following George's instructions. It took about as long as George had predicted, the thinned coat dried well enough over dinnertime, and he was about to start the second coat of varnish when Doc Witt showed up for coffee.

"Pretty sharp, pretty sharp. Seen all sorts of things made out of old ammo crates, and this has the mark of the best of 'em." Earl nodded in agreement, fumbling with his pipe. Raymond said nothing, but was looking at his work rather than staring into the distance as he leaned against the adjacent bench with the other two men, sipping. Realizing that he wanted to get back to work, they didn't try to construct a conversation with holes in it that he could fill if he were inclined but didn't sound ridiculous without his participation, left him to his work and went to theirs.

By the time Raymond had finished cleaning his brush and work area it was suppertime. First thing next morning, Rafe Bell helped him carry the nightstand across the courtyard and to his room, helped him rearrange what furniture was there so it could fit, and left him loading his gear into the drawers.

56. BEE BOXES

Not much later in the morning Earl looked around and saw Raymond standing beside him, a few sheets of unfolded paper, obviously been in his pocket, staring across the courtyard. He set his tools down where they wouldn't be knocked to the ground if someone bumped the sawhorses in his absence. "Let's take a smoke break and you can show me what you've got." He took the papers that Raymond was holding in one hand, rummaged in his pocket for his pipe with the other, and headed for the week's as-yet unbroken packing crates, the current available seating. Once they'd lit up, Earl looked at the papers. The first was a drawing of the components of a beehive; parts expanded enough to have space to write in dimensions, obviously copied from a book or magazine. The second showed the rip-saw cuts necessary to trim the pieces of wood from the standard dimensional lumber kept in the shop's racks. The third listed the hive components along with the amount of standard lumber that they required, some of the lighter bits listed as 'cut from crates,' and a total of each standard dimension required at the bottom of the page. Grimacing and keeping his pipe in a firm grip, Ralston let out a low whistle across his teeth. "You either been working on this for a while or you didn't sleep last night, doin' all that figuring." Raymond just sat and smoked, looking out through the doors into the courtyard. He had, in fact, spent one evening copying the first page, another doing his calculations, and the previous evening re-checking his math and making neat copies of those pages. "Not an enormous amount of material there, but enough that somebody nosing through the shop ledger'd raise his eyebrow if I just up and gave it to you. You go for an early dinner-break, maybe take a little nap, and I'll talk to a few people, see if we can't arrange something." Raymond headed off towards his quarters and Earl waved down the next tolerably-responsible looking person he saw in the courtyard. Saying 'good morning' and allowing about as short a time for response and a brief comment on the weather as could be considered polite, he got to the point. "I need to talk to Doctor Witt about one of his people. Spread the word over at the wards, please, asking for him to come and see me when he has moment." As his messenger walked off Ralston, thought to himself that he was perfectly willing to leave his work and go talk to the doc, but realized that an attempt at that professional courtesy would most likely be a wild-goose chase with him repeatedly arriving at places the fast-moving psychiatrist had just left. It wasn't twenty minutes 'till he saw Witt headed his way, looking a bit odd holding just his clipboard of papers without mugs and coffee thermos.

"Got the word about six times on the way over that you wanted to see me. Wonderful alert system. What's up?"

Ralston handed him the three pages that he'd kept weighted down on the sash with his hammer while he'd been cutting away rotted wood with a chisel pushed with the heel of his palm. "Mr. McCleary's got some ambition."

Witt shuffled through the papers, looking the longest at the expanded drawing of a hive, more interesting to him than lumber calculations. "Now it comes together a bit more. I was telling him one of my rambling stories the other day, someone's theory about why loggers drink to excess, and I noticed that he perked up a bit when I mentioned in passing that the family of the man who posed the theory had kept bees for generations. I was too deep in the tale to recall the significance of it. Raymond's last employer, who knew because he provided living quarters, told me that before he came to the hospital Raymond owned his walking stick, a pickup truck, an oak toolbox that he could unbolt from the bed and use as a footlocker, his clothes, his shoeshine box, half of a case of whisky and a book about beekeeping. His friends told me that most of his conversations about his family involved stories about his grandfather's having kept bees on the farm. If he's up to his carpentering ambitions, this just might be our chance to reconnect him with an important part of his life before the war. What can I do to help?"

"Cover our butts by signing off in the shopbook that materials and time that we give him are at doctor's orders."

"Where's the book?" Witt had his pen out and was unscrewing its top. Ralston retrieved the ledger from the little-used desk at the back of the shop, laid it in the sunlight on top of his half-mended sash , turned it to the current page, and stepped aside to give the doctor elbow room to write his prescription. Careful to stay clear of columns where totals had to be carried downward, he took two lines for his script, as on a school practice tablet: "Provide materials and assistance for Raymond Mc Cleary to construct such beekeeping woodenware as he can use. The hives shall be his personal property and he shall take them with him upon his recovery and return home. Farley G. Witt, M.D., Psychiatry, Attending. October 22, 1949." Witt capped his pen, pocketed it and turned the book so that Ralston could see. "Reckon that'll do?"

"Do just fine. Have to look back and see, but I'd bet there's nothing like it on any other page. Most Docs just figure carpenters as hired help to holler at when the roof leaks, not somebody who can help someone get well."

"Most docs don't realize how homicidal carpenters can become, push 'em too hard. Thanks for lookin' out for my man." Witt disappeared as quickly as he'd arrived.

"George! Oliver!" Ralston headed back to the workbenches, ledger under his left arm, Raymond's papers in his left hand, searching in his pocket for pipe and tobacco with his right. "We got us a doctor's order job, a patient pree-scription, not a ward repair number." George and Oliver came right over without the grumbling that would have slowed them if a doc had sent a note demanding that a job on his ward be given priority. He laid the ledger back from the edge of the bench, spread the three sheets of paper in front where both could see them, and gave his account of Raymond's appearance with the project and Witt's reasoning that it might be what it took to bring him back amongst them.

"First time for everything," Was George's response. "For sure better for the boy than tryin' to send him to farm with a bunch of patients when he won't look at anybody, much less talk to 'em."

Oliver was already planning the job. "Looks like production work to me. Lots of repeating things. First thing he needs to do is make a crate-wood pattern for each piece so he can trace out his work rather than laying out every tooth of his box-joints over and over."

The other men agreed. "There's that old toolbox some-body left under the second bench God knows when ago. We can give him that and whatever tools it has. Easier for you, Earl, if he ain't got half your stuff with him when you reach for it. The three of us got enough old tools hangin' around at home that we can fill out all he'll need."

"Yep," George agreed. "I've kinda taken a likin' to the fellow, hard and careful as he worked on that cra-zy-drawered nightstand." He chuckled. "We'll find out just how much his daddy learned him when we hand him a dull saw, tooth-set, and a file!"

"Probably no more'n yours or mine did either of us," Earl blew some smoke and laughed. "I remember on my first job somebody did that to me. No explana-tion, just put 'em down when I complained a saw didn't cut good. I had some notion why he gave me a file, but didn't even know what the set *was.*"

Oliver laughed, too. "Me neither! Reckon we'll have to go a little easy on him if he's to get anything done, since he don't talk, just asks questions by stndin' there, starin' off, but we'll have a little fun with him, bringin' him along."

The carpenters took their dinner break and were putting their buckets away and starting back to work. Oliver saw Raymond coming in and was right on him. "Mr. Raymond, we've seen your notes and have got ap-proval. I never knew a bee-man content to have just one box, figure you better do your layout work by making patterns you can trace around 'stead of measuring every piece before you cut it. Get some crate-wood over here and I'll show you how to glue it up wide enough to match what you're doin'." Raymond did as he was told and was Oliver's silent student for the rest of the day, interrupted just once, for his coffee break with Doctor Witt. After Raymond left for supper the three men dragged out the abandoned tool box, looked through what was there, and agreed what each would bring from home the next day to have him set up for his work.

The next morning, Dr. Witt happened by and saw Ralston working by the doorway by himself. He could see Raymond busy at bench in the back, close to George and Oliver and nodded in that direction. "Made some new friends?"

"'Pears so. Those two have kinda surprised me. Oliver remember an old tool box full of junk for him, we agreed on a couple of things we could each bring from home to fill it out, and durned if they didn't show up with the stuff this mornin' ! Never saw it in either one of 'em. Most things were dull or dirty, but they brought a good file or stone to set 'em right when he gets to needin' 'em. Plenty of stuff for cleanin' here without goin' into their tools." Earl grinned. "Boys are funnin' him a little, too, like any new man. Made sure that both the saws they brought were dull as harrow-teeth. They figure he'll know what a little triangle file can do, but are waitin' to see if he recognizes the saw-set, and if he does, waitin' to see if he has a clue of how to use it. 'See what his daddy learned him' -- that's as mean as they've got."

"Pretty mild so far as tradesman's tricks go. I remember horrible pranks from anatomy dissections in medical school. Know bout 'em from each end, figure I gave better'n I got! Might be one of the reasons I ended up messing around outside of people's heads instead of feeling and fingering the rest of 'em. Raymond was right quick on that nightstand. How long you figure the bee-box'll take him?"

"Hard to say. Certainly won't be as quick. The outer boxes should come along right fast, but as I understand his notes, the insides -- ten fiddly hanging frames in each, each frame outta' five pieces -- have to be made to an exact 3/8 inch tolerance for the bees to like 'em. He has those marked down to be made of crate-boards, which'll take considerable handwork and fittin'. Even then, I'm sure he'll be finished months before there's any bee-swarms around. I'll be happy if he can deal with those. Hospital full of lunatics and the air full of bees or a head-size clump of 'em settled anywhere, even up on the farm, ain't a good combination! Troublesome even when it's just citizens on the other side of the fence involved. By the time he runs out of work he'll have enough skill that we'll set him to something else. Maybe make him our coffin man. The plain boxes we make instead of toe-pinchers are a straightforward job, and there's a slow but steady demand to keep several sizes ready and stacked in the back."

"Coffin maker at an asylum. Think that reference'll do him any good when he gets well?"

"If he says he never got no complaints he'd be tellin' the truth."

"You're no better'n those other two -- just your funnin' is long-term. Long-term and fits what a homicidal maniac of a carpenter'd come up with!" Both men had a quiet laugh. "McCleary came up among working men, is bright enough, that he probably enjoys the little jokes, sees them for what they are, a mark of respect.

Keep talkin' to him, please. You and your buddies ask him about bees, ask him if he understands your answers when he comes up beside you with enough in his hands that you know he's stuck and needs help. Probably best not to try to force things by refusing to answer what you know is his question until he asks out loud -- that'd just break down the trust that he's been willing to show you.

"Gotcha, Doc. I'll tell Oliver and George how you want 'em to behave. Have a good mornin' over on the wards, just keep your hands outta your pockets and your back to a wall."

"Will do. Got my trusty clipboard to throw up between me and the spitters. I'm not so simple-minded that I have to look at everybody's papers, but lettin' them think so lets me keep her halfway there. Also makes the institution think I'm workin' at the edge of capacity. Kinda' like that half pile of shavin's you put in the red wagon with your toolbox when you sweep up at quittin' time, then throw down when you unload your tools each mornin." He winked before walking off. "Raymond ain't the only one payin' attention to what he sees."

The older man just shook his head and smiled to himself as he bent over his work. Yep, he thought to himself, like a lot of us in this world, he sees but don't cause anybody no trouble by talkin' 'bout it. Funny thing is, the fellers who'd get stirred up if somebody told 'em things are so busy with themselves that they don't see nothing.

Raymond worked steady on his boxes, won Oliver his bet with George that he didn't know what a saw-set was or how to use it, and amazed them both with how his total concentration enabled him to expertly sharpen any buggered-up old saw they could find to bring him. He did finish the boxes and frames before spring, doing a lot of hand carving to get the indentation on the bottom half of each frame's pair of side-pieces just right.

57. COFFIN-MAKER

Earl hadn't been joking about the coffins. Doc Witt said that it didn't surprise him that Raymond wasn't bothered by the assignment. "Farm boys," he observed, "know about life and death from the barnyard. On top of that, the man was a soldier. With relatives of both his parents strung out all over the state dyin' at a regular pace and them bein' expected to show up at every funeral, he was versed in all the rituals and proprieties from the earliest time he can remember. Might as well say he was raised in the Guilford County culture of death -- very different from my city upbringin' where there were black-edged letters, telegrams, and telephone calls giving word that someone had died a great distance off. Raymond's people'd say 'passed' or 'passed away", not 'died'. I was sixteen before I actually attended a funeral!"

"You're right. Things are a usually a little different that way in the country, though I'd bet there's a lot of similarities in big city neighborhoods where one man or whole families come over, then sent for their kin-people."

"Exactly. It's those extended systems where all sorts of traditions have a chance of surviving. Off to the wards. See you later." Doc Witt headed off.

Things moved along about the same, day-to-day for Raymond, the carpenters, the institution and its staff. "Institutional inertia," Witt called it. "Just keepin' things easy, not makin' trouble for anybody," that's how Bell and Weaver described it. Raymond continued to live and dine in his secluded quarters did his work, venturing no further than across the courtyard, remained hyper vigilant and said nothing. Said nothing, that is, until the second week of May.

58. THE SWARM

Tuesday morning of the second week of May, Raymond was just leaving the carpenters' shop, headed for his quarters to eat the dinner he knew that Rafe Bell had left for him just before the bell rang for everyone else. A couple steps from the door he heard an increasing commotion from the patients heading into the dining room, a couple of screams and different voices yelling "Bees!, Bees!". Raymond turned and as near as he could with a stick, ran towards them. Wasn't many steps towards them when he heard and saw the converging swarm up above, louder than the commotion.

"Stay calm!" he hollered, his voice loud and strong. "Stay calm and don't hit at 'em! Don't hit at 'em and move back this way! Don't hit at 'em and they won't sting you! Get back from the porch!" He got to the edge of the porch, where he could see the bees beginning to settle onto a branch of a big clump of lilac, turned and waved people away with both arms and his stick. Staff members had run from everywhere when they heard the frightened patients and Raymond, were taking up his cry in a much lower voice, and got everyone to the other side of the courtyard, two or three deep against the wall on both sides of the doorway leading to his room. The bees tightened up their formation, hundreds of them spiraling down and around Raymond heading for the lilac branch. Bees flew into him, bounced off of his face, got trapped under the brim of his cap then escaped, got tangled in the hair behind his ears and crawled free to fly on. Raymond stood still, a smile on his face, not swatting any of them, still talking softly, "take it easy, take it easy, nothin' to get upset about, go on with your buddies."

Rafe Bell figured that if Raymond was comfortable among the bees, he could brave them, and eased over within speaking distance. "Anything I can do to help, Mr. Raymond? You need anything to finish your work?"

"A paper box with a lid, about big enough for a basketball would be handy."

"Know just where one's at. You hang on, I'll send somebody for it." Bell motioned to another orderly, brave enough to meet him halfway across the courtyard. Spoke with him and the man ran back and disappeared into Raymond's hallway door. Now that the crowd wasn't at risk from the bees and the bees were no longer at risk from the crowd, Raymond half-turned so that he could watch the swarm settle on the branch, still smiling and talking low to them, watching the branch bending under their weight and concluding that it was strong enough not to break or bend so low that it touched the ground, either of which might have started them off again, looking for safer lighting spot where they could rest until their scouts returned with word of where they might make their new home. No way of telling whether that would be in two hours or two days. If

Bell's man didn't come back with what he needed, he'd send him to the carpentry shop and get the entire hive box trundled over on Earl's red wagon.

Bell's man came rushing back, carrying a ladies hat box. Tied shut with ribbon, covered in a thick coat of dust, it had vertical stripes and the name of Staunton's most expensive dress shop printed on its sides. "Just where you said it was in that storeroom," he reported, handing it over. Bell blew the dust off, pulled the ribbons loose, and uncovered a fancy piece of work, lots of silk roses and a sheer veil, pulled it out, tissue paper swaddling falling to the ground, and to the pleasure of the crowd, he plopped it onto the runner's head before he turned and carried the box over to Raymond. The other man pulled the hat off like his head was on fire and threw it to the crowd, where it was passed from head to head among peals of laughter. Staff, realizing that most of the patients had now forgotten about the bees, started directing them into the dining room through a side door and pantry hallway.

"Thanks. It's perfect. Pretty good show you put on, too," he laughed. "You'll have to tell me later how you picked your assistant!" There were hardly any bees in the air now. Raymond held the top aside with his left hand along the top of his stick and eased over to place the box immediately below the clustered swarm of bees. Still talking low and slow -- Rafe couldn't really hear what he was saying, just the murmur which he assumed was more of the same -- Raymond stood within arm's reach of the lilac branch, letting a few more bees settle. When he thought the time was right, he got a good grip on the bent-over branch above the bees, careful not to pinch any of them, pushed it down just to the top of the open box and gave the whole business a sharp shake. About two-thirds of the bees, the ones who'd been holding onto each other more than they'd been holding onto the branch, plopped into the bottom. Again surrounded by flying bees, he eased the branch back up without whipping anyone else off, then carefully laid the top over the box, the front rim propped across the sides, making it dark inside but leaving a gap of about three-eighths of an inch across the front. The gap immediately filled with bees milling in and out, more goinging in than coming out. A number of those coming out moved up to the peak formed where the rim met the flat of the top, raised their rumps high, held on, and commenced fanning their wings. "Yes, sir. She's in there." Raymond said out loud to himself and anyone else who might have been paying attention. As he pulled himself up on his stick he could smell the scent being fanned out by the messengers, unmistakable, sweeter than all of the flowers put together, calling the bees in the air and the few still clinging to the lilac branch, where it had been laid down half an hour earlier to settle the swarm there, home. He had hived his swarm.

Raymond limped over to the far end of the porch strips, sat down, leaning against the post, just like he had on so many evenings with Dave at Mrs. Russ's house, pulled out a smoke and lit up, relaxing. He'd been doing right much more standing, waving his arms about and shouting than he was used to. He was tired and his leg ached, but he was happy.

59. TALKING AGAIN

Rafe Bell, Dr. Witt, and all three carpenters converged on him from the different places from which they'd watched things unfold. Doc Witt fell in with the carpenters halfway across the courtyard. "Now's the moment of discovery, gentlemen. He spoke to meet the crisis. Now we get to see if he can talk with us."

Bell got there first, bringing Raymond's dinner tray from his room and setting it down on the step beside him. "Thank you, Mr. Bell. You didn't have to go to all that trouble, I'd have been happy to eat it cold after I finished up here."

"No point in you eatin' stone-cold meat later just because you're sittin' guard here now." Raymond carefully stubbed his half-smoked cigarette out against the side of the sole of his boot and returned it to the pack in his pocket to be finished later and commenced eating. Bell sat down beside him, taking up most of the middle of the step.

"Your box was perfect. So ancient that it didn't smell of glue, and the raw paper inside combined with dust and the old straw of the hat made it smell just like the inside of a hollow tree. Didn't take that queen bee but a minute to tell her folks everything was fine."

Earl and the other men came up, Raymond and Bell started to their feet. 'Keep your seats, keep your seats!" Witt spoke before Raymond had gotten a grip on his stick and the post and before Bell had done no more than turning half-sideways, one hand on the step, calf muscles just starting to raise him up. "Not enough room there for all of us to sit, you-all just stay comfortable." Dr. Witt's vocabulary had changed a bit, what with his time in the Army and at a hospital in Virginia. "Congratulations! You've got your bees and put on a show folks liked better'n a fight!"

"Thank you, Sir." Raymond pushed his cap back on his head, far from exactly the right angle so that the Doctor could see his face and eyes as he spoke. "That swarm clustered up just perfect, easy to reach, people moved away before enough bees got swatted to make 'em all mean, and Mr. Bell brought me the perfect box." Raymond leaned forward to look past Bell and confirm that the bees were still fanning and that stragglers were coming in. A steady line of foraging workers had already begun exiting one corner of the opening at regular intervals. "Mr. Bell, what's the deal on that hat and how'd you choose your victim to wear it?"

"That hat's been on the top shelf ever since I've worked here. What I was told is that there was some society lady sent here for a fright cure by her husband in hopes that'd make her behave. Must've took, because she went home a day or so later and never came back. Some lady friend, I guess figuring nothin'd pick her up like a new hat, had it sent to her. Arrived just after she left. Somebody wrote her a note asking her to send someone for it, but that never happened, so it just sat there 'till it was needed. The man I put it on was Thomas Jordan. Long time ago he did something that got people laughing at me, no need to go into what that was. I just let 'em laugh, thought 'Thomas, what goes around comes around,' and didn't let it ruin my workin' with him. Called him over to get the box 'cause I saw him at the edge of the crowd and knew he was reliable. Didn't even think about what happened back then 'till I had the hat in my hand an' saw his half-bald head right there. Didn't take me half a second to say to myself this business has come all the way 'round and clap it on him! Sweeter'n if I'd planned and schemed on it for days." The other men had another laugh at Jordan's expense and at Bell's moment of epiphany.

Raymond finished his food thanked Bell again for bringing it over to him, searched out the half-smoked cigarette from among the other Luckies and relit it. While Bell was gathering up the tray he asked Raymond if he needed anything else to finish up with the bees and promised to get it personally as soon a he'd gone by the kitchen. "A little beeswax would help me to get 'em to accept the move from the cardboard box to the hive. They probably have some in the cobblers' shop or to run their thread across"

"How's that?" Oliver asked. Bell stuck around to hear the explanation.

"See that stream of bees already coming and going? They've already started making wax for their combs, laying them out in wavy lines on the inside of the lid. You want 'em straight with the frames in the hive so that you can lift 'em out without tearing everything apart. Frames are made with a little strip that you nail down to hold thin sheet of beeswax stamped with a honeycomb pattern to encourage that. My Granddaddy showed me one year when he didn't have cash to buy foundation sheets how you dribble a line of real clean beeswax along the bottom of the top bar on each frame. Smells like home to 'em and saves 'em the work of tyin' into the wood fibers, so they usually follow the line and build straight. Not as reliable as the wax sheets, but a whole lot better'n just giving them a wooden box. Nobody knows what makes 'em line up their combs like they do on their own. The little curves back and forth give 'em strength like a serpentine wall, but the way they line up, who knows? Some folks say it's magnetic, like a compass, some say it's the moon, like the tides."

"Probably the sign they were in when they started work," Was Oliver's comment. He was a great believer in planting garden and cutting saw timber by the almanac.

"Or whether the bee-man drove a Ford or a Chevy and if the color was something other than black." George believed that the best use for an almanac was on the nail in an outhouse, a constant basis for their bickering.

"I sort of see how you can entice them into the hive box from the hat box, but how do you get them away from their favorite place here by the dining room door?" Doc Witt was looking beyond the morning's problem. "A hive of bees here is better than a naked swarm of bees, but still presents a problem for patients coming and going."

Raymond explained the procedure for moving bees. "Once they've gone into the hive for the night, we'll close 'em up tight and truck 'em as far away as we can, maybe out to the chicken-barn where I used to work. Leave them there a couple of days and they'll concentrate on learning their new surroundings, forget about the lilac bush. Once that's happened we could put them just across the courtyard and they'd never come to this side except to look for food. Don't move 'em far enough that first time and they'll just be confused and swarm away the next morning."

"Your Granddaddy teach you all this? You sound like a professor!"

"I followed him around as a kid does when he's not big enough to be put to work, and then I helped him when he got too feeble to lift bee-boxes. In between he talked to me a lot about bees. It was either bees or the War. Nobody else took much interest in the bees, I reckon the others could talk low enough and move easy enough for livestock, but nobody but me and Granddaddy had the feel for 'em. I came home knowin' I had the feel, but I was already crippled up like an old man, knew I couldn't do the liftin' work of makin' a livin' with 'em." Raymond looked sad and talked dull and low. "As for the professor part, I've gone to sleep every night since I left Sarah readin' and re-readin' Reverend Langstroth and Mr. Root."

Bell reappeared at just the right moment, a glass jar in each hand. "Got exactly what you need. Church wax! Cleaner'n sweeter'n anything the cobblers and binders ever get! I remembered that a long time ago a Catholic family didn't get here in time for a funeral. They spent a heap of time prayin' upstairs in the chapel and when they'd gone they left a little old flowerpot stand they'd pulled out of a corner up against a side wall with a couple of Saint's cards propped up and these two jar-candles burnin'. When DeJarnette heard about it, he had the candles blowed out quick, goin' on about the place bein' a tinderbox. Guess he was respectful enough, though, that he didn't order things thrown out. The stand got pushed back in the corner again -- that's where I found it and left it, two dusty Saints with a clean circle on the board in front of each of 'em. Blow the dust out, light 'em up, and once they're hot you can dribble beeswax lines all evenin'!"

"Well done!" Everyone agreed. "If I was to go back to soldierin' and wanted a rifle and bayonet, I bet Rafe would find 'em somewhere around here for me. Might be a spike bayonet, but he'd go through the heap and bring me a percussion cap weapon, not a flintlock; caps and ball, too. He'd have a desk-drawer pistol in his belt, but no extra rounds, unless he'd visited extra offices, 'cause those nervous types don't think to have any beyond what's in the cylinder or chamber 'n clip. I wouldn't be surprised if he topped it off with the Director's pretty quail gun and the case of shells reserved for entertaining politicians."

"And nobody," George winked, "would know nothin'. They'd be thankin' him for findin' them storage space or comin' by installin' the fine old desk lamp he'd found in the store-room, cleaned up and fixed the cord. Tickled 'cause it was a classier piece of work than what the supervisor had maneuvered to for *his* desk, by sweet-talkin' somebody in Richmond. So glad for Rafe's consideration, they wouldn't even think about him bein' in their desk requisitionin' a pistol. Wouldn't know a thing 'till the day there was such a ruckus that they peeped out the window, latched their door, and reached for what wasn't in the drawer, with Rafe Bell long gone and out of mind."

"Oliver, lets you and me get my toolbox off the wagon, load up Raymond's hive and bring it back here so he can wax his frames while he blocks the door and guards the hatbox and lilac." The two carpenters headed off, returned in just a few minutes with the hive, and unloaded it right by the hatbox but out of the way where anyone might bump into it. Trailing the red wagon, all three carpenters went back to their work.

Raymond pushed the candles across the step to where Witt was sitting against the other post. "Light these up for me, please, Doc." He grinned at Rafe, "everybody knows patients can have smokes or fixin's, but not matches." Witt blew the dust out from around the wicks and but had to ask Rafe for barn-burners to light them -- his Medical Corps Zippo couldn't reach the wicks. Raymond stood up, eased a step around the hat box, took the cover off of the hive and pulled out two of the ten hanging frames, then sat back down against his post.

Still standing, Rafe had been watching liquid wax pool around the base of the flaming wick in each jar. "I'll stay and watch you do just one, Mr. Raymond, then leave the rest of 'em to you and the Doctor to finish. I better go see who's still stirred up over things before they have to come back through here to supper."

Bracing his left forearm on his knee, Raymond held a frame upside down and tilted so that the side and bottom pieces did not interfere with the rim of the candle jar. Checking to make sure that he was beyond the toe of his boot if any wax ran over, he grasped the cool bottom half of the jar with his right hand and dribbled wax along the bar, where it immediately cooled into a long, low ridge. He looked up, cap still pushed far back from exactly the right angle, hair poking out under the brim "Thanks, Mr. Bell. Absolutely perfect."

"Glad to oblige. See you gentlemen at suppertime."

"You're talkin' now. What's it feel like?"

"Just like it always did. You want to do a couple of these?" Raymond put the two frames that he'd waxed back into the hive box and brought out the other eight, spearing them on his right forearm like the giant soft-pretzel guy at the fair holding his goodies on a stick. He one-hand fingered two off for Doc Witt without having to let go of his stick. Farley took a candle and slowly dribbled wax away from him along the first frame, then changed to the other candle, more fully charged with liquefied wax, and slowly dribbled wax back towards himself, then put the frames and candles down on the strep.

"Not bad work, so long as you don't have a whole truckload to do in an afternoon or some church feller ridin' you 'cause you filched his candles."

"Reckon so." Raymond finished the rest of the frames and blew out the candles. Took the top off of the hatbox, rapped it with a knuckle to knock the bees clinging inside off into the box. He moved the box far enough from the hive to lay the top, outside up, tight against the landing board entrance of the hive, schootching it down into the dirt a bit so that any bee smelling the wax they'd started to lay down inside couldn't get to it. He turned the hatbox upside down over the smooth expanse of entry board and box top and gave it the same shake he'd given the lilac branch before. The big ball of bees landed half against the entry slit and shrank as bees moved inside. He rapped the bottom of the box to at least make the hangers-on fly out and around for a bit. Leaned the box high against the hive so that plenty of light shone under it and he could see one side of the entrance board from his place on the step. He eased back down from mostly balancing on his good leg, propped his shoulder on the side of the post and fished in his shit-pocket for his smokes. Doc Witt accepted the proffered Lucky, tapped it on the face of his wristwatch to pack it down, then lit them both up.

Witt tilted his head back and tried, unsuccessfully, to blow a smoke ring, the effort thwarted by slight stirring of the air. "I know that you're making the transfer from box to hive, see how you've pushed the edge of the lid into the dirt to keep 'em from going back to their own fresh wax scent, but need you to explain the rest of it."

"Bees like a narrow entrance into dark place, that's why I set the lid the way I did at first. Now it's light inside the box and the attractive entrance is the hive. You can see the signalers lining up there, butts in the air and fanning, telling whoever's coming home of the change. They give off the distinctive, sweet but kind of sharp odor that you may be able to notice, the signal to 'come on in." The inside of the hat box still smells like the queen so that there'll be bit of confusion while that dissipates. Have to shake the two percent who never got the word off a couple of more times before taking the box away. Have to keep the box there until the foragers have time to come home to it -- they wouldn't recognize the hive all by itself. Propped it up high so'd there'd be more light than they like at home and so I could keep an eye on 'em from over here. When they swarm and settle they're not mean 'cause they're concentrating on staying with the queen and their stomachs are full of honey from the hive they swarmed out of. Don't want to fight anymore'n you do after Thanksgiving dinner. Now they have a new home, have used up most of the honey and are putting the rest into comb as fast as they can build it. When they've got settled enough that the scent-fanners go in, they'll post the usual guard-bees, who'll be kinda' testy after the move. That's why I'd rather watch from over here to know when to take the box completely away."

"Interesting. I wonder if anyone saved the hat and unclaimed property tag to be restored to the store-room."

Raymond gave a little chuckle and shook his head, but didn't say anything. He returned his cap to exactly the right angle and every now and then he looked over to check on the bees. Most of the time he just sat there, back against the post, stick between his knees, hands on top of the stick, chin on top of his hands, slowly looking from side to side throughout his range of vision. When the regular time came, Dr. Witt excused himself, returned with the Thermos and mugs and they drank with no more conversation than "more" and "thanks." Suppertime came and they made room for people to enter between them, single-file, with only a few cautionary words to those who looked as though they might reach towards the hive. Rafe Bell brought dinner for both Raymond and the doctor, which they were eating when Earl Ralston came by on his way home.

"Supper smells good -- lookin' forward to my own. I'll come back with my pickup to help you move 'em just before dark. Anything you need to get 'em ready to go?"

"I've got a strip ready to tack over the entrance, but need eight big staples to hold the boxes together to lift."

"No problem. I'll find somethin' that'll do and bring 'em back with me. Why don't you slip over to the shop and get your door-strip? The doc and I'll stand guard." Raymond headed off and Ralston looked in-quiringly at the psychiatrist.

"Stayed with him all afternoon. Ask him a question, he'll answer. Ask a question about bees, he'll give you a damn good explanation. Share a cup of whisky with him, he'll say "thanks" when you pour him more, but not a word more. Figured I'd better not push him. We sat and smoked most of the time, I just leaned back and watched him. Had his back against the post just like me, but he wasn't leanin' on it. Had his chin propped on his hands on his stick between his knees, anybody walkin' by would think he was half asleep. Wasn't though. Actively scanning all around him, no more looking into the distance and using his peripheral vision on the sly. Each circuit he'd pause and seem to relax a bit while he checked to see how the bees were doin', but the rest of the time the relaxed look was a good act. He could'a launched himself off that step like a bear trap snappin' shut if he'd wanted to. Our man's better, but he's not well."

60. MOVING BEES

"'Movin' these bees tonight, he said something to do with takin' them out to the place he came here from. I'm not too keen on haulin' him and his bees off of hospital property, and especially not there."

"Think you're right. A coin toss as to whether seein' the place would send him forward or back."

"When I come back after supper, I'll take him somewhere up on the farm instead." Ralston headed home for supper.

Raymond returned with the cover strip for the hive entrance, two small nails already started through, ready to clamp on tight with just two taps of the claw hammer he also held in his right hand. "OK if I stick around to see the move?" Witt asked.

"Sure," Raymond replied, but said nothing more. They had another smoke as it got darker. "No more foragers coming home." A bit later, "Guards easing back under the lip of the entrance." Raymond stood up, took the closure strip in his left hand, hammer in his right and swung around to the hive, balancing on his good leg. Brought the strip down over the entrance without touching the boards until the gap was closed, two taps of the hammer and all the bees were shut in. "Miss your move and brush the strip against something as you set it, you'll have a dozen guards hot on your hand and wrist, then headed for your face'n eyes. They know their business!"

Driving around the carpenter's shop, Earl saw Raymond sitting back down with the hammer in his hand and figured that he could pull the truck right on over to where the tailgate was even with the hive. He killed the engine and the lights dimmed, running on the battery. Killed the lights and for just a second or two the filaments glowed orange, the pupils of animal's eyes bulging out from either fender. Earl's pickup was really a mid '30's Dodge Brothers sedan, bought cheap after a storm-blown tree'd smashed everything behind the front seat, cut down to the frame, then built up with a box. Red, low and sleek seen from the front, and obviously a carpenter's job seen from the back. Rear wall of the cab was tight-fitting oak tongue-and-groove flooring with an oval window from God-knows-what vehicle or building, all the boards there and back to the tailgate gleaming with spar varnish like bright work on a yacht, every carriage-bolt head and brace pointed out in black

Jap. Doc Witt let out a low whistle. "Never would'a thought it of you. Car proud (Earl had, for years, arrived at work in a series of thoroughly used, unpolished vehicles, to which he added, not changed oil. Draining the sludge might have killed the bit of compression the engines had left!) Must keep that baby under a tarp in the shed on all but warm, sunny days!"

"I confess so. Raymond, I looked everywhere at home and couldn't find bigger'n a fence staple, but I think that these'll do the job if we're careful not to bump them sideways." He handed Raymond eight flat pieces of blued steel, shaped like the squared-off letter "U" with sharp points and broadly tapered legs. "Pinch dogs. Use 'em to draw the ends of boards you're gluing up together when you've run out of clamps or when the work's so dead true that you don't need but a pinch of pressure."

Raymond took the plates over to the hive and commenced hammering them in, joining hive base to body, body to top. "Have to be careful to point 'em in opposite directions when you nail each pair up, both pointing to center or each to a different end. If you don't and the box gets tilted front-to back, it'll slide open like the tray in the top of a tin tackle-box, and angry bees'll eat your ass right up!"

"'Make sure you get 'em right, then. Neither the doc nor I want to get et up! Thinkin' about what you said about taking the hive over to the chicken house. I'm scared it might do you harm to go back there, and know that if it did, our takin' you and your bees off of hospital grounds'd bring an anvil down on me and brother Farley." He looked over to the Doc for some support.

"Impossible to say what goin' back there might provoke. Might not make a bit of difference, but I'd sooner not take the chance. Much as I hate to admit it, Earl's right about trouble tumblin' down on us if we undo your progress in starting to speak again. Among the patient's you're now known as the bee man instead of the Army's hidden killer. Breaking out of your catatonia, you'll be the medical golden-boy of the hospital and hospital system for at least a week until something good or bad happens somewhere else to get their attention. I'll probably get my picture standing beside you published somewhere. I won't go into details, just tell 'em good care from all the staff did it. The guts of the hospital system would knot up trying to digest the combination of a safe room, afternoon coffee, tales of homicidal carpenters, and your assignment to coffin-duty. Don't let any bees sting your cheeks tonight, you gotta be pretty in the mornin'. Where else can we take those bees that'll be far enough away that they'll settle?"

"I can drive out the farm lanes to where they're building the new dairy barn, easy. That's almost exactly as far out on Richmond road as Mr. Hess' place, just out of sight on the south side behind a hill. You reckon that'll do, Raymond?"

"Sounds fine to me. Never been there, didn't realize that the Hospital had ground that far out. Since goin' there reduces the risk you fellows face of havin' to catch an anvil on my account, how 'bout helpin' me lift this hive onto the truck?" Earl lowered the end gate and the two men bent to the job, careful not to bump the pinch-dogs loose. Pushed the back of the hive up close against the side-boards and tied it off tight, into the bed far enough so that the dogs facing them couldn't brush loose against the gate.

Because the sedan had been one of the Dodge's first vehicles with a steering-column mounted gearshift, there was plenty of room for all three men in the front -- nobody had to bounce along with the bees. As he got in Raymond glanced down under the dash and saw a single cast section of a small steam or hot-water radiator with a valve on each end to prevent backflow in the summertime bolted to the firewall. Not, as in Bill Riley's big international, room for the entire array, but still far superior to any heater added as an option by the manufactures. The farm lanes cut straight through some of the pastures, but squared around land flat enough for farming fields -- all in all it was a longer ride than if they'd been able to drive out Richmond Road and cut behind the DeJarnette's Sanatorium steam plant, which the contractors for the new barns were no doubt doing, but the outside contractor was sure to have a gate with a lock on it, an aggravation and too many people to talk with to get through on short notice and only semi-official business.

The two new barns were being built according to the Department of Agriculture's latest enthusiasm. Not bank barns, typical of the Valley, but two long, level barns, the first floor made of concrete block with a quarter of the space devoted to a milking parlor and milk room. The lofts curved from bock sill to block sill, round, like a Quonset hut but without any of the simplicity of construction that let those buildings pop up in a matter of hours. Rather than being spiked through the corrugations into slits in arched steel frames, the sheet-metal roof of these barns was nailed to a tongue-and-groove roof deck that precisely matched their curve.

The design's purported advantage was that it wasted no space in framing. The roof had curved rafters at the normal interval extending up, around, and down from one sill to the other, at no point more than six inches deep because they were made up of dozens of small lengths, curved on one edge, scabbed together. Their assembly pattern was chalked on the loft floor in each barn. There was some attempt to follow the Quonset's example since all of the pieces in each arch except the two ends were identical and the carpenters could trim a standard piece to fit the sill. The parts for a vastly bigger barn could be cut off-site by either low-skilled labor or machine. Ship a sharp-looking barn in just a few boxcars, only thing that wouldn't fit neat into the car would be the curved sheet-metal, but the spaces left behind & in front of them could be filled with nails and hardware. Too bad that the jobsite was three miles from the nearest railroad spur. That spoiled the efficiency that had so impressed the folks in Washington when the job was written up. Good thing was that the customer was a state asylum. No dairy farmer to convince that he wanted barns unlike anyone'd ever seen on his place. That would be a tough sell, even to Quentin Baker!

Raymond picked a spot for the bees in the far side of a fence-corner away from the carpenters and truck traffic. They found enough cut or broken concrete blocks in the trash-heap to build a three-high base for the hive. "Gotta get them up off the ground to save your back and beat the skunks. Bees only have two natural enemies, bears and skunks. What bears do's obvious, skunks are more interesting. They'll scratch on the landing board, wait for one guard-bee to come out, smack him dead, eat him and walk on around the hive while anybody else stirred up calms down and walks back inside. Then they do it again. They'll walk a path in the grass doin' that all night. Folks used to blame witches or faries. After a few turns the guard bees are riled up enough from the smell of their buddies being crunched that a couple'll fly out rather than just walk on the board. If you raise the hive up, skunk's fur gaps apart, showin' his pink skin and he gets stung." They lifted the hive onto the stand, stepped back as Raymond held the cover steady and tight with one hand as he drew the nails with the hammer's claw. When all that held it there was the pressure from his hand, he made sure of his footing, then flicked it away and moved back as a whole squadron of angry and disoriented guard bees filled the space he'd occupied a second before. He eased back another fifteen or twenty feet. "Need to get well back while they settle. When they realize that you're not where you were, some'll zoom out any old way, lookin'. One of them finds and stings you, the smell brings 'em all on. I'd be happy to get in the truck, crank the windows up and go, 'less you-all want to hang around."

Earl had the truck started and Farley Witt had slid into the middle of the seat by the time Raymond climbed in. Dropping the hammer onto the floorboards and holding his stick between his knees, he wound the window up as quick as he could and they all heard a couple of bees against the glass as Earl eased off. Witt relaxed back into the cushiony sedan seat. "How long 'till they calm down?"

"Soon as our lights've gone and they don't smell us fresh anymore they'll start goin' back in. Be kinda cross for a few hours, but bein' in the dark and smellin' nothin' but themselves and the hive box the rest of the night they'll be calmed down by dawn. Come out here after breakfast and you could sit in a chair with your back to the hive and not be bothered so long as you took a minute to see what direction the foragers were working and were careful to hold your newspaper so it didn't mess with their path."

61. PLANNING A BEEYARD

"How long before you can move 'em back to the Hospital?"

"Two, three days. Let 'em have some peace to build comb and fill some of it with pollen and nectar, let the queen lay some eggs to take care of and the box'll be home, they'll stick with it most anyplace you put them after that."

Earl wheeled around a corner in the lane, lights sweeping the fields. "Where do you think they ought to go when we bring them back? I liked your just-the-other-side of the fence selection at the barn lot, but which fence back at the hospital?"

"I'm thinking the woven wire fence just up the hill from the dining hall building, the one that encloses the long, skinny bit of pasture below the upper wards. They use that ground to manage cattle waiting at the dairy after they've been walked in from the meadows. Set two posts and wire off maybe a twenty-foot square bee yard directly up from the courtyard, where we could keep an eye on it from the doorway of the carpentry shop."

"Makes sense. Pretty unusual for anyone to cut through there since there's path outside the fence at the north end of the lot and the service lane at the other end behind the dairy coming up to the far end of the wards. What do you think Doc?"

"I think that this afternoon proved everyone's respect for bees. Wherever you put 'em people'll shy away, and that's a spot without path, not on a direct route to anywhere in the daily course of things. I'll propose it at tomorrow's staff meeting -- know they'll be giving me a chance to talk and so happy to have a winner that I'll have a sympathetic ear." Earl pulled from the lane into the courtyard, let them out, and headed off to home.

62. DOCTOR WITT'S FORMAL ACCOUNTING

The Staffing Room was amurmur when Farley Witt eased the door open the next morning, clutching his overloaded clipboard under his left arm. The noise level increased as he made his way among the long white laboratory coats towards the coffee. Much of the noise was directed towards him, congratulatory comment vs or variations of the question 'How?' About the time he'd filled his mug and found a seat, things quieted down as the Director of the Hospital came in, took his place beside the Medical Director, and was handed his mug of Joe. The Medical Director got to his feet in deference to the big boss' presence at what was usually a pretty informal review of the previous day's happenings and each morning's plans. "Good morning, gentlemen. Dr. Witt, please start us off with a bit of case history and your observations on what we've heard happened with one of your patients yesterday."

Feeling like he was back in residency, when it was seldom best to be called on first, he began. "Yes, Sir. Raymond McCleary. He's a young man from a farm in North Carolina. He went into the Army right after high school, ended up in the Rangers, wounded in the attack on Normandy, one of the men who scaled the cliff, badly wounded in the leg soon after reaching the top. Convalesced at Woodrow Wilson Hospital, went home, decided there wasn't a place for him on the farm, came back up here, wound up driving an oil truck delivering to all the country stores -- joked that it was the only kind of truck that both loaded and unloaded itself, but soon found out it was more work, climbing and all, than he'd thought. Seemed to have a solid relationship with war-widow storekeeper he took up with, but was plagued with nightmares and drank considerable to cope with pain, has to walk with a stick. Broke up with her and left his driving job just short of being asked to because of the whisky. Took an isolated job running a chicken barn, kept more and more to himself, his friends brought him in after they found him catatonic, staring into the distance, unresponsive, as tense as a wildcat fixin' to pounce, mute and peripherally hyper-vigilant. He'd obviously been using considerable whisky for his pain, but wasn't intoxicated. His appearance was immaculate -- his friends commented on the habit, his boots and the 'just right' angle at which he wore his striped engineer's cap, perhaps a carryover from the discipline of soldiering. On admission he was passively cooperative, but still mute and rigidly staring into the distance, we kept him off of the wards for his safety and the safety of others should someone accost him. He is locked in overnight with meals in his quarters and frequent observation by staff. Nightly laudanum for pain and sleep. Afternoon whisky for pain. After a month or so he was coaxed out to sit, back against the wall in the courtyard, still with frequent staff contact and essentially constant distant observation. His friends visited and helped with his clothes, but he showed no more interaction with them or family on their one visit than with staff." Witt had to interrupt his report for a couple of long sips of coffee -- his mouth and throat had dried out. Everyone was patient and quiet.

Witt started up again, aware that he'd been talking about as loud and fast as he could and might need to ease the pace a bit. Someone got up and opened a window -- the room was getting fogged with smoke from numerous cigarettes and the cigar that the Director was enjoying. Farley Witt wanted to light one up in the worst way, but protocol wouldn't allow it, at least for a junior man. "On a hot day someone, don't remember if it was staff or a visiting friend convinced Mc Cleary that he'd be more comfortable on bench in the shade close to the carpenters' shop. That was likely the turning point. Earl Ralston, one of the carpenters likes to work outdoors on sawhorses rather than inside on a bench. He was within earshot, and I asked him to talk to Raymond, which he did, constantly. Didn't try to make eye contact or elicit a response, just talked. At my request, Ralston described in minute detail the work he was doing, usually repairing window sash; teasing McCleary in a friendly way about the differences between the barn carpentry he knew from coming up and the real carpentry that was being explained to him. Beyond that he talked about anything that came to mind. I told him that I'd gotten Raymond to smoke with me, so he took a lot of smoke breaks, first on the bench, then on a pile of wooden crates just inside the big doors of the shop when the weather pushed him back in there. It was Earl's idea to be real clumsy foolin' with his pipe and tobacco so that each break was long enough that Raymond went through the interaction of getting two cigarettes lit and smoked, still without a word. I came and talked with him every afternoon, gave him drink of whisky to ensure my welcome and ease his pain, which is still considerable. James Weaver and Raphael Bell, the two attendants that brought meals, medicine, and locked and unlocked his door had the same instructions to always have a one-sided conversation about something, anything, a give him the opportunity if something interested him enough to speak. Nothing did. Totally cooperative for months, totally silent, totally hyper vigilant, and always with his weight, feet, and stick positioned to launch himself into action should a threat present himself." Time for another sip of coffee for his dry throat. Witt wished it was afternoon coffee.

"The next sign of progress was the day after Ralston mentioned in passing that Raymond could use his tools if he wanted to make a night stand or something for is room using wood from the packing crates. Next mornin' Raymond showed up and wordlessly handed him a plan he'd sketched and measured out. Ralston got him started, the other carpenters took an interest enough to step over and show him how to do the next bit when they realized he'd slowed down or was just standing beside them staring, his way of asking for help. In a few days he finished a cabinet with a group of oddly proportioned drawers, but the aides pointed out that they were just right for the few personal things he has."

"Next morning he shows up and hands Ralston the drawings for a beehive, with table of materials worked out, listing what could be made from crates, what needed clear lumber. I remembered that his friends' told me that most of his comments about home had to do with his Grandfather keeping bees. One of the aides reminded me that a shallow drawer on his nightstand just fit a well-worn beekeeping book." As he paused to catch his breath Witt thought, but did not say, a contrast with the untold dozens of fingered but unread bibles about this place. "I signed off on the shop-book for the lumber, and he got to work. The carpenters found him an old toolbox and half filled it with their second- or third-best tools. He worked long and hard on the bee-boxes and their internal frames, which have to be made with complete accuracy to be useful. Still not a word, although he began to move his head to look around in the shop, returning to the distant stare only when idle. His hyper-vigilance eased up as he worked with the other three carpenters, but returned when he stepped away from them. The carpenters were impressed with his work on both of his projects and set him to work building coffins, not any more difficult than what he'd already done, and needed work that kept them from being interrupted when someone passed and the only box on hand was too short or the wrong size in every respect. That's what he was doing, going to his dinner break while building a coffin, when he heard the commotion over the swarm of bees and came out, shouting, to take charge."

"I stayed with him all afternoon and evening. He'd answer questions about bees in great detail, but was quiet otherwise except to thank the people who helped him. We smoked lots of cigarettes passing the time. He always thanked me for the light, but volunteered nothing else. When he appeared to be sittin' on the step learnin' against the porch post, his feet and stick were arranged to rise up fast, without any thought as to how, and he just stared off into the distance. At one point I asked him how it felt to talk again -- he said "just like it always did." I thought it best not to push him. I'm looking forward to going over to the carpenters' shop this morning to see if he's talking with those men. I've ordered that breakfast this morning be his last meal in his room. Dinnertime he'll be assigned a chair near a rear exit with his back to the wall, view of the main doors and just a few tablemates, all steady folks. He's not back with us completely, yet, not a well man, but he's made a big change."

The other doctors gave him a brief round of applause. Fortunately, nobody asked questions, perhaps because his narrative had been complete, made no claims of a cure, and explained what came next. That covered ground that he, like most medical students, had, at least early on, not considered as a structure for their presentations, providing prime opportunities for the ridicule and embarrassment deemed necessary for their proper training. He got some more coffee and lit a smoke, glad to be finished as the usual morning reports droned on, the Hospital Director eased out of this part of the meeting as inconspicuously as he could between speakers. The room relaxed a good bit at that point, and while everyone was shuffling out at the end of the meeting he got asked a couple of times what he thought made the difference with Raymond's case. "Good work from all the staff," was his reply. "Good work, especially, from the aides and carpenters!"

63. RAYMOND ENTERS THE PATIENT POPULA-TION

Earl Ralston was already putting shavings on the ground in his usual spot when Doc Witt got over near the carpenters' shop. He could see Raymond at work at a bench about halfway in, letting his hip carry a lot of his weight against the bench so that he had both hands free, his stick on the bench top where it could be grabbed quick as any tool, not leaning somewhere he'd have to reach for it. "Our boy talk to you this mornin'?"

"Said good mornin', polite, to each of us, then got right to work on that small box, fit an old lady or one 'a the smaller idiots when their time comes. Haven't heard a word since. Not quite time for a break, yet, so I really haven't had a chance to see what might develop -- probably bee talk."

"I'll go interrupt him a minute before I head for the wards." The doctor laid his clipboard in the middle of the bench a few feet from Raymond, turned his back to the edge and used his hands to hunch himself up to sit. "Mornin'."

"Mornin' to you, too. How're you doin'?" Raymond looked over briefly as he spoke, then back down at his work.

"Pretty well. Gave my speech about yesterday to the doctors and Director, but nobody's askin' to take our picture yet. Either they're waitin' to make sure you keep on talkin' or waitin' for the bees to get moved back here, make a more interesting pose. Maybe a little of both." Raymond had no comment, just kept measuring and marking his wood. "Don't know if Mr. Weaver or Mr. Bell told you at breakfast, but come dinnertime I've reserved you a place in the dining room. Back to the wall, good view of the whole place, just a few tablemates. Decided 'pass, the potatoes, please' would be good therapy for you."

"Reckon I can deal with that," Raymond replied without looking over.

"Good. Figured you could. I'll try to get approval for fencing off a bee-yard before I see you this afternoon. Tell you how that goes and find out who you ate with then. Careful cuttin' those boards. Don't want any bloodstains on 'em to make folks fear that you're one of those homicidal-type carpenters, hurryin' customers along to stay in work." Both men laughed as Witt hopped down, grabbed his clipboard and left. As soon as the doctor turned his back, Raymond looked after him, shaking his head and chuckling.

It didn't take much time for Witt to get approval for the bee-yard. The job wouldn't take much in the way of materials, fencing was already on hand and included in the farm budget. The ground he asked for wasn't productive, just a bump in the edge of an oversized cow lane. The farm supervisor said that he'd have some men put up the wire that afternoon. Witt suggested that he check at the carpenters' shop for exact direction. The man was obviously pleased at the prospect of talking to Raymond personally, and grateful, Farley knew, of having an offer that the carpenters would supply the gate to forestall griping from his crew, who could stretch or patch wire in a hurry, but didn't have much experience or patience for building gates, especially piddly garden-sized gates. All of the administrators were looking forward to some positive publicity. On his way to the wards, the doctor was sort of wistful that he couldn't tag some of the things on his wish list for those patients onto the coattails of Raymond's improvement. Perhaps the whole business would add some weight to his signature on the next supply requisition he submitted. Have to wait and see.

Raymond put down his work and looked up when he heard the dinner bell, uncertain exactly what was expected of him. The unspoken rule, 'don't cause nobody no trouble,' was on his mind, but he relaxed a bit when he saw Rafe standing right by the lilac bush, waiting for him. Set his cap at exactly the right angle, took up his stick and headed towards the man he trusted. He nodded to Earl, who wished him well as he passed, heading into and across the courtyard.

"You've seen these people a million times before, Mister Raymond, but never heard their names. Let me explain who you'll be at table with. First, there's Benny, biggest man you've seen in the yard, messed up brown hair, round face. He's an idiot, but has good manners because he lived with his grandparents 'fore they passed. Don't look for trouble, but don't know when to stop if somebody gets into him and that ain't pretty. We make sure that folks crazy enough to try him are kept away from him, just like we keep 'em away from you. Next there's Louise. She's kinda like the double strings on a mandolin, says everything twice, sometimes echoing off into three or four times. When someone answers her, she repeats the answer. People at her table have to talk about the progress of eating the meal or she'll get stuck at 'pass the turnips, please,' hold onto the bowl when its handed to her, softly repeating the request to herself and neglecting to take her turnips from the bowl and eat them – or pass the bowl along. Finally, there's Mattie Lou - Matilda Louise. Mostly she's just old. Has the daily order of things pretty good, but gets the years wrong. Conversation other than things concerns the meal on the table jumps five years from sentence to sentence, twenty years beginning to end. Her ability to come back as necessary to the food before her helps a lot in moving Louise along. Has a peg leg. Cut the real one on the edge a leaf running through a knee-high cornfield when she was a little girl, it got infected and they had to take it. Hard for her to deal with a bunch of jostling patients, she hasn't got your weight or shoulder strength, gets pushed off balance real easy. They made their way through the busy dining room to the small table at the rear. The table itself was barely visible because of Bennie's bulk in the chair nearest them. The two ladies were on either side, the chair with its back to the wall vacant for Raymond. Bell made introductions, then slipped away as Raymond was taking his seat.

Raymond sat down, lay his stick under the left side of his chair where nobody'd kick it and where he could reach down and retrieve it without thinking. The admonition 'don't cause nobody no trouble' was going-ing through his mind, as he took off his cap and placed it on the corner of the table at his right, combed his fingers through his hair, and raised his face to meet the eyes of his table-mates. "Hey, I'm Raymond. How're y'all today?"

"I know you, you're the bee-man," Bennie extended his baseball-mit hand across the table in greeting.

"You're the bee-man, you're the bee-man, you're the beeman."

"Watch out, Louise, here comes the girl with our meatloaf and green beans," Mattie Lou interrupted as they were set on the table.

"Green beans, green beans."

"Yes, thank you." Mattie Lou served herself some and passed them to Raymond. "Take some and help Louise get her share onto her plate."

It didn't take Raymond more than three repetitions of 'help Louise' to put his food onto his plate, then reach over and start helping Louise. "Here you go," he said as he spooned, the appearance of good smelling food at least temporarily silencing the echo.

Bennie had helped himself to a good portion of meatloaf and then handed the platter to Mattie Lou, who'd taken some and was reaching the dish towards Raymond, when Bennie said "Pass, the ketchup, please."

"Ketchup please, Ketchup please." Louise handed the tall bottle to Bennie.

"Bird," he said as he shook the bottle. "A parrot bird." He poured lots of ketchup on his meatloaf and put the bottle in the middle of the table where anyone could reach it.

Louise got the ketchup and began shaking it out into smallish dots all over her food "Parrot bird, parrot bird." She and Bennie laughed together at what was apparently a long standing joke between them.

Raymond was relieved when a different woman arrived with their bowl of mashed potatoes and a coffee pot. He silently held his mug out to be filled and found himself, out of habit and upbringin' smiling at her "Thank you, ma'am."

"Thank you, ma'am, thank you, ma'am, thank you ma'am."

"Louise, pass those potatoes to the two gentlemen and me when you've finished with them, please.

Lord," Mattie Lou rolled her eyes, "she's worse than usual today. Must be because you've joined us, Raymond."

"Must be, must be, must be" sort of dwindled off, muffled by mouthfuls of food. Raymond and Bennie ate in silence, hoping not to trigger another outburst.

"Raymond," Mattie Lou spoke between bites, "you'll get used to it, it's kind of like having a conversation with a friend at an auction when you're right far back in the crowd from the wagon. The crier keeps goin' but you don't really hear him 'cause you're listen to your friend. How much longer's this war going to last? I'm tired of the way rationing keeps our menu tied to what our farmers produce."

"War's over for a good time, Mattie," came quietly from Bennie, muffled by his mouthful of meatloaf and vegetables. Who learned you about bees?"

"Good time, good time, 'bout bees, 'bout bees."

"My Granddaddy kept 'em, I followed him around pretty close."

"Followed close, Granddaddy, followed close."

"Had a Granddaddy, too. Lived with him after Grandmaw died, after he was gone come here. Uncle got the farm but, he don't like me. "Dummy!" he said. "Dummy!" Only hit him once, he got up'n called the sheriff, brought me here before dark." Louise, despite all her craziness, had long ago smelled out the one word she'd best not repeat around Bennie. Raymond saw her cram into her food, mumbling so badly that nobody could tell what word she was stuck on.

Raymond finished his food as quickly as he could, reached with the appropriate hand for stick and cap at the same instant, scooted his chair back, and as soon as he got some purchase on his stick, stood. "Nice to meet y'all, but if you'll excuse me, they'll be lookin' for me back at the shop." In about forty-five minutes, he thought.
.

"Good to meet you, too, nice to have another gentleman."

"'Nother gentleman, 'nother gentleman"

Raymond moved away from the table as Bennie was grunting his farewell, got out the door and paused on the porch to set his cap at exactly the right angle before heading home to the carpenters shop. His mind was racing and he almost stumbled as he walked, looking ahead but straining to see what was just beyond a threatening distance on each side, listening for sounds behind him, and not processing any of the information in his normal, confident and controlled way. He was shook. The safety he'd come to feel in his well-defined world was fast leaving him.

Earl was already back at work just outside the doors, Raymond knew that he'd been watching him approach without staring -- Earl was just about as good at that trick as he was. "Not good?"

"No, sir."

"Here if you want to talk about it."

Raymond walked on, but as he neared his workbench looked back and saw Earl fumbling for his pipe and headed for the most comfortable-looking of the week's discarded crates. The attraction of a nerve-settling smoke was stronger than his inclination to stay deep in the familiar spaces of the shop. He turned and went back to join the older man. Earl already had his pipe going by the time Raymond sat down and reached a couple of matches from his pocket, holding them out without comment. Raymond lit up, took a long drag, held it longer than was comfortable, and sighed as he blew it out, elbows on his knees. Earl's crate had a single reinforcing board along the length of a joint on the bottom. He rocked gently back and forth with the resulting unsteadiness of the seat. Not as comfortable as a rocking chair 'cause it didn't have a back, but a pleasant, better diversion than whistling or telling some pointless story while he waited for Raymond to calm down, maybe say something to him. The two of them saw Farley Witt headed towards them -- coffee was early this afternoon, no doubt due to the doctor's curiosity for a first-hand account of Raymond's dining experience. They both knew that he came fully briefed by his troop of observers. "Coffee *and* smokes. No doubt both welcome to push away the urge for an after-dinner nap or other retreat from dealing with this world. Sure you won't join us, Mr. Ralston? I only brought two mugs, but the coffee's cool enough that you won't burn yourself sipping from the aluminum cup off of the top of the Thermos." He busied himself arranging a crate for his seat and another for his clutter of clipboarded papers, mugs and Thermos.

"Think I will, thank you. Coffee I had in my dinner-bucket today was a little off, didn't hit the spot."

Witt poured, and as the others started sipping, lit a smoke of his own, not taking up his mug until he'd enjoyed the first puff or two.

Braced by both smoke and drink and at once pressed and reassured by the patient silence of two men he trusted, Raymond finally spoke. "Everything went so smooth yesterday and last evening. Nothing bad happened at dinner, but having to sit with those people made me want to cut and run. Everybody here at the shop talks quiet and slow and to the point, that draws me into their kind of mood. The noise of the dining room and the talk of those three people, trying to be easy with them, be polite and have the amount of conversation to get the food passed around without aggravating their problems made my head spin, made me want to get by myself, quick, and make sure that nobody like them was close to easin' up near me! I know I still wake up screamin' every night, you have to bunk me in a brick cellar to keep me from wakin' folks and give me laudanum to sip at to get back to sleep. I know that 'cause I keep my stick handy and my eyes open the papers on the clipboard call me paranoid. I call it alert, sensible. You would, too, you'd been where I've been, done what I've done, and had done to you what I had done to me. Sensible if you'd and seen and heard it and felt it, and see and hear and feel it again every night of the world. Up until yesterday the papers said catatonic. I'd call that tendin' to what I have to tend to, not makin' no trouble for nobody, just like I was told when I got here, up until I saw those people about to get stung and those bees get hurt. I know I act different from most folks, but I'm not crazy, not yet. Make me endure that bunch three meals day and I will be, or say or do somthin' that'll cause trouble. I understand why you don't want me to keep on eatin' alone. I understand that you tried to put me in a safe place, with people that I'd be safe around, but it just won't work if I have to listen to that jabber. Let me come runnin' when the bell rings, I'll find a seat where I feel safe, I'll be happy if Bennie decides to sit with me or gets told to and I'll get along with whoever wants to join the two of us." Raymond had been looking off into the distance as he spoke, and didn't look to either of his companions for a response, just went about getting another Lucky from the pack in his pocket, his hands shaking as Earl leaned over and struck him a light. A long drag on the cigarette, a long drink from the mug, held in both hands, and he calmed down a bit, although he was still looking straight ahead.

"Hmm," Doc Witt mused, nursing his refilled coffee but foregoing a second smoke.

Not my place to say nothin', Earl thought, studiously ignoring both of his companions, focusing on refilling his pipe and considering the state of the stitching around the rim of his tobacco pouch. Doc's gotta' be the man to respond to that.

"Don't cause no trouble for nobody. Sounds more like the advice of a bunkmate to a new man in from the replacement battalion than advice to a patient here. Suspect that it stuck in your ear 'cause you'd heard it before, but probably good advice to a man in any new, mostly unknown situation. The shape you were in when you came here, eyes open and mouth shut, just made sense to continue. At first you spent a lot of time gone to where you were that morning over at Mr. Hess' hen-house. Then you began to slip in and out of it, when you started to scan this place's limited horizons rather than someplace we couldn't see. You were still coming and going, though not as much, when you got into the carpenters' shop. You're right when you say you'll always act different from other folks, but I believe that you're mostly stay with us, now. I don't think you're crazy, either. Just different and subject to goin' somewhere dangerous in your past. You realized it when you left Riley and went to work for Hess. You know bettern' us what works for you, so supper'll be done your way. With your permission I'll ask Bennie to find you so you'll have one familiar, easy talkin' face."

"Thanks." Raymond turned to face the Doc as he said it.

"Of just as much importance, when do we bring the bees home? I see that the yard's fenced off, just needs a gate. Earl, your truck available tonight?"

"Whenever you need it. Raymond said 'leave'm there a day or two.' Which is it?"

"Like to get them tonight, but it'd really be better to wait another day, not take a chance on 'em flyin' off again."

"Give us another day to get a gate up. Probably safer for the rest of the patients. You've gotta' know how to make gates, comin' off a farm, and I'll ask Oliver and George if they know of a couple of odd hinges and a latch, or at least a piece of chain to wrap 'round the post."

The men ended their break, to Doc headed off to the wards, Earl to question the other carpenters, and Raymond to measure the gap left by the fence-builders. Hinges and chain were found and Raymond set to work ciphering his list of materials in order to have a precise list before asking Oliver and George for help with the lumber rack, bolt bins and shop book. They'd been pretty easy on him recently, but he knew that if he asked for odd lengths or incorrectly described hardware he'd be in for a razzing. He planned to check the labels on the bolt boxes to make sure of the right words for what he recognized by sight. His diligence paid off, everything was drawn and entered in the ledger without negative comment. He commenced making the gate.

When the supper bell rang its first lick he did the minimum cleanup of shoving his tools into the box and hustled for the dining hall. Weren't many people there when he came in and he sat down at a good spot with his back to the wall. A couple of minutes later Bennie threaded his way between tables, headed in his direction.

"Hey, Mr. Bee Man. How you? Doc Witt asked me to look for you and sit if you wanted me to. Said you don't know many other folks yet that you like to talk to."

"I'm well, thank you. How 'bout yourself? Happy to have your company."

"I'm doin' good, hungry though. Been long time since dinner."

A lanky, medium-sized fellow came over and sat down. "Hey, Bennie. Hey, Mr. Bee-Man. I'm Thomas. No trouble to anyone 'cept banks and chain-stores, hope you're no connection with either of them."

Bennie leaned over and stage-whispered behind his immense hand. "He breaks windows, as many as he can."

"Pleased to meet you, Thomas, my real name's Raymond. Used to keep company with a lady storekeeper, and did my saving in a Prince Albert can, so we ought to get along pretty good."

"Glad to hear it. That means that we can talk about something else and I can enjoy my supper without gettin' all stirred up and bein' told to eat fast and quiet down."

The kitchen help had started bringing food out to the tables when a wild-eyed red-haired man rushed up and took the last seat at the table, looking back over his shoulder, towards a space where no one was visibly following him. "Hey, Red," Bennie called out while getting his share of the mashed potatoes. "The beeman's name is Raymond. You keep ahead of them this afternoon?"

"It ain't been easy, but yeah I have."

Raymond figured that if Bennie and Red knew who 'they' were, and Thomas either knew or didn't care, he'd just let it go and not risk starting something by asking. He couldn't help but think that the hospital was very different from any society that he'd ever been exposed to in that people were unashamedly open about the things that bothered them the most. Food was passed and eaten; most of the conversation was directed at him, questions about bees and particularly *the* bees to which he responded as directly as he could. A great improvement over his previous experience.

The same men sat with him at breakfast. They'd asked their questions the evening before, and now the conversation verged on normal, the food, the weather, where each was going to work or at least to be found that day. As Raymond left, he felt almost relaxed, paused on the porch to get his cap at exactly the right angle and headed across the courtyard to the shop, thinking of the couple of little things that he had to do to get the gate ready to hang.

64. DOC WITT CALLED UP AND MEETING THE PRESS

All three of the carpenters went with him mid-morning to put the gate in place. Since it was small and light, they each just took up a corner and carried it between them to the gap in the fence, the necessary tools in the free hands of those that had them, the 'L' shaped hanger bolts in Raymond's pocket. They held the gate up and one of the other men made the mark for the lower bolt hole, then handed the awl to Raymond to mark the top, which he did, recognizing immediacy that they were giving him another proficiency test. Earl augured out the pilot holes with a brace and bit, George wrenched the bottom hanger bolt in, and Oliver invited Raymond to do the top. He cranked on the bolt until they looked about even then held the long spirit level against the pivots to see if they were true, giving the top a couple of more turns but blocking the glass of the level so that the others couldn't see that he'd left it just a hair short of being plumb. "Put her up there, please." As George and Earl lifted both hinges onto their pins, Raymond could see Oliver reaching for the level to check his work. "Pull that top 'un off." George and Earl did, and Raymond wrenched the bolt around ninety degrees so that the pin stood out sideways. "Now hold the top of that hinge up at the end." George and Earl laughed as they did so and Raymond hammered the pin down into the hinge, completing the half-turn needed to draw the gate plumb and locking it place so that it couldn't be lifted off. Oliver laid the level gently on the grass, mindful of its glass vials, without even bothering to check the gate. He knew that Raymond had it dead on. "Figured y'all were layin' to catch me half a bubble off when Oliver carried that thing up here. Knew it for certain when you were grinnin' and tryin' to hang that thing with both pins pointin' up."

"George, I reckon we've gone about as far as we can foolin' with this feller. Gonna have to just let him be."

"Ha!" Earl exclaimed. "Oliver, you're not gonna let him be. You're just sayin' you won't try to trick him any more'n you're always after me 'n George."

Back down at the carpenter's shop they found Doc Witt sitting on crate, his coffee mug filled to the brim, probably not the sign of a first drink. He was holding the cigarette that he was smoking, or at least allowing to burn, in the same hand as an unfolded single-page letter. Oliver and George, still joking between themselves, went to their usual benches, carrying the tools they'd used on the gate.

"What's the problem, Doc?'" Earl and Raymond sat down opposite him, Earl filling his pipe one-handed, without looking down, about as quickly as Raymond could get Lucky form his pack, and they shared a light.

He was glad not to have to remember to perform the charade of clumsiness that had filled much of the silence when Raymond first became confident enough to join in a smoke.

"Called back up. Remember months ago when I was joking about the reserve unit of medical misfits, existing only on paper, that I'd been assigned to? It's real now. Off paper and assigned to a numbered building on one of the empty company streets covering Fort Ord's steep ridge half a mile inland from the beach and Stillwell hall, grandest Officers' Club in the West. Got to report there in fourteen days. Even with what's been in the news, war in Korea, the Seventh getting sent forward from occupation duty in Japan, then chewed up, it's a surprise. I really thought that it was just a paperwork drill, the last step of my demobilization. Turns out it's real, and with a long enough arm to claw me out of this mountain-bound asylum. Probably a positive thing professionally -- if I behave, I'll make major, lieutenant colonel, easy. Hell'uva thing that's happening to those boys in the Seventh Division, coming off occupation duty into a cakewalk start to a fight that sounds like the Little Bighorn!"

Earl reverted to the ploy of fumbling with his pipe because he wasn't sure what to say. He liked Witt, recognized that these circumstances gave him a chance to break away from the slide into alcoholic professional oblivion that would keep him at the Hospital until he died, but feared his leaving because of what he was doing for Raymond and hadn't yet finished. "We're sorry to see you go, but there's not much arguing with Uncle Sam. You could maybe go out back and work on one ear with an ice pick, but given that you're a doc and they want you, you'd probably just end up with a medical waiver ordering you to sit with the other ear towards your patient." Raymond listened, didn't say anything.

"At least I won't have to leave before getting my picture in the paper with the bee-man. Is tonight still the night to bring them home?"

"Yup. Move 'em just like before if Earl can bring his truck."

"No problem. I'll meet you here right after supper, just like before. If we have to wait for the last bee to come in we can just sit around up there, smoke, and tell stories."

Witt poured what little coffee remained into Raymond's mug and stood up to leave. "I know how to get along where I'm going. Enough going on that it'll all be interesting as long as they don't figure me for an administrative man. Not too likely!" He laughed. "I've liked working here, mostly because of you two gentlemen, have to admit it was less interesting, though, before Raymond came along. Good chance I'd have got too comfortable and become a permanent part of this place except for this call-up. Got to do the wards and slip off for a haircut and some shopping. See you this evenin'."

Raymond and Earl raised a pipe hand and mug in silent farewell as the doc headed off. Reckon he's like me, Raymond mused, his discharge uniform hanging dusty in the closet 'cept for the raincoat and garrison cap he's been usin' in bad weather. It's got droopy enough from being wet so often, I 'spect he's gonna have to buy a new one, first post he hits. "Bet you a dollar his shopping today includes a can of Brasso and a new tin of shoe polish! You really think that they're gonna' come take a picture of the bees?"

"I'm sure that the Superintendent is gonna have them here to take his picture with you and the Doc beside him and the bee-box in the background. Good publicity, maybe even be picked up in the big papers. Maybe I ought to take up your bet about shoe polish and make my own about how anybody else tries to crowd in on the Boss in the picture it'll be posed closer and closer to the hive 'til there ain't any more of them!" They both laughed, Earl pocketed his pipe and tossed back the rest of his drink as they separated and go on with their work.

Sure enough, Rafe Bell passed the official word to Raymond at dinnertime that there were going to be photograph taken and a meeting with reporters at ten-thirty the next morning. "Early enough that everybody'll look fresh," he said, "but late enough that nobody important would be inconvenienced, and that extra people'd be elsewhere about their business. Seen before how these things go."

Raymond finished the box that he'd been working on for the last day or so -- the speed of his production wasn't critical -- and got George and Oliver to help stack it at the back of the shop. They now had a reasonable inventory. Without an immediate carpentry task, he told Earl what he was about and went scouting around behind buildings and into corners looking for enough bricks to stack up a base for the hive high enough to protect the bees from skunks. Finding one here, one there and only able to carry three or four at a time under his right arm, the job took the rest of the afternoon and enough walking that when he was finished he checked back with Earl and went to his room for a nap before supper.

As promised, Earl pulled the cut-down Dodge to the edge of the Courtyard as dusk began to fall. Raymond, hammer in hand, and Farley Witt, sharp-looking after his haircut, climbed in for the ride up through the farm lanes to retrieve the bees. As soon as they got there, Raymond retrieved the strip of wood that he'd flung down as he freed the bees two evenings before, tapped the nail points back flush so that when the time came he could use it to close the hive entrance tight with one smooth motion, and laid it and the hammer on top of the hive. The carpenter and doctor were standing in the open doors of the Dodge, leaning their arms on its roof and talking. "How 'bout you-all backing that thing over here where we can sit on the tailgate and see when the bees stop flying?" Earl did as he was asked, Raymond ground-guided him into the right spot, let down the gate and the three of them settled down for a smoke.

"Well, Earl," Witt said after a good long drag and thoughtful blowing of smoke. "If I remember right, you said that we'd sit and tell stories if we had to wait for the bees to come in. Let's hear yours."

"First one that comes to mind was told to me by a carpenter, one of the men who built Mr. Hess' chicken house. Don't worry, Raymond, it's about the fellow when he was a boy, before he learned the homicidal tricks of our trade. I can't tell it as well or as long as Marvin himself does, but I remember the most of it. Marvin likes to tell stories and gave this one a good long time. That fact sticks in my mind because he told it to me one summer night just as he was leaving our house, screen door open, one foot inside, one outside on the step, his hand one the knob, refusing each of my invitations to step back inside with 'won't be a minute more, we both have to turn in' while the mosquitoes and candle-flies, drawn to the dark-yellow bulb by the door that wasn't supposed to attract them swarmed into the house."

"Marvin and Dewey's daddy and granddaddy had been wheelwrights, did enough of that work that they didn't have to farm on the side, just keep few chickens, a milk cow and fatten up a hog. The cluster of houses for their family, some cousins and in-laws, wheelwright shop, sawmill and lumber sheds, was about a mile east from the Mount Sidney railroad station. Folks called the whole mess, which it really was, just a mess of houses and buildings that growed without any plan or organization, 'Craig Shop'. The name stuck even after wooden wheels went out, the old man died, the boys' daddy took up carpenterin' and there was a lot less goin' on, just buildings closed up and settlin' back into the ground behind a screen of weeds and broke-down cars. When Marvin was ten or eleven, he was right keen on baseball and he played in the evenings on the field behind the Weyers Cave School. His momma didn't fuss when he grabbed leftover biscuits and some cold meat for supper rather'n waitin' to sit down with everybody else, 'cause that meant that if he hustled he could get over to Mount Sidney and snag a ride on the step of the caboose of the train headed down to Harrisonburg. The engineer knew that a good many boys'd do that, but they had an understanding that they'd drop off before the switch-tower at thee Harrisonburg yard so that nobody'd see them and the trainman wouldn't catch hell. Marvin'd drop off at the Weyers Cave station five miles down the road, play his game, loaf around somewhere for a while and then reverse the deal to get home on the last train headed up to Staunton. Worked out pretty well so long as the game didn't go into extra innings, there wasn't a double header, or he didn't lose track of time while hanging around the edges of the groups of older boys and young men at the pool table in the drugstore or the card game upstairs over the Post Office. A whole lotta' bugs got into the house while he stood there, elaborating on the charms of those two distractions. If he missed his train it was a long walk home in the dark."

"One evening he lost track of the time and missed his train, which everyone thought was hilarious. One fellow was making fun of him stumbling along the tracks, tripping on sleepers and falling on sharp clinkers dropped by the engines onto the ballast. "Can't laugh at me about that," he defended himself. "I'm gonna' walk home the short way, over past Westview School," an unused one-room school house along a side road from which he could cut across a couple of farms' back pastures, saving a good bit of distance. He'd only made things worse for himself. They lit into him again "ghosts gonna get you, blah-ha-ha-ha! Ghosts gonna get you, two cemeteries 'long that road, blah-ha-ha-ha" "I ain't scared of no ghosts," he replied, and set out walking."

"It was a little over a mile before he got to the first, larger, cemetery next to the Brethren church. Long enough to think it out. He'd known that the cemeteries were on his route, but hadn't thought the first thing about ghosts. Now they were all he could think about. By the time he reached the church he'd reasoned it all out. Ghosts came from unhappy dead people. If he was goin' by a place where there'd been a killin' or a battlefield it'd be one thing, but goin' by church graveyards where everyone had been laid to rest in sweet Jesus' arms, there shouldn't be a problem. He got past the graveyard without a twinge, but halfway up the next rise, towards Milller's place, hayfield on one side, pasture on the other, he felt the hair on his neck raise. He was sure somebody was followin' him. Maybe one of the boys from over at the 'Cave was behind, tryin' to make him jump or run, though he figured they were too lazy to come this far. He turned and had a good long look. Nobody. The feeling left him as he passed the house and stable, close up on the road, reassuring light in a window, the sounds of pigs grunting when they smelled him pass."

"He kept on walkin'. About a quarter mile up the road was the Union Chapel E.U.B. church and cemetery, but before he could continue the story, he had to digress into some commentary about how at the time this had happened to him as a boy and now, as a grown man, he couldn't much tell you the difference between a Church of the Brethren Christian and an Evangelical United Brethren Christian, but he had, over his lifetime noticed that each to offense if you misspoke and said that they were the other and were right quick to correct your error. Back to walking in the nighttime, the further he got from Miller's place the more the feelin' of being followed came on him. He *knew* that none of his buddies would've walked that far. He remembered the old saying and in fact whistled past the graveyard. Stopped whistling, felt that feeling on his neck, looked all around, saw nothing. Started walking again, still whistling, a quarter mile to the school, he felt it again. Whistle, hell! He began to sing, mostly first bars of hymns, nobody there to line out the full verses for him. Didn't run, but sure marched quick-time 'till he got to the place to crawl over the fence, hair still up on his neck. Just after he got into the pasture he passed some stock, brood cows and their calves, and the feeling eased off. By the time he crossed the fence into the next field and could see a light at home, it was completely gone. He ate the cold supper plate that his mother had left out for him and went to bed."

Next morning his father greeted him to the breakfast table, "miss your train last evenin', boy?"

"Said yes, sir," and told him about his walk home. Father said that he'd bet I was followed and to come with him in the Ford and show him exactly where I'd left the road before the dust got churned up. Didn't take but a few minutes to get there. He stopped short of the post I pointed out and scouted along the road real slow, pausing to lean on his stick and study the marks in the dirt. "Here!" he pointed with his stick. You were bein' followed by somethin' -- a lion, panter, whatever you want to call him. Moved up beside him and looked where he was pointing. Clear in the dust was my footprint, and over it a pug mark as large as the biggest dog's, but without any claw scratches. "Never saw one myself, only heard of one bein' killed here in the east side of the Valley when I was comin' up. Boy, you got a real story to tell your grandkids, one that you can say your daddy proved true, stalked by a panter."

"Gave him a couple of appreciative comments and the man finally let the screen door come closed, said 'goodnight' and went home. Took us three days to kill all the 'skeeters he let in while he was talkin.'"

Earl leaned back so he could see both of his friend's faces at the same time, looking for their reaction. "Good story about a man tellin' one. Literary people and editors probably have a word for doin' that, but I don't know it" was the doc's observation.

"I remember a couple of folks like that back home. Practically had to throw 'em off the place to get on with what you wanted to. Don't know a thing about mountain lions, if they'd come down huntin' like that. Do know that you're right about those double-priced yellow light bulbs, they don't work worth a damn. Gettin' almost dark, let's see how the bees are doin'." Raymond got up and stepped behind the hive where he could look up against the gray of the twilight sky and spot the black dot of any bees dropping down from their flying height to the entrance board. "Not many coming in, but still a few. About the time I think there're aren't any more, one'll drop down. We better wait a few minutes more. How 'bout you, Doc, you have any stories?"

"Well, as you know, I'm a city boy. Could probably remember something from there, but it'd be as long as Earl's, too long for the time we have left. Don't have any war stories of my own, never fired a shot, never got shot at or shelled. Anything I have would be bits of second-hand stuff folks told me-- listenin' to 'em was how I did my work -- and what I've read in reports, trying to know what other people said had gone on before I talked to someone the second or third time about what was givin' them problems. Amazing sometimes, the difference between what things were like for men fifty feet apart in a fight; crazy the difference between what dogfaces told me and what got written up at headquarters, things were always neater, organized, when they hit paper. Then there were the things that men didn't tell me, ashamed or scared to until we got to trust each other, or things they didn't talk about 'cause they couldn't bear to think about them. Lots of times they didn't even realize until later they'd been holdin' out on me. Sometimes I'd know more'n they realized 'n could back 'em into talkin', sometimes they'd just remember and start in themselves, remember for no more'n hearin' a particular sound on their way to see me or seein' some scrap of something on someone else's uniform in the corridor. Smells seemed like real powerful recallers. Had one fellow who'd passed a ward where they were cleanin' up a bunch of guys who'd just come in in real bad shape and there was a tub of uniform pieces and field dressings out in the hallway, the smell got him as he came into my office and he broke down, remembering or for the first time capable of telling me about being wounded, pinned down, waiting for the arrival of a relief column." Raymond moved away, over to where he could watch for returning bees against the sky. It was time to check them again, and Doc Witt, knowing it or not, was getting too close. "The fellows I worried about, still think about, were those who I thought were still struggling when they were shipped out, sent home or back to the line, without having told their full story."

"Nobody flyin' in for as long as I can keep from blinkin'. Time to close 'em up." As he had two days before, Raymond slid the door into place smooth and quick, sweeping the couple of guards on the landing board back into the hive without injury and tapped the two nails deeper into their holes than before so that there was no chance of them working loose. "If you two can help me, we can get 'em on the truck nice and steady, like we did before." Earl and Witt did the lifting and Raymond made sure that things were positioned so that there was no chance of the pinch-dogs being jarred loose, wouldn't have had to be as particular if they'd had staples, but the dogs were designed like bench-dogs so that it didn't take but a tap to loosen them when they'd been holding the end grain of glued-up boards. There were no more stories as they drove back to the main grounds, just a mutual running commentary on ruts, fences, gates, crops, and how well the bees looked to be riding, either glimpsed through the oval glass or viewed full-on by Raymond when he held onto the top of the doorframe and slid his ass up on the sill, head above the roof for a good look. Transfer to the brick pedestal in the bee-yard was smooth and the carpenter and doctor got back into the Dodge's cab, ready to drive off after Raymond flipped the door off to let the bees out and hooked the chain around the gatepost.

Earl didn't kill the engine as he threw in the clutch and stopped in the courtyard. "I'll be watchin' from the back row at picture time tomorrow, you fella's look good!"

"Righto!" they responded and headed in opposite directions to their quarters, both intending to spend more time than polishing their footwear before going to bed. Raymond didn't have much else to do other than lay out a clean shirt and the better of his two railroading caps, a present from his engineer buddy when he'd visited some months before. Witt's quarters were a jumble. He had little in the way of personal property; the odd collection of furniture was the Hospital's, so that he was primarily dealing with clothing and books. He had a footlocker on which he'd stenciled his name, rank, and next unit and duty station, a wooden crate on which he'd stenciled his younger brother's name and address, and a manageable, medium sized leather suitcase laid open and was in the process of sorting things among them in preparation for his departure at the end of the week. Books, mostly, was what he was sorting between footlocker and crate, trying to decide what medical books were useful and which were not, which other books were old friends that he needed to have with him, which were merely acquaintances who could pass a long visit with his brother. Every time he looked at the division he revised it. Raymond, he thought, had a much simpler life with only the one book on bees. Some of the medical books dealt with general medicine, not psychiatry, but he knew from the last war that push come to shove in a forward medical unit, all that mattered was the "MD" after his name and that he'd end up assisting in surgery or holding sick call while the surgeons slept. He'd learned more practical medicine during the war than in school, given his specialty. His one complete uniform was on a hanger on the outside of the wardrobe door, with bits and pieces of others folded in the footlocker. The suitcase had a couple of changes of underwear, his second remaining uniform shirt, his Dopp kit, open so that he had access to razor and toothbrush until his departure, and two bottles of whisky. Thrown on top of the shirt and skivvies was a leather portfolio big enough to hold his orders, a couple of magazines to read on the train, extra smokes, and an artfully slender silver pint flask that had come into his possession during the last war -- all that he had to make sure stayed to hand on his journey.

There was a good deal of bustling around in the courtyard after breakfast in preparation for the Director's mid-morning meeting with the photographers from Richmond and the local papers. Earl had, as usual, set up his work just outside the shop door and had a good view of the porch sweeping and litter collection. For the first time in his memory a crew was washing every ground-floor window within view. Some underling from the Director's office came through to confirm that Raymond was at the shop and available, even went back to say hello and give him the once-over, then scurried off to report that he looked presentable. The photographers arrived about half an hour early and decided that they wanted to shoot from the gate side of the beeyard so that the specks of bees coming and going would be visible against the sky above their subjects' heads and that the morning was far enough along that faces wouldn't be unduly masked by shadow. Having made their professional decisions, they grounded their gear and leaned against the open gate and fence posts for a smoke, laughing among themselves as they talked trade-talk, each brief story trying to top the humor of its predecessor.

About a quarter of, Earl sensed someone approaching and looked up to see Dr. Witt a few steps away, dressed in full Medical Corps uniform, although he was carrying his garrison cap under his arm on top of an unusually neat half-clipboard of papers rather than wearing it.

"'Mornin', Earl. I'll just set the thermos and mugs over in the corner 'till everything's over." Stepping back from doing so, he asked "How's Raymond today?"

"His usual self, said good 'mornin' and went right to work. Didn't say anything or act any different, but did have a sharper lookin' hat than usual -- kinda like you." They both chuckled. "I 'spect it's about time for you to get him over with the bees 'n photographers."

Witt walked back to Raymond's bench where he was curling off shavings with a bock plane, truing the edges of some boards to be glued up, checking the angle after each stroke with a try square, holding it up where he'd just made a cut to see if he'd hit what he wanted, then holding it up again in the length of the next stroke to know which side of the edge to favor or if he could just cut straight. "You're gettin' to be as much of a shavin' carver as Earl! I'd say that's a good thing if you've picked up his eye and hand."

"'Mornin'. No, it's not a bad thing, followin' after him. I sort of think truin' an edge is like sughtin' in a rifle. Go slow and easy, knowin' where each little adjustment's goin' and it's not long before you're there. Just have to consider the edge of a knot or a bit of hard grain like you'd consider windage. Ease against 'em, don't try to force things and jump too far."

"I see. Soldier carpenter rather than homicidal, although bein' so methodical folks could say you were just quietly makin' plans for the deadly move. Ready to dust off your hands and put on your bee-man look for those fellows out there?"

"Sure." Raymond laid the plane down on the bench on its side, dusted his hands against each other, brushed some shavings off of his shirt front, set his cap at exactly the right angle, took up his stick and swung around away from the bench. "I'll follow you, Cap'n." Witt, too, put his garrison cap on at just the right angle for a Medical Corps man. A bit off from regular Army but nowhere nearly as rakish as the former Air Corps officers.

The director was already up at the gate as they came out the door and around the corner. Halfway up the little hill, within easy earshot, he looked their way and threw up his arm in greeting. "I heard about your call-up, Doctor. Quite the transformation!" Dr. Witt's full uniform, dark jacket crossed by a Sam Browne belt balancing neither sword nor sidearm with several bright dabs of ribbon attesting to his former presence and good behavior in the European Theatre *was* quite a change from the threadbare kakhi trousers he'd habitually worn with civillian shirt and tie beneath his unbuttoned and flowing hospital-laundry lab coat. Comparison, should he be standing inspection, would have revealed that habitual polishing over the day's dust had darkened his brown army shoes to near-black, hardly a match for his belts and the leather bits of his cap. "'Mornin', Mr. McCleary! These folks are anxious to hear what you have to say about catching your bees. Anxious, too, to be a few steps further away from them once they have their pictures!" By that point they were close enough for handshakes and perfunctory introductions. "Son, how 'bout you step inside the gate, stand with your free hand on top the box. I'll back up against the hinge-post. Doctor Witt, step over here on the other side of me in front of the gate, just a bit downhill please. Let these men frame their composition on our bee-man and box, we'll cover the distracting lines of the gate. How's that gentlemen, satisfactory?" His question was met with a consensual murmur and clicking of shutters. Nobody there was aware that his father had been in the newspaper business and that childhood recollections of his father's evening, pipe-smoking comments from behind his competitors' upheld sheets about writing and photography had taught him how to draw focus to the subject of the article in a photograph yet still preserve the prominence of any potentially grateful notables present (his father's highest praise for the competition had been "that photographer they've got 'd convince 'em the governor'd been down on a stool with a bucket at the State Fair milkin' contest when he never even bent over low enough to count tits!").

Photos shot, the Director invited the visitors down to the dining hall for coffee. Everyone settled, he asked Raymond to tell what had happened just outside a few days before when the swarm of bees appeared. Raymond, thankful that things were informal enough that he could remain seated and sip coffee (*real* coffee) when his mouth got dry, did so without elaboration or a bee lecture. Someone asked him where he learned about bees – "followin' my Granddaddy around." Someone else asked about his stick – "the war."

The director stood and talked for a few minutes, suggesting that the most interesting part of the story was one that Raymond hadn't, maybe couldn't tell, that he'd been admitted to the hospital in a catatonic state, and that after months of treatment his first words, commands, really, had been to calm the other patients and protect them and the bees. Before asking Dr. Witt to comment on Raymond's treatment and recovery he said it was the most remarkable success he'd observed during his career in administering the State's asylums.

As he stood to speak, Doctor Farley Witt wished his coffee had come from the Thermos in the carpenters' shop, just as he had when speaking at mooring report the day after Raymond hived the swarm. As he'd said then, he claimed no successful medical intervention, gave credit to all of the everyday staff members who'd made Raymond feel safe enough to speak out. He made no mention of the disguised whisky ration that helped with Raymond's physical pain, no mention of the absurdities that had baited Raymond to interact with Earl Ralston, the carpenter with a red toolbox on a child's wagon. As the Director clearly desired, he let the reporters believe that there'd been what they'd no doubt write up as a miracle cure, chalking up score for the system. He did not voice his personal reservations, that yes, Raymond was markedly better, but that he was only well enough to function as he was, where he was, that he was not yet a well man, nor likely to ever be. What amazed Witt was Raymond's capacity for coping, transitioning from the cocoon of the Army hospital to the farm; from the farm to Bill's oil business; from family to Mrs. Russ' rooming house; to Sarah's; and as things got worse from Sarah and Bill to Frank Hess and the chicken barn, all the while avoiding total disaster. Despite the whisky and presence of the Nitro Hunter, he was alive, and had transitioned into the odd sort of confinement occasioned by his unorthodox arrival at the hospital. He had allowed himself to be coaxed into the social interactions of drink, tobacco, productive work and return to a farmer's pseudo-recreational passion. He was speaking, but the rest of his illness was still there, waking screaming in the night able to go back to sleep only after drinking the laudanum his aides put by his bedside each evening. He was watchful in the ordered, familiar confines of his room and the carpenters' shop, but hyper-vigilant elsewhere, sat with his back to the wall where he could see who entered the room, and kept his hand on or near his country walking-stick, cut to serve equally well as a support or weapon. Leave him alone when his immediate task was finished and his gaze was to the front, at no discernable object or distance, the muscle groups necessary to launch him into attack from any given posture primed and ready beneath a veneer of lassitude.

65. DOCTOR WITT'S LAST EFFORTS AND DE-PARTURE

Farley Witt wondered how long things could hold together for Raymond after his own departure, given that he had been the organizer of much of the interaction that had broken the spell. How would he deal with the pain in his bones without the extra whisky concealed in a thermos? How long before Sarah and Mrs. Hess tired of the ongoing charity of tending his clothes? Sarah had been sending things with others for some time now, not from lack of interest, he thought, but because of the pain each encounter brought her. How long before Bill Riley assuaged his guilt for having underpaid Raymond, became sporadic and then stopped his deliveries of liquor and cigarettes? Raymond's family, far away and with others at home to care for were now out of the picture but for an occasional letter. His parents were still alive, and there simply wasn't a place for a third person on the porch. Witt's file on Raymond was the largest in his drawer. He'd leave a recommendation that whisky and laudanum be generously prescribed, but had no assurance that his successor would have any understanding of war wounds, mental or physical. Whoever got the case might even turn out to be some sort of temperance man cast up on the strange shore of a system that, despite what was beginning to show up in the medical journals, medicines that acted on the mind, had nothing but purgatives, aspirin, opiates, penicillin (on rare occasions) and alcohol on the approved formulary list. Having given his little talk and shaken hands with the departing director and started to walk back to the carpenters' shop with Raymond, Witt was surprised at how quickly these thoughts rolled through his mind -- he must have been thinking them in bits and pieces and they'd pulled together as he carefully kept them out of the words he'd spoken to the press.

All three carpenters had seen them coming and had started their smoke break at the edge of the week's heap of crates, lamenting how many of them were now made with cheap-assed, already delaminating and useless plywood. Raymond found a seat and pulled out his Luckies, Witt pulled up a box between them to hold his cap, upside down on the clipboard and their mugs. "Brought an extra, if anyone wants to join us." George allowed that as there might be few remaining opportunities that he would. The Captain poured, then tended to his own smoke. "Heard the last bit about plywood crates as we were comin' in."

George put his mug down, licked his lips and then wiped the moisture on the back of his hand. "Yep, the change is gonna' cut us short of a good bit of material for little jobs, cut us short of firewood come winter, and make it harder to be accommodating, next fellow like Raymond comes hangin' around."

Earl scratched his head with one hand and further revealed his carefully suppressed talent, refilling his pipe with the other, none of the fumbling that had filled the silence early on with Raymond. "Reckon I've been around here longer'n any of you -- too long -- and it seems to me that the folks in the purchasing office in Richmond need some education. Make us keep a shop ledger in the same way that somebody required before the War, study it like schoolmasters whenever they're here to look for a pound of missing nails, but don't consider having requirements for shipping that would help us. Henry Ford did it. The battery manufacturers couldn't quite figure why he gave them specific dimensions and wood grades for packing crates other than the fact that the space they filled with sawdust mimized shipping damage. Took a while," he laughed, "for word to get back to them from folks that their trade names were prominently displayed on the bottoms of Ford floorboards!"

Everyone had a chuckle over the sly old bastard's ways, with a few more stories of his schemes passed around. "You're too hard on Richmond," George interjected. State got back on its feet after the War, so did the Tredegar Iron Works. Difference is it took until the 1918 war for Tredegar to change from keeping their official books in pounds, shillings, and pence. Our men in Richmond were really quite progressive, accepting central banking controls and the use of greenback dollars even before the Yankees got tired of keeping occupation troops on the streets. Oliver, I bet you wouldn't gripe about the quality of plywood if they sent you the scraps from the Brit's Mosquito airplane factory. Only problem you'd have with 'em would be that most of 'em'd be curved! That wouldn't bother the Brits though; they've been framing houses with ship's ribs for generations. Changing subjects, Raymond, how'd this mornin' strike you?"

"Not a big deal. Top dog got everyone lined up like he wanted, shook some hands and got his picture. Nobody gave a damn about the bees -- they were just an excuse. Suited me alright 'cause I didn't have to say much, nothin' people in the dining room hadn't already asked me."

"That's the way it looked to me, too. Give me a newspaper with my picture in it to show my new C.O. -- that won't hurt any. Kinda sad, but I don't think that any of 'em thought anything more about you than they did the bees. The Boss said it was the best thing he'd ever seen, that was good enough for them. None of 'em had any questions about how you got here, just figured you were war-crazy after being told you were a soldier. War-crazy's something the Army, the papers, and the medical profession don't like anybody talking about any more'n they want talk about men so blown apart and burned that they're gona' live out their days in unseen back wards of the biggest, most shown off Veteran's hospitals." Raymond looked down into his mug and shivered, thinking of the tankers during the pause Doc Witt took for a full swallow from his mug. "Those guys are gonna' use the word 'catatonic' in their copy 'cause I said it without knowing the difference between the medical term and the proper name for an Indian Ceegar tree." The carpenters knew the name and murmured their agreement, drifting off back to their work. "How do you think you're going to get through the day with your leg pain when my Thermos and I ship out?"

"Be alright. Climbed up and down off of the truck all day without it, leg isn't near as much trouble leanin' against a bench here. A person gets so they tolerate more pain than most folks think they could. Almost becomes a friend, a point of attention keeping your mind from going where it shouldn't. I'll miss the companionship of our frequent coffees, but don't think that not having the liquor'll make much difference."

God, what endurance this man has! Witt thought to himself, endurance and insight up to the point where everything shuts down. "Raymond, I know what you mean, except its usually old folks accepting what comes when it does rather than a man your age."

Raymond responded a bit sharply. "There are thousands of men my age, hurt the same way I was, just gettin' on with their lives, working, not complainin'. Some do a bit more drinkin' than before, but you just get used to the way things are, as far as pain goes."

"Agreed. Harder, though, to deal with what's inside, the nightmares and what keeps you tight and staring into the distance when you're not immediately occupied. Probably had you craning your neck to study every rock face on either side of the road past Ramsey's Draft when you drove to Highland and back for Bill Riley."

Neither man said a thing for a long time, both of them sitting and smoking beside each other, elbows on their knees, chins on their hands, staring into a middle distance -- someplace through the walls about halfway into the dining hall and kitchen.

"You realize," Farley Witt said as softly as he could, "that I've known how things went for your unit since the second week you were here. The papers at the time had one splash about the climbing, said you linked up with the rest of your unit, and then went on with all of the positive invasion news. Nothing in print about being pinned down. A couple of telephone calls to people I know and I got the full account. My guess is that's the story you had to tell the birds. Told it over and over, probably louder and more dramatically each time but, since hens don't talk, got no response. You couldn't help thinking about it except in your few hours of sleep when the nightmares of the ladders hadn't yet come. Eventually you got stuck there, standing watch on your part of the line, suppressing your pain and everything else, just like you had to for those days."

Raymond said nothing.

"The one thing I can't understand is why you never told anyone about it."

"Lots of things I never told anybody about. Came home and everyone had their minds full of the newsreel and newspaper version of the invasion. Knew of the climbers. Had their own images of hospital stays and broken bones. Young people hadn't any under-standing of pain or of a stick beyond something a fel-low needed to lean on. The old people figured that since I hadn't come home dead or missing a leg that I just had limitations like theirs, only with youthful strength to help me cope. It was easier for everyone if I just went along with their version of the story of my war. I couldn't see any advantage in correcting a picture that they thought was pretty bad, but that they could live with, by filling it out with details I didn't want to think about myself. My family welcomed me home and gave me time to figure where I fit in. I reckon if I'd wanted to I could've claimed Granddaddy's chair in the kitchen and on the porch. Didn't want to. I was lucky who I fell in with up here in the valley, good people who gave me work and a place among 'em as long as I could keep up. I couldn't and they got me here to the Hospital, didn't forget me even then. Y'all here helped me find a place inside that's bettern' most fellows'd have. Right now it's working for me, a safe place after I broke down under the best that could be found outside. Dictionary mean-ing of 'asylum' without the words 'Western Lunatic' in front."

It was Witt's turn to sit for a moment, not saying anything. He could understand a soldier not discussing his experiences because the memory was painful or disturbing. He'd never considered the fact that a man's family constructed a version of events based on limited information; the closest analogies they could construct based on their experiences; a conviction that morphine, corpsmen and doctors, ambulances and field hospitals were plentiful; and that the suffering of their loved one would be kept to a minimum. Not wanting to disturb those perceptions could, he understood, keep a man silent. He could also appreciate the outright inconvenience of working to disabuse folks of their more-comfortable-than-reality beliefs.

"It's maddening, too, that I was only in the fight for four days. Four days and I'm like this! Lots of fellows fought for years and they came home normal."

"Four days, perhaps, but the first forty minutes were extraordinary. At least your nightmares forced truth about them into the version of anyone close to you. Nobody came home the same as before. Some just have everything packed down deeper, festering, changing their behavior in more subtle ways than screaming in their sleep without waking up, which inevitably leads to some truths of the experience being told."

"I don't mind being gimpy, we all come to that eventually -- I just got old quick. At least I came home with both legs, lots came home with less or worse." Raymond thought, but said nothing about the burned tankers. "If I tried to talk, tell the story, walking with a stick is what people would understand. They'd just take me for a complainer, ungrateful for having got off so easy. Yeah, I got off easy. Patch it together good enough to save it, then come home to have it re-broken and cut apart and put back together a little neater. Two years of hospital wards, dope enough to keep me from waking everyone else up at night. I kept looking for a Ranger patch to talk to, but gowns, pajamas and hospital robes don't have any of that, unit insignia, you just have to listen and try to pick up where a fellow's form. I can probably talk to you some before you head out, I'd like that, but no disrespect intended, even you can't understand everything -- you were never on the line. I wish Granddaddy was still alive, he'd understand."

"No offense taken. My war was spent in field hospitals, a bit of shelling here and there, but no fighting. I did listen to a lot of men, though. Enough that my nights would be easier if I didn't remember the things they told me and the things that after a while I began to realize were just across the line from what they were willing to say. I was trained as a psychiatrist, but it took being behind a few battles to become an Army doc. Anybody who got sent to me'd experienced way too much war, so much that they stood out in their units or on the wards where other wounds were being attended to. 'Too much war' isn't a competitive sport -- what brought each man to me was sufficient for him, didn't matter where it fit in with everything else I'd heard, didn't matter how long he'd been fighting. If you can spare the time from your work, how 'bout telling me what you told the chickens?"

"Pretty good stock of boxes in the back; don't think Earl and the others'd mind my taking time to talk. This bein' a hospital," he laughed, "I reckon doctors, even if they are about to leave, rank carpenters." Raymond went into his story, talking until dinnertime, then for most of the afternoon. Doc Witt, he just listened.

"Other than the climbing, I've heard other men describe similar things, had men come close but not quite bring themselves to. Tell me the story a couple of more times before I leave. I think listening is about the best that I can do to help. Actually a good thing that I'm leaving. Makes me safe for you to talk to. Since you know you'll not be around me in the foreseeable future, maybe never again, you can let yourself say things about how you feel or felt that might make you uncomfortable if it was a sure thing we'd have our regular routine next week. Be like writing a letter making amends to a friend who's passed, then ceremonially burning it -- modern society's adaptation of ancient rituals."

Raymond was worn out and edgy after their log talk, had just enough time to clear his workbench and put his tools up before the bell rang for supper. He was polite to his table-mates but ate fast, his mind going back to bits of conversation with the doc whenever it wasn't kept in the present by a need to pass the potatoes. More vigilant than usual as he crossed the dining room to leave, conscious of the increasing number of unseen people behind his back with each step towards the door and conscious of his relief as he closed the door behind him and stepped off of the porch into the courtyard, where he'd hear the scuff of anyone's feet behind him. He set his cap at just the right angle and walked up to the bee yard. It was still early enough that they were flyin' pretty good, so he eased himself down onto the grass in the fence corner, leaned his back on the post, stretched his leg out to where it didn't hurt him, and just watched them come and go. Sittin' like that had been one of his Granddaddy's pleasures, a little hard for Raymond to tolerate when he was an active little boy but determined to stick with the old man. He now understood why his Grandfather had liked watch-

ing the bees going peacefully about their business. The regularity of arrival and departure was like the heartbeat or respiration of the colony, observation of the direction they took once they'd gained a little altitude and any pollen load they might carry on return gave evidence of where they were working and what was happening inside the hive -- more pollen meant more new eggs being laid, an absence of pollen a strong honey flow from a nectar crop. He chuckled to himself, thinking that only a bee-man could see a field or fencerow infested with thistle as a strong crop. Watching the bees didn't strain a man, but demanded enough attention that you couldn't worry about something else at the same time. Secure with his back up against a post, like a hound on the porch, he began to relax a little, focusing his thoughts on each bee as it came and went, watching the guard bees greet each returnee. Granddaddy's told him that the guard bees weren't as vigilant as you might think, that they'd let any bee with a load pass. Proved his point by slowin' down or stopping to point at any row of bee boxes they might see. One end box, sometimes both, would always be taller by at least one super. A bee tired from the heat or a day's flyin' would be tempted to land on the first front porch rather than flyin' down the row to home, and those guard bees'd hustle 'im right indoors if he had a full load, even if she didn't smell quite right. 'Till she jostled around unloading, she'd
Smell enough like the hive that nobody'd say anything when she came out again. Granddaddy said lots of those moves ended up to be permanent -- that's why it was important to think about where food and water were when you set out your boxes; if you wanted to be sure that they all did well. It'd been a long day, the Superintendent's show, then talking to Doc Witt. The Doc had been good about just letting him talk as it came out, didn't ask questions or interrupt to try to prove what he

understood or let on that he had anything in his past that
he could use for comparison. That'd made it easier, but
he was worn out. Worn out, but pleased with himself
that he'd got through it in a quiet voice without raging
or crying the way he had the last times he talked to the
birds as he did his work. Just as it was getting dark he
saw a commotion at one side of the entrance board,
three or four house bees dragging a weakly struggling
bee, either injured or dying, to the edge and tipping her
over the edge into the tall grass below to perish in the
night's chill and damp. No tolerance in their unit for
those who couldn't give a hundred percent.

As Raymond started to get up, he realized that
the chill and damp had stiffened him into his comfortable position. He braced his stick against the woven wire
fence where he could reach it when he got up, then
pulled himself up the way he'd been taught to use ladders and cargo nets, grasping the vertical wires, bracing
his fists against their union with the horizontal. The effort got him erect in a wallowing sort of way. He hadn't
considered that unlike rope ladders and cargo nets,
fencing isn't anchored above, but instead stretched lat-
erally, and the fencing crew hadn't seen much purpose
to leaning into their work on such a small enclosure
where the proximity of the posts would minimize the
droop of the weave and a single well-stretched strand of
barb above would discourage any curious stock from
necking things down. He stood, grabbed his stick and
paused for a minute to get his legs under him, and
headed off for his room. Once there, he locked the outer
door, poured and sipped on a glass of whisky as he attended to his boots; decided that the clothes he'd put on
for the photograph and hardy worked in the rest of the
day were good enough for the next day; laid them out
on and over the chair; swished the last of the whisky

through his teeth in lieu of brushing; and collapsed onto the bed in his skivvies, stick in hand.

Farley Witt carefully brushed and re-hung his uniform and located a clean lab coat in order to present a properly physician appearance to the new man, his as yet un- met replacement, that was to accompany him on ward rounds the next morning. It was Witt's plan to give him the clipboard and leave him to his own devices and the staff's care in the afternoon, which he planned to spend with Raymond. God, he wished the man had found his tongue sooner!

Witt's packing was becoming simplified to the extent that he was shopping for filler for the footlocker. It's book collection slimmed to what he actually remembered from the last war; a medium-sized dictionary, because every medical officer had anatomy books and none ever had a dictionary against which to check one's memory if a good crossword appeared; Ambrose Bierce's Devil's Dictionary to put things into perspective; a King James edition of the Bible, full of slips of paper marking all the usual soldiering stuff men had been preached on and which stuck in their minds and passages he'd been told by chaplains and soldiers to check as justification for either side of 'most any position; The Virginian, for when he needed a few moments escape into a world of clearly marked boundaries; two different translations of the Tao te Ching, neither of which was comprehensible by itself but when read side by side, compared and argued with himself, occasionally led to some helpful insight; and, finally, a pocket-sized, leather-bound and gilt-edged, turn-of-the-century engineering reference of which he hadn't the slightest idea of how it had come into his possession. Brief forays into the arcana of survey and load-bearing calculations provided absolute escape from psychiatry. Any of the books could be opened at random for a page or two of diversion. He'd gotten a couple of flashlights with spare bulbs and batteries. Two bottles of his favorite were swaddled in extra long underwear and socks -- supply could always provide shirts and trousers, but warmth needed by men on the line cost dearly one echelon back. He had room for extra, which cushioned his booze and would be a start in bartering for whatever else turned out to be scarce once he reached the field.

Going to bed, Farley Witt's mind was filled with ideas about his patient rather than questions about what he might face in the command to which his orders assigned him. He could delay his departure for just a couple of days. What could he accomplish in that time that might help Raymond but not hurt him when their interaction ceased? He'd never developed much rapport with any of the other physicians on staff. None of the other physicians even extended as much as the courtesy of a 'good morning' to the carpenters, the only staff beyond Rafe and Sam that Raymond trusted. It was likely that the other docs knew Rafe as a reliable and resourceful aide, but impossible to believe that they appreciated his depth of loyalty to Raymond or the role that he'd played in his treatment thus far. It was unlikely that his successor would build on these assets. Institutional inertia and Raymond's continuing nightmares and screams would probably keep him in his present room. The whole shop of carpenters would raise hell and probably stage a covert work slowdown if anyone tried to take their coffin man away, and Raymond was still a celebrity, the bee-man, so that he'd most likely remain secure at the Hospital, but he was unlikely to ever leave. He'd talk less, his hyper-vigilance would become more entrenched, and he'd continue to become more and more used to others doing the little things a man does for himself, like waiting for the dinner bell rather than thinking of what he might eat -- in a lot of respects like the old-man privates and sergeants who made the army their home, 'sojurin' ' as long as possible, finding that life's restrictions in some areas and unfettered range of tolerated behavior in others preferable to civillian life. Witt's conclusion just before falling asleep was to try and keep the man talking and remain as silent as possible, resisting the urge to question, make comparisons, and draw analogies. His role, he decided, was to keep the wound draining so long as he was there.

Doctor Witt met Doctor Jacob Hershberger at the next morning's medical briefing. As he expected, he was younger, newly qualified. Drawn to the Hospital job because it allowed him to maintain his family connections in the area, which, unknown to Witt, included kinship to Frank Hess' wife, Mary Frances. No military background. "Mostly they call me Jake;" he introduced himself after someone muttered to him and pointed Witt out as the man to pair up with.

"Farley Witt. Spent enough time in the Army that I jump when somebody hollers 'Witt!', either name or both suits me fine for conversation. Awfully glad to see you here. As you can imagine, lots more patients than docs. Would've been hard on my people if they hadn't found you right after I got called back up. The number of aides was way down when I came -- they'd just released the CO's then, but the place is pretty much up to where it should be on staff now that hiring's kinda' leveled off everywhere." They got their coffee, found seats, and listened to the morning report which included Dr. Harshbarger's introduction, met by quiet but genuine applause. "Come on with me," Witt got up started a step motioning with his clipboard for Dr. Jake to follow, "and I'll introduce you around your wards."

"What's the biggest part of ward work?"

"You've got to pay attention to what's going on, then it's mostly people management, try to prevent conflicts from developing, notice when some little thing makes people happier or function better and try to incorporate it into their treatment orders. There's a good deal of general medicine, even for us. A combination of preventive medicine, a keen eye for untreated conditions -- sick call conducted by charade -- and an awareness of how deterioration in condition, mental or physical, affects a patient's ability to cope with unnatural surroundings. Don't usually spend a lot of time with each patient, but you've got to keep an eye on everyone, know how they're getting along. When you step onto a ward, take a moment to scan the whole place even before talking to staff. You can pick out individuals who might need attention through some change in how folks are paired off, if there's an unusually animated conversation, that sort of thing"

"I know exactly what you mean. I came up on a farm and it's the same with livestock. Feeding time, stop at the gate and look the herd over before putting out the feed, you'll see who's standing back, who's buttin' at someone else, or who's limping, which you wouldn't see once they all had their heads in the trough."

"You got it. The saying amongst the more articulate old-timers here is 'don't cause anybody any trouble.' If everyone on a ward, or sharing sleeping quarters is functioning at about the same level, there're less likely to fuss or take advantage of each other. Sadly, so few people get well that it's a matter of figuring out why somebody's stirred up and trying to calm them down or get them extra staff attention so that things don't escalate. A lot of patients won't think to tell you or staff things like if there's a hole in their sock strangling a toe or a thin sole on their shoe with something sharp stuck and poking through. Just noticing that someone's walking different can prevent a festering wound; noticing that they're carrying themselves different can indicate a need for a different, less strenuous work assignment for a week." Witt chuckled. "You'll have to decide for yourself whether you're lucky or not. You're taking my place and since I was the last new man I was given the most wards. Good thing is that they can be run with the kind of social management we've been talking about. Bad thing is that so many people are involved that you don't have much time in your office. Odd thing, there's kind of a reverse hierarchy around here. The senior docs take pride in being in charge of a 'difficult' ward - - violent men are tops -- incontinent and idiot further down. The wards I'm showing you don't have much status, just require more time because of the number of patients. Truth is, staff does the heavy lifting on any ward, even the difficult ones, and the senior docs only get called out of their offices when there's a crisis. Give a couple of orders, calm things down and give a positive report at the next mooring's meeting. At home in their offices those fellows read the papers, make a few phone calls and write the occasional letter to maintain themselves politically both within the Hospital and in Richmond. Probably drink a little whisky, too, once they've hung the lab coat on the back of the door to keep the newsprint off their cuffs."

Doctor Jake didn't say anything one way or the other about Witt's view of medical seniority. After the farming comment, he just followed along as they walked through each ward, listening. He had a lot to absorb, what with staff introductions and Witt's commentary on each patient as soon as they'd passed out of earshot of each person or group of patients.

"I've saved the best for last -- a fellow, unusual combat experiences, leg shot up pretty badly. Brought in paranoid, catatonic, mute. Got a little toehold visiting with him with a thermos of whisky disguised as coffee -- he'd been drinkin' real heavy to cope with pain and the nightmares. Pushed him, with the help of the lead carpenter telling absurd stories and explaining each minute step of his work, to spend his days around their shop. You probably saw his picture with the Superintendent in the paper -- a swarm of honeybees settling in the courtyard jarred him into speaking. Still not a well man though. The business that gives him his nightmares and led to his catatonia is still unfinished. I'm trying to spend as much time with him as I can before I leave to see if he can make a start on that." They'd reached the carpenters shop by then, and Witt looked out of the corner of his eye to gauge Harshbarger's reaction to the bright-red toolbox and wagon as he introduced Earl. Just like everything else all through the morning, he didn't say anything, but Witt saw a twinkle in his eye when he spied the wagon. Maybe Doctor Jake'd get along with the carpenters -- it would certainly be to Raymond's advantage if he could. They started threading their way back to Raymond's bench, nodding and throwing up a hand when George and Oliver glanced their way. "I can't stress enough how crucial these non-medical men have been in Raymond's progress. They understood how much woodworking skill he had from growing up on a farm, realized how bored he was just sittin' and staring. They used their smoke breaks to cozy up to him. Thought I was going to have to go to bat for 'em with the maintenance supervisor they were taking so many breaks, but there never was any complaint. I reckon the work got done and I was with 'em as often as I could get over here. Even though he wasn't sayin' a word in response to anything, they suggested to him that he build a little nightstand to make his quarters – Rafe Bell'll tell you about where he lives and why. He built it without much assistance and the day after he finished it showed up with drawings and an accurately computed bill of materials to build the base, boxes and innards of a beehive. When he came here the friends who brought him in told us that he'd often spoke of his Granddaddy, who had been in the War and did the old man's jobs of looking after the bees and chickens on the farm. Turns out his prized possession is a bee-book thicken a bible. Made one of the drawers in his night- stand just to fit it. I signed the shop-book to authorize the materials he couldn't salvage from crates and he spent months last winter doing precision work with the second-or third-best tools the carpenters pulled together for him to use. They rode him as hard as any apprentice who could have talked back to 'em, an act of respect that I'm sure helped him along. Their favorite trick was salting his toolbox with tools never seen on a farm, usually with some important part removed." They reached Raymond's bench and introductions were made. Almost immediately Witt made his manners that he had to get Doctor Jake to the dining room before the dinner bell, to meet people. They left, winding their way across the shop. "Raymond's assigned to work with the carpenters. Mostly works by himself building coffins, all different sizes to have a good inventory. It's more common here at the Hospital to sign the shop-book for one o' them than to sign a purchase order for a train or bus ticket home." As he'd planned, Farley Witt used just enough flattery during dinner introductions to get Dr. Harshbarger into someone else's care for the afternoon. After going to his office to collect the coffee Thermos and a couple of mugs, he headed for the carpenters shop.

Raymond was gluing up the boards whose edges he'd been truing the day before, the pleasant pile of shavings that had been on his bench replaced with a spread of old newspapers and the simmering glue pot. "'Afternoon, Doctor. Let me get a couple of clamps on here to draw things in where my eye wasn't so good."

Witt made he comfortable sitting on an adjacent bench, feet dangling, and poured himself a splash while he watched Raymond working the clamps to make an even seam, scraping away the already congealing glue that was forced out of the joint. "Damn sight easier to get it off now than when it's hard. If I was workin' in a real coffin shop they'd spring for better timber and the only gluin' would be the joints to pinch the toes just right." He wiped his hands on a rag, turned down the heat on the glue pot, grabbed his stick and swung over to join the doctor. "Shortage of clamps makes a day with a lot of breaks. Glad you're here."

"Thought any more about what you were talking to me about yesterday?" He poured Raymond's mug about two-thirds full.

"Yes, sir. Probably haven't thought about much else. Went up and just watched the bees fly until dark last evening to calm myself down, think about them and what they were doing instead. Like you found out and I told you yesterday, the facts from back then are pretty clear. It's just that the facts fit different with different people and how I feel about that. Told you yesterday I let people believe how they think it went for me 'cause it was easier for them, but every time I did that, down inside I felt like a liar. Every time let them off easy, letting them think that my hospital time was as simple and painless as they wanted to imagine, I felt like a liar. Felt like a liar, but felt like I'd be asking for sympathy when lots of men suffered worse'n me if I told 'em. Part of me really wanted to explain, wanted some sympathy, but more of me didn't want to be a hypocrite or soft, so I just swallowed the lies that fit their imaginary stories. Those kind of mixed up feelings about yourself, about lyin' by not saying something and about both wanting some understanding and sympathy and not wantin' to seem like a complainer are hard to handle, 'cause they're all real and you can't bring yourself to tell 'em to anyone. I didn't even explain that to Sarah."

"Some folks ask you honest and want to know what it feels like to take a round in the leg. They're as sympathetic as they can be, some of 'em, the hunters or men who've butchered livestock even have some notion of what the impact of a bullet on flesh and bone looks like, but then they move on into their mind's comfortable movie version of how brave medics with unlimited morphine process you rearward into hospitals full of good-lookin' nurses with plenty of time to sit on the foot of your bed and chat. They're good folks, but you know you'd be pushin' 'em beyond their limit to tell them what really happened, so you lie by sayin' nothin, act pleasant and grateful that they asked, which isn't too hard at first because you really are grateful, but it gets harder as you go about your day thinkin' about the truth because you've crammed your head and guts full of courteous lies. How many folks want you to tell them it hurt like hell after each surgery, that there were never enough nurses to get around with more morphine in time before the last shot wore off, that I'd be talking out of my head or that they learned it'd worn off because I was screaming in my sleep and they heard it down the hall at the nurses' desk? Me and whole wards of guys. Safe back in England, safe just up the road at Woodrow Wilson with a nurse who just shot you up with dope cradling your head and shoulders, rocking and whispering 'Hang on buddy, hang on, it'll hit, it'll hit,' until it does and she feels you ease off. That's a senior nurse, sent as far back in the system as possible for a break from seeing and doing what she's had to. A nurse just out of training, there for a bit of experience before being sent forward might do the same if she's had her eyes and ears open. If not, there'd be a clattering of things easily carried in one hand on an enameled tray and 'there, that's done, you'll feel better soon.' Not her fault, really, too new to know. A damn lonely place." Raymond didn't say anything more, Witt gave him the chance by shaking out and lighting a smoke for each of them, but he remained silent. When he'd field-stripped his butt and crumbled it cold between his fingers, safe for the floor's sawdust he threw his weight onto his stick, pivoted to his bench, and started readying the next pair of boards for gluing, his back to the Doctor.

Farley Witt spoke softly, choosing his words carefully. He didn't have much more time with this man and couldn't afford the luxury of rambling around, voicing his thoughts until they coalesced into something even remotely useful. "I understand how it's easier, more considerate and practically a necessity for you to allow folks their mind-movie version of what's happened to you if you want to be able to deal with them. I think that you're right in figuring that knowing that you're telling lies of omission can't help but back up, filling, as you say, your mind and your gut. I'm amazed that you held out as long as you did."

"There's more. I feel like I let my buddies down by not fighting out the war with them. They never had a break, had to have had more points than 'most anybody else when they set the order of shipping home. My war was some training on the cliffs in England, one climb, and three days of laying in a hole shot up, hungry, thirsty and scared shitless. We were trained to fight hungry if we had to, thirst was worse. I'm lucky, I'm sure that a lot of 'em got hurt real bad or didn't make it, but for them, after a couple of more fights I might as well have been dead. Faced with what they had later, it couldn't have taken long to forget the guy they collected magazines from as they rushed by, forget the names of the wounded guys making a weak spot in the line. Maybe it's not guilt. Maybe I feel like circumstances robbed me of anything better with them to remember. I got a mind-movie newsreel, too. That's all there is to it, and it keeps going and going like it's been spliced into a loop, falling off of one sprocket of the projector onto the floor, then sucked up by the other, so short that it can't tangle and break."

Witt slid down from his perch and eased up beside Raymond, reaching out to steady the next pair of boards as Raymond began to smooth glue from the simmering pot onto their mating faces. "I talked with lot of men who fought right through the war. Hardly a one who wasn't still dealing with some recent crisis didn't remember and speak of the first time he faced the enemy. If we were lucky enough to get out of talking about the preset, most of those fellows remembered, often naming those who overcame their fear and moved out first. My recollection is that you and the sapper were out front after that machine gun. Apparently the habit of moving out first formed quickly, more like an instinct; too many of those conversations ended with my man shaking his head and reciting where the other had died. Your type was variously described as 'crazy as hell,' 'movin' like a fox,' 'bravest man I ever saw,' or 'a real soldier.' I believe that you'll be remembered by those who survived the climb and then survived the war. Given what the first four days were like, you may be fortunate to have been spared your unit's cumulative memories." Witt helped scrape the excess glue from the boards while they were still in the clamps, and then tidy the bench for the end of the day.

Raymond put his cap on at just the right angle and took up his stick. "Come up to the bee yard right after supper, while they're mostly still flying and I'll show you something special, something my Granddaddy showed me when I was real little."

Witt found himself following just a few yards behind Raymond as he headed up the incline to the bee-yard. As he expected, Raymond sensed his approach, turned and called out a greeting. As he came through the gate, Raymond motioned for him to stand to one side against the fence. "I'm gonna' show you what my Granddaddy called 'the golden chains.' Just put an emp-ty box on these ladies, so I'm sure that they're busy building comb in the frames. They produce tiny flakes of wax from a gland in their abdomen, combine them into workable amounts by hanging in long living chains, each bee combining her flake with what's been passed to her, chewing it to a workable consistency be-fore passing it along, eventually to reach the house-bees who butt it into the proper cell dimension with their heads. 'Most everybody's either busy building or still out foraging, you just ease over here to look when I tell you and you won't have trouble with anyone." Raymond slowly raised the outer cover so as to allow any bees underneath time to move to safety. He used the big blade of his pocket-knife to loosen the inner cover, partially sealed with propolis, and eased it up and off in the same way, putting both down on the grass without stirring up the guard bees by bumping against the hive. "I'll just pull this outside frame to give us some lookin' room -- the outsides are always the last place they work." He used the tip of his blade to raise one end of the frame from its rest high enough to grasp with his fingers, eased it out and laid it on top of the covers. He saw that nobody was working on the next frame, so he took it out as well. With his knife point he pried each end of the next frame's top bar just enough to break any stickiness on the rests, then inserted the blade between it and its inboard neighbor and twisted with his wrist, the blade levering the frames far enough apart for him to pinch the top bar at each end and lift. "Ease up and look over my shoulder." As Witt stepped forward Raymond slowly raised the frame, never lifting it entirely free of the box. They could see four distinct chains, one bee thick and glistening as they moved hanging down from the start of new comb following the line of church-candle wax that he'd run along the bottom of the top bar with a tin snuff can that he'd pinched far enough out of round that he could pour smooth line rather than dripping. The chains of bees had originally only hung the full fingers-of-a-hand span between the top and bottom bars of the frame, but as Raymond eased the frame upward and towards himself in the gap the bees standing further down the face of the comb below who'd been contributing their crumbs of wax to the job grabbed onto the worker being pulled out of reach and the chains grew, swaging across the gap where the other frames had been removed, fully twice as long as when Witt first spied them. "Show's over. Gotta put 'em back now." Witt marveled at how Raymond had judged just how far he could pull to make the chains longer without breaking, that he'd done it without stirring up anyone to fly out and sting, and at how he undid the trick, easing the frame that he held back into place at a rate which allowed each bottom bee to step back onto the comb below without interrupting the flow of wax flakes up the chain or causing anyone to fall out of line. Witt stepped back to the fence as Raymond snapped his knife shut and slid it into his pocket, then replaced the hive-covers and gestured with his stick to usher his friend through the gate. He'd handled the covers casually, beyond glancing at them to keep his hand from hitting a stray bee and not striking a corner against the hive, but the last half-inch of lowering them into place was a controlled motion, slow enough to allow any bees on the edges to step aside. Judging from the lack of any appearance of concentration in Raymond's expression, Witt concluded that the subtlety was habitual, having returned with the work.

"Let's stop for a smoke on the bench by your doorway -- comfortable to lean against the wall there, and the shops closed up tight."

"Okay by me." They got settled, lit up and relaxed against the wall, Raymond's cap pushed back and his stick across his lap. The doc's sleeves were rolled up and he'd pulled his right heel up onto the bench, cigarette-hand dinging over his knee.

"'Golden chains.' I guess your Granddaddy got the name right! An impressive piece of beemanship -- if that's what you call it."

"I reckon that'll do. It's knowing what's happening in that box and the best time to move in slow and easy to showboat. 'Bout the best way goin' to make a boy want to grow up a bee-man. Worked on me."

"Might have done for me, too. If Sherlock Holmes could retire and keep bees, no reason an Army shrink couldn't do it after his second war."

"You told me that your orders are for Ord. I know that was the biggest basic training base on the West Coast. Any idea where you'll go from there?"

"Given that the reserve unit they stuck me in was too heavy with psychiatrists for basic training sick-call, I imagine that unless I politic to stay at Ord or annoy someone so badly that I get assigned to screen folks trying to fake a nut-job discharge, I'll get shipped to a division hospital, then either be kept there or sent down to a brigade or lower. That's how it was last time, they spread us out where we were needed, moved us around as units got to stand down and tend to their people. Don't know that I agreed with their logic in waiting until then to send me to a unit. I think that I should have been further forward, at a mobile hospital that got moved enough to merit the name or even at an aid station. Seemed to me that I did better talking with soldiers who'd brought a buddy in and were determined to stay until they knew how things were going. That far forward I had enough gore on my coat from helping out that they just figured I was a regular doc on a break and they'd talk to me when they'd never knowingly talk to a shrink. I enjoyed that, occasionally had a chat with a commander late at night over what came my way. You know the Army, though. Take what you get, 'yessir, yessir, three bags full, sir!' You may find it hard to wrap your head around, but non-surgical MD Captains are about like privates in the Medical Corps."

"'Cept for not having to pull KP."

"Except for not having KP. More'n a fair share of Officer of the Day or Guard, though."
They both grinned knowingly at the difference between officers' and soldiers' ideas of burdensome duty, each pleased that they hadn't had to assume the other's.
"Those bees swinging in the air were beautiful, but a little bit desperate, too, hanging on because they had too. Can't help but think of you men on the ladders, see-in' them swing and eager to put a foot back down when they could."

"It'd never cross your mind if anybody else'd showed you that trick."

"You're right, but you showed me and I know more about you than I'd know about somebody else."

"Save you asking the question -- I've thought that too. Thought about it starting up the ladder. In my dreams they sometimes turn from one to the other. Sometimes I'm one or the other and may not match up with the rest of the column. If I'm a bee I'm wondering what the hell's going on with the line stretching and shrinking, moving about when it oughta' be hanging still. Crazy. Everybody's dreams are crazy, and at least those are easier to take than the nightmares where

there's no confusion about where I am and what's hap-
penin'. "

  "I'd be a professor somewhere rather than back
in the Army if I could explain dreams. I'd even understand myself. "A wry laugh as he lit up another smoke.
"Understand myself!"

  "Doc, you're leaving on the morning train. I've
got a feeling I'm never going to leave this place. I Got
out of the Army hospital, realized I'd drag my people
down on the farm, figured out something else and for a
little while it was working, even getting good, what
with Sarah, but then it all slid downhill, came apart.
Considering how many men got killed some folks'd say
I'm lucky to be alive, but I'm not so sure. The nightmares are as bad as ever, I've lost my girl and what I'd
gained in the community, and my freedom. I feel guilty
thinking it, 'cause I'm alive, but I'm angry over what
I've lost. Angry that it seems like nothing can be done
to get any of it back. I've got my eyes open enough to
see that people don't get well and leave here, just die.
Hell, my job is to make their box! When I came back
up to the Valley from the farm, I'd thought out a plan
and fell in with folks who made it work for a pretty
good spell. What kind of plan can I come up with here?
Carpenters've been good to me, but there ain't no place
out there for a half-trained gimp woodworker unless it's
a shop owned by his daddy or uncle. I was blessed with
Bill Riley and Mr. Frank Hess kinda' like that, but I
came to them outta' the Army and off the farm. That
luck won't happen again comin' outa' this hospital because of what happened in the war. Shit, people gotta'
whole new war full of soldiers to brush aside if they
come home not quite right, and we both know that
there'll be a mess of 'em. God knows I love the bees,

but a gimp can't run the hundred or so stands you got to have to begin to make a livin'. Bee man with a hundred hives would be even farther away from makin' enough to hire help and sure to fail if he tries to run the business from a pickup rather than getting sticky and stung. My carpenter work's accurate enough to build boxes and frames, but there's no competing with factories full of machines. Rich men'll pay for hand-made bird guns, but I don't know of any call for eight-hundred dollar hand-made bee boxes. I hit a slow place in my work, I admit I sometimes still stare off and find myself in the past. Doesn't usually start there, though. Usually it starts when I have some glue settin' or a hitch in my leg makes me have to stand straight on my stick for a bit for me to go away in my head."

"I catch myself looking out into the courtyard but not paying any attention to what I see unless it could conceivably pose a threat, which isn't often, even for a paranoid vet. I come back to where I am and start staring out there trying to come up with a plan, maybe use the GI Bill, but I don't know what I'd aim for, teaching, maybe, but I'd be last in line for hiring behind all of the guys graduated before me, gimped up and handing in an application that shows I've been here. Got my doubts about how pain, whisky and nightmares'd fit in with studyin' and how I react to things and people'd fit in with crowded hallways and classrooms where the safe seat with my back to the wall is a good ways from the door up front next to the teacher. It's right discouraging. Sometimes I think that I was better off layin' there waitin' for the rest of my unit to fight their way into where we were. At least I knew then that help was on the way. Sometimes it's real hard not to start going back to the way I was when I wasn't talkin', just let my head go back to focusing on listening and watching for the slightest change in my part of the line, not have to consider what the rest of my life will be."

Doctor Witt had put up his smokes and was just relaxing against the wall, thinking, sadly, that Raymond was making a pretty realistic assessment of his own prospects. "Can't argue with the points you're making. A lot of truth in all of them, I'd be lying if I didn't agree that the odds are right much against you." And, he thought to himself, not much likely to improve. "It'd be a mistake to give in to that urge to go back to starin' and not talkin', though. Talking and working with the carpenters will keep you improving your skills, trying to build up to as many beehives as you can handle will probably amount to some extra honey, which'll keep your connection with your friends in the community alive. Maybe time will be kind to you and let the nightmares ease up." Farley Witt stood and extended his hand. "My train leaves just after tomorrow mooring's medical briefing, so that this is likely it for us this time around. Good luck to you, my friend!"

Raymond rose, adjusted his hat to exactly the right angle, and relying on his stick as little as possible stood like a soldier as he shook Witt's hand. "Thank you, Sir. Best of luck to you, too, make it home safe!" As they broke their grip, Raymond took all of his weight from the stick, stood at attention and gave Doctor Farley Witt a smart salute, pivoted and headed into his hallway door. The doctor strode across the courtyard to his quarters without looking back, thinking of Raymond.   If, somehow, I stayed, could I ever get him out? Just like the old men in the ranks, the longer he stays here, the longer things are done for him, the longer his life is regulated and managed for him, the harder it will be for manage for himself. Witt had talked with too many old soldiers who'd left with their dreams and savings, only to reenlist weeks later, broke and broken, coming home.

Doctor Witt said his official goodbyes at the next morning's meeting and was sent off with courteous applause. The Director, or his assistant, was thoughtful enough to have a car and driver waiting to take him to the station.

66. HOW THINGS WENT FOR THE LONGEST TIME

Raymond remained on Doctor Harshbarger's list, but was left mostly to the care of the aides and carpenters. It took a while to adjust to losing his afternoon coffee, but he became more conversant with George, Oliver, and Earl, and got a padlock for his tool box which he improved with a compartment for a pint of whisky for days when his leg was acting up. As Doctor Witt predicted, modest honey production kept him in touch with his friends in the community and provided a few dollars to buy supplies like factory-rolled and cut comb foundation, a hat with a veil, a smoker and gloves. He did splits and caught another swarm, filling the small yard to capacity with four stands. Successfully keeping the bees kept him popular with the Hospital administration because it was a good thing to point out to visitors.

Bill died, but Dave stepped in to make sure that his laundry baskets had smokes and the two bottles of whisky, so that he wasn't reduced to the blue-bag state supplied roll your own tobacco. Sarah still helped with his clothing, although they never met or conversed, neither of them willing to risk the emotional turmoil involved. The story of his arrival at the Hospital began to fade from memory, he gained weight, looked less like a soldier, and his hyper-vigilance came to be seen as peculiar rather than a possible precursor of violence.

Dr. Jake, the newest-qualified member of staff, was aware of developing anti-psychotic drugs and made his mark by convincing the administration to add them to the Hospital's pharmacy on the grounds that their expense was worthwhile in terms of reducing violence, which allowed the maintenance of relatively constant staffing needs even as the patient census was growing. There was no doubt about the drugs' efficacy in making really crazy people docile, if a bit imbecilic, and low doses became more and more common throughout the wards. Some people who had family members assertive enough to keep them taking their medication regularly even went home and became acceptable members of their old households in their subdued state. Liquor and Laudanum, the old pacifiers were dispensed less and less frequently. Probably because of his value as the bee-man and carpenters' helper, Raymond was spared all but a brief trial of the new medication, which kept him from staring off and constantly scanning for danger, but which also clouded his thinking, affecting his carpentry and limiting his ability to manage and explain the bees to visitors, and did nothing to lessen his nightmares. He was quickly taken off of the drug, and given his old remedies, but few others were.

Changes in the agricultural industry moving away from low-skill labor broke the back of the always marginal economic viability of the farming operation. Similar changes and rigid improvements in sanitary standards did the same in the dairy. It became obvious that prisoners were more efficient book-binders and shoemakers, those jobs moved to the Penitentiary and the workshops were reconfigured as wards and filled with sedated patients. Shoes that needed mending were tagged, sent to Spring Street in Richmond, and usually reappeared in a few weeks, repaired but visibly untouched by awl or cording. Instead they bore the clamp marks of powerful electric stitching machines, the odor of strange adhesives, and evidence of heels ground to fit on an abrasive belt rather than having been crafted to size. Curiously, the staff at the hospital remained relatively stable. There was a regular turnover of strapping big aides to deal with admissions and the drug-resistant who moved on to safer, better-paying jobs, but a lot of folks, like the carpenters, liked what they did, had established homes, had already raised their families and simply didn't want the disruption and uncertainty of chasing higher-paying jobs that might not last. The Commonwealth might not pay high, but it paid regular. Some of the physicians at the Hospital shared the carpenters' views, especially those with enough personal wealth to maintain their social standing in town while doing a 'public service' that involved fewer hours than a small-town or country practice. Others enjoyed the opportunity to involve themselves in the political side of medicine, committees, commissions, connections with the Board of Medicine, legislators and the Governor's Office. A few, some quite talented, others right broken down, were there because they'd run afoul of precisely the same groups in Richmond, had their licenses restricted, and preferred the Hospital over working at the Penitentiary on Spring Street, some big-city jail or a TB sanitarium. If regulations specified a retirement age, they were regularly overlooked for aides with the knack for handling even a single especially refractory case.

67. WOKE UP DEAD AND TELLING THE BEES

Rafe Bell was edging into that latter category of older but indispensable men. He wasn't what you'd call an old man, but wasn't a youngster, either. He talked easy with the best of them, but like all attendants kept a worn towel draped across his shoulder. Somebody got past what good manners could handle, and his towel was lightning fast around the troublemaker's neck, tight, cutting off his wind and letting him down easy without a fight. If the big young aides, yet to learn the subtleties of applying that technique, had a problem they couldn't handle, they waited for Rafe to show up, as he invariably did, word getting to him quietly that something was getting out of hand. Raymond had become one his special charges when he arrived with all the soldier talk, catatonic and paranoid. Wound like a spring he could have been in danger or a real problem if some disturbed person had jumped him. Rafe Had looked after him then, when he'd needed it the most, now they were old friends with an established, mutually beneficial whisky smuggling protocol. Rafe checked on Raymond every morning, usually after he'd worked with other people who needed help with the start of their day, and made sure Raymond's laudanum was in place before leaving in the evening. One mooring he crossed the courtyard to where Earl was just setting up his work, looking real serious.

"We got a real problem."

"What's that?" Earl was unaccustomed to that sort of comment from the man whose reputation was that of the Hospitals chief problem solver.

"Raymond wasn't at breakfast. Went to check on him and saw he woke up dead this mornin'."

Earl set everything down and looked real carful at Rafe as he spoke, not wanting to be the victim of some practical joke. "Dead? You sure he ain't just playin' possum? Maybe we ought to find one of the doctors."

"Find all the doctors you want. One's gonna' have to sign the paper declarin' him although I just declared it to you. Looks like he fell asleep last night and woke up dead. I've seen enough dead that I recognize 'em, even if they've gone sweet and easy like he has. You and your fellows better brush off the right size box, I'll get a crew out to start diggin', then find a doctor."

"Aren't you jumpin' the gun a little bit? What if his people want him home?"

"Can't afford it. Last time I had 'em on the telephone I made like I was completing a form I had to fill out and asked 'em. They wanted to know what it would cost, I told 'em what the last one I knew about had been, there was a long silence and some whispering and they told me that they just couldn't do it. I told them that they didn't need to be ashamed of that, and that when the day came they'd get a call from one of the doctors."

Cost was the main reason the undertakers over in town didn't get called very often and that Raymond'd had steady work. There weren't many gravestones up on the hill, either, just two-foot concrete posts set deep, even with the top of the ground, each one with the next consecutive number cast into the top, made up as needed by the highway department fellows that made survey markers.

"Why'd you ask his people that? Seems kinda rough to have to talk about when they'd just been checkin' on him.'

"That's why I told 'em some fool'd come up with a new form. Damned sight easier on 'em knowin' what to expect than bein' called in from the barn to be told he'd passed and asked 'by the way, how's your bank account doin'?' I haven't done that but a couple times. You never can predict with farmers. Sometimes they have money from the last crop in the bank, usually they can sell a cow, but that can't happen in an instant, and they might not be able to lose any brood stock. Long way to carry him down there, it'd have to be expensive. Respected Mr. Raymond. Liked him and didn't want him lyin' around festrin' while everybody spent half a day wondering to each other what the arrangements might be until some office person got their nerve up or was told to call and ask. This way the doc can just read the note that I wrote beside the telephone number, call, make his manners over the passin' and easy-like make sure there's been no change in plans."

"Wise and considerate of you to have done that, Rafe. Deny that I ever said I was in favor of adding one, but maybe there ought to be a form like the one you asked questions for. Which other piece of paper deserves to die to make room for it?" He really didn't expect an answer, although he wouldn't be surprised if he got one later. "I'll just go take a look while you get things started."

It was as Rafe described. Raymond was in bed, next day's clothes laid out at the footboard, his boots, shined, by the chair ready to pull on and lace up. The medicine glass on a saucer on the night-stand was empty and Raymond's eyes were closed. At least he hadn't passed in the midst of one of his terrors. His stick was on top of the bedcovers right next to his hand, which was cold.

"'True what they're sayin' about Raymond?" George had come out to Earl's sawhorses and tool wagon.

"Must be -- there go a couple 'a doc's hustlin' across the bricks toward his door." Oliver had been only steps behind Earl.

"Just looked at him. I think he went easy."

Oliver looked at George. "Who's gonna tell 'em, you or me?"

"Neither one of you, or me either. We're carpenters. The docs are paid to do that, or push it off onto someone they boss around while they fill out the certificate."

"Not Raymond's people, the bees. Raymond told us one day that the rule since anybody could remember was that when a bee-keeper dies someone has to go right away, rap on the hive covers and tell 'em. Tell 'em respectful-like and ask 'em not to fly off, that there's a new man comin' to look out for 'em. He had that book memorized, but so much of what he knew about bees he said that he got from his Granddaddy, come down from the Old People, so it must be important. He didn't ever try to trick us that we know of when it had to do with handling the bees."

"Since he told both of you and left me out 'spect you'd better go together. Might be bad luck if you don't. I'll go wipe the dust off a box and you can help me carry it out when you get back." Earl headed into the shop and the other two men started for the bee-yard. Earl got a clean wiping cloth from the varnish shelf rather than picking up a rag from one of the benches. Slowing as his eyes took a minute to adjust the dim light in the back he thought about the service. 'Guess this'll be one for the Chaplin, won't be any local preacher comin' in.

68. EARL'S THOUGHTS ON THE CHAPLAIN

The main building of the Hospital had a large chapel, big enough for all of the patients capable of sitting still and quiet when it was built, back before the War. Couldn't come close to holdin' 'em all, now. It was a pretty place, lots of careful joinery in the woodwork, easy to see because since the chapel didn't get the hard use the rest of the place did, the edges weren't rounded and the joints weren't obscured by the layers and layers of paint covering every other touchable surface in even the 'new' buildings up on the hill. Being named Chaplin was probably a big thing back then, too, right up there with the doctors and directors. Chaplins these days weren't thought of so highly, when they were thought of at all. Tended to be odd ducks, either end-of-the-liners like the docs who weren't allowed to practice outside the fence or absolutely new fellows who'd been so improvident as to be ordained without having been able to line up a church along the way or those who fancied a brief time in challenging call as a career-starter, but had enough common sense to realize that the hospital presented a lower risk of premature death from tropical disease than conventional missionary work.

Earl had to think a minute to remember that the current Chaplin was a young one who, in general opinion, had arrived favoring public service at the Hospital over the Army. A practical matter rather than a matter theology, the basis for the difficult path taken by the CO aides during the last war. Being a chaplain was an easy route to a captain's commission like the doctors could get. Just sign on the line, put the brass on your collar, and right off you can buck lieutenants if there is a line for the officer's latrine. Problem presented, though, was that for freshly-made chaplain captains at the time this man had come to the Hospital, both the line and the latrine were in Korea. That decision made and the Chaplain settled in at the Hospital, Korea had since simmered down to a sort of standoff, but the Chaplain was having a hard time with his next step, figuring out how to leave.

It had to be strange, doing that job. Attempting to provide spiritual solace those able to ask for it but so disorganized in thought that further discussion was impossible. Conversing with those who knew that they heard God's instruction to at worst kill themselves or others or at best to engage in activities clearly not sanctioned by any Christian sect and known and accepted to few others touched upon in basic seminary training. Lots of Old Testament possession by demons and, of course, the problem of how to relate to those convinced that they were God, Jesus, or an embodiment of the entire trinity. The first group, along with the imbeciles and idiots were well served by a cheerful countenance and a kind touch. The other two, prone to be argumentative, required great patience in preserving a courteous demeanor while looking for a means of escape. The experienced aides were generally protective of the Chaplain in that regard, appearing on some pretext to allow him to escape, unless the day was so unusually peaceful that they had leisure to amuse themselves by watching his efforts to extract himself from his tormentor's clutches. Chaplains, just like other new staff, had to be quick learners Hard to say whether the professors back at the seminary would be amused or appalled at the urgent protestant murmurings demanded by those complaining of demonic possession. The more he thought about it, the more confident Earl became of the Chaplain's ability to do a good job. He'd been active at the Hospital longer than most -- the dead-enders were usually seen less and less on the wards towards the end of their stay -- and although he'd not been around him much, Raymond was good preaching material. Good material and well thought of by the Chaplain because even though he was older by enough years to matter, Raymond had respected the younger man's education and position and he'd always addressed him as 'Sir.'

69. PREPARATIONS

The two doctors reappeared and talking quietly between themselves went off to the forms cupboard in the administrative offices where they could get the certificate they needed to fill out to make their pronouncement official and look in the files for the number to make their call to Raymond's people. As soon as they'd left Raymond's room Rafe and a couple of other aides who knew the work turned the corner from where they'd been waiting to clean Raymond up, dress him and lay him out proper.

George and Oliver came back to the shop looking sort of serious. "Raymond acted like it was important," George told Earl as soon as he got close.
"Hope we did it right. Bees just flew in and out like
they didn't give a damn one way or the other."

"Gave me the chills" was Oliver's observation.
"I know he put right much stock in doin' things the old
way, the right way, just like in carpenterin', but it felt
strange, two grown men talkin out loud and serious to a
bunch of bugs. Maybe that strangeness was a connection with the Old People. Like George, I hope we did it
right."

"I'm sure that you did." Earl tried to reassure
them, marveling at how serious the two pranksters were
in latching onto what had probably been passing comment as a solemn duty. He reckoned that was their way
of showing respect for a man who had shared his unusual abilities. "If you'd done it wrong the bees wouldn't
have kept on flyin', they'd have got all over both of you.
Just don't go talkin' about it to folks who won't understand. Do that and you'll get told you felt strange 'cause
of what you had for breakfast. Let any church-ladies
know about it and you'll get called out for bein' un-
Christian, although I expect that you two have already
been called that and most everything else on their list!"
Bein' warned against church-ladies got rid of the serious looks, and with the usual atmosphere of the shop
restored, the three men turned to their work.

Maybe three-quarters of an hour later Rafe came
over to Earl. "Box ready?" he asked quietly. "We need
it now." Each man there took a corner, a light carry
over to the door into the hallway. "Just tip it up on end,

let me check it inside." Earl had done a good job, Rafe didn't even find a chip inside, but he knew the work well enough to make his final inspection outdoors, where the light was good and any dirt would fall to the ground. The wide doors made maneuvering inside easy, although with a man on each corner, the hallway was a close fit. Inside, Rafe and his men had set up two pairs of straight chairs facing each other about six feet apart, one pair by the bed, where they had to start, the other in the sitting room where they planned to end up. They put one end of the box on the seat of the chair at the head of the bed, the other on the seat of the chair at the foot, lifted the lid off and set it out of the way against a wall. One of the aides busied himself pulling clean rags from a bag and folding them into cushions topped with threadbare towels, fitting them into the coffin where he calculated the head, small of the back, and knees would fall. Rafe stood at the middle and bucked the coffin tight against the bed with his thighs and belly.

"Earl, you just pay attention to his head, ease it over and don't let it get bumped. You other men put a hand on where you can to push or pull and we'll ease him over to where his right shoulder, arm, and foot just are hanging in the air. On my count." "One." " Two." "Three." Everyone did what they were told and Raymond's body stopped precisely where it should. "Good. Now a couple of you get up there on either side of Earl where you can control a shoulder, one'll have to knee on the bed for the other. One on each side of me to take up the weight then let it down, all in one motion. One man knee on the bed and push at his hips, last man hold his ankles, lean back and then let him down slow and straight." Conscious of the fact that Raymond had put on considerable weight in the last year or so, people moved into position, hands on but not really gripping.

"On my count." "One." The men gripped. "Two." The men took up the slack in their own muscles and Raymond's clothing and flesh. "Three." Everyone pushed, lifted, swung and eased Raymond's body down onto the cushions just where it needed to be, then, as they caught their breath, reached in and neatened up the position of a hand, flattened out a wrinkle on the shirt. "Very, very good. Oughta always had carpenters help! Last thing, we need to get over into the other room 'till it's time to move to the chapel." Wasn't hard for six men to make the shift to the second pair of chairs. Earl laid Raymond's stick in by his left hand, went back and got his cap and set it where his right hand touched the brim, ready to put it on at just the right angle. "Lay the top on kinda loose, let a little air circulate but give that nice pine smell a chance to stick to his clothes and hair. Gather up our cleanin' stuff and we're done." Rafe was the first man out into the hall. As each of the others passed the doorpost, turned and took a step towards the bright light of the outside he held out his right hand to shake, murmured his thanks, and offered a pint of whisky with the top off with his left. Nobody turned him down. When they'd all passed he headed down the dim hall, taking a drink himself, screwing the cap back on with just the fingers of his left hand. Slid the bottle back into his pocket and climbed the winding stairs to use the telephone in the front hall to call Mr. Frank Hess.

Hess answered on the third ring. "Augusta Bank, Frank Hess speaking."

"'Mornin', Sir. Raphael Bell." Rafe gave his name for politeness, knowing full well that Hess recognized his voice. "How're you this morning?"

"Reasonably well. How about yourself?"

"Not too bad, Sir, but I've got some sad news. Raymond passed last night. We just finished laying him out."

"Sorry to hear that. He was a remarkable young man. Any idea what it was?"

"He went to sleep and just didn't wake up. Looked real peaceful when I found him. Haven't seen a death certificate. 'Spect it'll say heart failure. Get right down to the end of things, that one's always accurate and doesn't ruffle anybody's feathers."

"Know what you mean. 'Respiratory failure's' popular too, under the right circumstances. Glad to know that it looks like he went easy, rather than your findin' him on the floor with the bedclothes all torn up from one of his nightmares. They'd still write 'heart failure' but there's a world of difference."

"Couldn't agree more. I'm calling to see if you and Mrs. Hess might be able to go out and tell Sarah."

"Be glad to do that. Woman deserves more than a phone call. Not so busy this morning that I can't leave early for dinner. Just as soon as we drop off I'll call Mary Frances and ask her to be ready to go with me. What about his people, have they been called?"

"One of the doctors is doing it. Don't believe any of them will try to come up on the trains tonight -- too many farms, too many milk-cows, too many children and old folks for them to get those sort of plans movin'. I asked 'em some time back, pretended I was fillin' out a new form, if they planned to have him brought home and they said no, they couldn't afford it, so we didn't call the undertaker, just took care of him ourselves like we do for most folks that aren't local. Reckon the funeral' be tomorrow afternoon. Usually have 'em at three o'clock so as not to cut the day too short for those who come, but early enough that the men doin' the work aren't kept from supper." They made their manners hangin' up, Frank called his wife, picked her up and they headed out to the Westview store.

Sarah was helping a customer at the counter, moving from shelf to shelf, retrieving cartons and cans as the list was read, but she threw up a hand towards the couple as they came in. They wandered over to chairs on either side of Oscar's rocker and paid their respects to the aging cat, which purred but didn't arise to stretch. Busy as she was, Sarah wondered what brought her friends to the store on a weekday morning. They weren't on vacation -- Mary Frances was wearing gardening sort of clothes, but Frank was in a banker's suit. There wasn't any point in trying to read Franks face, she knew that it wouldn't reveal anything of what was on his mind. He'd of made one hell of a poker player, but having religious scruples against gambling, soldiers casting lots for the garments and such, he confined himself to a chief teller's inscrutability in the face of any matter presented, and the most harmless sort of practical joke when he wanted fun. Mary Frances looked distraught, taking comfort from her interaction with Oscar, but that wasn't telling either. A lovely, kind lady, her moods were unpredictable, transparent and most often unrelated to what was going on. If she woke up happy she made every effort to savor and share each moment of happiness. If she woke up sad nothing could change it and she struggled to accomplish what she had to do, often avoiding others in an effort not to spread her misery. That's just the way she was. Figuring up the bill, bagging the groceries sending the customer politely along interrupted Sarah's chain of thought and it wasn't until they'd exchanged greetings and she'd lifted the flap in the counter to join them with Oscar that things came together. They'd been friends and customers for years, but in recent times their biggest connection had been her and Mary Frances' tending Raymond's clothes. Frank had left the bank mid-morning, didn't want to face her alone and brought his wife who'd been hiding among the roses. Sarah slid both hands under Oscar, picked him up, sat in the rocker and smoothed him back into position atop her lap before she spoke, as evenly as she could, fighting imagination and emotion in a way Mary Frances would understand. "Y'all have to be here about Raymond. Is he worse, hurt, sick?"

Frank cleared his throat and Mary Frances moved her hands along Sarah's on the black cat's flank. "We're sorry, Sarah, but we've come to tell you he passed last night. Seems to have gone easy, no sign of a nightmare, his eyes were closed when Rafe found him after he didn't come to breakfast."

Sarah sat silent. Not because she couldn't speak, but because there was too much to think, much of it contradictory, much of it inappropriate to mention in the moment. She was sad that Raymond was dead; she was glad that he was finally free of his torment; she was angry that they had been robbed of their happiness; she felt the old wound open and was torn because of John, reliving the shock of the news of his death; and angry that despite losing wonderful men on three occasions -- Raymond's decline and hospitalization made him count twice -- she was still damned to float like a helpless angel behind the blacked-out, burning bomber. "Thank you both for coming to tell me in person rather than having someone call." She gathered Oscar up to her bosom and buried her face in his fur, breathing in his warm cleanliness and letting her mind ride his purr. Frank and Mary Frances reached over and held hands but remained silent. They'd both known and felt the difference between a friend's silent presence in hard times and the chatter of an acquaintance seeking relief from his own discomfort. Sarah spoke after the whole surge of emotions had passed through her mind a second time. "I guess the funeral'll be pretty quick. Will any of his people be able to come?"

"Tomorrow at three. Hospital Chaplain. According to Rafe none of his family are going to be able to come."

"That's understandable. I know from the little bit that we've kept in touch that their days just get fuller and fuller and that money for train tickets might grow from the dirt but isn't in hand 'till the crop comes in. Even the old reliable 'need somthin', I'll sell a cow' isn't much help in catching that night's train." Sarah fell silent again, her previous troubling thoughts increased by sadness and anger over how easily Raymond's family, who she knew to be good people, had let him slip out of their lives. More things she shouldn't mention. Customers came into the store, Sarah re-settled Oscar, straightened herself, put an arm around both of her friends, and gave them a hug. "Thanks for coming to tell me, lots easier finding out than when I was alone. I don't know if I can handle a funeral -- I'll think about it and give you a call." She went back to work and Frank and Mary Frances went home to dinner and the few moments of a workday easy-chair nap that, at least for Frank, followed.

Word spread quickly of Raymond's death. Some patients could only say "bee man's dead!" sometimes prompting the response "they get him?" Hand-picked bunches of wildflowers, really any weed that had anything remotely resembling a blossom, and some that didn't, like sweet-smelling bunches of mint or catnip accumulated on the lid of the coffin, slid down so that visitors could see Raymond's face. An extra couple of aides kept people moving so that the room and hall didn't get crowded and hot, and had opened doors and windows in the hall other rooms and the stairwell so that some fresh air pulled through.

Chaplin Harris was crouching over his desk, alternating between writing a few lines and leaning back with his feet up and his hands clasped behind his head to think. Once in while he'd crash his feet down and lean forward to strike or blot out a word or an entire line and substitute another. Other times he'd come down slow and easy, write a word or two, and then go back to thinking. This was the most challenging ministerial task he'd been put to at the Hospital, and he intended to do it right. Seminary exercises had only dealt with writing formulations for ordinary congregations, which he'd made do until now, but this time he knew he had to please the administration and be understandable to a congregation of lunatics, but mostly he felt a need to do right by a man he'd only met a couple of times but who'd treated him with more courtesy and respect than anyone else in the whole place.

The carpenters had remembered a bit of brass plate in the jumbled hoard beneath the workbenches and spent the morning working to make the coffin different from any other up on the hill. True to his love of the shape of the back window in his pickup, Earl showed the others how to use string, a pencil, and a narrow scrap of wood with two small nails in it all tapped down even on top of the brass rectangle with a bench dog to lay out the biggest oval they could fit in the space. They decided that rather than sawing it out, hard to do with carpenter's tools, they'd cut it with a freshly-sharpened cold chisel normally used to edge loose large screws that were too tight to move. As they worked along, they used the same chisel to stamp a border line all the way round. Once they'd done that, which took a long time to do, keeping each stroke even, and filed the edge completely smooth, they'd each brought their little tins of number and letter stamps out of the dark corners of their toolboxes and keeping them in separate groupings, taken regular turns striking each letter and figure into an otherwise uselessly shaped scrap of brass to determine whose was sharpest and clearest. Each man's own initials always, of course, came in last. They laid out the lines and stamped in Raymond's name and dates. In a column of four lines beneath they stamped 'Bee Man,' 'Soldier,' 'Carpenter,' 'Friend'. Outside, curving along the double lower line of the oval, they stamped their initials and those of Farley Witt, M.D. It didn't take long to polish it up, and maybe twenty minutes for a coat of shellac to dry. Over in Raymond's room it didn't take but a couple of minutes for Oliver and George to position the plate and screw it to the lid. Pine's soft. Didn't need pilot holes, just a mark from an awl to start each screw. While they did their work Earl rummaged in the shallowest drawer of Raymond's nightstand. As they stepped back to admire their work Earl straightened up from his search, stepped in front of them, got something from his pock-

et, and started doing something with both hands on the
lid in front of himself, out of their sight.

"Hey, we can't see!"

"What you doin', anyway?"

"Just hold your horses."

In a minute or two Earl turned around and handed each of them a sheet of writing paper with a blue
tracing of the plate. He'd found paper in the drawer,
torn the winding off of the blue lumber-marking crayon
in his pocket and rubbed its flat side across the sheets of
paper laid on the plate to copy the inscription. He
turned away from them again, hands still busy. "Somethin' for you-all to fold up and keep in your Bibles.
Maybe mark the part about good things comin' to those
who wait. You can wait another minute or two for me
to rub another for me, one for Sarah and one to send to
Doc Witt." The other two men apologized for rushing
him; allowed as he'd just done something they would
never have thought of doing; and were pleased with
both the gift and Earl's understanding of its importance
to everyone he was making them for.

Things were finally coming together for Chaplain Harris. He figured that he could start with the mys-
tique of Raymond's arrival and the severity of his illness, details unknown to newcomers, then move on to
the bee incident, known to most everyone, and present
it as a near-miracle. He could move on into Raymond's
having found a place in carpentry, hit a bit on Joseph
and Jesus having been carpenters, point out that there
was a place and purpose in this world for everyone,
glossing over the fact that some folk's place was in an

institution and their only possible purpose was as a point of comparison for those outside or better or worse inside, and end up with being called peacefully home at the end, probably the highest aspiration of most of the congregation. He could praise the actions of each level of staff in connection with Raymond's progress without ruffling any political feathers among the medical staff because Dr. Witt was out of the picture. Best of all, Raymond's behavior at the institution had been exemplary, he never caused anyone any trouble, an object lesson for patients and staff alike. He could end with a positive recitation of remembering him for the virtues that, unbeknownst to the Chaplain, the carpenters had just finished chiseling into a coffin plate, bee-man, soldier, carpenter, friend. Wouldn't be too long or two short, and best of all he could talk it from a brief outline on a couple of note cards. There'd likely be some sort of after-the-fact press coverage because, after all, Raymond had been the bee-man, already a page in the file in the morgue of several papers, one of which might send a photographer. A good opportunity for someone to take notice that he was preaching with his head up and the couple of cards indistinguishable in his gesturing hands. Raymond's exit could prove to be the best chance he'd had yet to get his ticket out of the place punched.

Sarah was more than a little distracted for the rest of the workday. When no customers were in she sat rocking with Oscar rather than cleaning or re-stocking shelves. When anyone asked about it she told them about Raymond. The responses varied from the kindness shown by the Hesses to the abrupt and unthinking, 'I figured he went back to Carolina years ago,' 'no idea he was still alive,' to unthinking and downright hateful, 'I reckon he done himself in. A wonder he lasted this

long, what with his drinkin' so bad Bill Riley let him go
and those nightmares I heard he had." She either said
'thank you' or acted as though she hadn't heard the oaf-
ish comments, unclenching her teeth enough to make
her manners and usual customer farewells. Oscar subsequently heard her soft, loving voice as she stroked
him damning those last customers to rot in hell. Peculiar, but a singularly effective way of venting steam that
she had picked up from her father as a small child. He
always talked to a cow as he milked, leaning his head
into her flank and talking soft and easy with the rhythm
of his hands. Usually his talk amounted to random
comments on the work strung together, 'good gal, that's
it, stand easy, don't want that tail slappin' me, let's give
the cat a squirt, give 'im another he caught that one just
right, watch your hoof, don't want it in the bucket,
slowin' down now, 'bout ready to stop.' A big enough
girl to go to the barn with him, she liked that because
she could lean against a feed barrel and listen, hold her
doll or play some make-up game in the bits of hay and
grain on the planks of the feeding-room floor. Big
enough to walk hand in hand with her father, she was
still small enough that looking over the wall of the feed
through to see him was a hands-on-top-stand-on-tiptoe-
and-pull proposition. The rims of the feed barrels were
impossibly high. Sometimes she heard her name, her
father telling the cows they'd better behave because she
was there or telling them what they'd seen and done on
their walk from the house. If he was happy, he said so.
If he was tired or down he explained that to them.
Sometimes he used words she didn't know, but that
didn't matter, she and the cows all liked the rhythm and
tone. It was only when she was older and had come to
understand the differences between barn language and
house language that she realized that her father had occasionally forgotten that she was there and, used the

steady talk to release his anger or frustration about something or someone, sweetly and rhythmically voicing his opinions, saying things that would never have passed his lips in the kitchen. Oscar was as pleased as the cows had been with the stroking and the talk, and Sarah knew that because he was an old cat who'd seen and heard a lifetime of what passed in the store, not a little girl or a cow, he agreed with her every word. Oscar, had, after all, been the one who, by staying in his lap while he sipped those late afternoon Cokes and Nehis and she tended the rush of customers, had told her that Raymond was a good man.

Mary was over at their parent's house and took the call from Dr. Jake. She was glad that her mother was spared the shock, and although she figured her father had been expecting the call from the day Raymond stopped talking, she was glad that he hadn't picked up. Given his poor hearing, he'd have given the doctor the courtesy of attempting to hear him out without interruption and thank him, then summon her or her mother to have it all repeated to make sure that he hadn't missed anything of importance. She started spreading the word to the family, the preacher, and a couple of others, but it wouldn't really get around until folks came in for dinner. Some of them would probably make over after supper to visit.

Raymond wasn't, she thought, a black sheep of the family, it had been a couple of generations since anyone had really earned that name and Grandfather had confined himself to saying as much about one of his brothers when the begats were being recited of an evening when she was a girl. Maybe father knew the details, but he'd never volunteered them. Raymond wasn't forgotten, but it was hard to define his place in the order of things. Neither dead nor alive, almost always referred to in the past tense except when Sarah might have called or when someone other than father said grace and felt the urge to seek the blessings of the almighty on specific individuals (one of the few disadvantages to befall the family upon welcoming the children's spouses). The nieces and nephews had little understanding of him other than the previous owner of the truck with the funny-looking grille or the central figure in a few humorous stories. He stuck in her mind the way he'd been on his visit with Sarah, coping well with his physical disability, cheerful and joking, and unhaggard by his obvious problem with nightmares, largely, she figured, because of Sarah's help and reassurance. Mary had not been out on the porch with Father and Raymond that late evening as they shared their fears that he was becoming one of the men Grandfather had talked about who came home from the War in body but not in mind.

After supper all of the remaining children were there to visit, but none of their spouses or children. The preacher came to call, and it was decided that an obituary and mention at next Sunday's service were all that was needed. Mindful of whose roof he was under, the preacher accepted the proffered drink of whisky without protest and kept his prayin' to a minimum, asking only the Lord's care for a Gold Star Mother whose bereavement came years after they'd stopped mailing out banners and for a family who's loss had come over the course of years rather than in a single afternoon's telegram. Amen.

Word spread among Sarah's friends before the death notice appeared in the next day's *Morning News Leader*. Folks started coming towards the end of the day with enough food to feed her and Oscar for a week. Mrs. Russ and Mary Frances Hess came out to the store after supper with a spray of flowers to hang by the door so that other folks would understand why it was closed the next day. When Sarah told them that she'd insofar as she hadn't been able to face visiting Raymond at the Hospital after that one time with Bill, she'd decided that she couldn't bear going to the funeral there, the two ladies offered to come sit with her for the day. "Frank and Lee can be there for us. We'll each bring a book and some handwork so that you needn't feel like you have to entertain us, and if any callers appear to be getting anywhere near tiresome, we'll just push them out the door and down the stairs. If you don't want callers, we'll put a chair at the bottom and take turns expressing your gratitude and expressing them away unless you open the door and tell us different."

Sarah hugged her friends, accepting their offer. "I don't know how well I'll sleep tonight, but me 'spect it's time for both of you to be getting home. Thank you for coming this evening and for planning to be here tomorrow."

Candor comes easily riding in an automobile through the dark countryside. "Mary Frances, I hope she makes it through the night. First she lost John, the she and Raymond couldn't make it together no matter how much in love they were, she had to watch him slipping away until the day he stopped talking and could only respond with a single tear from each eye when she came. Lord bless her for not abandoning him, helping you with his shirts and things, Lord knows how she found the strength to stay away from visiting him later, keeping one step away from having her heart broken again by seeing him held up as a great medical success for just functioning in that place, surviving largely on account of the friendship of a bunch of carpenters, a burned-out Army doc who'd blown up there when no place else would have him, and a Colored man who decided to look out for him, which included helping you-all smuggle in enough whisky to dull the pain and get back to sleep after his nightmares." The road from Westview came right into Beverley Street. Mary Frances stopped without having to pull over and let her friend out at her front walk.

"I'll call in the morning and we'll set a time to go out. Goodnight."

70. THE FUNERAL

Just after one o'clock the next afternoon Dave the engineer walked around the end of the main building by the kitchen and headed across the courtyard towards the group of men gathered at the door of the carpenter's shop, where the Chaplain was checking details. "Did the gravediggers finish this morning?"

"Yes, sir," Rafe replied. "Got the timbers in place and the rope laid out nice and even."

"Don't need to worry about either of 'em." Earl filled and lit his pipe. "It was years ago I signed the book for 'em to have good straight stuff that'd hold the weight of a giant and were long enough that a little crumbling along the side of a grave wouldn't let a box slip. An ass-whippin' the time somebody 'borrowed' the rope outa' their shed has done a good job of guaranteein' that the one they have now is clean, dry, and not frayed." Everybody had a chuckle over the system that preserved gear unprotected by ledger from agricultural misuse. "Hey, Mr. Train-Driver," Earl held out his hand. "Glad that you got here."

"Started switchin' off with the right men soon as I heard.   They were all real good about gettin' me up here."

"I know that Rafe does it regular and the diggers know to work with him. I want him as a pall-bearer on a back corner where he can tell folks what to do. Who else? You, Mr. Hess?"

"Thank you, Reverend, but I'm not very tall and my right hand shakes from toting up too many columns of an evening when I started bank work. I'd say that with Rafe, Dave, and these three carpenters you're set to load up here. Somebody else'll step forward as the sixth man when you need one later."

Recognizable by sound before it made the turn, the head of the digging crew wheeled the Hospital's just-hosed-down Ford pickup around to the hallway door. Used mostly for errands, the black truck wasn't as beat-up as one from the farm. Even Earl knew that this was not the time for his baby. Oliver slipped a hammer into the loop on the leg of his overalls. "I reckon we just as well go ahead and move him up to the chapel. Dave, you want to see him private before I tack the top down halfway?"

"Thanks. I appreciate that." Dave walked off and the others hung back, and then went over to talk to the driver, giving him as much time as he wanted.

"Roomed with him across the back hall at the boarding house," Hess told the preacher, indicating with a nod of his head towards the door that he was talking about Dave, who was already inside.

"I was wondering about the connection. Think there'll be many folks from town?"

"Probably not. Maybe a couple of his old oil-route customers. His old boss, Bill, he's dead, maybe his boy'll come. Can't say, don't think he and Raymond were close. His girl, Sarah, just hasn't been able to handle seeing him after she came to visit when he couldn't talk. She won't be here, my wife and his old landlady're sitting with her this afternoon. I think that Mrs. Russ' daughter, Lee'll probably come in her mother's place. Might be someone from the paper -- I wrote them up an obituary in time for the morning paper. Raymond did his work and kept pretty much to himself otherwise. Sarah was one of his customers, the Westview store. I reckon Dave is about the only friend he had other than these men here and Doctor Farley Witt."

Dave came to the doorway, cap in hand, nodding towards the group to come on in about their business. Oliver noticed the smell of cigarette smoke as he came into the room. Taking a brief look inside before tacking the top on the coffin by driving the already started box nails about a third of the way home, he saw a new pack of Luckies, opened and with one missing, tucked into Raymond's shirt pocket. The trainman's hat next to his fingertips looked less faded than he'd remembered, and he saw a fingermark of oil on its brim.

"Truck driver'll make six men down here, Mr. Hess, let's you and me go up the inside stairs rather than walking the long way 'round with the truck." He led the way down the hall and to the left, and then left again into the steep, twisting stairwell. "This'll be the first funeral I've ever preached in the Chapel," he spoke back over his shoulder to the man he could only hear following a couple of steps below. In fact, it was to be the first proper, sanctuary funeral he'd preached since seminary. Funerals at the hospital were graveside affairs, with little to be said beyond some identifying remarks and reading the Service for the Dead. After his fourth or fifth, he'd gone home and told his wife at supper that the cumulative experience made him feel like a sailing ship's captain on a long voyage with an aged and sickly crew rather than a proper preacher.

As the six men with the truck and coffin knew, there was a practical reason for the small number of chapel funerals. Carrying an occupied coffin up and down the expanse of stairs from the front drive to the main hall was tiring, and completing the trip to the second-floor Chapel was exhausting, even though it was the only broad staircase in the building and had a landing halfway up large enough for everyone to stand level with the load on their shoulders, get their breath, and relax their balancing arms and hands for a moment. There had been some unfortunate incidents, especially on the way back down.

There were a pair of trestles set up in the front of the Chapel, purpose-made to be unobtrusive under the coffin. Looked a lot more proper than the chairs, Oliver thought as he pulled a thumb-sized block of wood from his pocket to use as a fulcrum beneath the claw hammer's head, not marking the lid and easing the nails out unbent, so that he could be sure of driving them home true, without embarrassment, when the time came.

George had disappeared as soon as they had put the coffin down, but came back, huffing a bit from the stairs carrying a folded United States flag. "They mailed this to us after our boy was buried in France, saying it was 'symbolic' of the one they'd used there. Package was postmarked from somewhere here in the states, so they knew that they had to say that or be caught right out as liars. Meant a lot to the wife before she passed. I never told her that I knew that they were still damn liars. Precious few individual graves dug in France. Those graves registration boys used those little farm Cats where the driver's on a steel tractor seat sprung low behind the back and a blade no wider'n the tracks to push long trenches laid out with survey stakes. Other lines staked out at right angles and with a string pulled so there'd be no mistake from eyeballin' as those GIs pulled boxes rougher'n this one off the truck and spaced 'em out by chalked number for the markers to go up if we won. Closest my boy's coffin came to a flag was when the two-ton drove past the pole at the gate." He paused for a minute. Nobody said nothin'. "Earl, please, gimme a hand so we get this thing laid out straight."

The service went superbly. Medical staff and administration were in attendance, even someone from Richmond, in town for a couple of days to consult with the Superintendent. As suspected, the same newspapers that had covered the bee story years before were there, probably as a result of a call from the Superintendent's assistant. The few people that he didn't recognize he surmised were, as Mr. Hess had mentioned, customers from the oil days or kitchen folk from what had been Woodrow Wilson Hospital. The sermon came off just as Chaplain Harris had hoped. Hardly had to glance at

the two cards in his gesturing hand. He gave the benediction and asked the congregation to head down the
stairs first to make the pallbearers work easier and to
give them time to walk or take their cars to the cemetery on the hill southeast of the main building.

George whispered to Dave to help him with the
flag. Motioning Dave towards Raymond's head they
lifted the flag, sidestepped a bit to clear the coffin,
snapped it taught and folded it twice so that Dave had
stars top and bottom on his end. George remembered
the drill, folding just enough of his end forward onto
itself that the subsequent side to side angular folds left
Dave with the right amount left to tuck the grommeted
edge into a fold, leaving a tight triangle formed by the
union. Dave handed the folded flag to one of the administrative people in the front row, whispering "It has to
go back to George -- it was his son's"

Chaplain standing beside him, Oliver lifted the
top over Raymond's face and let it down gently. Two
light blows each, even though he could've set the light
box-nails with one heavier blow, he worked his way
around. Finished, he slipped his hammer into the loop
on his leg and assumed his position as Rafe's partner on
the rear. At the chaplains slight hand motion the other
pallbearers moved forward into position, leaving the
side post nearest the remaining congregants, mostly
medical staff and the superintendent, who was in no
hurry because he knew that his car and driver were out
front behind the pickup. Wordlessly the Chaplain gestured to the open spot then swept his arm broadly across
the pews, a questioning look on his face. There was a
momentary pause, people looking at each other to see
who might move, deciding whether or not decorum or
position required or prohibited their rising. To the sur-

prise of many, Doctor Jacob Hershberger rose, handed his hat to his neighbor, and stepped forward. Rafe was relieved, because medical training had not robbed Dr. Jake of his farm boy shoulders and he was confident that there'd be no unexpected shifting of the load on the way down with his strength in the middle.

Up on the hill the pallbearers let the coffin down onto the two timbers spanning the grave. Rafe bent down and gave one side of the rope a twitch, moving it into the gap between the a fully functional cross-brace beneath the bottom boards of the coffin which tied into the sides, and their dummy twins, shorter and out of sight, of little structural value but invaluable in keeping the coffin from slipping from the ropes if someone stumbled and it took a moment to catch the slack.

The smaller group that had come to the grave-yard stood bareheaded as the Chaplain read the Service for the Dead, held one hand high and gave his benediction. As his hand came down, Rafe and George stepped to the far side of the grave and took up the sides of the loop of rope extending around behind them, each backed up by one of the gravediggers. Two by two the other pallbearers took up the ends of the rope on the near side of the grave, pulling in the slack until it was snug between the twinned cross braces. The other two men from the grave-digging crew knelt with their hands on the timbers, ready to pull them away once the rope had the weight of the coffin, their faces turned towards Raphael, who spoke no louder than necessary.

"On my count." "One." "Two." "Three."

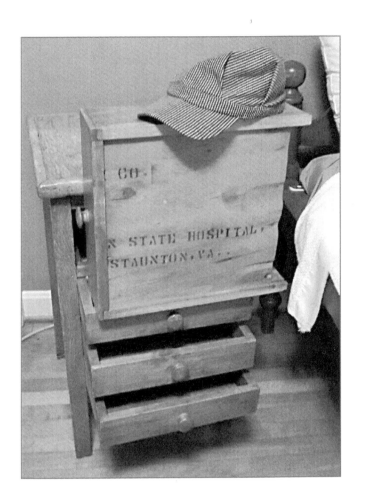

Made in the USA
Charleston, SC
12 July 2014